BLOOD & BOND

The Shard of Elan, Book 2

Laura VanArendonk Baugh

Æclipse Press
Indianapolis, IN

For Luca's ladies,
Becky, Bethany, Kate, and Kayla,
for always keeping the support flowing.

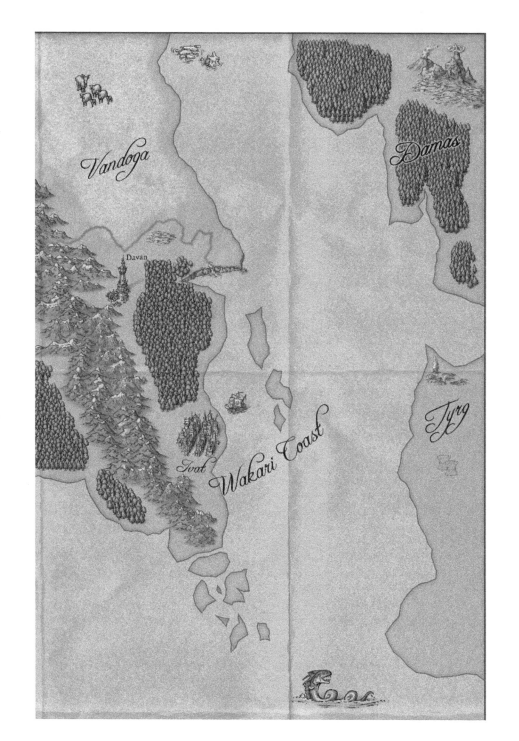

CHAPTER ONE

Shianan hesitated in the shelter of an empty trellis, a dozen paces from the palace entrance. Guests streamed steadily through the brightly lit doors, oblivious to him in the dark as they shared conversation and called greetings. He tugged fretfully at his unaccustomed clothing, making the metallic gold and silver geometric bands in his doublet flash with reflected firelight. Overlapping black leather belts, one tooled with indigo and one with burgundy, shifted unfamiliarly over his hips without the weight of a weapon.

It was too much, really. The entire ensemble had been a gift from his majordomo and new estate of Fhure when Shianan had come into possession of a title, but it was too extravagant. Even as a count, Shianan had little reason to wear formal or rich attire; he appeared at court functions rarely and briefly, more often present in a military capacity than in his comital rank. He had put away the fancy trappings and nearly forgotten them.

But he could not appear in his usual serviceable gear to such an invitation as this, and he had retrieved the bundled outfit from the rear of a chest. It fit well enough and was not far out of fashion, and it was his only hope to be admitted gracefully. But...

He adjusted the cape's textured edge and fidgeted once more with the pointed collar, his fingernail flicking a tiny dangling stone. He wasn't sure he wanted to be here at all, in these clothes or any other. But royal invitations were not to be spurned. He straightened, exhaled, and started for the entrance.

"Commander," said a familiar voice. "Good evening."

Shianan peered over the collar at General Septime with a weakening stab of relief. "Oh, sir, good evening. I'm glad to see you."

Septime nodded at the guards flanking the door as they passed together. A second rush of relief swept through Shianan; he'd been half-afraid someone would challenge his right to enter. But the general was unconcerned. "You, too, commander. I didn't know if you'd be here."

"I received an invitation," Shianan answered too quickly. *Steady. No need to be defensive.*

"Of course." Septime paused as a brightly dressed slave

9

appeared to take his cloak. "I only meant I hadn't pegged you for a dancing man."

Shianan chewed at his lip. "Perhaps I only haven't had the opportunity." There had been few dances at the plains outpost, after all, and few women to partner.

But there were women here. The great hall was filled with people, dazzling in their finery and bright with laughter. In the center, the elite swayed and dipped to the merry music provided by liveried musicians in the balcony above, as encircling courtiers joked or gossiped or complimented or politicked or observed or posed. It was a brilliant and terrifying scene.

Septime had already moved into the crowd, greeting and laughing with acquaintances. Shianan blinked into the hall, suddenly quite alone. A part of him wanted to flee, to return to the dark night and grieve for Luca and stay safely away from this unfamiliar gaiety. But another part of him wanted to remain, to see what might be in this strange and fascinating society.

He moved hesitantly through the crowded room, smiling faces gliding past him on either side, and took refuge in the lee of a decorated column. Around him the music played, and people laughed and called to one another. He pushed his shoulder against the column and watched, trying to look as if he were waiting for someone.

"Your Highness!" A lady gestured for Soren to join their group. "Come and see what Glynde has brought!"

Soren allowed himself to be drawn in. "What have you found us now, Glynde?"

"Look at this." Glynde offered a stiffened paper to him. "What do you see?"

It seemed to be a mash of black and red, dots and lines swirled together. Soren frowned. "Nothing much. Perhaps an accident at the colored glass workshop."

"Ha, the glass workshop!" Several in the group giggled more than the weak jest deserved, and Soren found himself annoyed.

Glynde shook his head with a smile. "No accident, and how curious that you mentioned colored glass."

"Now try these!" urged a girl—young Lady Fanshawe?—as she thrust binocles at him, set with pale red glass.

Soren held up the binocles, feeling faintly foolish, and looked at the paper. The colored glass muted the red ink, and now he could see a leaping horse. He was impressed despite himself. "Very clever. Where did these come from? Who thought of such a thing?"

"There's a craftsman in my march who first brought them to me," Glynde explained. "Very clever, as you say. Here, look at this one."

Again, viewed by itself, the card was an uninteresting blur. But with the colored binocles, Soren saw a lady having her hair coiffed by a slave.

A surreptitious nudge at his arm interrupted his viewing and he glanced over his shoulder to glimpse Ethan. He nodded and turned back, presenting the card and binocles to Glynde with a smile. "Duty calls," he said lightly, and he withdrew from the group amid a flurry of bows and curtsies.

Ethan waited a short distance away at the edge of the wide stair landing. He handed Soren a fresh goblet of wine and murmured, "He's here, my lord."

"Where?" Soren looked over the hall from their vantage point. It was hard to distinguish a single face in the blur of dancing and socializing.

"At the far end. Near the oak leaf column."

"There! I see." Soren took a drink of the wine. Shianan looked lost, even at this distance. "How long has he been there?"

"He came only a few minutes ago. I had his arrival from a slave taking cloaks."

Soren nodded. "I have another task first. Keep an eye on him, if you would, please. I'll want to find him later."

Ethan made his typical small bow and Soren left him. He threaded his way down the stairs, as much a gathering place now as a means of ascent or descent, and moved through the crowd. Along the way he smiled and nodded and promised to return, never pausing as he worked toward the knot alongside the dancers.

"Your Highness!" A hand landed on his arm, a bit forward for catching the attention of the prince-heir. "Will you join us? Bansbach has just wagered that Barstow will ask Lady Selina to dance, and Barstow swears he will but he's as reliable as a skinny chef or a fat mage—"

"I beg your pardon," Soren inserted politely. "I'm on my way to my lord father. Could I come back to you in a few minutes, perhaps?"

He slid into the cluster of courtiers that marked the king's presence and smiled his way to the center. He seized a moment when his father was taking a drink and leaned conspiratorially close. "That was well done, Father."

King Jerome glanced at him. "What's that?"

"Bailaha's here. That will clear up any questions regarding your faith in his innocence and his commission." Soren nodded approvingly. If manipulation was a tool of royal governance, he would use it toward his own end and general benefit. "I was perplexed as to how to reassure the court and troops of your trust in him after the trial, but this will quell any rumor. That was brilliant."

"He's here?" King Jerome's eyes jerked about them. He kept his voice low. "Where—"

"Didn't you think he'd heed your invitation? He's there, at the end, by the column. Waiting for someone to join him, by the look of—"

"I didn't send for him," whispered the king.

Soren knew that. "You didn't? Someone must have supposed you meant to. And it will only help—"

"Get him out." Jerome's hand fell heavily on Soren's arm. "Your mother's here."

Soren went suddenly hollow. "I—she came? After all?"

"She did." The king's voice was tight. "If she sees him..."

"I'll watch him," Soren said quickly.

Jerome nodded. "And be sure that—"

"Your Majesty," someone gushed drunkenly, turning to them, "may I tell you how lovely this occasion is?"

"I'll see to it," Soren murmured, and he withdrew.

He fled toward the stairs, ignoring the greetings and cheerful hails. His mother had come? He hadn't expected it—not this time of year, not without letting him know, not tonight—

He took the steps two at a time, heedless of the startled glances as he passed. If he had any luck at all, she would be in the north wing. He glimpsed Ethan at a distance as he spun around the balustrade at the top of the wide stair.

The door was open to admit the hall's music. She was in what had once been her favorite room, waiting as a maidservant sponged a spot from her gown's skirt. She glanced up in surprise as he burst through the door. "Soren! How good to see you—but what's wrong?"

He shook his head to calm her worry and took a few deep breaths. Surely his condition wasn't that poor; he was only breathless with alarm. "Nothing's wrong, my lady mother," he answered, and he approached her, making a courtly bow before taking the hands she offered him. He kissed first her knuckles and then her forehead. "I ran because I only just heard you had come. I did not know you would."

She gave him a fond smile. "How could I not come? Celebrating the renewal of the shield that protects us—it's a worthy cause, at least, unlike so many silly balls." Her face took on a resigned look. "And I'd thought, when I set out, they were trying the bastard for it. I heard on my arrival that he'd been released."

Soren nodded. "I was at the trial, Mother, there was no evidence for it. He's the one who recovered the Shard, in fact."

"I know, I know." She sighed. "I only hoped it was true." She glanced down at her skirt. "Is that spot gone yet? I want to go out."

"I'm just finishing, mistress."

Soren fidgeted inwardly as the maidservant blotted the skirt dry.

"There, mistress, bright as new. Is there anything else you require?"

"No, thank you, Eve. My son will see me downstairs." She glanced toward Soren as the maid gathered the cleaning items. "You will escort me, won't you?"

"Of course, my lady mother." Soren bowed and offered her his arm. "It's been too long since our last visit."

He was fond of his mother, though now he saw her only rarely. He did not want to have to deceive her now, and concealing Bailaha felt like a kind of deception. Still, having her encounter him unexpectedly might be worse. She had left Alham when he had been called to the city. Any interaction between queen and bastard would be a public scene, no matter how stiffly formal she might be.

They moved down the corridor and to the stair. Soren glanced down to the wide landing and saw Ethan waiting, nodding. Becknam was still visible below.

Someone jostled Ethan, throwing a dark look, and Ethan bowed his head respectfully as he tried to press further into the worked stone balustrade. Soren frowned. "Ethan!"

The slave worked his apologetic way through the crowd and came to Soren's side. "Bring Her Majesty a drink," Soren directed. Ethan bowed and disappeared, safely out of the disdainful crowd.

They descended slowly, smiling and nodding around them, and paused on the landing. Queen Azalie looked over the bright hall, smiling. "Such a glad group. Happy, and with reason. I'm afraid I don't know everyone as I should, though, as I've been so long at Kalifi. Who is the gentleman in red, down there?"

"That's the Marquess of Stowmarries. He came into the title only last year; before that he spent little time at court."

Soren glanced toward the end of the hall and saw Shianan, now picking a path through the crowd, a mostly-full drink clutched in his hand. He paused and spoke briefly to someone who laughed, nodded, and then moved on. Shianan rotated slowly to look across the room, fully visible from the landing. Soren swore mentally. "Mother, did you know that—"

"One moment, Soren, I'm enjoying the view. We don't have so many balls at Kalifi, and you should let me enjoy my ogling. That's a pretty couple, don't you think? It's too bad he's contracted to wed her cousin."

Ethan arrived with two iced drinks on a tray, and Soren handed one to the queen before seizing the other. He gulped too large a mouthful before catching himself. Should he simply tell her Bailaha was present? Would that be worse than hoping she somehow did not see him?

She was sipping the drink, gazing over the hall. "You'll have to dance with me, Soren, at least twice. Everyone else is so unpleasantly formal, and of course he's an awful dancer. Always has been." She smiled.

"I'll be glad to dance with you, Mother." Soren took another drink.

"Are you all right?" She gave him a concerned glance. "You seem nervous."

He forced a smile. "It's been an eventful few days." Would it be better to escort her to the main floor, where her vision was less sweeping, or to keep her here, where she would not meet him as they passed? Perhaps he should simply tell her. But not here. He'd have to find a private area.

"I suppose so. I heard you went out to find Alasdair, too, when he was lost." She shook her head. "Somebody ought to do something about that boy."

"Well, you are his mother."

"He wasn't my idea." She raised an eyebrow at Soren and then laughed at his dismay. "These things happen."

Soren chuckled. "Spare me the sordid details, Mother. I trust we were born, and that's as far as I care to know." He turned his head and caught Ethan's eye before glancing significantly toward the main floor. *Go and take him out of sight. Find an excuse.*

Ethan understood—there was a reason he had been with Soren for a dozen years—and started down the stairs.

"Who is that? In the dark doublet, standing apart?" Queen Azalie nodded toward Shianan Becknam, standing alone below them. "Handsome man. He favors you a little, which helps of course." She laughed.

She did not know him! But of course she wouldn't. She had not seen him since he was a child.

Soren hesitated, but he had to give an answer. "That—that's..."

She looked at him, caught by the change in his tone.

"He's no one, Mother. No one."

"No one?" Her lips thinned. "You seem oddly upset by this person of no consequence." She looked toward Becknam again. "He is—but I said he favored you, didn't I?"

Soren's stomach rolled. "That's the Count of Bailaha, Mother. Commander Shianan Becknam."

She did not move. "Is it? I didn't know him." She hesitated. "I have not seen him since... He must have been three, perhaps four. Four, I think."

"Mother..."

"Oh, Soren, don't be a fool. I'm not going to scream or faint or embarrass anyone." Her fingers shifted on the stone. "Do you know him?"

"A little."

"What do you think of him?"

"I—I think he's an interesting man."

She gave him a critical look. "Safely spoken."

Below them, Ethan had nearly reached the commander, who turned and addressed a passerby, probably some military associate. Ethan hesitated, unable to interrupt their conversation, and glanced apologetically toward the landing. Soren shook his head; it was irrelevant now.

The corners of the queen's mouth quirked upwards. "You really were afraid of me seeing him, weren't you?"

Soren shifted. "You have been very careful to avoid him."

"Yes."

She stood very still, only her eyes moving as she watched the count. Soren's stomach clenched as her mouth pinched.

"Soren," she said, "please call back Ethan for me."

CHAPTER TWO

Shianan smiled, made a polite comment, and watched as Escher moved away through the crowd, leaving him alone again. This was miserable, he should never have come...

"Shianan!"

He whirled, his ears burning, and Ariana leaned toward him to be heard over the music and chatter, her face bright with exertion and excitement. "I did not know you were here! I've been trying to see you for days—but how smart you look! This really suits you."

She was in a gown of deep red, her dark hair arranged high and cascading down her back. Above her left breast was a gauzy black scarf twisted into a perfect circle and pinned into place, denoting her honored position. Her eyes ran over Shianan, possibly admiring his extravagant clothing or possibly looking for evidence of his beatings.

"I—er—thank you," Shianan stammered.

She laughed. "You needn't say it like that. I did mean it. You never believe a compliment, do you?"

"I'm sorry. I'm not really myself at the moment." He shifted inside the prickling collar. "Welcome back. Welcome home."

She sobered. "Yes. Thank you. I'm glad I had the chance, before the shield was recreated."

He caught his breath. Did she know? Did she know what he had done to save her?

But she smiled and continued, "At least I had the chance to participate this time."

No. No, she did not know.

He stood there, absolutely still in the whirling crowd, uncertain of what he could say. Her eyes shifted, looking over his shoulder to some excitement beyond him, and in sudden panic he sallied, "So we're safe, then? No more Ryuven?"

This somehow seemed to sadden her. "No more Ryuven," she repeated. "We're safe. No more war."

"Most think that a good thing," he answered, trying to tease back her cheerful expression. "No more war with the Ryuven, no more massacres, no more fighting or starving."

She nodded, still a little wan. "That's right. No more soldiers dedicating their lives to danger and dying to protect us. You can live a normal life."

Ice lanced through Shianan. No more soldiers... But that was all he was. He could not have a normal life, not the bastard. Every honor, every recognition, every scrap of praise had been hard-won by military accomplishment. Without the war...

"You can all live normal lives," Ariana said with determined relief. She tipped up her chin. "Do you dance, Shianan Becknam?"

He blinked. "I..."

"It's a simple enough question. Do you dance?"

"Not well."

"Good," she declared. "Then I won't feel too ill-suited for you. Come with me?" She grasped his arm and pulled him into the maelstrom of music.

Shianan had little time to consider refusal, and they were promptly surrounded by swaying couples barring his escape. She transferred her grip to his hand and began to pace with the others, giving him an encouraging smile. Shianan moved haltingly, stiff with uncertainty and hot with embarrassment. But Ariana kept hold of his hand and matched his pace, and gradually he began to move more freely. She twirled and came to face him, her hands resting on his forearms, her face lifting toward his as she laughed at her own play, and he caught his breath. She was so near, and so joyous, and they were both alive.

"You're not doing so badly," she told him.

His hands ached to slip about her waist, but this was a different style of dance, and that might be too forward. He tightened his fingers about her arms and leaned nearer to her. "My lady mage..."

The music ended with a pipe trill and the dancers about them paused to breathe, laughing and speaking. Ariana hesitated a moment in his grasp, looking at him, and then she drew away with a quick, shy smile. "That was a fine dance, once you began. Thank you for partnering me." She plucked at her skirt.

Shianan swallowed. "My lady mage, you—you're beautiful," he blurted. Horror swept him. "I mean, you look absolutely beautiful tonight." That was hardly better. "I mean..."

"Your lordship." A voice came from behind him.

Shianan tightened his fingers on Ariana. "Yes?" he asked, turning his head over his shoulder.

But it was Mage Hazelrig who smiled disarmingly back at him.

"Only a moment." He held out two decorated cups. "I thought the two of you might want something to drink after that."

"Er, thank you," Shianan accepted awkwardly. He took the cup which Hazelrig offered and drank. Chilled watered ale, safe enough.

He looked again at the older mage, dressed in a doublet of rich midnight blue. It made a stark contrast with the white scarf pinned to his chest, twisted in an exact circle.

"Your scarves are too perfect," Shianan commented. "Mere cloth shouldn't be able to hold that shape. Are they magicked?"

Ariana laughed aloud. "No, no. They're wrapped about a metal ring. See?"

Hazelrig was amused. "We needn't use magic for everything. That would be both difficult and wasteful."

Shianan chuckled. "I suppose that's true." He took another sip. "Thank you for the drinks."

Ariana nodded and looked about. "Linner was asking me to dance," she said in a lower voice, "but I don't see him now. Which is just as well, because I'm hoping someone else will ask me for the next one." She tossed a pointed glance toward Shianan. "After all, I issued the last invitation."

Shianan caught his breath and glanced toward Hazelrig, but the mage only smiled at his daughter. Shianan looked from the White Mage, unconcerned about the bastard, to Ariana, sipping her watered ale to hide a grin, and for just one moment life was perfect.

"Excuse me, your lordship," cut in a polite voice. "One moment?"

Shianan turned to a bowing slave.

"If you please, your lordship, I am instructed to bring you."

The slave straightened, his eyes respectfully below the commander's, and Shianan's brief joy shattered into icy crystals. This was Prince Soren's personal servant—Allan, or Efren, or Ethan, yes. Had the prince seen him dancing with Ariana? What did he want?

"My lord?"

Shianan gulped. "I—yes. I'll come." He turned to the two mages, who looked concerned. He must not have guarded his expression well. "Please excuse me."

Ariana reached for his arm. "My—Shianan," she began, her voice quiet and urgent, "is it the king?"

"Prince Soren has sent for me." Beside him, the servant gave a small cough.

"Will you—will you come afterward? To dance?"

'Soats, she saw right through him. She was worried for him.

He forced himself to smile. "I'll come when I may. Enjoy yourself." He bowed to the two of them and turned to follow the waiting slave.

Ethan led him through the crowd and out a heavy, carved door. They would be meeting in private, then. They made two turns in the corridors and Ethan paused to knock at another carved door before opening it. He bowed and gestured Shianan inside.

CHAPTER THREE

Shianan's first thought as he entered was that someone had moved the great portrait from its prominent palace corridor. Then he saw she was no portrait, and he realized he had entered the wrong room. He fell into a bow and retreated a step, hoping for quick escape, but Ethan was already closing the door behind him.

No, he had been brought deliberately to this. He collapsed more than knelt and dropped his head low over his knee.

"Good evening, Bailaha."

"Your Majesty," he forced.

"Thank you, you may rise. I want to see you."

He did so, keeping his eyes on her feet. Silently he cursed. How had he come here? How had he even received an invitation when the queen would be present? He drew in a breath, awaiting the worst.

Ethan was gone. Shianan was alone before the queen.

"I did not expect to see you here tonight," she said neutrally.

"I—I did not know Your Majesty would be attending. I offer my deepest apology—"

She rose from her chair and started toward him. Her movement silenced him, although it should not have.

Shianan straightened and clenched his jaw as when he'd awaited an eviscerating scolding from his captain, as when he'd been verbally flayed by the king. At least if he was to be scorned and humiliated now, there was no one else to see it.

She stepped to one side and tipped her head to regard him. "You would not have come tonight had you known of my presence?"

He stared stiffly at the chair she'd vacated. "I would not have troubled Your Majesty."

"Troubled?"

Offended, then! he thought madly. Why did she torment him? "I know Your Majesty would not be—pleased to see me." He blinked and hoped she would not see fit to correct his understatement. *Not pleased? I hate your odious form.*

"No," she agreed, "I was not. But you were a boy when I saw you last. Before you were sent away."

"I was, Your Majesty," he answered the chair.

She sighed. "Am I so fearsome as that? You needn't look so—so military. I'm not one of your generals. I wanted to speak with you, not hear monosyllabic agreement."

He did not know how to respond to that. He glanced momentarily at her, a fleeting impression of Prince Soren's eyes, and then looked forward at the chair again.

She sighed again. "I suppose that outpost or wherever left its mark. Very well. What are you now?"

"I beg your pardon?"

"Tell me something about yourself. I want to know something about you."

"I..." Shianan faltered. How could he answer, when every promotion he'd earned, every position he'd held was an affront to her?

She waited a moment, watching him, and then she turned back toward her chair. "I think I believed you would be like Lucien. He was never acknowledged, but we inside knew it. The duchess's extra son. He was an insufferable little pustule." She stopped and looked at Shianan again. "He, at least, would not have been utterly tongued-tied when asked to speak of himself."

"Oh, Bailaha can speak, my lady mother," Soren offered as he entered by the far door. "He can wax quite eloquent on the subject of ugly pigherds, for example." He came to stand beside the queen as Shianan bowed. "But I never knew old Baron Lucien was illegitimate."

"You weren't meant to know," she answered. "And you probably believe he died in battle, too. Well, that much is true, at least, but we don't know for certain whether the guilty blade was theirs or ours."

Soren was visibly startled. "He was killed? For his birth?"

"It's possible, though I rather think it was for for his wretched personality." She seated herself again and gave Soren a significant glance. "For example, he was often inserting himself where he wasn't wanted."

Soren acknowledged the reprimand with a chagrined expression. "I only thought to drop in and see how you were getting along. After you borrowed Ethan—"

"I am quite capable of managing without you. You have guests. Go see to them."

Soren made her a bow before retreating. The queen looked after him curiously and then glanced at Bailaha. "Well, he did say he found you an interesting man."

22

Shianan did not know what she meant by this, but he felt somehow more vulnerable now that the prince had departed.

Queen Azalie put two fingers thoughtfully to her chin and regarded Shianan as if he were a portrait to be approved. He stood utterly still, almost without breathing, wishing he were anywhere, anywhere at all but here.

"Shianan Becknam," she said finally. "That is it, isn't it? Your own name?"

He opened his mouth and found his voice had fled. He nodded.

"Commander Shianan Becknam, Count of Bailaha." She blew out her breath. "I must admit, I was furious when he ennobled you. I raged in Kalifi." She quirked her mouth. "I overreacted."

If there were a way that he could flee, without flagrantly disregarding all conventions of respect and obedience... If only there were an attack on Alham that required his defense—if the Ryuven were to besiege the Naziar Palace—if Pairvyn ni'Ai himself were to burst into the room—

"Shianan Becknam," said the queen, "I have something to say to you."

Shianan's knees obeyed before he could think. He knelt and bowed his head, awaiting her scorn or her orders or her warning.

"I have been a foolish woman. It is not the first time I have been, and it is not the first time that my foolishness has cost another." She paused. "What are you doing on your knees again?"

His throat worked frantically. "Your Majesty..."

"Get up, man. You cannot kneel to hear my apology, that's hardly fitting. Stand and listen to me." She watched him get to his feet.

His thoughts whirled. For decades he had been trained to avoid the queen, and he could not navigate these waters.

"Shianan Becknam, I once hated you. I hated you because you were not a person, in my mind. I never thought of you as a person. You were a living sin, a name, nothing more."

Shianan swallowed against the stone in his throat.

"But you did not have a part in your birth, and now I see you for yourself." She looked at him with cool eyes. "I do not pretend that I know you and like you. I do not pretend we shall be friends. I only know that while I hated the concept of you, you were in fact only a boy, a young man, a soldier, a courtier, and I have wasted myself in spite." She shook her head. "Part of it is hearing his bragging, of course. It's cruel to praise a bastard to the mother of your children, isn't it? But that is another of his crimes, not yours."

Shianan stared at her in disbelief. "Your Majesty...?"

"And Soren likes you, so that says something for you as well. I didn't know; he's never spoken of you. Perhaps he was worried for my reaction. Regardless, I hold his opinion in high esteem, so there must be something worthwhile about you."

Shianan's knees were weak. He could not speak.

"Bailaha?"

"I—I never meant to offend you—I never wanted..."

She gave him a small, grim smile. "It was never a matter of what you intended. But it seems you are determined to prosper here regardless of my favor, so I might as well grow accustomed to the idea. Perhaps you're not the horror that I thought."

Shianan bowed low. "I shall try not to be, Your Majesty."

"Good. Now go out that door, but slowly. It won't do for the prince-heir to be caught listening at keyholes."

Shianan could not think of a safe answer for this, and so he bowed again and backed to the escape of the door.

As he closed it safely behind him, he saw Soren waiting a dozen paces down the corridor. "I'm sorry," Soren said immediately. "I'm sorry. I had no idea she would be here. I tried to keep her from noting you..."

Shianan shook his head, confused and alarmed at the prince's consternation. "No, no—my lord, Your Highness, it is my fault for coming here."

"No," Soren said firmly. "It is not your fault. You were invited, weren't you? Then you should have come." He looked down. "It's all right. I'll talk with her later. I'll tell her something." He glanced at Shianan, almost nervously. "Was she—did she challenge your invitation?"

Shianan shook his head. "No, my lord." In fact, he was stunned at how—indifferent she had been. He'd never thought to meet the queen face to face and walk away intact.

Soren relaxed a little. "Still, I'm sorry for that."

Shianan didn't understand why the prince would apologize for such a thing. "No, it's all right." He hesitated. "If it pleases Your Highness..."

"What? Oh, certainly. Go back to the ball." Soren gestured up the corridor. "Good evening."

Shianan bowed. "Good evening, Your Highness."

24

He was nearly at the hall when he heard Ariana's voice. "Thank you, but again, no. I'm waiting—"

"Yes, darling, I heard, but you're still here. He can't be worthy of you if he makes you wait so long. Come dance with me."

"No, thank you, I will wait."

Ariana. Shianan's spine elongated and his shoulders squared as he exited the corridor. Ariana and a young baron glanced at him.

Shianan pointedly ignored the young man. "I beg your pardon, my lady mage," he pronounced as he bowed to Ariana. "I was detained, and I apologize."

"Oh, you're nearly forgiven, your lordship," she answered smoothly. "Linner did not leave me alone."

Linner squinted as he tried to work out if he'd been insulted or complimented. Shianan straightened and put an arm casually against the wall over Ariana's shoulder, leaning near her. "How thoughtful of him." He looked at the baron for the first time. "Then he'll be glad of the chance to return to his other friends."

Linner stared back, startled. "What do you mean to say?"

Shianan loosed his practiced commander's glare. "I owe Lady Ariana a dance yet, and she would appear rude if she left you here alone. No thoughtful gentleman would put a lady in a position to appear rude."

Linner visibly swallowed. "I see, your lordship." He bit out the honorific with hardly concealed distaste. "Then I will leave the lady to your care for now." He made a stiff bow to Ariana and none to Shianan before he merged into the crowd.

Ariana cleared her throat, and Shianan self-consciously withdrew his possessive arm. Before he could decide how and for what to apologize, she shook her head and smiled. "He wasn't so bad as to deserve that," she scolded gently. "But he's probably none the worse for it."

Shianan exhaled. "I'm sorry for overstepping."

"I had him in hand, but I appreciate the gesture." She tipped her head. "How are you?"

"I'm sorry?"

"I don't know if I have the privilege of prying, but I saw enough to wonder."

His gut clenched. "What did you see?"

Ariana's eyes widened. "Don't look like that! I won't ask any more, if you want. I only wanted to—"

Shianan shook his head. "No, I'm sorry. What did you see that concerned you?"

"Only what was obvious. When the summons came, you looked as if someone had poured snowmelt down your collar. You walked away as if going to your death." Her voice was pitched low, careful no one else would hear.

Shianan winced. "Was it so plain?"

"Only to those who were looking." She hesitated and then touched his arm. "If I can do anything..."

"No. No, it was the queen." Shianan took a deep breath. "The queen sent for me."

Ariana's fingers tightened on his arm. "She's here? Did—are you all right?"

He didn't know how to answer her.

The prince emerged from the corridor beside them, and Ariana pulled away from Shianan to curtsey. Shianan half-turned and made the obligatory bow.

When he straightened, Soren was smiling faintly. "That didn't take long." His smile broadened as he turned to Ariana. "Are you enjoying the ball, my lady mage? It is, after all, partly in your honor."

Ariana was not practiced in speaking with royalty, but she made a valiant effort. "Oh, no, Your Highness. I'm only the most junior member of the Circle."

"Ah, but the Black Mage is a part of the Circle, yes?" Soren grinned at her. "Enjoy yourself this evening. Bailaha, may I expect you in the morning?"

"At what time, Your Highness?"

Soren glanced over the swirling gaiety and one corner of his mouth twitched. "Nothing too early, I think. Or rather, nothing early to my pampered eyes, as early to a commander is probably not even within my cognition. Come when you will. Tomorrow I have no appointments before noon."

Shianan bowed. "I will, my lord."

Soren excused himself and went out into the ball. Ariana watched him and then looked toward Shianan. "You don't look apprehensive at that."

Shianan realized he did not feel apprehensive, either. But he was not sure he felt much of anything at the moment. The dizzying exchange of joys and despairs of the last hour had left him exhausted. "No."

She waited a moment and then faced him. "Well, then, my lord, will you pay your dance debt, or must I go and chat with my dear friend Lady Bethia Farlyle?" She nodded toward the striking young woman casually intercepting the prince's path.

Shianan looked at Ariana's expectant expression and a little of the weariness left him. She was trying to distract him, but he did not mind. And perhaps he could feel something, after all.

He bowed. "Forgive me, my lady mage. A man must always pay his debts. And I think the Lady Bethia would prefer that you not join her and the prince-heir."

Ariana raised an eyebrow. "You've heard?"

Shianan attempted a smile. "It is quite the rumor, if even I've heard their betrothal will be announced before long."

"No rumor, I had it from Bethia herself. It's the most open secret in Alham." She extended one hand to him, her chin raised in mock imperiousness. "Enough court gossip. Let us find music."

CHAPTER FOUR

Tamaryl came gently to the ground, his wings stretching pleasantly as they flexed against the air. It was good to be himself again, his own Ryuven form. A warm breeze brushed over him, welcoming him from the cold human world.

His first duty was to report to the Palace of Red Sands. He had stayed longer in the human world than expected, and he should explain himself. He must also find a way to break the news that the shield was renewed. After Oniwe'aru had finished being disappointed in him, Tamaryl would go to his house and see how Maru fared, and whether Daranai'rika had thought to bring formal complaint against him for breaking their betrothal contract.

He sighed. There was much to do here, so far to go, but in the end, this was his home. He could do good here. He'd studied what he could find of human agriculture, wrestling with books on crop diseases and treatment in his hours away from assisting Ewan Hazelrig. Their flora was not identical, but there were similarities and shared species, and he hoped for new insight on the problems which had led to so much. They could work away from their dependence on the human world.

He folded his wings against his back and started toward the palace. The guards knew him and directed him to the aru.

Tamaryl entered Oniwe'aru's audience chamber and dropped to one knee. "I have returned, Oniwe'aru."

"So I see. I had expected you before now."

"I apologize, Oniwe'aru. I wanted only to be sure that there was nothing more to be done."

He had evidently interrupted a conversation. A rika stood near Oniwe'aru. Her emerald-black hair was bound in a high tail which dragged over her wing and shoulder as she turned her head toward Tamaryl. He recognized her, and the cobalt sash she wore from right shoulder to opposite hip.

Oniwe'aru nodded. "At least you are taking your duties seriously. Edeiya'rika, you will pardon us?"

"Of course, Oniwe'aru. And I will set more guards on the storehouses." Her eyes flicked to Tamaryl as she left, as if assessing

29

him. Given the sash she wore, she might well have been. Tamaryl would have nodded respectfully to her had he not already been on one knee.

"Rise, Tamaryl'sho, and tell me why your steward begged so politely to decline on your behalf my invitation for you and Daranai'rika to dine with me."

Tamaryl's chest tightened. "Ah. Er, I'm afraid I am not sure how best to explain... I wish to break our betrothal."

"Break it?" Oniwe'aru frowned. "That is a significant step, especially after so many years."

"I was not here for most of those years."

"All the more reason to be cautious now. You left her in contract, locked in a partnership without a partner, unable to negotiate a new joining. Even when her house faltered, even when her aunt died, she did not ask to be freed of the contract which could not be completed with you in exile."

"She wanted the position of a prince-doniphan's mate more than the prince-doniphan," Tamaryl snapped.

Oniwe raised an eyebrow. "I remember once you were pleased."

"I was. I was glad such a beautiful and vivacious match was chosen for me. I could do far worse." Tamaryl took a breath. "But I have seen what she is, and I won't be joined to her."

"Strong words, Tamaryl'sho." Oniwe'aru scratched at his chin.

Tamaryl had to be careful how he presented his complaint. Ending a betrothal severed a link both familial and political, and discipline of a nim was hardly a crime, even if the nim was Tamaryl's friend. "She is unhappy in this betrothal, and cruel in her unhappiness. She has taken nim as lovers, and against their will."

"There are many nim who would not argue at the chance to share a rika's bed."

"That may be true, but those who did protest were coerced into acceptance."

"What did she do to your friend?"

Oniwe saw so clearly through him. "He would not lie with her, and she tortured him for it."

Oniwe'aru frowned. "As I recall, you left him in her household while you were away, and she has the right to discipline a servant."

"Not for refusing to bed his lord's betrothed. And it was not the typical minute or so of *fup*; she was stripping his power from him."

"I did the same to you, if you recall."

"I was a condemned outlaw. You were quick and efficient about it—not that it was pleasant, and by the Essence I would be pleased never to taste it again, but it was different. This was a slow process, intended to force him into submission." Tamaryl tried to keep his voice level. "At first she lied, saying he'd assaulted her, but—"

Oniwe'aru snorted. "Maru, attack a rika? Not at his most foolhardy, and never successfully."

Tamaryl was relieved at his agreement. "She blamed me and my absence. She resented me and—and you. I think she might be as glad to be done with me."

"Oh?"

"She called herself the traitor's betrothed. She was caught between position and notoriety." Tamaryl was unwilling to defend Daranai's actions but obligated to express her frustration. And if he emphasized that the engagement should have been long ended, perhaps it would be simpler to end it now. "I know my duty, but I cannot condone her taking lovers by force. Nor one bound in service, which is too near force."

Oniwe blew out a long breath. "Daranai'rika was not often present at court, though I heard of her frequently. I had thought— well, I was wrong, I see." He eyed Tamaryl. "But you won't repeat that, will you?"

Tamaryl tried to gauge the ruler's humor. "I will forget your confession the moment my betrothal is dissolved."

Oniwe'aru gave a small chuckle. "Bravely spoken." He drummed his fingers absently. "But the law allows. You are certain she wants to be free of you as well?"

"I do not know. She may not know herself. I believe she wants to be matched to someone, especially someone with privilege, but whether she favors me over another is uncertain."

Oniwe'aru nodded. "I will speak to her."

"I am afraid she will not have kind words for me."

"I am not interested in her kind words," Oniwe'aru answered shortly. "I am interested in whether she wishes this betrothal ended." He looked frustrated. "With the deaths of her aunt and father, she became less of a political benefit. If she is unhappy with you and you with her, there is no reason to pursue this."

Tamaryl felt relief, mixed with a faint fear that Daranai might refuse only to spite him and retain the powerful association of his house.

Oniwe'aru sighed. "I wish she had said something to me before now. Or you, Tamaryl'sho. You never led me to believe you might want someone other than her."

Tamaryl eyed the floor. It had never occurred to him that he might, either. He had always known that he would conjoin for the good of the court and clan, and he had never considered an alternative.

Oniwe'aru gestured toward the open doorway. "You know Edeiya'rika?"

"By reputation, and briefly—long ago—but not well."

Oniwe'aru raised a significant eyebrow. "You should. She will likely be Edeiya'silth in the future." The leader of the Ai.

"I see she is Tsuraiya ni'Ai now." The cobalt sash marked a hard-won prestige, one that would be useful to carry her to the head of the Ai.

"Indeed, and most respected in that role."

Tamaryl considered his next words. "While conjoining the Pairvyn with the Tsuraiya, who may become silth, would indeed be a coup, I observe that entering a new betrothal just as one is dissolved might be—"

Oniwe'aru laughed. "Be at ease! Even I wouldn't throw you into a match so abruptly. And Edeiya'rika takes her duty very seriously; I doubt she would accept a mate tainted by humans."

Tamaryl frowned. "I am not so corrupted as that."

"You might explain that to her," Oniwe replied, chuckling, "but not near my fragile valuables, if you please."

Tamaryl sighed. He had known he would be doubted. It would pass. Eventually.

Regaining his abandoned position had not been simple, and Oniwe's assignments were a simultaneous punishment for his long-ago treason and probe for his present loyalties and abilities. But they had been necessary and practical tasks, Tamaryl admitted. Oniwe was not wasting him in petty make-work, and Tamaryl could be proud of what he'd done since his return.

He was less proud of what he must do next, but it was necessary for the welfare of his struggling people.

"Oniwe'aru, I have brought something more from the human world."

CHAPTER FIVE

The Palace of Red Sands had one of Tamaryl's favorite gardens, a small jewelbox of fountain, moss, and vivid flowers cascading across and down from a few thin overhead chains and down a wall, providing both color and a modicum of privacy in the roofless space. Tamaryl slipped into it and sank onto a narrow stone bench, warm with the sun. Safely out of sight, he slumped and put his face into his hands, his wings hanging low behind him.

"Is it so terrible to be home?"

He jerked upright and twisted on the bench. It took him a moment to identify her form through the tumble of flowers. "Edeiya'rika. I am sorry, I didn't mean to intrude."

She shook her head as she came around the vines. "I usually find this place empty, too. That's why I like it." She sat on the edge of the fountain, facing him. "I'm sorry I disturbed you."

"I was only thinking, and it probably needed interrupting." He blew out his breath in a long stream. "It was something about you in a way. About your duty, I mean. To be perfectly honest, I was envying you."

She cocked her head, her emerald-dark hair falling over the crest of one wing. "Oh?"

"You know each of your fights is right. You fight only for defense, and when is it wrong to defend your home? So you can face battle, or thoughts of battle, with confidence and a clear conscience."

She nodded. "It is one of the joys I find in my duties as Tsuraiya. Most of politics is not nearly so clear."

"I want it, some part of it, some piece at least, to be clear."

She waited, watching him, inviting him to speak if he wished.

Words he had not been able to speak in Alham tumbled free. "Before I left—I was focused on the fighting, I suppose. Yes, I knew the crops were poor, I knew there were shortages, but I was the Pairvyn, and what I saw was the raids themselves. I saw sho strategize to maximize their own glory. I saw che sabotaging tactics to put warriors at risk so that they could come in later as heroes and win recognition and reward. I knew this war would undo us, and I decided I could not fight it."

She nodded, though of course she knew all this.

"But I saw only what was immediately before me. I did not see how severe the famine was growing. I did not realize that by refusing to participate in the sho's and che's petty competitions, I was sacrificing the people I had pledged to aid. When I returned... I saw with fresh eyes." He looked at her, expecting to see judgment.

But her expression offered a sad empathy. "You were not as blind as you think. In truth, it has worsened considerably since you left, despite our best efforts. People are growing more frightened. There was a riot at one of the Union storehouses a few days ago."

Tamaryl winced. "I can't bear to think that I helped to cause that desperation. But I don't want to undermine social stability and set inexperienced che to oversee fields that aren't producing and yes, kill human farmers who are also just trying to survive. I can't focus on only my duty. I don't know if I can be the Pairvyn as I should." He forced an unconvincing chuckle. "I'm not sure why I am, to be honest. I didn't hazard to ask, but shouldn't I have been replaced after so many years?"

"He didn't dare." Edeiya leaned back, dangerously near the splashing water. "As you've seen, the situation has been worsening, and Oniwe'aru manages his ministers tightly. He could not afford to place a representative of another family as Pairvyn, not when he needed to consolidate power."

"Was there no one in the South Family to serve?"

"He did consider Gann'sho for a time, but then Gann'sho died in a raid, so that effectively ended his candidacy. After that, he could choose someone from one of the other families or keep the position of champion empty under your name. Which is what he did." She shook her head. "It's been a dangerous field, and I am frankly impressed that Oniwe'aru has managed so well the last few years without the Union recalling his vote."

The four ruling families voted upon a silth or aru, who would serve for the next thirty years—if he or she safely navigated the three confidence votes at the conclusion of the first, third, and seventh years and then governed well enough to avoid a recall during the ensuing reign.

"It sounds as if no one else would want to take his place, not with things the way they are." Tamaryl looked at her. "Though I have heard you are a candidate."

Edeiya did not downplay it with false humility nor puff up with pride. "I am one. Frenses'sho of the West Family is another, and I do

34

not know if the North Family has settled on someone, or if they mean to put anyone forward."

Tamaryl remembered how Edeiya had, with a quiet observation, smoothed tensions between Ariana and Oniwe while simultaneously destroying Daranai's social standing. He did not know if she had done it because of Daranai's assault on Maru or for another reason, but it had been subtle and efficient. "You will be a formidable silth."

She smiled. "I am honored that you think so."

"Do you have any hope for this?" Tamaryl asked, and the question came out more urgent than he'd intended. "I'm sorry, I meant to say, I expect you have ideas to help mitigate the suffering here."

Edeiya sat up, looking somber. "I wish I did. We can expand attempts to magically infuse the fields to help speed growth before the blight strikes, but that's been only minimally successful so far and I'm not sure we can rely on it. To be honest, I believe there will be more riots and protests, and I don't think we can survive without the raids to bring supplies." She turned toward him, hair swinging. "But you have been too long in the human world, and this bothers you."

"If we do not raid, we will indenture more nim, and we will turn on each other for ever-diminishing resources, and we will starve. And if we do raid, we will fight and perhaps kill people I love."

She bent toward him, elbows on her knees, shifting her wings away from the fountain's splash. "A leader should choose the greatest efficacy with the least harm. But when there is no perfect solution, and there rarely is, something will have to be sacrificed."

Tamaryl closed his eyes. "I know. I thought before that it could be me, that I could sacrifice myself, stay away and not contribute to the harm. But that isn't so."

She tipped her head again, regarding him. "So you came home. You chose."

He took a breath. "I chose."

CHAPTER SIX

Luca folded his chained wrists to his chest and rested his forehead on his knees. It was cold in the slave stable, making the warmth of his breath valuable, and burying his face let him hide the tears from the silent slaves around him.

Shianan had sold him away. It did not matter that it was to Luca's own brother—he had not even asked Luca whether he wanted to go. That was his right as a slave's master, but it was not what Luca had expected. It was not what he had believed.

Jarrick had not come to the caravan staging ground where Luca waited with the other slaves. Luca had sat in such a stable before, weeping and praying his father or brothers might come for him, but they had not. They had left him, then as now, chained, helpless, alone.

He heard himself whimper and tried to disguise it with a shiver. It was no worse than before, he told himself. At least now he was free of that despicable Furmelle collar, no longer marked a dangerous rebel. Perhaps he could be fortunate enough to find a reasonable place again.

Or, if Jarrick came, Luca could go home with him. He could live upon the Wakari Coast, watch the ships again, maybe return to his father's accounting—

His stomach writhed like a provoked serpent. Would they welcome him? Would—would he be glad to return to them?

Jarrick had searched for him, he'd said. He had at least searched.

Luca shivered, a real shiver this time. His cloak had been left in Shianan's office, and he could see his breath when he lifted his head. Thin moonlight through high windows showed the dark forms of other slaves, huddled together or curled tightly as they slept. There was a clink of metal as someone shifted in the straw.

Someone began arguing outside. "Let me...!" snapped a voice before it dropped again. Luca glanced toward the door. Jarrick? He wasn't sure. There was a sharp exchange of voices, indistinguishable, and then silence.

Luca dropped his forehead to his knees again. If Jarrick did not come, then he would be a nameless and helpless slave once more. If

Jarrick came, he would have to face the family that had abandoned him. If he had stayed with Shianan, he would have remained a slave forever, while if he went home to the Wakari Coast, his family could free him...

He sighed. He did not even know what he would choose—but he did not have the power to choose. Shianan should never have remade him into a thinking, feeling entity once again. It had been cruelty to enslave and brutalize Luca the first time, but it was beyond cruelty to offer him friendship and then return him to what he had been.

But no, Luca would not think of Shianan. Not now. He would not think on the friend who had betrayed him at his most vulnerable.

He would sit here, passive and silent, and wait for what would come.

Luca woke, stiff with cold, as the stable door opened. He picked his way to a corner to relieve himself, glad they had not chained his wrists behind his back.

The overseers moved through the stable, addressing their various tasks. A boy of eight or ten started down the aisle with a bucket of mush and a shoulder bag of wooden cups, dipping each cup efficiently and dispensing them among the slaves. Luca accepted one with his bound hands and gulped at it, though it was cooled and thick. He knew enough of caravans to take breakfast when offered, and quickly.

Indeed, a moment later an overseer went to the stall beside Luca's, jangling keys and chains. "Up, now! On your feet. Move it." There was a general shuffle as the slaves were directed toward the wagons.

Luca sucked the last of the viscous mush and rose with a few other slaves as another overseer came to their stall. The overseer muttered and toed a body still curled in the straw. Luca's stomach tightened; this was all too familiar. He shoved his hands before him and waited, eyes on his wrists.

The overseer reached him and hesitated. "You're a tack-on, right?"

Luca hesitated. "I'm sorry?"

"You're not ours, you belong to a passenger. Who's your master?"

Was Jarrick coming after all? "I served Commander Becknam until yesterday, when—" His voice broke as he discovered a slave could learn yet new humiliation.

The overseer didn't seem to notice. "Don't know your new master yet? You'll go in the line." He nodded toward one of the wagons being pulled into the yard.

Luca glanced hopefully at his wrists. The overseer scowled. "No one walks free in the line. Go."

Luca obediently moved toward the indicated wagon, where another overseer linked his wrists to a long chain which stretched from the rear of the wagon. The weight pulled lightly at his arms.

Luca recognized the slave chained opposite him but did not speak until the overseer had moved on. "Andrew?"

The slave glanced at him. "Oh, you. The commander's servant."

Not anymore. "Luca. What happened?"

Andrew shrugged. "They didn't need as many hands in the kitchen, I suppose. Lent me to the warehouses for a day, then another, and then decided they could do without me."

Andrew had only one wrist chained; Luca had not done well to struggle in Shianan's office. "Will you sell as kitchen help or labor?"

"I don't know. I think they—"

"Move up!" came the order. "Into line, now, let's go!"

The wagons were shifted into formation, the slaves evenly distributed. The boy was coming down the lines now with a heavy bucket of water, offering the ladle to each slave. A movement caught Luca's eye, and Jarrick hurried into the yard. Luca's throat closed.

Jarrick addressed the nearest overseer while scanning the closest line of slaves. The overseer pointed toward Trader Matteo and Jarrick hurried toward him, followed by a slave bearing a roped chest on his back.

Luca watched as Trader Matteo pointed Jarrick's slave—other slave—toward a wagon to stow the cargo and nodded for an overseer to take charge of him. Few slaves traveled loose with a caravan since Furmelle.

Jarrick asked the trader a further question, but the trader shook his head impatiently, busy with the final organization of the caravan. He gestured at the wagons, and Jarrick started for the far end of the line. Jarrick's name formed in Luca's throat, but he knew better than to call.

Knew better than to let Jarrick ignore his call.

An overseer directed two more figures alongside Luca's line. Trader Matteo signaled and they paused as he drew near. He studied them for a moment, appraising them with an expert eye. One was a thin, dark-haired man, the other broader with fair hair, both with their hands shackled behind them. Troublemakers.

Trader Matteo looked at the thin, dark one. "You're not strong enough for a single, I hear. But you had a good price. We'll fatten you a little and see if you can't be motivated for a multi-hitch. Put him behind number three." He turned to the broader man. "And you're the overseer who didn't work out."

The man licked his lips. "I did as told, master."

"Orcan says you embarrassed him in front of his patron and a dozen others. Says you make a better draft than overseer, from his trial." Matteo frowned. "Bend over."

The slave hesitated. "Master..."

"Bend over."

The slave eased forward gingerly, his face tight. Matteo sighed. "Orcan's sharp about that, anyway. You'll go in the line for a day or two, give your back a chance to close, and then we'll move you to draft. Number three."

The two slaves were fastened behind Luca and Andrew. Neither spoke, and the thin one seemed to lean away from the other, stretching at the end of his single wrist chain. The demoted big slave was pushed into line and chained by both wrists. Luca turned his eyes away from the overseer.

And then Jarrick was running toward them. "Luca! Trader, that's my slave. I want him released."

"Released?" repeated Matteo from the next wagon. "Why?"

"He doesn't need to be in the line. I want him with me."

The boy with the water reached Luca's line. Andrew took the ladle.

Matteo shook his head. "You can manage for a week. I've got a reputation of never having lost a one, and I mean to keep it. If you need him for some chore, let me know, but he'll walk with the others."

Luca shook his head as the water boy came to him, intent on the conversation at the edge of his hearing. The boy regarded him curiously and then offered the ladle to the dark-haired slave.

"But—but he's my..."

What excuse would he give the trader?

"He's my brother. I'm taking him home. Let me have him,

please."

The broad slave fumbled the ladle in his bound hands, spilling. The boy glanced nervously at him and dipped another.

Matteo stared at Jarrick. "Your brother, eh?" He shook his head. "You say that, but to me, he's responsibility. He's a slave, and a slave until we cross the border. If I free him before then, I break the law."

"But just to unchain him, to let him ride with me—"

"Hey!" An overseer came from the other side, a switch in his hand. "What are you about there?"

The water boy jumped and snatched the ladle back from the big slave, retreating.

"One ladle each, runt. Don't waste time." He scowled at the demoted slave. "And you—think you're something special?" The line of slaves ducked and flinched away in unison, but the switch landed solidly on the slave's broad shoulders. "You're common labor, now, and you'll act like it."

Luca cringed, afraid the switch would descend again, but the overseer moved on. He looked back toward Matteo and Jarrick, who were walking away together, still in conversation. Jarrick glanced back over the trader's shoulder and their eyes met.

Luca, Jarrick mouthed. *Hold on.*

Luca's stomach clenched. It was no different. *Endure, Luca.*

The final checks were completed, the cargo of feed and supplies confirmed, and the orders came to move. Luca shuffled forward with the others, chains ringing and pulling at his wrists.

Endure, Luca.

CHAPTER SEVEN

Tamaryl consciously flattened his wings, worried their restless tension would betray him, and looked down the line. Mostly nim, one or two che per group. It should be enough. He hoped it was enough.

He hoped this was the right choice.

To his right, Edeiya'rika landed gracefully and walked to stand beside him, her eyes on the gathered nim. "You came to watch them?"

He nodded. His chest was too tight to speak.

"I know what this must cost you," she said softly, her eyes just darting to him and then moving quickly back to the others.

He wasn't sure that was true, but he appreciated her effort. He clasped his hands behind his back, attempting a more open posture. "I heard about the raid last night."

"A Hentu attack on our westernmost repository. They came in force, but we were able to drive them away. They suffered significant casualties; I hope they will not return soon."

"Thank you for your service."

She nodded once. "Two days ago the Lian made a probe to leap the between-worlds, testing the shield, but of course that was unsuccessful. We did not even bother to shoo them away, letting them carry back word that it would be futile to try again."

Tamaryl nodded. "And the storehouse protest this morning?"

Her face was somber, her eyes directly ahead. She'd known he was working toward the question. "I handled that myself. It was unpleasant for all. But we distributed enough to calm the panic and buy time."

Tamaryl drew a slow breath, exhaled it, unclasped his aching fingers. "I hope it is enough."

Soren yawned and shifted beneath the heavy blankets, already sensing the tingle of cold outside the bed. He heard the subtle creak of his door and the soft sound of someone crossing to the fire, stirring and fueling it. Soren said nothing; he did not want to admit to being awake yet. The ball had finally dissipated sometime around dawn, and he had only then made his way back to his rooms, dropping his formal clothes to the floor and falling into bed. If he remained still, he might slip back into sleep...

How did Ethan do it? He'd dismissed the slave sometime before dawn, but surely Ethan had seen to other duties before going to his own bed.

A hand caught the edge of the hanging curtains and drew them back. Soren squinted against the light and turned his face into the downy pillow. "Not yet," he mumbled into it. "Go away."

"I'm sorry," answered Ethan, "but you're called."

Soren groaned. "I specifically told the commander not to come early."

"No, master. It's His Majesty."

Soren twisted, cool air shocking his bare chest as the blankets fell away. "Find me something to wear."

He stumbled out of his room with his doublet over one shoulder, Ethan doing up the sleeve lacing while Soren ran fingers through his uncombed hair. By the time he reached the private sitting room, the doublet was over both shoulders, fashionably unlaced at the collar, and his leggings were tucked securely into his boots. He glanced to Ethan, who nodded to confirm no escaping shirttail betrayed him, and then he raised a hand to signal the page beside the door.

King Jerome was seated at a table set for a meal, but without any food. He had a sheaf of papers before him, several in one hand, others scattered about the place settings. "Soren, good morning, come in," he said, barely looking up. "I thought you could join us for brunch."

"Us?"

"Your mother and brother will be coming shortly. We can take care of some state business before they arrive."

"Certainly." Soren waited for his father's gesture and then took a seat.

Jerome raised a handful of paper. "I see the embargo situation has not been dealt with. How is that?"

"My lord, you know I've been bending on that task for—"

"Too long, far too long. We are losing revenue, the merchants are losing trade, and I am losing patience."

Soren took a breath. "Sire, the route in question has been in dispute for over thirty years. I cannot arbitrarily order a resolution, and I must be seen giving consideration to—"

"Are you fretting about your image?" demanded the king. "Worried what the courtiers might think of you?" He shook his head and deposited the papers in another stack before rising from the table to pace. "You have two lords locked in disagreement, and you cannot let them wallow in their past contentions. Speak with them, understand them, and then do what must be done."

Soren stood as well. "I will review our work with an eye toward more immediate resolution."

The king paused, and something changed subtly in his expression. "Bailaha dedicated himself entirely to retrieving the Shard."

Soren was cut. "As I am working toward this end."

"Our trade routes are critical to our thriving despite Ryuven predation. See that it's resolved."

Soren bowed, stung. "Yes, sire."

"Good morning," said Queen Azalie as she entered. She eyed their respective positions on opposite sides of the table. "Let's sit down together, shall we?"

The king and queen took seats sharing a corner, a little distance apart but facing one another amiably. Azalie lifted her cheek for Soren. "It's not too early for you, is it?"

Soren grinned. "I stayed with the last of the guests, I'm afraid." He moved toward her and kissed the cheek she offered.

"What did I interrupt?"

"Nothing much," the king said. "We were talking about Shianan Becknam. I had not expected him last night. I am sorry."

"It wasn't so bad as that," Azalie answered. "I had not seen him since he was a small child. But I was surprised he appeared so boldly at an event to celebrate that which he was accused of destroying."

"He was acquitted," Soren said quickly.

His mother smiled, a personal smile of acknowledgment; he had revealed something to her in those few words. She did not play him like his father, but she could always ferret out what he hadn't meant to say aloud.

But he had no time to think on it before the king continued, "I won't have him inserting himself. The queen has long troubled herself to be rid of him, and then he, without invitation, took our royal hospitality while the touch of the High Star was still on him. His wings must be clipped."

Soren's heart quickened. "Father, I said last night it was good he'd come, that it demonstrated your faith in him after the trial and acquittal. I complimented you on his inclusion. Don't you remember—"

"We did not invite him!" snapped Jerome. "And when I find who did, there will be dire consequences, even if it is Alasdair who did it." He frowned and looked at Azalie. "You don't suppose it was Alasdair, do you?"

Soren had never dreamed his mother would come, that there might be any trouble with his sending Shianan's invitation.

"Most likely he came of his own initiative," the king muttered. "Without an invitation. The fools at the door neglected to confirm his entry, and he sought to appear a member of the court again."

Soren shifted. "Er..."

"Is he so presumptuous?" The queen rang for food to be brought. "But then he was certainly alarmed to see me. Perhaps he'd gambled on attending—"

"He's not presumptuous," Jerome interrupted gruffly. "Bailaha sacrificed himself to recover the Shard—sacrificed his standing with the public, the guards, his men, even with me. He should have told me his plan, but he was wholly dedicated to his project."

The familiar jealousy stabbed through Soren. *I am sorry that my work does not permit me such glorious triumphs.*

For a moment he wanted to shout that Shianan had lied, that he had indeed stolen the Shard—but it would do great harm and, he saw now, mean little. Now that he had seen the trick of it, he could recognize the manipulations, if he did not allow himself to believe them.

He must not allow himself to believe them.

"The man would have been killed if his plan had not succeeded," the king continued. "That is confidence. And his dedication—'soats, did you see him when they brought him to the Court?"

"I saw him," Soren answered.

"Then you saw what he suffered for his work."

"The king does not attend the Court of the High Star," Soren ventured. "How did you see him?"

"I observed when they first brought him back to Alham—as was only natural, being curious about potentially so great a treason." The king's answer was quick, his voice pitched too casually, his eyes darting to the queen who was carefully folding her napkin.

Slow suspicion formed in Soren's mind. The king had been truly grieved but had not dared to show his concern for the bastard. He took a breath but hesitated, unsure how to broach the question. "Father—"

"He wants to earn his place. That's his best characteristic, his willingness to please. Makes him useful. But he'll do anything to catch one's eye, even risk offending my queen."

Willingness to please! Soren pressed his lips together.

"Maybe that's his crime," Jerome continued. "He was uncertain of his place after the trial, and he came to the ball to show he'd lost no position. No, he's not presumptuous, but he is ambitious—"

The door opened and Alasdair came inside, one hand on his swaggering hip as he swayed to show off a new doublet. "Good morning, everyone," he greeted, making a brief bow toward his royal parents.

"Good morning, dear." Azalie glanced back at Jerome. "What will you do with Bailaha, then?"

Alasdair made a face. "Bailaha."

"You don't like him?"

"He's a sniffy soldier who thinks he's one of us. He walks around and calls himself a count, but he's nothing but a bastard."

"Alasdair!" snapped Soren, nearly in unison with their father. Even aside from his cruel disparagement, to mention Shianan's birth before the king and queen together—!

Alasdair frowned, sulky but unabashed. "He thinks he's better than he is. He's annoying."

"Rather like some little turd who barges into other people's conversations?" muttered Soren.

Alasdair started to turn, half-hearing and sensing insult, but his mother spoke first. "Let it be, Soren. Why do you say so, Alasdair?"

He faced her, eager for an audience. "He was rude to me! He criticized me for coming home without Clemb and losing the deer when I fell in the ravine."

Soren sighed. "I doubt Shianan Becknam is so foolhardy as to insult you directly. And if he did criticize your decision to abandon your guide during a night storm, then I suppose he had the right, as he was the one to find your soggy hide."

"He was the one?" Azalie asked Alasdair, surprised.

Jerome cleared his throat. "If not for Bailaha, we might have lost our younger son." He frowned, watching for the effect of this statement which simultaneously justified his siring of the bastard and criticized Soren for not finding Alasdair himself.

"He was so rude to me!" Alasdair protested. "He actually

turned his back on me!" He delivered this with an air of finality.

"If you mean that he led the way to—"

"No, no, it was deliberate. He made me help a slave, pull him up, I mean, and then he deliberately turned his back on me while we were speaking and walked away." Alasdair jutted his chin toward Soren.

Azalie exhaled sharply, her brief forbearance toward the bastard overturned. "Even if we allow that Alasdair might have been somewhat...shrill, perhaps, in his distress, he is still a prince and he is to be treated as one—most especially by those who might sometime consider themselves deserving of the same rights. This is intolerable, Jerome."

Soren rarely heard his mother address his father by name. The king nodded in agreement. "He can't be suffered to presume upon the princes' rights and privileges. I'll see he understands his place."

Soren fumbled for words. "But, my lord, consider what censure at this time would mean in the court. If you want your soldiers to have faith in their leaders—"

"Confound it, Soren, I am not a fool! I can manage my own well enough. I will see him privately."

Privately... Soren's unease grew. There was something about his father's dealings with Shianan Becknam which shamed the commander, rather than honoring him as a private audience should. Becknam had deflected questions with a poor jest, and his slave had begged not to answer. *The commander is merely a slave to the king.*

Azalie nodded, frowning toward Alasdair. "As you say."

Soren remembered Becknam's discomfort and stiff conversation in the cleft that stormy night. He had no doubt Becknam had been equally distant with Alasdair, but not openly rude. But he could not disprove Alasdair's report, and he was helpless to defend his friend.

"Oh, Soren." Azalie held out something which barely filled her palm. "This is for you."

It was a miniature portrait of a young woman. Soren's stomach twisted; he did not recognize her, but he knew who it must be. He accepted it slowly, almost reluctantly, and studied the dark-haired beauty, all careful brush strokes on catobelpas ivory.

"What do you think of her?" his mother asked.

It was hardly a fair question. "She's very pretty," he replied neutrally. "Though I wouldn't expect anything else from a court painter."

She chuckled. "True enough. Well, keep it for now. Lord Adoniram left it with me when he came to Kalifi."

Soren nodded. "Thank you, madam."

He looked at the face in his hand—flat, empty, a false smile on a false face. The painter had given her beauty without expression, a face without a soul. Perhaps there was little soul to portray.

He looked at his mother, smiling expectantly, and nodded again. "Valetta is a lovely name," he offered gamely. "I shall wait for further word."

CHAPTER EIGHT

Shianan knocked at the black-painted door and heard a muffled, "Come!" He entered and found Ariana stretching between her workbench and storage shelves, trying to push a half-fallen book back into place on a high shelf with one hand and cradling a bowl with the other.

"Oh, good!" she gasped. "You can help me."

Shianan dashed across the room and reached for the bowl. "Here, I'll take—"

"No!" she snapped, but without jerking back. "No, don't touch that, it's nearly pure phlogiston. Can you take the book?"

He reached over her and pressed the book into its place. "Got it."

She relaxed but kept the bowl steady. "Thanks. I caught my foot on the table leg and threw myself against the cabinet to keep from falling with the phlogiston, which seemed like a good idea at the time. Then I was terrified of dropping the book into it or spilling on the whole shelf." She grinned. "Thanks for saving me."

Thanks for saving me.

Shianan stayed still, faintly smiling, as her flippant words lanced through him.

Ariana had already turned away toward the rear room. "I just stopped in to separate some of this for Mage Tadak. Give me one moment to put it safely away and I'll be ready to go."

Shianan shook free and moved away from the shelf. He took a folded report from his wallet and read it again, letting his mind fret over more familiar worries.

"What's that?" asked Ariana, returning. "It's making you frown."

"Just a patrol that got into trouble." Shianan folded and replaced the report. "Nothing to worry your fair head about."

Ariana placed her hands on her hips. "Shianan! I'm a Mage of the Circle!"

"Don't talk down to mages," advised a new voice. "They can turn you into an alley rat if you annoy them."

They turned toward the open door, where Mage Parma stood

51

in her silver robes.

"I wasn't speaking down to her," Shianan said, a little defensive. He'd meant the comment to subtly carry his tentative compliment, but now he could hear and regret the dismissal in his clumsy attempt. "It's a military concern, and the Circle wouldn't ordinarily be involved." He tried a grin. "Besides, I'm pretty sure she can't really turn me into a rat."

Ariana snorted. Mage Parma smiled. "That's probably true. Ariana's only the Black Mage, after all." She raised an eyebrow significantly.

Shianan hesitated, uncertain how to respond.

Ariana laughed aloud. "I think we'll be fine without any rats today, thank you. Was there something you wanted?"

Mage Parma stepped inside. "The larger treatise on Gehrn history is gone from the library, and I thought you might have borrowed it after recent events."

Ariana shook her head. "Not at all. I'm happy to remain ignorant about them. What do you need a history of the Gehrn for?"

Mage Parma waved her hand in dismissal. "A question about the ongoing trial. Nasty, exhausting business all around. Perhaps your father has it. I'll keep looking."

"I'll let you know if I happen across it," Ariana said. "Shall we go, Shianan?"

He offered his arm, and she took it, and it was splendid.

"One moment," Mage Parma said, and Shianan's stomach tightened. But she only plucked a piece of string from Ariana's dark shoulder. Then she took a step back to allow them through the door. "Have a good morning, wherever you're going."

"The paper market," Ariana answered. "I need some new packet slips, and I want to introduce Shianan to a friend."

Shianan hadn't known they were meeting someone. The news that she wanted him to meet a friend warmed him.

The market crowd was swollen even so early, and they had to squeeze their way through past some of the more popular stalls. Ariana purchased a bundle of small sheets which could be folded into powder packets, and then she led Shianan to a bookbinding shop. "Hello, Ranne!"

"Ariana!"

The two women embraced as Shianan stood awkwardly, and then Ariana turned to him. "This is Ranne, and we've been friends for years and years. Ranne, this is my friend Shianan. Well, the Count of Bailaha, I'm sorry."

"Shianan will be fine," he said quickly. The bastard had no ground to parade status; his title was only armor to be used among the court. "I use my military title more than my noble one, and you're exempt from soldiers' discipline."

Ranne laughed and put out her hand. "Nice to meet you, Shianan, then."

The words hung pulsing warm in the air. Only a few months ago he had told Ariana there was no one to call him by his name, and now he was being introduced by it. "It's good to meet you, too."

"Military, eh?" Ranne smiled, and he saw she was working hard at not recognizing him as the bastard. "So what will you do, now that the war is over?"

The question struck him as if for the first time. What would he do now? He was a soldier, a commander, a defense against the Ryuven—but with the shield restored, what need was there of these?

Ranne must have seen the change in his eyes. "But of course you'll be protecting us from bandits and the warlords to the south." She glanced at Ariana.

"Oh, Shianan," Ariana said, smiling, "with the war ended, you can be anything you want."

He made his head move up and down, but it was not a nod. She did not understand. He had never been what he wanted, would never be.

Ariana and Ranne were already talking again, and they did not notice when Shianan turned to examine a stack of unbound books waiting for covers. He needed only a moment, and then he could face them again.

How quickly his mood could swing, when he was with her, from elation to despair. She weakened him, opened him anew to emotions he had long controlled, and he could not understand why he liked it.

CHAPTER NINE

Shianan knocked at the courtyard door to the prince's office and jerked at his tunic. This time Soren would not turn him away. He would keep his promise.

"Commander!" came a voice behind him, and Shianan glanced over his shoulder as the door opened. The servant at the door looked from Shianan to the approaching soldier and waited. The soldier jogged toward them and then drew himself up to face Shianan. "Sir, there's a messenger at your office asking for you. You're summoned to the king's presence."

"Who's keeping the door open?" came a voice from within.

The slave stepped backward and answered the voice. "It's Bailaha, master."

The soldier and Shianan executed twin bows as Soren came to the door. "Becknam! You've come. Please, come in."

Shianan hesitated. "Your Highness, I've just received word the king has sent for me." He gestured to the soldier beside him.

Soren looked sharply at the soldier. "The king?"

"He's sent for the commander, Your Highness."

Something shifted in Soren's expression. "I see. Well, Becknam, last time I found myself unable to meet as promised. This time, it seems you have duties which call you." He hesitated. "Will you come and see me when you are finished? This afternoon?"

Shianan was surprised and somewhat unsettled by the prince's tone. "I will come to you when I can, Your Highness. As soon as I have answered the king."

Soren nodded. "This afternoon," he repeated, making Shianan wonder at the urgency. And then the door closed, leaving Shianan to blink at it.

He had little time to wonder, however; the king had called him. Had the queen complained of him last night? He swallowed against his unease and asked, "Where am I to attend the king?"

"In the old wing, sir," came the answer.

Shianan's stomach sank. She had complained of him. Protests that he had not meant to offend her, that he had not known she would even be present, all would be in vain. The king would be angry, and he would tell Shianan how unwelcome he was at royal events.

Shianan took a deep breath. Unkind words had not killed him yet. There would be nothing new in hearing the queen despised her husband's bastard and Shianan should keep his offensive self out of sight.

There were few courtiers; the king was not holding other audiences or meetings here. Shianan was admitted and knelt inside the door as the king waved the servant outside.

"Rise, Bailaha, and come closer. We have business with you."

The king was not alone. Prince Alasdair was seated at a table with him. Surely the young prince would not be involved in chastening Shianan's attendance of the ball?

"Bailaha, you have served us for years."

"From my childhood, Your Majesty. I surely was not much use as a boy, but I have been allowed to serve more in recent years."

"In positions of authority granted in reward for your loyalty," agreed the king. "And you claim you are a loyal servant."

Shianan bowed his head, partly in respect and partly to hide the sting of the words. "You know I am, my lord."

"And are you loyal to our line? Will you serve the next king with equal fervor?"

"My lord, I am a faithful servant of the throne. I have fought beneath the royal banner for our people, not merely for one man, however deserving."

"Hmm." King Jerome rose from his chair and came around the table. "Then why do you show disrespect to our prince? How can you disdain your rightful lord?" He beckoned Alasdair to join them. "You shall honor and obey Prince Alasdair as you would any other royal."

Shianan stared, feeling a treacherous expression of confused incredulity break over his face. "I—Your Majesty, what have I done to—"

"Be quiet." King Jerome jerked his head toward the floor. "Kneel."

Shianan obeyed, his mind spinning. He had not even seen Alasdair since the night of the search, and the next morning the king had seemed pleased. What could have happened? What story had reached him?

"You will apologize to your prince for your ill manners," said Jerome flatly.

Shianan was stunned. "My lord, when did I show ill manners to the prince?"

"Denial will not serve you! You will apologize."

Shianan blinked up at them, seeing the king's stern face and Alasdair's smug smile. He dropped his eyes to the floor, as much to block the view as to demonstrate respect, and fumbled for words. "My lord prince, if I have treated you out of accord with your station, I humbly apologize and beg your forgiveness." It galled to abase himself further before Alasdair, but there could be no further protest to the king.

Alasdair made a tiny sound nearly like a giggle. Shianan shifted on his knee, hoping for permission to rise. Was this why he'd been called? To apologize for a slight to the spoiled young prince?

"Very good, Bailaha," allowed the king. "And now, you will swear your oath to him."

The words shocked Shianan. He lifted his head and stared in open amazement at the king. "Sire?"

"You will remember your place!" snapped the king. "You may believe because the Court of the High Star did not condemn you that you are privileged above your circumstances, but that is not the case, Bailaha. You will acknowledge and respect the distinction between your position and the prince's. If you are trustworthy as you claim, you will swear service and obedience to my son."

The words cut Shianan as if to draw blood. For a moment he could not respond.

"Bailaha!" The king was displeased by the hesitation. "You will pledge your fealty to your prince."

Shianan licked his lips and clenched his fingers on his bent knee. "Your Majesty," he began carefully, "I honor my prince as I do my king. But it is you, sire, who are my lord and master."

"Fealty to your prince will not conflict with fealty to your king."

"But I am meant to serve as a soldier, for the good of Your Majesty and the kingdom, and I cannot in good conscience pledge to obey a boy who may not comprehend—"

The king's kick caught him in the chest as he knelt, taking his breath and shoving him backward. "Mongrel!" snapped Jerome. "Swear!"

Alasdair's eyes jerked wide and his smile vanished. Shianan stared in hurt shock as he gulped air. "Sire..."

"Will you deny your king's command? Is it true your ambition makes an enemy of your prince?" The king kicked him again, this time striking his shoulder as Shianan involuntarily shrank backward. "Is that why you seek recognition in the court?"

"No!" protested Shianan breathlessly.

"Then swear your obedience!"

Shianan fell forward, his eyes on the floor before their feet. He slowly resumed his formal posture. *You are a slave to your master. You do not choose your master; he is chosen for you.* "I..."

"Swear now, or declare yourself a traitor."

You must obey your master's commands, even when you would not. You are a slave. Shianan licked his lips. "I am a loyal servant of the throne," he began, hearing his voice quiver. "I solemnly pledge my service to the crown and to those who might yet bear it. I hear and obey my lord the king and then his—son, my prince." He gulped. "I swear obedience to my lord the Prince Alasdair Laguna." *You must obey without question the orders of a master you cannot choose.* "I pledge my service to him, as it pleases my king."

He swallowed against his closing throat, terrified his humiliation might spill into sight. Above him, he could just see Alasdair's face slowly lose its horror at his father's violence and regain its pleased gratification as Shianan, shamed, swore to obey him. Shianan clenched his teeth and his fists, wanting only to flee—flee the room, the fortress, the city.

The king nodded stiffly. "That is acceptable. Now I have your word to respect my son as he is due. See that you keep it in your daily actions."

Shianan only nodded, not trusting his voice.

"You take too much upon yourself, Bailaha. You presume to appear at our court ball although your presence is not wanted while your queen was here. You treat your prince with disrespect. You recover the Shard in a way to draw the most attention and laud to yourself instead of correctly reporting your suspicions to your superiors, as if you craved glory and advancement. Is your word good?"

Shianan closed his eyes against traitorous emotion, his face bowed toward the floor. "I am your servant, my lord."

The king did not move. "I wonder if I did not make a mistake in bringing you here." He sighed. "Bailaha, I have seen you serve faithfully in my army—but within the capital, when you move through the court..."

Shianan swallowed. "I am ever your servant, my lord."

"You may go, Bailaha."

Shianan nodded tightly before opening his eyes. He rose and, keeping his head bowed, backed to the door.

Once safely outside, he passed a hand over his face and started briskly down the corridor. He wanted to be away, he didn't know where, he wanted to be away from the castle and the fortress. He wanted to see Ariana, to hear her talk of things which had nothing to do with the king's sons. Any of them.

He brushed again at his face. At least Luca had found his freedom. One of them was no longer bound.

Luca came to a grateful halt as the wagon's wheels stopped. Beside him, Andrew stumbled and jostled him. "Sorry," he muttered. Kitchen work had kept him busy but not conditioned for the foothills.

They had the additional misfortune to be alongside the former overseer, whom Matteo's overseers seemed to have singled out for punishment. With Andrew's slow feet and the big slave's sore back, their line had lagged behind the wagon and the switch had visited them all.

Luca was thirsty. He'd missed his opportunity for water that morning, and the road's dust clung to his throat. He started to lower himself to the ground, but an overseer was approaching their line.

"Where's the cookslave?" The overseer frowned at the line. "Which of you is it?"

Andrew raised his free hand. "I am."

The overseer came to unfasten him. "Hand out bread while we change teams, and you'll make the mush tonight. Meal's in the fourth wagon, boy can fetch water with you." He released Andrew and gestured him on his way. Then he paused and looked critically at the big slave. "And what are you looking at? Keep your eyes down!" The overseer moved back a step and the line flinched as one. The switch struck the slave's back, making him grunt. "You'll lose that sniffy look or we'll skin it from you. Go ahead, stare again—got your eyeful?"

The slave shifted under the residual sting of the switch, eyes on the ground. The overseer stomped on, faced with too many tasks to linger and torment them. The slave crouched and went carefully to his knees, grimacing.

"They don't like you much," observed Luca, sinking to the

ground as well.

The slave shook his head. "They can't. It's one stroke of bad luck that keeps them from my place." He threw a dark look at the slave chained beside him. "It's easier to believe I deserve it than to face that they could be here in the span of a bad day."

Luca nodded. That made a sort of sense. The former overseer was strong, well-spoken—if he could fall from a master's capricious grace, so might anyone.

Even Luca.

Another stockman passed and, without warning, struck the man again. He grinned at the yelp and snapped, "Get out of the way. We want room behind this line." He brought down the switch once more, and this time it bit across Luca's shoulders. "Move up!"

Luca and the others obeyed, bunching against the rear of the wagon. Luca shrugged against the sting, wishing he had a hand free to rub it. Still, the hurt was not what the switch was on bare skin, and almost nothing to the whip skimming flesh from his bones. He would endure.

CHAPTER TEN

Ariana looked around her office and workroom, breathing deep the familiar scents of clay and ink and the pungent perfume of arcane materials. It would be good to settle into routine again. She had spent much of the morning with Ranne and Bethia, giving them a carefully told version of her adventure—keeping the role of the slave boy Tam artfully minimized, repeating the supposition that she had been released out of respect for the Circle as worthy opponents—and then recounting the ball with Bethia for Ranne, and letting them spoil her with sweets and welcome. But she had been away from her work for long weeks and, as glad as she was to have returned to her own world, she was beginning to feel uncomfortable with all the close attention. She had always thought to earn her place in the Circle and her respect there, rather than to fall into it by ill chance and a concealed Ryuven.

She closed her door, guarding herself against the string of well-wishers and curiosity-seekers who would certainly start again, and turned to her table.

A part of her wished she had stayed with Ranne and Bethia. She felt a subtle unease here in her workroom, which made no sense. That was just the disruption of her absence, and everything would fall into place again now that all was normal once more.

Where to start?

There were a number of projects waiting for attention, including a new ink Mage Renstil had suggested, infused with energy to speed arcane tasks. That might be fun to experiment with.

But they were always in need of healing amulets, long to form, thirsty for power, and familiar in their execution. She could start a fresh set of amulets in her sleep. She pointed at her athanor and sparked the little furnace to life.

Or she tried, but nothing happened. No power leapt at her guidance.

She looked at her hand, as if it had betrayed her, and at the athanor. She closed her eyes, envisioning the magic more clearly than she should have needed, and tried to light the tiny fire.

Nothing happened. She felt nothing.

Confused, she opened her eyes and tried to raise a small flame in her hand. Then she turned and tried to push a stack of papers from the table. She groped for power, feeling as if she were grasping in the dark for an elusive strand. There was nothing there.

The magic was gone.

Her heart raced. What had the Ryuven world done to her? But no, she'd worked magic since returning—she had helped with the creation of the renewed shield.

She hurried to the board of colored crystals in the corner of her room, brushing the white crystal to harmonize with the matching stone in the White Mage's workroom. But without a little flare of power, she touched only her own stone.

Air wheezed in her throat. She was the Black Mage, a Mage of the Circle, and her power was pledged to the good of the kingdom. She had trained all her life for this, this was to *be* her life, and she had nothing.

She left her workroom and started for her father's office, forcing herself to breathe slowly—a count of four in, a count of four out—and to walk instead of drawing attention by running. She knocked and let herself in without waiting for an answer.

He looked up and saw her expression. "What is it, darling? What's wrong?"

On the edge of panic, she raised an unsteady hand and gestured uselessly at the items on his desk. "I have no magic." Her voice shook. "*I have no magic.*"

Ariana huddled in a chair at her father's table, her arms wrapped about herself. She wasn't cold, but she somehow felt she should be.

Someone knocked at the door. "Ewan?"

Her father opened to admit the Silver Mage and locked it behind her. Elysia Parma went directly to Ariana and sat beside her. "Oh, Ariana. Tell me."

Ariana had to lick her lips to speak. "It's gone," she said simply. "I reach for the magic and—and it's not there. I can't see it, can't feel it. There's nothing. It's like I'm not a mage."

"Show me. Spark that candle."

It was a simple task, a beginner's lesson so ubiquitous as to be a joke, and Ariana teared up to think that she could not do it. Obediently she raised a hand and pointed at the candle, and obediently she called the spark. Nothing happened, not so much as a glow on the curled wick.

Mage Parma's face betrayed no trace of disappointment, and Ariana wasn't sure if she loved or hated her for it. Mage Parma asked, "When did this start?"

Ariana shook her head. "I don't know. I suppose it has to be something from the Ryuven world." She sniffed. "The magic there— it's so strong. It nearly killed me. That's why they drugged me, to dull my senses." She tried to clear her closing throat. "But when I needed the magic, to help Maru, I let it all in, I let it run through me. I must have burned myself out."

Mage Parma sat back. "And did you use any magic after that, while you were there?"

Ariana shook her head. "Only a little, and it didn't always go right." She remembered a moment of alarm as a shield failed to coalesce around her. "But I didn't try much. I didn't want to do anything that might appear to be a threat, not when Oniwe had only left me alone because he thought I was helpless and useless."

"That was wise," her father said. "You were the first human mage to survive. They might well have ensured that you didn't."

"But we can't be sure exactly when this started," Mage Parma said. "Though you helped with the shield."

Ariana licked her lips. "I did."

Mage Parma glanced at Ariana's father, who leaned forward. "And?"

Ariana should have felt shame at the admission, but all other emotions were buried beneath the loss of magic. "I was afraid. When the shield came up, and I saw it rushing toward me—just like that day when it collapsed."

Her father nodded. "That's understandable. But you did the magic with us?"

"It was hard. I did it, but it was difficult. I thought at the time it was just because it was such a large spell, requiring so many mages, but was it perhaps because I was losing my magic?"

Mage Parma pursed her lips.

"Can you see anything?" asked her father.

Elysia Parma scented magic, and the Amber Mage felt it through the skin, but Ariana was a seer. She watched the Silver Mage cup her palm, as if preparing to throw a bolt, and she closed her eyes.

She looked, she hoped, she wished.

"Nothing," she choked. "Just my own eyelids." She opened her eyes and looked back and forth between them. "I'm only the Black Mage," she said, her voice unsteady, "and I haven't been in the Circle for long. You can replace me."

"Replace you?" repeated her father. "What are you—"

"The Circle is supposed to be the best mages, the most useful in case of need. I'm not even a mage now."

Mage Parma put a hand on her forearm. "You are a mage. You have been a mage for years. Now something has happened, and yes, it's something we haven't seen before—but we can work to learn what it is. Don't give up so easily on yourself, or on us."

"But the Circle—"

"Needs mages who can keep their heads through surprise."

"Surprise? This isn't a surprise!" Ariana shook her head. "I have lost my magic. I was only barely in the Circle anyway, and—"

"Why do you say that?" interrupted her father. "You are a full Mage of the Circle. Didn't you hold Mage Callahan in awe when he was the Black?"

She almost laughed, and it came out as something like a hiccup. "Not just for being in the Circle."

Her father smiled. "Now be kind. He's a bit... intense, but that's all."

"Ariana, listen," Mage Parma said. "If we determine that nothing can be done, that you really have lost all magic, then we'll make the necessary decision at that point. But we are not yet at that point. Don't you remember a time when you couldn't light a candle? And didn't you work your way past it?"

Ariana looked at her in incredulous despair. "I was a child then."

"And when Mage Odderman broke his leg and could not walk, just like a child, didn't he work to get better?"

"This isn't a broken leg!"

"Obviously not. You're tough; you wouldn't whine so much about that."

Ariana blinked at her and then looked at her father, who did not quite betray her by smiling but did nod in agreement. "Don't panic," he said. "Let's see what's to be done."

She took a breath, trying to calm her racing heart. Magic required concentration and focus, and agitation would work against her. "How?"

"Let me look over my notes from your return," Mage Parma said. "I'll see what I can come up with. Let's talk tomorrow. For now, go outside, walk around, breathe. I know it's an impossible task, but at least try to get your mind off this. Clear your head so we can start fresh."

CHAPTER ELEVEN

Ariana closed the black door behind her and checked the latch. Then she glanced up the hallway and, seeing it empty, placed her fingers over the mechanism.

Previously, the bolt had always flashed a bright yellow in her mind's eye and seemed to interlink with the jamb. It was probably foolish for the Black Mage, lowest of the Great Circle, to attempt a magical lock on anything within the Wheel. The higher mages could unwork her spell in a moment. But she liked to think her workrooms were secure from any patrolling soldiers or passing grey mages who grew curious, and it could do no harm.

Today, however, the latch was only a latch, the bolt only a bolt, and there was no arcane lock overlapping the ordinary one.

She swallowed her panic and turned toward the exit, holding her chin rigidly high.

She left the Wheel and started across the courtyard toward the gate. There were vendors within the grounds, of course, but there would be a greater variety of offerings in the city markets. *Clear your head*—as if such a thing were possible.

A hooded figure, head bent against the weather, was crossing the courtyard. Despite the billowing cloak she recognized his movement. "Shianan! Wait a moment!"

He must not have heard her through the wind, for he didn't slow. He was going toward his office and quarters, and she cut the angle to meet him. "Shianan!"

His head lifted and turned slightly toward her, but the sheltering hood shaded his face. "My lady mage."

"Oh, don't be so formal. We're old friends."

Speaking would make it too real. She couldn't say it yet, and not in the street where all could see.

"I was going for something to eat. Do you have a few minutes?" She took a step around him, trying to find his eyes. "Here, stand still. I can hardly see you."

"No," he began, and his hand moved from beneath the cloak. But Ariana had already caught sight of his expression. He blinked and looked away. "No, I'm afraid I won't join you in a meal."

"You look as if someone had died," she said bluntly. "What's wrong? Did your meeting with the prince go badly?"

"The prince?" Shianan repeated. "Oh, no, I could not meet with him, after all; I was summoned elsewhere." He glanced down. "I'm sorry, I didn't mean to frighten you. It's nothing."

"I am a Mage of the Circle," Ariana said firmly, pressing down her quick doubt, "trained to face rampaging Ryuven, and the sourest expression you might produce could not frighten me. And don't lie to me. If we're friends enough to call one another by name, we're friends enough to be honest. This isn't nothing—you look like a kicked dog. What happened?"

Shianan winced and then sighed. "I'm sorry, my lady mage. Ariana. I'm not at my best presently."

Her stomach clenched as she remembered what she should never have seen. She reached for his hand and folded it in hers. "Then come with me and think of something else for a few minutes, at least. Have you eaten?"

He made a face. "I'm not even close to hungry."

"Well, come with me while I find something, anyway, and we can at least keep one another company." She gently tugged him after her. "You don't even have to talk, if you don't want to. I can tell you all about distilling the dust of inferior gems and ordinary inks into a new ink to draw out runes and sigils without the need to finish them magically. Isn't that fascinating? Isn't that worth staying in the weather to hear?" She gave him a self-deprecating grin.

He smiled tiredly. "Of course, my lady mage. And at the moment I could listen to you recite the runic alphabet, if there is such a thing."

"There is, but probably not in the way you're thinking of it."

"I don't care. You can say it backward and I won't know the difference. Just keep talking." He glanced down at the hand she still held. "I think I'm glad you spotted me."

She gave his hand a squeeze. "If you're not eating, would you rather watch me eat a pork pie or the leg of some sort of fowl?"

He hesitated and then gave a long sigh. "The little goodwife with the cart at the northeast corner outside the gate has an excellent mutton pie. I'd recommend that. And you need a cup of ale from the Hawking Babe."

"I haven't been there. Is it so good?"

"Very good." He flexed his fingers within hers and finally

curled them about her hand. "I'll treat you to a taste."

Ariana desperately dredged her mind to chat amiably of unimportant things as they walked, about the ink they were developing, new pendants to hold mage healing for future use, how she was frustrated she had nothing new to contribute and longed for some magical breakthrough that would make them all notice her. That veered dangerously close to her fresh fear, but she fought to keep her tone light, pretending all was as it had been that morning. He had just come from a private meeting with the king; she couldn't break her news to him while he was in such a state. "Ranne and Bethia gave me a lovely welcome party, a little late but official by their declaration— you know Lady Bethia, Duke Devinne's daughter. She wanted to test for the Circle, but there was only one opening and it went to me. And she's been quiet about it, but I know she thinks I must have achieved everything at last. I know because my own goal was always to become the Black Mage and finally join the Circle. But now that I'm a part of the Circle, I'm just another low-ranking mage again! So I wish I could develop something really outstanding and be recognized."

Her throat closed. *I wish I could keep my magic and stay in the Circle.*

Shianan nodded. "To be recognized, and appreciated, and to be really indispensable."

She squeezed his hand, chiding herself for her self-pity. No matter what happened with the Circle, her father loved her. "More or less, yes. Are you sure you don't want a pie?"

He shook his head.

They walked on, and she became aware of his gaze, beginning now to observe her instead of avoid her. "I thought you'd be in the Wheel at this time," he said, and she thought his words were deceptively light. "How is your work progressing?"

"It's fine." And now she'd lied to him, quick and unthinking. She grasped for something that was less false but not yet the awful truth. "I thought I'd go out for a walk, even in the wind, and try to clear my head."

"Are you tired?"

"No, I—I haven't been sleeping well. I have dreams, but I can't remember them." That was true at least, if incomplete.

"What kind of—"

"I can't remember them, I said," Ariana interrupted, more sharply than she'd meant to. "Look, there she is!"

The short vendor gave her a warm pie and a friendly if gappy smile, and they started for the tavern Shianan had mentioned.

"It's been a long while," Ariana said, breaking off a piece of the pie and watching the released steam curl into the air. "Maybe you could come some night for supper again."

"You're inviting me?"

"I thought you were buying me an ale. Can't I then invite you for supper?" She proffered the chunk of pie. "Would you like a bite, at least?"

He started to answer, hesitated, and then gave her an embarrassed grin. "It does smell good."

She felt better now he'd relaxed enough to accept food. "Take it. And tell me how the soldiers are doing—in their training, I mean. Don't you have some sort of royal review coming soon?"

"Yes, for the Founding Festival. They'll need to present themselves well, and most of them I think will do it. There are only a few I might need to assign to clean privies that day, to keep them from sight." He paused and glanced at the sign over them, a painted raptor bearing a chubby infant on its back. "Here's our tavern."

He ordered two ales and led her to a corner away from the midday press. She tasted her drink. "This is good! I'm glad I found you."

He glanced at her and then down at the table. "So am I. I mean, for lunch. And—well, as you saw, I wasn't in a pleasant mood. Thank you for tolerating me, and for helping to alleviate it."

He was helping her at least as much. "What did he want? Or may you tell?"

"Who?"

"The king." She hesitated. "If it's something you can't discuss, or don't wish to, that's fine, of course."

He stared at her. "I didn't think I'd told you I'd seen the king."

"Only the king could call you away from the prince." And she had seen him in a similar despondency once before.

"Clever." He sighed. "It's—nothing to trouble you. Please don't worry over it." He smiled wanly and took a drink of his ale.

She wouldn't press. "So when will you meet with His Highness?"

Shianan frowned. "I was going back to my office. He said to come when I could and, well, you saw my state of mind."

"But if—that means the prince-heir gave you an open invitation, Shianan! That must mean something. You should go."

He looked thoughtful. "You think..."

"I think if Prince Soren asks you to visit when you may, you certainly may. He seemed friendly enough last night, no?"

Shianan nodded. "I have only paperwork this afternoon, and that's even more distasteful than waiting upon royalty."

Ariana chuckled. "And with that bald confession, I know we're truly friends. Let's finish our drinks. You should go to the prince, and I should test my ink."

They walked back to the fortress without speaking, but it was not the terse silence of before. Ariana glanced at Shianan and thought unexpectedly of their journey across the mountains to bring the Shard. She had not thought then that the cool, upright commander might become a trusted and trusting friend.

Except they were each keeping secrets from the other even now. Not because she did not trust him; rather, she craved the normalcy of being with him and not thinking of what had happened, without him looking at her differently, and she couldn't pour her grief over his depression. Still, it felt like she had trusted him more when she had known him less, burying dead farmers in the mountains.

But he had shown glimpses of his true nature even then. He had come to rescue her when Tamaryl was first revealed, risking himself and the Shard, and then refrained from killing at Ariana's urging. He'd treated Tam's wounded shoulder though he knew the boy was a hated enemy.

Tam... She'd been trying very hard to avoid thinking of Tam. She missed him a dozen times a day: returning to her home without his boyish welcome, visiting her father's workroom without its short famulus, thinking of the Ryuven. He had been a part of their household for as long as she could remember, and then he had been a family secret, and then he had been a friend in a distant, hostile world.

And he had hinted at feelings for her, but he had gone before she could even determine her response. She felt unsettled, as if they had unfinished business—but that did nothing to assuage the aching hole he'd left as the friendly young member of her household she'd known all her life.

Shianan's fingers brushed hers and retracted. She glanced at him, unsure if the contact had been deliberate, but he looked straight ahead as he asked, "Would you like me to walk you to the Wheel?"

She shook her head. "The prince's office is nearer. The Wheel is out of your way." Belatedly she wondered if she should have accepted, but she had been thinking faintly of Tamaryl's discomfiting final words to her.

Unfinished business. Aching farewell. Tam and her magic, both gone. She swallowed against the rising lump in her throat, and her pulse began to pound in her ears. Irrational feelings, grief for what had not died, coming when she was unprepared—

Shianan nodded stiffly. "Then I'll turn off here." He stopped at the stone arch which marked the end of the common yard and faced Ariana. "Thanks. For walking with me, I mean."

"It was my pleasure, thank you. And now I must get back to work. Magical ink, you know." She mimed busywork and forced a grin she did not feel. "Now that the shield's up and the war's over, we'll have to make ourselves useful in other ways. No more Ryuven to fight."

Shianan's eyes flicked away and he swallowed visibly. "How's Tam? Is he gone?"

The question struck Ariana hard. "He's—" She gulped, her throat closing. "He's gone—oh, no." Tears brimmed at her eyes and she rubbed at them. "I'm sorry, I don't know why—"

"What?" Shianan looked almost frightened. "What's wrong? What happened?"

Everything converged at once upon the fragile dam she had put up, and the humiliating tears broke loose. "Oh, this is awful!" She turned away. "I shouldn't cry, not for this. Not for Tam." Her words blurred in her uneven breathing.

Shianan's hands reached for her but hesitated, hovering uncertainly. "What happened?" he repeated.

"Everything! The shield and the Ryuven world and everything. My magic—helpless." She shoved tears from her eyes. "And he said—no, I can't say—and when the shield—and he kissed me, and I wasn't expecting—I was off guard... The mages were at the door, but he just—and I can't talk about it, not even with my father, because I don't think he knows, and—"

"Ariana!" Shianan seized her upper arms, fingers squeezing too hard. "Ariana, did that Ryuven touch—did he—to you...?"

Ariana stared at him for an eternal instant, unable even to sob as she tried to comprehend what he asked. He thought—he thought Tam had—

He heard nothing she said, only his own twisted imagination of what Tam had done, that it had been like the terrible attack on Maru—

She threw her arms out, shoving him backward. "How dare you?" she demanded. Tam would *never* hurt her as Daranai had hurt Maru. "How dare you accuse him so!" She could not speak beyond that. Angry, helpless, useless tears overcame her and she bolted, fleeing across the courtyard and pulling her concealing hood close as she went.

CHAPTER TWELVE

Shianan stared after Ariana, jaw hanging, the stinging in his singed palms nothing beside his pained confusion. He wanted to call after her, to follow her, but he could not move.

A scuff of leather on stone broke his trance and he wheeled. Behind him, Soren hesitated, a look of chagrined embarrassment on his face. They each froze.

The prince spoke first. "Do you want me to walk away and return as if I've only just arrived?"

Shianan blinked at him, unable to think, and then something seemed to break within him. He sank against the stone arch. "No," he managed.

His knees weakened as the day's wrongs overwhelmed him. Some part of his brain recognized that he owed obeisance to the prince, but his body moved too awkwardly.

Soren swore. "What happened? It's none of my business, of course. But you—what magic did she do? Are you hurt?"

The wall was cold against Shianan's cheek. He wanted to sink into the stones and be gone forever. What humiliation was possibly left to him this day?

Soren seized his arm, making Shianan jump. Before he could speak, the prince leaned close and said fiercely, "Oh, no, don't even think of it. Your life is in the service of the crown, isn't it?" He squeezed Shianan's arm. "Isn't it?"

"Yes, my lord," answered Shianan dully. *More than ever.*

"And you wouldn't abandon your duty, would you? Or rob the crown of your service?" Soren's voice grew sharper. "Would you?"

Shianan blinked, startled by the prince's intensity. "No, my lord."

"Good." Soren released him. "Then come with me. I have something which, if it won't put everything right, will at least make the world spin the other direction for a few minutes. Let's go."

Shianan obediently followed the short distance to the rooms where the prince conducted his political business. He was numb with accumulated disappointment and shame, and it hardly mattered what happened next.

"Ethan!" called Soren. There was no response. Soren kicked the door behind them and gestured Shianan toward the open room on the left. "Go on, I'll be there in a moment. Ethan!"

The servant appeared in the far doorway opposite them, his eyebrow raised and a significant look on his face. "What is it?" asked Soren. Shianan took a step into the left doorway.

"Soren!" called a female voice. "I've been waiting for you. Why didn't you answer my—" The voice stopped suddenly as Shianan looked with horror at the queen, seated in the prince's sitting room. "Oh. I see."

Shianan's demoralized knees gave way and he dropped to the floor, nearer a collapse than a conscious decision to kneel. His lips moved, shaping the words, "Your Majesty," but he could not produce a sound.

"My lady mother," Soren said in dull surprise behind him. "I didn't expect you."

"Obviously not," she replied coolly. "You told me you found the commander distantly interesting. You never said you were in the habit of inviting him to your private sitting room." Her voice grew acidic. "Are these all the manners he has been taught? He tends to fall to his knees whenever I see him."

"Mother, please!" snapped Soren.

Shianan licked his lips. "Your Majesty, I swear the prince has not—this is the first time. If it pleases Your Majesty, I will go—"

"I would be pleased if you'd stay," Soren said firmly. "My lady mother, I respectfully request that while you are in my office you show a measure of respect to my guests. Surely you trust me enough to have some small faith in my friends?"

Shianan closed his eyes, not daring to witness the queen's response. He should not have seen her rebuked. He could only pretend he was a piece of statuary, a tile in the floor, a slave without social presence.

"Is that how you see it? That I should trust your invitation to this man, of whom we've heard recent complaints?"

"Considering what you know of me, my lady mother, are you justified in assuming I invite a viper into my chamber? Or is it possible I might have reason to believe this Bailaha is not all that you've heard?"

Queen Azalie hesitated. "If you say I should judge your word against Alasdair's, then I suppose I should wait and listen. And you are quite right, it is the worst of manners to insult your guests in your rooms. I apologize. Stand, Bailaha, and join us."

Shianan didn't think he could move.

"Bailaha?"

"Peace, mother. I brought him in part because he needs something strongly medicinal. Ethan? And something softer for Her Majesty, as well." And then Soren's boots were before Shianan's blinking eyes. "Give me your hand, Becknam."

Shianan lifted his head and gaped at the prince for an eternal heartbeat, and then he grasped the prince's hand and was pulled to his unsteady feet. The prince left him within comfortable distance of a sturdy table and turned back to the queen. "I'm sorry. I'd not received word you were coming when I'd asked Becknam to come for a talk. I think I'm safe in assuming he would be happy of a few minutes to himself while he waited on our business. Ethan can see him settled in my office."

Ethan slipped beside Shianan and proffered a tray. Shianan took the drink before thinking that the queen and prince should have been served first. He glanced at the slave, but Ethan was standing immobile behind him, watching the two royals expressionlessly. Shianan eyed the drink in his hand, wondering if he dared taste it before they were served.

"No," answered the queen, "don't send him away. In truth, I came largely because of him, so he might as well be present."

Shianan hastily took a gulp. Liquid fire scorched down his throat and he choked, coughing as the drink burnt through him.

"Steady," he dimly heard Soren say. "I promised something that would make the world spin the other way, yes? Mother, I'm afraid we don't have your favorite Cheerling. If I'd known you were coming to Alham, I would have laid in a supply."

"Thank you, Soren, this will be fine." The queen accepted a drink of a different color and sipped genteelly at it.

Ethan glanced at his master with a questioning look and Soren shook his head. "I haven't decided yet. Have you got speech again yet, Becknam? That will shear the tongue from your mouth if you're not careful." He looked seriously at Shianan. "What business did the king have for you this morning?"

Shianan froze, staring at the cup in his hand. "My lord..."

"Did he ask you to keep it in confidence?"

"No, my lord."

"Can you not, in good conscience, tell us what business he had?"

Shianan closed his eyes and swallowed. "After this day, I have no pride to spare. He wanted my loyalty to His Highness, Prince Alasdair."

There was an awkward pause. "Of course you would be expected to be loyal to the princes," the queen said slowly. "Is that all he asked of you?"

"That is all. He bade me kneel and swear my obedience to Prince Alasdair, who accepted it with all the dignity of his position."

"Alasdair was there?" Soren sounded surprised and— something more. "He swore you to Alasdair directly?"

Shianan saw the queen's eyes flash dangerously. Her voice was terse. "Soren, have you..."

"No, Mother. No, I have received no oaths. Not while my king lives." He exhaled in a long stream. "Ethan, I think I'll have what the commander is having."

Slow realization came to Shianan's jangled mind. The king had ordered an oath of allegiance to the younger prince, not the elder. Some might see it as the first act in arranging the succession to pass over the elder prince.

Shianan had seen it as his own complete humiliation, but now he recognized it as an affront to the only prince who had been civil and even kind toward him. "I'm sorry," he began, hardly hearing his own voice. "I'm sorry, Your Highness. It wasn't—"

"It wasn't your doing," Soren interrupted, almost annoyed. "Mother, do you—has he said anything?" He turned to face the queen. "Has he said anything at all?"

Shianan blinked at the plaintive note underlying the prince's words. But that was hardly surprising from a man who had thought to be king one day, suddenly learning that perhaps he would not.

I still resent you, commander. I hate you for every big and small victory the king hangs over my head to show me just how far short I fall. Soren, the elder prince and apparent heir, fought for the king's eye just as Shianan did. He was unsettled, even frightened, by this news.

"He's said nothing to me, Soren," the queen answered quietly. "I hear only of your accomplishments and his pride. But perhaps this conversation should be continued another time."

"Your Highness," Shianan tried, "I would not—I protested that a military commander should not be sworn to a mere boy—" He faltered.

Soren turned with a grim smile. "You protested? I am almost glad to hear that, though it could not have done either of us any good. How did the king respond?"

Shianan glanced down, flinching at the hot, shameful memory. "His Majesty..."

But Soren must have read something in his hesitation, for his eyes narrowed. "And Alasdair," he muttered.

"Who was present?" asked the queen.

Shianan swallowed. "Only His Majesty and His Highness, my lady. And myself. No one else."

"Not even a slave?"

Only myself. "No one else, Your Majesty."

"Then, Soren," she said thoughtfully, "it's possible he meant only to straighten this morning's affairs. This was not a public gesture, this was a bit of housekeeping. It may not have been intended as a slight against you at all, though it seems he wasn't especially thoughtful about it."

For most of Shianan's life, one of his greatest fears was to be thought of as a political pawn, as that potential defined his danger and alienation. Now the king himself had drawn Shianan into the devices of succession, and he was helpless to escape.

"If he meant this only to ensure recognition of Alasdair," continued the queen, "then it will be simple enough to arrange for you to openly receive oaths from a few key nobles and officers. If the generals swear publicly their fealty to you, who can give more credence to a private vow from a commander?"

Soren hesitated. "If he was... But yes, you're probably right. He probably was caught up in our talk about Alasdair, and he did not intend a public..." His voice faded and he glanced toward Ethan. "Still—leave the queen's wine, Ethan, and send a note to His Grace that I'll want to see him at his earliest convenience tomorrow. I want to have that trade route agreement finished."

Ethan bowed and left. Shianan bit at his lip and stared at the chair beside him. The prince, too, needed accomplishments. Shianan felt ashamed to have seen his insecurity.

"Then," said Queen Azalie with a sidelong glance toward Shianan, "let us talk of something else entirely. You say this is your first visit, Bailaha?"

Shianan jumped. "Er, yes, Your Majesty, it is. My duties do not usually bring me here."

"You did not tell me much of yourself last night. Will you do so now?"

Shianan was utterly unprepared for a conversation with the queen. He could hardly think, reeling from the day's events. "Your Majesty could not be interested in the concerns of a mere soldier, my lady."

She raised an eyebrow. "You might be surprised what could interest me, Bailaha. But if you won't tell me of yourself, tell me of something else. I want to hear you speak."

Shianan hesitated. What was safe for conversation? What would she want to hear? When would she release him?

Soren smiled. "He has a slave of whom he's fond, like my Ethan or your Eve. What's his name? Luca?"

"Luca," repeated Shianan softly. Without warning his throat closed, and he had to blink firmly. "Luca is gone."

Soren opened his mouth in surprise. "He died?"

Shianan shook his head.

"But you would not have sold him? I thought—it seemed you liked him."

"I did." His throat swelled and closed. "But his brother came from the Wakari Coast to redeem him."

The queen looked from Shianan to Soren. Soren's face softened. "You let him go?"

"His family wanted him." Too late Shianan realized the danger of that thoughtless statement.

The queen, at least, seemed to have understood both possible meanings. She stiffened in her chair. "Well, it was good of you to send him to where he was wanted."

Shianan flinched and stared at the drink sloshing thinly at the bottom of his cup. He wanted to escape, to flee to his quarters, cold now without Luca to stoke the fire in anticipation of his arrival, and to hide within his room, safely away from king or prince or queen.

"Er," continued the queen in a softer tone. "That was hardly in the spirit of my words last night. I shall try not to take offense from your impersonal comments." She glanced at Soren. "Besides, you are still the guest of my son."

"He was freeborn?" asked Soren. "Your slave?"

80

Shianan nodded. "He was enslaved for debt." They did not need the details. "His brother came to Alham on business and—they recognized one another. I sent Luca home with him."

"A touching story," commented Queen Azalie. "But shouldn't a Furmelle commander be more cautious in relating how he freed a slave?" She smiled.

Shianan shook his head. "I did not, Your Majesty. I merely transferred him to another man. What his new master does with him once they cross the border is none of my doing."

"Oh, I meant no harm," she assured him. "I think it a rather grand tale, myself."

It had hardly been a grand life for Luca, but Shianan did not protest.

The queen stood, brushing her skirts into place as the two men straightened. "I will not keep you from your business. No, Soren, you needn't trouble, I can return by the palace passage."

Shianan bowed deeply as she passed, remaining still a moment longer than the prince. Only after she had gone did Shianan straighten.

Soren gave Shianan an empathetic look. "It's been a difficult few days, I see. The Shard, the Court, and Luca. My lady mother. And today the king, and then the mage... What happened, dare I ask? May I?"

Shianan sighed. "I misunderstood. I was moved to defend her, but it seems she needed no defense, and—well, my erroneous assumption was not appreciated."

Ethan, returning, collected the queen's cup.

"Sit down, Becknam, please." Soren gestured Shianan to a chair as he took a seat himself. "I'm sorry to hear about your misunderstanding." He paused. "She doesn't know, does she?"

"Your Highness?"

"About the Shard. The reason it disappeared."

Shianan's stomach clenched. "I don't know all the purpose behind the theft of the Shard. Perhaps they intended to ransom it to the kingdom—"

Soren waved a hand imperiously. "Oh, no, no. I don't intend to try and overturn the Court of the High Star's ruling; think how that would look. But I believed you more the first time." He lifted his drink and gazed at it. "Though your Luca, when I asked, did a splendid job of protesting how the merchant had tried to kill you. One almost forgot, listening to him, that he'd not answered about the Shard itself."

Shianan sat very still, wondering if he were expected to respond to this indirect accusation.

Soren sighed. "I'm sorry you lost him. I could see you valued him." He drained his cup and held it toward Ethan. "What about you, Ethan? Do you have any freemen family to take you?"

Ethan approached and refilled the drink. "No, master. I was bred for royal service."

"I thought so. But would you wish for ransom?"

Ethan paused. "Had I a different master, I might."

Soren smiled. "Are you being truthful or obliging?"

"Both, master. May I speak freely?"

"Please do. Becknam is not likely to act on anything you say."

Ethan nodded, his expression thoughtful. "A slave always wishes to be free, and I cannot deny I have dreamed of being my own master. But my position here is better than that of many impoverished freemen, and my service is such that I would exchange places with few. My master is both fair and generous."

Shianan stared down, seeing nothing. *I'll never do better*, Luca had said. *I want to stay your servant.*

Soren was grinning. "Generous, you say? What do you have your eye on?"

"If Your Highness could spare me, I would like an afternoon or evening..."

Soren's grin widened. "Paying a visit to the lovely Clara?"

Ethan returned a nod which managed somehow to be simultaneously obedient, conspiratorial, and prurient, and Soren laughed. "See which day has the fewest appointments here and take it. I'll have work enough to keep me occupied, but if I need anything, a prince should be able to find help somewhere."

"Thank you, master."

"Not at all. Please fill Becknam's cup again and then you may go."

After the slave had left, Soren glanced at Shianan again. "You have not answered my question, but I suppose it no longer matters. As far as the annals are concerned, the Shard is recovered and that is the end of it. But if I can help in any way to soothe this recent misunderstanding, please let me know. 'Soats, after facing that this morning, you deserve a little luck in your love."

"Your Highness...."

"Becknam—even a king can err. Between us, I'm sorry for it."

Shianan looked at him wonderingly, but Soren seemed absorbed in his own thoughts. He turned in his chair, one leg propped upon the other, chewing at his lip.

The fire in the cleft, the Kalen baths, even the awful night on the wall, all had shown Shianan aspects of the prince no one else had been present to see. Prince Soren was no longer a resented entity to be hated for his privilege, but a thoughtful and deliberate man conscientiously working through his tasks. He would make a good king.

Shianan set his cup down and rose to his feet almost without thinking. "Your Highness," he began, surprising the prince into looking up, "is it true you have received no formal oaths of allegiance?"

"As I said."

Shianan took a step and knelt before the prince's chair. "I would be honored, my lord, if you would accept my pledge as your first."

"Becknam...!"

"My lord, I solemnly swear my loyalty to you and to the kingdom which will be in your hands." The words tumbled earnestly from him as if by their own will.

"Becknam—"

"I pledge to follow my prince."

"Becknam, you needn't do this for this morning's—"

"That had nothing to do with it," Shianan interjected. He swallowed and continued. "I can think of no other master I would rather serve. This is my oath to Your Highness—I have sworn to obey Prince Alasdair in the letter of the law. I swear now, not to obey but to serve Prince Soren, with spirit and heart."

Soren straightened in the chair, leaning toward Shianan. His expression, when Shianan lifted his eyes, was intense. "Do you know what you're saying?"

"I believe so, my lord."

"In the event the king really is positioning Alasdair to inherit, you have just committed yourself."

"I would be honored to serve you."

"'Soats, Becknam, I am not looking to assemble a personal army, not now. I don't want to draw attention to the succession. If rumor goes out that the prince is—"

"There will be no rumor, my lord," Shianan interrupted quietly.

"I seek no public witness for a declaration. This is between my prince and his willing servant."

Soren gave him a long, appraising look. Something in his eyes softened. "You don't have to do this."

Shianan held his gaze. "This oath, Your Highness, I make of my own will."

Soren nodded slowly. "Then, I thank you. I accept your pledge and in return I swear to honor your service." He exhaled. "Rise, please, Becknam."

Shianan did, standing taller than he had in days.

"Why?" Soren looked at him. "I, for one, am not worried about any attempt you might make on the throne. And if I feared military support for Alasdair, I would be more jealous of the generals' oaths than yours. Why?"

Shianan shifted awkwardly. "Ethan likes you."

"What?" Soren made a wry face. "A man's slave is the truest judge of his character, is that it?"

"No one spends more time with you, and he respects you but does not fear you. If even your slave likes you... And I have had the unique privilege of seeing you without a gallery of courtiers. You are a good man without spectators, too."

Soren eyed him. "One of those privileged instances was when I was beating the bloody snot out of you," he said dubiously. "Am I to believe you considered me a good man then, too?"

"The fault, my lord, lay in your zeal for your responsibilities. The destruction of Caftford, that was the catalyst. Remember, you also came to my defense when I was first taken before the king. I did not expect anyone to speak for me."

"Because I came first to protest your arrest, I am absolved of pummeling you while you were chained and wounded?"

"It was the price of my actions, my lord. You did as you thought best for your kingdom, and I had some sacrifice as consequence for my own choices."

"Some sacrifice." Soren stared at him, shaking his head. "King's sweet oats. No wonder they call you the demon commander."

"What?"

The prince smiled. "Yes, I get some of the common soldier gossip as well. But now I almost believe their nightmarish stories." Shianan blinked, and Soren chuckled. "While you were watching servants for clues to my character, I was gathering information on yours."

A moment of panic struck Shianan. Whom had he asked? And who could give a fair report of the bastard to the prince-heir?

"Curious? The recruits call you the demon commander, but they have a reluctant admiration for you, I think. The veterans unhesitatingly answer that they would follow you again into battle, that they would rather have you than another. All call you fair and even-handed." Soren smiled. "They did not know to whom they were reporting, of course."

There was a peculiar warm hollow in Shianan's stomach as he listened. He had not heard his troops' opinions so plainly before.

The prince stood. "And what if the king chooses Alasdair to succeed? What then?"

Shianan took a slow, deep breath. "Then I must break an oath. And the one I made of my own volition will not be the one I break."

Soren gave him a long look, his expression shuttered. "And in the end," he said finally, "I do want you on my side." He reached for Shianan's forearm, clasping it in the ancient sign of solidarity. "I am only now beginning to know Shianan Becknam, but I know I want him beside me."

Shianan blinked, and the spreading warm glow began to radiate through him. He gripped the prince's arm in return, unsure of his voice.

Soren swallowed and blinked. "We both—king's oats, man, I can't—Becknam, I find myself dangerously close to believing you, to thinking you really don't intend a political move. No one plays his politics according to the opinion of a slave! Do you mean it?"

Shianan was surprised at the question. He'd never thought the prince might doubt his friends as much as the bastard. "I play no politics, my lord, save to serve my king as best I can. I knew long ago anything more would be dangerous for myself and for others. I never asked for my title. I am not a courtier..."

"And that is why your oath means more," Soren said firmly. "I know, at least, you are no threat to the crown. A bit misguided perhaps, in your efforts to help your friends, but no threat to the succession." He smiled, not the practiced smile of a very public prince, but an honest smile.

There was a knock at the outer door, and Soren made a face. "But as much as I would prefer to linger and talk all the afternoon with you, we both have other duties, as I was saying, and I'm afraid I must let you go." He blew out a breath, almost unhappy. "Do let me know if I can help with your mage's misunderstanding in any way—flowers from the royal hothouse, or fruits, whatever you think might win her fancy and a hearing for your apology."

Shianan could feel his face flushing. "I will try something, my lord. I never meant to give offense."

"Offending a mage could be dangerous," Soren warned with a wry smile. "You might consider whether you want to pursue this." Outside, they could hear a servant admitting the newcomer. "Becknam, I have my duties, but I hope to see you soon. Don't hesitate to contact me if you need anything."

"Thank you, my lord." Shianan bowed and backed appropriately away.

As he returned to the office awaiting him, he thought of the stacked paperwork rather than the bleak and empty room containing it. Something had changed, but invisibly, like a plate of bedrock which had shifted but left the grass growing above. He was still only the bastard, a commander in the army and a stranger in the court, but he had a new master and he was not quite alone.

CHAPTER THIRTEEN

"Trader Matteo!" Jarrick pointed toward the front of the caravan. "I'd like the slave from wagon three."

The trader frowned. "I said you could manage for yourself on this trip."

"You also said if I needed him, I could ask."

"And you need him?"

Jarrick clenched his jaw. "He is my brother."

"So you say." Matteo gave a grim smile. "I've heard every variant of every story. I think my favorite is the one where the slave knows some secret treasure and must be questioned in private. As if I can't guess what jewels they're after... You want him sent to you privately, no doubt?"

Jarrick's breath caught and he felt his face go scarlet. "He is my brother, truly. We will sit in the sight of others, if you—"

Matteo made an annoyed gesture. "Keep your explanations and promises. But he'll be chained again. I won't lose my record to your... brother."

Jarrick nodded, thinking it better than to argue and risk the chance of speaking with Luca. What they had to say could not be said before others. "Thank you." Some part of him was galled to thank the man for releasing his own brother to him, but the merchant in him knew the value of smoothing the way for future negotiations.

He went to the fire where two slaves crouched. One scraped at a nearly empty pot with a wooden implement, and the other dished up a bowl of steaming soup and handed it to Jarrick. It burned his tongue, so he waved the bowl gently in the air as he went for a drink. A small slave was determinedly hefting a water bucket to his shoulder, but he paused long enough to let Jarrick dip a drink before shuffling toward the rear of the caravan.

Jarrick took a tentative mouthful of soup. He was not sure how to approach Luca. He had not really spoken to him—only those few words in the baths, when Jarrick was mad with relief and Luca dizzily resentful with illness, and all witnessed by Luca's master whom Jarrick had earlier obediently attempted to murder. There had been no understanding there, no reconciliation. No healing.

The soup wasn't good, but fine meals weren't a priority in a caravan of human merchandise. He started toward the wagon he would share that night with the trader.

The trader was not there, but Luca was. He sat in the empty bed of the wagon, arms crossed over his drawn knees, chin resting on his upper wristcuff. His face was without any particular expression, his eyes hollow.

Jarrick was suddenly afraid to speak. He stopped and looked at his brother across the short distance. After a moment Luca's eyes blinked and he raised his head. "Jarrick."

Jarrick swallowed. "Luca."

Luca's eyes shifted. "Or, I should say, master." He licked his lips. "After all, I am your property now."

"Don't, Luca." Jarrick felt as if he'd been punched. "You know that isn't what I want."

"No?"

Jarrick wanted to pull his collar away from his neck, but it was already loose. "Come away a little distance, where we can talk."

Luca's jaw tightened. "As you order."

Jarrick, stunned and hurt, watched him unfold his legs and ease off the rear of the wagon. He did not know what to say, so he led Luca silently to the edge of the camp, where they were in plain view of anyone caring to look but shadowed enough that their conversation could not be read. Jarrick sat on the matted grass and stared at his cooling soup.

"I waited—I didn't think our first talk should be in front of all the others in the line." After a moment Jarrick realized Luca was still standing. He looked up at him. "Sit down, won't you?"

Luca made a stiff bow and obeyed.

Jarrick's heart sank. "Luca... I am not your master."

"Trader Matteo and the others think otherwise."

Had the trader said something to him, too? "I don't care what they think. I am not your master."

"Then what are you?" Luca kept his eyes on the fallen leaves, but his voice was angry. "You take me away without consulting me, you have me chained in the stable and the line, you—"

"That was none of my doing! I could not get into the stable last night, I tried. And you saw yourself I wanted you out of the line this morning. Trader Matteo worries too much over losing you to escape. He hardly believes we're brothers."

Luca flinched.

Jarrick softened. "Luca—I'm sorry. For all that happened, I'm sorry."

Luca said nothing. Jarrick could see little of his face, bowed as it was, and after a moment he took another mouthful of soup, just to occupy himself. Luca glanced at him and then returned to the leaves again.

"I couldn't wait for another caravan," Jarrick said. "The names of all our conspirators are on a single sheet of paper, in my handwriting. And Shianan Becknam told me himself he wanted me out of the city by dawn."

"Because you tried to kill him."

Jarrick had no answer which he had not already found insufficient. He stared at his soup. "Have you eaten?"

"Had mine already."

"You want some of this?"

Luca shook his head. "I'm not hungry."

Jarrick tried to take another sip, but it was tasteless. He set the bowl aside. "You want to tell me about it?"

Luca crossed his arms and hunched forward.

"Luca, talk to me."

"Is that an order?" came the strained answer.

"Flames, Luca, I said—"

Jarrick froze with sudden insight. Luca was not grinding Jarrick's nose in his unhappy position. He was keeping Jarrick at arm's length and testing, even begging, perhaps unconsciously, to be told he was not a slave but a brother.

Jarrick's ire melted and he moved impulsively toward his younger brother, catching him as Luca looked up in surprise. Jarrick threw his arms around him and pulled him close. "Luca, I'm sorry. I asked everyone I could find, but Trader Matteo won't be moved. As soon as we cross the border, I promise— You are my brother, Luca. I'm so sorry I did not find you. I'm sorry I did not stop them that day. I didn't know—I couldn't react... Luca, I'm sorry."

Luca, stiff in his arms, softened. "I..."

Jarrick gulped and released him. "Tell me, Luca. I should hear it all. It's my penance to hear it."

Luca drew back. "I don't know that I want to tell you all."

"Then tell me what you can."

Luca crossed his arms. "At—those first days—I kept waiting.

I was in one of the little closed stalls where they put rebellious slaves to stew and starve, or where they put freshly enslaved soft merchants' sons to realize the world has utterly changed. I sat there in my own dirt with my wrists clamped together, waiting for Father to come for me." His throat worked. "Then they put me to work grinding grain, and I was so relieved when the trader warned I shouldn't be whipped before my sale." He gave a little bitter mockery of a laugh. "I didn't realize that left the switch and anything else the stockmen could think to use."

Jarrick clenched his fists. "We thought you'd make a clerk, that you'd have a soft place doing numbers."

"Sandis didn't want that. He wanted to see us debased."

"I know."

"It did not happen, though. A man came looking for a slave to draw his children's cart and I begged for the work, promising I would tell them histories as we went. That stopped him. He didn't believe I could, of course, but when he tested me I knew everything I'd claimed."

"You were always reading histories."

"It saved me. He thought me a bargain, an educated slave for the price of an unconditioned mill-grinder, and he took me as a tutor for his son and daughter." Luca took a deep breath. "It was not a bad place. I was a slave and that galled, but I was fairly used. I thought I had hard work then, though later I knew... But I'd gone to Furmelle."

Jarrick nodded. The Furmelle slave uprising had scattered lawful citizens in flight and dumped hundreds of captured slaves onto the market, drowning the labor economy. Their house had observed and profited well by those events. "What happened then?"

Luca shrugged. "It was all nightmare. My master's family hid in their home behind locked gates. I was taken by soldiers one day on the street. My master would not claim me; they were afraid. Of all of us." He hesitated. "As a merchant, you must know what happened. There was enormous supply and little demand for rebellious slaves, even cheap ones. We wasted and rotted and starved until someone purchased my lot at an obscenely low price." He smiled weakly. "I should have been insulted."

Jarrick cleared his throat. "I looked for you, Luca. Really, I did. But there were so few records."

Luca shook his head. "You would never have found anyone in that chaos." He licked his lips. "You want more?"

90

Jarrick clenched his fists. "I asked for everything."

Luca cupped his hands about his knees. "Cheap labor goes to hard, menial work. I was set to pick lettuces. But we'd been chained for weeks, and at the end of the day, they called me too soft for the work and sold me in the twilight to a passing tinker."

Jarrick waited. "And?"

"And I lived the next year and more chained to the cart's shafts. He was afraid. I was a Furmelle slave, no matter what I hadn't done, and he was ill. So he kept me chained where I could not escape and could do no harm." Luca gave a sad, bitter smile. "Actually, he may not have been a bad man, if not for the pain and the drink he took for it. But I didn't have him without the pain and the drink. I went over most of the Faln Plateau chained to that cart."

Jarrick nodded slowly, only half-rejecting the image of his brother shackled to an angry drunkard's cart. He could not avoid this. What was painful to hear had been horrific to live. "Go on."

"And then he finally died, working on some tools for the Gehrn. The Gehrn high priest took me." Luca drew his knees to his chest.

Jarrick knew he was staring but was unsure of what else to do. "What then?"

"I wanted to die." Luca nearly whispered, his eyes fixed on the ground. "I would have been happier never to wake in the morning. You know the Gehrn are a militaristic cult? He treated me as an animal—I half became an animal, too ashamed even to think of myself as myself." His body was rigid. "I hated it until I didn't have the will even to hate anymore."

Jarrick's mind reeled with possible horrors, but he didn't have the courage to ask which were true.

"Then Shianan Becknam came for the Shard of Elan, to create a shield against the Ryuven. When the high priest went to Alham, he brought me to serve as usual. He—I was also—I was also a component to a ritual for the Shard, which needed the blood of a prisoner of war. Since I had come through Furmelle, I sufficed, and he flogged me."

Jarrick sat immobile, thinking of the stripy scars on Luca's unconscious body.

"The shield collapsed—I suppose you heard about that. Master Shianan took me from the prison, kept me himself instead of letting me be sent to auction again."

Jarrick saw again the injured commander flat on his stomach, sobbing with the effort to pull a sodden corpse from the river. "He thought well of you."

"We were friends. He was my master, but he was my good friend."

A sudden, desperate fear stabbed Jarrick, that Luca might attribute higher qualities to his savior of convenience than to the brother who had searched across countries for him. "Masters don't befriend their slaves. You were glad to be away from the high priest, surely, and—"

"Shut up, Jarrick." Luca's voice was flat and acidic. He closed his eyes. "He remade me. He gave me a chance to escape and be free, though I couldn't recognize it at the time. He—he promised never to sell me. Until you." He opened his eyes again and glared at the dead leaves.

Jarrick tried to swallow against his closed throat. "Me?" He gulped. "Do you mean you would have—you can't have wanted to stay. He was kind enough to you, but you were a slave there."

"And what will I be in Ivat?" demanded Luca. "You might take the cuffs from my wrists, but I have been sold once already there. How can I go back to those same people—"

"They are not the same people." Jarrick's head drooped and he blew out his breath. "Nothing is the same, Luca. Father's changed, very changed. He drinks, and he eats viante. There are stretches in which he is nearly himself, his old self, but then there are periods when he hides in his rooms and will not open the door." Jarrick rubbed at his treacherously damp eyes. "Thir manages things now, when Father is—unable. Sara will be married soon. It isn't the same, Luca. They will be glad to see you."

"Will they?"

Jarrick's chest spasmed. Would they? He had not even thought to question that. Surely they would want to see Luca back home. Surely they would welcome him as a son or a brother, not a reminder of their most shameful moment. "Of course they will. Don't be ridiculous."

Luca clenched his fists and looked across the grass. "Why didn't you come for me?"

Jarrick stared at his stony profile. "What do you mean? I followed you to Furmelle, I asked everyone in the auction house, I looked in the records—"

"You looked in the records! But if our house had sent around that you were seeking—if after you started ascending again, after word had gone around about Sandis and people knew—if you had offered a reward..." Luca bit off the words.

Jarrick could not respond. He could not explain that no one ever spoke of Luca, no one mentioned what had happened, not their father, their brother, no client, no worker, no peer in the shipping industry... It was as if Luca had never existed. But Luca was right. If they had summoned the courage, if they had used the first fruits of sympathy's profit to offer a reward, they might have found him.

"And then, when I finally return, I'm dragged back on the end of a caravan chain, thin and footsore and filthy and beaten, and everything they see confirms I am nothing but what I was then, a pawn and a slave without merit or dignity." His voice shook a little, as if he did not quite trust that he could say the words.

"You were never..." Jarrick's voice failed. He could not protest when Luca's point was too clear. He had been sacrificed.

For years he had wanted to bring Luca home. He had never thought Luca might fear to come with him. But he had been a fool; how could he have thought that Luca would be as overjoyed to see them?

"How would you come, then?" He forced a smile and tried to lighten the question. "I cannot afford to let you triumphantly ride a horse through the gates. We're faring better, but not that much better."

Luca acknowledged the weak joke with a minute lift of his mouth. "No."

Jarrick laced his fingers together and propped his chin on them. "Think on this, then: I have a friend with a small house outside Ivat, a little retreat in the lower mountains. He has generously offered to let me use it if I wish. I could take you there. You could rest a while, let— let the marks fade from your wrists, get your feet under you. You could come home when you felt ready."

Luca nodded slowly. "That might be good." He rubbed unconsciously at the cuffs on his wrists.

Jarrick exhaled unsteadily. "You don't know how I did try, Luca. I did. No matter where I was, in what land, no matter who was with me, I couldn't help but look at every black-haired slave we passed. I thought so many times that I'd recognized your walk or saw your profile, or... Luca, I thought you were dead, and still I couldn't help but look for you. And then I heard your voice, and a moment later you were dead again." Tears broke through his thin control. "You don't know how glad I was, only you were so barely alive, and I was afraid that if you lived you would hate me. And I was so afraid he would not let you go, or he would ask so much that—but I would have to pay it, no matter what the price, and..."

Luca sniffed. "Jarrick, I don't hate you."

Jarrick threw a hopeful glance at him. "No?" He impulsively leaned toward his brother and embraced him again. "Thank you."

Luca wept quietly, and for a long moment they held one another.

The sound of a forced cough made both Jarrick and Luca jump. Jarrick turned as Luca hurried to his feet.

"It's late," Trader Matteo said gruffly, a dozen paces away. "Time to get back."

Jarrick turned to Luca. "Tomorrow, I'll walk with—"

"No," Luca said. "Not where I'm chained. I don't—just don't."

Jarrick nodded.

Luca threw a quick glance at Trader Matteo before starting toward the third wagon.

Jarrick rose to face the trader. "Wait," he said, keeping his voice low. "Can't you let him free? I swear I'll tell no one. Your reputation won't suffer."

"Not yet. If you've waited for years, you can wait a few days more."

"If I waited—then you believe now we are brothers?"

Matteo smiled without humor. "I've known since the commander-count first charged me with taking the slave."

"But why didn't you let me have him?"

Matteo shook his head. "A man does not become a slave incidentally. Men fall from honorable humanity through some act. When we collected him, there was mention of a brother, which matched your claim, but that did nothing to assure me your brother had not been enslaved for crime or debt, or that you were not another criminal come for him. I have no wish to be robbed or murdered, and I took precautions."

Jarrick stiffened. "You know I am a merchant of an upstanding house."

The trader gave him a disdainful glance. "I know that's the name you use." He shrugged. "Though I'll grant, you might or might not be Jarrick Roald, but you're either a supreme actor or a shame-ridden brother—elder, I'd guess. And I'd put my money you're not an actor."

Jarrick stared at him. "I am the elder brother. How...?"

"You're a merchant; you study faces for a living as well. Perhaps I need to see more, to know which slaves will work well and which will require restraint or coercion. It was simple enough to watch you together. If you'd invented this play, you would not be so boneheaded in going about it. You would be more of a hero to your brother and less of an arse."

Jarrick blinked. "What—how can you—"

Matteo shrugged. "I don't pretend to be privy to what goes on between you. But your brother isn't overjoyed to be rescued, if that's indeed what's happening. I don't think he trusts you. And that's reason enough for me not to trust you either, which is why that slave will remain in chains until we reach our destination."

CHAPTER FOURTEEN

The overseer nodded toward Luca and Andrew as well as the big demoted slave and the thin man who'd arrived with him. "Up front. You'll pull the next leg."

Luca's stomach sank. As a privately owned slave, he'd thought he'd be exempt from the caravan's draft work.

"Move!" A hand slapped the back of his head and shoved him forward.

There were crossbars for four draft slaves, in pairs. Luca and Andrew were directed to the wheel positions, with the big slave directly before Luca. Andrew was footsore and tired even in the mornings, and the overseers were particularly hard on the big man; they would be watched closely and driven hard.

Chains were run from the crossbar through the rings on Luca's wrists. He glanced over his shoulder, hoping to see Jarrick arguing with Trader Matteo, but there was only another overseer taking a switch from the wagon bed. Luca caught his breath and faced forward.

"Move out," came the order, and Luca leaned into the crossbar. His wrists flexed and swelled against the cuffs and there was an awful moment when the wagon hung motionless behind them, but then the load shifted and began to move. Luca hoped it would roll easily, that it had just been difficult to start, but the weight dragged behind them.

Andrew made a small sound, and when Luca glanced at him, his face was tense with strain. "I can't do this," he breathed. "I can't do this all day."

"Keep your weight low and forward," advised the big slave in front of Luca. "Yesterday's soreness will loosen in a few minutes. Keep breathing, slow and deep. Shallow will hurt you."

Luca's legs were beginning to burn. Privately he shared Andrew's fear he would not last before the heavy wagon. Renner's tinker cart had not been so solid. He shifted his hands on the crossbar and wondered where Jarrick was in the caravan. Did he know Luca had been pressed into labor?

Big drops of rain began to fall, chilling as they splattered over shoulders and arms. They were all breathing hard now, blowing in unison as they stepped together.

The rain increased, a steady downfall which made their drenched clothing cling to their tired legs. Luca ducked his head and pushed blindly, trusting the slaves in front to keep the pace and distance from the line before them.

The road angled upward, and Andrew gave a small despairing moan.

"Keep with us," Luca told him with more encouragement than he felt. "We'll manage." Andrew nodded, his breath puffing white.

Luca licked his lips, tasting rainwater, but it did not satisfy him. When had they stopped to water the draft slaves the previous day?

A faint whistle gave a split second of warning before a switch fell across the big slave's back, spattering Luca with water and making the slave jerk and gasp. Luca recoiled from the switch so near his face, and the overseer snapped, "To work!" and struck Luca, the switch biting through his sodden shirt to his cold skin. Luca yelped and threw himself forward. He had not even heard the man's approach in the rain.

"No slowing," grumbled the overseer. He struck the big slave again. "Move!"

Luca sucked air between his teeth. It would sting hotly for minutes yet, and on his cold back it seemed to bite deeper. He hunched his shoulders, trying to ease the feeling, but it only made pushing more difficult.

Trader Matteo came alongside the wagon, wrapped in an oiled cloak. "There's a steep run ahead," he told the nearest overseer.

Luca's heart sank. Steep? How steep?

"I expect some trouble with this lot. That lean one in front had trouble moving a single, which is why I had him for so little. The other of course is more used to directing than to pulling his own weight, so keep an eye on him for shirking."

"I'm doing my best," the slave volunteered from the shafts.

The overseer slashed the switch across his shoulders. "Keep to your work."

"Easy," chided Matteo. "You can strip the shirt off his back if he gives you real trouble, but save your strength until then." He splashed off through the slick mud. "Keep them moving."

This was not one of the good army roads, but mixed dirt and gravel, becoming sticky without a drainage ditch alongside. Luca slipped and caught at the crossbar, missing a step with the others. He stumbled and found the rhythm again.

"...how you fare!" The thin slave was saying something to the big slave. It was hard to hear over the rain and the mud sucking at their feet. "...mud and the wagon..."

The big slave gave him a dark look. The road turned and Luca's heart sank as he saw the first wagon above them on the hill.

The thin slave bit off a sharp, sibilant epithet and the big man threw him a furious glare. Andrew began to pant as they tackled the incline, and the wagon grew heavier in the mud. The overseer glanced to the rear of the wagon. "You in the line! Push!"

Luca bent over the crossbar, his chest nearly against his shackled wrists. He heard the dull slap of the switch in the line behind them. Sharp fear cut through his torso and tasted of steel in his mouth. The wagon dragged.

Andrew was lagging. Luca glanced toward him. "Come on." Andrew rolled his eyes toward Luca in worried reply, his breath coming too fast to speak. There was another snap and yelp behind them.

"How do you like it?" growled the black-haired slave unevenly. They were no longer breathing in rhythm. "Slipping in the mud, the switch about your ears—how now?" He stumbled and caught himself.

"Shut up," panted the big slave. "If you'd been worth half—"

"Faster!" The switch whistled into the big slave's back, making him and Luca flinch together. "Put your backs in it!"

The switch cut through Luca, biting deep. He gasped and stumbled. The chains jerked against his wrists as he missed a step, and the switch lashed across him again as he tried to regain his footing and tempo. Then it stretched across and struck Andrew. "Get to work!"

Luca scrabbled in the mud and strained at the crossbar, his panicky mind capable of nothing beyond escaping the switch, moving forward to make it stop, make it stop...!

There was a cry from several voices behind the wagon and then a tremendous jerk as the wagon dragged backward. The overseer wheeled, cursing, and started for the rear. "Get up! Get untangled! What's the matter with you stupid clumsy—"

They heaved at the crossbars, trying to restart the wagon's progress uphill. Luca's breath scraped in his throat. The big slave grunted as he pushed, looking about him for help or the switch.

The thin slave slipped in the mud. "This is your doing, all of it! I hope they flog—"

The big slave twisted and lunged, catching him at the range of his chains. The wagon hesitated as he jerked the slave toward him and drove his face into the crossbar.

Luca shrank back in horror as the slave fell away from the bar, eyes rolling. The big man seized him and punched him, his movements short and confined. He struck again and once more as the other tried to shield himself with shackled arms.

The overseer was shouting beside Luca, flailing the switch. Luca ducked against the shaft, hiding from the fight and the wand that cut indiscriminately over them. More voices joined the shouting and bodies closed around them. Someone kicked Luca hard in the thigh. Then there was a roar of general triumph and the space over Luca cleared.

"Got him!"

"Bring a whip."

"If he'll attack another in harness—"

Blood ran over Luca's cheek where the switch had caught him.

"—come right at someone—"

"He came with his back—"

Luca cautiously raised his head and looked into the enraged eyes of the big slave. He'd been dragged over the crossbar so he now faced the wagon, his crossed wrists tangled in the chains so he hugged the bar awkwardly. A man was twisting a belt about his folded leg, bound about the ankle and thigh, leaving him precariously balanced. The slave looked over his shoulder, his face contorted and reddened. "Get off me!"

"Here." One of the overseers uncoiled a whip with a toss of his wrist. "Master said we could strip his shirt if he gave us trouble."

The slave snarled. "Do your worst! You'd never dare if I weren't chained."

"Do it now. The line's already stopped."

Luca shrank back, but he was chained in place. He would be face to face with the bound slave as he was flogged.

The slave twisted, but he had only one leg to balance, and he fell against the crossbar. Chains tightened and scraped along his arms as he swore. The gathered crowd spread apart a little distance and the overseer swung. The lash whistled and buried itself in his back, making him grunt.

"Strip him!" someone called.

The second blow ripped fabric as the lash came free. The slave writhed and fell, dangling from the crossbar and the chains about his forearms. The whip came again and wrapped about his torso.

"Stop!" cried Luca, clawing at the crossbar. "Stop it!"

Someone laughed. "He's not even tasting it himself." The whip lashed the slave again.

"Stop! Please!" Luca gasped for air. "Don't do this."

"And why would we listen to you?" Someone stepped forward and reached for Luca. "We can knock you down a few pegs, too."

"No!" Luca jerked his head from the grasping hand. "No, I'll buy him. Let him be."

There was a moment of stunned silence and then a sudden outburst of howling laughter. "You'll buy him! If you had the means, you'd have yourself out of those chains, huh?"

"I am in earnest!" Luca's voice shook. "Where is the trader?"

"I'm here." Trader Matteo pushed forward from the crowd. "I'm curious—what's your proposal? And it'd better be good, or tack-on or no, you'll pay for interrupting fair discipline."

Luca gulped. "Let me buy him. I'm good for it—or Jarrick is, you know that. I can pay for him, especially what he'll be worth when they're finished with him. You'll lose money on him like this. Sell him to me."

The overseers had fallen silent, amazed their master had even answered. They stared between them.

Matteo seemed amused. "You're a slave until we cross the border. You have no property to offer and can own no slave yourself."

Luca dug his nails into the crossbar and held Matteo's eyes. "Jarrick!"

There was a long pause, a pause which iced Luca's blood, but then Jarrick answered from the side. "I can act as his agent today and hold the slave in my name."

Matteo nodded once to Jarrick and turned back to Luca. "I paid eight hundred for him."

Luca took an unsteady breath. "He won't sell for half that if he's freshly flogged. Six hundred for him as he is."

Matteo laughed aloud. "Look at the man, haggling over price from his own chains! I have to admire your audacity—but even that is not worth a difference of two hundred. I could keep him until his back closed and sell him at a profit. He has muscle enough, and with proper training I might even sell him again as an overseer or stockman. That could be two thousand, if he learns his lessons well."

"If he learns his lessons well. But he's under the whip even now, and only a few days after his previous master sold him freshly beaten for intractability. Will you pay for his keep and recovery on the hope that you can recoup your costs, or will you take the sure sale now?"

Matteo grinned. "I could argue further with you—or, slave, I could use other advantages in this market. But we've delayed long enough, and I would just as soon be rid of something with an unhealthy temper. Eight hundred, so I lose none of his price, and his labor until we arrive, to pay the cost of his feed. What do you say, from your chains?"

Luca forced words through his tight throat. "Eight hundred and his labor. But he will be less useful freshly whipped, and I'll want him to do his share of the work rather than leave me to do it without him. He continues his labor directly."

"And if he proves troublesome again?"

"Then I'll see to him, or I'll turn him over to your overseers, paying the usual fee for their service."

Matteo laughed and nodded. "Good enough. Put that rock-brained hothead back in his place beside his new master and get these wagons started again. Water break on the downside of this hill, if anyone even needs it in this wet." He glanced up the hill road. "No, it's this cursed mud. We'll change everyone at the break. Tell them they've only to make it to the top, and then we'll change." He waved. "Move!"

Two overseers stayed to unbind the slave's leg as the others scattered. He glared at them, jaw muscles visibly clenched, and tensed.

"Try it," sneered one overseer. He freed the short cudgel in his belt. "Come on, then—try it."

"Hey!" Luca tried to interrupt.

One of the overseers turned to him. "You're still chained here, pulling this wagon, too."

"So I am." Luca squared his shoulders. "But in a few days, I'll be out of these chains. And then I might take it into my head to buy you, too."

The overseer hesitated and then turned with a huff back to the slave. "Watch your step. You owe good labor, and we won't stand for any stupidity."

The other moved to retrieve his switch from the ground. "And you," he addressed the dark-haired slave, "you'd better work proper, too."

The slave rubbed blood from his nose, smearing it beneath his swelling eye.

"Now, get to work, and if this wagon doesn't get up this hill, I'll skin you all, no matter what you are. Move!"

Luca's legs seemed locked in place, and for a desperate moment he thought he couldn't take a step. Then he moved and they nearly collapsed beneath him, and he clutched at the crossbar to steady himself. But the fear and horror and bravado ran liquidly out of him, and he bent to his work as before.

CHAPTER FIFTEEN

Ariana knocked on the silver-painted door and hoped Elysia Parma was not in.

Unfortunately, the Silver Mage answered the door and beckoned her inside. "Come in, Ariana."

She obeyed. "I'm sure you have many important things to do," she said, trying to gesture and cross her arms at the same time. "And—"

"I do, many important things, and this is one of them," Elysia Parma said firmly.

This line of protest would be futile. "Then—but what if this doesn't work?"

Mage Parma led the way to a table with an array of objects and turned to face her. "What if it does?"

Ariana had no answer to that.

"Sit down, and let's start."

The objects on the table were an unlit candle with a blackened wick, a book, and a collection of colored beads. Ariana recalled similar items from her earliest days of training, when she had to kneel on her chair to see the surface of her father's work table.

"You said magic in the Ryuven world was overwhelming," Elysia Parma said. "You had to be protected from it, and then you finally used it, but only on a large scale. You manipulated great amounts of overwhelming power. No fine control work."

"That's right." Ariana rubbed her palms across her robe. "Do you think I burned out my ability with Ryuven magic? Is that possible?"

"We wouldn't know if it's possible," Elysia said gently, "until it happened, and you would be the first, as you are the first to survive the Ryuven world's magic. But I don't think that should be our first assumption."

Ariana realized she had unconsciously folded her leg beneath her, as if to boost her height, and she adjusted her position.

Mage Parma continued, "I think you learned to protect yourself by shutting off your skill, so you would not be buried by the more powerful foreign magic. Now that you are home, where magic is more subtle, you have blocked yourself from sensing the more delicate strands."

Ariana shook her head. "I don't think that's the case. I helped with the shield."

"Where you suffered another fright—with good reason—and probably strengthened whatever barrier you'd erected. And you said the magic was more tiring, perhaps because you weren't drawing power enough for it?"

Ariana did not want to think on this. "You're telling me this is all in my mind."

Mage Parma quietly snorted. "All magic is in the mind, as is every other intention we have. If you were unwilling to put weight on a broken leg, that would also be in your mind, but it wouldn't mean it was without cause." She tapped a stack of papers into order. "But neither should one assume the leg could never be walked on again, without teaching the mind to test it and assess it and progress on it."

Ariana sighed. "What do you want me to do?"

She had tried to light the candle previously, so they ignored that for now. Mage Parma started with one of the simplest of tasks. She opened the book and flipped some of the pages, leaving a fan of onion-skin paper. "Rustle the pages," she said simply.

Ariana should have been able to do this with a flick of her finger, hardly looking at the book. Instead, she fixed her eyes on it and concentrated, stretching her fingers wide and cutting horizontally through the air, like scooping the top layer from a cake.

The onion-skin papers did not move. Ariana strained, her eyes aching with the effort, and imagined herself pulling the papers back. She closed her eyes, trying to visualize the magic, but there was only dark.

"I can't," she said.

"Keep trying."

Ariana squeezed her eyes shut, though that had not helped her in years, and imagined she pushed and pulled at the open book. Not so much as a glimmer of magic lit her dark sight. "Mage Parma, I—"

A pillar of white-hot fire leapt up beside her, and Ariana flinched backward, dropping her tentative reach for the book. She gave a little cry as she fell over her chair. She opened her eyes and saw the ceiling, the table, Mage Parma's concerned face. No fire.

"Your magic," Ariana gasped.

Mage Parma nodded, closing her hand and snuffing out the

energy couched there. "So you really can sense it."

Ariana caught her breath and thought about what she had said. "Yes, I could see your magic. But not mine."

"But it means you have not become insensitive to magic. You can sense it still, if it's powerful and close. The question is, why not when it is small?"

"Because I've burned it out," Ariana completed. "That's logical."

"If you persist in this line, I shall have to begin rolling my eyes," Mage Parma said dryly. "Aren't you prepared to do hard work here in the Wheel? This is it."

Chastened, Ariana nodded. "All right."

Ariana closed her eyes, and Elysia Parma flicked magic about the room in stronger or weaker bolts for Ariana to identify. It was difficult, and frustrating in its difficulty; Ariana should have been able to point out the various energies like brightly colored balls sailing through the air, but it felt more like watching for mice in tall grass at twilight. When at last Elysia called for a break, Ariana was exhausted and perspiring despite having stayed still in her chair.

"I don't know," she said, rubbing her face. "I feel like I'm not making any progress. Is this worth the effort?"

Elysia Parma raised a critical eyebrow. "This is exactly why I was sure to take data instead of letting you rely upon your tired emotions," she said with kind firmness. She held up her pages of notes, full of tally marks and occasional lines of commentary. "In the beginning, you could recognize only the strongest energy, and you often missed those which weren't near the last one you'd sensed. But by the end, you were catching them regardless of location, and many of the smaller ones as well."

"Really?" Ariana was grateful for her reassuring tally marks. "I didn't feel at all as if I was improving."

"Weariness does that," the Silver Mage said.

"But I still can't use—"

"Ariana Hazelrig, do not complete that sentence. Are you better than you were this morning?"

Ariana nodded.

"Will you return tomorrow to improve again?"

She nodded again, a little afraid to do otherwise.

"Good." Elysia Parma leaned over the table. "The uneducated think magic is all about words of power and secret phrases which will unlock the universe. We know that is foolishness—mostly. Magic is a science, not secret phrases. But we also know that words are powerful with their own sort of magic, and they influence not the universe, but our perceptions of it, and thereby our actions and even our abilities."

"You're saying if I can't recover my magic, it's because I said I couldn't?"

"It's not so simple as that. I'm saying if you say you can't recover your magic, you prepare yourself to accept failure, and you resist expending as much energy on what you believe to be a futile endeavor."

Ariana thought about this for a moment before she nodded. "And that makes failure more likely."

Elysia Parma stood. "Good work today, Black Mage."

Ariana forced a weary smile. "I'll come back tomorrow. And tonight?"

"Rest tonight. No games to test yourself! Give yourself a chance to recover. Remember how hard magic is physically, and you were a long time away from practicing even without considering the extraordinary effects of the Ryuven atmosphere. Take a rest."

"You really think I can just rest and it will come back?"

For answer, Mage Parma called a pillar of power into her hand, and Ariana flinched away before she could stop herself.

"You're afraid," Mage Parma said gently. "Understandably— but afraid." She turned back to the table and lit the candle with a gesture. Her hand hovered near the flame. "If I want to pass my hand through the fire, how should I do it?"

"Just push it through," Ariana answered. "Straight through."

Mage Parma nodded. "And what happens if I hesitate? Start, stop, hold back?"

"You'll be burned."

"And then it will be that much more difficult for me to attempt it properly the next time. Or, in the imprecision of desperation, I might shove my hand into the wick or upset the candle." Mage Parma snapped out the flame. "That is why I don't want you practicing on your own, and not just for the obvious concerns of safety. Let's take this at a measured pace, and let's not risk letting you burn yourself."

Ariana caught her breath. "You think—you think it could get worse."

And with magic, she did not risk a singed finger. Uncontrolled magic, as every carefully supervised apprentice knew, could kill.

For the first time she could remember, Ariana saw Mage Parma turn away from a question. "We don't know enough to know that."

Ariana made herself take another breath, long and slow. "But you think it can get better."

This time Mage Parma smiled. "We have already seen it get better."

Ariana felt a little encouraged as she left. She was still powerless, still a fraud within the Circle, but she was not entirely senseless.

CHAPTER SIXTEEN

Someone moved beside Luca, and he flinched. But it was Jarrick, pacing him in the mud and rain. "Are you all right?"

"I'm fine."

"Your face is bleeding. And—and..."

Luca shook his head. "I'll be all right."

Jarrick was clearly torn. "Are you—I'm going to go see Matteo. I'll be back."

The slaves at the rear of the wagon pushed with them, all efforts renewed at the sight of the concerted punishment available, and the caravan moved up the hill once more. Luca's legs trembled with strain, and the gap between the second and third wagon grew larger. The overseer barked a warning and struck Andrew with the switch.

Please, sweet Holy One, give us strength, prayed Luca. His back hurt with the welts, and inches before his eyes he saw the torn shirt and bloody stripes from the whip. *Let us make it.*

They did, somehow, and crested the hill. The overseer directed them to the side of the road and they stumbled to a halt. Andrew was wheezing with effort and hunched with fresh blows, and the two front slaves hung on their crossbar. Luca dropped to the road but found the chains were shorter than those of Renner's cart, and he could not quite sit but had to kneel.

He was shaking with fatigue. Surely Matteo would keep his word about exchanging draft slaves.

"What was that?" asked a breathless voice. "What gave you to think I wanted your help?" The big slave looked over his shoulder. "Did you really—did you really buy me? How?"

Luca nodded. "I am a slave only until we cross the border," he panted. "My brother's taking me home. Once I am a freeman again, I have the rights of a freeman." He smiled tiredly at the slave's puzzled expression. "I know it sounds farfetched and confusing, but the end is, you're now with the Roald house."

"And so you are my new master now?"

"Or my brother, technically." Luca shifted his aching legs, cold mud squelching around his knees. "What's your name?"

111

"Cole." The slave hesitated. "That is, Cole, master."

Luca nearly laughed, but for his physical and emotional exhaustion. "I am on my knees in the mud and in chains myself."

Andrew was staring. "You'll be a freeman?" he asked in a soft, wondrous tone.

Luca felt a quick wash of sympathy. "Yes, I—"

Luca's words were cut short by the overseer's arrival. He unchained them curtly and motioned to the rear of the wagon. The thin slave shrank from Cole as he moved away, but Cole ignored him. Perhaps he was too stunned by his change in fortune to waste thought on the other slave.

"Luca." Jarrick was beside their wagon. "Come back with me."

"But during the day—"

"I've just paid Trader Matteo for your new slave, so he will not argue over what we do now. And you're bleeding. Come with me."

Luca's tight shoulders slipped. "Thanks, Jarrick." He glanced over his shoulder. "Cole, too."

Jarrick's wagon, shared with Matteo, featured an oilskin cover and blankets within. Luca climbed inside and began to shed his sodden clothes, scraping his fresh welts. Jarrick caught his breath. "Luca..."

Luca shook his head. "I've had worse."

"Let me find you some oil or salve. Surely there's something here."

"For him, too." Luca beckoned to Cole, who waited at the tail of the wagon. "Come inside and take a blanket."

The oil Jarrick located was not so efficiently numbing as the salve Shianan had once used, but it helped. Luca rubbed it into his shoulders, keeping his eyes away from Jarrick's unhappy stare.

"Luca," Jarrick ventured finally, "I didn't know you were pulling today."

"One of the overseers. There was no chance to argue." He nodded toward Cole. "Take off what's left of that and let's see the damage."

Cole was reluctant. "I can see to it myself, master. There's no need to trouble yourself." The words seemed awkward in his mouth.

Luca rubbed oil gingerly into the swelling cut on his face, his arm shaking. "It will be more trouble if you're not fit enough to keep the trader happy."

Cole backed against the wall and peeled his wet shirt off, revealing the bloody weal on his abdomen.

Luca frowned. "Are you meaning to hide something from me?"

Cole's eyes shifted, confirming Luca's suspicion. Jarrick looked from Luca to Cole and back, shaking his head. "Flames, Luca, what have you done?"

Luca blew out his breath. "You'd best let us see."

The slave rotated in the narrow wagon, exposing his back to the watery light. The four torn stripes stood out clearly among the crisscrossing bruised welts of the switch, but beneath those was a mass of half-healed wounds and faded bruising, and fainter scars extended over his ribs and arms. He'd been no stranger to punishment even before recent beatings.

Jarrick sighed a curse. "What have you done, Luca? I've just paid twice or thrice what anyone should for a slave who fights his work, fights other slaves, fights his masters..."

Luca ignored his brother and spoke to Cole. "I know how it is to be judged on what others have said and done. I was a Furmelle slave. Remember, I've seen you work as no master has." He looked at Jarrick. "He was honest in the wagon shafts, pulling his share or more. He's been a favorite target since he came, I've seen it. He didn't deserve all he took today. I would like to hear his own explanation."

Cole's head bobbed unhappily. "I have been a draft slave and then an overseer, now draft again," he confirmed. He took a breath and spoke more rapidly. "But I do mind punishment, no matter what they may tell—I'm as eager to avoid it as any reasonable man. But it takes me, and I just can't... My blood runs black." He looked at Luca. "The one beside me today, he drew a single cart in Orcan's caravan. It stuck in the mud."

"Wait," said Jarrick. "I remember you. In Alham."

Cole looked at Jarrick. "Were you the merchant master then? Orcan said if I didn't have it out of the mud, he'd loosen both our hides, and that was no idle threat. When it didn't come free, I—I panicked." He shrugged.

"Panicked? You had that man screaming on the ground."

"To stave off worse." Cole glanced away, resentment underlying his miserable expression. "And then you came, and you criticized Orcan."

Trader Matteo's comment returned to Luca. "Orcan said you'd humiliated him before a client."

Cole nodded. "Yes, master. I tried to avoid a beating and so earned it." Something dark colored his voice. "It's a sick and bloody game we can't win, so why play?"

Jarrick looked as if he wanted to answer, but he glanced at Luca and kept silent.

Luca had thought of trying to flee Ande, before he'd learned to give up all hope of escape. "And today?"

"And today, on the hill—no matter how I pulled, and when he said—I only saw red. He's why I'm here now, and..." He flattened his mouth and ground out, "Thank you, master, for sparing me."

Luca shook his head. "Those cuts need oil."

Cole took the small bottle and looked toward Jarrick. "When the wagon was stuck in Alham, you went to that puny draft and spoke to him. Only criticism for me." Cole checked himself. "Beg pardon, my lord. It's only—I wondered for hours, while I waited for Orcan to come... I suppose as something to distract myself. But I wondered why you had a word for him when he was at fault."

Jarrick shook his head. "He had black hair." He crossed his arms, his eyes on the rain outside. "I had to look."

Luca went hollow as he stared at his brother. The herbal scent of the oil filled the wagon. Luca impulsively leaned forward and embraced his brother. "Thank you, Jarrick," he said hoarsely. "For being there today. I did not even look for you—I knew you would come."

There was a shout from outside and then the wagon shifted, rumbling forward. Luca glanced around. "I should go—"

"No. Stay here."

"But Trader Matteo—and the ones pulling this wagon..."

"I told you Trader Matteo will not concern himself with us today. As for the road, it is a long downhill slope here, and you will not trouble the draft slaves too much if you stay. If you insist on worrying, I'll step out and walk myself."

"But—"

"But you'll stay. You need rest, or haven't you seen yourself lately?" Jarrick ventured a half-smile.

"I'll go, masters." Cole looked anxious to be away from the brothers. Jarrick nodded, glad to be free of him as well, and he eased over the wagon's tail and started away.

Jarrick looked after him a moment, wondering whether he'd made a mistake in supporting Luca's desperate rescue. Being inches from a flogging would affect anyone, of course, but he could not afford to spend so much on an impulsive purchase, especially one which might be near worthless in the end.

Still, he could hardly have refused. He looked at his brother. He would find it difficult to refuse Luca anything for a long time. He wondered how that would affect their future.

Luca had changed, as much as their father or anyone. He was no longer the annoyed and annoying younger brother, watching his elders from a distance and complaining occasionally over his work. He was harder now, quiet, with an expression that expected nothing of life. Aside from that initial heated argument when he awoke in the Kalen baths, Luca had been quiet, invisible, submissive—a slave. When for the first time again he'd shown vitality, Jarrick had to act on it.

If buying a worthless slave restored his brother's trust, it was cheap at twice the price.

"You can stay, Luca. You don't have to go."

Luca shook his head. "It isn't that I'd rather not stay." He sighed and shifted his shoulders. "But if I don't walk loose tonight the morning will see me hardly able to move. Even if I'm not pulling, they'll switch the line for lagging."

How straightforwardly he said it—not as if it held the horror for him as it did for Jarrick, and not as if he meant to shock or rebuke Jarrick with it. It was merely fact, a fixture in his life, no more shocking than tides to a sailor.

No, he would not be able to refuse much to Luca. Not for a long, long time.

CHAPTER SEVENTEEN

"Got another one." Captain Torg dropped the report on Shianan's desk. "Four killed, planting seed taken."

Shianan reached for the report but did not look at it. "To the northwest again? Do we know of any established bandits there?"

"Due west this time, too far to be the same bandits on foot. Survivors insist the raiders were Ryuven." Torg delivered the news levelly, though frustration showed in his pinched mouth. "But Ryuven can't come here, not with the shield again."

"Exactly. So why would these people lie?"

Torg scratched his beard. "I don't pretend to understand the magic of it, but couldn't the shield work both ways? With the shield, the Ryuven can't come—but they can't leave, either. Maybe there were some who were trapped in our world?"

"It's possible. But in multiple places?"

"I suppose we wait to hear if anyone spots them. They can't fly too much without being seen, so that will slow their travel."

"True. But if they're trapped here, why take the seed? Why not something more, I don't know, immediately useful, like ordinary robbers?"

"They're doing what they know," Torg suggested. "But if they've got nowhere to go, we just wait until we have a lead on them and then pick them out like lice. Now, you want to hear what fourth squad will be drilling again?"

Shianan made a show of putting his face in his hands. "What have they done now?"

It was the longest week Ariana could remember.

By day she sat in her workroom, pretending to work on the new ink while in fact she stared at her utensils and books with a slow, sick dread. For an hour each day, she went to Mage Parma or her father or the two together, attempting simple exercises in magic as if she were a child, struggling to master the simplest of fundamentals which had come more easily to her the first time.

It was worse than being a child, in fact. When she had been a

117

young girl, propped on her knees and leaning on her elbows to concentrate on a blackened candle wick, she had been thrilled with each small success. Now that she could remember practicing magical combat, creating an amulet to heal a broken limb, sealing Tamaryl's Ryuven essence—now each tiny success was a fresh cut to her pride, salting anew her terror that the others would learn, would find she was more an impostor than ever, would cast her out of the Circle.

By night, she hugged herself in her bed and choked on sobs that were harder to fight down in the dark.

She had told no one else. After her first desperate grasp for help, rushing to her father, she was afraid to speak of her loss. If the other mages of the Circle learned, she would lose what standing she had in their eyes. Worse, she might be removed from the Circle altogether.

Nor could she tell Ranne, who had been so supportive and so proud of her. Or Bethia, who had lost her own chance at the Circle when Ariana became the Black Mage, who could only be insulted to learn Ariana was no longer capable of it.

And Shianan. She was ashamed to recall her outburst, ashamed to have lashed out at him when she knew he had just come from the king and that something, *something* had happened. She should have gone to him, should have apologized and asked—but she wasn't supposed to know what happened in the king's private meetings with the bastard, and she didn't know how to ask without humiliating Shianan too.

So she avoided her friends, letting them believe she was buried with Great Circle work while she sat useless in her workroom.

It was late in the week when she achieved for the first time the newly difficult conquest of lifting a silken scarf tossed into the air. The effort exhausted her and left her trembling, but she had done it. Mage Parma's look of satisfied pride was salve enough for Ariana's raw nerves after a long session of struggle.

"Now take the day off," Mage Parma told her. "Don't push any further just because you accomplished more today."

Ariana shook her head, her muscles like water. "No worries there. I don't have the strength."

"Just bask in your glory, then." The Silver Mage turned to her table and began to collect the array of training items.

A knock sounded at the door, and Ariana went rigid. Mage Parma called for the visitor to enter.

A woman in orange robes came in. "Sorry to bother you, but I wondered—oh, hello, Mage Hazelrig. Sorry to interrupt."

Ariana nodded tightly.

"Mage Tadak?" prompted Mage Parma.

"Oh, I'm just out of dark shield paper, and I need only one, and I thought you might save me a trip to the market."

"Of course, help yourself." Mage Parma nodded toward the shelf of supplies.

"Thank you." Mage Tadak smiled at the half-cleared table. "I remember those days well enough. Looks like you're starting a new apprentice?"

Ariana's breath snagged in her throat. Mage Parma only shook her head. "No, not at the moment. Do you want to take some extra shield papers, just in case of need?"

"Thank you." Mage Tadak gave them each a friendly smile and let herself out.

Mage Parma turned to Ariana. "What was that about?"

"I don't want her to know." Ariana's face burned. "I don't want any of them to know."

Mage Parma waited.

"They won't—they won't look on me as if I'm one of them. Because I'm not one of them. And they will put me out of the Circle."

Mage Parma scooped the last of the training items into a shallow wooden box. "Do you think so?"

Ariana couldn't think to answer. "The Circle is supposed to be the best of mages, the elite. The Circle is supposed to be a polished unit, a cadre working together, each member reliable and accountable to the others. That's not me."

The Silver Mage set her hands on the box's sides and waited.

Slow dread rose in Ariana's torso, twisting her stomach and reaching up to choke her with her own words. "Oh. Oh, no. I have to tell them." Her throat closed, but she forced her voice out. "I can't keep this from them, or I'm not a failure, but a traitor."

"I wouldn't have put it in quite those words." Mage Parma's eyes were soft, sympathetic. "But you should tell them."

"Tell them what? That I'm no longer a mage, that I must leave the Circle?"

Mage Parma tapped her notes from the session. "Tell them you have experienced effects from your exposure to the Ryuven world, show that you are rebuilding your skills, and report what progress you have made thus far."

"And am I making progress?"

Mage Parma gave her a stern look and tapped the notes again.

"All right, I am. But is it enough?"

"Just be careful," the Silver Mage cautioned. "If you try to rush ahead, you might set yourself back. Don't, in your eagerness to prove yourself, make your hill into a mountain."

"It feels like a mountain already," muttered Ariana, but she nodded. "I'll be careful. No outside practice."

Mage Parma smiled. "Now go and treat yourself to something special. You earned it today."

In the corridor, Ariana squeezed her eyes shut against silent, burning tears as she returned to her own office. She would have to tell her friends first—they shouldn't hear it from Circle news or rumors.

Ranne was in the market. Shianan was closer, if in his office instead of with his soldiers. He would understand if she told him.

It would be so hard to tell him.

CHAPTER EIGHTEEN

Shianan looked down the slope of the hill to the village nestled at its base, smoking from too many places. The granary stood open, its door damaged, and a child had been stationed to shoo sheep and goats from the remaining stores. The livestock had grasped their advantage, and each time the child ran at a clump of raiding animals, a few opportunistic sheep and goats darted around for mouthfuls of spilled grain, only to retreat when the frustrated keeper charged them and gave others a chance.

Shianan blew out his breath. "How many?"

"Three dead, sir, and one seriously wounded. She'll probably pull through."

Shianan did not need to descend to the village to know what he would find, but his duty here was only partly to identify and counter the danger. He also had to represent an official response to reassure the frightened populace. He nodded for the sergeant to signal the soldiers and started downhill.

The attack was easy to read, from the blood spatters on walls to the magic burns on two of the corpses, laid out on the threshing floor as the village was too small for a meeting house or a temple. Shianan knew what the survivor would say even before he went to see her, bundled in blankets in her bed.

"They were Ryuven," she rasped. Bruising marred the side of her face, red and purple streaking downward from her eye like bloody tears. "Six Ryuven, come for our grain and vegetables."

Shianan did not insult her by asking if she was sure. "Did you see them arrive? Crossing the between-worlds?"

She shook her head. "No, but Brooker did. He's the one who first raised the alarm."

"Can we see him?"

"You already did. On the threshing floor."

Shianan sighed. "Right. Thank you, Alys, for your help, and take care of yourself."

Alys kept her eyes on him. "I thought there was supposed to be a magical shield to protect us."

Shianan fought down the unease. "We're working on it, and

121

we'll have things set right as soon as we can." Then he stood and escaped before she could ask again.

Surely this was too much to be a few trapped Ryuven.

Shianan had purchased the Shard of Elan from the Gehrn with his townhouse and a foothold in Alham. He had sacrificed his escape from torture to return the Shard to the Circle. He had given his property, his honor, and very nearly his life to help bring about the shield. How could there be Ryuven raiding in Chrenada?

Ariana kept her eyes down as the meeting proceeded around her, shifting to ease the ache in her lower back. This week's Circle business was nothing out of the ordinary—yet. In a few minutes, she would have to explain that she was the first member of the Circle to be powerless.

Not powerless, Mage Parma would have reminded her. But no longer qualified for the Circle.

Despite her intent, she had not told anyone else about her loss. Shianan had been out of the city on a military assignment. Ranne's shop had been closed when Ariana visited, and no one had answered at their home. Ariana felt she was betraying her friends as much as her colleagues, trying too late to tell them, and now she faced the Circle without the practice of explaining.

"The next item is somewhat sensitive," the White Mage said, and Ariana's heart quickened. "It concerns the other Mage Hazelrig."

She stared at the table, wondering if her stomach might force itself up her throat.

"Due to the difficult nature, I will give a brief introduction, and then if there are specific questions, Mage Hazelrig may answer."

Ariana slid her eyes toward her father, who nodded once without looking directly at her. Bless him—he was saying the hardest words.

"Since her return from the Ryuven world and her exposure to its dangerous magic," he said, his voice thick with emotion, "Mage Hazelrig has experienced a precipitous drop in ability. For a time, she was unable to manipulate energy at all."

A susurrus of sound ran around the table, and Ariana pushed her eyes down again so she wouldn't see mages turning to stare.

"She has been working through it, however, and is regaining her ability. Presently she is at the level of a beginning apprentice. We anticipate she should continue to improve with practice."

There was a long, pregnant pause, and at last the Crimson Mage, Ademar Carrock, cleared his throat uncomfortably. Ariana could hear his chair creak between his hesitating words. "How quickly is this improvement progressing?"

Ariana's breath caught. She had been good at magic the first time. Yes, it had taken time, but it had come steadily under her father's tutelage. Forced to regain the same ground, struggling for each success—she knew, in rational thought, she knew she was improving, but was it fast enough? Was it good enough? Was it enough?

After a moment, her father answered. "It is hard to be exact with a figure, but she has reached the level of a novitiate apprenticeship in a little over a week. That does not necessarily indicate the rate of future progress, which could be faster as her skill improves."

"Or could be slower, as we don't know what caused its loss in the first place." This was Mage Renstil, the Forest. "I am sorry, but someone must say it—the Great Circle is the cornerstone of defense for Chrenada and its people, and I don't know that we can afford to have a mage without ability."

Ariana's faced burned so that she thought it must be shedding its own light.

"Let's speak of that defense," Mage Parma said. Ariana did not look at her, but she knew the note of confident challenge in that voice. She had heard it enough of late. "What is the Great Circle to defend against?"

Mage Renstil did not immediately answer.

"The Ryuven have been our greatest threat, all would agree. But we have renewed our shield against the Ryuven—which Mage Hazelrig assisted us in doing, at the apparent cost of her last magic— and we are now protected from them. Who else brings immediate threat to Chrenada? The Wakari Coast? We are on good terms and in fact are presently negotiating a marriage alliance. The warlords of the south? They are still in Heege, which, for all that it is a disputed territory, is a pebble of little worth, and it's unlikely the warlords will leave their swamps to assault Alham. We face no immediate threats, and it is my opinion, having seen Mage Hazelrig's progress thus far, that we may take some time to assess her recovering ability and make an informed decision."

No one answered, and Elysia Parma's words hung in the air.

Sweet all, did they want her gone? No, surely not—Ariana was one of them. It was only, this was her dream, her whole life, and what if they did choose to replace her...

"Perhaps we should hear from Mage Hazelrig herself," suggested Mage Fallat, Scarlet. "Since it is her position we are discussing."

Ariana did not want to face them with her face burning so red and tears brimming her eyes. She forced a deep shuddering breath and blew it out softly through her pursed lips.

Shianan had faced the king and the courtiers time and again, with a far more hostile moderator than her father. She could be brave like Shianan.

She stood and fixed her eyes on the far wall. "I understand your concern, and it shows your fidelity to your duties and the Circle's purpose." She paused to take another breath. "The Circle, though it has duties as a whole, seeks to balance its strengths. I was admitted not for my battle experience but for my theoretical knowledge and efforts in research. For myself, I can say that my theoretical knowledge is undiminished and indeed, I am daily more and more immersed as I return with a more advanced eye to more foundational subjects." She tried to smile, as if it were a jest, but wasn't sure her face succeeded. "I will of course understand if you choose to remove me from your ranks, as it's evident I could not join the Circle if I were to test today for entrance." She tried not to feel Mage Parma's eyes heavy on her. "I know this should not be a decision made on the basis of emotion or other connection. But for what it's worth, I am working hard, and I want more than anything to stay and earn back my place."

She tore her eyes from the far wall and made herself look around at them. "Unless you have any questions for me directly, I will excuse myself to allow you all more latitude to discuss the situation. Thank you."

When no one raised a question, she took measured steps, counting them to keep her pace orderly, and then fled through the door and into the corridor.

There was nothing to do but wait. Ariana stretched her tense neck and leaned against the cool stone wall.

The wall was cold against her back, but the draft coming around the Wheel chilled more, too. The sensation between her legs was strange but distantly familiar, and after a moment of startled confusion her heart sank. With a glance toward the door—surely they would not be ready to recall her, not so quickly—she went down the corridor to a privy.

She was bleeding. She had not even recognized the pain in her back; it had been so long since she'd had cramps. Magic used the body hard, so that male mages rarely sired children and female mages usually had to take a hiatus to bear a child to term. Like most women practicing magic regularly, Ariana had bled rarely and lightly. She stared down at the rusty-brown betrayal, yet another vivid sign of her fall.

Of course there would be no sachets of blood sphagnum in the Wheel; none of the Circle's women would need them. She would have to go down to the market once she'd heard the Circle's decision on whether to keep her.

She beat her forehead into her palm and growled.

"Mage Hazelrig? Ariana? Are you in here?"

Ariana jumped and snatched at her clothing. "Just one moment!"

It was Mage Marie Tadak who stood in the corridor outside. "I couldn't find you," she said, her tone apologetic. "I hoped... I hoped you were only in the privy."

Ariana hunched her shoulders against the corridor's draft. "What did the Circle have to say?"

"I'm supposed to invite you back to hear, but we voted to keep you provisionally, until it should become apparent that your magecraft is not returning. We have some tests of proficiency we want to see, milestones for your continued progress. It will be explained." She smiled. "So that's good."

Ariana nodded, only partially relieved. "So long as I keep improving."

She had others to thank: Mage Parma's challenge had done well for her, and her father's assertion of her progress. She could not disappoint them, could not fail them and herself.

She thought irrationally of Tamaryl eating chocolate to restore his depleted magic and wondered if she might find some in the market when she went down.

CHAPTER NINETEEN

Ariana's father did not answer her knock, but it was possible he was busy with a project in the workroom, and years ago he had set a charm on his office door to recognize her. Ariana let herself in, embarrassed to be proud she could manage the minimal working of the charm.

He was not in the rear workroom, either. She blew out her breath and settled her troublesome ink and brushes on an empty surface.

Maybe she should try the ink again, waiting for him. Mage Parma had cautioned her against pushing too hard with her magic, lest a setback occur, and Ariana was hesitant to experiment beyond previous successes without another mage to steady her in case it went wrong. Still, she might try once more. She wanted to help with the ink research, to feel as if she were still contributing to the Circle's efforts, and it felt so childish to ask her father to supervise her attempt with a new spell.

Oh! The fragment of broken Shard, the subject of his initial investigations into the Shield—it could augment energy. It might help both to boost her weakened power and to stabilize the ink's transformation process. She turned to his storage cabinet, but the piece of crystallized ether was not on the shelf where she had seen it. Someone must have borrowed it for an experiment.

On the shelf below sat her own sketched map of the Ryuven city where she had stayed. It was incomplete and rough, but it was their first glimpse of the Ryuven world. The lines were blurred, however, and she realized it was not her own drawing, but a tracing on onion paper lying atop her own map. Why had her father bothered to trace her incomplete map?

She turned back to her ink and brushes. She would try the ink again anyway. It was a small spell, not too risky.

Ariana carefully inked a rune and blew to dry it. Shifting the paper to a separate worktable, judiciously away from the inkwell, she placed her hand over the figure and began to form a spell. In her mind's eye, thin strands of color began to wrap together, forming the shape of the rune and knotting into—

Flame burst from the paper and licked at her palm, making her yelp and jerk her hand away. The half-finished magic spiraled away and a shelved bottle shattered. Ariana gasped and recalled the spell, collapsing it upon itself and absorbing the errant energy. It tingled up her arm as she upended a jar of sand over the burning rune.

The damage curtailed, she stepped back and sighed miserably. She confirmed that the flames were extinguished and then scooped the sand together to scrape back into the jar.

"Hello, Father," she said to herself in a mocking tone. "I came for help on a containment issue. Sorry about the mess."

A clear liquid dripped from the shelf and broken glass. She picked up a rag, hoping the spilled contents had not been too valuable, and went to check the label.

A shock wave rolled across the room, staggering her. She whirled as jars and bottles rattled around the workshop. She was certain the fire had been out, and surely a single rune could not cause this—!

Pressure squeezed at her eardrums. Ariana gulped and raised her hands, though she hardly knew what magic to form or what would actually come. It could not be Ryuven—the shield was raised, it was perfectly functional, it could not be Ryuven...!

The ceiling seemed to open, timbers rippling in bending light, and a flash of membranous wings made Ariana blink and shrink back. Ryuven! It was impossible, but somehow, somehow they had found a way through the shield.

There was no time to call for help—her father's board of harmonic crystals was across the room, beyond the appearing enemy. The shield had slowed the Ryuven's entry, but he was coming, and this moment of stretching between worlds was her best chance to attack. She raised her hands, eying the winged form between her outstretched fingers, and reached frantically for magic.

And then the ceiling wavered and she saw his face.

"Tamaryl!" She dropped her hands, dissipating the frail magic, and rushed forward. What was he doing? "Tam!"

He seemed to push downward through an invisible boundary, becoming clearer to her vision and lowering slightly beneath the ceiling. She could see now the lines etched on his face, concentration and determination as he fought his way, layer by layer, through the shield. His eyes were squeezed tightly shut and his teeth gritted, exerting all his considerable strength.

"Tamaryl!" She reached for him, but her fingers passed smoothly through his clenched fist. He cried and jerked his hand away, and she watched as the skin seemed to trail behind the quick movement, resolving itself once more as it caught him.

The mages! Surely they would feel the arrival of a Ryuven so near, especially one so powerful as the Pairvyn ni'Ai! But as she started for the door, she realized she felt no telltale swell of power. The disruption of the shield was specific to the point of intrusion, and all of Tamaryl's natural essence was feeding directly into the shield, masking his arrival.

She stood unhappily, afraid to attempt to help, unable to move. He dropped another few inches, his face twisted with effort, and he clawed at something invisible between them, ripping at air. Iridescent strands appeared around him, streaming backward from his arms, his face, his wings, pulling like taffy into the outer plys of the shield. They stretched impossibly far, clinging to him and drawing him back, but with a final grunting cry he broke forward. The strands whipped backward and vanished, and Tamaryl dropped leadenly to the floor.

Ariana rushed forward, kneeling and reaching for him but, remembering how contact had hurt him after the sealing, not quite touching him. He had made no effort at all to catch himself. Had the shield killed him after all?

She could not help him without touching him. She tentatively took his shoulder, noting blood at his ear, and rolled him from his prone position. Blood streamed from his nose as well, though that could be from the fall, she reasoned desperately. And the other ear, and his nose, and—and tiny rivulets of blood showed in the corners of his half-opened, unseeing eyes.

The shield was designed to penetrate a crossing Ryuven and shred his innards or leave them outside as he came through. It was only by Tamaryl's massive expenditure of power that he had impressed it and finally punctured to the center. He had not been able to blunt its effects entirely.

But he was not dead yet. Ariana looked at her father's shelf of medicinal supplies. There weren't many—the White Mage was more occupied with innovative magical defenses and theoretical experiments than routine healing—but she should be able to render some help.

She did not waste time with the few healing amulets. They worked in harmony with the natural healing of a human body, and she did not know how they would interact with the wildly different magical healing of a Ryuven. She remembered Tam lying broken at the base of a steep valley, beaten by hateful Ryuven and drained by Oniwe'aru. Maru had given him power, raw power, to let his body begin healing.

Power, then. She looked about her father's workroom. Raw power... Over months they compressed power into amulets, creating a reservoir which was then magically manipulated toward the appropriate system. That was one way to handle raw power...

She took down a jar of deep emerald salve. Maru had directed his power into Tamaryl's face, but he was a Ryuven, presumably more comfortable with the transfer of power than Ariana in her first attempt. She would not dare to experiment so near the brain, and the damage was likely to be worst in his torso, as that was where the shield had hurt him when they'd first created it. That was where it was designed to kill.

She scooped out a handful of the glistening salve. His skin was feverish as she first touched it, and then as she spread the salve she hit icy, clammy patches and then hot again. She didn't pause to wonder at the mottled temperature but spread the ointment evenly, making sure it was level across his skin. She did not want to concentrate power into one area over another.

The salve would draw the power she generated, pulling it like a lodestone drawing needles or honey trapping a fly. Usually they used only a tiny dab on an amulet—her father would not be pleased to see so much of the precious material gone—but she needed to do in minutes what they usually infused over months. She needed to generate a phenomenal amount of power and she could not lose a particle of it.

A phenomenal amount of power... She had been warned. But she could not watch Tamaryl die. There was no time to weigh the risks; she had to save her friend.

If only there had been a way to store his own power she'd drained during the binding...! But there was no time to regret the impossible now. His shallow breathing was taking on a wheezing, gurgling sound, and she did not want to think about what fluid was filling his lungs. She spread her hands over him and concentrated.

Power sparkled around her when her eyes closed. She began to gather it, condensing it within her illusory grasp, funneling it downward toward the emerald ointment which sucked at her weak stream like thirsty cloth, wicking it into Tamaryl's ravaged organs. She pulled at the atmosphere, keeping a steady drizzle transferring to the inert body.

She steadied herself, balancing the collection of power, and spared a quick internal glance at Tamaryl's form. There was no shining power there, as there had been when she'd drawn it from him. The thin stream she fed into him was diluted instantly in the magic-hungry Ryuven. There was not even the flickering light which had struggled in Maru. He had no magical signature at all. It was as if he were human, or dead.

Not dead. She could, if she drew back from funneling power, hear the bubbling gurgle of his strained breathing. It was worse than before. In a moment, he would drown in his own blood—

If only she had the nearly unlimited magical atmosphere of the Ryuven world! If only she had the ability she once had. If only she could open herself somehow again, as she had done to save Maru, and command so much power...

Oh no—Holy—please— Thoughts slipped brokenly in her mind.

She gulped and braced herself, throwing wide her arms. Magic was dangerous. All of her magical training had been about control, about safety and preservation. But she had unthinkingly done this once before, in another world with other magic—

Brilliant sparkles of power flew across her closed eyelids, burning her skin where they struck her. A bright stream coalesced around her and spiraled downward, plunging into Tamaryl in an ever-widening torrent of energy. Ariana gasped for breath as power spread through her, an endorphic exhilarating rush that fascinated and terrified her.

Ariana. She heard her name whispered from a long, long distance. Tamaryl? Her father? Shianan?

Abruptly another flame of power rose beside her. The cataract of energy twisted, bending to the direction of this second will, and she felt the power tamed, no less than what it had been but now under greater control, diving into a ready channel now rather than splashing over the well which could not admit all at once. The emerald ointment sucked up the energy and poured it into Tamaryl.

And then the channel was filling, and the power began to rebound. Tamaryl could absorb no more. The second will ceased to direct the stream, letting it spread where it would. *Ariana...*

She stopped drawing the cascade and tried to close herself to the influx. But the power would not be deterred—it pressed upon her, prying into her pores, filling her beyond capacity and stretching her painfully—

An audible *crack* shattered her concentration and she gasped, falling backward. But arms caught her as she fell, pulling her close to white robes. "Ariana," breathed her father. "Ariana, can you hear me?"

"Father?"

"Oh, sweet Holy One." He embraced her close. "You—I can't—oh, Ariana. Can you hold yourself? Are you all right?"

She did not understand his concern. She felt well enough. Well, her skin hurt in a peculiar way, as if it had been inflated around her, stretched uncomfortably and still too large, but that was all. "I'm fine."

"We'll see about that." He looked down at Tamaryl's unmoving form. "He came through the shield?"

She nodded. Her head felt a little loose as she did. "I was waiting for you, and he came—I saw him break through the shield, but it—well, you can see."

"Only the Pairvyn ni'Ai," he muttered. "You had the right idea, anyway. I'm sure it saved his life."

She looked at him. "But he's not moving. Shouldn't he..."

"I doubt he will move for quite some time," Hazelrig said. "We put a tremendous amount of power into him, true, but he is rebuilding himself from the inside outward. Only someone so powerful could perhaps have come, and I doubt a silth or aru would heal more quickly. Let me get him on a table, where we can deal with him more easily."

Ariana tried to stand as her father lifted the Ryuven, but her legs were wobbly and disobedient. He left Tamaryl supine on a worktable and turned back to her. "You," he said firmly, "know far better than to ever do such a thing. Especially when your ability is so tenuous! If I hadn't come—if I hadn't cut your magic and risked injuring you..." He checked himself, looking older with worry. "I know you were thinking of helping him. But what would it have helped if I'd come to find two bodies instead of one? And one my own daughter?"

She understood. She had been caught in the stream of her own magic, unable to control it and unable to end it. It would have poured through her until it killed her, just as every instructor warned novices with dire stories and threats. Her father had saved not only Tamaryl's life, by directing the raw power, but hers, by ending her wild spell.

"I'm sorry." Her voice was subdued to her ears. "And thank you. For helping both of us."

He nodded and hugged her again. "Now, let's make him as comfortable as anyone with half a kidney and a pulverized liver can be."

They wrapped him warmly in their mages' cloaks, cushioned his head gently on some workroom towels, and bathed away the blood, which mercifully had stopped streaming from every orifice. Ariana turned her back as her father stripped and cleaned the wounded Ryuven, thinking again of Shianan's inference. Of course they had not—Tamaryl had not tried to force her. How could Shianan have believed such a thing?

"You may turn back, Ariana," came her father's voice, and she did. Tamaryl's breath still wheezed in his chest. Hazelrig frowned. "I don't like the sound of that. Let's turn him onto his shoulder. Have him? Ready?"

As Tamaryl's head lolled toward the edge of the table, more blood began to drain from his mouth. Ariana stared in sick fascination as a thin gleaming rivulet ran from the corner of his lips. "He looks like a slaughtered pig," she whispered.

"We'll hope that he gets over that." Her father sighed. "Why did he come back?"

"I don't know."

"Don't you?" He gave her a piercing look.

Ariana stared back at him. "No, he couldn't say anything—" She stopped, wondering suddenly at the look in her father's eyes. She thought back to Tamaryl's final words to her before departing for his own world. No, his final action—when he had bent and kissed her, leaving her with only the taste of him...

"No," she protested, only half-meaning it. "No, he said he never wanted to see us again."

"Seeing us again would have been in battle." He gave her a narrow, paternal look. "But I wasn't the one he kissed."

She flushed hotly. "I—I didn't—he never..."

Her father had mercy and turned his piercing eyes away from her. "Let's not speculate until he can speak for himself. In the meantime, we'll have to keep him protected. We can't move him in this condition."

Ariana looked down at him. She had been helpless and in pain in the Ryuven world, and Tamaryl had somehow kept her safe.

She had used her magic, had pushed it dangerously beyond what she should have. Somewhere too deep to really feel it yet, fresh terror seized her. She had done the worst, had destroyed her magic.

She did not have time to think on it. Tamaryl's breath burbled wetly and then he began to cough.

"Get a towel," ordered Hazelrig, reaching for him.

Ariana turned to find one as spatters of bright blood struck her dark robes, disappearing into the black. She turned back and held the towel over his mouth, catching the droplets and gobbets of gore as he tried to clear his lungs.

Her father seemed pleased. "That's good. At least he's trying to breathe now, and has the strength to do it properly."

Ariana left him with the towel and took another to mop up the scattered spray over the table and floor. Too many questions hung over her, smothering her.

When Tamaryl's breathing had steadied and quieted, Ariana and her father covered him and then looked at each other. They had a Ryuven again, one who had to be hidden.

CHAPTER TWENTY

Cole was struggling, Luca observed. It had to be disorienting, for a man accustomed to a dizzying mix of authority and responsibility and vulnerability as an enslaved overseer, to find himself reduced to the lowest of common labor and then sold to a fellow slave. Now Cole was trying his best to be careful of the man chained beside him, taking care to avoid jostling Luca in the line and calling him "master" despite the snickers of the slaves around them. Luca guessed he had weighed their present derision against the weeks or years which lay ahead under Luca's authority and judged it better to ingratiate himself.

The thin, dark-haired slave was the worst. He made a point of repeatedly stepping into Cole or Luca, and when Cole meaningfully bumped him in return, he whined and stumbled and earned Cole a switch across the shoulders. Cole waited until the nearest overseer had gone behind another wagon, and then he did something Luca could not quite see which drew a gasp and whimper, a tiny movement which kept the other slave at bay for a few hours. Luca was uncomfortably reminded that Cole had been an overseer, a driver, one of the enemy.

"I'll find you," the thin slave muttered as they stood close while a front wagon was rocked out of a hole. "I'll earn my freedom, and then I'll find you and I'll make you pay."

Cole snorted. "You won't."

"I knew a litter bearer who was freed when—"

"Oh, it happens, sure, but not to you, and anyway you'd be a slave again inside ten days," Cole sneered. "I saw it, slaves brought in to have cuffs pulled off and next month we'd have them back to sell to someone else."

"How is that?" Luca's slavery on the road and with the Gehrn had been more isolated.

Cole checked most of his disdain to answer his new master. "Most slaves are too stupid to manage their own selves. I've seen them given their own price and more with their freedom, and they're bashed with coin. They drink it and whore it and eat viante or worse until they're starving in a gutter and get picked up, or even sell themselves back."

"But, if they have money..."

Cole laughed. "Master, you should see them. I watched a man handed two thousand pias on his release. Two thousand pias! He'd been some favorite cook or table server or something. Three months later he came through again on a caravan to Vandoga, draft and half-skinned. He'd spent it all and lost his own self in a dice game. There are people too stupid to be freemen."

"How can someone lose two thousand pias?" Luca was calculating food and rent and how long it might take to find new work.

"I can think of a few ways," Cole said with a grin. "Would be a fine way to go down. But they're stupid, and so they land themselves worse than they were."

The thin slave's lip curled derisively. "Says the overseer now pulling draft."

Cole moved fast, stomping on the slave's foot as he caught the wrist chain and snapped it downward, yanking the slave's face into his upswung knee.

"Stop!" Luca tugged Cole back.

"What's all that?" called an overseer from the front as the line split around the attack.

Luca ducked his head, willing them to move on, his hand still on Cole's arm. The other slave was stunned quiet, blinking and probing the side of his face. Then the tilted wagon shifted and the overseer turned back, and they were forgotten.

"You can't!" Luca whispered furiously. "You can't do that or they'll come for you."

"Let them," Cole growled, but he turned away from the slave, who had shrunk to the end of his chain.

The wagons began to move again, and the line started forward. The thin slave limped but kept his muttered threats quiet enough to be ignored.

Andrew moved close to Luca, keeping a wary eye on the others. "I'm not ever going to be free," he whispered, "but please, couldn't you purchase me too?"

Luca looked at him, uncomfortably helpless. He should have expected this. "I don't know. I don't have any money of my own, and Jarrick was none too pleased about my bargaining for Cole..."

"Please! Don't let me go to the mines or be chained to an oar. Please, won't you do it?"

Luca's heart sank. Andrew had been kind to him when he had

first come to Alham. "I'll see what I can do," he promised, guilt pricking him. What he could do might not be much, but he had to give Andrew some hope.

When they curled up for sleep that night, grouped tightly for warmth, Andrew wriggled close to Luca—whether to influence him by lending body heat in the cold night or to reassure himself of Luca's thin promise, Luca couldn't guess.

But the nights were not so cold now, and the mornings no longer showed frost on the grass. The protected waters of the Wakari Coast mitigated winter. The scent of the sea returned on the warmer breeze, and Luca's pulse began to quicken as he thought of the border, freedom and home.

And then one evening, as the wagons came to a heavy halt, Trader Matteo waved for an overseer to join him as he approached Luca's line. Jarrick was already coming for his nightly talk with Luca.

"Congratulations, Luca," Matteo said. "That checkpoint this afternoon marked the end of Chrenada's law. If your brother keeps his word, you're a freeman now."

"Yes," Jarrick put in. "Release him!"

Matteo nodded to the overseer, who blinked in silent surprise and ran the chains out of the cuff rings. "We don't travel with a full smithy, of course," Matteo said, "so we can't do anything about the cuffs until we reach my stable. But for our purposes, you're a free man, Luca."

"Thank you," Luca said automatically. And then he straightened tiredly and looked at the trader. "I'll be joining my brother in the caravan, then?"

"It will be a tight squeeze, the three of us freemen. I won't even charge you the accommodation. Consider it my gift to a very fortunate man." He motioned for Luca to step out of the line.

Andrew made a quick, hesitant motion as if to catch Luca's arm as he passed. "Luca..."

"Watch your manners," warned Matteo. "You should know more than to address a freeman by name. Is there anything else you need, Roald—either of you?" He shifted his eyes from Jarrick to Luca. "Your slaves will be remaining in the line, of course?" He indicated Cole.

"He will work," Luca answered flatly. "Could I borrow him for a few moments tonight?"

Matteo shrugged and nodded to the overseer. "Just see he's

back for his supper."

"He'll have it." Luca avoided Andrew's searching, anxious eyes and led Cole with Jarrick a short distance from the line. His back to the trader and overseers, he folded his arms against his torso and hugged himself.

Free! It was something he'd given up even dreaming of, something he had surrendered forever somewhere on the Faln Plateau. He gulped the evening air, stinging with the faint tang of salt. *Free!*

When he paused, Cole circled to face him. "Master."

It was awkward to hear such words addressed to him. It couldn't be possible that he could leap from chained slave, shuffling out of the overseers' way, to receiving the obeisance of another in so short a span.

"Cole," he said, "they'll use you as draft labor tomorrow or the next day."

Cole's shoulders tightened.

"I know. I know what you fear." Luca licked his lips. "It's justified. They will be looking for excuses."

Cole's shoulders rose another half-inch and his jaw clenched.

"You have to hold yourself, Cole. Keep your head, keep your temper, and endure it. Make it through the day without giving them reason, and you'll walk away in Ivat."

Cole nodded. "I will try, master."

"Trying is not enough. Clench your fists, grit your teeth, think of pressure bearing down on a stone, whatever it takes—but keep your head."

"Yes, master."

Jarrick said, "Cole, get back to the line. Let's not start with any jealousy over privileges."

"Yes, my lord." Cole started back.

"Do you think that will be enough? Just a word of warning?" Jarrick asked.

Luca looked after the slave. "It will have to be."

"I don't know. Perhaps the whip would improve him."

"A whip improves no one," Luca answered in a voice which surprised himself. "It may give the temporary strength or compliance of fear, but it cannot make him truly stronger or more willing."

Jarrick turned to face Luca, looking as if he would speak. He hesitated and then reached suddenly to embrace him. "Luca," he said softly, "I'm sorry. I'm so glad you're here again."

Luca hugged him in return. "Thank you for looking for me."

"Come on. The meals are awful, but maybe better than what you've been eating."

Luca was hungry, and there would be time later to mention Andrew. For the moment, he was for the first time in years in possession of his full name and capable of taking his own supper.

Ariana and her father kept the door to the rear workroom closed, in case of visitors to the White Mage's office, and after Ariana made a quick trip home for supplies, they spent the night with Tamaryl's still form. He was recovering, Hazelrig reported as he probed magically, but he had not yet awoken. "He's utterly exhausted. Drained completely. It will be some time before he has even a pitiful strength. But it is only exhaustion, and he should recover."

Still, Ariana could not forget the horrific image of Tamaryl bleeding from ears, nose, eyes. As the first day passed without any motion from him, she became more worried.

He had helped to design the shield; he'd known what it would do to him. As powerful as he was, she didn't think he was so arrogant as to believe that he could pass unharmed, and it had seemed he expected to be in the Ryuven world forever. What had brought him back?

Her father's implication pressed at her, and Ariana squirmed mentally. She did not want to be the cause of his injuries...

She pushed the thought from her mind, walking briskly through the marketplace.

She stepped into the bookbinding shop and nodded a greeting to Vaya, Ranne's mother, who gave her a friendly wave in return. Ariana went directly to the supply room.

Ranne was there, binding a book. She stopped tapping a block of pages into place and glanced up as Ariana entered. "Oh—Ariana! What's wrong?"

Ariana hesitated. "Wrong?"

Ranne set the half-bound book down. "Don't pretend, not here. Did something go wrong at the Wheel? Are you feeling ill again from the Ryuven world? Did you have a fight with your illicit love?"

Ariana startled. "I—illicit love?"

Ranne smiled. "That was just to get you to talk." She took

Ariana's arms, concerned again. "So what is it?"

All Ariana's words froze up like ice piling in the river. She had wanted to tell Ranne, wanted to share everything and plead for something, she couldn't even say what—or anything.

Ranne tipped her head to the side. "Ariana?"

Ariana couldn't tell her, couldn't say that a Ryuven was hiding in the Wheel itself, that he was a friend of many years, that he had kissed her. That she had lost her magic, started to regain it, and might have burned it all away to save a Ryuven.

She shook her head. "I don't know, I just... It's too much. I know the shield's raised again and..." She wanted to say she had argued with Becknam and was ashamed of her emotional outburst, but Ranne might ask what they had argued about, and anyway a fight sounded too much like they were sweethearts instead of friends.

There was too much to say, and so she couldn't say any of it.

Ariana sighed. "Can I just stay here for a while? Watch you bind books?"

Ranne gave her a squeeze. "Of course you can. Pull up a stool, and I'll put you to work hammering folds or something."

CHAPTER TWENTY-ONE

Shianan was rounding a crowded corner when suddenly the men before him drew themselves to the side and straightened or bowed. Shianan just had time to step aside as Prince Soren came into view. Shianan bowed.

But the prince slowed as he passed. "How did your apology fare, commander?" came a low question.

"I have not yet ventured," admitted Shianan.

"Delay will win you nothing," Soren warned, and then he was gone.

Some hours later, a knock sounded at Shianan's office door. Outside was a slave shielding a wrapped bouquet of flowers in full bloom. "From the hothouse," reported the slave through chattering teeth, taking his cloak from about them and pulling it over his shoulders. "I was told to deliver them to your lordship."

Shianan looked them over. *Sunshine on flowers.* Perhaps she would hear his apologetic explanation.

He set aside the sheaf of papers which awaited his approval and eyed the flowers. He wrapped them in a spare tunic and started for the Wheel.

Ariana slipped inside her father's office and nudged the door closed behind her. "How is he?"

"There has been no real change, though I think he's breathing more easily." He sighed. "I wouldn't have imagined a Ryuven would take so long to heal, but he seems to be steadily improving. I suppose he'll wake when he can."

Ariana set down the luncheon tray and passed to the rearmost room where Tamaryl, lying still on the table, was padded with blankets smuggled from home. He would move occasionally now, a muscle twitching as fibers rejoined or his torso shifting as he cleared healing lungs, but he had not regained consciousness. It was frightening. "He will wake, won't he?"

"That he is alive at all is a miracle. If he has not died yet, I think we should believe that he will eventually wake." Her father put an arm

141

around her shoulders and smiled. "Be patient, my girl. Now, come away from the table." He gestured to the open space.

Ariana did, not understanding.

"Show me a little colored light."

Ariana opened her fingers, hesitated, quested for magic and immediately flinched. She could sense the magic just out of reach, almost see it hanging in the air. But it was beyond her.

Her father put his hand atop hers, stilling her attempt. "What did you do for him?"

She thought it was a rebuke for risking her magic. She looked back at the table. "I had to," she defended, justifying the loss to him and herself. "Even though I knew it was dangerous. He was dying."

"And did you hesitate?"

Ariana chewed her lip, and he let her work through her thoughts. "It was different," she said at last. "When I was practicing with you or Mage Parma, I was afraid of failure."

He nodded.

"But just then, I was afraid of the consequences of failure. If I didn't give him magic, Tamaryl would die. So I couldn't hesitate, I had to put my hand in the flame." She looked at her father. "You're going to tell me that I thought about what I wanted to do instead of what I was afraid of not doing."

He raised one shoulder in smug acknowledgment. "Why should I repeat what you've just said?"

Ariana made a face. "You sound like her."

He nodded toward her hand. "The light."

Ariana looked down at her hand and recalled that she had channeled an unreal torrent of pure energy through her body. It had been foolish, it had been dangerous, it had been thrilling, and her father was beside her to catch her if she fell into the torrent again. She brought up her hand and watched a spiral of light form, shining pink and white, and spin over her palm.

She stared, her mouth slightly open, delighting in the simple trick of light.

Her father clapped his hands once and laughed. "I knew it!"

Ariana let the light dissolve and then she sank onto a stool and took a long, relieved breath. "But what if I had tried to help him and failed? If Tamaryl had died? How could I bear that?"

Her father smiled that smug, knowing White Mage's expression. "If you had tried and failed, then it would have been exactly as if you had not tried. Tamaryl would have died." He bent close to her and whispered, "Exactly as if you had not been here at all."

Ariana struggled to grasp his words. "You're saying—are you saying I couldn't have made it any worse? Or that not trying would be like not even being here?"

He kissed her forehead and straightened. "I'm going to go make—"

A ragged breath from the table interrupted him and their eyes focused on the Ryuven. Tamaryl's throat worked, as if something had caught in it, and he dragged air into his lungs. "Rrrru..."

"He's talking!" Ariana gasped.

"It's not necessarily speech," her father cautioned. "It may be only another spasm."

Tamaryl's eyes blinked suddenly open, his face tensing in stark contrast to the loose expression of his long sleep. His lips jerked.

They leaned over him, uncertain of how to help him. He stared unseeingly upward, his face twisting as if in fear or pain. "Mm..."

"We're here, Tam," Ariana told him desperately. "It's all right, we're here."

His fingers worked and then, as if he'd exhausted his meager strength, he fell still again.

Hazelrig placed a hand on his chest, listened for a moment, and then gently smoothed the bent fingers. "He's fine; he's just away again. He'll return to us." He hesitated. "Still... Still, I think he could use another dose of jackwort."

Ariana nodded. Tamaryl's expression, brief as it was, had been distressed.

Neither of them were trained healers, but a mage educated for battle had to know at least a smattering of medicine. Hazelrig turned to the shelf and took the jar, frowning as he lifted it. He shook it and then removed the lid to glance inside. "There's not much here, perhaps half a ration. Did you give him some last night?"

"I did, but I thought you had another supply."

"No, that was all." He shook out the dried leaves into a shallow wooden dish beside Tamaryl. "I'll borrow some from Elysia."

"Won't she ask why you need it?"

"No one questions a man of middle years wanting an anti-inflammatory herb in winter," he replied with a smile. "Why do you think I had only a small stock left?" He swung his white outer robe over his shoulders and started for the door. "Give him what we have. I won't be long."

"Take your soup," she called. "It's still warm."

"Not anymore," he answered from the front room. "Put them on the athanor and I'll have it when I return."

Ariana was already pulverizing the jackwort. The soup could wait a moment. When the leaves were evenly smashed, she poured oil over them. Fresh jackwort was more effective and quicker to act, but it was difficult to find in winter. Only a few herbalists kept it growing in their protected shelters, and most had to make due with cheaper dried leaves.

She froze at the knock. Who—but anyone might knock at the White Mage's door. If she waited a moment, he would go away.

But then she heard the latch shift. "Mage Hazelrig?" called a familiar voice. "Are you here?"

The office door wasn't locked! Ariana rushed to the front room, nearly slamming the workroom door behind her before he could see the bundled Ryuven. "Shianan!"

He looked surprised, and he took a few steps into the office. "I went to yours—then I came here, because you weren't—well, obviously, you weren't there, and—I thought your father might know where I could find you."

"And do you always make a habit of entering where you haven't been admitted?" she demanded, tense with worry at Tam's near exposure.

His face fell. "I thought perhaps—if he was in the rearmost room... I would not have come inside without..."

She crossed her arms, recalling their last meeting. Things were unsaid and she did not want to talk with him, not with Tamaryl lying unconscious just behind her, when she had not explained her weakness, when he could not be here.

Shianan seemed to wilt. "I only meant to ask where I could find you."

"And what was so urgent?" She watched him glance at the bundle in his arm, his expression uncertain. He picked at the cloth wrapping—was that a tunic? Ariana let an antagonistic note creep into her voice. "You brought your laundry?"

His jaw tightened. "No, my lady mage, I did not." He hesitated, his eyes averted. "I'm sorry," he muttered finally. "I have made a mistake."

Even angry and preoccupied as she was, it upset her that they faced each other so contrarily. Things might have been different without the pressing presence of Tamaryl, half-dead in the room behind her, if she were certain he had not nearly killed himself only to reach her... Shianan could not stay.

Shianan walked to the nearest table, never meeting her gaze. "These are for you," he said gruffly. "Accept them or not as you will, but I have no use for them elsewhere." He pulled the tunic away from an armload of flowers and dropped them on the table before turning back toward the door.

Ariana stared at the flowers, colorful and bright in full bloom. He had come to apologize. For her irrational tears and anger. She could hardly think of how to respond. "Shianan..."

He did not answer her as he continued toward the door.

"Shianan, wait..."

He was at the door now, never looking at her, reaching for the latch.

She flung a small burst of power to slam the door from his grasp. "Shianan, wait!"

He recoiled, startled at the door's movement, and glanced uncertainly at her.

She looked from him to the door and back. "I did it."

Shianan reached for the door again.

"Shianan!" She hurried forward and caught his sleeve as he tried the door. "Look—I'm sorry. I'm—stay a moment."

She had pushed the door closed, against his grasp, from across the room. Achievement thrilled in her even as shame twisted around it.

He did not look at her. "Let me go, my lady mage."

"No. Please wait." Her face was hot with humiliation. "You were bringing those to me?"

He nodded.

"I'm sorry. I was—I can't explain it right now. But I'm sorry."

Shianan stared at the door. "No, I was bringing them to apologize. For what I said the other day. I didn't mean... I never meant to offend you."

Trusting that he would not bolt, she released his sleeve and edged toward the flowers. "Wherever did you find fresh flowers? They're beautiful."

His shoulders dropped marginally. "Sunlight on flowers, you

said once. I couldn't do much for the weather..."

She burned with shame. "I'm sorry, about the laundry. You were only keeping them from freezing, right?"

He shifted. "I was anxious to find you before they spoiled. I did not know how long they would last."

"They're not so fragile as that! With some water and care, they'll last for days." She turned and scanned the room. "Where is that pitcher...?" She eyed the shelves and then remembered leaving it beside Tamaryl's makeshift bed when they had last bathed him. She started for the door and then swiftly corrected herself, turning back toward Shianan. "Well, I can find it. They'll last a few hours as they are." She smiled brightly.

Shianan pulled back a chair at the table. "May I?"

"Oh, yes, please."

He sank shakily into it, looking anxious. He laced his fingers and leaned his forehead against them. "I was only worried for you, that day. I never meant that you would—that you—I only worried that someone might have hurt you." He flushed.

She took the chair opposite him. "I should have known your intent."

"We are friends, then?"

"Of course."

He exhaled slowly, deeply, as if releasing a great pressure. He lowered one hand, leaving the other to prop his tired face. "You're having company?"

"What? Oh." Ariana's eye fell on the three mugs of soup. "I forgot that I needed to warm these. Father is coming soon, and he— he might be bringing someone." She scooped up the mugs and arranged them over the little burning furnace, where they could gently heat sensitive potions.

"Oh?" Shianan's eyes followed her. "I thought your guest might already be here."

"Father left only a moment before you came. You might have passed him in the corridor."

"Then who is in the back room?"

She froze. "What?"

His voice was quiet, weary. "You closed that door rather sharply when I came. You thought about opening it for the pitcher and then chose to leave it closed. You have soup for three here. And I thought I saw, just for an instant, something long like a body wrapped

146

on a table before you closed the door." He gave her a long, sad look. "Please, not now. I have hoped and hurt too much these past days, I cannot face a puzzle. Please, if there's something—you know I will help you if I can. We are friends, are we not? Shouldn't friends be honest with one another?" He offered a weak smile. "Haven't I proved I will keep your secrets?"

Ariana's breath caught. "Some secrets are harder to keep." She looked down. "Or to tell."

"Ariana. Trust me."

She stared at him, and all the words clustered together, making a knot which bound in her throat. "My magic," she said, a brutal truth easier to tell than the Ryuven behind her. "My magic had—"

A dull crash sounded from the rear room. Ariana spun as her heart leapt into her throat and she ran for the rear room. Tamaryl—!

Tamaryl was stirring on the table, shifting in his blankets. He had knocked the bowl of crushed jackwort to the floor. Ariana rushed to the table. "Tamaryl?"

His fingers seized her sleeve and twisted into it, clutching her close. "Shh!" he tried, his eyes blinking and wide. His wings worked weakly over the edge of the table.

She stared at him, seeing him awake for the first time since his return.

His hand shook in her sleeve. "Shhinn...!" he hissed urgently.

"Shianan?" she ventured. "Do you mean Shianan?"

"Mmmmaru!"

"Maru?"

"Maru!" he confirmed, and he seemed to weaken, his message conveyed. As he stilled, Shianan's hand closed over his, peeling the fingers from Ariana and laying the hand on the table once more. Then Shianan stepped backward, unspeaking.

Ariana hesitated, seeing Tamaryl was slipping into sleep, and then turned slowly to face him. Shianan's face was shuttered, and he said nothing.

"He came back," Ariana offered. "Through the shield—it almost killed him. He hasn't spoken before. I don't know what—it must have been something important to make him risk it..."

Maru, he'd said. If he had come for her, would that be his first word? But why had he come only to say that? What did he mean?

Shianan finally spoke, with seeming effort. "What did they do to coerce you?"

147

"What?"

"How many are there?"

"What are you talking about?"

Shianan's jaw set, but his voice was strained. "I do not want to bring you trouble. But my first duty is still to protect Chrenada from the Ryuven."

"Protect from what? It's just Tamaryl, come just—I don't know why. Not yet. But it had to be urgent."

"Urgent," he repeated. "Did you know I've been out of the city, visiting raid sites? I am writing a report for the Wheel, to ask how there could be Ryuven raiding through the shield."

Ariana stared at him. "That's impossible. It must have been bandits."

"I know the marks of a Ryuven attack well enough. And there were survivors to describe them."

"But the shield is up."

Shianan's eyes moved from her to Tamaryl and back to her.

"No! They might not be the same Ryuven at all—I know there are different clans. Or maybe some Ryuven were here when we erected the shield and now they cannot go home. I don't know! But Tamaryl's only just arrived through the shield, and it nearly killed him. If I hadn't been here, hadn't helped him, he would have died. He only made it at all because he's so powerful—" She stopped.

"He's the Pairvyn ni'Ai," Shianan finished. He stared at her. "You knew that."

She nodded.

"You know what he is, and you still shelter him?"

"I know him," she said unhappily. "He is not what the stories say. He took care of me in the Ryuven world. He saved me in the mountains, remember? That's what exposed him. He left the Ryuven in the beginning because he couldn't agree with the war. You knew him, for a time. Didn't you see that he's not a heartless murderer?"

"Tell that to the widows of Caftford," snarled Shianan. He glared at the still form as if he could kill with a glance. "Tell that to the families I've just left."

"Shianan, you can't tell anyone. Please, you can't. They would kill him."

"As he killed—how many? Hundreds? Thousands?"

"You said you would help me!"

He took a breath. "You commit treason for him? You risk your life for him?"

"He protected me," she protested. "He risked his life for me."

"And so did—!" Shianan stopped, looking quickly away. "And so you will protect him while he is here." He crossed his arms, facing the shelf on the wall. "What did he mean? What did he say?"

"Maru is the name of his friend. Maru cared for me while I was ill there."

"And why would he come here to discuss Maru?"

"I don't know."

The outer door opened and Mage Hazelrig entered. "I have the—ah, flowers. How nice." He came to the workroom door and stood, looking seriously at each of them. "Your lordship. Good day."

Shianan's voice came strained. "My lord mage, I did not know you had a guest."

"Bailaha..."

Shianan made a short, terse bow. "My lord mage, forgive my intrusion. By your leave, I will go and leave you to your work." He made an identically quick bow toward Ariana and then pushed past Hazelrig, hurrying to the door. Ariana took a quick breath, and then the outer door slammed.

She stared at her father, her heart pounding. "He came—he saw the soup, he guessed—I didn't mean..."

"It's all right," he replied heavily. "He will say nothing."

"I'm not sure. He knows Tamaryl is the Pairvyn ni'Ai."

"And that tears at him, I'm sure, but he will say nothing."

"How can you know?" she asked, ashamed that her father had more trust in her friend than she did.

"He dares not," came the quiet answer. "He knows my treason, and I know his." He shook his head and extended a paper packet to her. "More jackwort."

CHAPTER TWENTY-TWO

Luca stretched his arms overhead, savoring the luxurious freedom of movement, and paused at the top of the slope. Beside him the wagons rumbled on, the slaves grabbing quick breaths as they shifted their weight to steady the loads on the downward slope. His eyes, however, were on the town at the base of the foothill.

Abbar was a village lying outside Ivat, providing a less expensive resting place for those who couldn't afford the city. Ivat was visible up the coastline, but Abbar's smaller docks welcomed enough traffic to make the village a bustling, successful marketplace.

A shout from the line drew his attention, and with a stretch of his neck he started forward again. He jogged ahead, deliciously aware that he could change pace as he chose, and slowed to match the third wagon.

Cole was in the second pair this morning. Luca fell into step alongside him. "We'll be leaving the caravan in Abbar. At the base of the hill. It's all downhill, then." The joke was weaker than breakfast gruel, but he grinned anyway.

Cole nodded, still catching his breath from the final climb.

An overseer stalked along the line, scowling. He snapped an order to a slave at another wagon. Cole's fingers clenched on the crossbeam.

Luca's throat closed. The overseer continued toward them, his eyes on the team beside Luca.

"I—" Luca's voice failed, and he coughed and tried again. "I will need you close in Abbar," he said quickly. "I'm not sure yet what work Jarrick will have for you, but I'll need to find something, anyway. And Abbar is only a short walk from Ivat, which is where I was born. I think I'll be staying in Abbar for a time. I hope the weather holds." He was babbling, he knew it, but he forced himself to keep talking, to say anything at all. "The docking fees are less in Abbar, but there are fewer warehouses and storage can cost more if there's much demand, and so quite often there's no real benefit to using Abbar over Ivat. It depends. But we always had our own warehouses as well, so we did most of our business in Ivat, although there were times when we had to use Abbar, and then we had to run back and forth between our offices—"

151

"Hold up, you lot," barked the overseer. "You, big brute in the back, do your part! You're rolling too fast." The switch twitched in his hand. Cole bent his knees and pulled on the crossbar, but the wagon did not change speed. The overseer took a step. "I said, slow it!" The switch rose.

Luca raised his chin and envisioned his master holding a staff. *Hold your ground, Luca. Use your weapon.* Luca's fingers clenched, wanting the feel of a staff to give him strength. But he did not flinch as the overseer moved toward Cole. "Sometimes then I would remain in Abbar and they would send runners, sometimes two or three before the first could return, and—"

The overseer hesitated, eying Luca. Luca gulped and forced his voice to steady. "You aren't thinking of using that over me, are you?"

The overseer did not quite know how to speak to the slave-turned-master. "If you'd step aside..."

"I think no one can complain if I use this time to instruct my new servant?" Luca returned, trying to imitate Master Shianan's tone. How had he spoken to the soldiers who had first toyed with Luca? "I own his ears, after all." He thought desperately of Shianan. "You would not interfere with the orders I give my own slave?"

The overseer gave him a flat stare. "No." He glared at Cole, irritated at Luca's scant protection but uncertain of how to safely circumvent it. "Not until it interferes with our orders."

Luca drew himself upright. "There's no trouble here."

"That's mine to determine," grumbled the overseer, but he moved down the line.

Luca sagged, his shoulders dropping with released tension and all his breath escaping in a rush. He passed a hand over his face, rubbing at his eyes and forehead. His legs tingled.

Cole had said something. "What was that?" Luca asked breathlessly.

"I said, thank you, master." Cole kept his voice quiet, and the words were reluctant, if sincere. "There was no reason..."

"Quit mewling," another snapped. "He didn't face him down for us. He was flaunting his own place."

Luca gave a tiny laugh of disbelief. "Face him down?" He took a deep breath. "I was shaking."

Cole looked at him. "You held your place."

Luca glanced at the paved road. "I owe much to my old master, then."

"Your brother?"

"No." Luca answered before he could think. "I mean, perhaps my brother, but... I wasn't thinking of him."

The caravan came to a slow halt on the level road just outside the outermost buildings, before the traffic thickened. "Change out," ordered Matteo. "Fresh draft."

Luca started toward the trader, trusting that Cole would follow in a moment. Trader Matteo turned to face him. "Yes, my fortunate young man?"

"I'm interested in another of your slaves." Luca gestured toward the line.

Matteo crossed his arms. "Some of these will go to the auction block, some will be sold for a set price. Let's see which you're favoring."

Luca turned and pointed to Andrew, who was extending his wrists for an overseer. Apparently he was being rotated into the pulling team. "That one."

"Him?" Matteo made a face. "I can't see your interest. He's not much, I'll grant you."

"Auction or fixed price?"

"I tend to deal in labor—slaves for pulling, lifting, carrying. Warehouse workers, dock slaves, mill slaves, mine labor, oarsmen, litter bearers, plowmen, you see. He's a little reedy to bring a good price, though he might do for the narrows of a mine. Still, I'd likely sell or trade him to a friend who hawks lighter labor and servitors, to be cleaned up, given some proper manners and sold at a profit." He eyed Luca. "What's your take on him?"

"He was a kitchen drudge," Luca answered. "He's not worth the price of a draft slave."

"What do you think he's worth?"

Luca shifted uneasily.

Matteo chuckled. "Been a long time since you saw the other side of the block?" He nodded toward Andrew, now waiting unhappily behind a crossbar. "He'd auction for maybe three hundred, if he were in the middle of my line, because I'd have a crowd expecting big useful brutes. In Gregor's line he'd fetch maybe four and half. He's not much to look at, so no one's going to fight over him to serve at table, and drudges are easy to come by."

"And what would Gregor pay you for him?"

Matteo burst into laughter, making several heads turn. "If ever I doubted you were a merchant's brat from birth, boy, that would put me straight. All right, I'll be honest with you—if we did coin instead of trade, I'd get something about three hundred for him. It's possible I could do better at auction, but I might not, and it's not worth annoying my customers with an untrained reedy runny-nose when I can be rid of him more quickly."

Three hundred... Luca wished he had money, wished he didn't have to beg Jarrick for this. "And so if I offer you three hundred, and you don't have even the trouble of taking him on or haggling with your friend, you'll be satisfied?"

"Near enough." Matteo grinned. "Friend of yours?"

"I suppose, in a way. We knew one another."

"You going to free him?"

Luca had not even thought beyond the purchase. "It is my brother's money," he answered uncomfortably. "I can't say where he will be put."

"Well, good luck to you." Matteo nodded. "You'd best hurry to your brother. We're ready to go again."

Luca looked around and saw Jarrick with his own slave. Cole stood a few paces from them, watching Luca. "I'll be one moment," Luca said, and he started for Jarrick, trying to find the right words.

Jarrick was not pleased. "Three hundred for another slave? Luca..."

"I won't make a habit of this, I promise. But I've known Andrew—he won't go to a good place, Jarrick. Look at him, he's not going to make anyone a handsome servitor or litter bearer. The only place he'll go in Ivat is to the mines or to someone who couldn't afford proper labor, and they'll kill him in months." He paused to breathe. He hadn't realized this meant so much to him. "Jarrick, that could have been me. That *was* me. I've been there, after Furmelle. Please, not to someone I know."

Jarrick swore. "Take the money, Luca. As if I could—go get him. But what are you going to do with him?"

Luca was already moving back toward Matteo, who received the payment amiably and motioned for Andrew to be released. The slave nearly ran to Luca, relief plain in his features. "Thank you, Luca, I mean, my lord, thank you..."

"That would be your master," Matteo corrected easily. "Get on, then. Luca Roald, I am not quite certain, but I think it has been a pleasure. I hope I never have to negotiate with you from equal ground, but if we meet again, remember I took no unfair advantage of you."

Luca gave him a small bow. "Thank you for your consideration." He turned toward Jarrick, with Andrew following.

Jarrick was ready with a plan. "There's a good chance we'll find Isen at his office here. He splits his time between Ivat and Abbar. We'll go to a local smith and then try his office. Han and Cole, and your new one, will wait for us at the Red Sail— they have a room for servants— until we've finished and can go up to Isen's place. That's where you'll stay." Luca thought Jarrick's voice changed subtly. "You can stay as long as you want. But I'm sure they'll be glad to have you home again when you—"

"Where is the nearest trader?" Luca interrupted. His stomach had clenched at Jarrick's first mention of home.

Jarrick seemed taken aback. "Up the street, if you remember. What's wrong?"

"I'm just nervous about the cuffs," Luca muttered. "I want to have it done."

"Then let's go."

The Red Sail was a nicer tavern than many in a coastal village, a few streets away from the docks and aimed more at merchants than their hired men. There was an additional space behind the public room, where several slaves loitered while their masters drank or made deals in the front. Jarrick directed their slaves there, bought drinks for himself and Luca, and checked the wallet at his waist. Luca stared at the ale, remembering another tavern, another drink...

"Luca?"

He jumped. "Sorry." He pushed away the ale.

"Not to your liking?"

"Have it yourself," Luca replied quietly.

Jarrick watched him for a moment and then finished his own. "Whenever you're ready."

"Let's go."

The slaver's was not far, and after Jarrick spoke with the smith, Luca bent over the fitting table for the fifth time. *Must be something of a record*, he thought wildly as he turned his eyes from the workman's hammer.

The cuffs came free without much trouble and Jarrick paid the slaver as Luca stood, rubbing his naked wrists. He was truly free now. Truly free.

Jarrick clapped him across the back. "Welcome home, Luca." He grinned over Luca's faintly bewildered relief. "Let's go find Isen, shall we?"

Falten Isen was a merchant and a good friend of Jarrick's. Jarrick was certain he would welcome Luca.

"Does he—know me?" Luca asked. "Does he know who I am?"

Jarrick hesitated. "He knows I had another brother, yes," he answered obliquely. "I don't know that he would know you."

"Could we not tell him?"

Jarrick looked at him. "Don't you think he might wonder why I need to hide someone?"

"You're not hiding anyone! We're just using the house as he would, for a respite. I don't want word getting back first..."

"How would word get back before I did?" asked Jarrick. "Or didn't you... I thought I would tell them right away. How could I not tell them?"

Luca had no answer for that. How could Jarrick not tell the family that Luca had been found?

How could Luca return to the family which had sold him?

"I'll tell them tonight, all right?" Jarrick sounded as if he were trying to convince a child. "And Trader Matteo knows, anyway. Word might spread regardless."

Luca could not argue.

"Don't you want to come with me? Shouldn't you be there when they first hear?"

"I don't know." He shrugged and looked down at himself, muddy, weary, marked, in filthy and crumpled clothing. "Not like this, anyway."

"I see," Jarrick agreed. "What would you like?"

During the first year or so of Luca's enslavement, he had comforted himself in the night with visions of his return home. Sometimes he had earned his freedom, either by a great heroic deed— saving one of the tutored children was a common device, from a falling crate or from bandits—or, less often, by finding additional work and saving to redeem himself. Then he would appear unannounced at home and his family would fall upon him, sobbing and begging his forgiveness.

Sometimes, in his hopeful dreams, he earned his freedom and set out to further earn a fortune, secretly buying his father's debts. Then, when the house was on verge of collapse, Luca returned triumphantly, restoring his family and receiving their gratitude and pleas for forgiveness.

Sometimes he secretly purchased the house's debts and then revealed himself, but he did not save them—instead, he savored their screamed apologies and craven begging as they were dragged away in chains as debtors, while he resumed his old place.

Never had he imagined himself brought back by one of his brothers, facing them almost as the slave he'd left.

Jarrick led the way to a clothing market and gestured for Luca to look over the wares. The fashions were somewhat different here, and Luca spent a few minutes staring at the array of options, almost paralyzed. He had chosen nothing for himself, made no decisions for himself for so long...

"I think this blue is nice," offered Jarrick. Luca glanced at him, wondering if his brother had seen through his hesitation, but Jarrick seemed to be merely browsing and chatting. "Your coloring would be served well."

Luca found his voice. "Do they all have these ridiculous shortened sleeves?" He held up a tunic with sleeves that ended midway between elbow and wrist.

"That's the style. Alham will have it next year, you'll see."

The shortened sleeves would betray the mismatched coloring and scrapes of Luca's newly unshackled wrists. Jarrick seemed to follow his thoughts. "You could wear a longer shirt beneath it. There are a few who choose a layered effect. Could you find such a shirt, please?" he directed the vendor.

The shirt sleeves were not as long as Luca would have liked, but it seemed the best he would find. He slipped self-consciously between two hangings to change, keeping his back to a wall lest someone catch a glimpse. Then, dressed in fresh leggings, braies, shirt, tunic, a new cloak, and unscuffed boots, he looked at Jarrick anxiously for approval.

Jarrick nodded. "Splendid. We probably should have visited the bathhouse first, but you look wholly different. Better."

Luca felt a whisper of encouragement. "Then I suppose you'd better pay for these."

But he caught the merchant eying his wrists as they paid, and he flushed with shame. The clothes did not make him different.

"The ragpickers will be glad of these," commented a shop assistant, and he tossed the discarded clothing into the street. Luca hesitated, an unvoiced protest on his lips. The shirt had been Shianan's, and it felt wrong to cast it away. But bitterly fighting children set on the clothes almost as they landed and they were gone in seconds.

Jarrick had not noticed Luca's dismay. "And now, to Isen."

"One more, please," Luca said quickly. He pointed to a sash of the same pale linen as his shirt. "I'd like that, please."

Jarrick gave him a curious look but nodded, and the shopkeeper handed it wordlessly to Luca.

"I'll go find Isen," Jarrick offered, replacing his wallet. "Shall we meet at the Red Sail?"

Luca returned to the tavern and sat in a corner, only a few paces from the door to the slaves' area. Alone in the shadow, conscious of Cole's and Andrew's eyes, he methodically tore the sash into strips. Then he wound the strips about his palms and up his wrists, tying them awkwardly. They slid and slipped about his fingers.

"I can help, master," offered Cole. He was bare-chested, working a repair in his whip-torn shirt with a fishbone needle and thread teased from an edge.

Luca turned toward him. "Please do."

Cole twisted the strips and bound them securely, so that the signs of the cuffs were completely hidden. Luca braced his elbows on his knees and looked at the result. He looked something like a street entertainer, wrestling for a few coins, but less like a slave, he thought.

He glanced up and saw a man across the public room staring directly at him. He quickly averted his eyes. What had he seen? Did he think Luca looked familiar? Had he known him when younger, or did he know his brothers? Luca bit at his lip and then slowly pulled his hood over his hair.

And then Jarrick was coming toward them with another man. Cole retreated to the rear room and Luca slid to make room at the table. "This is my friend Falten Isen," Jarrick introduced. "Isen, my friend Dom Nerrin. He needs a place to relax for a few days."

Luca felt a quick rush of gratitude. Jarrick had not called him by name after all. Luca did not yet need to face the pitying, assaying stares of those who knew he was returning to the family who had rejected him.

"Relax?" repeated Isen with a grin. "He looks as if he needs a place to hide."

Luca's heart froze, and then he realized the man was only joking about his garb. He slid the hood back from his head. "Sorry," he said sheepishly. "Habit. From the sun."

"You've been in the east, then?" Isen nodded knowledgeably. "After much of that sun, you'd need more than my humble house to recuperate. Well, if Jarrick vouches for you, you're welcome there. Someone ought to keep an eye on the silver."

"He'll be there intermittently," Jarrick put in. "He'll come with me at times."

"I hope you won't need too much in the way of hospitality," Isen said. "I've left just one servant there, to keep away the dust."

"I need very little," Luca said. "An empty house would suit me." Belatedly he realized he had servants of his own.

"Well, it's near enough." Isen slapped the table. "Let's go up, then. The gate will never open to you alone. She's too cautious for that."

Luca nodded, thinking of Marta, the plump mistress who did the accounts for Fhure. She was level-headed and certainly would open no doors without good cause. He rubbed at his eyebrow.

The afternoon sun was bright as they ascended the hill road, and to maintain his thin story Luca drew his hood up again. It actually felt good, in some way, to hide anonymously within his hood. He was a turtle, secure within his mobile shelter.

Isen had a faint limp, but it did not slow him noticeably. The three slaves followed them, silently taking turns with Jarrick's chest. Luca was glad of that, as it demonstrated to Jarrick the servants he'd brought weren't useless. They left the road and took a narrower track to a walled garden, set against the steep rise of the mountain which lay behind Ivat and Abbar. Isen pulled a cord and a bell sounded pleasantly within.

A moment later a door slid back in the gate, showing dark eyes behind a lattice. "Welcome, master."

She was younger than Luca had imagined, less like plump Marta and more like what Sara must be like now, if he let himself think of her. He pushed his sister from his mind and looked about the garden as they entered.

A fountain played before them, with hardy autumn flowers wilting about it, the last of the Wakari's late season. The rest of the walled area was filled with flowering vines, fruit trees, and vegetable plots, but most were withering with the onset of winter. In the center stood an upright white house, two levels and a flat roof. Somewhere behind the house, a goat bleated.

"I never meant to entertain here," Isen said, "so there isn't much for hospitality. Please use my room, of course, and help yourself to whatever has been laid in for winter. Except, of course, for Marla." He laughed in a good-natured way, but there was warning beneath.

Luca nodded, caught off-guard.

"What about the slaves?" Isen turned. "Which are yours?"

"Two, but I will have little need of them here. I thought to send—"

"I will take the smaller one for a time," Jarrick interrupted, "but I think you should keep Cole. We haven't the work for him, and you said you'd rather not send him to the docks. He can work the garden here or help the girl with any lifting in the house." He dropped his voice. "If he doesn't kill you in your sleep."

Isen nodded. "There's a hut in the rear for a gardener, or he could stay in the back room downstairs." He looked at Marla. "As you've guessed, this man will be staying here for a time. Please render him your appropriate service. Nerrin, is there anything else you need?"

"No, my lord," Luca answered before he could think. He licked his lips, hoping no one would notice the slip. "No, I think I will be very comfortable here. It has the privacy I seek, and I don't require much else. Thank you very much for your generosity."

Isen nodded. "My pleasure, for a friend of a friend. I'm sure you can find your way inside, and Jarrick and I should be on our way if we are to keep the light down the mountain."

Andrew took a quick step forward. "I will go with my lord's— friend, then?" His voice was worried.

Luca nodded. "Go with Jarrick, Andrew. He'll find a place for you." He looked at his brother. "He'll do well in a kitchen, if you can put him there. Thank you for taking care of him for me."

Jarrick nodded. Andrew bowed again. "Thank you, my lord."

"I'll come by later," Jarrick promised solemnly. "Until then, Lu—Dom Nerrin."

CHAPTER TWENTY-THREE

Snow had begun to fall, clinging to Shianan's cloak as he crossed the courtyard, but Shianan had no eyes for it. He tore open his office door and stalked inside, casting a dark glance at the soldier leaning against the edge of his desk. "What are you doing here?" he demanded.

The soldier jerked to attention. "Sir! I had reports, sir, and I—"

"And you saw fit to wait in my office?"

He faltered. "I'm sorry, sir, I thought you wouldn't mind... It's snowing..."

"So I see." Shianan shook the flakes from his hair and ripped his cloak from his shoulders. "I seem to have survived it, myself."

The soldier straightened. "I am also to tell you, sir, that Sergeant Parr would like a word with you before our next assembly, regarding the upcoming review."

"Can't he organize a handful of turnip-headed—" Shianan stopped himself and took a slow, shuddering breath, raking his hand through his damp hair. "Anything else?"

"No, sir."

"Then get out."

"Yes, sir."

Shianan slammed the door behind him and snapped the bolt into place. He would see no one else that afternoon. He went into his sleeping quarters, locking that door too behind him.

He dropped heavily into a chair and let his head fall backward, eyes closed. His stomach clenched into a sick, wretched knot.

Useless. All of it, useless.

She committed treason for the unconscious Ryuven—she risked her life for him. All that Shianan had done for her, she did for the Ryuven—and not just a Ryuven, but for Pairvyn ni'Ai, the nemesis of legend, their enemy above enemies. She sheltered him, protected him, risked her life for him.

He groaned miserably. She committed treason, betrayed all that he had done for her, and he knew he would never speak a word against her. Jealousy would not make him overturn his effort to save her. And that hurt nearly as much as the betrayal.

161

He did not try to conceal his conflict. There was no one to see it. His quarters were empty, chilly with an untended brazier. No one would see.

No, it had not been quite useless... At the least, she had survived and come home to their world, safe from the Ryuven. Hadn't he told himself that he would be satisfied with that? Wasn't it enough to know she was not dead, or the helpless prisoner of some depraved Ryuven?

He set his elbows on his knees and buried his face. And he could take some small vindictive pleasure, if he tried. Ariana could no more openly claim her choice of lover than Shianan could have done. He had always known his desire was a fantasy, that the bastard would never be permitted a Mage of the Circle. And a Mage of the Circle could never wed the Ryuven champion. He choked a bitter, contemptuous laugh.

He wanted to go and find the strongest drink money could buy, to gulp it until his throat burned and his stomach scorched and he could not recall even his name, much less the details of his unhappy existence. He missed Luca keenly. He had not guessed how stark his quarters would be without the slave. Before Luca's coming, Shianan had not known what he lacked. And he missed the White Mage, whom he'd barely known but had grown to like during their brief conspiracy. It was too awkward to speak with him now.

He rubbed savagely at his eyes. He could not afford to drink, not now. The last incident had scathed a warning deep into him, and while he had little pride left to preserve, he'd rather not sacrifice the rest before the court. Given his luck, the moment he picked up a bottle, the king himself would walk through the door. Even Prince Soren couldn't save him then.

He sagged another inch. The prince might well ask him how the apology had gone, and Shianan had no reasonable lie. He would have to answer that the Black Mage preferred someone else to him. He sighed. At least he could be spared explaining that his rival was such in every sense of the word.

Marla eyed the stranger warily. He was swathed in a cloak, which he kept pulled close about him as if cold, and when she caught a glimpse of his hands, hidden within his cloak despite the moderate temperature, the wrists were wrapped to the arms. What was this man? Had her master brought a leper?

Her master and the others were leaving, and she followed them to the gate and bowed before locking it behind him—locking herself with the cloaked monstrosity and his big slave.

She turned and moved to within a dozen paces of her master's guest. The slave was speaking to him. "Where will you have me sleep, master?"

"Do you prefer the dignity of the house or the privacy of the hut?"

The slave inclined his head. "I've not been a personal servant, master. I'm willing, but I will need instruction."

The cloaked figure laughed dryly. "I've no need of that, Cole, none at all. Sleep where you will. You are at this woman's disposal for our time here."

Marla nodded respectfully. "The hut and the quarters in the house will be equally available for him, master. I have my quarters in another room." *Please, please don't say that I'll be sleeping with you.*

"Then, Cole, do as you please. I only want that I won't be disturbed." He looked at Marla, freezing her blood with his shadowed face. "Is the master chamber upstairs?"

"It is, my lord."

"Is there a bath?"

"Beside the kitchen, my lord."

He nodded, the movement barely perceptible within the hood. "I would like a bath. Very hot. In private."

She nodded. "And supper?"

"After the bath, if I am still awake... But Cole will need something, and yourself as well. I'll have a portion of whatever you're having."

She hid her perplexity with a small bow. What an odd man he was. Perhaps, if he did have an illness, it sapped his appetite. "I'll go and heat your bath, my lord."

The sun faded quickly, slipping behind the mountain, and by the time the bath was full, the room needed candlelight. She set out a number of lights, checked the supply of soap, and went to the front room where he seemed to perch uncomfortably on a chair.

He'd removed the hood, and the cloak had fallen back a little, giving her a better view of his wrapped arms. She had not expected his face, much younger than her master's, serious and deeply thoughtful. "Your bath is ready, my lord."

He followed her to the room, now comfortably warm with steam. "Thank you." He crossed to the curtained doorway opposite and lifted the dark fabric, peering into the dog-legged storeroom beyond.

In private, he had said. What was he hiding?

"Cole will need a healthy ration tonight. His meals have been lean of late." His words slipped together, as if he were barely drunk or very tired. "Can you see to him?"

"Of course, my lord."

"Thank you." He checked the latch behind her.

Marla went to the kitchen and set another pot to boil, this time for their supper. She glanced out the window, where the slave Cole had fallen asleep on a stone bench beside some frost-killed flowers. She liked that stone bench; it held the sun's heat for some time. He might stay until she called him in.

The water was still quiet in the pot. She glanced again at Cole—he did look a little underfed—and then went to the kitchen end of the dog-legged storeroom. The stranger hadn't guessed it had two openings. She could creep to the far end and learn what sickness was in the house.

There was a tiny gap between the curtains near the floor. He was sitting outside the tub, his cloak folded neatly behind him. His clothes were new and of a moderate cut, well-made but not extravagant. He was leaner than she would have guessed with the cloak. As she watched, he unwound the bandages on his right arm, staring as he did so as if he expected to find something unpleasant. But when the wraps came free, there was nothing distinguishable to her eyes.

At least it isn't leprosy.

He unwrapped the other arm, equally whole, and then he began to work his tunic and shirt over his head. As the fabric slipped over his bare skin, she caught her breath. Even in the candlelight, the stripy scars showed plainly.

The stranger had been flogged. He was a criminal or a slave.

She slipped silently backward as he stripped his leggings and braies and got into the steaming water. The bandages over his arms... They might serve to conceal the marks of wrist cuffs or shackles, indistinguishable in the dim candlelight. Which was he—a criminal, a runaway slave, or a freed slave? Was he dangerous?

She returned to the kitchen and glanced at Cole, still sleeping

164

in the garden. Did he know what his master was? Would he tell, if she dared ask?

When the water began to boil, she added handfuls of cut vegetables and meal. She had been startled by his bald statement that he would share the slaves' meal, but now that she had seen his history, she understood that he would be satisfied with their fare. She glanced again at Cole and took down a sausage to cut into the pot. Then after a moment of thought, she took another. The stranger had been thin beneath his clothes as well.

The supper had been ready in the pot for some time when Cole came into the house, looking sleepy and vaguely guilty. "Was I called?"

She shook her head. "He's still in the bath."

"Still?" He rotated his neck stiffly. "I suppose he had a lot to scrub away."

He knew something, but she did not think it prudent to ask. Instead she indicated the covered pot warm beside the fireplace. "Food's ready. He told me you'd need an extra ration, so there's plenty."

"He—? I see." Cole looked at the pot, his face concealing some inner thought.

She took a polished wooden bowl and uncovered the pot herself. "Have you been with him long?"

He shook his head. "Only a few days."

"I suppose he wants you fattened to his standard, then." She handed him the bowl. "There's a spoon behind you."

"Thanks," he said gruffly, as if the word were disused. "He—he could use an extra helping himself, if you made enough. I mean, you should make enough."

"I already considered that," she answered blandly. "I wouldn't short my lord, don't you worry." She looked at him. "So who are you?"

He swallowed a mouthful of thick meaty porridge. "I'm Cole."

"I'd heard your name." She watched him shove another spoonful into his mouth. "He picked you up a few days ago?"

He nodded. "Pike, woman, this is good," he mumbled through chewing. "I've been living on the chunky colored water they give out in caravans. You say there's more?"

"Glad you like it, though it's naught too special. And it's Marla." She scooped another healthy portion from the pot.

"It's special enough, woman," he answered, wiping his mouth with the back of his hand. "I haven't eaten my fill since I went in the

165

line."

She halted the ladle over his bowl and eyed him. "Marla."

He blinked, a little surprised, and then seemed to understand. "Marla." He had the sense to look sheepish. "Sorry. I—I'm used to—it's Marla."

She plopped the porridge into his bowl. "Have all you want. I can make more. Didn't he ever feed you?"

"It's only been this day." He took another bite.

"I thought you said you had been with him a few days?"

"He made my purchase then," Cole said awkwardly. "Out of a caravan line. But I stayed until—it was only today we came to the town below this place."

"I see." So the criminal or escaped slave had purchased another slave, though he seemed to have no real need for him, and come to her master's house to hide. Curious, indeed. Some men might need someone in their power, to assure themselves of their new higher place, but that didn't seem consistent with what else she'd observed.

She glanced out the window. The garden was dark. "He's been a long time. His bath will be cold." Cole said nothing as she levered another pot from the fire and wrapped a rag about the handle.

She did not take the short passage through the storeroom but went into the corridor, tapping at the bath's door with her foot as she held the heavy pot away from her. "My lord? I've brought hot water."

There was a quick rippling splash and then a voice called, "Yes?"

She took that as admission and nudged the latch with her elbow. He was in the narrow, upright bath, sunken to his chin, his back pressed to the wall. Concealment, she recognized. He looked startled. "What do you..."

She realized he hadn't understood her. "I've brought water to heat your bath. I thought it would be cooling by now, and you'd said you wanted it very hot."

She tipped the pot over the tall bath, steam rising over both of them. He shifted quickly beneath the water—covering himself, she thought, or hiding his wrists. Perhaps he was a eunuch as well. At least with his shyness she did not have to worry that he would call her to his bed. "Is there anything else you need, my lord?"

"Is Cole settled?"

"He's eating now, my lord, and then we'll make a pallet for him. Is there anything you require of him?"

"No."

"Would you like me bring your supper? It's plain fare, as you said, but I can—"

"No," he said quickly, and his arms dropped another inch beneath the water, rippling with candlelight. "No, thank you. Please leave a tray in my room."

He was afraid for even a slave to see. Perhaps Cole did not know, after all, or only suspected. "As you wish."

CHAPTER TWENTY-FOUR

Luca woke with a strange disorientation. For a week of dawns, he had been pressed tightly between Cole and Andrew, all coiled to conserve warmth in the mountain mornings. They had shaken themselves stiffly to their feet, relieved themselves in the road's drainage ditch, and taken the cups of gruel offered by the boy, numbly facing another day of walking. Once freed, he had taken refuge with Jarrick, still sleeping in a tight coil for warmth, but now back to back with his brother instead of another slave.

This morning, however, he found himself beneath a pile of comfortably heavy blankets. Sunlight streamed into the room, warming the stone wall set opposite the windows to absorb and radiate heat. There was no heavy tread of an approaching overseer, no cold breeze, and no distance to walk through the coming day. He lay still, hardly daring to move lest he wake from the dream, savoring the soft bed and thick pillow.

The light moved across the wall, and at last his bladder urged him to rise. He stood, comfortably free of itching fleas and old dirt, and stretched. He had not felt so physically good in—what? Months? Years?

Then his eyes fell on his wrists as he reached for his clothing, and his happiness faded. He was not wholly new. Even after the white bands tanned to match his arms and the scrapes healed, he would still bear the scars on his back—and in his soul. They would never fade entirely.

It doesn't matter, he told himself fiercely. *I can be Luca Roald once more. So I may never visit a public bath again—what is that? I am a freeman, I am a merchant, I am my own man.*

He'd left his clothes on a cushioned bench across the room, a sort of narrow couch without arms. He dressed and, turning, found himself facing a mirror he had not noticed the previous night. It was not so large and grand as the one in the Kalen baths, but it showed his face plainly enough. He still needed his hair cut, ragged in its tail behind him. He thought he looked less wary than before. Perhaps his few days of freedom had already begun to fade his term of slavery.

He would find work. Accounting, or even tutoring. And Cole

169

could work as well. They could together earn enough for a small living. He would think on it.

He wrapped his wrists—not as smoothly as Cole had done, but it would do for a time—and descended the stairs. No one was in the sitting room or the corridors, so he glanced into the kitchen. The slave glanced up from the basket of beans in her lap and gave him a respectful nod. "Good morning, my lord. Would you like some breakfast?"

How easily she said that, as if all he had to do was desire breakfast. "Yes, please." He could see a curtained doorway beyond her, which probably led to the slaves' quarters in the rear of the house. "Where is Cole?"

"He's still sleeping, my lord. I didn't think you'd left him any chores, so I didn't see fit to wake him."

"He's slept this late?" Luca took a seat at the large worktable. "He must have been tired from the trip. As was I." *Or, as I was, he's lying somewhere in the joy of being able to merely lie somewhere.*

The servant set aside the beans and went to the fire. "You traveled together then, my lord?" She dropped a large block of butter into a black pan.

Luca nodded. "From Alham."

She took eggs from a basket—three of them!—and set them on the hearth before crossing the room to slice a thick rasher of bacon from a hanging slab. Luca's stomach growled and he pressed his arm against it. "Where is Cole?"

"He's in the hut in the rear garden, my lord."

"No, my lord, I'm here now." Cole looked rumpled and puffy-eyed, but he stood erect as he came through the doorway. "I didn't wake... I'm sorry."

Luca shook his head. "No, no, it's obvious you've been in harness rather than livery. Never draw attention to your error. Your master is not so stupid that you need point it out. Instead, hurry through the door as if you've just barely completed your previous task and beg, how may I serve?"

Cole blinked once before his face softened into a faint smile. "Yes, my lord. How may I serve you?"

"Have your breakfast," Luca said.

The female servant looked at Luca.

"The same for him." Luca knew of masters who took care that their slaves did not eat the same food or at the same time—he'd had

170

them—but sitting here in the kitchen, it seemed petty and futile. "And right away."

The scent of frying bacon wafted through the kitchen, making Luca salivate. He folded his arms across his stomach in an attempt to smother the growling. He had eaten little last night, exhausted physically and mentally, and now he felt a slave's keen hunger. He wondered if he might shame himself by drooling. To distract himself he asked, "What needs work in the garden?"

Marla poked a piece of bacon to the side and cracked an egg into the pan. "There are a couple of plots which need turning, and the dead stalks can be trimmed for the winter." She broke another egg. "There's not much planting over the winter, as the bulbs are spreading nicely."

"Cole can help with the heavier work. Use him as you will. He has no other tasks."

"Thank you, my lord. He will be a help."

A moment later she set down two plates and a pitcher, and they tore into the meal ravenously. She went back to picking through the beans, apparently finding nothing unusual in the master and slave eating together in the kitchen. Perhaps she had seen men more pragmatic than hierarchical.

Cole finished and rubbed the back of his hand across his mouth. "Good—Marla. Where do I start?"

She set aside the basket. "I'll go out with you. These can wait."

They went out into the garden, and Luca sat by himself in the kitchen. He looked around, feeling it alien to him. He had rarely needed to enter his kitchen at home, as the family was served in the dining room. He had come late to a full household in Furmelle and was lodged with the litter bearers outside, coming inside only to give lessons or for some other task. He had spent more time in the Gehrn kitchen, but it was a massive affair like the military kitchen in Alham, as much a place of toil as a mill. This kitchen, on the other hand, was small, cluttered, warm—cozy. Comfortable.

He thought of Andrew and wondered how he was faring, whether he had gone to the family kitchen after all and what he thought of it. He wondered if Andrew found it more comfortable as well.

Abruptly a lump rose in his throat. He hoped Andrew was glad to leave Alham, as glad as Luca himself was—glad to return to the familiar Wakari Coast, to see his brother again, to come home to his own family, to leave behind the taunting soldiers, the hated stigma of Furmelle, the constant grating disdain reserved for barely human slaves...

He swallowed a sudden, unwanted sob. Alham was also where he'd left his friend, his best friend, the only man who had seen *him* and not a slave. They had shared a common pain and a common need, and somehow they had forged a friendship beyond what anyone could have expected of a military commander and a Furmelle slave.

Luca had loved Shianan as the brother he should have had, and he had left him in Alham with everything else. He had nothing left of his friend, not the gifted cloak, not even the castoff shirt, nothing at all.

No, that wasn't quite true. Shianan had given him something no one else ever had. Luca blinked his damp eyes and pushed himself back from the table.

Cole and Marla were working alongside the house. Luca ignored them and started through the garden, his eyes sweeping the ground. The plantings were well-maintained and mostly for the kitchen; he might not find something suitable.

"Master?" Cole paused with his fork in the earth.

"I'm looking for something," Luca answered, somewhat embarrassed.

"Can I help?"

"I want a stick, so long or longer." He gestured. "Sturdy, straight."

"Like a trader's staff," Cole guessed dully.

"Yes," Luca admitted. He smiled to allay the slave's flat, wary expression. "But without the trader."

"A staff?" Marla straightened from her cutting. "There are two or three staves in the storeroom. They were a soldier's, not a trader's, but one should serve your purpose well enough." There was a question in her eyes.

Luca answered it. "It is for my own exercise, nothing more. I wanted privacy, not stagnation..."

"They're in the kitchen storeroom. I'll fetch one for you."

"No, no, I can find it." He turned and went into the house again.

The curtained doorway led not to the slaves' quarters but to a storeroom, he noted, and from there to the bath room. He found the staves lying along the base of a wall, held in place by several boxes and knee-high jars of preserved fruit. He eased one out and rubbed the dust from it.

It would serve perfectly.

The slaves were outside in the garden, and Luca felt self-conscious at the thought of practicing where they might see. The furnished rooms were of course impossible. He glanced up and climbed the stairs.

Yes, like many houses near the coast, the flat roof was a paved terrace. He ducked under the low cover for the stairs and walked out onto the sun-warmed tiles. A waist-high ledge enclosed the terrace, walling it like a smaller garden, with leaf-shaped holes along the base to drain water. It was perfect.

He returned to the center of the roof and stood still for a moment, balancing the staff in his hands.

"Take it."

"No! Master Shianan, I cannot. I am a merchant's son, a bookkeeper—"

"Are you? I thought you were a slave. My slave, bound to obey my orders. Pick it up."

Luca closed his eyes and saw Shianan standing opposite him, his fingers deceptively loose on the staff. His master had ordered him to defend himself, had forced him to hold his ground. The military commander had ordered the Furmelle prisoner to learn to fight.

The imaginary Shianan before him attacked. Luca moved the staff and brought it into the first posture he'd learned. Again. Again. He fell into a rhythm—fifty repetitions, Shianan had said. But fifty thoughtful, correct repetitions. And then there was another movement to practice, and then another.

The wrappings over his wrists were hot and irritating, so he slipped them off before continuing. The actions came more easily to him as he concentrated, recalling his lessons. He began to sweat freely; the walled terrace trapped the sun's warmth just as the walled garden did below, prolonging the growing season. He stripped first his tunic and then his shirt, knowing no one could see him here. It was good to stretch his muscles, to move as he wanted, to smash unseen enemies and be victorious each time.

He smiled to himself and recalled Giusto's arrogant figure. He brought his staff up to deflect and then shifted his hands, bringing the tip over his shoulder, toward the tiles and forward, directly into the blustering soldier's groin.

He had been so terrified, then. But Shianan had laughed. Luca

grinned and did it again, just for fun.

He was far from being a trained fighter. He had only to recall Shianan's whirlwind defense against the swordsmen's ambush to see the difference between them. Mere weeks of training could not make him competent to really fight—but they had given him a glimpse into something he'd forgotten, or possibly had never known. They had given him the strength to hold his place before the overseers, to bargain for Cole and then to protect him.

He spun the staff, still pleasantly surprised that it moved in his hands as it had in Shianan's. He pictured the road and ambush. The man on the left had come first, and Shianan had checked his charge with a wide sweep...

He moved forward, recreating the battle as best he could recall. A sweep, a jab to the torso—wait, he could not have done that without reversing the staff—turning to the new threat, rotating as the stick shattered with the sword hit— Luca remembered that well, certain it was death—a blow to the temple...

He lunged, extending the staff horizontally to catch the swordsman's descending elbows, and then he drove the tip into the invisible swordsman's throat. He moved with more deliberation than speed. Slow practice could pick up speed more easily than sloppy practice could pick up accuracy, Shianan said. He whirled to face the next threat and saw a human form.

She was standing on the upper stairs, stooped to clear the small angled roof, holding a tray. Luca drifted to an uncertain halt, letting the staff spin down and clatter on the tile.

For a moment neither of them moved. Luca forgot he was master here, forgot he owed her no explanation. He could only stare dumbly and wonder what would come next.

And then she moved forward, onto the roof, and straightened. "I brought you some refreshment, my lord."

He stepped over the fallen staff. "Thank you."

She offered him a cup filled with some sort of fruit juice. It was sweet and amazingly good, a delicacy as he had not tasted in years. He gulped it, thirsty and suddenly greedy for the sweetness.

"I did not know you were working, or I would have brought more. I will bring something else, if you like." She glanced at the staff. "You are a soldier, my lord?"

He laughed. "Oh, please, no. No, I was never a soldier, and I'm not much of a fighter of any sort. This was—this was tribute." He sobered.

"Tribute?"

"To a friend." He cleared his throat. What was she thinking?

She took the empty cup. "I am sure he would be honored." She hesitated. "Would you like those treated?"

He knew she had to have seen, but still the mention made his throat close. "I'm fine."

"I can help so—"

"I'm fine," Luca repeated, hearing a note of desperation in his voice.

"As you wish. I'll bring more to drink."

When she returned, he was fully dressed, toying with the strips of linen. There was no point to them now. He would stay in the sun and let the skin color to match the rest.

This time she had both water and juice, which she left before returning silently downstairs. He drained the water and then sipped the juice, enjoying its rich sweetness.

There was another narrow bench at the end of the terrace, and Luca sat on it and looked over the small garden. The house's position against the face of the mountain created a series of hothouses, trapping the sun first before the mountain, then within the garden walls, and then within the terrace walls. It was a simple and ingenious design.

Cole was still turning earth below, his movements unevenly slow. He was tiring, Luca guessed, or his back was paining him. Cole jabbed the fork into the ground and straightened, reaching over his shoulder and plucking at his torn shirt. It clung to his back.

Marla crossed toward Cole. He didn't see her at first, but when he did he hastily released his shirt, feigning an indifferent stretch. She was not fooled. She went directly to him and asked a question Luca could not hear. He answered evasively, and as she handed him water she ran the tips of her fingers lightly over his back.

Caught, Cole blustered indignantly, but as she spoke he surrendered. She went behind him and carefully teased the fabric from the healing wounds.

Luca swallowed and looked away. He hadn't thought to ask the condition of Cole's back before sending him to work. Was he the same as any other callous master? What would Cole and Marla think?

175

She left Cole's back, asked him a question, and then returned to the house as he drank his water. Luca saw him set the cup aside and return to his work, moving a little more freely but still tentatively. Luca would tell Cole that the rest of the day was his own. He rose from the bench and started downstairs.

Marla was in the kitchen, checking a pot beside the fire. "My lord," she said upon seeing him, "will a capon be acceptable for supper? I can start it early, and we might have a light lunch now."

Luca's mind was not prepared for such questions. "That sounds fine," he answered mechanically. "I'll call Cole in."

The slave saw him as soon as he came around the corner, so Luca merely gestured and returned to the kitchen. Surely the house had a dining room, but he did not want to use it. He wanted to be here in the kitchen, with Cole and with Marla.

Cole came, nodded to his master, and sat across the table. Marla gave them each a bowl of soup, a cooled blend of vegetables and cream, probably from the goats in the rear. It was good after the morning's exercise. The three of them ate in silence, but it was not awkward, Luca thought.

As he finished his soup, he glanced at Cole. "You needn't finish that plot today, Cole. I don't want you opening anything."

"It's late for that," Marla said. "With your permission, my lord, I'll see to his back."

Luca blinked. "Of course."

Cole looked worried. "Master, I—I don't need much..."

He was easier to correct. "Let her see to you, Cole."

"I wasn't slacking."

"I know that," Luca said quickly. "I also know there's no hurry, and you could use some rest. It will be there tomorrow."

"Good." Marla rose from the table, collecting bowls. "Then you can pluck the capon this afternoon."

"What?" Cole asked bluntly, as if she had spoken in a foreign tongue.

Marla chuckled. "Pluck the capon." Cole started to rise, but she pressed his shoulder, holding him in the seat. "Slip off your shirt. I'll get the salve."

Luca retreated to the next room. Through the open door he could see Cole sitting stiffly at the kitchen table, his shirt across his knees, his shoulders rigid. Marla's offer must have seemed an unfamiliar threat.

No matter, Luca thought. It would be good for him. He could do with having his expectations overturned, with discovering that not everyone meant to wring what they could from him.

Marla stood behind Cole and gently pressed him forward to expose his back. He resisted tautly. She ignored this, rubbing her hands briskly together and then placing them on Cole's shoulders. Luca saw her fingers move, and then her hands, and then she was pressing deliberately over his neck and shoulders. Cole gave a little, and then another inch, and then he bent like a reluctant willow as she eased him forward. Marla continued massaging one hand over his neck as she smoothly scooped a globule of salve from a wide, squat jar and gently slid it over the first stripe.

Luca slid back in the chair, drawing one knee to his chest. Yes, it was good for Cole to find that he needn't be wary of every interaction. He was relaxing under Marla's ministrations, physically and mentally. She was treating body and mind, all that Cole needed.

All that Luca wanted.

Cole saw to the weal across his stomach himself—he had not relaxed so much—but when Marla stepped away, Luca thought he was disappointed. He rose slowly from the table, as if he wanted to linger. "One moment," the slave woman said, and he was rooted to the stone-paved floor.

Marla left the kitchen through the rear door, and a moment later there was a frantic chorus of squawking from outside. She returned, brushing dust from her skirt, and handed Cole a dead chicken. "The capon. Pluck it in the rear, so the feathers don't litter the front garden."

Cole was visibly disconcerted. "How...?"

She demonstrated, making Cole flinch. "He's dead, he won't feel a thing. And he'll be good eating." She smiled and closed his hands on the bird. "Out back, please."

Luca smiled. Yes, Cole's world had changed.

Had his?

Marla gathered the medicinal jars into a basket. Then she came into the sitting room, where Luca sat with his heels on his chair, his arms and chin resting on his knees. "My lord?"

He shook his head. "I didn't call. Don't let me keep you from your work."

"I have nothing that cannot wait." She looked at him with calm, appraising eyes. "I could see to your back now, if you would."

177

He looked at her. "I..." How had she known? "Yes, please."

She nodded, unsmiling. "I'll bring my things to the roof, my lord."

Luca had not expected that, but he saw no reason to protest. He stood and started up the stairs, loosening the laces of his tunic. On the roof, warm with the captured afternoon sun, he sat on the bench and looked out. Three goats moved lazily on their tethers, ignoring the chickens which had gone back to scratching.

"Your shirt and tunic, please."

He drew them off, the air cool against his skin until he grew accustomed to it. "They are not fresh," he said awkwardly, unsure of why he'd consented to her attention.

"These welts are not old, only a few days, perhaps. Not severe, but there is no reason to ignore them."

She folded his tunic and shirt at the end of the bench before him. Then she took a thin, upright jar from her basket and poured oil onto her fingers. Luca felt something almost like disappointment. The oil Jarrick had given them had not been so helpful as the ointment Shianan had. Probably a soldier by necessity found better products. At least this smelled pleasant, like almonds.

But Marla did not immediately apply the oil to the faintly sore welts. Instead, she rubbed her hands to warm the oil and, fingers spread wide, eased them into his shoulders with a sweeping, circular motion. Luca, surprised, shifted, but her hands followed him smoothly. "Don't fret, my lord. You saw how it helped your servant, didn't you?" The motion spread over his back. "And shouldn't a master receive as much care as his servant?"

Luca was softening under the steady motion. "I don't..."

She shifted to include his upper arms, making the nerves tingle down to his hands with released tension. "Please, lord, trust me. If afterward you think I have done wrong, then deal with my master as you will. But give me a chance to help you."

He did not answer. Indeed, the simple strokes were soothing, steadying. Her hands were warm, firm, calming. He began to slump.

"Right, my lord," she whispered. "Lie forward and let me work."

Luca did not argue as she pressed him chest-down onto the bench, pillowing his head on the folded clothing. He'd experienced massage before, of course, in the baths as a young man, and he'd seen it offered to rich and poor everywhere, at varying prices and in varying skills. But it had never reduced him so quickly to quiet compliance.

She added more oil to her hands and began a deeper pressure, working across the rigid muscles and coaxing them to loosen. Luca ceased to worry about the massage and let her dig into his tight places, smoothing them. For long minutes there was only a steady thrumming contact over his back, working from shoulders to hips. At last, he felt her remove one hand and trace a sore welt with something cooler than the warm oil, but her other hand kept an even, soothing motion over his shoulder blade and he couldn't summon the effort to brace himself for the salve's application. He needn't have bothered; he barely felt it. He barely felt anything but the gently insistent rolling...

A moment later, she shifted both hands to one of the welts, moving across it rather than along it. "Does this hurt you, my lord?"

"Hm." It was surprisingly difficult to talk. "Hnyeah."

"It's unpleasant?"

She must have been practiced at interpreting half-blissed subjects. "Mm. Not quite good."

"They need a few more days, then. That will help it to heal with less of a mark, when it's comfortable." Her hands slid smoothly to another place. "What about here?"

"Mmmm."

"These are older." She fell silent again, and Luca wondered for a moment if she was trying to guess at the scarring. But he couldn't maintain the worry and, sighing at last, he let her knead him into pliant jelly.

Luca was not sure how long she worked. He slipped into a waking dream, where sounds and colors danced about him indistinctly. But gradually he became aware of the distant splashing of the fountain, and of a faint muttered curse from Cole regarding feathers, and of Marla's hands moving gently over his back as they had started, no longer pressing deep.

She seemed to know when he had returned to coherence. "How do you feel, my lord?" The soothing hands changed to a small towel, wiping away the remaining oil.

He wanted to speak, but his face was heavy and damp against the folded clothing. He wondered briefly if he'd wept or drooled in his removed state. "Nnthya..." With effort he lifted his head and drew himself up on an elbow. "Thank you."

She ceased working, leaving one hand lying warmly between his shoulder blades. "I did salve the welts, and I worked across the older scars. They are recent enough that they can be helped if you choose." If she wondered at them, she had tact enough not to ask. "I took the liberty also of helping you to relax somewhat. My master said you were here for solitude and retreat, and he instructed me to serve you to that end. I hope you are not displeased."

Luca managed a smile, which felt odd on his limp face. "Displeased?" He sighed. "I'm sorry I ever thought to stop you."

She chuckled. "Thank you, but that was only a portion. If my lord wishes, I can work more completely, perhaps tomorrow?"

He dropped his head and looked under his arm at her. "Your master won't be angry that you...?"

She laughed aloud. "No, my lord, you misunderstand. I am a trained aelipto. That is my primary purpose here. Nothing more."

Luca flushed. "I didn't mean..."

"I didn't think you did. I am sure my lord is perceptive enough to recognize the difference between a touch which lays him blissfully down and one which brings him happily standing."

Luca blushed hotter and gave an embarrassed laugh. She was free with her speech. It was obvious no one could be angry with her after she'd performed her ministrations. He liked her. "And your master keeps an—what did you call yourself?"

"An aelipto, one trained in specialized healing massage. You don't know my master well?"

"We met only yesterday. We share a friend in Jarrick Roald."

Her voice deepened slightly. "My master was a soldier before he was a merchant. He was wounded, twice seriously, in his back and hip. There are days when he needs my help to leave his room." She turned one palm up. "Other days, he does very well. But he needs care."

Luca's breathing seemed deeper than before. "Thank you again for your help, beyond what I asked." He sat up slowly, letting her hand fall from his back, and rubbed at his face. The air was cooling, and he picked up his shirt. "I might..."

She understood. "If I can serve my lord, you need only ask." She retrieved two or three jars and returned them to her basket. "And now, unless my lord objects, I will go to see how Cole is faring with the capon."

Luca stayed on the bench for a few moments, dressing slowly, unwilling to move and disrupt the hazy contentment that he had, just for now. But as he descended the stairs, feeling startlingly tall and— yes, assured, that was it—self-assured, the contentment followed.

CHAPTER TWENTY-FIVE

Sara caught sight of them from an upper window and hurriedly skipped down the wide stone steps to hug her brother. "Jarrick! It's been ages. I missed you."

His arms were tight around her, as firm and solid as ever. "I missed you, too, Suri."

She smiled at his pet name. Only he called her by it, and she had not heard it in months. "Come in, come in." She glanced at the man beside him. "You too."

Falten Isen laughed and shook his head. "No, I have some calls to make. I only came because I love to watch Jarrick welcomed home. It makes me ferociously envious."

Sara laughed. "Come, Falten, surely someone would be glad to wait for you. I've offered before to recommend you."

He smiled and made a tiny bow. "I know, and I am always surprised that you would condemn one of your friends to life with me." He chuckled. "Goodbye, my dear, Jarrick. Perhaps we can dine together some time." He turned and limped away.

"It's bothering him?" she asked softly, watching him.

"We walked from his house above Abbar. It started giving him trouble halfway here."

"I don't know why he doesn't use a litter like everyone else in Ivat."

"The healers told him that a litter would let it worsen. The exercise hurts but keeps it from crippling him."

"He still thinks no woman will have him, doesn't he?" She turned and hugged Jarrick again. "We'll worry about him later. I'm so glad you're home. Come in and sit down." She glanced behind him. "I remember Han. You found someone else while you were away?"

"This is..."

"Andrew, my lord," offered the slave.

Sarah frowned. "Did you come home through a mine, Jarrick? They look terrible."

"Actually, I traveled with a slaver's caravan. Not my first choice, I admit, but that's why everyone's a little footsore."

"Footsore? I think they forgot to feed this one. Andrew? I'll

181

have Marcus take you back to the kitchens for something, and then—"

"Then he can stay in the kitchens," Jarrick said. "I'm told he's a fair drudge."

"I was going to say he could wash up, which I think might be a good idea if he's going to stay in the kitchens." Sara tipped her head. "You brought a kitchen slave all the way from—where?"

He looked discomfited. "I was asked to take him. By a friend. I'll explain later."

Sara gave him an odd look. "Right. A friend asked you to take a kitchen drudge." She shrugged. "Both of you, get inside, get cleaned up, and get something to eat. If Jarrick has anything else for you in the next hour, I overrule it. Move."

"Yes, mistress," answered Han, bobbing with the chest on his shoulder, and he led the other to the side of the house.

Sara took Jarrick's arm. "Come on, it's cool out here. Thir's at the docks, settling something between Hart and Elg, and—"

"Father?"

"He's with them." Her voice dropped a note. "It's a good day."

Jarrick nodded silently. There was something in his face, something she couldn't quite read.

"Anyway, I've got you to myself for a couple of hours, because Hart and Elg have been building up to this for weeks. You can tell me all the really good stories and when they come back, you can give them the boring bits they want to know about." She laughed.

Jarrick didn't laugh with her. "I don't have much I can tell you, Sara."

"You were away for three months and you have no stories? Bah, Jarrick, I should toss you back into the street. You're a boor and a tease."

He made no jest in return, and Sara felt her happy mood touched with shadow. She paused and looked at him.

He started, suddenly aware of her eyes. "I'm sorry. I'm just tired, I suppose."

"Then you'd better come and sit down. Don't argue, you can bathe later. The dirt's not going anywhere." Sara gestured to a passing servant and ordered warm drinks. "Come, brother, you worry me."

She had a suite of rooms at the end of the house—her father and brothers preferred rooms overlooking the sea, where they could keep an eye for incoming ships—and she led him to his favorite chair while she dragged a wide couch to adjoin it. "Did something happen on the way home?"

He shook his head. "No."

The slave brought steaming drinks and Sara dismissed her promptly, sensing that Jarrick needed privacy. "You want to talk about whatever didn't happen?"

That, at least, brought a faint smile. He rubbed at his face, looking tired and, perhaps, older. "This was a difficult trip, Suri. For many reasons."

"You didn't get the Alham contract? But we knew they might not want someone so—"

"I have the Alham contract," he interrupted gently. "If that were my only concern..."

She leaned forward, elbows on knees. "So there is something else."

Jarrick hesitated a long moment, seeming to hover on the steam of his drink. Abruptly he turned and set the mug on a low table, keeping his eyes from Sara. "I think I'll go wash away the road grime. I'm tired."

She was taken aback. "Jarrick..."

"I'm going to sleep after my bath. Tell Father and Thir we have the army contract." He withdrew a flat leather wallet from inside his tunic and unwound the safety cord that held it to his belt. "The papers for that and the others are all here." The wallet slapped to the table beside the untouched drink. "If I don't wake for supper, then let me be." He rose and went to the door.

"Jarrick! Wait!"

But he went on without pausing, leaving her alone with the documents. She started to follow him but stopped. If he truly meant to leave her behind, he would do so, and harassing him would help nothing.

She picked up the leather wallet and withdrew the sheaf of contracts and miscellaneous sensitive data. Thumbing through it, she saw nothing extraordinary, nothing that should have him worrying how to break the news that he'd lost an important client or had seen a captain sign with another shipper.

She drank her own tea, folding her feet onto the wide sofa. He might be better able to talk after a bath and sleep, after all. She would go to him then.

But when her father and Thir returned, Stefan was with them.

She could hardly be upset—Stefan was her betrothed—but it meant Jarrick would be unlikely to talk openly over supper, and she would have no chance to speak with him privately afterward.

But she could not resent Stefan for coming. She had been anxious when their fathers had first struck the match, and when they'd first been introduced he had been stiff and taciturn, reciting memorized compliments and stepping on her toes as they danced. But as the party wore on and the parents and well-wishers turned to their own merrymaking, leaving the betrothed couple to speak between themselves, she'd discovered he was actually as nervous as she, and that once he was not trying to appear older and bolder before his parents' friends, he was actually sweet. It had not been long before both of them were anticipating their wedding.

"Marcus said Jarrick had come home?" her father said as she exchanged smiles with Stefan.

"Yes, but he was tired from the journey," she said. "He went to bathe and sleep."

"Did he say anything about the Alham contract?"

"He has it." The papers were still in her room. "Everything's fine there."

Jarrick did not appear for supper, and midway through the meal Sara motioned a servant to her side. "Jarrick will need supper in his room."

"Yes, mistress. I believe Marcus has already seen to that."

Good old Marcus, dependable steward without equal, who thought of most things a moment before his masters. She wished she could take him with her—but he was needed here, as he had a brilliant way of working around her father's bad days.

Her father and Thir seemed mildly disgruntled at Jarrick's absence, but they had a guest, and Thir commented that Jarrick would be awake in the morning and the reports would not be stale before then. After supper, Stefan chatted a few moments with his future relatives and then, his social duties paid, joined Sara on a moonlit balcony for more private pursuits.

Breakfast was usually an informal affair, taken singly as they began their various days, but her father and Thir were already there when she arrived the next morning, apparently waiting for Jarrick to make his appearance. Sara noted with dismay that Marcus stood behind her father, instead of beside him. It would not be as good a day as yesterday.

"Where's Jarrick?" he asked irritably, confirming her observation. "Isn't he coming?"

"I'm here," Jarrick answered from the corridor. "Good morning, Father. Hello, Thir, Sara."

Thir nodded and clapped his brother on the shoulder. "Welcome home."

"Indeed, son. So, Jarrick, what have you brought?"

"We're profiting." Jarrick slathered butter over bread. "Overall, it was a very successful trip. We have reduced port fees in Boabrimtown, we have an exclusive deal for cotton in Madigan City, and we have the Alham army contract for grain delivery."

"Excellent."

"How was Alham?" asked Thir conversationally. "I was there once, three or four years ago. Cold in the winter."

Jarrick nodded. "It was cold."

There was a pause. Thir seemed to expect more, but Jarrick kept his eyes on his plate.

"Did you get the message from our friends?" asked their father. His fingers slipped on his tea. "About Alham?"

Jarrick glanced quickly at Sara. "Father..."

Thir shook his head. "We can talk about that later, Father."

"I want to know how the alliance views us," he said stubbornly. His eyes had the faintly unfocused look Sara hated. "Did Jarrick satisfy them or not?"

Jarrick set his cup down firmly, sloshing tea over the table. "The alliance is gone," he said sharply, "or it will be in a few weeks. We'll make our own way."

"Gone?" He blinked. "How can it be gone?"

"Do you really want her to hear this?" With a start Sara realized Jarrick was angry, angry beyond what she had seen for years. His rage burned beneath his tightly controlled speech. "Or do you even care? Can you even think clearly enough to know what that would mean?"

Sara flinched in her seat. Thir gave a low warning. "Jarrick..."

"They tried to kill the man who uncovered the scheme. That was their great plan, to kill the man who found it. As if no one would be scrutinizing in the future, if he were only dead! But Bailaha isn't that much a fool, and they're not much as assassins. He found them out and arrested some of them. He has the names of the rest. It's a miracle we aren't a part of it."

Sara couldn't understand what he was saying. Alliance? Assassins?

"And to make it all the more ridiculous, the man they sought to kill was the man I needed for our contract. Imagine that, if you will— I need his seal, and they want his death, and they claim to want our profit! I tell you, the entire thing is maddening. Or mad."

Thir was watching him warily through calculating eyes. "Then the Alham contract..."

"The Alham contract is sealed! Done! Everything we asked! Don't ask me how, I claim no credit for this one. I want no part of it."

"How," began their father, staring from his chair, "how can the alliance be gone? Some of the greatest merchant houses in the middle lands..."

"It's gone!" Jarrick snapped, dropping his fist to the table. "Gone! Houses disappear, Father, even great ones. You of all people should know that!"

Sara caught her breath. Jarrick ventured near a topic which none of them dared to mention.

"The alliance is broken, and when Bailaha reaches its leaders, some of the houses will be gone, too—and nothing is going to save them, Father, nothing. We have to leave them and make our own way again. And if—" his voice broke—"if you can't lead us there, Father, then we'll have to find it ourselves." Jarrick shoved himself from the table and hurried from the room.

Their father looked after him in uncertain equanimity. "Why...?"

Sara could feel her jaw hanging. She looked at Thir. "What did he mean? What was he talking about—what alliance?"

"It's a kind of merchant guild," he answered quickly. "I don't know what he meant about murder."

But he was lying. She could see that even if he was not so close to her as Jarrick. She dropped her finger-crushed napkin and ran after Jarrick.

He was on a balcony, gripping the railing, his head bowed as if in prayer. He was breathing hard, as if he had just run a long way. She slowed and stood behind him. He would know she was there.

After a moment he spoke without turning. "I'm sorry, Sara. I shouldn't have—I didn't want you to hear that—not in that way..."

She stepped closer and wrapped her arms around him, his back against her cheek. "We've been trading illicitly?"

186

"Not all of it. Not even most of it. But enough." He was trembling, just barely. "Our partners were defrauding the Chrenadan army. Handsomely. It's been going on for years, and we joined them three years ago. After—after..."

"After we nearly lost our house," she supplied softly.

"When they were discovered, they turned to murder." He shivered, distinctly this time. "They told me to kill the Count of Bailaha."

"Jarrick!"

A hand slipped over hers. "I didn't. But—I tried. But it didn't happen."

She squeezed him tightly. "No wonder you were upset yesterday."

He shook his head. For a long moment she hugged him, thinking wild thoughts. Why had they joined such an alliance? Had they known of the fraud when they joined? Had they pressed her brothers to do other things before? What would Stefan think?

Was Stefan already involved?

Jarrick exhaled and turned in her arms to embrace her. "Your Stefan is not involved," he said softly, a smile in his voice. "Nor any part of his house." He chuckled. "I could smell your worrying."

"Thanks." She bit at her lip. "What are you going to do?"

"Do?"

"About the—alliance. Whatever it is."

He sighed. "If nothing splatters in our direction—meaning no one names us when they're taken—then I mean to be an honest merchant all the rest of my days. Father and Thir won't have a choice, as there won't be an alliance in a few weeks."

"So you're an honest man now?"

He gave her a brave smile. "A little tarnished, if you will, but my intentions are shiny."

"What if—what if the others name us? When they're arrested?"

Jarrick squeezed her. "I don't know, Suri. If... I don't know."

Sara slipped away and leaned on the balcony railing, the sea breeze tugging at her hair. No one was on the patio below. "Is there anyone near enough to hear us? Thir, slaves, anyone?"

He glanced around. "I don't think so."

"I'm going to break a rule." She tightened her fingers about the rail. "There is a forbidden subject in our house, one so forbidden that we can't even say aloud that it is forbidden."

Jarrick turned away, leaning on the rail beside her and looking to the sea's horizon.

"You know what I mean, Jarrick. I know you think of it, too." She paused. She had not yet dared to say it aloud. She swallowed and took a breath. "If we joined the alliance after... We needed capital. More than—for Luca." She licked her lips, frightened at her own words which made all of it real again, not just the memory of a nightmare. "I still think of Luca, sometimes. I wonder where he is, and why he hasn't written us to tell us. And I think that maybe, if I had been in his place, I wouldn't, either."

Jarrick was silent, unmoving.

"But then I think maybe I would write. He's a clerk, or a scribe, or a bookkeeper; it's not so different from taking a position outside of the house, really. Surely he would write—and then we could bring him home now, couldn't we?" She clenched her fists. "It's not right. Father and Thir and everyone don't ever speak of him, not even you, Jarrick. No one mentions him. It's as if he never existed. And if he would only write, only tell us where he is, then they would have to read his letter! They would have to!"

Jarrick's shoulders sagged. "You say he should write, Suri. But what if he couldn't?"

"What do you mean, couldn't?"

"Suri, after—after that, I went to look for him."

She looked at him sharply. She hadn't known he had tried, too.

"We all thought Luca would be a clerk or something similar. But Sandis saw that he was sold as common labor. To strike further at us."

She gasped. "But—how could—then he wasn't a clerk? He isn't?" Her mind reeled. "He might be—plowing? Rowing? In the mines?"

"Suri, listen—"

"How could you know this and not tell me?" she demanded, letting fury protect her. Luca was not as she had imagined him, safe and scribing— he was chained, sweating, maybe even beaten. "How could you not tell me?"

She shoved herself from the railing and ran, knowing she would cry and too angry to allow him to comfort her. He tried to catch her but she was too quick, and she ran through the door and down the corridor, leaving him as he had left her the night before. All the hopeful tales she had told herself were lies. Luca could be hurt, he could be sick, he could—he could have died. Many slaves lived hard lives, and few lived long ones. She imagined Luca, shirtless and bent beneath a heavy bale on the docks, and she sobbed at the horror.

Her maid stared as Sara burst into the room, and she shrieked, "Out!" Then she threw herself on the couch, beating her fist against the carved arm, wanting to shock herself from the nightmare. Luca was her brother. He had left some years ago, when their business was failing. He was a clerk somewhere, a talented clerk, someone who was valued and protected and appreciated...

The door to her sitting room opened. "Suri, you have to listen to me."

"Go away!"

"This is important." Jarrick closed the door and knelt beside the couch. "I have to tell you."

There was a curious excitement in his expression that stopped her. She hadn't seen him quite like this before. "Tell me what?"

"Suri, while I was in Alham, I—"

She gasped. "You found him," she breathed. "You found him?"

He nodded intently. "I did."

She threw her arms around him. "Where is he? Is he safe? What's he doing? How did he get to Alham? When is he coming?"

"Easy, easy." He gently removed her arms so that he could hold her eyes. "I found him wholly by accident. He was with the man I went to see. It was complicated, but—but in the end, he came back with me."

"He's here?" Her voice was too loud, and she clapped a hand over her mouth. "He's here? Where?"

"Near Abbar. Isen's house. Hush! No one else knows, you understand? Not even Isen. He thinks he's just a friend."

"Let's go! I'll get my—"

"Sara, listen." He was having trouble choosing his words. "Suri... It's been three years. And while you and I have been living here, living like this—he's been a slave, Suri. Not a clerk at a desk, but a working slave."

Slow horror crept over her. What was he trying to tell her? "Like Han?"

"Like Andrew, the other one I brought back. He knew him. Like—like the dock slaves."

She recoiled. "Not Luca..."

He clasped her hands. "If we go, you have to be prepared. He won't laugh and hug you, Suri. He was afraid to come here, afraid of Father and Thir and all of us. Do you understand?"

No, she didn't understand. Understanding lay in a great black crevasse which threatened to engulf her if she leaned to peer into it. She didn't understand... But she clenched her jaw and said, "I want to see him."

CHAPTER TWENTY-SIX

Ariana woke, heart racing, and stared into the darkness. But it was wrong—her bed was wrong, the sound of her breath was wrong, it was—

No, she was in her father's workroom, she remembered. Already the dream was slipping away, leaving only its unrest and breathlessness and exhaustion.

Ariana pushed herself upright and muttered into the darkness, regretting the lack of window in her father's workroom. That was to the benefit of his experiments, his privacy, and the current welfare of Tamaryl, but it made spending the night inconvenient. She fumbled after a candle, wondering if she would be able to light it without a firesteel.

"Good morning, my lady," came a voice through the dark.

She nearly dropped the unlit candle, grasping for magic with the other hand. "Who's there?"

"Don't you know me? Don't tell me I look as awful as I feel."

Relief ran through her. "Tam?" She lit the candle—with her will—and hurried toward him. "Tamaryl, how are you? Will you be all right? Why are you here?"

"One moment. Help me to sit up, please." He clung weakly to her arm and tried to push himself to lean against the wall. He looked at her and smiled thinly, breathless with effort. "Isn't this ironic?"

"I'd thought of that." Ariana heard the outer door close. "There's Father."

"Good, he will have the best chance of knowing." He bent his neck and slowly, carefully, stretched his wings. "Ouch."

"What's wrong? Are they damaged?"

He chuckled. "No, no. Only, trust a human not to know how to lay someone on his own wings."

"I'm sorry, it didn't come naturally to me," said Hazelrig as he came through the door. He closed it behind him and immediately crossed to Tamaryl, embracing him gently. "Welcome, my friend. I am so glad to see you awake." He released him. "You worried us. We've been taking turns to sleep here with you."

"That long?" Tamaryl looked distressed.

191

"Why did you come?" Ariana asked again. "You could have died! Did something happen there?"

"Not exactly," he answered. "I came to find Maru."

"Maru? But, he's there. Isn't he? We left him there."

"So we did. But he—Maru came back here, to the human world."

"What? How?" Ariana shook her head. "The shield nearly killed you, and Maru couldn't withstand more, could he?"

Tamaryl looked unhappy.

It was Ewan Hazelrig who answered, with a resigned tone. "Unless he carried something to negate the shield's energy."

Tamaryl turned, and for the first time she could remember, Ariana thought he looked afraid to face her father. "You know?"

He shook his head. "I didn't. But I've been looking for the chipped-off bit of the Shard, asking if anyone had borrowed it. No one had. And we're receiving reports of Ryuven raiding parties." His expression was pained. "I thought you wanted the shield as much as we did. You helped to develop it. I thought you wanted to end the war."

Tamaryl's eyes fell to his lap. "I did. I do. But—but I hadn't seen, not until I went back with Ariana, how bad it's become." He looked at Ariana, as if hoping for her confirmation. "The crops are failing worse than before. My people are starving. This war may have started as much for prestige and profit as for food, but now it's for food. There is a chance we can save our crops, and I still hope for that. But in the meantime, we need the resources your countryside can offer."

Ewan Hazelrig held his eyes. "So you stole the chip, so that you could continue the raids even through the shield."

Ariana's fingernails dug into her palms. Tamaryl—but he couldn't. Not Tamaryl, not the sweet boy she knew, not the brave man who had carried her to his world to save her life and then carried her back at his own risk. Not Tamaryl, who had fought so hard to create and protect the shield to end their war.

In your world, my lady, I would obey you. But here, I am Pairvyn ni'Ai.

"Oh, Tamaryl," she breathed, and he flinched under her disappointment.

"So where is Maru now?" asked her father, pragmatic as ever.

Tamaryl nodded. "A few nim were entrusted to retrieve

supplies. No sho, few che."

"So we would not sense the more powerful Ryuven as they crossed."

"And to prevent larger conflicts! If they were not here for you to sense, there would be no mages and soldiers to wage battle against the sho, and no sho to wreak more harm during the raids."

"Only our common people would be harmed."

"My common people are dying." Tamaryl's face was conflicted and ashamed, but his voice was firm.

There was a moment of cold silence, and Ariana at last prompted, "What happened to Maru?"

Tamaryl seemed to refocus. "But this last time, the group was broken apart, and the two who returned did not bring Maru with them."

"And so you came to find him."

Tamaryl nodded. "He could not have leapt home alone through the shield."

"And then you'll carry him across the shield like this?" Ewan gestured to Tamaryl's fractured body. "You'd kill him."

Tamaryl's mouth tightened but he answered, "I would not abandon him here. I would find a way."

Hazelrig softened his tone. "And if he died in the fighting?"

"Then I will learn what happened to him." Tamaryl turned back to Ariana. "But that is not certain. He could have run away, could have hidden. He could have been taken prisoner."

Ariana thought of Shianan's reports of Ryuven raids. The commander had never mentioned prisoners.

It was too easy for Tamaryl to read that she had no hope for him. He turned to the White Mage. "Nor even you? You didn't fight him?"

He shook his head slowly.

Tamaryl's hopeful, desperate face fell. "Oh. I—I see."

Hazelrig put a hand on the Ryuven's shoulder, and he hesitated before speaking. His words weren't the saddened consolation Ariana expected. "There is one possibility."

Tamaryl seized on this, but cautiously, fearful of disappointment. "Where? How?"

"I will undertake to look for him—"

"Would another mage have helped him?"

"Not as we did you, hiding you in another, less vulnerable

form." Hazelrig looked uncomfortable. "Ariana, would you bring something for him to drink? He's had only soup these past days."

Ariana kept her eyes on her father as she reached to the watered wine on the next table. She poured some and set the cup down, holding his gaze and daring him to send her away again.

He relented. "I will tell you both, but I ask that you pledge your silence. There are very few who know this, and it was my hope that neither of you would ever be among them."

Ariana leaned on the table beside Tamaryl.

"No matter what you think, what you feel," her father continued, "you must be silent on this. It is a secret of the Circle."

"But I'm a part of the Circle now," Ariana protested.

"Oh, Ariana." Her father laughed mirthlessly. "There are circles within circles." He looked at each of them. "Swear for me."

Ariana felt unsettled but slightly excited at the prospect of secret knowledge, and a little guilty at her excitement in the face of Maru's disappearance. "I swear, I'll say nothing."

"Thank you." He looked at Tamaryl. "This will be more difficult for you. If you prefer not to give me your word, you may take mine that I will search for your friend on your behalf."

Tamaryl took a slow breath. "You have never given me reason to distrust you, my lord mage. I will trust you further and pledge my silence."

Hazelrig nodded unhappily. "I hope you do not regret that." He sighed again and drew a chair toward the table. "The war has been devastating to your people and ours. Especially since Luenda, you know we have been trying to find a way to end it in whatever way we could."

Tamaryl nodded. "The shield."

"Not just the shield, though that was a part of it." Hazelrig folded his fingers together uncomfortably. "Offensive magics as well."

Tamaryl and Ariana exchanged glances. This was not new to them. What was he trying to say?

"Test subjects were needed. How could we devise a shield to repel a Ryuven heart unless we had a Ryuven heart?" He looked at them pleadingly. "Do you understand? We needed Ryuven blood to work the spell to create the shield."

"You said the Ryuven blood was from Luenda," Tamaryl protested.

Hazelrig bowed his head. "I did not actually say that. I allowed you to believe it. I'm sorry."

Ariana stared at him. "But that's what we thought, too. All of us."

"Most of you," he corrected. "There are a few in the Circle who know that some Ryuven prisoners are kept below the Naziar."

Tamaryl tensed against the wall, his wings shifting. "Prisoners?"

"Only a few. We did not want or need many, and no one wanted the people to fear what was in the cells." He bowed his head. "I'm sorry, Tamaryl. I did not want to deceive you, but you can see... I had been sworn to that secret long before we met. And it would only have upset you to know."

"And that gave you leave to imprison my people?" Tamaryl demanded in a choked tone. "To use them?"

"It was war, my friend," Hazelrig reminded him. "Your people took prisoners as well."

"How—how many times..." Tamaryl shifted on the table, trying to push himself higher. "You were my friend!"

Hazelrig sagged in his chair. "I am sorry, Tamaryl. I truly am sorry."

"How could you do this?"

Hazelrig raised his head. "Your people took human prisoners, at Luenda and since. Did you release them when you took Ariana to your world? Have you returned them to us since?"

Tamaryl hesitated. "I had no authority..."

"No mage ever taken by your people has been returned, Tamaryl, not by goodwill, barter, or treaty. Is that so different?"

"Mages die," Tamaryl muttered bitterly. "We would not return corpses."

"Then why did you take them?" demanded Hazelrig with a pained tone. "Only to let them die?"

"They could be questioned!" snapped Tamaryl. "And those who died in our world would not kill us later!"

"And the others? The soldiers, those who weren't mages?"

"All right!" Tamaryl's voice broke. "Yes, it was war, I agree. We are all at fault. I understand that. But how can you ask me to know they are here and not to act? They are my people nonetheless! Could you sit in my residence and not move to help your human soldiers?" His wings snapped against the wall. "What if one might be your oldest friend?"

"We will find if Maru is among them," Hazelrig promised. "If he is, I swear to you that somehow he will be freed."

Ariana clenched her fists. "Maru took care of me, Father. He watched me and sat with me while I was ill, while Tamaryl was away."

"I will do all I can for Maru, my dear. Believe me. But you two must trust me. There are only a few who know of the prisoners, but all of them are powerful. Tamaryl could not go before Oniwe'aru and demand the release of all human captives, nor can I free all the Ryuven. We must go carefully."

CHAPTER TWENTY-SEVEN

Sara shifted in her seat—carefully, so as not to affect the litter bearers—and began to toy with a strand of hair in place of picking at the thread on the seat cushion. The climb to Falten Isen's house was far too long for her anticipation.

That morning, Jarrick had announced he had a meeting in Abbar, and Sara had casually mentioned she would go with him to shop in the village. Jarrick had insisted they not tell their father or Thir about Luca, not yet.

She leaned to look out the window, trying to see the house, and felt the litter dip as one of the bearers did not adjust quickly enough for the weight shift. "Sorry," she called. "But can't we go just a little faster?"

"We're climbing a mountain, Suri," came Jarrick's gentle chiding. He dropped back beside the litter so he could smile at her. "Be patient a little longer; we'll get there."

"I feel I could run up this mountain."

"And ruin your complexion for your wedding?" He grinned. "Only a few minutes more."

He was right; she could see Isen's house after the next bend. She drummed her fingers nervously and imagined, for the hundredth time. "Luca!" she would cry as she entered.

He would look up from his book—of course he would be reading, he was always reading—and his face would light at seeing her. He would stand, but she would already be reaching him, throwing her arms about him and hugging him close, so close that he could not slip away again, and he would hold her tightly and say, "I missed you, little sister," and she might cry...

They were nearly at the gate. Only a few minutes more.

There was a tiny wrinkle in the sheet below Luca's cheek, but he could not be bothered to shift for it. As he had hesitated that morning, wondering whether he would ask her after all, Marla had, with her basket of oils and salves, matter-of-factly asked if he would have his massage in the room or on the roof. He had now been

197

facedown on the narrow bench long enough that she had worked nearly to his toes, soothing pains he hadn't even been aware of until she began coaxing them out, feeling world and worries slip to a distant, negligible memory.

Now she was rubbing firmly at right angles to the stripes on his back, doing something she'd explained would reduce the scarring. He didn't quite understand, but he had no reason to protest. Her touch was warm, reassuring, comforting, and the soothing of his tense muscles seemed to peel away some of the shame he carried.

A bell chimed distantly, and the steady pressure slowed. A moment later it chimed again, and her hands paused. "One moment, my lord. Stay in the sun. I'll return quickly."

"Mmn," he agreed. The sunlight was warm across his back and legs, bare for her work. He sighed comfortably and slipped back to the hazy consciousness of near-sleep.

Jarrick rang the bell three times before someone opened the small grate. "I was on the roof, my lord, I'm sorry," said the woman who looked through at them.

"I'm Jarrick Roald, you'll remember. We're here to see Luca."

"My lord?"

"Dom! Dom Nerrin." He chastised himself for the slip. "I brought him here with your master."

The servant opened the gate. "Of course. Please come inside."

Sara hardly waited for the litter to settle on the tiles before leaving it. "Where is he?"

"My lady, I—"

"Where is he?" she repeated excitedly.

"On the roof, my lady, but if you—"

Sara was already running, handfuls of skirt gathered out of her way. Behind her Marla started forward. "My lady! Please!"

But Jarrick was faster, and he reached the stairs before Marla, inadvertently blocking her as he hurried after Sara. Marla hurried after them. "But, my lord, wait!"

Luca heard distant voices, but they seemed a part of the little world which did not concern him, far as it was from the blissful

198

sunlight. He felt himself sinking through the padded bench into a pleasantly dark sleep...

"Luca!"

The voice ripped through his stupor and tore at him. He twitched and tried to rise, but his mind responded more quickly than his muscles.

"Luca, I'm—" Her voice cut off abruptly.

He seized handfuls of the sheet and rolled off the bench, stumbling as he hit the floor. He pulled the sheet to shield himself and stared at her.

Sara had frozen mid-syllable, her mouth hanging uncertainly. She had seen. She was completely stunned.

Angry humiliation rushed over Luca. Why was it like this? Why would it always be like this? He clenched his fists in the sheet. "What are you doing here?"

She seemed to start from a trance. "I—I came to see you, Luca."

"To see me? As an exhibit?"

That seemed to confuse her. "No—no, I came for you."

You are years too late, he thought, but he managed to keep the words behind his teeth.

"Luca," she started, and her voice was both pitying and pleading, "you—you..."

Behind her he saw Jarrick, watching mutely, and then Marla, coming up the stairs with an unhappy expression.

Sara gulped. "Why didn't you write?"

For a single instant Luca was too numb to respond, and then a great hot sphere of emotion burst within him. "Why didn't I *write*? Did it not occur to you that it might be awkward to scribe a letter with one's wrists shackled, even if paper and ink were readily available in the trader's stable?"

She shook her head, her eyes wide. "No..."

"Did you think it was my own responsibility to inform you that, yes, I was still enslaved? Something along the lines of, 'Dearest sister, I have a new master this week, and I won't be writing for a while because I am chained to a wagon in the middle of the Faln Plateau?' And how exactly did you expect me to send a letter, after I'd stolen ink and paper, given that a slave has no money of his own? Was I to, while on my knees begging mercy from the stick, also beg that my letter be carried?"

"Luca..." she whispered.

Jarrick stepped forward. "Luca, think a moment. She only meant that she missed you."

"Missed me?" Luca was scraped hollow by the words. "As if I were on a pleasure trip or away on business?" He gulped as his throat closed. "If she missed me, why didn't she come for me? Why didn't any of you come? I was in Trader Laren's stable—not so far! I was kept what, three days before going to the block in Furmelle? And no one came. No one ever came."

"I would have needed money," Sara protested. "Where would I have gotten money?"

"Sell yourself!" Luca snapped. "You were willing enough to sell me! Sell Sara, and you still have her when it's over."

"Luca!" Jarrick snarled as Sara recoiled.

"Isn't that what's happening right now?" Luca demanded, too enraged to be deterred. "What is this marriage if not a transaction? It's well and good to make her a whore for the sake of the house, but she mustn't diminish her value merely to buy back her brother?"

Luca spun away from them, aware he'd said too much but incapable of stopping himself. Behind him there was an awkward, shocked silence. He wrapped the sheet around himself and shuffled toward the terrace wall. "Go away." His voice was ragged. "Please go away."

Sara was crying. His stomach twisted further within him. Well, let her cry! Hadn't he wept again and again? He'd given her nothing but words. Words didn't hurt, not like deeds.

But he couldn't turn back to face her. He heard her sob something to Jarrick and then she retreated to the stairs. He glanced hesitantly over his shoulder, afraid she would leave and equally afraid she wouldn't. Jarrick's arm was about her shoulders, his head bent over hers. Neither of them looked at him as they began to descend.

What had he done? And yet they had not argued, they had not protested, they had not bothered to defend themselves, to insist that they had really sought him. All he wanted, all he really, desperately wanted, was to hear them insist they'd wished to save him, and they could not be roused or prodded into it.

But what had he done?

He pulled the sheet more tightly about him. If only she had not first seen him bared, his past naked to see. If she'd come to *him* first, and not his stripes, or if she had not begun with such a ridiculous demand...

"My lord?"

He shook his head. He did not want to speak to anyone now.

"My lord, I tried to stop them, but they were quite excited. I'm sorry, but I could not stop them."

"They wouldn't have heeded you," Luca mumbled. "It would not have mattered that I was undressed and asleep. They think they own me as much as any master. I am theirs, and at their call." He sighed, miserable.

"Would you have me serve them refreshment, my lord, while you dress and recover yourself?"

He stared at his bare toes. "That's your suggestion, I see." He turned slowly. "I wish we could start again, where I could receive them with some dignity, instead of being found stripped and striped..."

"I will make them comfortable in the sitting room, my lord, until you are ready for them."

"I don't know that I'll ever be ready for them." He looked at Marla, seeing her shock behind the servant's obedience. "I'm sorry. I didn't mean to be like that."

"My lord owes no apology to me."

Her words and voice were perfectly pitched, but the implication was there. Luca sighed. "I loved Sara. We're only a year apart. She was always closer to Jarrick, but I did love her. When—when—it had to be someone, Father said, and he didn't want it to be Sara..." He gulped and shook away the memory. "Go and see to them, please. I'll dress and—be down in a moment."'"

Marla was looking over the edge of the flat roof. "They are departing now."

Luca turned and saw the litter swaying through the gate. "Wait!" he protested, not loudly enough. "Wait!" But Jarrick, walking beside the litter with his head inclined as if speaking to the occupant, gave no sign of hearing. Cole, abandoned by the hastily summoned litter slaves, stood silently to one side and watched them exit.

Luca slumped further. What had he done? He retreated to the bench and sank upon it, pulling the sheet about his neck. They were all that he had, all that remained, and he had driven them away.

"Marla," he said gruffly, "where does your master write his letters?"

CHAPTER TWENTY-EIGHT

Maru drew a hissing breath, trying not to shiver. Shivering pained his wing. He leaned forward and pressed his bare arms against his legs, drawn to his chest to conserve warmth. His bruised wrists shifted against the shackles, making him wince.

He did not want to be here. He was not entirely certain where *here* was, exactly, but he did not want to be anywhere in the human realm. Unfortunately, it was growing more and more certain that he would not be going to his own world again, nor even anywhere else in the human realm.

He had tried to defend himself, of course, and to escape, but his scavenging party had been surprised where they had expected no resistance and they had scattered, leaving him alone against a handful of furious farmers and mages. The consecutive bolts brought him heavily to the ground, and immediately three or four surrounded him and directed spells to Subdue him. The innate power was ripped from him, and Maru lay gasping and helpless in the mud.

Slaves had brought a large chest carved and painted with sigils and runes and symbols in varying depths and several colors, and the human fighters hauled him upright. "In the box, monster. We want to store you under the bed."

Maru did not move, unable to comprehend, and the men closed on him. He recoiled, reaching reflexively for magic that did not respond, and they overpowered him easily. They lifted him and pressed him into the chest, pushing hard when the fit was tight and scraping a large patch of skin from his shoulder. One wing was trapped awkwardly beneath him.

"All the way!" someone muttered, and they crammed his other wing roughly into the chest, bending it where it should not. Maru struggled, trapped against the unfinished wooden walls, but the hands did not release him. Light bones bowed and snapped as the lid closed, shutting out the light and making Maru's cry echo dully.

He could not move in the cramped dark, could not shift his broken wing or seeping shoulder or aching limbs. The box swayed as it was lifted, pressing him alternately against the wall or his wings, and hours crawled by in the stifling atmosphere. Would he die for want of air? Could they not have killed him more efficiently?

Eventually they'd brought him to this dank cell, where he was shackled—as if muscular humans needed to fear Ryuven strength—and left him in the dark. Stone formed three short walls, the dripping ceiling and the floor, while vertical iron bars, rusted with moisture and age, separated him from the walkway where humans passed and gave him cursory, hateful glances or sneered or occasionally prodded him with their polearms. There was no sheltering barrier to shield him from his captors; he had no choice but to shiver or sleep or relieve himself within their view. At intervals, they shoved a bowl of slops through a creaking gate in the lower barred door. Once a day? Twice? Without natural light, he had no way to be sure.

He was not alone. There were other Ryuven in the cellar—he thought it was a cellar, with the musty smell and the dripping stone—in similar cells to his right. They spoke when there were no humans nearby, but Maru had learned little. They were prisoners, captured in battle or upon crossing the between-worlds, all Subdued and restrained.

There had been more, in the empty cells to his left, he learned. Some were bled occasionally, for unknown purposes. Some had been subjected to magical experimentation, testing new spells for combat. Some had been removed and never returned. All had died when the shield had been restored. The two who remained had been protected from the expanding shield by the rune-shielded chests like the one Maru had been brought in.

The humans did not bother to experiment with Maru, coming only to push bowls of soft meat and brown vegetables through the tiny gate. Maru huddled in his cell, miserable and in pain, knowing he could never cross to his own home again.

CHAPTER TWENTY-NINE

Luca raked his fingers through his hair and stared at the words covering half a sheet on the desk before him. This was hard, this was excruciatingly hard. How could he hope to convey the depth of his apology and grief through mere paper?

But paper was safer, of that he was certain. Paper could not betray him, could not come upon him suddenly, could not interrupt him mid-sentence with words that would disrupt his meaning. If he were to make a proper apology, it must be through paper.

He absently pushed his hands through his hair again and read over the lines. *My beloved Sara, dearest sister, I cannot begin to convey my regret. I owe you the greatest apology. In the hundreds—thousands—of times I imagined meeting you again, never once did I think I could say such things to you.*

That was not a very good beginning, but it was the best he had managed thus far.

If I had been prepared to meet you, I think it might have been different. I would not have chosen to present you first with such a graphic view of my years away. But as it was, my first thoughts were of deepest shame, not of my joy at seeing you. And somehow I lost the moment, lost that I was seeing my sister again at last, and all I could feel was my own humiliation, and the fear and the pain and the resentment— yes, I would lie to deny it—and I could not think of anything but escape. I don't ask you to understand, Sara, because I'm not sure I understand it myself. But I need you to know that I did not mean all that I said.

Marla entered and set a mug on the desk beside him. "Soup," she offered. "Take some."

He brushed back the hair which had fallen over his eyes as he read. "Thanks."

He heard Cole enter the kitchen on the other side of the wall, dropping firewood noisily into the stack. Then the slave came into the room, dusting his hands and tunic. "I've raked out the goat shed and cut back the vines. Is there anything else, my lord?"

"No, Cole," Luca sighed. "Not at the moment. I hope to have something for you later, though. Go and bathe."

"Where?"

Marla straightened. "We always use the bath beside the storeroom. Go ahead."

Cole nodded. "All right. I'd wondered, since I'm not staying in the house…"

"Why did you choose the shed?" asked Luca distantly, rubbing his aching temples.

Cole glanced at Marla. "She put me there, master," he answered with the faintest trace of indignation. "Made me up a nice pallet, sure."

Luca looked from Cole to Marla, whose mouth twitched faintly. Ah, that made sense; the lone female slave might well place the large stranger in an outbuilding. He nodded dully. "Go and bathe, then. Your clothes, too, or see if you can find something else to wear. I don't want to send you wearing goat dung."

Cole nodded. "Yes, master."

Luca reached for the mug and held it for a moment, savoring the warmth on his fingers as he pinched at his forehead with the other hand. Whatever peace and comfort he'd felt that morning had evaporated with Sara and Jarrick's arrival, and his head was pounding with unhappy thoughts. He closed his eyes and saw the letter dancing before his mind.

"My lord?"

He shook his head, opening his eyes. "I'll be all right," he answered wearily. He took a drink of soup. "It's only—I wish this morning had never happened." He sighed. "But then, I could wish a lot of things had never happened."

"If my lord will excuse me." She leaned over the desk and rubbed a cloth over his hairline. "You've inked your forehead."

"What?"

"Probably running your fingers through your hair." She smiled gently. "You've done that a few times."

"I have?" He hadn't been aware of the habit. Had he always had it? He remembered watching Shianan rake at his hair. Had he adopted it?

"Would you like anything in addition to the soup?"

He sighed. "I doubt you can supply what I need, but thank you."

She left and he stared at the letter, adding lines occasionally as he considered. He had somehow to ask to meet Sara again—to meet both of them. The thought made him cringe, but he could not hide here forever. He had to face them.

I will come to supper tomorrow night, if you will have me. I do want

206

to see you again, Sara, and talk with you. Will you admit a boorish once-slave, if he vows to comport himself in a more civilized manner?

"I've brought some tea, my lord," Marla said. "The soup was not to your liking?"

"What? Oh, no, it's fine, I just haven't gotten to it yet."

She gave him a skeptical look. "It has been two hours since I left it."

He was gnawing at his thumb. That was another trait Shianan had displayed when nervous.

"Is there anything I can offer you, my lord?"

"Aside from a brilliant solution to my miserable morning?" He bit down on his thumb. "I was monstrous this morning. Heinous. And I don't know why I'm saying this, you saw it yourself, and it's nothing to do with you."

She blew out her breath. "My lord... As you've already spoken, may I suggest a point?"

"What? How?"

She tapped the desk. "Write something to the effect that you understand and appreciate what she meant to do. She needs to know you saw her intentions were true. Her fault today was that she was too eager to see you again to hear a slave's protest."

He stared at her. "You've guessed at it all, haven't you? We've all said enough, and you know everything."

"No, my lord. I heard only a little, and I know only as much as you will that I should."

He tapped the letter. "And you know I'm writing to her, not to him."

Her eyes shifted nervously. "I'm sorry, my lord."

Perhaps one became inured to humiliation with repeated exposure. He merely set the pen aside with a sigh. "It will be less awkward if you aren't reading over my shoulder or upside down from across the desk. And please, go ahead. I clearly cannot afford to refuse help."

"My lord..."

"Please. If you can help me to reconcile myself with my sister, I'll be in your debt."

She gave him an odd look and then turned to the letter. He watched her start again, her lips moving occasionally as she tested a phrase. Finally she took a slow breath. "I do not know my lady," she began cautiously.

Luca made a gesture of futility. "Clearly, neither do I."

"I think, though, you have made an admirable attempt. There are a few small changes you might consider, my lord, and then the assurance that you do understand her intention..."

Luca took up the pen. "Please, help me. I cannot let this morning stand."

Half an hour later, he finally blotted and folded the letter. "Shouldn't I recopy it?" he asked.

Marla shook her head. "No, this one looks real. Honest. The ink blots show you were pausing, considering, worrying about what you wrote. You don't want to send a clean sheet that looks rehearsed and unfelt."

Luca sealed it and wrote *Sara Roald* across the outside. "Cole!" he called.

The slave entered, fidgeting with his faintly damp clothing. "Yes, master?"

"I have a letter for you to carry. Take this to the house of Roald in Ivat and give it to the young lady. See yourself that she has it directly; don't entrust it to any of the servants."

"Yes, master. Will there be a reply?"

"I—I don't know." He extended the letter. "Be careful of it."

"I will, master."

The slave left for the gate. Luca slumped wearily. "Thank you," he said numbly to Marla. "I appreciate your help."

"Of course, my lord. I only offered my humble opinions. I hope they serve."

"We'll see." He sighed. "So, an aelipto is trained to read and write as well as to treat muscles and ligaments?"

"Actually, I was chosen for training because I could already read and write. Master Thalian was looking for bright new students."

"He buys common slaves and sells them as aelipto?"

"After training, yes. It benefits all involved."

Luca nodded. "It was education that saved me, too. I should have been a field slave, coarse labor, but I was able to recite a snatch of history and found myself a tutor instead. It kept me out of the wagon shafts for a while, anyway, until Furmelle."

"You were in Furmelle, my lord?"

"Unfortunately." He glanced at her and then slid down the short bench. "Please, sit. You know what I am. It's foolish to pretend otherwise."

208

"You are a freeman and a master now."

"And I was once before, too, until my circumstances changed. Please sit."

She did, facing carefully forward on the bench, her back straight.

"How did you know to read before your training?" Luca asked. "Were you freeborn, too?"

"Oh, no, my lord." She gave him a quick, embarrassed smile. "No, I had some schooling from my mother, who was also a born slave. I'm not sure where she'd picked it up, but she was always clever with it. We were part of a country estate, you see, until the old master died without an heir. For a couple of years after that, a proxy steward managed things. Then rumor came that the estate would go to someone else, a reward to some royal favorite, and our steward knew he was going to be replaced. He made it a point to squeeze as much money from the place as he could before he left, including selling off a number of us."

"Your mother was still with the estate?"

"Yes, my lord. I was, if you'll allow the telling, terrified, sure I'd end up in a brothel or a rich pervert's bed. But Master Thalian found me first, and I became an aelipto." She looked at him. "We heard stories about Furmelle, many stories."

"Whatever the worst were, they were true." Luca hunched his shoulders. "Be glad you weren't there." He paused. "Why don't you say what you think?"

"My lord?"

"Your master brought you a flogged man whose siblings sold him into slavery. Most people would be at least startled by this, and yet you say nothing."

"It is not my place to comment on my master's friends."

"You were free enough in your speech at other times, teasing my ignorance—not that I minded. And you act as you will, offering help even when I didn't know I wanted it. You are not timid, you merely hold your own counsel."

She glanced down, suppressing a smile. "I—at first, I guessed you were a leper."

Luca gaped and then laughed aloud. "A leper? Because I hid myself?"

"Exactly."

"Your master would never permit it. I suspect an aelipto is too valuable to risk."

"An aelipto is somewhat costly, but I couldn't imagine why else you were wrapped and cloaked."

"A leper." He chuckled again. "I've not been that, yet."

"I've never actually seen a leper," Marla admitted. "I'd only heard stories from old Gehrnzarse—" She gasped and put a hand to her mouth, as if to catch the word before it had gone too far.

Luca grinned. "Which one was that? The proxy steward or your instructor?"

"Master Thalian," she confessed, blushing. "I'm sorry, my lord."

"I am not your master. I won't mind what you call them."

"We actually liked him, we did. He was very fair, patient, never touched the women nor the men in training. But we called him that because that's what he said whenever he did get irritated." She smiled with the recollection. "It took us months to learn what a Gehrn's arse even was. The Gehrn are a cult—"

"A militaristic cult, worshiping war, specifically strength and the display of it. Their central citadel is in Davan."

She sobered; he must not have kept the bitterness entirely from his voice. "You have some experience with them?"

He hesitated. "Some." He glanced down at his fingers, clenching white in his lap. "I have seen them, yes." His fingers spasmed. She would have needed to be both blind and stupid, and she was neither. "If ever Falten Isen takes it into his mind to sell you, and you think you might go to the Gehrn, break every law and run."

His eyes were on his white fingers, so he did not see her expression. But her body shifted nearer on the bench as she turned to face him. "I'm sorry."

"No," he said quickly, "I'm sorry. I didn't mean—it's only—this has been a day of unpleasant memories and worse speech. There was no reason for me to say such a thing."

She smiled. "Fortunately, I believe my master has no inclination to be rid of me. And it seems unlikely you will ever see the Gehrn again, either."

"Not one, at least. The high priest is in prison in Alham." Luca relaxed marginally.

"In prison? Did your brother do that?"

Luca snorted. "Jarrick? No. Jarrick came to Alham on business, that's all. Flamen Ande was arrested when the shield collapsed during his ritual."

"The shield?"

"You've heard of that, surely. The Great Circle made a magical shield to repel the Ryuven. It stretched over all of Alham and beyond, over the kingdom, maybe the entire world, I don't know."

"Yes, we'd heard of that. You were with the high priest when it collapsed?"

He grimaced. "The Gehrn ritual required a prisoner of war, and I was a Furmelle slave. Near enough."

She caught her breath. "I'm sorry."

"Don't be. I'm glad of it, in a way." He exhaled. "After the shield collapsed, Master Shianan took me from the prison. He treated my wounds and he made me human again. If not for the ritual, I would have stayed with the Gehrn, I would never have known my friend, I would never have seen my brother."

"Master Shianan?" she repeated. "That's an odd..."

Luca smiled faintly. "It is indeed Master Shianan, not Master Becknam. He—we were friends, really. More than a master and slave. Nearer brothers."

"He is not the one who came with you? Who brought my lady this morning?"

"No! No, that's Jarrick, my brother by birth. No, Master Shianan is entirely different."

"He is the one you honored by practicing on the roof."

He glanced at her, surprised. "Yes."

"He must have been a fine man. And then your brother found you?"

"He came for business with Master Shianan, and—and I recognized him."

"You must have been so happy," Marla supposed. "If I saw my mother here..."

Luca bit at his lip. "I did not know if I was pleased. It was my own family which sold me. I wanted to go home—but I was afraid of them." The words surprised him. "Yes, afraid of them. That is why, this morning..."

"But you came with your brother."

"I had no choice." Hot, dark emotion flooded him. "Master Shianan sold me to Jarrick. *Sold* me! After he'd promised that he would never... Yes, it was my brother and not a trader for auction, but—but he knew I was unsure. He knew I was afraid to go home."

"Perhaps he knew, but wanted you to be with your family. If his family is close—"

"Ha," Luca snapped. "He has no family—he never has. He is a bastard son. His father won't acknowledge him, his half-siblings disdain him, his father's wife hates him, I've never heard any mention at all of his own mother. That is what we were to one another, both rejected. His family is not close. He doesn't have a family to be close."

Marla spoke softly. "And your brother wanted you."

Luca stared at her, and gaping understanding opened before him. "I hadn't thought—you're right." He heaved a great sigh. "Of course. And only the Holy One knows what Jarrick said. How could he have refused? He would give his own blood for a word from his father or brothers. He would never have kept me from—he must have thought he was giving me the chance he could never have."

"He was a good friend to you."

Luca nodded silently.

"You could write to him."

Luca nodded again. "But—not yet. Not until I can say I am settled here."

They were quiet a moment. He could feel Marla's nearness, aware of her in a way that he had long thought he'd forgotten. He glanced at her and wondered.

He felt comfortable with her, of course—not only in submitting to her healing touch, but in speaking with her, in telling her too much, in chuckling as she gently mocked him. He'd craved her stability and calm. He could be good friends with her, he knew. But there had been a charged tingle when her hair brushed his skin, a tension of more than mere friendship.

But he had hardly thought of such things. Yes, he'd entertained fancies and dreams when he was a tutor in the Vadis household, eying the pretty female slaves, and then had come the failed and gruesome rebellion. And then he had gone to the Gehrn... A man did not indulge in fantasies when he lived in daily fear.

Marla looked at him, a slow recognition dawning in her eyes and, with it, a faint wariness.

"No." Luca clenched his fists. "No, you needn't worry on that, I swear. I have been a slave myself, and I will not take advantage." He gulped. "And I would not dare to ask you. I am free, they say, but I feel myself a slave still. I only..."

Marla shook her head. "It was only a moment, my lord. You were thinking of other things, and you made no approach to me. I accepted the offer to sit beside you and was caught in the heady rush of privilege. We neither of us—"

Luca's hand twitched toward her, wanting to catch her but not quite daring to touch her. "Wait. Please, if for just one moment you were not a slave and I were not a freeman—would you...?"

She glanced down, and her head moved slightly. "No. I'm sorry."

His breath caught, and embarrassment scorched through him.

"And I am married."

Luca blinked. "You are?"

Marla gave him a quick, mocking smile, herself again. "Slaves do marry, you know."

He gestured, glad for the excuse to look about the room. "You were alone here... I assumed..."

Her mouth stayed in a smile, but her eyes shifted away. "We were separated."

Luca's stomach sank. He should have guessed. "I am so sorry."

Her face tightened, pressing her lips together. "I keep a hope that I will see him again. It's possible. Why shouldn't it happen?" Her throat moved.

Useless, helpless sympathy chafed at Luca, and he wanted to reach out to her, to offer comfort. But he dared not move toward her, not after his tentative advance, and she would not want it. "I am sorry," he repeated. "Maybe you'll find him." He needed something more to say. "Where is he? Er—what does he do?"

"He's a clerk," she said. "My mother trained him; that's how we met." She took a breath and then exhaled sharply. "Enough, that's no interest to anyone." She slid from the bench and made a hasty bow. "I will go for my lord's supper."

She was upset, but not angry. He had carelessly stumbled upon a hurt, and there was little to be done for it.

Luca was left alone in the darkening room, feeling the tangible absence of Marla, of Cole, of Jarrick, Sara, Shianan. He twitched restlessly on the bench, feeling hot disappointment and frustration mix with his bitter loneliness.

Had it been easier as a slave? No, no, of course not—he had only to think of any single day under Ande to know that, or to recall again the constant weight of the chain linking his wrist to the tinker's cart. Even as a tutor he had chafed and fretted, though if he had known what lay ahead, he would have been pathetically grateful to face only moody children and petty fellow slaves.

But he had known his place, at least. He had known that nothing was available to him, that he dared not hope. As the youngest son of a merchant house, he had been nominally respected, but the attention and prizes had always gone to his elder brothers. He had contented himself with their leavings, entertaining the client's less-fair daughter or attending the lesser gatherings, but the bright hope of *more* had always teased him. As a slave, he'd learned to expect nothing, and he had never been disappointed.

And then Shianan had given him more, surprising him wholly, and he had begun to dream again. And then he had come here, where he was more than a slave but less than a freeman, excluded from slaves' conversation just as he no longer moved comfortably among the free.

He stared at the remaining paper and ink, but there was no one to whom he wished to write. He clenched his fist and rose, shoving the bench back. He could not sit quietly, could not be idle after years of forced activity, could not be still with thoughts whirling within him. He climbed the stairs to the roof.

CHAPTER THIRTY

Maru did not know how long he had sat in the cell. There was no sunlight to mark the passing of days, and the guards' schedule was irregular, he guessed. They were largely unconcerned with the Ryuven, and aside from the inconvenience of bringing food and water, the guards barely troubled themselves with the prisoners. Once in a while they brought a bucket into which he could empty his soil pot—not often enough—but if there were still experiments as the other prisoners had described, Maru was not taken for them.

His broken wing ached in the cold. He could not fold it, but it was tiring to hold it above the chill, damp floor. He braced an edge against the wall, wincing at the pressure but losing less heat to the stone. His good left wing he kept partially extended, wrapped about his shoulder and arm for warmth.

There was another Ryuven in the cell to his right, and one beyond that, nearest the door. No one ever went to the empty cells to Maru's left. There was no physical escape through the stone and rusty iron, even with the reduced guard, but he could call to the prisoner beside him.

"Cilbitha'sho." They did not bother to whisper. There was no one to hear them.

There was a grumble from behind the wall. "I was trying to sleep."

Maru pressed his fingers against his arms. "There's plenty of time to sleep."

"It's the only way to pass the time. Do you think I want to listen to a nim's prattle?" There was a sigh. "What did you have to say, Maru?"

"I—nothing in particular. I just—it's so silent. So dark and silent."

"Like we're buried. Maybe we are. Maybe this is dead."

"Shut up, Cilbitha," came a more distant voice. "Look, lad, can you move?"

Maru extended his good wing an arm's length, until it bumped the opposite wall. "Yes."

"Exactly. You ever seen a corpse move? We're not dead, then, Cilbitha."

"Of course not," snapped the Ryuven between them. "But we might as well be. And given their failing interest, we might be soon. If they don't kill us, they might just forget to feed us."

"That's so," admitted Parrin at the far end. "I don't think they remember as often even now."

"How's your wing, nim?"

"It hurts." Maru shifted. "I keep hoping—they say Subduing can wear off after time."

"I've heard that too," said Parrin. "But I've been here a long time... Sometimes it never comes back. You're just burned out and empty forever."

"And what of that?" Cilbitha snapped.

"It would hardly make a difference to me," Maru added. "I'm only nim. No one would notice if I were Subdued forever."

The others laughed with the grim humor of the condemned. As the cells fell quiet again, Maru blinked unseeing into the dark. What he'd joked was untrue; nim had the least power of any Ryuven, yes, but they could heal themselves of many injuries, given time. There were moments when they chose not to—one never augmented healing of a wound given by one of a higher caste, for example, at least not within the other's sight—and magical injuries were easier to heal than physical, but ordinarily even a traumatic injury like his snapped wing should have troubled him no more than days.

Without his innate magical ability, though, his wing was knitting too slowly, and anyway it was not the type of injury which should be left alone to heal. A bone could join, but if misaligned, it still could leave its owner a cripple.

Maru choked back a sob and pressed his fist hard against his mouth, lest the others hear his distress. It did not matter whether his wing healed properly or not, whether he ever recovered his natural abilities—he was trapped in a tiny, cold, wet world without sunlight, and he was as good as dead. Nothing else could matter.

A rattling of iron echoed to them, as hinges creaked and a flickering light crept down the corridor. Maru instinctively leaned toward the bars, as a plant might bend toward light, and his wing twinged sharply.

"We just got the three of them, my lord mage," a gruff voice explained. "We was told we wouldn't be needing the rest, anyway."

"I understand." The footsteps sounded sharp in the damp atmosphere. "Bring the light. I want to see them." One set of footsteps hurried as the other stilled. "Good afternoon."

"Afternoon, is it?" came Parrin's dry tone. "I wouldn't know."

"I'm Ewan Hazelrig, White Mage of the Great Circle," came the even reply. "I'm looking for a Ryuven."

"You've found one, it seems."

Maru's heart quickened. The White Mage Ewan Hazelrig... This man had known Tamaryl. This was the man to whose office door Maru had carried the letter.

"I was rather hoping for one in particular," the mage answered. "I want a nim."

There was silence from Parrin's cell. The guard cleared his throat. "What's a nim, my lord mage?"

"It is a common Ryuven," answered the mage absently. Maru thought he sounded vaguely annoyed, as if he disliked being distracted from his business.

"Common, my lord? It's a type of Ryuven, then?"

"Yes. Most of the Ryuven who came here were nim."

"Common like a garter snake?"

"If you please, guardsman, I have work here."

"Yes, m'lord mage. Sorry."

"I may assume, then, you are not nim?"

It was Cilbitha who answered. "What do you want with a nim?"

The White Mage came further down the corridor, followed by the guard with the torch. The light hurt Maru's eyes. "You're nim?"

"I'm sho. I'm worth good ransom, if you'd only think of it." The veneer of bravado in his voice began to crack. "Take us out of the dark, mage. If you know we're of rank, you know we could have higher accommodations. We're no good to you down here, none at all."

"I will mention that to the Circle," answered the mage levelly. "But my purpose here today was only to ask for—"

"I am nim," Maru blurted. *Please—I nursed your ill daughter! But what do you want with us?* "I am nim."

His heart hung in his throat as the mage approached his cell. Did the mage know that the Ryuven who'd helped his daughter was here? Or had he come for one of the experiments which had claimed other prisoners?

The White Mage looked narrowly at him, frowning through the bars. Maru flinched from the unshaded torchlight. At last the mage spoke. "I am looking for one who has some experience in carrying messages."

Did he remember the letter Maru had left beneath his door? But he could not have known it was Maru. Did he want someone to carry documents of war to Oniwe'aru? No, they would want a sho or rika for that. "I..."

"My name is Ewan Hazelrig." The mage drummed his fingers on his crossed arms. "What are you called?"

Maru gulped. "My name is Maru."

The simple words did something to the mage. Maru could see the shift in his shoulders, and the crossed arms loosened. "I'll want you for my work. If you—"

"No!" Cilbitha struck the rusty bars at the front of his cell, inches from Maru and invisible behind the stone wall. "You'll kill him as you did the others!"

The mage did not turn his head. "If I wanted merely to kill him, I could do it here. And I don't want him for—"

A pale arm stretched from beyond the stone partition and clawed toward the mage's throat. The torch bobbed as the guard jumped, startled, but the concussion was already spreading, rolling over Maru with a percussive burst through his skull, chest, and wings. He grunted with the diminishing force of it and opened his eyes to see Cilbitha's arm falling, dropping to the damp floor with a weight which implied it would never move again.

"'Soats, my lord, that was fast," breathed the guard, staring at the body.

The mage had hardly moved. "They are fast."

"But you... He's dead, my lord mage."

"I'm aware of that," the mage answered flatly. He looked unhappy. "Spend thirty years on a magical battlefield against a superior foe, and see what reflexes are left to you." His eyes shifted to Maru. "What's wrong with this one?"

"What?"

"He's injured. How?"

"I don't know. He's been like that, I guess. We just feed them, that's all."

The mage crossed his arms again. "I need to disable the ward at the gates. When I'm finished, I'll want to take this one to my workrooms."

"What? Er, my lord mage, we were told they wouldn't be going anywhere. Most of the work's done, eh?"

"And do you think," the mage demanded, peeved, "that with the shield, the responsibility of the Circle ends? That we mages will simply sit back and wait for age and death to creep upon us without accomplishing any more?"

"No, my lord! I didn't mean that."

"I'm glad to hear it."

Maru stared at the pale, singed arm. Dimly he realized that the White Mage would take him from the prison. He glanced up worriedly.

"I will return shortly," the mage said clearly, looking at Maru, "with my servant Tam. I trust you'll be ready for us?"

Tam! Was that Tamaryl? Had Ryl sent the mage to find him? Was it too fantastic to believe—had desperation and hope made him guess too wildly?

"Someone will be here with the keys," the guard answered promptly.

"Good."

CHAPTER THIRTY-ONE

Marla glanced through the window to the front gate again, but the repetition didn't bring Cole home. The slave had not yet returned, and given that it was three hours' walk to Ivat, without counting time to ask directions and find the Roald house, he might stay the night and not return until morning. He had no duties to demand otherwise.

She bit at her lip. Without Cole, she was alone with her master's guest. Even if Cole returned, his presence in the outbuilding meant nothing. She had to navigate this shoal alone.

This afternoon had frightened her—not only because of how familiar she had been with the visiting freeman, but because of how comfortable she had been doing so. It wasn't until he pulled back that she realized exactly how comfortable she had been—and yet, she couldn't say it had happened without her knowledge. It had just felt... natural, as if they were friends rather than acquaintances of only a couple days. Rather than freeman and slave.

She had not spoken of Demario to many. Her master knew, but few others did. She wouldn't have mentioned him today if not for the guest's tentative overture... but she was waiting still for Demario. She had not lost hope.

This man would not press her, though. She was sure of that. He knew too keenly a slave's helplessness, and he did not seek to salve his own hurt by inflicting it on others.

She stirred the pot, noting the thickening consistency. She could not delay any longer, if she wanted to serve a decent meal. She drew out a wooden tray and picked up a bowl.

She did like him. He was a freeman, a master of slaves, and yet he wore humility where most wore pride and superiority. He had been wronged, but he was not wholly bitter, only wounded and uncertain of how to reconcile himself. He had not used atrocity to justify his own offense but had sincerely regretted his lack of judgment. In short, he was a principled man, and that he had been a slave made it easier to think of him as an equal, one of her own. She ladled stew, thick with remaining chicken and winter vegetables, into the bowl and began to slice the crusty bread. She would not mind his friendship, if a freeman and a slave could be friends.

She loaded the tray with stew, bread, and ale, draped a cloth over it to keep the warmth, and left the kitchen.

He was not in the sitting room, nor in her master's tiny office. She did not find him in the garden or the sleeping chamber. Finally she climbed the stairs to the roof. "My lord?"

He was there. She stopped, sloshing the ale, and stared at him on his knees, scrubbing at a stain on the tiled terrace. He sank back onto his heels and let the brush drop splashing into the bucket beside him. "Hello."

"My lord," she stammered. "What are you…"

He looked ashamed. "I just couldn't sit still, and so…" He shrugged. "I think I did well enough, though. I didn't make more work for you."

"No," she answered numbly, "no, it's fine." She approached him, still holding the tray. "I've brought supper…"

"Supper," he repeated. "I'd not even thought of supper." He looked about the rooftop. "When I was newly a slave, only a few months into my first place, I was told to scrub a patio. I protested that a tutor—that was my position—a tutor should not be given such a menial task." He rested his arm on the lip of the bucket, faintly smiling at his foolish pride. "Our steward disagreed, and he said I shouldn't eat until the chore was finished."

"I think you're near enough, my lord. Will you come downstairs to table, or will you eat at the bench here?"

"I haven't quite finished. I want to have it done." He looked a bit sheepish. "It's ridiculous, I know."

"My lord…"

"I would have preferred an enormous table of ciphers, but there was none handy." He gave her a self-mocking smile. "There's nothing like arithmetic to set the order of the universe right."

"My lord, please eat something."

"If you insist."

The tile was drying in the evening air, showing matte patches in the shiny damp surface. Luca sat on the bench and Marla set the tray beside him. "I will go down and——"

"No." His voice had changed, quiet, pleading. "Please, don't leave me."

She hesitated.

"This afternoon—I'm sorry for what happened. I didn't mean to frighten you, or to touch on private matters. But, if you can

222

overlook that, I would very much like to speak with you." His words were coming faster. "You're the only one here who hasn't seen someone else in me. Only myself." He looked away. "I am not asking you for anything. Only conversation. I am neither slave nor master; let me be someone for a short time at least."

She hesitated and then sat down at the far end of the narrow bench. "What would you like to converse about, my lord?"

"Anything. Tell me a story from your childhood, I don't care. Only say something."

Marla smoothed her skirt. "A story about me as a child, or a story someone told me as a child?"

"Whichever pleases you more."

"You're not eating, my lord."

He surprised her by chuckling. "See, I am no respected master, if you admonish me so. You needn't be formal—Marla." He tested her name tentatively. "I need no honorific, please."

This was unfamiliar and dangerous ground. "But—"

"Please. I want to be Luca, for one evening. Not a slave, not a former slave, not a pathetic cringing drudge, not an inconvenient and shameful younger brother, not a freed slave who should be grateful, not a freeman who must be confident in everything, not anything but Luca."

She looked at him, thinking that perhaps she understood. "If you like." It was a heady rush to leave *my lord* from the address, a daring flaunting of position and convention. "But you'll have to eat your supper."

He laughed, a quick release of nerves. "I eat, I eat." He dutifully tore a piece of bread and dipped it into the stew.

"When I was a little girl," Marla began, "my mother taught me my numbers, of course. She was educated and saw that I was, too. And she taught me how to count to thirty-one on one hand—"

"Oh!" cried Luca through a mouthful, startling her. He gulped and then continued, "No, you can't surprise me with this one. I was a trained accountant, and I know all your number tricks." He held up five fingers and wiggled them. "One, two, three, four, five, six—"

"All my tricks?" she repeated, raising one eyebrow. "I'll bet not. Think of an animal, and—"

"A chicken," he supplied.

"No, don't tell me! That will spoil the joke. Think of another animal and keep it to yourself." She grinned. "Now spell it out in your

223

head and count the number of letters."

"And you're going to have me add them together, right?"

"Not in this one! Not yet, anyway. Multiply by nine and subtract five. Got it? Now sum the digits."

He hesitated. "Wait... they'll all work out to four, eventually. So your trick must be based on that."

"Oh, you are clever, aren't you? Try this one, then."

It was not so hard to forget Luca's station. As he was caught in the game, he leaned forward and his eyes shone with delighted laughter, resembling not at all the self-important men who came to her master's main house to talk of business. Nor did he resemble the shrouded, taciturn guest who'd followed her master through the gate. He was nearly one of her fellow students under Master Thalian, joking over some lesson.

The sky darkened into night, and the air grew chilly. He noticed when she rubbed briefly at her arms. "I'm sorry, are you cold? We should go down."

"Oh, not for me. I'm all right."

He shook his head. "No, I promised you I would ask nothing, and yet we're sitting beneath the stars. Whether I intended it or not, that could be seen as... We must go down or it will compromise my word."

"And sitting before the warm hearth no less so?" She tipped her head back to look at the starry sky. "No... I love the stars. I cook every day when I'm alone. The kitchen fire holds no romance."

"I'm afraid the stars don't move me," Luca replied, leaning backward himself.

"No? How could they not?"

"Too many nights under them and nothing else, and they never answered my questions." He straightened. "But we'll both be warmer by the fire, and I'll try to keep my indifferent mood from beneath the indifferent stars."

"The kitchen hearth is more moving?"

He sobered. "Yes," he said. "But I don't quite know how to explain. It's very... warm. Not from the fire, but—it's comfortable."

She busied herself straightening his tray. "My mother used to tuck me in before the kitchen fire, and brush my hair, and sing songs for bedtime. Is that what you mean?"

There was a long pause. "I think so," he said finally, his tone thoughtful. "I think so." He picked up the tray before she could. "Let's go."

The fire had burned low, so she built it into a merrier blaze than was strictly necessary after the cooking was finished. She turned to find that he'd dropped two bags of meal from their high storage against rodents and had settled on the floor against them, stretching his legs before him. "I've never done this," he mused. "I've never sat on the floor in a kitchen and watched the fire."

She sat on a nearby bench and propped her chin in her hands, looking at him. "No? Not in either of your lives?"

He smiled sardonically. "My two lives; that's one way of putting it. And no. A merchant's son does not loiter in the kitchen, and I never served in a capacity which kept me there."

She stared past him to the fire. "What was your best situation?"

He didn't hesitate. "Serving Master Shianan, of course." He glanced up. "It was cleaner work being a tutor, I suppose, but if I had to choose..." He shifted his legs. "I'm not quite sure what to say. He remade me after the Gehrn."

"He was a soldier?"

"He is a soldier," Luca confirmed. "And he was instructing me in the staff. Teaching a slave to use a weapon, and he was at Furmelle—can you imagine it?"

"He must have been a fine man, as you said."

Luca nodded. "I will write to him, of course. Only, I want to tell him good news. I'll wait until then."

CHAPTER THIRTY-TWO

Ewan Hazelrig could feel the tension in Tam's slight body, stiffening as the heavy door ground open before them. He wondered that the guard did not grow suspicious—but then, a prison guard was hardly likely to give a second glance to a slave. If he did note the boy's discomfort, he would attribute it to a rational distaste for the deep prison itself.

The guard picked up a torch and gave Tam a glance, making Hazelrig's chest tighten. But he said only, "He coming with us?"

"The Ryuven is injured," Hazelrig said, seeing Tam's shoulders rise another notch. "Ryuven aren't heavy, but this one is filthy with captivity. I don't want to carry him, if he needs help. The boy can handle him."

The guard nodded, satisfied. "I guess a mage's boy knows how to keep his mouth shut." He turned and lit the first steps.

Tam followed a half-step behind Hazelrig, but the mage could see his expression tighten as they descended. Ryuven were creatures of air, and the dark underground must seem a very tomb to them. It was disconcerting enough to Hazelrig himself.

Torchlight flickered down the narrow corridor between cells, and something long and pale showed in the path. Hazelrig extended his hand to block Tam and halted. "Why is he still there?" he demanded quietly.

The guard looked at Hazelrig and then at the arm of the dead Ryuven, stretching between the iron bars. "I hadn't got to him yet," he answered defensively. "He wasn't going nowhere."

"So you left a corpse alongside—between—the remaining prisoners?" Hazelrig could hear a cutting edge in his voice. This was difficult enough for Tamaryl; he did not want additional indignity and abuse. "Leave the key and take care of him. Now."

The guard blinked, but he'd heard the edge in Hazelrig's voice as well, and he did not argue with the White Mage. "As you say, my lord mage." He fingered through his ring of heavy keys until he found the one he wanted and went to unlock the second cell. Tam stared in silence, unmoving. The guard returned and handed the key to Hazelrig, and then he went to retrieve the body.

Hazelrig stepped to one side, making room for him to pass with the dead Ryuven. He touched his hand to Tam's shoulder—a master guiding a slave boy out of the way, or the conciliatory touch of a friend—but Tam had eyes only for the marred corpse as it passed. He watched, stone-faced, as the guard passed, and he continued to look as the guard carried the dead Ryuven up the steps.

"He died by magic," Tam said at last. His voice was flat, incongruously young in the dark.

"He attacked me."

Tam made no answer. Hazelrig half-expected him to protest, to argue, but he said nothing.

Hazelrig extended the iron key. "He's in the third cell."

The words broke Tam free from his seeming spell, and he snatched the key with a strangely boyish alacrity. Hazelrig remained where he was as Tam hurried past the empty second cell and spun to face the bars of the third. The mage turned to one side, but he could not avoid hearing the draw of breath. "Maru!"

The Ryuven rose toward the bars. "I... Ryl!"

They clasped arms through the bars, and Hazelrig closed his eyes, glad of their chance at reunion without the guard's presence. He could hear their excited, pained exchange, low voices of surprise and outrage. Hazelrig wished again that he had found Maru unharmed instead of crippled as he was.

But at least he was alive.

He could hear Maru's amazed questions. He had needed only a moment to recognize his disguised friend, but the guise was strange to him. Tamaryl had drawn on Hazelrig's power to change his shape, and there had been no need to seal his own pathetic strength. It had been easy enough to bend temporary cuffs about his wrists, giving him a slave's invisibility.

They left the cell and came up the corridor, and Hazelrig turned back to them. "My good Maru," he said quietly.

The Ryuven regarded him warily. Hazelrig didn't blame him. He had seen the White Mage kill a fellow prisoner with one quick bolt. Tamaryl's presence would not be enough to assure him just yet.

"Will you kill him, too, mage?" The voice seemed to echo aloud Hazelrig's thought. He turned to the first cell, where a Ryuven hunched over his knees without looking at them. "What torture or death awaits him?"

Tam looked at the remaining Ryuven for the first time. He left

Maru and went to the cell, crouching to peer between the rusted bars. He looked dazed, as if trapped in some terrible dream. "You too..."

The prisoner raised his head with a sullen glare. "Leave us or kill us cleanly. What experiments do you practice upon us? Do even you assist in our torment, slave boy?"

Tam looked as if he desperately wanted to speak but could find no words.

The Ryuven blinked and looked uneasily at Tam, his glare giving way to wary wonder. "Who... who are you?" he asked suspiciously, rising into a defensive crouch.

Tam's throat worked visibly, and then Hazelrig felt a minute shift in the atmosphere. For an instant, power thrummed through the air, a single quick pulse, and then it faded.

It was enough for a sensitive Ryuven. The prisoner's eyes widened. "Pairvyn," he breathed. "Tamaryl'sho, what are you doing here? How are you in such a form and place? How did they—"

"I haven't time to answer," Tamaryl answered unhappily. "But understand, I am no prisoner. My strength will return."

The Ryuven lowered one knee and knelt. "Parrin, Tamaryl'sho."

"Parrin'sho..." Tamaryl seemed suddenly to recall the iron keys he held numbly. He lifted them and began searching for the cell key. "Come with us—"

"No." Hazelrig's voice was unexpectedly loud against the stone. He winced, wishing it had not sounded so sharp. "I'm sorry, but we cannot risk it. Taking one prisoner can be explained, but taking both that remain will invite questions we cannot afford. It will endanger all of you further."

Tamaryl turned flashing eyes upon him. "But he is—"

"We cannot draw suspicion! There are no experiments now. The safest place for him is here." Hazelrig sighed, knowing he was right but hating his words. "We will come for him later. We can find a way." He swallowed. "I'm sorry."

Maru looked at the floor uncomfortably. Tamaryl turned back to the imprisoned Ryuven, his shoulders drooping. "I am sorry. I trust his judgment. We cannot risk suspicion."

The Ryuven looked over Tamaryl's shoulder. "He is the White Mage."

"He has not failed me yet."

The Ryuven took a slow breath. "Pairvyn ni'Ai, I am yours to command, if you have need of me."

"Not yet. But I hope soon to order you out of this cell." Tamaryl clenched his fists against the floor. "Wait a little longer, Parrin'sho. I will not forget you. I'm sorry. But wait."

A clang above them indicated the guard's return. Tamaryl rose with obvious aching reluctance and, slowly, turned from the cell and the kneeling Ryuven. He looked at Maru, who took a step toward him.

"My lord mage?" The guard tramped down the stairs. "You still down here? Is that one giving you trouble?"

Tamaryl blinked and stepped behind the White Mage, subtly becoming nothing more than the slave Tam.

Hazelrig shook his head as the guard drew near. "No trouble. Take back your keys. We're going."

CHAPTER THIRTY-THREE

Shianan did not have to wait long; Connor Kudo was not important enough to keep him waiting. "My lord commander?"

Shianan took a seat at his desk. "How are the audits progressing, my lord?"

Kudo exhaled a long, exasperated breath. "We very much appreciate your discovery of the fraud, of course, and it's all to the good, but that is a lot of accounting to check." He rubbed at his eyes and gestured at the ledgers stacked on the end of his desk. "I'll be reconciling numbers into my grave."

Shianan produced a sheet of paper and spread it upon Kudo's desk. "Would it help if you knew exactly where to look?"

He had recopied Jarrick Roald's incriminating list so that the man's handwriting could not be recognized. It would do no good to send Luca home to a family just before their arrest and collapse.

Kudo held the paper at arm's length and squinted at it. "Is this a list of defrauders?"

"These are the merchants I am confident you should look at most closely." Shianan leaned conspiratorially over the desk. "And as I did not learn this by my own accounting and I should like to protect my source, I ask that if you should add any name to this list, please confirm it with me first to avoid exposing my informant."

Kudo nodded eagerly. "Given the months of effort and headache your informant has just spared me, I will gladly spare him. As far as I am concerned, this list is complete."

"Thank you, my lord."

Shianan returned to his office, glad of his strike against the murderous alliance but also freshly wounded. Jarrick's list had not been Luca's price, but it was too near the loss.

The outer door opened without a warning knock, and Shianan raised his head from his paperwork, prepared to snap at the soldier who entered without permission. But it was Ewan Hazelrig who came through the door, swathed in his white cloak, and Shianan bit back his rebuke. No matter his mood, he could not vent it on the White Mage.

"I hope I'm not disturbing you," Hazelrig offered by way of greeting, raising an eyebrow.

Shianan smoothed his expression into what he hoped was a polite mask. "Not at all, my lord mage. Please sit."

"Thank you." Hazelrig seated himself, settling his official robes. "Blasted things," he complained amiably. "Such a nuisance. Show every little speck." He raised his eyes to meet Shianan's. "Have you a few minutes, my lord commander, for us to speak in private?"

Shianan's spine stiffened. "My lord?"

Hazelrig did not so much as blink. "Have you? Or should I come another time?"

Shianan swallowed, nervous for no reason he could define. He rose and locked the door behind the mage. "We won't be disturbed. What may I do for you, my lord mage?"

The mage looked at him steadily. "I thought you might have something to say," he began mildly. "I came to make it convenient for you, if you wished."

"Convenient?"

"To ask your questions, your lordship, without danger of being overheard in the Wheel."

Shianan took a breath. "It is not the place of a commander to question the White Mage."

"I believe it was you who said we could not afford to stand on formality."

Shianan bit back a curse. "Then, if we must be blunt, that was when we shared secrets, my lord mage. We traded one secret for another, and that concluded our contract. I did not even know you had such a prize in your hands now."

Hazelrig shook his head. "You observed that I had a guest—not a prisoner."

Shianan clenched his fist. "Pairvyn ni'Ai is no guest in this land."

"The Pairvyn ni'Ai has been a guest in my home for much of your lifetime," the mage replied, a hint of acidity creeping into his voice, "and I owe him the life of my daughter twice over—which is once more than I owe the same to you, my lord commander, grateful as I am."

Shianan could not answer.

Hazelrig settled again in his seat. "Tamaryl returned to our world to seek a missing friend," he explained, his voice smooth again, "who is now found. I owe Maru my gratitude as well, as it was he who nursed Ariana through her illness in the Ryuven world."

Shianan swallowed against the lump in his throat. "I do not disregard the service to you and your daughter," he muttered. "But there are Ryuven raids happening around the countryside."

"I assure you that Tamaryl is not leading them."

"The Circle seems to believe that they are isolated bands of Ryuven trapped within the shield."

"They do." Hazelrig's face was impassive.

Shianan clenched his jaw. "I am sworn to defend this land against the Ryuven—as are you, my lord mage."

"Then when my guests show themselves a threat, we will respond together," Hazelrig answered. "Until then, I am more concerned about why the only pitcher in my workroom is filled with a bunch of wilting flowers."

"My lord mage?"

"You were a more frequent visitor before you risked your life to give my daughter a chance at coming home. After proving your friendship and admirable devotion, you have been to the Wheel only rarely, and to our home not even once. Why?"

"Why?" Shianan looked down, growing warm. "You need ask? There is a Ryuven in your workroom, which I cannot condone, and more, your daughter loves this Ryuven. Why would you have me come nearer to witness my defeat at the hands of my bitterest enemy? There is enough cruelty in this world, my lord mage."

"Of course she loves him. Why should that stop you?"

"She sheltered him when he breached the shield," Shianan said angrily. "She risks her life every day he is here, just to watch over him! She is committing treason for him! I can see that she loves him—there is no need to make things more difficult for us all."

Hazelrig looked at him gravely. "There are different kinds of love," he said after a moment. "The slave you sent to me, Luca—he risked himself in leaving his rightful master and going to you while you were under guard, all for your sake. He loved you, but not in the way you love Ariana." He gestured vaguely. "She grew up beside Tam. He is like family to her. She loves him, in one way, and I think she could grow to love him in another. But you are a military commander, your lordship—would you leave the field to your opponent and then merely hope for victory?"

Shianan stared at the inky surface of his desk, the grain marred by scratches and stains. "I would not enter a battlefield without a reasonable hope of success."

"If you are looking for promises and guarantees, my lord, then there are few in this world. And I do not pretend to know my daughter's mind. But there is a makeshift vase of flowers in the very room where she hosts your rival." He rose and drew his white cloak about him. "There will be two Ryuven staying with me for a time. The second is a prisoner of war, perfectly legal, so you needn't worry about that. I hope they will both be safely gone soon. In the meantime, consider yourself invited to supper." He went to the door and nodded toward Shianan's speechless form. "Good day, my lord commander."

CHAPTER THIRTY-FOUR

Luca turned in the blankets so that they wrapped about him. His fingers clenched on the pillow and he made himself release it. Cole would eventually return, and there would be time enough then to—

There was a quiet knock at the door. "Master?"

Luca thrashed as he twisted to face the door. "Cole! Come in."

The door opened, admitting the muscular slave. "I left before dawn, knowing you were waiting, master. Here is the return message."

There was a hopeful note in the voice, and as Luca sat up and stretched for the message he nodded. "Thank you, Cole. You did well." He wet his lips. "I only hope this note..." He hesitated. "Did you have something to eat? Marla should be in the kitchen, I think." She undoubtedly had been up for hours, while he had been wasting time here, trying not to think. He squeezed his fingers, denting the folded paper, as Cole made a short bow and left the room.

The reply was written across the bottom margin of his own letter. It was Sara's handwriting. He smoothed the creased paper compulsively.

My dear brother, I think I, too, was not wholly prepared for our reunion. But, like you, I believe we are capable of better. Please come to supper tonight. Jarrick invites you, too. Tonight we dine as a family again, a family of five.

She had signed it simply, *Your loving sister.* He had not lost her. She still wanted him.

Luca slumped with relief. He took a slow, deep breath, the sunlight warm across his shoulders. He would see her tonight.

He would see all of them tonight. A family of five, she'd said. Sara, and Jarrick, and Thir, and their father. He would see them all.

He slid out of the blankets and reached for his clothing. He would need to leave early, to give himself plenty of time to—he stopped and looked at his clothes, the new outfit Jarrick had bought. It needed washing, and it would need time to dry. He wished he had something that would cover his arms more fully, to hide the remaining marks on his wrists, but there was no help for that.

"Marla?" he called, descending the stairs. "Marla, is there—"

She stepped out of the kitchen. "My lord?"

235

He hesitated, suddenly self-conscious. "I want to wash my shirt... Is there something I can wear in the meantime?"

Marla looked startled. "I can do the washing, my lord."

"I know that. But then I would have nothing to do but wait, and..." He grinned nervously. "You'd find me scrubbing the roof again, and naked."

She laughed. "We can't have that, my lord. I'll find something of my master's for you to wear."

The robe she brought him was clearly that of a traveling merchant, an exotic tight weave which managed to feel silky and warm at once. He undressed in the storeroom, tying the robe about his waist, and carried his clothes into the kitchen.

Marla glanced at him sitting between the fire and the squat washtub. "It's good news, then?"

"Yes. She's invited me to supper." Luca could taste the words. "I said I would be in your debt if you helped to reconcile us."

"That was only my just service to my master's friend."

He gave her a serious look. "No, Marla. I sincerely thank you."

She kept her eyes on the blade she was sharpening. "My lord."

The clothes were not filthy or stained, and it did not take long to soap them. Luca hung them evenly near the kitchen fire where they would dry without becoming smoky and then bailed the washtub water into the garden. "And now a bath," he told himself. He could not present himself looking like a slave. He set water to heat, glad of the snowmelt-fed fountain which provided fresh water for each task.

He scrubbed every inch of his skin, wishing for the perfumed salts of the Kalen baths. He ducked his head and scoured his scalp until it stung. He was not satisfied until the water cooled. Finally he rose and wrapped himself again in the warm, silken robe, squeezing water from his hair.

There was still time to fill after his bath, and he doubted his clothes would be dry. He went into the sitting room and watched his fingers jump restlessly from chair arm to lap to handful of robe.

Isen had several books shelved neatly against the wall. Luca reached for one, reveling in the feel of its leather binding. He had longed many times in his servitude for the solace of a book, once his constant pastime, but he had only the children's schoolbooks in his tutoring and then of course, nothing at all. He opened the unmarked cover, finding a short treatise on military history.

But he could not make his eyes sit still on the page. Though history had been his passion, the words jumbled together and made no sense to him. He worried briefly that he had lost the habit of reading but quickly corrected himself. He was merely too nervous to focus properly. Sitting still would not relieve him; he needed movement. He set aside the book. Had he left the staff on the roof? He couldn't remember. He went to the storeroom and retrieved another before climbing the stairs.

The drills Shianan had taught him were simple and repetitive, but the motion helped burn the nervous energy which had plagued him. As he concentrated wholly on each repetition, immersing himself in the movement of the moment, the worry eased, and by the time the shadows had moved across the floor, his muscles were loose with work. He paused and sat on the sun-warmed tile, leaning on one arm and resting the other on his knee. The loose robe shifted and gaped over his chest, but the cool air felt good and he did not move, closing his eyes.

Sweet Holy One, thank you for this chance. Thank you that I've come this far. Please give me strength and wisdom for this night.

"My lord?"

He opened his eyes and raised his head as Marla came across the rooftop. He got to his feet without thinking.

She held folded fabric in her arms. "My lord, I must beg your forgiveness. I was clumsy enough to jostle your drying tunic and it fell into a basket of cut fruit for preserving. I was able to wash it clean, so it will not stain, but it won't be dry in time for your departure."

Luca pulled his robe closed, self-conscious. "It's a long enough walk that it should dry."

"I went into my master's storage, my lord, and found a replacement. It is of an older cut, rather than the new style, and I apologize, but if you wish..."

She lifted the tunic in her arms, letting the folds tumble out, and held it for him to see. The body was very much like the current cut in Ivat or Alham, but the sleeves were longer than the ridiculous Ivat fashion, and one showed the overlong fabric turned back and buttoned in place, concealing the entire arm and probably part of the hand, as well.

Luca stared at it a moment. His back and wrists would be wholly covered. There would be no physical sign of his shameful years, no marks demonstrating he was less than his siblings. He would not be the former slave, he would be merely Luca. And she had done this for him.

Impulsively he moved forward and embraced her. "Thank you," he breathed as she stiffened in surprise. "I am twice in your debt now."

"My lord," she protested, drawing back, "I only rectified my own error—"

"Did you?" He grinned and took the garment, holding it against his chest. "Did you really? Or is my own tunic stored safely away?"

She flushed. "One sleeve is a little damp. For truth's sake. But only a little."

"You're a jewel, a shining ruby. No, a sapphire. An emerald!"

"I'll take half in coin," she answered, smiling. "Please, it was a simple thing. I did not want to embarrass you by suggesting... I only hope I was able to air the storage herbs away."

He draped the tunic over his arm. "Thank you."

She smiled, a shy, honest smile, and he thought it might be all right.

Sara clapped her hands as she entered the dining room, needing to do something with the restless anticipation within her. The sight of the table, set already for supper, thrilled her.

There were five places. Once there had always been five places at their table, their father at the head, Thir and Jarrick on one side, Sara and Luca on the other. The night Luca left, however, Sara had descended to find only four places set—her father and Thir across from places for Jarrick and herself. That was how she first learned that Luca was gone, that she would never see him again.

But tonight, he would be in his old place beside her. She laughed aloud and spun, nearly colliding with Marcus. "I beg pardon, mistress," he offered, stepping back. "Is there something else you wanted for tonight's guest?"

"I don't think so. You gave the menu to the cooks?"

"Of course, my lady."

"And I want whoever is serving tonight to be discreet. I don't think he'll like ostentatious or obsequious service."

"As my lady is so anxious, I plan to serve the family myself," Marcus said with a smile.

"Oh, thank you! Marcus, you're a dear." She clasped her hands and squeezed her fingers tightly. "And now I suppose there's nothing to do but wait. Oh, I hate waiting."

"Will the master return in time for supper? We have set for five, but—"

"I hope he does," Sara replied urgently. "He and Thir both. They don't know anyone's coming; they had already gone last night before the messenger. But they should be back by this evening..."

Marcus gave her a sad smile. "I'm sure he would return for your guest if he knew its importance to my lady," he said gently. Sara heard the underlying meaning beneath his words as well. There were days when many things might be different if his mind were clear.

She nodded, suddenly unhappy. "Thank you, Marcus."

He nodded respectfully. "Mistress."

CHAPTER THIRTY-FIVE

It was a long walk to Ivat, but it seemed this day to stretch as if Luca were walking to Alham once more. Luca had more than enough time to review again and again his failed reunion with Sara, his awkward conversations with Jarrick, his tangled hopes of home. He thought of Thir, always older and distant and apparently indifferent to his youngest sibling. He thought of Jarrick, who had wordlessly watched him dragged away but who had guiltily sought him afterward. He remembered his father interrupting his reading one evening, explaining worriedly that they had defaulted on their final creditor, that Sandis had extended their loan upon one cruel condition.

"You would not have me sell your sister, would you? She is a beautiful girl, and very young. She would not fare well on the auction block, and if she stays—if I come through this somehow, she might marry, and our house needs an alliance, Luca."

"Sell her...?" breathed Luca, not yet comprehending.

"Thir is my heir, my firstborn, and he must inherit whatever I can salvage for him. I cannot sell him to save a house for his younger brothers. Jarrick has served me for years. You are the youngest brother, Luca."

And then the men had come from where they'd lurked in the doorway, seizing Luca and forcing his wrists between two crimped iron bars. He'd struggled and nearly broken free, but he had stilled in shock as his father took hold of him.

"Luca, you must do this," he said, as Luca stared dumbly. "There is no choice. Do not make things worse for yourself by resisting."

Tears broke over Luca's cheeks as he stared at his father. "Please, don't do this. Please."

His father tightened the bolt which locked the iron sheets across his wrists. "He's secure."

The slave trader moved forward to fasten a rope through an accommodating hole in the shackle. A wild burst of terror shook Luca. "Father!"

His father seized his forearms, holding Luca still. "You are no base field slave. You will find a good position. Do your best, Luca. It

241

will be all right. While you yet breathe, Luca, there is hope. Don't forget that." He stepped back, his face immobile.

While you yet breathe, Luca, there is hope. The words had haunted him for years, taunting him, mocking him. Lying in the dark, aching from Ande's malicious cruelty, he had wanted to claw the lying words from his memory. But in the end, dawn had come to the horrific night, and there had been Shianan, and then Jarrick, and even Marla and Cole. In the end, there had been hope.

But his father hadn't known anything about Shianan, or Jarrick's search, or Luca's fellow slaves. His father had lied as he sold his youngest son for debt.

Buildings appeared on either side of them, and traffic increased as they neared Ivat. Then the streets narrowed and the crush of hasty mercantile traffic squeezed them. The mingled shouts of overseers trying to make up time, of stewards, of stock men, of dock workers, of sailors on leave, of ships' mates collecting sailors late to return from leave, of whores and vendors and beggars and street performers all merged together into a single cacophony which rang both loud and familiar to Luca.

Cole was looking at him, perhaps wary of his master's dark mood over the last hours, perhaps waiting to offer the directions he'd asked the night before. But Luca knew the way, and he led them unhesitatingly through the main and side streets, slipping through a thin alley swept spotlessly clean and into a small paved plaza.

There were several houses opening onto the plaza, each built in the typical Wakari style of wealthy bourgeois homes with steps climbing to a main gate. Beyond the gate lay a small courtyard, often larger in the homes of the nobility, and around this patio sat the house and the slave stables. Luca turned to the house on their right. He knew every step of that one, had known it from the days when he ran through the corridors and patio, when he complained of Jarrick's teasing and when he quietly watched Thir from a distance, when his mother was still alive and would laugh and scold him for playing in the fountain...

He realized he wasn't walking, only standing beside a wall in the shaded plaza. Cole stood just behind his shoulder, close but silent. Luca swallowed against the lump lodged firmly in his throat. "Cole," he said, his voice sounding disused, "do what you will while we dine. There will be something for you in the kitchen, I'm sure, and if you'd like to go out, you may. Only—only don't be long, because I may want to leave early. I don't know. Or I may stay the night, if all goes well." He rubbed his hands down his legs. "Just take my cloak when we go inside, to lend me an air of respectability."

"Would you rather I stay close at hand, master?"

"No," Luca answered wistfully. "No, take some rest in the kitchen."

A moment passed, and Cole shifted his weight. "Did you mean for me to go ahead, master?"

Luca blinked, startled at his voice. "No—no, let's go." He touched his collar, which did nothing for the tightness in his throat, and started for the gate. Cole stepped around him to ring the bell.

There was a moment when nothing happened, when Luca thought for one horrible moment that it had been a horrifically cruel jest, that they would not open to him. Or perhaps in their financial crisis they had left this house and moved to another—but Cole had delivered his letter, and so if the door did not open it could only be because they would not—

The bolt slid with a grating sound and the gate opened. "Please enter, my lord," said a bowing slave. It was Marcus, their steward. Ordinarily a steward wouldn't come to the gate himself. Why was he here?

Marcus straightened, his expression concerned as Luca remained in the gate. "My lord, is something—" He froze. "Ma—master? The young master?"

Something rippled through Luca. "Yes..."

Marcus struggled visibly, surprised and even pleased. "I—my lady said we would have an important guest, and—but I did not know it would be you, my lord." He bowed again, but it did not obscure his wondering and glad expression. "Welcome home, young master."

Luca stared, his knees weakening. He had not imagined their steward would welcome him home. "Thank you, Marcus. Thank you." He felt faintly unsteady. "Sara called me an important guest?"

"She did, my lord. Please, come in. She is very excited about this evening, and now I understand why." Marcus was definitely pleased. "Come in, young master, come in."

Luca did, feeling as if he moved through an invisible barrier. Slowly he turned as he entered, looking about the familiar courtyard. It was not exactly as he had left it; some of the plantings had changed, and repairs had been made to some of the stonework since his departure. They were doing well enough, it seemed, since—since then.

Someone cleared his throat softly, and Luca realized the two slaves were waiting beside him. He glanced at Marcus, who smiled and gestured across the courtyard. "I believe you know the way, my lord."

Luca nodded, not trusting his voice, and started for the door. Marcus opened it for him, and he paused within the entrance. Cole stepped close, anxious to perform his single task, and Luca shed his cloak reluctantly and handed it to him. Some part of him wanted to keep the concealing, protective cloak.

"Is he here?" Sara's voice called. "I heard the bell!" She hurried around the corner, eyes wide, and slid to a halt on the polished floor. "Luca..."

They stared at one another, balanced precariously on the edge of guilt and longing and hurt, and no one seemed to breathe. Then Luca gulped and moved forward, his heart pounding in his throat so that he could nearly taste it, driven only by the greater fear that he might fail again. They stared at one another apprehensively, and he reached for her hand as he dropped to his knees. He bowed his head, a slave's natural posture, but this time offered not in fear but in humble apology. "I cannot express how much I regret my words yesterday," he began, careless of the slaves behind him. "Please believe that it was shame and—"

"Luca, don't." Her voice shook. "I don't want that clouding over our evening."

"Nonetheless, I beg your forgiveness." He kissed her knuckle. "I'm sorry."

She tore her hand from him and flung both arms about him as she dropped before him. "Luca, Luca," she breathed, "we're both sorry. Please—don't say any more. Let's not catalog our faults. Don't make me apologize for three years of—" Her voice broke. "I'm glad you're home."

He dropped his forehead onto her shoulder, wanting to sob with relief. There was a soft sound of footsteps beside them and a hand fell on his shoulder. "Luca," Jarrick's voice came, gruff but gentle. "Thank you for coming."

Luca lifted his head, blinking back tears. "Jarrick, I owe you—"

"You owe me nothing," Jarrick said firmly. "I should have been more careful of your privacy—which was, after all, the reason for your stay there." He seized Luca's arm and pulled him in, embracing him. "Welcome home."

When he released Luca, the two slaves were turned away, silently keeping their eyes from their masters' emotion. Jarrick cleared his throat. "Marcus, we'll want something to drink. Something celebratory. And—flames, Luca, you brought that one?"

Luca looked back at Cole, who stood immobile and expressionless. "He's done well these few days," he said defensively. "I told him there would be supper in the kitchen."

Jarrick nodded. "Marcus?"

"Right away, my lord." Marcus gestured to Cole, who followed obediently.

Jarrick turned back to Luca and Sara, a hand on each of their shoulders. "Father and Thir haven't returned yet, but they shouldn't be long."

They did not take him to the formal sitting room where they received guests but to the rear room where the family spent idle moments. Sara dropped carelessly to her favorite couch. Luca hesitated, looking around. This was where they had come for him, where his father had surrendered him. He ran his fingers over a comfortably upholstered chair, grander than anything he'd been permitted for years, and sat uneasily. He wondered briefly if he'd chosen poorly, if he'd cursed his uneasy homecoming. This was the chair in which he had been reading when his father came.

Marcus came through the door, making Luca jump, and displayed his serving tray to Jarrick, who raised his eyebrows appreciatively. "I did say celebratory," he conceded. "Please pour."

The wine was dark and rich, deeply flavored and mellow with age. Luca wanted to gulp it after his walk down the mountain, but he knew better. He hesitated, looking at the wine in his hand.

Marcus paused, his eyes on Luca. "Would my lord prefer water alongside his wine?"

If ever he found himself a slave again, Luca told himself, he would be like Marcus, making himself invaluable. Masters did not sell or abuse slaves to whom they were perpetually grateful. "Yes, please. Thank you."

Sara sat forward eagerly on her couch. "You're home to stay, Luca, yes? You don't need to hide at Isen's retreat. We can manage for tonight, and then—"

Luca ducked his head. "I haven't thought that far," he admitted. "I'm not sure."

"But where else would you go?" she asked reasonably. "This is your home, Luca. Everyone will be thrilled to see you've returned, you'll be the talk of Ivat, and—"

"He won't be a social novelty, Sara," Jarrick said firmly. "Let him find his feet."

There was a cup of water beside him now. Luca held the wine tightly for a moment longer. "How can I suddenly come back? What did you tell everyone? Won't they just stare at the—won't I just shame the house?"

There was an exchange of voices from the corridor, and they glanced at the door. Thir walked through the open frame, still wearing his cloak and pulling at his gloves. "Evening. It's brisk on the—"

His voice choked off as he stared across the room. Sara started up from her couch, beaming, and Luca froze like a startled rabbit.

"Sweet Holy One," intoned Thir breathlessly. "Dear, sweet Holy One."

Luca got to his feet, tried to speak, failed, and tried again. "Hello, Thir."

Thir seemed to have similar trouble with his words. "Luca, I— you—he will—"

He was interrupted by the entrance of another man, shouldering past Thir as he called for a servant. "Blasted thirsty wind," he grumbled, looking at the hands he rubbed together as he started across the room. "Sucks the life right—"

"Father," Thir interrupted dully.

Their father paused and looked up, glancing at Thir and then across the room. His eyes met Luca's, and for a long moment the earth did not move, Luca's heart did not beat.

Sara broke the spell. "Isn't it splendid, Father?"

"What?" The question was distant, detached.

"Father," Jarrick prompted, "Luca's come home. Luca's come home to us."

Luca licked his dry lips and forced words through his closed throat. "Hello, Father. I—I've returned."

"Luca," he repeated. "That—that is not Luca."

Thir started visibly. "Not—Father!"

"That is not Luca." He lifted his chin. "Luca is dead. That is an impostor."

Something tore within Luca. "Father, you know me. You must know me."

246

"It is an impostor, here to try for a part of our fortune," his father snapped. He turned sharply, nearly jostling the tray from Marcus' hands. "Marcus, you—my aged Nariya wine! You fool, I had that as a gift from Lord Silmar himself!" He glared indignantly at the steward. "Put it away, you faithless—no, it's opened, the damage is done. We'll have it with supper tonight."

"There won't be supper tonight," Jarrick cut in fiercely. All eyes fell on him. "I will be dining with Luca, Father, so I'm afraid I won't be at your table."

Sara turned wide eyes from Jarrick to their father. "What's wrong with you? Father, you—you can't be like this..."

Luca cringed, a slave pleading for mercy. "Father," he begged, "you know me."

But he turned away stiffly. "Luca is dead," he pronounced. "Luca died years ago." He pushed past a silent Thir and left the room.

For a moment there was utter silence. No one wanted to acknowledge the awful words which hung in the air. Finally, Thir swallowed audibly. "I'll go," he said thickly, and he fled through the door.

Luca blinked again and again at the floor, not daring to lift his eyes where he might see Jarrick's or Sara's shocked, pitying gazes. The woven pattern of the carpet blurred dangerously as tears scalded his eyes. No, curse all, he would not weep for this—he had wept a thousand tears for his father's first betrayal; it would do no good to shed more for a second.

Sara clenched her fists. "Marcus!" she snapped, her voice brittle and sharp. "We'll be taking supper in my sitting room, if you'll see to that."

"Yes, mistress."

Sara whirled and seized Jarrick's arm. "You and Luca will come, won't you? To my rooms?"

Jarrick hesitated. "I won't speak for Luca. He'll say where we go, here or a public house or..."

Luca swallowed. "Sara will be a fine hostess, I think."

Sara nodded. "Then let's go. I've had enough of this room."

Luca followed her numbly. It was eerie, moving through the house. There were lights flickering brightly against the painted halls, a sign they'd overcome the poverty which had kept them in darkness in the last months before his—departure, and the rooms they passed were clean and well-kept, evidence they had no shortage of servants now. But a silence hung over the house, and a maid's distant laugh was quickly hushed. The servants knew, as they always did.

Sara's room was comfortably furnished with several chairs and a couple of couches, space for friends to talk together while their fathers transacted business. She flung herself down on a pillowed chair. "How could he?" she burst. "How is it even possible?"

"Suri," Jarrick soothed. "He's not right—we've known he isn't right in his thoughts..."

"He wasn't like that tonight," she protested. "He wasn't. He was just—just—I haven't even a word for it."

Luca lowered himself onto an upholstered couch. The room seemed unreal to him, a bit distant, as if all of this were happening around him but he were not a part of it.

"Luca? Are you... Would you like something to drink?" Sara pushed herself from the chair.

"I'm fine. It's just—it's odd to be here again."

"You're not fine," Jarrick responded darkly. "How could you be fine? None of us are fine, not tonight, not here in this—this house." He clenched his clasped hands. "None of us are fine."

There was a soft rap at the closed door. "Mistress?"

"Marcus! Please come in."

He did, carrying a tray with two bottles and fine glasses. Behind him came two servants bearing wide serving tables with short legs. "I've brought the supper, my lords, my lady," Marcus explained unnecessarily. "And drinks."

Luca's throat seemed to close. "I don't..." he tried, but his voice seemed a whisper.

But Jarrick was already accepting a glass from the steward. He took a swift drink, even before Sara and Luca were served, and he blinked in astonishment. "Marcus! This is the Nariya!"

"I beg your forgiveness, young master. I thought it would be suitable for your private celebration. I will bring something else if you prefer."

"Marcus, you know Father will be furious."

"The master said it should be served with supper," Marcus replied.

Jarrick smiled. "Good enough, Marcus."

"Thank you, my lord."

Aromas wafted through the air from the tables the servants were arranging behind Jarrick's seat. Luca sniffed, wishing the complex scents could appeal to him. He felt no hunger, only a pained hollow ache in his stomach which no food could appease.

But then Marcus was offering him a plate. He glanced up, startled, and saw that Jarrick and Sara already held plates in their laps. Luca started to decline and then inhaled. "This is her pork…"

Sara was pleased at his surprise. "I made a list of what I remembered you liked… I couldn't decide which to choose, so in the end I tossed dice." She laughed at her own absurdity.

A wave of heat washed through Luca. She had arranged a favorite meal for him, and he had not expected that. He had always thought of this as their mother's pork, though he knew now it was a popular dish. The garlic and rosemary and olive oil blended perfectly with the tender young white pork, and it tasted of home and summer and laughter on the terrace.

He took the plate and ate a mouthful as Sara watched. It was food, merely food, and yet… It was everything.

She seemed to expect him to say something. "The rosemary in Davan and Alham was almost always dried," he managed. "It's better fresh."

"Then you'll have it every day." She stopped herself. "You will stay, won't you?"

Jarrick looked away. Luca hesitated, stared down at his plate, opened his mouth, but no words came. He shifted his eyes to the carved table beside Sara. "How can I?" he asked softly. "How can I stay, when the master of the house does not even—"

"Leave him," Jarrick cut in sharply. "You make your own decisions."

Luca blinked at Jarrick, surprised at this mutiny, and glanced back at his plate. He could not think—not here, not in the very location.

Jarrick seemed to understand. "You don't have to decide tonight," he muttered gruffly. "But you're welcome, if you want. Sara has the only private sitting room, but my bed's wide enough, and—"

"Thanks," Luca answered quickly, fighting a rush of panic. "I'll think about it." But his pulse quickened, and he did not know what to think. They had not mentioned his old room; what had been done with it?

"So," Sara began, her eyes casting about. "I suppose—how did Jarrick find—how was your journey from Alham?"

Jarrick ducked his head, and Luca smiled faintly. She had tried, anyway. "It was somewhat awkward. By law, not until the border..." He faltered.

"We were glad to reach Abbar," Jarrick supplied. "I know so much has changed. I told Luca you were engaged to be married, but I don't know if we had a chance to speak at all of Stefan."

"Oh. You know him, I think—the Drawnes' middle son? He's really—I'm very pleased, Luca, and I'm so glad you're here. Our wedding will be next month."

"Stefan Drawne?" Luca repeated, trying to recall a face. "Isn't he fairly, well—"

"Not at all! He's a little shy, maybe, until one knows him. I'll have to introduce you anew, Luca, so you two can be friends."

Jarrick had chosen well; Sara was glad to speak of her betrothed and leave uncomfortable topics well alone. They ate two servings each, along with the vegetables and crusty light bread Marcus had brought, and then the steward served honeyed fruit to end the meal. Luca savored it, a little embarrassed at his enjoyment. It was a wholly different life.

One of the candles guttered, and Luca glanced involuntarily toward the popping wick. It was growing late, and the tentative spell which held them would end soon. He did not know what he would do then.

Sara seemed to read his anxious thoughts. "Would you stay here tonight? I know my couches aren't large, but one of them should accommodate you for a night. There are pillows here, and I can have blankets brought for you. Then tomorrow..." Her voice trailed and died.

"You can't expect him to sleep in a girl's sitting room," Jarrick chided gently. "Luca won't want frills and ruffles. My own room hardly deserves the term, Luca, as I spend as much time away as in it, but it has a wide bed and it's at the rear of the house, away from the noise of the main rooms."

Luca smiled. It wasn't the noise they spoke of at all. "I don't know about tomorrow, but the couch will be fine. Thank you."

"You're sure?"

He did not want to share a bed with his brother, not in a place where he should have his own. Sara's sitting room was at least a neutral ground, an obviously temporary setting instead of a grating reminder that he had no place of his own. And he did not want company this night. "It will be fine, thank you."

250

Sara and a maid brought blankets and additional pillows, layering one of the couches in thick swathes of fabric. Sara hesitated as she turned back to Luca, and then she reached for his arms and leaned to kiss him on the cheek. "Goodnight. Sleep well."

Luca's throat closed suddenly, and before he could speak she was moving toward her own bedchamber, closing the door behind her. But whatever wrong he had done her had been forgiven.

Jarrick's hand rested on his shoulder, startling him. "Don't think about the morning," he advised. "We'll find something then. I told you, he's not always himself."

He did not seem affected tonight, Luca thought before he could stop himself. *He knew me. I know he knew me.*

Jarrick's eyes met his. "Tomorrow," he said firmly. "Get some sleep."

CHAPTER THIRTY-SIX

The room was not quite dark, as two windows on one wall admitted light from the swollen moon. Luca lay on the couch, musing that the makeshift bed with its half-dozen blankets and surplus pillows was far more luxurious than his pallet in Davan or sleeping beneath Renner's cart or even his low bed in Shianan's quarters. He thought of the room he'd shared with the litter bearers in Furmelle and Falten Isen's comfortable bed in his mountain retreat. He did not think of the tearing moment when his father had turned away, declaring him dead.

But he had worried too long the night and day before, and he had little strength for another night of it. Sleep came as moonlight crept across the floor, marking the hours.

He woke blearily with an impression of light, though he could not say why. The windows still admitted a cool moonlight, but it should not have been enough to disturb him. He wondered if he was awake or merely dreaming. Then he thought he saw a flicker of yellow-orange light, a seeming reflection of flame on the wall beyond the open door to the corridor, gone before he could fully recognize it. Hadn't Jarrick closed the door behind him?

Luca closed his eyes sleepily. But some sense honed under Ande prodded him awake and he opened his eyes again, feeling the presence of another. He gradually discerned a figure in the doorway. It was a dark shadow, nothing more, only faintly backlit by weak light from behind the wall. He blinked, trying to make his tired eyes focus. Who was there?

The shape was familiar, etched into his mind over a dozen sweeping emotions. *Father.* He could not hear his own voice. He shifted on the couch, wanting to wake and yet afraid to disturb the dream. "Father," he whispered.

The figure vanished.

"Father," breathed Luca, suddenly afraid. He pulled himself upright and shoved blankets aside. A dream? He stood, cold in the sudden chill, and stared at the closed door.

It had been only a dream. He had wanted to see his father, and so he had. He stared unhappily at the door and then felt fading sleep pushed further by surprise. The door was not closed fully.

He crossed the room in two strides and opened the door. The corridor was empty, without even a hint of light at the end to mark a retreating candle. He paused, embarrassed by his suspicion and his hope, and shifted. His bare toes brushed a little mound of cooling wax.

Luca dropped to one knee and pressed his thumbnail into the puddle, finding it soft and warm in the center. Someone had stood in the corridor, tipping a candle behind the wall to shield its light, watching him. And someone had fled when Luca recognized him.

Shock iced through him, chilling his bowels. His father had come to stare as he slept, but he would not see Luca awake. He had refused...

Hot rage pounded over the shock, and Luca stood abruptly, swaying unsteadily. He owed no filial duty, he owed nothing to such a man. He stalked to the couch and jerked clothing over his limbs. He would not stay in the house of such a man, not even until the morning.

He drew on his boots and started down the corridor, leaving the door open behind him. He reached the front door before recalling his cloak was with Cole. He hesitated, wondering where the slave had been housed, and then started forward again. He did not want to wander through the dark rooms. Cole could come in the morning, and Luca would hardly feel the cold, shielded by the heat of his fury.

He unlatched the gate and went out into the street, silvered by moonlight. He would need no torch to light his way, and a torch would only alert any late thieves to his passage, anyway. He would be safer in the dark. He stalked through the empty streets, fuming.

How could he have come to where Luca slept, have come that far, and refused to speak with him? How could he turn away his own son, deny his own son? How could he tell his son to his face that he was *dead*?

There was a faint gleam of frost over the paving stones, unusual for Wakari winter. It recalled walking through midnight streets with Shianan and of seeing his brother Jarrick try to kill his master. He clenched his jaw angrily. His family had done nothing right, nothing at all.

His gut twisted with the memory. There wasn't much he could actually recall. He remembered tensing as the archer spun toward him and seeing the arrow jerk in his direction. He had recoiled, trying impossibly to escape, and then something ripped past him as he fell. The edge of the bridge had scraped his ribs and then there was a sickening drop and a sudden, shockingly painful cold—

He clenched his fists. He had nearly died for Jarrick's stupidity, just as he had suffered a living death for his father's pride and betrayal. He wanted nothing to do with them.

The city gates were closed, but the postern was open with a sleepy guard standing a nominal watch, barely nodding as Luca passed. Luca folded his chilled fingers beneath his arms and set a furious pace down the road.

It was an hour before he began to regret leaving his cloak. The winter air, even moderated by the seacoast, bit at his exposed skin. But he shivered and pressed on. He could not return in the middle of the night, even if he had the desire.

It was another hour before he recalled that Isen's gate would also be locked for the night.

He was numb despite his panting as he hurried up the mountain, finally chilled through. He pulled the cord at the gate and heard the bell within. A moment passed without response. He glanced at the sinking moon and the thin line in the east, promising dawn. When did Marla rise? Would she hear him? He rang again, and again.

The shutter slid back and Marla's sleepy face peered suspiciously out. Her eyes widened as she recognized him. "My lord!"

The bolts slid back with a solid metallic *thunk* and she pulled the gate back. "Come in! What are you doing here? Are you well?" She held a blanket around her shoulders, but as she saw his hunched and shivering posture she spun it off and draped it around him. "Come inside, and I'll warm something for you."

Luca followed her inside, where she stirred the banked kitchen fire. "I'll have some tea ready in a few moments," she promised, "and some soup... What happened? Why—" She caught herself. "I'm sorry, my lord."

Luca leaned close to the fire as she set water to boil. "No," he breathed. "Well you might ask." He stretched his numb fingers close to the coals. "My father—he..." His throat closed, and he could not speak it.

Marla paused and looked at him. "I'm sorry."

Luca dropped to the floor, propping his cold feet before the flames and resting his elbows on his knees. "Don't be. It was foolish of me to go back. I should have learned the first time." He flexed his fingers. "I owe him nothing, not even the courtesy of spending a night beneath his roof."

"I'm sorry." She put a small pot of cold soup beside the kettle and folded herself to the floor. "But you must have stayed a part of the night."

"He said I was dead. I am an impostor of myself, he says. And yet he came to spy on me while I slept, but when I saw him... He fled." He swallowed and closed his eyes.

Warm fingers worked slow, gentle circles at the base of his neck. Luca shook his head, his eyes still closed. "I don't think you can rub this away."

"I don't expect to. But it's what I can do. You needn't carry it all over your shoulders."

"I didn't choose it," snapped Luca. "Do you think I asked to be sold into slavery? Do you think I wanted my own father to chain me for the traders? Did I ask for my family to deny my very existence?"

"Your brother and sister did not seem to deny you."

"My father ran from me!" He felt her jump at the sound of his voice. "He would not even speak to me. Don't you think I'm justified in a little resentment?"

Her voice was guarded. "Yes. But this is not a little resentment."

He gave a grim chuckle. "I suppose not. I'd be happy to hear he died of his viante-eating. If I have died, it's only fair that he die too, right? And what would—"

"I asked once if you would have the scars on your back healed," she interrupted, her hands stilling on his shoulders. "You chose to help them heal."

"What does that have—"

"You have that same choice again," she said sharply. "What scars are you willing to heal?"

"That has nothing to do with this!"

"It is everything to do with this!" Her fingers clenched on his rigid shoulders. "What is done is done. Someone wronged you—you may dwell on it a thousand years and it will not alter a thing. It will not relieve you." Her voice wavered. "A master may choose your actions, but you choose your thoughts. If you let someone else dictate your feelings, you are more a slave now than ever."

"Are you saying I should not mind that my own father would be rid of me?"

"I'm saying you, not he, should choose your way. You dislike his actions, and rightly so—why let them determine your new life?" She

256

hesitated. "And you're not thinking at all, not now."

"To the contrary, I'm thinking very clearly."

"Then why can't you see that your father fears you more than you fear him?"

Luca spun out of her hands and stared at her. "You have no— that man destroyed me. He would not even speak to me."

"He *cannot* speak to you," she answered with deliberate enunciation. "He cannot bring himself to face you now. He has to deny it. You said yourself he ran away. Why do you think he came while you slept? Why would he come at all, except that—"

"No!" snapped Luca. "No, don't defend him!"

"I'm not defending him. I'm defending a man who in desperation called his sister a whore."

The words struck Luca like a blow, and for an instant he couldn't move. Then wrath took him, but before he could spurt his indignant rebuttal she had turned for the door. He stared after her. "Marla!"

"I am not your slave, my lord," she replied without looking at him. "I have set tea and soup for you, and I am returning now to bed."

A kind of panic took him and he leaned as if to reach after her. "Marla."

She heard the plaintive note and hesitated. "My lord?"

"Marla, I—stay, please. Don't—not you, too." His anger faded, leaving him hollow on his knees as his head sagged wearily. "Stay, please."

She came, her shift whispering as she crossed the floor. "I'm sorry," she offered. "That was harsh. But you... you weren't the man who came here."

"I don't know what I am," he confessed. "I am not Luca Roald, he says. I am not a slave, I am not a merchant's son, I am not—"

"I don't care what you are not," she interrupted gently. "And you needn't decide what you are this very night." She glanced toward the fire, where the kettle was beginning to steam. "Sit a moment."

He watched her pour hot water over the dried leaves, wondering at her words. Had his father hidden in the dark for fear of facing him? Even if that were so—and Luca did not find it easy to believe that his father hid in fear—didn't that still leave him with no place in the old house? Where could he go?

He glanced at Marla, holding a mug of tea tightly and leaning toward the fire. "Here," he said suddenly, recognizing her posture.

"Take the blanket. You're not dressed to be out of bed. I'll be fine. And have some tea yourself."

She glanced self-consciously at her shift. "I think I had better go, if my lord has no further need..."

"No, no," Luca said firmly. "I will sit here quietly and eat my soup. Take the blanket, I don't need it."

She wrapped the blanket about her shoulders and sat beside the fire, a little distance from him. "I'm sorry about what happened, with your family."

He nodded, pressing the warm mug between his fingers. There was nothing to say.

CHAPTER THIRTY-SEVEN

The bell at the gate rang, and Luca tried to calm himself. It could be Falten Isen, returning to his house. It could be someone looking for Isen, a friend or neighbor.

It was Thir.

He left his litter at the gate and came across the little yard, with Cole following. Luca gulped as they passed the fountain and took a step backward in the tiny entry. "Thir," he said weakly. "I..."

Thir came into the shadowed entry and looked hard at Luca. A moment passed, and then he released a long breath. "Flames."

Luca shifted, his gaze wavering.

Thir shook his head. "You're a different man." He rubbed his forehead with a finger. "Though of course you'd be; how could you not?"

Luca licked his lips. "Different..."

"Not different the way he meant it," snapped Thir. "Sweet all, I know my own brother." He shook his head again. "Luca, I can't believe it. No, I do believe it, but..."

The slaves were watering at the fountain. Luca made a tentative gesture toward the house's interior. "Will you come in?"

"I can't. I lied about an extra appointment and worked the bearers hard to reach you as it is." His face was lined and tired. "Last night—I wouldn't have left of my own accord. Flames, Luca, it was a shock to see you, but I was glad. Most glad. But Father is... I went with him to see that he didn't—come to harm," he said gruffly. "To keep him safe. I thought to speak with you in the morning."

Luca stared at him with blurring vision. "I couldn't stay."

Thir looked at him. "What passed between you?"

Luca started. "What?"

"I found him taking—he eats viante now, did Jarrick tell you? Ever since—but I found him taking it in the dead of night. He said... I thought he'd seen you. And then you were gone."

Luca clenched his fists and turned to hide the treacherous emotion. "We didn't speak."

There was a long pause. "He's not well," Thir's voice came finally.

Luca could not answer.

Thir sighed. "I have to get back," he said heavily. "But I had to see you, and I had to bring you this." Thick paper rustled against leather. "I wrote it out and marked it this morning. It's wholly legal."

Luca rubbed at his eyes and glanced back. "What is?"

"This is your inheritance." Thir held out the sealed letter. "After Sara's dowry, this is one third of our house."

Luca stared. "But—but he doesn't even recognize me! How can I be an heir? And even if I were, one third is—"

"The house has been his in name only for two years now," Thir confessed. "My signature and seal are binding. You are not living as a younger son in our household, so I won't see you given only a younger son's share. And I won't see you make your way with nothing from us." He pushed the letter toward Luca. "Take it. Our credit is good again. You can exchange that nearly anywhere."

Luca's hand seemed to move without his volition, reaching for the letter. The heavy paper was richly textured; Thir had used the best quality. His throat closed.

Thir gave him a sad, heavy look and placed a hand on his shoulder. "Write to us," he said solemnly. "If you won't stay—and I understand that—then write to us. We do know our brother."

Tears came hot to Luca's eyes and he couldn't speak. Thir's fingers tightened on his shoulders and then he turned, going out into the yard and calling to the litter bearers. He never paused, leaving them to scramble together and hurry out the gate behind him.

Luca stared across the table, his chin resting on his hands folded across the wood, hardly seeing the lettering on the envelope. The ridges in the wax seal seemed to deepen in the slanting evening sun from the window.

An entire life lay before him. He did not know what a third of their wealth might be, but their house had obviously recovered and fared well enough at the moment. If they thought they could sustain a contract with an army... Whatever that envelope represented was enough to allow Luca a small home and a reasonable start wherever he liked.

Where did he want to be?

Cole cleared his throat from the door. Luca dragged his eyes away from the envelope without lifting his head. "Yes?"

"I've finished."

"Nothing else, then," Luca answered flatly. He looked back at the envelope. "Your time is your own."

"Would you like something to eat, my lord?" another voice asked. He hadn't seen Marla behind Cole. "You've not had much today."

"I don't want anything." A moment passed. "But, you two, go ahead and eat. Don't wait on me."

The bell at the gate rang, sending a thrill of apprehension through Luca. Who now? He rose and placed the precious envelope on a high shelf, weighted by a jar of honey. He could hear indistinct voices from the garden.

He met them as they passed through the entry. "Luca!" Sara threw herself at him. "Where did you go? Why did you leave?"

Luca held her automatically, looking first at her and then at Jarrick behind her. "I... I couldn't stay." He glanced over his shoulder. "Come in, please."

Marla was ready with drinks, and she served them silently and then retreated to the kitchen. Luca saw Cole pass the sitting room doorway and continue without pausing. He looked back at his siblings' anxious faces.

"What happened?" Jarrick asked simply.

Luca folded his hands, resting his elbows on his knees. How could he tell them? "I saw Father. He—he wouldn't speak to me."

"Still?" asked Sara in disbelief.

"I couldn't stay in his house! Do you understand? How could I stay in the house of a man who won't even—"

"But it's not his house alone!" protested Sara. "It's your home!"

Luca shook his head. "Not anymore."

Sara hesitated, bowed her head, nodded. "It's not mine, either. I'm marrying Stefan—now, I mean, not next month. I'm staying in Abbar tonight, and then tomorrow we'll have a justice there."

"Tomorrow?" Luca echoed. "In Abbar?"

She nodded. "Thir gave me my dowry today. After what Father said last night—I understand, Luca. I don't want to be a part of that, either."

So Thir had spent the hours before dawn writing out the dissolution of his family. Luca turned toward Jarrick questioningly.

Jarrick shook his head. "I've already made my stand. I won't be a part of the mercantile alliance anymore, or anything like it. Thir knows that." He sighed. "I'll stay on with Thir. There's nowhere else for me to go, and he'll need help. Father will be little use in a few years." The bitterness was heavy in his voice.

"What about you?" Sara asked Luca. "You could stay with Jarrick and Thir. I know they'd have you."

Luca shook his head. "I'm going to find a place where no one knows my history."

Jarrick nodded slowly. "I have some money saved. I can give you—"

"Didn't Thir tell you? He gave me money, too. My inheritance."

"Your blood money," Jarrick muttered. "Good, I'm glad you have it. Where will you go?"

Luca chewed at his lip. "I haven't decided yet."

Jarrick looked at him steadily. "Wherever you go, you write. Do you understand? I don't want to lose you again for his actions."

Luca nodded. The strands between them were tenuous, but holding. "Will you take care of Andrew?"

"Of course."

"Come tomorrow," Sara urged. "Come to the wedding. It will be nothing like we'd thought, but I don't care for that, and Stefan understands."

"You told Stefan? About me?"

"In part." She looked at him. "Don't you want it known that you've come back?"

Luca hesitated. Did others need to know? Deserve to know? He tried to think of his first days in slavery, chained in Trader Laren's stable, waiting desperately to hear his father's voice ringing down the aisle. He had barely thought of his friends, those with whom he passed his free hours. Of course, he'd had fewer friends as their fortunes slipped, and they had not come for him, either. They had not been so dear as they pretended.

And he did not want to be a social oddity, the once-slave now paraded through Ivat's homes and held at arm's length for observation... He shook his head. "I don't want to announce myself."

"But Stefan and I will know, right? And you'll come?"

He felt his stiff face fold into an awkward smile. "I'll come. Where? When?"

CHAPTER THIRTY-EIGHT

Tamaryl fretted. He had been trapped in the White Mage's house for days, avoiding windows, hiding from Mother Harriet during her regular visits, drumming his fingers impatiently while Mage Hazelrig and his daughter worked in the Wheel and left Tamaryl and Maru to wait in their house.

Tamaryl had hidden fifteen years in this house. He did not want to hide here now.

Maru's wing rarely pained him now, but he was understandably ill at ease in the human realm. But even if Tamaryl's strength returned, he could never carry them both safely home, much less the Subdued Parrin'sho as well.

That strength was a liability. If he recovered his power, he would need to be bound and sealed to remain hidden. It should not chafe him so after he had spent fifteen years without his natural ability, but he did not particularly want to be bound again—powerless before Ariana's eyes and helpless before Shianan Becknam's.

The bastard was besotted with Ariana. Everyone could recognize it, Ariana and Ewan Hazelrig and perhaps even Becknam himself. Tamaryl did not want to admit his own feelings for her, feelings which embarrassed him both for their inconvenience and their root, which he was just beginning to suspect and shied away from exploring.

Regardless, alignment with the commander would set Ariana against the Ryuven, and against the Ryuven friend she had known most of her life.

Maru entered the kitchen. "Ryl, where are—you're washing dishes?"

Tamaryl looked at the suds. "Why not?"

"You're sho. You're the Pairvyn ni'Ai."

"Both mean little here, and I've washed these dishes for years and years." He scrubbed listlessly at a platter.

Maru crossed the room and took up a towel to dry the stack beside Tamaryl. "What are you thinking?"

"Nothing."

"That's not so."

Their best hope was to find a raiding party carrying the broken-off bit of the Shard of Elan, to return home through the shield with them. But there was no way to predict where the next raid would come, or to travel safely to meet it. Reports delivered to the Wheel had suggested the raids were growing larger, striking erratically across the countryside, with more and more nim and che crossing to challenge larger targets, and were correspondingly meeting more resistance. Tamaryl had helped to craft the end of the war, had sabotaged it, and had created the identical situation, now with his friend injured and trapped with him.

Tamaryl did not want to say this aloud. "I don't know how we'll get home. And I don't want us to stay. I had the choice once, and I made the decision to leave. You never had a choice."

Maru was silent.

Tamaryl voiced the questions he wished Maru weren't afraid to ask. "What if we can't go? What if we've exiled ourselves forever?"

"The mage'sho says we'll find a way." A moment passed. "Oniwe'aru will be furious when you return."

Tamaryl smiled sadly. "I appreciate your optimism, but you needn't pretend for me. Once, I thought I might be here always; I suppose I should face that again. At least I am not alone this time." He pushed a plate through the suds. "You, myself, and Parrin'sho..."

Maru set aside a dried dish. "Will we have to hide as humans?"

"We cannot stay in this house forever."

"I hope they think my human disguise very handsome. Irresistible to human women."

Tamaryl laughed.

"And you too—we'll carouse together."

"I think I'll leave the women to you."

Maru sobered. "After Daranai'rika?"

"No! No, I don't miss her. I regret what happened, on all parts, but I don't regret losing her."

"Then it is Ariana'rika."

Tamaryl gave him a level glare.

"I like her, too."

He sloshed suds over a cup. "I have watched her grow from a child into a woman. She is special. But..."

"But?"

Tamaryl shook his head. "No."

Maru wrapped the drying towel between his fingers and

squeezed it until his knuckles whitened. Tamaryl sighed and nudged him with a wingtip. "I'm sorry. It's all right. And I'll find a way to contact the raiding parties."

Maru shook his head. "Maybe not."

Tamaryl stopped scrubbing the cup and looked at him. "What do you mean?"

"I've been listening, Ryl. The reports were of raids happening every two days, occasionally three. But the last few reports were delayed, speaking of old raids. No one has actually crossed in over a week."

"That... may not mean..." But Tamaryl did not believe his words. There would not be a shift in pattern without reason.

Maru said it. "Maybe they're not coming anymore."

That would mean the raids had stopped, as he'd wanted. That would mean the fighting had ended. That would mean they were trapped forever in the human world.

The cup slipped from his wet fingers and bounced against the tub's edge before shattering on the tiled floor. Tamaryl stared at the fragments and groaned, grateful for the inane complaint. "That is Mother Harriet's favorite tea cup. She uses it while waiting for a meat pie to finish. She would scold me blue if she knew little Tam had broken it."

Maru set aside the dish he was drying and crouched to scoop together the pieces. "Surely we can repair this one."

"Not before she comes this afternoon."

"Can't we replace it with one that looks similar? Isn't there another cup with this pattern?"

Tamaryl went still, staring past the dishes, seeing the cellar of the Wheel, the Shard of Elan, a bloodied slave. "We should look for it."

Ariana rolled the sticks between her palms and then dropped them to the table. Three showed red, two black. "Yes!" she cheered. "I can take your footsoldier."

Maru groaned as she seized the game piece. "I'm finished. I can't come back from that."

"You've still got three pieces left," Ariana said cheerily. "It's possible I could cast four straight failures."

Maru gave her a patiently disbelieving look, and she laughed.

"Well, I'm not out yet," Tamaryl said, collecting the

throwsticks. "Four red, four red, four red!"

The throwsticks came up five black.

Tamaryl turned up his hands and sat back from the table. "I do believe Ariana is cheating."

"I am not!" But Ariana was a little pleased at the accusation. She had made great progress and had acquired nearly all her previous skill, and she sometimes wondered if her aptitude in magic had actually deepened with the second passage.

Maru laughed and leaned forward to collect the pieces. "I will concede, and we can start again. Would anyone like something to drink? We really should have some *philios* for this."

"Is that a Ryuven drink? We have wine, both grape and plum, and cider, and apple brandy."

Maru looked up, confused. "So many kinds?"

"Well, I didn't mean you should drink them all at once."

"That's not what he meant." Tamaryl straightened from his posture of defeat. "In Ryuven society, different drinks are used for different occasions."

"We do that here, too."

"Not nearly to the same degree. *Philios* is drunk to seal or renew bonds of friendship, at gatherings like this. *Muruka* is for business transactions. There are others which are drunk only at births, or only at ascensions, or only to celebrate milestones."

"Really? Not by taste, but by occasion?"

"There is even a wine made only for the bonding of a former silth bonding to an aru, and other for a former aru bonding to a silth— but to be honest, I think that's a relic of more extravagant times when minute details of etiquette were a form of ostentation."

Ariana raised an eyebrow. "Were?"

Tamaryl cast her a petulant rebuke.

Maru was still looking between them. "You mean, you just drink whatever you want, whenever you want? No sense of decorum or propriety?"

"There's certainly propriety," Ariana hurried to say. "Being drunk in a street and drunk in a night tavern and drunk at breakfast are all viewed very differently."

Maru looked unconvinced.

Tamaryl laughed. "Men defending while women stay home, and people drinking beer or wine or ale as it pleases them. Poor Maru must feel quite adrift. Don't ask about the magic."

266

"What about the magic?" Maru promptly asked.

"What's wrong with our magic?" Ariana followed. "I mean, it's not thick enough to choke a human, like yours, but we've done all right with it, I think."

Maru looked between them. "What about the magic?"

Tamaryl smiled. "Lady Ariana, please tell Maru how you began training."

Ariana shrugged. "When I was about four, I began to comment on the pretty sparkles that happened around Papa when he was working, and that's when he knew I had inherited the ability. I then—"

"Sparkles?" repeated Maru.

Ariana nodded. "I'm a seer."

Maru blinked at her.

"You know, I sense magic visually? Others perceive through another sense, hearing it, scenting it—"

"But why do you *see* it?" Maru asked.

"No one knows why some people perceive through one sense and some another. It doesn't seem to be hereditary."

"But—it's magic, it doesn't have a color or a sound, it has an aspect. How can you *hear* it?"

Tamaryl was grinning broadly at them.

"Aspect?" Ariana repeated.

"Yes. Its... its emanation."

"Emanating what? Do you feel it on your skin?"

"No, of course not."

"Then what does it feel like?"

Maru opened his mouth, hesitated, closed it, drew his eyebrows together, tried again. "It just—is. How would you describe what it feels like to breathe? Is there a sensation to that?"

Tamaryl held up his hands to stop them. "Humans don't have a natural sense for magic. Just five, and so one is pressed into additional service in mages."

Ariana and Maru looked back at each other with awed half-smiles. "Really?"

"Then how can you use magic?" Maru continued.

"It was hard for them in the beginning," Tamaryl said. "So unnatural."

"It's unusual, but not unnatural," Ariana protested. "Clearly we can use it."

"The old stories say you stole it," Tamaryl said archly.

"What old stories? And we did not!"

Tamaryl laughed. "Don't be so quick to protest what you don't understand. But, in fairness, I don't know that we know the truth, either. It's just said that humans stole magic shortly before or shortly after the Burnings. The tales vary."

Now Ariana jerked upright. "The Burnings!"

"Yes, your father was very keen on that, too. The Burnings is the time of our oldest history, when history is myth—and yours also speaks of the Burnings."

"That's shared history," gasped Ariana. "In separate cultures. Separate worlds."

Tamaryl nodded. "Unfortunately, I couldn't offer him much more than that. I am not a scholar of myth, and I had not thought to bring texts on ancient stories with me to fight in the human world."

"Still. That must have delighted him and then tantalized him."

"It took him two years to finally accept that I couldn't offer him any more than I already had and stop asking."

His tone was light, but Ariana heard the faintest of undercurrents in it. Tamaryl was still struggling with her father's betrayal, as he saw it, of keeping secret the Ryuven prisoners in the Naziar. How he weighed that against Tamaryl's own theft of the Shard's fragment, or whether Tamaryl blamed himself as well for the rift, she couldn't guess. She was glad he was trying to put on a more agreeable face.

Maru must have heard it, too. "Well, lacking *philios*, I'm going to bring some indecorous cider. Ryl, will you reset the game, so that Ariana'rika cannot cheat this time?"

Ariana made a face at him. "Bring some of Mother Harriet's sweet smallcakes and I'll let you cheat a round."

"Done!"

CHAPTER THIRTY-NINE

Shianan stood at the door, beside the branches he remembered the boy Tam trimming. He stared at the decorative nails patterning the wood, taking a moment to gather himself. 'Soats, but he'd rather face an armed opponent than knock on this door.

The latch rattled and the door swung back, startling him. "Come in, my lord commander," invited Hazelrig with a smile. "We saw your approach through the window."

Simultaneous rushes of relief and irritation hit Shianan. "Thank you, my lord mage, I will."

Hazelrig led him to the little gathering inside. Shianan stiffened. Tamaryl sat on a tall stool, his wings folded behind him, holding a drink. Beside him Ariana rose from her chair. "You did come!"

"I did, my lady mage," he answered automatically. But he could hardly look at her for the Ryuven. Even when he had been here before as the boy Tam, he had not arrogantly displayed his own enemy form.

Tamaryl inclined his head in greeting.

Shianan turned abruptly to Ariana. "Thank you for having me here tonight, my lady mage," he said formally, bowing.

She laughed. "There's no need for that; we're all friends here. Have some wine. Father, is your drink empty? Bring it here." She moved into the next room.

Shianan rotated to face Tamaryl, still on the stool. "Good evening," he said shortly. "Don't the Ryuven rise to greet other nobles?"

Tamaryl's cool smile flickered. "I thought there was little advantage in pretense, now that you know my true rank."

Shianan's neck grew warm. "Then I must apologize for failing to bow to you. Truthfully, I hadn't expected to find you here, not with so many outlying villages resting complacent and vulnerable in the belief there are no Ryuven within the shield."

The Ryuven's eyes narrowed. "And——"

"Bailaha, Tamaryl, please join us," Hazelrig called. "I am told supper is ready."

They moved apart, watching one another warily, and went into

269

the dining room where Ariana was in conversation with a second Ryuven. Shianan stared.

Hazelrig smiled. "Maru asked to serve our supper. He felt our notable company deserved service, and he pointed out rightly that no human servant could be admitted here." He gestured to chairs. "Tamaryl, if you please, and Bailaha, there."

Ewan Hazelrig sat at the head of the table, and Tamaryl took the seat to his right. Ariana sat on her father's left, with the strange Ryuven standing between them, and Shianan beside her. He felt a tiny triumph at having the place nearer to her, but he resented Tamaryl's place of honor by the mage's right hand.

Maru looked at Tamaryl and then turned to a sideboard. One wing hung behind him, not folded as tightly as the other. Shianan wondered at the obvious break, which a Ryuven's unnaturally quick healing should remedy. But then, Hazelrig had called him a prisoner of war, and so he must have been Subdued.

Tamaryl was saying something, Shianan realized, which he'd been ignoring.

Hazelrig cleared his throat. "We'll find a way."

"We can't go back through the shield," Tamaryl said firmly. "Even if I could do it again, it would kill Maru. It bled every shred of power for only myself."

"Don't surrender hope yet. We might be able to use amulets as energy reservoirs to push you through."

Shianan blinked. "Are you instructing the Ryuven on how to penetrate our best defense?" he blurted.

Four pairs of eyes fell on him—even the Ryuven servant turned to look. Shianan glanced at the colorful vegetables, dressed in a bright sauce to hide their softening with winter storage. "I'm sorry," he bit angrily. "It's not my place to speak against the White Mage at his own table. But—Pairvyn ni'Ai!"

"I think—" began Hazelrig gruffly.

"It would not benefit us in the end," Tamaryl said, speaking over the mage. "We need no amulets to store power and so the Ai don't have the skill of making them. And no number of amulets could bring an army through the shield."

"The Ryuven don't manufacture amulets, no. But didn't the servant boy Tam help Mage Hazelrig with his work? You know the method of them now, don't you?"

Tamaryl's face tightened. "I have opposed this war for years. I helped to develop the shield. Do you think I'd help to defeat it so easily?"

Hazelrig gave Tamaryl a sharp look.

Ariana set her flat hands on the table. "We all want a world without war."

"That is true," Tamaryl said, "but some also want other things, and more. Some make their living by it, others live by it."

"That's ridiculous," Ariana said flatly. "They can find new ways to live."

"Can they?" Tamaryl's mouth quirked as he glanced at Shianan.

Shianan sat absolutely still, offering no resistance as the simple words knifed through him.

Ariana caught the glance, but not its meaning. "The war is over."

Shianan found his voice. "The war is not over! Not while there are Ryuven raids still happening, and Ryuven still in Alham." He fixed his eyes on Tamaryl. "But be assured, I will end it."

"And then what?" Tamaryl raised an eyebrow. "What will you be then—commander?"

Shianan's heart spasmed.

"You forget, I know this world. You are honored—tolerated—only because they fear us more than they dislike you."

"Tamaryl!" Ariana gasped.

Shianan stared at him, unable to respond, his soul's terror peeled bare and raw before his enemies and his friends.

"You need us, commander," Tamaryl said, "and you need us here."

"Tamaryl." Mage Hazelrig's steely voice did not need to be loud. "You are both guests in my home."

Tamaryl raised a hand. "Forgive me. That was more than I should have said. I only meant to illustrate that it is not always so simple as saying a war should end. My people are starving. Without raids, they die. And both Ryuven and human fighters earn their positions in fighting. Even if someone wanted to end war, not all could surrender his own standing and worth."

"No one could put his own desires above the deaths of civilians and children," Shianan said, his jaw moving stiffly.

Tamaryl gave him a significant look. "I feel the same."

"So you want the raids to continue? To feed your children on

271

the blood of our farmers and soldiers?"

Hazelrig raised his hands. "Gentlemen, friends, we are not covering any new ground. None of us wishes for war, but none of us has found a way to end it."

Shianan was not ready to be placated. "How are you even here? You are a traitor to your own professed cause. The shield is still in place. How did you come through it?"

Tamaryl gave him a disappointedly patient look. "I am the Pairvyn ni'Ai. I am more capable than the average Ryuven."

Shianan gave him a hard look. "We've confirmed the recent raids are Ryuven. The farmers killed some, we have Ryuven bodies."

Tamaryl met Shianan's eyes steadily. "And do you think, if I had been there, farmers would have prevailed?"

"You were injured and hiding in Mage Hazelrig's workroom."

Tamaryl tipped his head in incredulity. "You think some farmers could have done that?"

"Anyone can have a bad day." Shianan knew it was incorrect—the Ryuven lying supine on the workbench had been destroyed by magic, not physical attack—but the shocked affront in Tamaryl's eyes was worth it.

Tamaryl raised his spread hands, palms toward Shianan, touching the tips of the thumbs before him. "I spoke too harshly before, but now I swear to you by the Essence, I have not participated in these raids."

"Then how are they happening?" demanded Shianan.

"They may have stopped happening," Ewan Hazelrig said. "We've had no new report for nine days."

"That's not long enough to prove anything. There aren't supposed to be any Ryuven here at all, and yet there are raiders to the north and two here in this room. Why?"

The room went uncomfortably quiet.

At last there was the sound of a throat being tentatively cleared. "I was trapped here," offered the second Ryuven, Maru. "I could not get through the shield to return home."

Relief flooded Shianan like warm water after chilling wind. Torg's supposition had been right; the resurrection of the shield had trapped some Ryuven in the human world. Those remaining were dying off, which was why reports had slowed. There were no gaps in the shield. "And why did Tamaryl come here?"

"To find him," Tamaryl answered for himself. "Maru is my

friend. I came to bring him home."

"And you think you can take him home without any of your officers asking questions about the shield?"

"Tamaryl'sho is strong enough to have carried himself through it," Maru said. "As for me, I will have been missed in my duties, but I can simply say I was shirking—"

"Even a runaway slave draws notice," Shianan interrupted.

"Nim are not slaves," Tamaryl snapped. "We don't—"

"Enough!" shouted Ariana. "You both are beyond squabbling at your host's table. This is ridiculous."

Shianan hesitated, stung. He looked at Ariana and then across the room, avoiding Tamaryl just as the Ryuven avoided him.

"Do either of you believe my father would let harm come to this kingdom or to his friends?" she demanded.

Shianan looked at the vegetables on the Ryuven's plate.

"Do you?"

Shianan licked his lips. "I do not believe the White Mage would knowingly bring harm to us."

Tamaryl's answer was more eloquent. "I have trusted the White Mage with my life for many years."

"Thank you," Ariana said shortly. "Then, if you've finished bickering like schoolboys, Maru might hand around the bread."

Hazelrig coughed, and Shianan saw the telltale smile lines above the concealing hand.

"I apologize," Shianan said gruffly. "I should have known that you have a plan for the Ryuven."

Hazelrig shook his head. "I don't always have a plan. You have seen when I was lost and grieving, unable to think. And I don't have a clear plan now to return Tamaryl and Maru to their home. But if we cannot return them safely, I will see them settled safely here. They can be hidden as Tam was once hidden. I won't have them endangered or beleaguered."

"I see."

Tamaryl shook his head. "We have to return. There must be a way."

Ariana nodded. "We'll keep working. And I still have hope that we might be able to end this war in another way, more formal than a shield."

Hazelrig nodded, chewing on a sprig of herb. "I think we can all agree that we want peace and prosperity. Will you drink to that and end this talk?"

They drank, divided in nature yet united in this wish at least. And then Hazelrig spoke of other things, leading them into less inflammatory topics.

Ariana was animated and attentive, listening to Shianan's words with interest and adding ideas of her own. Shianan would have been glad, but she showed the same courtesy to her Ryuven guest.

Maru was quick and unobtrusive despite the broken wing, and Shianan found himself enjoying the well-prepared food. With argument implicitly forbidden, the conversation was a little forced but not unpleasant. Hazelrig led them neatly between stories of their travel over the mountains and comic tales of magic practice gone wrong or other lighthearted adventures. Shianan was finishing a story of bumbling soldiers trying to complete a task they had utterly misunderstood when Maru brought a dessert wine to pour.

Ariana lifted her glass, the dark liquid swirling. "To friendship," she offered suddenly. "Between ourselves and our peoples. May we find a way to share stories over a meal again."

A sudden and intense need took Shianan, the longing that he would sit again at a table with the White Mage and his daughter. He raised his cup. "May we find a way."

CHAPTER FORTY

Tamaryl lay on his bed—less comfortable in his natural form than it had been for the boy Tam—and regretted.

He should not have said the things he had over supper. His assessment of the commander's position was accurate enough, but to say it so plainly would drive tender-hearted Ariana to Shianan's support. Nor was it appropriate behavior as a guest in the Hazelrigs' home.

Edeiya'rika had neatly incised Ryuven society with a single, quiet observation and extracted Daranai to be cast out like the cancer she was. Tamaryl wished he had that skill.

He wished a lot of things. He wished he had not learned his friend of so many years had kept such a secret from him. He could, if he checked himself for a moment, understand; Ewan Hazelrig had been sworn to keep the secret of the Ryuven prisoners before he had ever met Tamaryl, and what would the boy Tam have done even if he had known? But that did not touch the hurt.

And any thought of betrayal raised shame and a deeper hurt. Tamaryl had not planned clearly to take the fragment of ether; he had grabbed it on impulse as the finality of his leap home pressed upon him. He had not even been certain it would work. But had he even then acted on a desire to keep a secondary plan open, a possibility of returning not only to his friends, but to a sure source of supplies for a starving population?

He did not know.

What was certain: He had worked for fifteen years in partnership with a noble man trying to save his own people and then had betrayed him. Now that man had rescued Maru and was sheltering two Ryuven in his own home. Yet his betrayal and Tamaryl's had driven a wedge between them, and Tamaryl hated it even through his anger.

It was easier to resent the commander. Shianan Becknam had no just claim to Ariana. His was a pathetic attraction, the grasping love of a man who was ostracized from most social contact and had latched frantically onto the only woman to be kind to him in his loneliness.

...And no, that wasn't Tamaryl's situation, it wasn't the same at all. He *knew* Ariana, knew her better than Becknam did, and he had rejected another already betrothed to him, so it certainly wasn't that he wanted any sweet comfort, desperate for any feminine sympathy.

Memories of Daranai'rika's pliant lips and teasing hands came unwelcome to him, and he writhed angrily into another position on the unaccommodating bed, grunting as he pinched a wing.

"Ryl?" Maru whispered blearily from the other side of the room.

"It's nothing," Tamaryl said, hunching his shoulders and compressing his wings.

He had to get home, he had to get Maru home, he had to fix this. He didn't know how he would rectify everything—didn't know how he could—but he would start by going home.

Ariana cradled the sealed jar, emerald glass and stoppered with gold, and marveled at it. She had never noticed it before in the Circle's archives, but today she saw its runes, set by Wakari pirates centuries before, and knew it instantly for what it was.

She pierced the soft gold seal with her thumbnail and spoke. "Come forth and do my will."

Green-black smoke poured from the jar and billowed into a nebulous serpent, its features difficult to distinguish. "My lady mage and my mistress. What do you desire?"

She did not hesitate. "End this war between human and Ryuven."

In truth, it had been more than a week since they had a report of a Ryuven raid, which had been coming every two or three days. That was a good sign—but it was not peace.

"No more fighting?"

"No more fighting. And—men shouldn't enslave other men. End our slavery, too."

The misty snake roiled and shifted. "When you turn, it will be done."

So simple? "Thank you," Ariana began, but the smoke was already dissipating. She clutched the bottle, wondering if she should have done something to retain the creature, but it was gone.

She took a breath and turned.

The world shifted about her and she was standing on a market square. Around her, vendors called to potential customers and voices rose in barter. The market stalls were full of bright vegetables and plentiful bins of grain. She saw no one in cuffs, no slaves cringing beside masters. No one watched the sky in fear. Children ran by, laughing. She drew a deep, satisfied breath and smiled to herself.

There was a rumble of wheels, and she turned to see a freight wagon round the corner. Her heart dropped as she saw that slaves drew the heavy wagon, chained to the shafts and slipping on the cobblestones as they strained. A driver lashed at them mercilessly, making them cry and stumble. There were four of them—no, six—a cluster, all pleading for relief, and she started forward in protest. "No, you aren't supposed to be here, there are no slaves anymore—"

They were Ryuven. Their slender limbs were chained in place, and the roots of their wings ended in bloody stumps amidst welts and stripes. She gaped in silent horror as the wagon drew slowly past her. Behind it stretched a line of bound Ryuven, wretched and weak and crippled with scarred stumps in place of their graceful wings. Human overseers moved up and down the line, plying switch and whip and rod and strap, and Ariana dropped to her knees.

The line shifted and one Ryuven burst free. He still bore wings, and he tried to take flight as he broke from the others, but an overseer grasped the chain on his shackles and jerked him savagely to earth. He landed before Ariana and reached desperately for her.

An overseer placed one knee on the Ryuven's back and seized a beating wing. Ariana wanted to move but was frozen in place. The overseer's arm moved with a flash of steel and the wing collapsed as the Ryuven shrieked.

Ariana could not breathe. The Ryuven wailed and looked directly in her eyes, pushed his chained hands toward her. "What have you done?" he demanded, gasping. The overseer chopped his second wing, making him scream and convulse. He twisted as the overseer dragged him upright, bleeding, and snatched at her arm. His eyes held her like magic or shackles. *"What have you done?"*

Ariana screamed and shoved him away. She pushed herself backward, stumbling away from the line of mutilated Ryuven, and tripped over a severed wing. She crawled and screamed and screamed.

Someone caught her and held her arms, and she gasped for breath. The hands on her tightened, and someone said tersely, "Don't shake her! Ariana! Ariana?"

She gulped air and blinked, aware suddenly of her bed and her room and her father holding her tightly. She choked and looked up at

Tamaryl, crouching wingless beside them.

She screamed.

"Ariana!" Her father pulled her close, enveloping her. "Breathe deep, darling. You're awake now, and everything is all right. It's all right." He looked down at her. "Are you with us?"

Sweat poured from her, and her pulse was loud in her ears. "I— was dreaming," she said weakly.

Her father forced a humorless laugh. "We'd guessed as much."

Tamaryl had moved back when she recoiled from him, and she saw now his wings were still there, hanging low behind him. Maru was there, too, standing to one side. At the sight of his broken wing, a rush of nausea swept over her and she grasped for the washbowl on the nearby stand. Her father released her, and she only just made it.

Hands gathered her hair and held her shoulders as she hung above the bowl, trembling. "Ariana..."

She spat and sat up. "I'll be all right." She shivered and slid into the bed once more, rubbing at her mouth with an arm.

Tamaryl took the empty pitcher from the stand and passed it mutely to Maru, who departed promptly. Tamaryl approached the bed again, his face anxious. "What was it?"

Ariana took a shaky breath. "I don't..."

"You don't recall the dream?"

She shook her head. She did recall it, too vividly. It was far clearer than most of her dreams, unnaturally clear. It terrified her.

Her father kissed her hair. "It was just a dream, darling—albeit quite a dream, apparently. You frightened us all."

She took another breath. "Could it be more than a dream?"

"What do you mean?"

She looked at Tamaryl. "I wished for the war to end, for the fighting to be done, and when it was granted, the Ryuven were enslaved."

Her words frightened Tamaryl, she could see that. That frightened her more.

"How did you achieve this wish?" asked her father.

"I—I found an entrapped wishing spirit. In the archives." She felt foolish as soon as she spoke. How could she admit to fear of a child's fairy story?

Her father smiled. "Well, if you do not commit your wish for peace to a make-believe spirit known for trickery, it seems unlikely your nightmare will be realized," he said reasonably.

Ariana glanced down at her arm, red with weals where she'd clawed herself free of the clinging Ryuven. "It did not seem like an ordinary dream."

He squeezed her. "I believe you."

Maru returned and poured a cup of water for her. She rinsed and spat, and then she drank a cup. Her throat burned from screaming. "I think I'd like to read for a while."

"Would you like someone to stay with you?" Tamaryl offered with a glance at Mage Hazelrig.

She shook her head. She appreciated the offer, but she did not want to sleep again, not even with someone watching. "No, I think I'll go downstairs and read. I'm sorry to have disturbed you all. I'm terribly embarrassed." She gave them an uneasy smile.

It did not matter what they thought—the dream had been terrifyingly real and horrific beyond anything she could have invented. She remembered this one, but there had been others, ever since she had returned. She had to find a peaceful solution to the war, something more than the shield.

CHAPTER FORTY-ONE

Luca breathed deep, feeling his muscles slip loosely as he moved down the street. He could just detect the lingering scent of Marla's embrocation. She had caught him as he hesitated near the door, fussing at his sleeves in a final delay before starting down. "You'll be seeing them," she had said simply.

He nodded. "Only Sara and Jarrick. The wedding won't be a public affair."

"But you're thinking of it already. I can see it in your shoulders."

He shifted his arms self-consciously. "Is there anything you don't see?"

It was eerie, how easily she could read him. Luca had thought he'd learned to keep his thoughts to himself in his years as a slave. But worry, he supposed, was clear to see, and she was a close observer. She had smoothed the tension from his shoulders with a few minutes' work and sent him on his way with a clearer head.

A shout warned him, and he stepped aside as a freight wagon rumbled dangerously close. He let himself drift to the side of the street, not in such a hurry as the mercantile traffic. He had some time left before the ceremony, and he was still reluctant. If he had not promised Sara...

A column caught his eye, familiar after his long absence. Luca glanced at the small building of white stone set behind the column. He'd passed this temple each time he came to Abbar. It was meant to be a respite from life, but today it was a respite from traffic. He turned into the tiny semicircular courtyard and lowered himself onto the white steps, warm in the winter sun.

The traffic continued, separated from the yard by the column. Luca watched and sighed. Was this the wisest choice, attending his sister's wedding? What would Stefan and his guests think of Sara's once-enslaved brother? She had done well to make such a match after their financial disaster; would he spoil her chance at a happy marriage and respectable social standing?

There were letters carved into the column, wrapping around the base. Luca couldn't remember ever actually reading them as he had navigated traffic. He let the patterns distract him from his unpleasant thoughts, absently running his eyes over the words faded by salty sea wind. A tingling shock raced suddenly through him—*while you breathe*, his mind had registered.

His stomach tightened with long bitterness. *It's so simple to lie.*

But he could not stop himself from trying to work out the rest of it. It was difficult to make out the weathered letters, and he leaned to one side trying to follow them around the column.

"*You are his poem*," said a voice behind him. He jumped and glanced over his shoulder at the priest standing above him on the white steps. "You know the passage?"

Luca shook his head, wary and vaguely embarrassed.

The priest descended the steps, and Luca caught himself shifting his weight. The Gehrn had patterned their robes on the Wakari temples' designs, and while Luca knew they weren't the same, his reactions did not.

The priest sat on Luca's step, but at a comfortable distance. "*For you are his poem, and despair has no hold for those who do not wrestle with the artisan. Know that while you breathe, he is yet elaborating his careful craftsmanship in you, and so you may hope.*" He glanced at Luca. "You look as if you take some issue with that."

Luca wondered when his face had begun to betray him so regularly. "No, not exactly. 'While you yet breathe, there is hope.' Someone told me that once."

The priest nodded. "A proverbial form, unfortunately common."

"He lied. He used that to justify—and it was a lie." Luca was startled by his own voice, by how quickly his anger had swollen into view. What business of this man's was it?

But the priest merely nodded again. "I'm sorry you were hurt. Would it help to talk?"

"No." Not here, not after that reunion, not to a stranger, not to someone in those robes.

The priest did not seem offended. He rested his elbow on his knee and watched the traffic flow by, wagons and carts and baskets and bundles all streaming to market or home or docks or caravans. The noise filled the silence between them.

"He lied to both of us." Luca wanted to justify his protest, but spoken aloud his words were part anger, part discovery. "He used those words to excuse what he did, and he lied to each of us."

The priest flicked a finger to indicate across the street. "You see that man accosting passers-by? Beside the fountain? He'll tell you, if you wander near enough, he is collecting money to relieve the suffering of Ivat's orphans. He's not, of course. He's worked that corner for years, and he lives well enough and drinks the surplus. He dresses in the colors of a temple priest, and many are taken by his words. But compassion itself is no less worthwhile for his lies. Compassion may be tarnished in his hands, but underneath it is still pure silver."

Luca shifted uncomfortably. "My sister is waiting... It is her wedding today."

"Then don't let me delay you." The priest gestured and offered a friendly smile. "Be well."

Luca escaped into the traffic. His father had lied—had *lied!*—to excuse the sale of his own son. No protesting priest could argue that. Luca could not shed his resentment so easily.

The Drawne home was not much farther. Luca entered by the open gate and passed through the garden, avoiding a few chatting groups which must be Stefan's family and slipping into a side room where servants were assembling serving trays. One glanced at him, but Luca shook his head hurriedly and looked away. He wanted only to hide from the guests.

Long minutes passed, and the servants seemed to decide he was an unpopular cousin avoiding the family quarrels and they left him alone. Luca fidgeted. He should not have come, he should never have come...

And then a woman came into the room and spoke to the serving slaves. "Have any of you—" She noted Luca. "Pardon me, my lord, but could you be Luca Roald?"

He nodded, surprised.

She gestured with a dull flash of wrist cuff. "Come, my lord! My lady has been asking and asking for you. Please, this way."

Luca went with her numbly into the garden, which now seemed filled with people. Luca's stomach clenched. *She never said so many!*

"Luca!" Sara caught his arm, startling him. She was gorgeous, dressed in bright blue and green and radiant with excitement. "I've been looking for you!" She embraced him.

He gave her a tight smile. "I'm here now."

"My lady?" A steward prompted.

283

Sara gave him a quick nod and glanced back at Luca. "Come on, now we're ready to start." Then she turned and went into the center of the garden.

Stefan Drawne had matured since Luca had seen him last. He didn't recognize the young man dressed in matching green and blue until he moved forward to take Sara's hands. As they faced one another, the onlookers gathered in a circle about them. Luca glanced self-consciously from side to side, and when he saw the witnesses joining hands he shrank back to stand in the shadow of a vine-wrapped pillar.

A justice in the red robe of his office place one hand over Stefan's and Sara's and raised the other. "Stefan Drawne, Sara Roald, do you both swear to be one in the eyes of law and of justice?"

"We do."

"Do you swear to be one in flesh and to belong one to another, until you breathe your last?"

"We do."

"Do you pledge to lead one another to the best of you?"

"We do."

"I hear your solemn vows and I witness that you are husband and wife in deed and law. Seal your pledges with a holy kiss."

To judge from Sara's embarrassed giggle, Stefan's kiss was a little more than holy. The circle closed in a torrent of good wishes and blessings, and Luca caught a glimpse of Jarrick, looking uncertainly pleased as his little sister joined another house.

Jarrick might have felt his eyes, for he glanced toward Luca. He disengaged himself from the circle and came to stand beside the pillar. "You came after all. We'd thought you'd given it up."

Luca shook his head. "I didn't think anyone would be honored by my mingling."

Jarrick cast him a reproving look. "You know Sara is glad you're here. And no one is thinking on anything but the happy couple."

People were moving past them now, disappearing into the house for food and wine and dancing and rejoicing. They flowed past Jarrick and Luca, laughing and embracing, a cheerful rushing stream.

And then Stefan and Sara were beside them, clasping hands and smiling. "Jarrick," Stefan greeted, extending a free hand. "My new brother."

Jarrick grinned and took the offered arm. "My best wishes to you."

Sara opened her mouth, but before she could speak Stefan turned to Luca. "And—Luca?"

Luca nodded, his mouth dry.

Stefan extended his hand. "Thank you for coming." His voice was soft but sincere, and his eyes were warm with both happiness and sensitivity. "You are family in our home."

Luca hesitated, stunned by the earnest greeting, and then he grasped the bridegroom's wrist firmly. "Thank you," he said hoarsely. "I appreciate it."

"Will you come inside with us?" Sara asked. "There are more than I thought— Stefan's family couldn't not come—but you're more than welcome..."

Luca licked his lips. As welcoming as Stefan was, he could not be certain that the rest of their guests would be pleased. And even if they did not resent Luca's intrusion, the discovery of the lost Roald brother would draw attention from the wedding couple, and that was hardly fair. "Not today. But—thank you."

Sara leaned forward and kissed him. "I understand," she whispered. "Thank you for coming."

Stefan and Sara moved inside to join the guests. Jarrick turned to Luca. "Where will you go?"

"I haven't decided."

Jarrick nodded. "But, write." He clasped Luca's shoulder. "I'll go; we should have someone to represent our family." He moved forward to embrace his brother. "Take care, Luca."

CHAPTER FORTY-TWO

Shianan was tired and faintly sore from a full day of drilling, but a note from the prince-heir was not to be ignored. When Ethan opened the door, Shianan gave him a weary smile. "Hello, Ethan. Your master sent for me."

"Yes, your lordship. Please come in." Ethan took the cloak Shianan shed and gestured toward the sitting room. "His Highness will come shortly. Please make yourself comfortable."

Shianan eyed several wide leather chairs, grouped together for conversation. The leather was glossy and new on all the chairs but that nearest the door. Shianan chose a gleaming chair and sat low, resting his head against the back. He was tired. The royal review was in two days. No new reports of Ryuven raids had come in, but there was no explanation yet for the previous ones.

"You look something like I feel," came a voice, startling him. Shianan blinked and jerked upright, embarrassed that he'd missed the prince's entry. He was halfway to his feet when Soren waved for him to remain where he was. "Keep your seat, Becknam. I won't tell."

Shianan hesitated and then straightened. "It's not about appearances, Your Highness."

Soren smiled tiredly as he dropped into the scuffed chair. "You have nothing to prove to me. But I appreciate your conscience." He waved Shianan into his seat again. "I'm sorry I'm late, and for my own invitation, too."

Shianan lowered himself, eying the fatigued prince. "Your meeting did not go as smoothly as expected?"

"You could say that." Soren glanced over his shoulder as Ethan brought a tray with drinks. "I wanted to finish that trade agreement, but as soon as the duke recognized I was anxious, he became more demanding." He sighed, taking a cup. "We had to work out new percentages and shares, new rates of exchange... I have no skill for that sort of tight accounting."

Shianan accepted a cup, wine cut with unfermented juice. "Nor I. My earnest sympathies."

Soren gave him a skeptical glance. "This from the man who single-handedly uncovered years of bookkeeping fraud?"

287

Shianan silently cursed his slip. "Not single-handedly," he allowed.

Soren smiled. "I'm pleased. I'd thought I had one more thing to resent about you." He grinned. "Your secret is safe with me."

"Resent?"

"If you excelled at accounting as well? You're already the demon commander, admired leader, esteemed fighter, and the hero who found the missing Shard." Soren ticked items on his fingers. "Do you know how they speak of you, the man who gave himself to the Court of the High Star to flush the real thieves?"

"But—but..." Shianan did not know how to protest.

"What I would give for your charisma," Soren said mildly.

"You have it, whatever there is of it," Shianan answered, hiding his self-consciousness with a half-grin. "I have sworn all of me to your service."

Soren gave him a serious look. "And that is something I cherish. I think of that, sometimes, when I cannot guess how I'll manage. At least someone believes I have a good chance of muddling in the right direction." He sighed. "Still, I wish I had your gift."

"My gift," Shianan repeated.

"'Soats, man, your men would follow you nearly anywhere, would fight for you against insane odds. That's what I need, if I am to be king. That's what I want."

Shianan stared down at his wine. "You have it, my lord."

Soren gave him a quick, startled look. "Becknam..."

"Why else would I swear myself to you, after my king demanded a pledge to your brother?"

Soren blinked and smiled. "I suppose you're right." He sighed, relaxing marginally. "Then perhaps I'll soon see His Grace pledging his trade to my purposes, right?" He chuckled.

"We can hope." Shianan lifted his cup. "To your trade agreement."

"Thank you." They drank, and then Soren held up a finger. "Ah, but we cannot drink to my project without drinking to yours. How have you fared?" He raised an eyebrow. "Did the flowers help?"

Heat flooded Shianan and he glanced away. "Er..."

"Come, man, confess. You did give them to her, yes?"

"I did. I did, thank you." Shianan bit at his lip, remembering the awkward scene and his gut-wrenching discovery of the Ryuven. "She did like them..."

"You sound uncertain. She liked the flowers but she hated you?"

He shook his head. "No, not quite... No, we haven't seen quite eye to eye again, but she doesn't... Her father seems to think that she's even fond of me, but—"

"Ho!" Soren waved his drink. "Her father, you say? And did he mention this while warning you away or urging you to press your courtship?"

Shianan had not thought of it so simply. "He invited me to dine with them. But do—"

"Did he?" Soren grinned broadly. "Then, my friend, you are faring well thus far." He laughed and lifted his cup. "To Shianan Becknam and his pursuit of a mage!" He drank.

Shianan smiled obligingly. "Yes, Mage Hazelrig is—we have spoken occasionally, and he is a good man to know. And perhaps he is friendly toward me. Be that as it may, my interest in his daughter will be fruitless."

"Don't be so bleak. You're not an heir, bound to marry by the will of the kingdom. You can choose your own way, your own..." Soren's voice trailed off.

Shianan stared at him, incredulous. "Your Highness, I was sent to a distant outpost for military training when I was four years old. I did not choose my career. I did not choose to come to Alham and be named a count." He shook his head. "I can bring no complaint; I am skilled, as anyone started so young should be, and I don't know that I should have made a better tanner or chandler or baker. But I have chosen precious little."

Only Luca. He chose to take Luca from the prison. And he chose to risk himself for Ariana. He chose to trust Ariana and Ewan Hazelrig, staying his hand from killing the injured Ryuven when Tam had been first revealed. He chose to trust Soren, after their rainy meeting and bitter exchange. And he had chosen to surrender Luca to his brother.

"No," he corrected quietly. "I have chosen for myself. As have you, my lord."

Soren looked at him warily. "We are both bound by our positions."

"You chose to speak to the bastard. That night, in the rain— you could have sent me away. You could have allowed me to leave, as I would have done. But you chose to call me back and speak with me. You chose to defend me before the king. Your birth called you to spurn me, but you chose your own path."

Soren shrugged, embarrassed. "No one should be so heartless."

"Some are, but you chose to be different." Shianan nodded toward the office beyond the door. "You chose to pursue this trade agreement. You choose to win his favor."

"I must do that, if—"

"Must you? Would you not still be prince if you were to recline on your couch and let nubile slave girls dangle fruit into your open lips?"

Soren chuckled. "What an image. Yes, I would be prince, but I might not be king—and I would not be prepared to be a good king."

"Why does that matter?"

"What kind of question is that? It matters! We need a good king. Slave girls dangling fruit would not help this kingdom or its people."

"Then you have chosen to pursue what is important. Instead of sacrificing the throne for leisure, you have sacrificed your leisure for the throne."

Soren tipped his head and considered. "I see." His eyes fixed on Shianan. "And what have you chosen to pursue?"

"What do you mean?"

"I'm asking you, Shianan Becknam, what you are willing to sacrifice. Is your pretty mage worth your trouble? Or will you sacrifice her in the name of being quiet and obedient and forgotten?"

Shianan tensed. "That's different. I am only remembering my place."

"Your place, Bailaha, is that of a count. And you are a highly regarded commander, which is no small station of its own. So how then can you say your place keeps you from a woman who is, though a lady by family skill, not even nobility?"

Shianan clenched his jaw. "She has been a lady much longer than I have been a lord."

"What does that matter?" Soren frowned. "I do not believe you consider her birth to be an obstacle."

Shianan looked away, conscious he was growing angry. "Her birth has nothing to do with it."

"Yours, then?"

Shianan clenched his fists, biting down his reaction. This was still his prince. "Yes, mine."

Soren gestured in curt frustration. "Speak to your mage. Then go to the king and—"

"Go to him?" Shianan tried to cover his shock with a failed laugh. "Just like—I have never gone to him, never. He sends for me when he wishes."

"You can request an audience, can't you?"

The idea had never occurred to Shianan. His gut clenched even at the thought of it.

Soren eyed him. "'Soats, does he scare you that badly?"

Shianan jerked out of his chair and moved away. He stared hard at the wall, seeing nothing at all.

Soren's chair creaked behind him. "I'm sorry." A hand settled on Shianan's shoulder. "I did not mean—I should not have said such a thing."

Shianan swallowed, flexing his fingers, still staring ahead. "My lord, I apologize."

The hand tightened. "Don't. It was my mistake." He paused. "He really is not such a formidable person. If you had seen him elsewhere, going to hunt or reading a story..."

"But I have never seen him there," Shianan bit out fiercely. "I have never walked with him, hunted with him, sat beside him to listen. I am nothing more than a tool to him—a tool mistakenly produced, an error in the smithy, but serviceable for the moment, anyway."

"Do you think that is how he sees you?"

"Isn't it?"

"I told you, he brags of your achievements."

"A tool must be useful. And he is ready enough to punish failure."

Soren squeezed his shoulder again. "I know. I should have guarded my words." He released Shianan and crossed the room. "But I believe you have nothing to lose by seeking your mage, if that is what you want and if she will have you. If denied, you'll be just where you've placed yourself now."

Shianan said nothing, rooted in place with his thoughts whirling within him.

"Ask to meet him. He'll speak to you privately, won't he?"

Shianan's shoulders rose another quarter inch. "At times."

There was a pause, and then Soren continued, "Perhaps after the review. He'll be wanting to congratulate you on that, won't he? It might be an opportune moment."

Shianan drew a slow breath. It was true that the king had been pleased in previous years, offering precious praise for the troops' good show. Would he be gratified enough to consider Shianan's request?

Was it even worth asking? What would Ariana think?

Soren returned deliberately to his chair. "Think on it, anyway. You're too worthy a man to deny himself everything without a hope."

Shianan forced himself to breathe. Could he risk the king's denial? Dare he?

Would he?

Perhaps he might test his footing with Ariana. If she favored him, then he would have to decide whether to venture a petition. But if she did not want him, there was no reason to torture himself with wondering at the king's mind.

He turned and looked at the wine he'd left beside his chair. What kind of drink would he need to whip his courage to speaking so frankly with Ariana?

CHAPTER FORTY-THREE

The Silver Mage nodded a hello as Ariana passed her in the Wheel's outer corridor, and Ariana hesitated. She crossed her arms, hugging herself. "Do you have a minute? Can I speak with you?"

"Absolutely." Mage Parma went ahead and held open her silver door. "Come in. How is your practice coming along?"

"Pretty well." Ariana picked up a paper packet on the floor and went to the nearest open chair. "It's as hard as learning it all the first time, but at least it's going more quickly."

"That's good to hear." Mage Parma locked her office door and then came to sit across from her. "What's wrong?"

Ariana handed her the packet. "This had been slipped under the door. It's from Flamen Mennti, so one of the Gehrn, I suppose?"

Mage Parma took the sealed paper and, without looking, spun it with lazy precision into the little fire burning in the hearth. "Now, what's wrong?"

Ariana looked after the burning letter in surprise.

"Ariana?"

She bit her lip. "This may sound ridiculous."

"The door is locked, and I'll try not to laugh."

Ariana couldn't summon a smile for the jest. "Do you... do you believe in dreams?"

Mage Parma raised an eyebrow. "In what way? I've had dreams myself, if that's what you mean, so I think they exist. Or do you mean hopes and dreams?"

"Mantic dreams," Ariana blurted. "Do you think dreams can tell the future?"

Elysia Parma did not laugh. She pursed her lips and frowned thoughtfully. "What's this about?"

Ariana took a breath. "I had a dream, and—it was terrifying. Horrifying. I woke—I was ill, I was so afraid. And I want to know... I want to know if it could be real."

"Do you want to tell me about it?"

"No." Ariana regretted the blunt answer. "That is..."

Mage Parma shook her head. "We don't have to discuss it yet, if you're uncomfortable. Let's speak generally, first."

There was a knock at the door, and with an apologetic glance she rose to answer it. "Hello," she said, opening the door only a few inches so that Ariana and the visitor could not see one another. "I'm terribly sorry, but something urgent has come up, and now isn't a good time. Could we meet later tonight? Over supper, perhaps? Yes, the Hawking Babe will do. Bring your notes. Thank you."

She returned to Ariana and folded her hands on the table. "It's my belief that most of our dreams are just that, dreams. But that doesn't mean they don't hold meaning, or that we cannot learn from them. What I am about to say may sound patronizing, but I mean it sincerely: you have been through a great deal of late, Ariana, and there is much on your mind. What worries you will influence your dream, and the weight of your waking concern will make the dream more substantial. Then when you recall the dream, the terror of it will lend your concern additional import. Each experience fuels the other in a kind of perpetual impetus." She held up a hand. "Now, understand I absolutely do not mean to belittle either dream or emotion, but let us work through it as a dream, first."

Ariana hesitated and then nodded. "Every time I think of it, I feel ill again."

"Did you dream of the Ryuven?"

Ariana nodded.

Mage Parma's expression softened. "Did you go back?"

Ariana shook her head. "No, it wasn't about that. It was... about the war."

"Which has of course been on your mind," Parma granted gently. "And did you dream of an unfavorable outcome? Or something happening in connection to the battle?"

Ariana nodded mutely.

"There's no surprise you would dream of something so serious. All our thoughts are bent on this issue." Parma folded her hands. "So the question of your dream was likely this: what can you do to influence the conflict with the Ryuven?"

Ariana felt foolish. "Well, of course. That's all we've been working on."

"And your dream seemed greater than that? But is it possible you were just thinking of this worry in a different way?"

Ariana rested her chin in her hands. "I want to see this war ended. And I feel there has to be something other than the fighting we've tried for so long. There's something we're missing..."

"So like your father." Mage Parma sighed, but without exasperation. "My duty is to defend against the Ryuven. I have not put the effort into exploring other solutions because my efforts are bent on defense.'

"Like the shield."

"Like the shield, and others. But if you wish to explore other avenues than fighting, then don't think of it as a war. Look from a different angle entirely, like your dream."

"What do you mean?"

"Well, let's work through this systematically. A loose map of sorts can be useful for choosing an oblique approach. What is the first of the five material sciences?"

"Botany, zoology, chemistry, physical philosophy—"

"One at a time will do. Let's start with botany. What do you know of things botanical in this concern? Anything at all."

Ariana considered. Failing crops had started the raids and had prompted Tamaryl to abandon his conviction to the shield. "The Ryuven are starving. Better harvests might reduce or end the raids. But I have no way of guessing what plagues their crops, nor even what plants they grow."

"Still, it's something less often discussed than open battle. Let's continue with this line of thought."

Ariana was accustomed to this style of guided discussion from her apprenticeship with her father. "The Ryuven cannot buy from human growers without some sort of common currency." But she had already wracked her brain for a potential trading commodity. If only she knew what plants the Ryuven used...

She thought of the bag of medicine Maru had sent with her. "I have a tiny sampling of Ryuven flora. What could that tell us?"

Parma's eyebrows rose. "I think that's more than we've had to study in the last hundred years," she answered readily. "It cannot hurt to examine it, and ask for help if you need it."

Perhaps Mage Parma was only giving her makework to distract her. "You think looking at their medicinal herbs will help me understand what's blighting their food crops?"

"Only if the herbs also suffer blight. It's hard to say what you might find. But it would be foolish not to examine what you have. And if it reveals nothing, there's zoology and chemistry to consider next." Parma rose and went to the array of crystals near the door, reaching to the one labeled *White Mage*. Instead of tapping it, however, she held her fingertips against it. "Ewan, are you there?"

Ariana stared. A moment later her father's voice returned, flattened but recognizable. "Yes?"

"Who is the best arcane botanist you know?"

"Callahan, of course."

"I thought so, too. Thanks." Parma released the crystal and met Ariana's eyes. "There you go."

Ariana ignored her words and pointed to the crystals. "I didn't know that was possible!"

The Silver Mage glanced back at the plaque. "No? To be fair, it's a scant handful who can do it. It's hardly a practical communication tool, limited to so few. But it's useful among ourselves."

"How? How does it work?"

Parma smiled. "Now really, you should be able to work that out for yourself. The concept is not nearly so difficult as the execution."

Someone knocked at the door. Ariana rose. "I'm sorry to take your time. Thank you for listening and for your suggestion. It probably was just my worry, after all."

Parma nodded. "I'm glad to talk, Ariana. If you need anything, anything else, come see me."

Ariana nodded and excused herself.

CHAPTER FORTY-FOUR

When Luca returned to Isen's home, there was a litter sitting to one side, a single unfamiliar slave rubbing it clean.

"The master is here—the master of this house, I mean," Cole explained. "He arrived maybe an hour ago."

Luca's stomach tightened. "I see." If Falten Isen had returned, Luca would not be able to remain long. He would have to decide soon where he would go with his new life.

He ascended the stairs, passing by the bedchamber where he'd slept, and went onto the roof. It would be pleasant to think over his plans there in the evening sun.

But the roof was occupied, he saw. Falten Isen lay face down on the narrow bench, his back bare. Marla bent over him, working hard above his hip. Neither noticed him at the corner of the roof.

Isen tensed, a small sound of discomfort escaping him, and Marla reached for a bottle with one hand as she continued the pressure with the other. Then she bent further, leaning into her pressure, and Isen's leg spasmed on the bench.

It was healing work, not sensual, yet Luca felt awkward at having happened upon the scene. He was turning to go when he heard Marla murmur something to Isen. The merchant shifted his head slightly. "Nerrin?"

Luca needed a moment to recall that Jarrick had introduced him as Dom Nerrin. "Forgive me, I did not mean to interrupt."

"No, please." Isen's eyes closed. "I apologize for my unexpected return."

Luca smiled. "It is your house, my lord."

Isen chuckled and then winced as Marla struck something, and the rhythm of her hands changed. "I'm afraid I'm not much of a host at the moment."

Luca was near enough now to see a livid slash of scarring across the lower right of his back. Marla's thumbs were on either side of it, nudging the damaged muscle. "Please don't trouble yourself for me. Cole and I will finish some work in the garden."

"Oh, no," Isen protested mildly. "My guest may enjoy my garden but not work it. Please relax. I will be finished here shortly."

Luca descended and went out among the plantings, wandering between the ornamentals, cut back for winter, and the vegetable and herb beds toward the rear of the house. The fountain splashed noisily. It rarely grew cold enough to freeze on the coast, and the fountain would play through the winter. He sat on a brick border and rested his chin on his cupped hands.

After a moment, he felt he was not alone, and he glanced up to see Cole watching him steadily. Disconcertingly. When their eyes met, Cole spoke. "I talked with the drudge, the night you left me in Ivat."

The words were mild, the tone mostly level, but the sentence carried an undercurrent of meaning. Luca hadn't considered that Cole might have resented being left behind, unexpectedly abandoned in the house of a man who disliked him.

"He said the first time he saw you, you had a Furmelle collar."

A thin wire of fear lanced Luca, the long dread of association. "Yes."

At the word, Cole's hard expression turned to awe and even admiration. But as he looked at Luca, it faded to disappointment and then quiet disgust. "Oh."

Luca squeezed his fists, muscles clenching all through his arms and legs. Furmelle had been his first introduction to terror, and blame and retribution had trailed him from Furmelle across the Faln Plateau to Davan and then to Alham. He was humiliated by his fear, but he did not deserve Cole's disdain.

"That's why you haven't freed me, then. I suppose in Furmelle you were with them." Cole regarded him with a pinched, downturned mouth, resentful. He rolled a shoulder and spat into the bed of empty stalks.

Cole would have fought in the revolt. Again, the recognition stirred that Cole had been one of the enemy, and Luca tried to quell his sudden unease.

"I wasn't with anyone." Luca closed his eyes against the memory. He had lived horrors with the Gehrn, but they were different horrors than the fighting in Furmelle, the brutal murders of women, children, slaves, freemen, anyone caught in the streets by any prowling band to whom they hadn't sworn fast enough.

But memory could not be stopped by the dark, and Luca had to open his eyes, fixing them on the broken stalks of the garden. He licked his lips and repeated, "Free you."

It had not occurred to him, in all his worry, that they *could* free

Cole. The law permitted it here. Luca had grown too accustomed to helpless acceptance of how things were.

But Furmelle was a wound, and Cole's derision was salt. "You haven't mentioned Andrew's release. Are you arguing your principles or your wants? Would you free the slave you'd bought?"

"Your brother can afford it."

"That's not an answer."

Cole scowled. "I would free my slave if I were as rich."

"And if money were scarce? That's how I became a slave, when scruples became a luxury for the rich."

That stung Cole into quiet, if not into contrition.

Luca turned his head, irritated with both Cole and himself. Cole had been an overseer and enjoyed its power. For all his contempt about Furmelle, he was less concerned with opposing slavery and more with opposing his own. But Luca, too, had thought only of his own situation.

What would Cole do if freed?

What would Luca do, entirely on his own and without another voice, even a distant, subservient one?

Still, chained to the tinker's cart, he would have given anything for a chance at freedom. He could not in good conscience neglect to offer that to Cole.

"My brother paid eight hundred for you. I'm sure he'll take the same. I can help you earn that to buy your freedom."

The slave's eyes snapped to him. "How?"

"I'll seek work in accounting or clerking. You can come with me and hire yourself out. I'll want forty pias a month for your keep, and the rest you can keep toward your freedom."

Cole scowled again, but with less force. "So I would be your slave—and working?"

"I won't have much use at home for you. I hardly need a personal servant, and I don't think you'll want to help with clerking. If you can hire out—"

"I could bring as much as eighty pias each month, in overseeing, or thirty or forty in lesser labor. If I do well, I could be free in under two years."

His ready calculations surprised Luca. "What is your basis for eighty a month?"

"My master before Orcan, Master Barbame, let us keep a tenth part of our hiring price, if hired outside, and we could earn a share of profit if we did his work well enough. I did very well. Some of the others drank their earnings, but I wasn't so stupid."

Luca nodded, encouraged.

"I'd saved about six hundred before Rand started cheating—he swore the dice weren't weighted, but it's not natural to lose like that. I lost nearly four hundred fifty in a week. You know that's got to be bad dice."

"You gambled it all?"

"I lost some to the dice and the rest when Barbame sold me on to Orcan. I gave a third to a fellow overseer, to—to use the whip lightly. The balance my master took back."

"That was a considerable loss."

Cole nodded with a barely perceptible scowl and wince.

Luca tipped his head. "Yes? Go on."

Muscles twitched in Cole's jaw. "I was angry. I wanted my savings, and—I argued with my master."

"You argued with him?"

Cole looked across the garden. "I struck him. More than once."

Luca winced too. "You paid for that."

"Yes, master. And I did not have another hundred to spare my back a second time." He smiled grimly. "But Barbame did not tell Orcan of it. He wanted the price of a reliable overseer. So I didn't fall as far as I might have."

"You have now," Luca answered frankly. "You're a common laborer, and you've lost your savings."

"But my price has fallen from two thousand to merely eight hundred, so I am nearer than ever." His mouth turned up in a wry smile.

Luca laughed. "That's true. Does that mean you like the offer?"

Cole's smile faded. "Two years is a long time."

Luca rubbed his earlobe and said nothing.

"It's longer some places than others." Cole looked back at the house, and then he took a handful of dry stalks from the beds. He rolled them over one another in his fingers. "Who would hold the money?"

"What?"

"The money I earned. For myself. Who would hold it, you or me?"

It meant little, in fact; a slave had no property, so any money Cole earned would legally be the Roalds'. But there was a pledge to be made. "It would be your money, Cole. You hold it until you have enough."

Cole nodded once, a tight motion that did not dislodge his frown. After another long moment, he snapped the dry stalks with a savage motion. "Do you remember when I said some slaves were too stupid for freedom?"

This was a moment to tread carefully. "I remember you telling how some had no practice in managing for themselves."

One corner of Cole's mouth quirked, acknowledgment of Luca's charitable weaseling. "I'll say it plainly, then—I earned more than six hundred under Master Barbame. But six hundred was the most I had at once."

"That's a good sum." *Until you gambled it.*

"Until I gambled it." Cole chewed his lip. "I can't afford to miss this chance. I'll never be so close again. If I can land a good position— it could be a year and a half. I can't drop this." He dropped his head and blew out his breath. "You must think me stupid. Another dumb brute who can't control himself."

Luca shook his head. "I think planning around temptation is excellent management."

Cole didn't look at him, but Luca saw his expression soften.

"I'd be happy to hold it for you. And if you choose, I can help you invest it to bring returns."

Now Cole looked at him, mouth open. "I don't understand much of that."

"It was just a thought."

"No—no, I'd like that. More money, sooner. I'd like that."

It was the largest statement of trust he could give, obliquely committing his freedom to Luca, and it gave Luca a swell of pride such as he had not felt in long years, long before his own enslavement. Luca breathed deep, feeling taller even as he sat on the planting border.

Now he had only to settle his own life.

Luca took one of the fallen stalks and began to fidget with it. "Where would you go, Cole?"

"Master?"

"If you had the choice, if you could go anywhere, where would you go? Say whatever comes to mind. Where would be a good place to make our way?"

"Not Fersiam," Cole answered, as if reluctant to speak it aloud.

Luca smiled grimly. "Not Fersiam," he agreed. That was the site of the largest concentration of iron mines. "Nor Ginar, nor Kinnau, nor Salfield." Silver ore, gold ore, and the salt harvesting flats.

"You're a good man, master."

"Hn," Luca snorted. "Neither of us wants that labor, that's the truth." He propped his chin in his hand.

Isen's voice called from the rear of the house. "Nerrin? Are you here?"

"Here," Luca called, leaping to his feet and barely keeping himself from adding, "my lord."

Isen rounded the corner. "I'm sorry to have surprised you this afternoon. My trip did not last as long as planned."

"As I said, it is your home. I can hardly complain if you return to it."

"It's your friend Jarrick Roald who influenced my return," Isen said amiably. He glanced toward Marla, following with juices, and sat down opposite Luca. "He and his brother are revising their house's interests, and they've asked me to be an agent for them. Thank you," he told Marla. "And stay for a moment, you'll need to hear this."

Marla nodded and stood a few paces from Cole.

"I've agreed to be the Roalds' agent. So I'll be leaving Ivat and Abbar."

Marla gasped. "Where, my lord?"

"They just signed a major supplier in Damas."

Marla wrinkled her nose in dismay. "Damas? But that's a horrid place. All pinewood and nomads and burnt rock."

"And the best wool prices for five hundred leagues," Isen added.

"Cheap because it stinks of sulfur," Marla said uncharitably. "Nomads don't have public baths. How will you fare there, my lord, without your soaks?"

"Eh, you make a good point," Isen conceded. "Then I suppose it's a good thing that we're not going to Damas, but to Alham."

"Alham!" Luca and Marla said together.

"The Roalds have a new supply contract with the Chrenadan military," Isen explained, "but Jarrick said he needs someone else in Alham to manage it."

Luca smiled a little. No, Jarrick would not return to the city where he had betrayed his co-conspirators to trade with a man he had tried to murder.

Marla's smile lit her face. "Oh, that's wonderful!" Then she made a ferocious scowl. "Damas, you said."

He laughed, and she grinned and returned to the house.

Luca hadn't realized he was staring after her until he noticed Isen watching him. He jumped and tried to look as if he hadn't been looking, which of course only made it more obvious.

"Are you thinking of my aelipto?" Isen asked. "Have you been disregarding my single injunction to you?"

"No!" Luca blurted before he saw the joking smile. "No, I haven't. She did work on my back, but she offered—"

"Easy, friend," Isen offered. "I can see well enough she's at ease about you. But you are thinking of her, yes?"

Luca hesitated. "She was kind to me, when I came here. She has been very—useful." His words sounded awful in his ears.

"Useful." Isen separated his hands and drummed his fingers. "She is that."

Cole remained very still, unobtrusive.

"Well." Isen set his hands on his knees. "I had better go and speak with Marla about when we can leave." He rose cautiously, favoring one side, and smiled sadly. "She does good work."

Isen and Marla, the nearest he had to new friends, were going to Alham. Everything Luca wanted now was in Alham.

CHAPTER FORTY-FIVE

"Good evening," Isen offered, approaching from the rooftop stairs.

Luca glanced up from his book. "Good evening! I'm sorry, I didn't hear you coming. I hope you don't mind that I borrowed from your library."

"I told you to make yourself at home. What did you choose—a military history?"

"A hobby."

"Only a hobby? You were fighting with the staff, I hear."

"What?"

"Marla told me you have been practicing here."

Luca's cheeks warmed. "Yes, sometimes."

"You have been a soldier?"

"Oh, no." Luca would be ashamed to let a wounded soldier think he was something of the same.

"A bandit, then?" Isen grinned.

"No, I had a friend who was teaching me, that is all." His fingers twitched. "I was only practicing what he'd shown me."

"Had you trained long?"

"I'm afraid I didn't have time to go far in my training. I would have liked to progress, I think, but it wasn't to be."

Isen considered this, nodding. "Your friend was a soldier?"

"Yes."

"I'm sorry."

A moment passed before Luca understood. But Shianan hadn't died—he had only sent Luca with his brother. "Oh, he—"

"Let's go a few rounds, then."

"I beg your pardon?"

"My physician has always advised me to exercise. If I don't exert myself, he says, I might find myself a cripple. Today I used a litter, and if I do not take some exercise tonight, I will need Marla's help to rise in the morning. More, my physician has been chiding me that merely walking is not enough, that this is the reason I have been pained." He grimaced. "I don't know that I agree—it's not as if it doesn't hurt when I do exert myself—but for what I pay the man, I should at least consider his advice. And it would be good to have someone to train against."

Luca did not know how to respond. "I don't think..."

"Oh, come, Nerrin. You're a young man. Humor me."

Luca hesitated. "My lord, I'm not sure..."

But Isen was already retrieving the two staves from the edge of the rooftop terrace. "Didn't your soldier friend engage you in some friendly sparring?"

"No," Luca answered honestly. "The difference between us was too great."

"He was that good, was he?" Isen chuckled. "Or you were that bad?"

"Both, I think," conceded Luca.

"Then we won't spar yet," Isen allowed. "But you will run through some drills, won't you? It would help me."

Luca could not refuse his host, as he knew his host knew. He exhaled and took the staff Isen extended to him. "If I may be of use, my lord. But I know little enough."

"We'll see." Isen spun the staff in his hand. "Will a slow drill do? You may lead, if you like."

Luca could not move. How could he strike, even in slow practice, such a man? A respected merchant, an injured soldier, his host, a freeman?

"Come on, then," Isen prompted. "I'd like to work through it before supper."

Luca lifted his chin. It was not Falten Isen standing before him, but Shianan Becknam. *As you like. I am going to swing at you; you may block or not as it pleases you.* Luca shifted his grip and lifted the staff.

Isen met his slow attack without hesitation, moving without speed but smoothly and powerfully. He did not seem to use much strength, but the weight of his body was behind each movement. Shianan would have approved. Luca responded as best he could, struggling to match Isen's movements. Minutes passed as they moved about each other in a slow rhythm of patterned combat.

And then Isen paused, tipping his staff upward. He was breathing hard and a sheen of sweat covered his face. "Flames, I am not fit for this." He laughed, panting. "I may not be able to call that physician a fool to his face after all."

Luca smiled. "Are we finished, then?"

"Not yet, if you please. I only want a breather." Isen leaned on his staff. "After this I'll need Marla to piece me together again."

Luca glanced away.

Isen scratched at his chin, thoughtful. "Fine woman, Marla. I hope she kept you well during your stay?"

"Of course." Luca examined the grain of his staff, wondering if he dared ask the questions in his mind.

"You're in merchanting, aren't you?" Isen moved stiffly to the bench and faced Luca as he sat.

Luca's resolve stiffened. He could not give up such an opening. "Actually, I know the man in Alham who signed the contract with Jarrick Roald."

"Do you?"

"I was thinking of going to Alham myself, finding a place there in business," Luca said, hoping he did not sound nearly so awkward as he felt. "I thought—I wondered if you might need an assistant, maybe just to start, when you go."

Isen did not seem offended at the question. "Well, if you already know the city and the man I must work with, that would be a help."

"I know Commander Becknam, but I suspect you'll be doing most of your trade with someone else. He was only the man to sign the new contract—but he's a fighter, not a bean-counter."

Isen laughed. "Good to know. I hear you can't pull anything over on him, though."

Luca smiled despite himself.

"I don't know that there would be enough work to require a partner—"

"Assistant."

"—at least at first. But I see no reason we couldn't travel together, and you could introduce me in Alham."

Luca's stomach sank. He could not introduce Isen in Alham, not to anyone who mattered.

"And we could see what might work out, as far as working together goes." Isen smiled.

Luca tried to return the smile, but it felt weak on his face. He should not have asked, should not have pretended to be more than he was. Now Isen would expect more, now Luca would be humiliated when they got to Alham, now Luca must find an excuse to retract his words.

Isen moved the staff in his fingers, watching it. "Let's spar, something nearer a real fight."

Luca's heart quickened, and he waved away the words with a false grin. "Oh, no."

"I'm in earnest. It would be good for both of us."

It would be good for neither of them. "But I may not fight you, my lord."

"Certainly you may. Half-cripple against half-trained; it's a fitting match. Do you agree?"

Every law of hospitality compelled him to agree. Luca resigned himself to a quick loss. "Just one round, my lord."

"Good enough." Isen stood slowly, his weight on his staff. "Are you ready?"

Luca lifted his staff so that it paralleled the tile floor, one end tipped toward Isen. "I'm ready."

Isen's staff whipped from its place as his crutch and spun into Luca's, jarring it loose in Luca's grasp. Luca recoiled, clenching his staff and jerking it to vertical to block Isen's backswing as he backed away.

His knees had been unprotected when Isen attacked—the man had chosen to surprise Luca into movement without striking him.

Luca retreated across the roof, blocking Isen's blows and acutely aware that he was not fast enough, that his opponent was deliberately pulling his attacks to allow Luca time to respond. Luca's mind was empty, he could think of no action to oppose or counter the onslaught. He could only react, and too slowly.

And then Isen whirled his staff overhead and swept it downward toward Luca's head with a sharp angry shout. Terror took Luca. His legs folded and he dropped to the tile, cringing. Air brushed his ducked face as the staff hissed past. Isen reversed the staff and brought it against Luca's naked neck, arresting its movement so that it just rested there.

Luca could not move. He could not make himself move. He could feel the staff against his neck, but he dared not shift, dared not—

"Oh sweet fate," Isen murmured. He withdrew the staff and stepped closer to Luca, extending a hand. "Here, son."

Luca stared numbly at the open hand.

"Here, come on, then." Isen flexed his fingers and nodded. "Up."

Luca reached obediently for the hand and stood stiffly, muscles cracking with the movement.

"Breathe, son," Isen prompted, his hands on Luca's shoulders. "Breathe."

Luca stared at Isen. "I—I..."

"Sweet fate, I didn't know it would be like that. Here, walk a bit."

Luca pulled away, hot with shame. He had collapsed and cowered, nothing more than a slave to be beaten.

Isen sighed and started forward, leading Luca about the roof. "I thought—but I did not think it would be—I'm sorry, son. I am."

Luca tried to swallow, but his dry throat constricted.

Isen leaned on his staff. "Who gave you your training?"

Why did he ask?

"You had a good instructor, for what you had. Your defense is not fluent, but it is accurate enough, if slow. I wondered who it was who taught you."

Luca took a steadying breath. "Commander Shianan Becknam, in Alham. He is also called the Count of Bailaha."

"Becknam?" Isen moved deliberately away and sat on the bench, giving Luca space. "I thought the man who trained you had died."

"No," Luca said quickly. "He hasn't died. I only left Alham."

"And the man who signed the Roalds' contract is the man who trained you. That's how you know him."

Luca nodded.

"Well, that makes sense. But I thought you had been in the east? Or was that after you left Alham?" Isen's voice suggested that he already knew the answer.

"I was not in the east," admitted Luca.

"I see." Isen sat back on the bench. "You were not a soldier under Becknam."

It was not a question. Luca shook his head unhappily.

"If you were not a soldier, why was he teaching you to fight?"

He knew. Surely he knew. "I—I don't know, my lord."

"He did not give you a reason?"

"He said once that he did not want someone helpless at his back, that it was no protection. But I do not know..."

"That was a generous offer, from a military man." Isen held Luca's eyes.

Luca slumped. "And one who was at Furmelle." There was little left to hide, it seemed.

For a long moment, neither of them spoke. Luca's breathing slowed, and his legs seemed more stable, but the humiliation threatened to smother him.

At last Isen broke the quiet. "When you left Alham and ended your training—did you come with Jarrick Roald?"

"Yes."

The next words were gentler in tone. "Did you know that Jarrick Roald had a younger brother?"

Luca swallowed. "Yes."

Isen's expression softened. "Is your name truly Dom Nerrin, son?"

Luca shook his head.

Isen sighed. "I'm glad for Jarrick. He's hidden it well, but he's worried over you since—you left. Welcome home, I should say."

"Home is not welcoming," Luca muttered.

"I see. I am most sorry for that." Isen sighed again. "Marla knows."

"She told you?"

"No, she didn't. But her certainty of your character made me wonder about you. Your covering yourself, your deference—you do say 'my lord' when you're unprepared, are you aware? I'm only a merchant, you know, as are you.

"And then I thought of Jarrick's brother. I only guessed this hour. I saw that faint band yet marking your wrists. It's nearly gone, so I could have been mistaken. But then in our match..." He shook his head. "Flames, I'm sorry. I did not mean—I would not have—I'm sorry."

Luca closed his eyes, his face burning with shame. "I'm not much of a fighter, you see."

"To the contrary, your commander did a splendid job. I meant what I said about your defense. But you did not spar with him, and you did not learn how to face down intimidation." He smiled. "But you did remember to shield yourself with your staff as you—fell. And your defense never collapsed into flailing. In what capacity were you with Commander Becknam?"

"I was his personal servant."

"How did you find him?"

"My lord?"

"Hear yourself? But I meant to ask, what kind of man is he? I have heard many stories."

Luca straightened. "He is a good man, a very fair man. He deserves better than what he has. He is an excellent soldier by others' accounts, but I am no judge of that."

Isen smiled. "A hero off the field as well, eh?"

"I'm going back to Alham," Luca said suddenly. "He is my friend—my only friend, it seems. Now that I have no obligations here or elsewhere, I will go to my friend."

Isen looked at him. "May I speak bluntly?"

Luca smiled bitterly and gave an exaggerated shrug. "I think it's clear I have no pride to protect."

"Well, then, if you have been a slave in Alham, why would you return there?"

Luca drew a slow breath. "I have been a slave in Alham and in Furmelle, in Davan, across the Faln Plateau, and here on the Wakari Coast. It is not my place on the map which concerns me, but my place in this world."

"And you feel that is in a foreign land."

"I feel I am a stranger here in my homeland."

"I see." Isen offered neither criticism nor pity. "I hope, then, that your commander will recognize and welcome you, though he knew you only as a slave."

"He will know me," Luca answered confidently. "I only worry that he will be angry at my return. It was he who sent me from Alham."

"And yet you want to rejoin him?"

"He knew I could be freed beyond the border. It is illegal to free a slave there, since the rebellions."

"I see." Isen regarded Luca. "Then I hope to one day give Commander Becknam my regards. I never met him in our joint efforts against the Ryuven, though I heard much of him. And I will tell him, if you like, that I think he is an excellent instructor as well."

Luca gave a sardonic smile. "Even though I clearly failed in our match?"

"It was an unfair match, son. Your instructor may have been a commander, but you yourself are no soldier, and your opponent was once a captain." He smiled gently. "That move is intended to disrupt and intimidate."

Luca glanced down, humiliated. "As it did."

Isen shook his head. "Don't feel too bad, son. It sounds as though you've had a steep week. And if I may say for myself, facing

Captain Isen, even as a cripple, is no simple task."

Cole appeared at the steps. "Your supper is ready, my lords."

"Thank you," Isen said after a moment. Luca realized dully that he should have been the one to respond, as Cole's duty was to him, but he had unthinkingly waited for Isen. He clenched his fists, disgusted with himself.

Isen rose, leaning on his staff. "Thank you for helping me to exercise. Come, let's go down and dine."

CHAPTER FORTY-SIX

Luca drummed his fingers as he stared unseeing at Isen's desktop. Surely in Alham there would be someone who needed an accountant or bookkeeper. And with Cole's additional forty pias a month, they would be able to afford a small set of rooms.

Cole was seated in another room with a needle and thread, repairing his torn shirt more properly. Luca didn't know what work the slave would find, but he would do his best, working toward his freedom.

Isen glanced up from his book as Marla entered. "You didn't need to bring anything, but thank you."

"I included some willow bark with yours," she explained, offering him a steaming cup. She turned to Luca. "And this is for you, my lord."

"Thank you."

She turned back to Isen. "If we're going to Alham... That's not so far from where I was born, just a day or so. Could I go and see my mother? And see if there's word of Demario?"

"Of course, if it's so close."

"Thank you!"

Isen glanced to Luca. "Have you decided, yet?"

He didn't know how to admit he was deciding solely by his friends' residency. "Alham's the place that makes most sense. I don't know any villages other than Fhure, and I don't—"

Marla's eyes widened. "How do you know Fhure?"

"My former master's home. Well, not his home, his seat. He lives in Alham, but after he was made a count, he was given Fhure."

Isen looked interested. "What is Fhure, Marla?"

"It's where I was born." She seemed to be struggling for words. "I was raised there, I married there, I lived there until I was sold and eventually went to Master Thalian." She focused on Luca. "You've been there?"

Luca stared at her, realization dawning. "Are you Marta's daughter?"

"Yes!" Marla beamed. "Yes! You know her? Is she well?"

"She keeps the estate's books. She's the one who taught you the number games."

"Yes!"

Isen closed his book. "What a striking coincidence." He looked at Luca. "So, it's Alham, after all? Then we'll be neighbors."

Luca glanced up at Marla's smile, and for the first time since leaving Alham, he felt he was making choices for himself, and they would be good choices.

Tamaryl cupped his fingers about the stubby candle and concentrated. Ordinarily he would not need both hands to guide the magic, but he had little power to command now. Beside him Maru sat very still, watching intently.

Below them, they could hear the pleasantly off-key wordless singing of Mother Harriet as she worked downstairs. They had to be quiet while she was in the kitchen; if they could hear her, so she could hear them. The bedrooms would have been less audible, removed so the family would not be disturbed by the servants in the kitchen, but Mother Harriet serviced them as well and they did not want her walking in on them with an armload of linens.

The candlelight flickered and darkened—not weakening, but changing color. The flame's orange deepened to red. "Nice, Ryl," whispered Maru.

Tamaryl nodded, trying not to let the color ebb as his concentration shifted. There had been no further reports of Ryuven raids. If they were to go home, they had to find their own way. That meant practice.

"It is not so difficult," Tamaryl replied haltingly, "to color fire to red. Let me see if I can take it the other direction." The flame wavered and lightened to fiery orange again, then yellow. Tamaryl took a slow breath and adjusted his fingers about the little candle.

Pale green streaked through the yellow, spreading gradually until the flame was a uniform grassy color. Maru held his breath. The green deepened and sank into blue, a darker blue, until the flame danced bright at the wick within the gem and a lovely sapphire hue at the edge.

"Beautiful." Maru reached a finger toward the tiny fire. "I wish I—"

The flame guttered and burned its ordinary orange. Tamaryl sighed and looked at Maru. "You wish what?"

Maru looked sheepish. "It was foolish. I can't do even simple things, now." He shrugged. "What good to turn a candle flame colors when you can't heal a broken wing or go home—no, I didn't mean that the way it sounded."

Tamaryl gave him a wan smile. "I know you didn't. And a caesious fire isn't terribly useful, is it?"

Footsteps sounded on the stairs, and they fell silent. There was no reason for Mother Harriet to enter the little storage room, and they would give her none. She went humming down to Ewan Hazelrig's chamber.

"But when we go home," Tamaryl continued softly, "we'll have Nori'bel see to you. She'll take care of your wing and your power."

"Can Subduing be reversed?"

"Sometimes. Often enough to be worth trying."

"But what if it—can't be done?"

Tamaryl closed his eyes. "If we stay, there will be no magic for either of us," he said quietly. "Let's get home."

CHAPTER FORTY-SEVEN

Luca shifted from foot to foot as Marla settled her small travel chest in the wagon. Isen leaned over the side. "Everything's tight?"

"Everything's fine, master. Stop fussing."

"Goodman," an overseer addressed Luca from one side. "We've had an injury. Will your slave be needed straightaway, or may we start him in the shafts?"

Luca looked at Cole. "I hadn't thought to lend him."

The overseer followed his gaze to Cole as well, appraising his muscular build. "Not to lend him? But... We'll be wanting a fee for a passenger, then."

Luca licked his lips. "Then I'll speak with Remio."

The overseer nodded curtly and started away.

Isen set a hand on Luca's shoulder and led him gently a few paces from the wagon, away from Marla and Cole. Luca braced himself for reproof. "I know I should have given him Cole, but—"

"Let me speak," Isen said firmly. He faced Luca. "You are your own man, and one with means. Jarrick Roald would never argue with a slave; nor should Dom Nerrin or Luca Roald." He smiled and spoke more gently. "To hesitate is to invite questions. Confidence inspires agreement. A merchant should know this."

Luca looked down. "I did know that, once. And once I could act on it."

Isen tightened his fingers on Luca's shoulder. "You'll do well, son," he assured him. "It is only practice. And Cole is your slave. If they take him as a draft slave, he's built for it, and he'll spare you some coins. But if you have reason to keep him out of the shafts, then as a paying customer you may state your will as if you expect to be obeyed."

Luca nodded. "Yes. Thank you."

Isen smiled and released Luca's shoulder. A few overseers called orders, and the wagons began to rumble forward.

Ariana fairly danced in place, knowing she looked like a giddy child but not caring. "Father! Aren't you ready yet?"

He called down the stairs. "I have one shoe on. You know the booths won't be open so early."

"I want to be sure of a good place to watch the parade! We'll need room for everyone."

"Go on, then, and don't wait for me. I know where to find you."

"See you there!"

She went out through their front door, past the bare fruit trees hoping for early spring, and though the ornamental gate. The morning was brisk and she tugged her black robes, worn for today's ceremonial tone, closer about her.

The streets were already busy, but it was still quick passage to the bookbinding shop. Ariana waved a greeting to Vaya, who was showing a customer a selection of leathers, and went directly to the supply room. "Ranne? Are you ready?"

Ranne glanced up as Ariana entered. "Oh—Ariana! Shut the door, quick!"

She was not alone. A man in expensive festival garb was beside her, mouth slightly agape as he stared at Ariana. Ranne's hand was in his.

Ariana closed the door. "Ranne, what is it?" She looked at the man, who stared back.

Ranne looked embarrassed and guilty and excited all at once. "I'm so sorry, Ariana—I meant to send you a message this morning, but—"

Ariana waved away the excuse. It was clear enough what had happened. "You have another companion for the parade viewing today."

Ranne's face wrinkled in conflict. "Oh, Ariana, I wanted to tell you. I only was so afraid it might get out. If you had told anyone..."

"Don't be silly, I wouldn't have said anything! But if you're going out to the festival together, it won't be much of a secret."

"It's not a secret any longer," Ranne said with a giddy rush. "Ariana, this is Connor Kudo."

Ariana had guessed as much. She had not met the baron's son, but she knew Ranne had been seeing him clandestinely.

Connor made a smart little bow to Ariana. "It's a pleasure to meet you, my lady mage. Ranne has told me so much about you, all of it complimentary."

"Except for her faith in my discretion, apparently." But she smiled and made a small curtsy.

"That may have been my fault, I'm sorry. I've urged secrecy. Father has in mind that I should marry among the nobility, but I set my eyes on a mercantile bride. He'll come around, though, I'm sure. I've been quietly warming him to the idea."

"But promise not to tell, Ariana, not yet," Ranne said. "We are going to speak to his father today, announce what we've done."

Ariana looked between them. "What have you done?"

Ranne clasped Ariana's hands. "Connor and I—we're married. We married this morning, it's all legal, but we're going to have it recorded officially so there can be no dispute. Then we're going to go to Connor's father tonight and tell him. He'll have to accept it if it's all done and everyone has seen us together at the festival."

Ariana couldn't speak for a moment. They were already married. A simple handfasting and exchange of vows was all that was strictly needed, but it was wiser to let a frustrated baron seethe against official records rather than their own word.

"Bethia's been such a help to us," Ranne continued breathlessly. "She's lent us messengers when we couldn't meet, and that's one of her men right now, keeping Mama busy. Mama—she knows about Connor, of course, but not about the marriage. I knew she'd worry about the baron, but now it's done, and she can claim ignorance and I hope be safe from retribution. Will you watch her, please? For a day or two? She'll take it well, being Mama, but I don't want her to worry. You can tell her where we are if she needs to know."

"She's your mother; of course she'll need to know." Ariana gave Ranne a quick hug. "Go on, then. I'll take care of her. Enjoy the day. And I'm so happy for you! I really am. Connor, it's lovely to meet you, and be good to her."

"I will, my lady mage!"

They exited the rear door into a narrow alley and started for the street. Ariana went back to the shop's front room. The customer made his selection and bade Vaya a good day.

Ariana took a deep breath. "Vaya, I—Ranne has..."

Vaya turned and met her eyes. "Ranne has married that baron's boy, hasn't she?"

Ariana nodded mutely, surprised.

Vaya smiled wistfully. "I thought as much. It was clear something was afoot, and then no one comes on a festival morning to look over every piece of leather we can show." She sighed. "I was hoping she'd tell me, but..."

"She was afraid the baron would blame you if you knew. She didn't want you to worry about him."

"Of course I'll worry! From what I understand, he wasn't hoping for a daughter from merchant stock. But he's not likely to send men to smash our windows. Where has she gone?"

"She and Connor Kudo are having their marriage recorded, so there can be no dispute, and then they'll go to Baron Kudo." Ariana hesitated. "I didn't know anything of it before, I'm sorry."

Vaya laughed. "I know. You could never keep a secret, Ariana, dear." She sighed. "Well, she is safe, and she is happy, and I'll have her again in a few days. Things could be much worse. It's not what I would have chosen, but I'll make the best of it, and it's not so bad as that, really. Give me a hug, Ariana, and then let me close up. No one will want bindings during the festival, and I should celebrate for them, even if on my own."

Ariana felt stunned as she walked home. She'd collect her father and then go to hold their viewing spot, now for fewer people. Ranne, married! And so suddenly! She was happy for her friend, but not as happy as she thought she would have been, had she known Connor and shared eager support for their union. She felt a little guilty for that, and a little resentful that Ranne had not told her.

Not that Ariana had any ground to resent keeping secrets, even secrets of inappropriate romantic overtures.

Ariana had misjudged Bethia, it seemed, whom she would not have guessed to help a merchant girl marry into a noble house. True, Bethia was friends with both Ariana and Ranne, neither born to nobility, but she had always felt... conscious of the difference between them, Ariana thought. But perhaps that had been more Ariana than Bethia.

You could never keep a secret, Ariana, dear.

The worst part of keeping a secret, Ariana reflected, was that she could not even tell Vaya she was wrong.

CHAPTER FORTY-EIGHT

Shianan tugged at his uniform, assuring himself there were no wrinkles. He felt for the buckle of his dress cape over his shoulder, checked that it was secure, and then went out to face the chaos.

The assembly yard was busy and loud, filled with laughter and shouts and milling soldiers. Captain Torg gave him a harried glance before turning back to a clot of men. Shouted orders rang through the yard as the captains and sergeants noted Shianan's arrival and called for order. The men moved into their lines, but it seemed achingly slow. "Soldiers!" he barked at three men jesting about their scrubbed appearances as they moved. "Assemble!"

They jumped, looking startled, and Shianan took a breath, cautioning himself. It would be too easy to be harsher than necessary in his agitation, and that could lead to more trouble. Nothing could be permitted to go wrong this day.

But they were gathered now and silent in their ranks. Torg fell into his place beside Shianan. "They're excited today, sir," he said softly. "A little anxious, I think."

Good man, Torg, to recognize it in both his men and his commander, and to warn without rebuke. Shianan was grateful for him. "I see. We'll try to steady them. Where's our advance?"

"Already out, sir, and watching for us."

Shianan nodded. "Any word from the palace?"

"Not yet, sir, but it's early."

"Right. Well, let's be ready. Presentation check."

Torg averted his head slightly, so that he shouted away from the commander. "Presentation check!"

The sergeants along the ranks faced the troops. "Presentation check! See to your fellow. Is his uniform neat and clean? Is his sword in place? Is his helmet correct?"

The list went on, as each soldier reviewed the next in line. It was faster than requiring an officer to look over each of them, and the pressure kept them cleaner; a soldier who helped another correct a fault was lauded, while one who was later found in disarray brought consequences to both himself and to the one who had checked him.

"Horses!"

Shianan turned and saw the animals approaching. Behind him he heard appreciative sounds from the nearer soldiers.

The foremost horse tossed its head and danced sideways, tugging at its lead. The sun shone on its burnished bronze coat. Shianan felt a quiet awe himself. *Beautiful creatures*, Ariana had called them. *So exotic.* He moved to meet them.

General Septime strode toward the horses and Shianan as they converged in the open space before the front ranks. "Good morning, Philip," he greeted the man standing alongside the horses. "Good morning, commander."

Philip made a small bow to each of them. "My lords."

"Which one is mine this year?"

"This one, my lord," Philip answered, turning to the bronze horse. He reached to straighten its dark forelock, his sleeve shifting to reveal the narrow cuffs on his wrists. "Be still on him, as he's young and excitable."

Septime nodded uncertainly. "I'll behave if he will."

Two more joined them, and Philip and Shianan bowed respectfully. "My lords."

Chancellor Washe nodded acknowledgment. "Good morning." He looked at the horses. "They look good."

"Thank you, my lord. I have the grey ready for you. And for you, my lord, the chestnut."

Uilleam, Grand Chancellor of the Realm, nodded stiffly. Shianan supposed privately that the man did not appreciate this part of his office. General Kannan had flatly refused this year to ride, citing a troubling old injury.

Shianan would never decline such an opportunity.

Two slaves stood at the head of each horse. They would walk beside the animals, ready in case of accident and careful to protect the valuable horses from any mishap. Philip was a royal slave, charged with the royal horses. He was privileged, but he carried a great deal of responsibility.

Philip gave an order, and the slaves turned the horses, one holding each head while the other moved to the opposite side to steady the animals. Philip himself offered his hands for mounting, first to the Grand Chancellor, who stepped into the cupped hands with a grimace and heaved himself reluctantly onto the back of the red horse. The mare flicked her ears with annoyance.

Chancellor Washe mounted more smoothly and stroked the

grey's neck as he settled into the saddle. Shianan watched motionless as Septime stepped into Philip's hands and onto the horse.

One day, he would ride a horse for the review, he vowed. One day, Ariana would see him on a horse.

"Sir." A breathless soldier jogged to face Shianan and saluted, one arm across his chest.

"Yes?"

"The king and his counselors are ready, sir."

Shianan nodded. "Thank you. Find your place." He glanced at the mounted men. "With my lords' permission?"

Septime nodded. "Go ahead, Becknam."

The front rows of soldiers noted the runner's arrival and fell still. The yard quieted as the effect rippled rearward. Shianan walked out to the center of the arrayed front line, feeling hundreds of expectant eyes on him. Nine hundred heads swiveled to follow his movement.

Shianan faced them. "Today we display ourselves to our king, demonstrating our strength to His Majesty, our people, and ourselves." He paused, looking over the erect, attentive soldiers. He smiled. "Do it well."

He turned and started back to his place. There was a brief moment of silence as the men waited for the rest of the speech, and then as they realized that was it, a cheer went up. Shianan allowed himself a grin as he reached Torg.

"Quick and neat, sir?" the captain asked cheerfully.

"A long speech is traditional, I suppose," Shianan admitted, "but if there's anything lacking, I can't instruct them in a few minutes. And if they've learned it well, they won't be improved by my lecturing." He glanced back at the laughing soldiers. "They're good men."

"That they are, sir." Torg straightened. "Ready?"

Shianan nodded. "Spears up."

"Spears up!" shouted Torg, and the order was repeated down the ranks. The soldiers shifted into parade posture, their weapons displayed proudly. Shianan watched the three horses move out and then followed at a respectful distance. Torg marched on his right, a half step behind, and Captain Alanz on his left. Behind them the first ranks moved forward, an array of trained might.

Their path would take them from the assembly ground to the broad thoroughfare beneath the palace, where the royals could look down upon the army, past the Wheel of the Circle, and then out into Alham's street, where the people could cheer and buy treats in a festival air.

Nobles, servants, merchants, and soldiers not included in the review flanked their path, calling cheers or jests. A few boys made taunts and then ran, secure in their belief that the soldiers would have forgotten them after completing their parade. They reappeared a moment later, emboldened by their success, and threw a small hail of pebbles.

"Alanz," Shianan prompted.

"My pleasure, sir." The captain stepped out of the line and started toward the boys, who yelped and bolted.

Shianan's gut tightened as they approached the royal balcony, decorated with banners. His men were under orders to keep their eyes forward, but he could not resist the urge to roll his own upward, straining at their sockets, to see what he could of the king's response.

They were all there—King Jerome, Queen Azalie, the two princes, flanked by solemn servants. Alasdair was pointing and saying something to the others over his shoulder. Shianan ignored him and tried to see the king, less visible behind the railing. He looked sober but pleased, Shianan guessed.

Alanz rejoined them. "Problem solved, sir."

And then they were past the balcony and marching toward the Wheel. As they circled the round building, Shianan scanned the crowds for Ariana or her father. They should have been easy to pick out, but there seemed to be black and white everywhere that he looked.

Now he could see the advance soldiers a short distance ahead, clearing the streets of over-excited children and indifferent vendors. Beyond them, the gates opened to Alham itself and packed streets of people glad of an excuse for festivity.

Septime's horse leapt to one side, startled by something, but the two slaves quickly brought him back to a prancing trot. The horses rarely saw real battle, of course, though in war the highest officers might have a horse for rapid movement behind the lines, but they made a good image for the people.

They passed through the gate and into the loud streets. The waving crowd alarmed the horses, but the slaves were skilled and kept them under soothed control. Shianan allowed himself a smile. These were the ones they worked to protect, these people who trusted the king and the mages and the soldiers to keep them safe from Ryuven and invaders. Even the boys who threw stones—all of them, he served them.

The parade marched on, and Shianan relaxed. They had looked good before the king, he thought. It had gone well. Now they had only the public sparring this afternoon, and he trusted that would go smoothly.

There! Ewan and Ariana Hazelrig, dressed in their mages' robes and waving and cheering from the side of the street. They gave Shianan broad smiles. He felt himself grin in return, and it didn't fade as he passed them.

The parade march ended without incident back at the assembly ground. Septime and the chancellors dismounted, and the horses were led safely away. Septime came to stand beside Shianan, who straightened. "Sir?"

The general glanced at the departing chancellors. "How'd we look?"

"Very good, sir, I think."

"I hope so." Septime looked over the ranks of waiting men, still at attention. "Any reason we can't release them?"

"None, sir. They've earned it."

"Then we'll see them in two hours." He gave Shianan a significant look. "Make sure you eat something this year."

"Yes, sir."

Septime departed, and Torg frowned at Shianan. "You missed a meal last year?"

"I was busy," muttered Shianan. "I didn't have time to eat. I ended up beside the general during the sparring, with him and me both listening to my stomach rumbling."

Torg suppressed a smile. Shianan returned a tight smile of his own and turned back to the soldiers. He had indeed been busy last year. He'd also been too nervous to eat. He cleared his throat. "Men dismissed."

Torg relayed the order, and the released soldiers began to disperse. Shianan sighed with relief. Good so far, and he thought the selected men would perform well in the sparring. He could perhaps eat something after all.

He didn't pause long, though, simply taking a meat pie to nibble as he went to the exhibition site. He checked the posted matches, confirming all he'd chosen were listed. But then he saw his own name at the base of the sheet.

He turned abruptly and nearly collided with Septime. "Sir! I was just on my way to find—"

"Is it about your participation?" The general glanced toward the list. "You were specially requested, Becknam. You do have something of a reputation."

Shianan hesitated, surprised. "Requested?"

"Defend us well, Becknam." Septime smiled and moved on.

Shianan hadn't planned to fight, but it was no great hardship. He could acquit himself well against the others in the list. But who had requested his inclusion in the demonstration?

CHAPTER FORTY-NINE

The crowd was cheering, but Shianan could see quick openings where one participant was tiring; the match would end soon. Then Shianan would be called to the dais for his own match.

In a flurry of movement the fight was over, a wooden sword pressed to a man's neck and a quick hand signal to yield, and the watching crowd cheered approval. The display was nominally to inspire confidence in the army's skill, but it was as much entertainment as anything else.

Shianan pulled an arm across his chest to loosen his shoulder. Drummond had won, so Shianan would face him for the next match. Drummond was quick on his feet, but he was typically wide in his defense.

"Commander Shianan Becknam, Count of Bailaha!" announced the ring steward, his voice booming across the plaza. "The Demon Commander, they call him, the hero of Dalm Valley, the feared and fearless officer who saved the Shard of Elan, the slayer of Ryuven, this is your Commander Shianan Becknam!"

"You don't have to make all that fuss about it," muttered Shianan as he climbed to the dais, his ears burning.

But the crowd liked it, cheering and shouting approval. The steward eyed Shianan. "Go on, give them something," he urged. "They want a show."

So Shianan hesitantly waved. The cheers grew louder, liking his reluctance. His ears continued to burn.

A long, shrill whistle cut through the noise of the crowd, falling into a series of trilling notes. Shianan turned and saw Ariana jumping and waving, her face bright with enthusiasm over her black robes. He felt himself flush hotter.

"A weapon for the commander!" called the steward, and someone threw a wooden sword for Shianan to catch. "And a worthy opponent!" He gestured widely to the deeply tanned swordsman climbing into the ring. "Begin!" He backed out of the way.

This wasn't Drummond. The strange swordsman was tall, broad, and in no mind to patiently assess Shianan or the ring. He lunged immediately and swept his wooden blade through where

Shianan had been standing. Shianan edged away from the wooden rail, giving himself room to move. Who was this challenger?

The swordsman moved again, fast and fierce. Shianan parried and the impact stung his hands. He did not return a counter-attack before the swordsman swung again, and Shianan slid out of range with a defensive thrust meant only to guard his distance.

He came with an overhand downswing, moving fast. Shianan sidestepped, using his feet more than his blade, and watched the swordsman beat his waster into the rail with an alarming crack of wood. Shianan caught his breath. This was no friendly exhibition match with pulled blows and measured attacks. Even a wooden sword could be deadly with such force.

But that blow was an opening. Shianan's waster cut at the man's back over the loose vest and rang against steel. Shianan leapt back as the man spun, unfazed by the blow. There was a slim cuirass beneath that loose vest, Shianan noted grimly. He wore light leather himself, to pad any connecting blows, but steel was another matter. Who was this man?

Shianan circled to the center of the ring and watched the swordsman come again. Forego the torso—there didn't seem to be any armor on the man's legs. He watched as the man moved and then lunged, slicing toward the thigh. The blow connected and he was rewarded with a wince from his opponent. "What is this?" Shianan hissed as he retreated. "What are you doing?"

A gasp from the crowd saved him. He whirled and barely parried a wide swing from a second swordsman, backing desperately so that he could see both of them. What was happening? Was this some sort of test, or did they really mean to injure him? Could he stop them somehow, demand a halt? At least the first seemed momentarily slowed by the blow to his leg, but that would pass.

He could not face them both with a sword, that was certain. No matter their intentions, a single sword could not defend against two. He thrust at the nearer of the two and risked a glance over his shoulder. There, at the edge of the dais, between the railing and the crowd... "Kote!" he shouted. "Spear!"

Kote grinned and threw the polearm butt-first. Shianan snatched it from the air, letting the wooden waster fall, and in the same continuous motion dropped his weight behind the spear and drove it into the second swordsman. He grunted with the impact, his own waster passing harmlessly before Shianan's face. Briefly Shianan regretted that he'd had only the butt of the spear.

No, he corrected himself. This was an exhibition match, entertainment for the masses. Kote was grinning. He did not think the battle was real.

Kote wasn't facing the strength of those blows himself. There was something more here.

Shianan whipped the spear to a more versatile position and faced the first swordsman, who hesitated at the new weapon. A polearm had greater reach than a sword and could be faster. The man glanced at his companion and edged to one side, separating to gain advantage.

They would wear him down a bit at a time, wearying him between the two, or they would converge at once and crush him. He had to take one of them down first. Shianan shifted his grip on the spear and attacked.

The first must have expected the sudden appearance of another opponent to have stymied Shianan, for he was not quite prepared to defend himself. Shianan snapped the spear downward over the wooden sword so that it rapped against the dais and stepped in, reversing the spear and dropping it into the man's neck—but he ducked away and the spearhead cracked against the steel hauberk. Shianan did not take the time to strike again but spun to face the second swordsman he knew would be coming. Shianan could only deflect his counter-attack before slipping away from the first swordsman again.

Blood roared in his ears, drowning the calls of the crowd. This was no mere match, this was battle. The world contracted around them.

He feinted high, letting the swordsman raise his weapon to meet the spearhead, but the other end of the shaft flew into the man's thigh. Shianan snarled—he'd meant for the knee. He started for a blow to the head but realized he had no time, whirling instead behind his opponent as the second came at him. He shoved the first man, who stumbled but avoided the second. Shianan jabbed the spear to buy himself distance and saw the swordsman's free hand reach for the shaft.

Was that a cuff on the man's wrist? He seized the spear and gave Shianan a savage grin.

Shianan fell backward, away from the first swordsman, and cranked the spear like a gear. The man's arm twisted with the motion and Shianan shifted his weight, his eyes on the vulnerable joint just below the iron cuff—

The world exploded with a deafening crash. Shianan felt himself falling but could not seem to catch himself. Where was the swordsman? He reached out with his free hand, keeping a tight grip on the spear with the other, and brushed wood. His sword! He tried to grab it, but it whirled away.

Hands took him and he reacted, throwing his arms out and trying to duck. But he could not find his balance and the arms moved with him. "Steady, steady," Torg's voice came near his ear. "It's all right. Just stand."

Shianan blinked, willing his vision to return. What had happened?

"...And that is the power of a Mage of the Circle!" pronounced the ring steward cheerfully. Shianan heard the crowd murmuring and cheering tentatively. He looked around, seeing fuzzy shapes moving.

"Take a bow, sir," Torg advised. "Careful—keep your arm on me."

The world swirled again as he dipped his head and clutched at Torg's sleeve. "Where are they? Who are they?"

A figure in black moved beside them as Torg drew Shianan to the edge of the dais. Ariana clapped her hands over her head, smiling broadly, and a geyser of golden sparks burst over the ring, cascading over the crowd in a glittering shower. There were sounds of delight.

"Steady down the side, sir."

Shianan eased himself over the edge, wondering why he felt so dizzy. He realized the two swordsmen were beside him, rubbing alternately their eyes and ears. Soldiers ringed them all, keeping the crowd back and creating space as they started forward. They did not have far to go. The first door they met led to a storage area which General Septime had seized for his purpose.

"Get in here!" he snapped. Shianan straightened and drew himself to attention, still blinking. Septime swore viciously. "What was all that?"

Shianan was struggling for how to explain what he didn't understand, when he realized Septime had turned on the two strange swordsmen. They cast him resentful looks. "Don't take on with us," the first one protested. "We were doing just as told, and we want paid for it."

"Told by whom?" demanded Septime.

"Our orders," he answered irritably. "You don't think we'd come this far for this kind of thing without an agreement, do you?" He nudged his companion. "Give him the letter."

The second swordsman withdrew a folded paper and passed it wordlessly to Septime. Shianan noted the wrist cuffs.

Septime looked at the unfolded paper. "This is a royal seal."

The first swordsman nodded. "I know. And you'll note we're to be paid?"

Septime turned his eyes on Shianan, who stiffened. "What do you know of this?"

"Nothing, sir. I did not know even that I was to participate until this afternoon, as you saw." His mind was spinning. A royal seal on orders to fight him in the exhibitions? But the king would not... would he?

The ring steward raised his hands and began shaking his head even before Septime turned to him. "I had only a note saying Becknam was to fight. Nothing else. I thought it was from Becknam."

"From me?"

"You did not bother to confirm that?" Septime's expression showed what he thought of this. He turned back to the swordsmen. "How did you receive this?"

The first took back the letter, passing it to the slave. "Just a runner. We weren't far, as we'd stopped in Birmingtown on our way to find fresh service. We thought a royal seal would be trustworthy."

"Only the king may use this," muttered Septime. He looked hard at Shianan. "Why would the king be bringing mercenaries to fight you publicly?"

Shianan shook his head, bewildered. "I don't know, sir."

"Becknam, if you've—"

The door opened and Ariana pushed inside. "Is he all right? What was that?"

Shianan looked toward her and then remembered the general, jerking himself to attention again. But Ariana had already seen him and started toward him. "What happened? Are you all right? I was worried about the concussion, but it wasn't... What's wrong? It should have worn off by—"

Shianan flicked his eyes toward her and then to Septime again, hoping she'd understand. She hesitated and looked to the general.

Septime sighed irritably but his voice was even when he spoke. "My lady mage, thank you for your help. Obviously our own efforts weren't going to interrupt anything safely, and your display made a nice finish to the exhibition. However, we're facing a muddle of orders at the moment."

"It's not so muddled," disagreed the swordsman. "It's plain we were hired to come and fight. Someone needs to pay us our coin, and then we'll go."

"Your letter says to fight Shianan Becknam," Septime read. "Two hundred fifty pias."

The first swordsman shrugged. "Not bad money for a single fight."

"But it says only Shianan Becknam," Septime repeated, frowning. "A proper dispatch would have called him the Count of Bailaha, or at minimum Commander Becknam."

The swordsman frowned. "Are you saying that isn't the royal seal?"

Septime shook his head. "No, it is. But I don't know why this would be written so."

Prince Soren had taken to calling him Becknam, a more personal use of his own name, but he would surely still use his proper titles in correspondence, and he was not authorized to use the royal seal, anyway. The king called him Bailaha, the title he had bestowed upon Shianan; it seemed unlikely he would have left it out.

Septime straightened. "I think you should remain close until we have clarified this," he said meaningfully to the swordsmen.

"Oh, we aren't going anywhere 'til we're paid properly," answered the first swordsman. He eyed the soldiers about the room. "You don't need to worry about that. We did a job, and we want paid."

"Then you won't mind going with these men, will you?" Septime smiled tightly. "That way we'll know where to find you when we have your payment."

The second swordsman tensed, throwing a quick glance at the first, who hesitated a moment and then gave an uneasy grin. "Why not make it simpler?" he agreed with false amiability. "Lead the way, gentlemen."

Septime turned to the rest of the room. "Clear out, all of you. Where's Petar? Becknam, stay here—I want to talk with you."

"Yes, sir."

Ariana cast a quick look at Shianan, her face worried. He tried to give her a reassuring smile, but his face didn't seem to move. She flicked her eyes toward the general and then mouthed something

Shianan couldn't catch before she followed the soldiers out.

Septime turned to Petar, who'd worked his way to his master. "I desire to speak with the king at his convenience. And 'soats, get that to him before he gets a summons to us. Move." Petar nodded and left hurriedly.

The storage room was empty of people now but for Shianan and Septime. Shianan stood still, waiting for the general to speak first.

Septime released his breath. "Did you know, Becknam, that the king was watching our exhibition matches?"

Shianan twitched. "No, sir, I did not."

"I thought not to tell you, when I saw that you were on the list. I thought it would be easier on your nerves." He smiled grimly. "You're a good man in battle, Becknam, but you're half a man before the king. I guess that's to be expected. But I did not want you folding in your match."

Shianan flinched. "I'm sorry, sir."

"And now I have to go before His Majesty and explain what fiasco took his match. Either we interrupted a contest he arranged for you, or we lost control of our exhibition and covered it with a magic show." He frowned. "I assume you did not hear our orders to stand down?"

"No, sir, I didn't. I was thinking only of the fight."

"I thought as much. It would have been a messy finish without the Black Mage." He sighed. "Come on, then. I want to be there when the king agrees to see us."

"Yes, sir." Shianan followed obediently.

Half a man. Sweet all, did everyone see it?

They met Petar coming back along one of the upper corridors. "His Majesty will see you now, my lords."

CHAPTER FIFTY

Septime bowed to King Jerome. "Your Majesty."

"General." The king's eyes shifted to Shianan. "And Bailaha. Proud of your little escapade?"

Shianan bowed. "Sire, I did not have—"

"Bailaha." The king's voice cut through his protest and he gave a significant glance to the floor.

Shianan's temper flared. This had been no fault of his. Even if the king had brought the swordsmen to fight him, Shianan had risen to the challenge and faced them both. He bit his lip and bowed low, but he did not kneel.

"Your Majesty, I am sure you saw that the exhibition this afternoon did not go as we had planned. Commander Becknam was—"

"Trying to show off for his friends?"

Septime hesitated. "I don't believe so, Your Majesty. In fact, neither Becknam nor I expected his opponents—either of them. And when we questioned them, they had a letter from you, it seems."

"What?"

Septime produced the relevant paper. "It has the royal seal."

"Let me see that." Jerome frowned at the paper. "I did not send for them!"

"Who could use the seal for such a thing? And if someone had forged a seal, why waste it on a simple exhibition match?"

The king's eyes widened. "I—the little—I have an idea of the answer." He scowled. "I know this writing."

Alasdair. Alasdair had stolen his father's royal seal and hired two mercenaries to challenge Shianan in the exhibition match.

For one moment Shianan wondered if they'd been meant to do more, but he dismissed the thought. The letters had mentioned only a fight, and they had not seemed as agitated as they should have been if apprehended in killing a man. No, they were meant to defeat Shianan publicly, that was all. And if he had not borrowed the spear and if the match had not ended abruptly, they might well have done it, publicly and painfully. Those blows, even with a blunted blade, could have shattered his arm.

Septime had not yet grasped it. "Your Majesty?"

"I'll take care of it," Jerome answered irritably. "So Bailaha did not know he would face two swordsmen when he fought?"

Shianan grasped at the hint of approbation. "No, sire. Not until they were both in the ring."

"You got that spear quickly enough."

"I knew I needed another weapon if I was to defend myself successfully." Another weapon, and perhaps some armor of his own...

"Could you have defeated them with your second weapon, had you not been interrupted?"

Shianan hesitated. He wanted desperately to present himself well to the king, but caution overruled. "It is difficult to say, my lord," he hedged. "An exhibition match is not a battlefield, and neither is certain."

King Jerome eyed him distantly. "I see."

Shianan looked down, wondering what he should have said differently.

Septime cleared his throat. "We have the strangers, but it seems they have committed no crime. They will be released."

The king nodded. "I suppose we cannot fault them for answering what they believed was a royal summons."

"They were quite insistent on their payment, Your Majesty. What should be done about that?"

"What did he offer them?"

"Two hundred fifty."

The king's face darkened. "Presumptuous! But it's over our own seal... Pay the men, and I'll take it from his allowance."

Shianan looked away as Septime nodded.

"And we should give something to the Black Mage. She did well, interrupting the fight and gentling the spectators with a display. We should send her a gift." He frowned. "I am unsure what would be appreciated."

"Flowers," put in Shianan quickly. "Fruit and flowers, from the hothouses. They are difficult to find fresh in the market." His face grew hot.

Neither man seemed to notice his embarrassment. "Yes, that's an idea," Jerome agreed. "Good. See to it." He looked at Shianan. "And I should compliment the two of you, as this morning's presentation went well. Our army is something for pride, and our people know it. Thank you."

Shianan flushed again. He glanced at Septime and bowed low with the general. "We are glad to serve, Your Majesty," Septime answered. "But as usual, it was Becknam who saw to most of the review."

"Bailaha," Jerome corrected mildly. "And he did well."

Shianan bowed again. Straightening, he caught the king's eyes, which flicked significantly toward the floor again. Shianan bent his head and dropped to one knee. He owed obeisance to his king.

"I only wish you had soundly defeated the two swordsmen," the king continued. "After so much rumor of the commander's abilities, it would have been satisfying to see it."

Septime glanced at Shianan. "We did not know the intentions of the two strangers, my lord, and thought it better to control the situation rather than allow your exhibition to become bloody."

"Of course. It was only a thought. Is there anything else, General?"

"No, Your Majesty."

"Then you may go."

Septime bowed and backed away, and Shianan rose and followed. Once safely out of the audience room, the general turned to face Shianan, looking as if he wanted to speak. Then he turned and started away, ignoring the pages and secretaries cluttering the antechamber. Shianan trailed him.

The king had been pleased with the morning's presentation. That was good. And he'd relented after he'd learned it was Alasdair who was responsible for the strange swordsmen and not Shianan. Shianan didn't know what to make of the king's disappointment in his failure to defeat the strangers immediately. It wasn't so simple.

Septime went to his own office, waving away the aide who tried to address him as he entered. "Close the door, Becknam."

Shianan did, his heart sinking. Then he turned and straightened before Septime.

"Fate above, man, what have you done? Why should the prince be working to shame you in public?" Septime looked agitated. "What were you doing?"

"I've done nothing, sir, nothing I can think of."

"Are you saying that Prince Alasdair simply woke one morning and decided to put mercenaries against you, without any provocation? That he had no reason to set a public challenge for you?"

Shianan had no answer.

"That was almost a disaster today—what if they had injured you? Or if you'd killed one of them during what was supposed to be a friendly entertainment for the people?" He eyed Shianan narrowly. "We can't afford a rift between the military and the prince. If he is trying to reach you, it will affect all of us." Septime crossed his arms. "You will not put the reputation or the efficiency of this army at risk because of your personal animosities."

Shianan clenched his fists, hiding them behind his legs. "Sir, I have not done anything to—"

"There must be something, Becknam. The prince did not choose this at random." He made a vague gesture. "Go. We both have work. And stay well away from Prince Alasdair."

"Yes, sir." Shianan left the office and closed the door, letting his hand rest on the worn wood a moment. The injustice of it burned, but there was nothing to do. Even if the general believed he had done nothing to antagonize Alasdair, the instructions must remain the same—do not allow a rift to form between the prince and the military.

He dropped his forehead against his hand on the door, closing his eyes. How would he ask now for permission to marry? Was the king pleased enough with the review that he would overlook the fight? Worse, did Shianan dare risk that somehow Alasdair would learn of Ariana—that he would find some new way to torment Shianan through her?

He wanted to see Ariana. He wanted to sit for ten minutes and be himself, nothing to anyone, neither commander nor bastard nor soldier. He missed Luca.

"Commander."

The voice made him jump, and he turned to see Torg standing a few paces away. He offered an embarrassed smile. "Sorry," he said unnecessarily. "I was just tired, after this morning and then the match."

Torg did not look convinced, but he did not offer to argue. "Do you have time, sir?"

Shianan exhaled. "What now?"

Torg shook his head. "No, sir, I only thought that I hadn't seen you take a proper meal." He shrugged. "It was the general's order that you eat. It's the duty of a captain to help his commander carry out his orders, and I thought I might buy us each a plate in the pub."

A bit of tension leaked from Shianan's shoulders. "Would that meal include ale?"

"At least two pints."

"Done." He ran his fingers through his hair and gingerly met Torg's eyes. "Thanks."

It was not late enough for the usual crowd, but the festival atmosphere had sent many patrons to the public rooms and taverns early. Torg and Shianan found a narrow table against a wall in the Brining Tankard and waved for service.

Shianan rubbed at his eyes, wondering if the ale would soothe his building headache. Torg gave him a concerned look. "How did it go? With the king, I mean?"

"The royal seal had been—borrowed," Shianan said softly, trusting the clamor of the room would keep the secret.

"Then it wasn't the king who hired the mercenaries?" Torg seemed oddly relieved. "You're sure?"

"Why would the king hire mercenaries against me? I'm his own commander."

Torg hesitated and then shrugged. "But king's oats, who would have the 'nads to use the royal seal?"

"Alasdair, though of course no one will know that."

Torg whistled. "Holy—and what did you do that he—"

"I didn't do anything!" snapped Shianan. "King's oats, I haven't done anything." He ran his fingers savagely through his hair. "He…" But he couldn't tell Torg that he'd been sworn to Alasdair's service, that the prince had seen him violently humiliated by the king, that Alasdair had no reason at all not to view Shianan as a ripe victim for bullying.

Torg shifted in his seat. "Sorry, sir. I didn't think that maybe you'd been asked that already."

Shianan shook his head. "No, I'm sorry. But I haven't done anything." He rested his forehead on his fists. "I was born, that's all."

"Look who's here." The first mercenary slid into the table next to them. "The great commander drinks with common men?"

"I drink where I please. Obviously they let you go."

The mercenary looked over his shoulder at the slave swordsman behind him. "We hadn't done anything wrong, after all." The slave moved and took a seat across from the first.

Shianan nodded toward him. "You know the Brining Tankard doesn't serve slaves?"

"Doesn't it? Well, it's fortunate they don't rate fashion, neither, and Mallach can keep his sleeves hanging long." The mercenary wore his own weapons now, and his motley assortment of mismatched clothing and weaponry bespoke his trade more clearly. He drew one foot onto the chair and rested his elbow on his knee. "So you're the demon commander. Odd. They talk you such a hero elsewhere, and almost the first I see you is getting chewed out by your officer." The mercenary bit at his thumb. "Aren't you a hero here? They said enough on it when they called you up today."

Torg bristled. "What you saw was just the general trying to sort out what you yourself had—"

"Oh, I don't mean it malicious. I was just thinking maybe they don't see things the same way. Wondering why." He put out a hand. "I'm Mannig. For hire, if you know anyone."

Shianan accepted it warily. "Mannig." He was trying to evaluate the man, who seemed somehow amiable in his rudeness. "Shianan Becknam."

"And you're lord of something, too."

"A count," Shianan answered evenly. "Bailaha."

"Nice." Mannig indicated the slave with a flick of his thumb. "This is Mallach. He's a good man, and I'm awfully glad you didn't break his wrist today."

Shianan raised an eyebrow. "You saw that coming?"

"Flames, I had it myself once." He held up his left hand. "Still not quite right. Never been glad to be leveled by a mage before, but it interrupted something that was going ugly quick."

Mallach nodded solemnly.

Mannig looked at Torg. "I mean no disrespect to your commander, here. He's got quite a name."

"I've known the commander a long time," Torg answered. "And I've known a lot of mercenaries."

Mannig grinned. "Some of us aren't as bad as all that." He took a deep drink of the ale as it arrived. Mallach drank, too, a bit of sleeve pinched between the tankard and his palm so it couldn't slip to show the cuff.

Shianan looked at his own ale, recalling another slave in the Brining Tankard.

"Commander." Mallach's voice was deep and unexpected. "You fight well."

Shianan looked at him, startled.

"What he means is," Mannig interjected, "we've heard a lot about you and we weren't sure we wanted to sign on for this. They say you're good, you know." He nodded toward Mallach. "He was supposed to come in a little faster, but he didn't. Said he felt bad coming behind in what was just a match for show, where you didn't have a reason to watch your back." He shrugged. "Can't say I blame him. But you didn't need much, did you? Flames, it was plain enough to see when you weren't fighting for show anymore." He grinned. "It was an honor to go with you, commander, your lordship."

Shianan felt he needed a moment to sort through Mannig's words. "Er, thank you."

"Your king has a lot of faith in you," Mannig said, sipping at his ale. "It's not many who would hire a couple of outsiders to surprise his champion in public. We didn't have orders to lose, you know." He shook his head. "Just odd to see your officer angry like that. I suppose the king straightened him out, though." He grinned. "But I guess you don't have to worry about that, do you? Got some extra help there?"

Shianan stiffened and looked away. "Not so much as that."

"Oh, nothing by that. Forget it."

Their meals arrived, and Torg made a sound of approval. Shianan took a long drink of ale.

Mannig gestured to their empty cups and the serving woman nodded. Then he turned back to Shianan. "That was a juicy cut of loin what came after you, though, fleshed out for a magicker," he said appreciatively. "Pike, I'd be glad to pack her! A tumble there would make up for a bit."

Shianan's shoulders went rigid. "Leave her be."

Mannig held up his hands in laughing placation. "Easy, commander! Nothing by that, either. Just admiring." He gave Shianan a narrow look. "Or don't you..." His voice trailed off and he took a quick drink.

Shianan was uncomfortably aware of Torg's eyes shifting between them. "Ariana Hazelrig is a Mage of the Great Circle."

"The Circle, eh? Pike. I suppose in a tiff she could scald off your stones easy as spending a penny." Mannig took a casual drink. "Still. Handful in all the right places, and she's got a tender place for you. Hard to resist tapping that cask."

Shianan turned his head, but Torg was already speaking. "Do you usually try to pick these fights? Or do you mean to finish what was interrupted this afternoon—one on one?"

Mannig's jaw tightened. Mallach shook his head subtly. Mannig took a breath and turned it into a sigh. "I can see I've stumbled upon something more than I thought. My apologies, commander, captain." He eyed his drink. "Still, must be awkward. Defeat the Ryuven, defend the kingdom, save the Shard, save the world, but can't take a woman to please yourself."

Torg started to speak, but Shianan gestured. They didn't need a public argument. The mercenary's comments were too ridiculous to merit response.

Defend the kingdom, but you can't please yourself.

That would change.

Mannig nodded toward Mallach. "We're off east, next. Mallach found something possible on the Wakari Coast for us. But if ever you need extra blades, lordship, we'd be more than honored to fight with you."

"We don't often call mercenaries," Shianan replied diplomatically, "but I'll keep you in mind." The Wakari Coast! But they would have no reason to know Luca, or his family.

Mannig caught the serving woman's eye. "Bring another round," he said. "We'll stand everyone a drink—even you, captain." He grinned. "Just to show we're not so bad."

CHAPTER FIFTY-ONE

Ewan Hazelrig hesitated as the crowd shifted and pushed, and he glanced over his shoulder. It was foolish, he knew. Tam knew the city, and if his slave boy form were delayed in the busy street, he could find his way home quickly enough. But Ewan felt a renewed responsibility for the Ryuven who had found his friend a prisoner.

That was part of the reason he had offered to help Tamaryl become Tam once more, to go and select himself the books he thought potentially useful from the Wheel's library. Ewan could have gone on his behalf, but he wanted Tamaryl to feel they were doing all they could. He had shared the reports on the last Ryuven raids, agreeing with Tamaryl that they seemed to have halted. When the Founding Festival had ended, Ewan wanted to follow up on those reports, particularly the last.

With most of the Circle outside for the festivities, there was no one to wonder at a slave poring over the priceless tomes. Tam had browsed many of the volumes as Ewan's famulus, and within an hour he had chosen those to carry back for further reading. Only one had Ewan forbidden; the Claire Ledger, chained to its lectern, was too rare and precious to leave the library and would be missed immediately. Most of the others Ewan could justify taking home, where they would research Subduing reversal and a possible escape through the renewed shield.

He felt a sharp corner from the books in Tam's arms as the slave boy was jostled against him. Tam murmured an appropriate apology to the passerby and tried to navigate to Ewan's side. "I always forget the crowding."

Ewan nodded. "The festival's a bit more festive each year. And the fights should be just ending. Some of this traffic is from that, no doubt."

"Lady Ariana went to watch?"

"She did. She's never seen real battle. Staged exhibitions still excite her."

"And the commander will be watching as well, no doubt." Tam did not quite conceal the bitterness in his voice.

"Yes." Ewan didn't spare him. "In fact, I saw he had been added

343

to the list of participants."

"Splendid," commented Tam sourly. "So he will fight a mock battle against mock opponents and come out a glorious victor, no doubt. How thrilling."

Another passerby stumbled against Tam, nearly knocking the precious books from his grasp. Tam scrabbled for them, keeping them precariously balanced in his arms, and the man growled a reproach as he cuffed the boy's head. Ewan turned to intervene, but the man was already moving away, talking with a companion. Tam, squinting against the blow, braced his chin on the books and shifted one back into position.

"Steady!" Ewan turned back anxiously. "Do you have those?"

Tam's face tightened. "I will not drop them, master."

The rebuke stung. Generally Tam had used the slave's address only when others observed them. Ewan knew the Ryuven was unhappy, but how could he blame him? And mentioning it would likely make him more uncomfortable. Instead he tried, "If you need a hand..."

Tam's reply was interrupted by a horn blast across the wide plaza. A man gifted with extraordinary lungs began to shout over the crowd. "This is your last opportunity, ladies and gentlemen, goodmen and goodwives, fishmongers and slaves! See the last Ryuven alive here—and see him die!"

Tam and Ewan came to a staring halt, ignoring the press around them.

"Here he is, the last Ryuven in all Chrenada! Your prisoner, and today you'll see him executed! No more bloody raids, no more—"

Tam started running, his fair hair flailing. Ewan bolted after him.

Parrin'sho was pushed onto the railed platform, staring wide-eyed about him. He seemed to be fighting for composure, his folded wings shifting frequently. His arms were securely shackled, chained to a heavy iron ball and a guard, so he would not escape into the air.

"Stop!" gasped Tam.

A half-eaten pie splatted against Parrin's face. The Ryuven recoiled, and a few other missiles flew onto the platform. A stone cut the Ryuven's forehead and opened a bleeding gash. The attached guard whirled as another vegetable struck him and snarled a warning at the jeering mob, which subsided as additional guards moved about the base.

An axeman climbed onto the stage, and the crier gestured to him. "Here for your—"

"Stop!" shouted Tam, shoving between the pressing crowd. "Stop!"

"Stop!" called Ewan, running after him and waving at the crier. "Wait, you can't—"

Two men seized Parrin and pressed him onto his knees, taking a handful of hair to bend him over a stained and jagged block of wood.

"Don't!" Tam shoved hard against someone in his path and the priceless grimoires tumbled to the ground. He seized spectators' clothing and tore himself through. "Don't do it! You can't!"

The axeman heaved his weapon overhead.

"No!"

The axe fell, and the mob screamed and cheered. Tam shrieked. Ewan made a desperate lunge and snatched the boy's tunic as the axe rose again. The guards holding the Ryuven turned their heads to avoid the spatter of blood. Ewan dragged Tam back, thrashing, and crushed him in his arms. The axe rose a third time and thudded dully into the wood.

"No," gasped Tam raggedly, beating his clenched fist into Ewan's chest. "No, no! This wasn't—he was supposed to be safe! You promised he would be safe!"

"I didn't know anything of this," Ewan tried, but he knew his explanation couldn't be heard, not now.

"Why didn't you stop them?" Tam bowed his head and struck Ewan again. "You're a mage! You're a *mage!* Why didn't you..."

Ewan held the boy among the scattered books, while around them the crowd called and cheered. Slaves carried the dead Ryuven away separately, a grey mage filled glass vials with blood, someone tripped over a book and cursed. Tam, partially concealed within the white sleeves, alternately pushed at Ewan and clung to him, and Ewan held him with the apology he could not say.

CHAPTER FIFTY-TWO

It felt strange to stand beside the road while other slaves worked at the wagons. Cole glanced at his master, a few paces away and preoccupied. Cole seemed to be left to himself for the moment, which suited him.

He lowered himself to the dead grass, his back to the road, and laced his fingers through the dry thatch. A few stalks of dried garlic flowers lay across the grass, no doubt dropped from a passing wagon. Remio's caravan included spices as well as furniture, foodstuffs, cloth, and more. Cole breathed deep, grateful he was not in the line behind him.

A part of him thought he should have served as labor in the caravan. If his master had meant to pay for his passage, perhaps he could have kept the difference as his first funds toward redeeming himself. Another part, though, relished his reprieve. He would work hard enough in their new home to support his master and his own precious savings.

For the dozenth time, he reviewed potential positions and what he might negotiate in hire. With his master's generous offer, he might achieve his freedom while young. He wouldn't be one of the broken and toothless old men sold for mere coppers, scraping seeds or other minor work until their eyesight failed and they were herded panicking into battle to slow the charge of an opposing army.

They had been traveling two days, and the hills were far less steep than when Cole had struggled with a heavy wagon. Only a few days more until he returned to the life of a draft slave, but the respite was welcome.

The wind carried a snatch of voice toward him, and he glanced to where his master stood in conversation with Marla. Cole didn't understand Luca's strange behavior toward the slave woman. Even if he did not savor rough love, it would not take much to convince her that she wanted it. It would be simple enough to avoid Isen's gaze; the man slept hard. But they had not, so far as he could tell, closed the distance. Cole shrugged. Perhaps his master waited for the privacy of their new quarters.

Wait—what was this? Cole grinned. Luca and Marla were

walking as they talked, moving along the road further from the forming camp. Perhaps they would choose the relative shelter of the woods. "Good fishing, master," Cole wished him under his breath. Lucky dog.

But they stopped, and Luca turned to face Marla, putting distance between them as he did so. Cole realized he did not mean to take her this time, either. "Pike, what a waste," he muttered. He shifted uncomfortably. He certainly wouldn't turn down any friendly accommodation.

He glanced in the other direction, still faintly nervous about sitting idle. A few dozen paces away, two of the caravan guards were in close discussion. They paused and looked toward him, and Cole averted his eyes. He was shirking nothing, he had done nothing wrong...

"You, slave." One of them approached and gestured. "Over here, near the line."

Cole hesitated, torn between avoidance and obedience. "But I am not a part of the line."

The guard's tone sharpened. "On your feet, brute, and in your place. I don't care that you haven't been in the line, you're in it now."

Cole got to his feet. Didn't they recognize him as Luca's servant? "My master is—"

The guard drew his sword and grinned. "Your master is Garl Asher now. Get in the line."

Cole stared, stunned and confused, as men began streaming from the woods, shouting and brandishing weapons. Other caravan guards cried with surprise and anger and ran to meet them as the slaves bunched together behind the wagons. Asher seized Cole's arm, shoving him toward the wagons. Then he impartially slashed the hamstring of a passing guard. "Esar! In the rear!"

Falten Isen stood against two attackers, holding them at bay with a scavenged polearm, and they could not seem to summon the courage to penetrate his defense. But a third bandit circled and struck him from behind, driving a sword up through his back. Isen gasped, fell, convulsed. Cole saw him die.

The second guard pointed. "Look there."

Cole followed the pointing finger and saw Luca and Marla running for the woods. Asher swore. "I thought everyone was in camp!"

Luca and Marla were beyond the ring of bandits and defending guards, trying for the sheltering trees. But Asher was far more swift. They were passing the first wagon when Luca pushed Marla forward with a shout and whirled, seizing the trader's staff which stood ready in every caravan wagon. He crouched to meet Asher.

Even at this distance, Cole could read his master's uncertainty. He would never stand against the charging guard—

But then Luca whipped the staff overhead and ran hard at Asher, forcing him to pause in his chase after Marla and defend himself. He blocked the first strike with his short sword and drove directly into Luca, who retreated with his staff flashing. Cole could not tell which of them had the advantage. But then Asher stepped inside the blurring hemisphere of Luca's staff and smashed his pommel against Luca's temple.

Luca dropped as if struck by lightning, his staff bouncing away. Asher stepped over him and followed in the direction Marla had run.

Steel jabbed at Cole's ribs and he jumped. "Move," snapped a bandit, safe at the end of a polearm. "In the line and on your knees."

Cole raised his hands. He could not see his master's body from the center of the camp. The point raked his ribs and he flinched away, kneeling as his pulse pounded hard through his ears. For a moment he thought of surging upward and choking the man, but there was the length of a polearm between them, and what difference did it make to a slave who led the caravan?

Around him caravan guards fell to bandits or the traitors. The draft slaves pressed close together, huddling beneath a wagon to avoid the fighting. Travelers who had bought caravan passage for comfort and safety shrieked and bunched close, clutching small valuables or makeshift weapons. When the bandits finished with the guards and converged on the group, most threw down their weapons in terrified surrender. A few charged desperately, and as Cole watched they were efficiently suppressed.

The attackers did not kill, though, if they could simply disarm or disable. In moments the fighting ended, and bandits began prodding together the slaves and freemen alike. "Give up your riches," came the call. "Coins and jewels!"

"You!" Cole jumped and looked at the guard Asher, stalking toward him. "On your feet, I have work for you. You, too, over there. I want those wagons gathered close. Esar! We need to sort the most valuable cargo into two or three wagons. I don't think we can afford to move more than that."

"But Asher, we've got all these to use."

"Too slow," Asher snapped. "Get to work. You slaves, with me."

Cole and another slave obediently got into the shafts of the outlying wagons and dragged them together, panting with the effort of moving a four-man wagon with only two, but it was a short distance and Cole thought Asher would brook no protest. He scanned the road's shoulder but saw no sign of Luca or Marla.

Asher caught him looking as he finished with a wagon of bales of cloth. "Wondering what happened to him?" He jerked his chin for Cole to follow and went to the next wagon. Cole stood a few paces back, glancing worriedly as Esar came to stand beside him. The second traitor guard looked impassively at Cole and then announced, "That's everyone."

"Except that girl," Asher growled. "Pity, she would have sold well." He reached into the wagon and seized a handful of cloth, rolling an unresisting body over the rear. Luca hit the ground hard, his limbs twisting under him or sprawling to the side. Blood marred one side of his head. Cole stared. Was he dead?

No, not dead. Luca moaned and stirred. Asher grinned. "Doesn't look so important now, does he?" He drew a knife and bent over Luca.

"No!" Cole gasped.

Asher laughed. "Nah. He's no profit dead." He slit the laces of the shirt and reached inside. "This, though, this is profit." He withdrew the flat wallet, cutting the cord which held it to Luca's belt. "What have we here? Some coins, nothing much, and what's this?"

Asher withdrew the parchment from the wallet, making Cole tense. That was Luca's...

"Inheritance?" Asher squinted at the paper, frowning at the more difficult words. "Flames, we've got a rich prize here." He grinned.

Luca's free arm moved weakly to his chest, as if feeling for the wallet. Asher glanced down. "You looking for this?" He kicked Luca, making him grunt.

Cole stood immobile. This was no different than observing a beating as an overseer, he told himself. No different.

Asher looked at Cole. "This one was your master, right?" He grinned. "You've probably dreamed of doing that yourself." He kicked Luca again, who moaned and curled to protect himself. "Want to try it?"

Cole made himself speak. "What will you do with us, my lord?"

Asher liked the honorific. "Profit off you, of course. Auction you away. Not much change for you, just a change of scenery. Benefit, really." He sneered at Luca. "Too bad for him, though. Must chafe to wake up and find yourself a slave."

Cole would be sold again, as draft labor most likely, away from his new master and his chance at freedom. There was little chance of salvation.

Asher tipped his head to regard Cole. "He's a big enough beast," he said to Esar. "Our contacts in Salfield would like to see him."

Cole's chest tightened. "I am a trained overseer. I'd bring a better price for that."

"Oh? You're right, that's considerably more profit. And of course you'd rather hold the whip than sweat under it." He grinned. "An overseer, though? Or you just trying to avoid the salt flats?"

"I have been an overseer ten years under three masters, my lord," Cole answered quickly, "in caravans and in site labor."

"I see. Good." Asher nodded toward Luca's huddled form. "Then get this out of my way and into the line. We'll cuff him tonight, and I want him sold tomorrow." He turned and moved away to the next wagon.

For one insane moment, Cole considered flight, but the armed men around him dissuaded him. He walked stiffly to Luca and crouched beside him. "Master? Can you hear me?"

Luca groaned. "Far..."

Cole didn't know what he meant, but at least he was partly conscious. He looked over Luca with an overseer's efficient eye: no broken limbs, only the bruising from the kicks and the head wound. Assuming his brain was intact and the kicks hadn't ruptured anything, he would recover.

"Cole..."

Cole grasped his master beneath the armpits and heaved. Luca cried—had Cole missed a broken bone?—and choked as he righted. Cole swore as he swayed, unable to keep his feet. "Master! Do this!" He looked toward the growing line of captives. "This way."

He more than half-carried Luca and deposited him on the edge of the group. Eyes followed them, wide with apprehension. The overseer in Cole noted they would be easy to intimidate into obedience.

Luca groaned. "I want to be sick," he breathed, collapsing as

351

Cole lowered him. He bent so that his forehead rested on the trampled grass. "My head."

"Give it time," Cole advised, but he knew almost nothing of healing. What if the blow to the head had damaged Luca permanently?

"New overseer!" barked a voice. Cole turned and saw Asher waving to him.

He rose and went to the bandit. "My lord?"

"Prove yourself and keep out of the salt harnesses. I want these new slaves tied and orderly. We'll reach a friendly forge tonight and cuff whatever's not done already. I want to make the noon auction at Cascais." He dismissed Cole with a jerk of his head. "Move."

Cole hesitated. "The injured won't make good time tonight. If they're put into wagons—"

"Did you bother your previous masters with petty details?" Asher snapped. "Get them in cuffs and to Cascais, and I want them on the block. This isn't your typical trade stable and I have no interest in keeping anyone back for a higher price later. I need to change evidence into hard coin, and quick. You can move them, or you can be one of them. Is that clear?"

"Yes, my lord."

"Then go."

CHAPTER FIFTY-THREE

"Your lordship," Ewan Hazelrig greeted with mild surprise. "Becknam. Do come in. I heard about the demonstration fights—there's nothing more wrong, I hope?"

"No, it's fine. In fact, that's part of why I've come." Shianan looked at Ariana, who'd come to the entry passage with a welcoming smile. "These are for you." He unwrapped the flowers—the hothouse workers had done a better job of it than he had—and held them up for viewing.

"Oh, they're beautiful! Wherever did you find them?"

"They're not from me," he said, almost regretting his honesty after her pleasure. "They came from the royal hothouses, along with these." He lifted a little box of fresh fruits. "They're a gift, in gratitude for your actions this afternoon, interrupting the fight and entertaining the spectators." He grinned sheepishly. "Apparently I was difficult to distract."

She laughed. "You had other things on your mind, yes. But are you all right? I was worried when they marched you all away."

"That was General Septime trying to sort it out. I'm fine, thank you."

She gathered the flowers. "I'll find water for these. And you may have some credit for carrying them." She went into the kitchen.

Hazelrig cleared his throat. "There's a rumor the king hired mercenaries to challenge you. Is there anything to that?"

Shianan shook his head. "No, it wasn't the king." He dropped his voice. "It's nothing about—that. The Shard."

Hazelrig nodded. "Good."

Shianan shifted uncomfortably. "I don't see—Tamaryl, and the other one."

Hazelrig's expression faltered. "The last Ryuven prisoner was executed today. Tamaryl didn't take it well." He looked toward the kitchen. "Ariana was distressed by the news as well, but she's putting on a brave face at the moment."

Shianan's stomach clenched. His errand was difficult enough without the burden of an execution.

Ariana returned with a vase overflowing with bright flowers.

"Let's put them here, I think. Won't you sit down?"

"Actually..." Shianan's muscles tightened. This was not the day, not after the match and the reprimands, but if the king had liked the review, then Shianan had to act quickly to take advantage of his good favor. He would defeat the Ryuven, he would defend the kingdom, he would save the Shard. He would act on his own happiness.

He looked toward Hazelrig. "Actually, I'd hoped to speak with Ariana privately."

Hazelrig raised an eyebrow. "Oh?" One corner of his mouth twitched. "I suppose I have enough work in my study to keep me occupied for a time." He nodded to them. "Good evening."

Ariana looked after him and then back at Shianan, her eyes widening. "Do you want to sit down?"

He shifted his weight awkwardly. "I think I couldn't," he confessed. His palms were sweating. Dear Holy One, what would he say?

She licked her lips. "I think I'd better." She perched on the edge of the nearest seat, where Shianan had sat the first time he came to their house to speak of Tam.

He could not afford distraction now. He had to risk it, had to speak with her. "My lady mage," he began, his voice odd in his ears, "I must—I must be utterly frank with you. May we speak plainly?"

She nodded.

"My lady mage, I—"

"Ariana."

He blinked at her.

"Ariana. I'm Ariana, and you're Shianan. You cannot keep an honorific between us at this late stage. You said you would speak plainly."

"Ariana." He gulped. "Ariana, I said before... I must know— what is between you and the Ryuven."

That wasn't at all what he'd meant to say, and he nearly cursed aloud. Yes, of course, he was anxious to know why she helped Tamaryl, whether she favored the Ryuven or Shianan or indeed either of them, but that was not what he meant to ask, and not at all how he would have asked had he meant to.

Ariana was visibly taken aback. "What do you mean? I was there for only... Or do you mean Tamaryl?"

Shianan pushed at his hair. "Yes, Tamaryl. What is he to you, that you'd risk yourself and your father for him?"

Ariana straightened. "He is the friend who risked himself for my father and me—and for his own friend, trapped here within the shield." Her tone grew suspicious, defensive, indignant. "What exactly do you mean?"

He was such a fool. "I mean, if I thought of asking...."

Now Ariana looked angry. "I will have whatever friends I please, Shianan Becknam, regardless of whether you approve of them. I know you must hate the Ryuven, and I wish that weren't so, because I do love Tamaryl even if he is the Pairvyn. He is my dear friend and I owe him my life. Maru, too, cared for me when I was helpless in the Ryuven world, and now he is helpless here in my world. They deserve better than a public axing to please a festival crowd. Is that what you wanted to know? Did you mean to ask if I would distance my friends?"

"I—"

"I won't. I would no more abandon them than I would abandon you when some brute refers to you as the bastard. I hold my friends more dear than that. Do you understand?"

Shianan looked at her a moment, his chest burning, and then he looked away and began to chuckle sadly.

"Shianan!"

"Yes, my lady mage, I understand." He did. It was clear now why he was fascinated by this woman who stood too passionately by her convictions while he bowed to pressure. "I am sorry to have upset you, Ariana. I did not mean to do so. I would not ask you to give up your friends, even the Ryuven."

"Then what did you mean?"

He shook his head. "I wish I had your bravery."

She caught his hands. "You are brave," she said, and her voice was low and serious. "I don't mean only in fighting the Ryuven, though obviously that's true. But you face—every day, you have—with the king—" She hesitated, open-mouthed and wide-eyed, as if she feared her own words. "Just, you're very brave, Shianan. And I am in awe of it."

He stared at her, unprepared for such open admiration. "I..."

She smiled at him, open and kind and strong like he wasn't.

He looked down and fought for breath. "I am not brave, or I could speak right now."

"I think sometimes we most fear those we most cherish," she said quietly. "It is easy to speak to someone whose opinion may not matter. But to someone whose respect we want, that's an entirely different consideration."

He blew out his breath. "I do care about the king's opinion. Perhaps too much." He tried to swallow. "But if you think I am brave, I will find a way to speak to him."

Her eyelids flickered. "About?"

Sweet all, he could not bear the shame of facing her if she accepted him now and then the king forbade it, leaving him helpless to act. He wanted desperately for Ariana to see him victorious, to see him with the strength she had, to stand by his own mind, and that meant he could not bare his vulnerable desire until he knew he could act on it.

Energy flooded him like the start of a battle, mixed with a new heat that flushed his entire body. He leaned close to her, breathing the scent of her. "I will speak to the king. Let me be brave and speak to the king."

Her eyes threatened to engulf him. "And then you'll tell me what it is you want to say?"

"I promise." He squeezed her hands between his. "I'm going now. Please, don't call me back. I am not brave enough to walk away from you."

She smiled. "Then I will wait until tomorrow." Her smile broke into a wide grin.

He wanted to kiss her—but he was not that brave, not yet. After he had conquered the king's audience. "Tomorrow," he confirmed, and then he reluctantly dropped her hands and backed away. "I'll come to your office in the afternoon, or possibly the evening. Good night!"

The chill night air bit at his flushed skin, but he hardly felt it. Now, he would prepare. He took a deep breath and closed his eyes, blocking the quiet street around him. The king could be generous toward him, yes, his title and Fhure proved that.

Tomorrow. He would chance it all tomorrow.

Maru eased back silently, hoping the floor would not squeak and betray him. He had not meant to spy, but the commander and the rika had been intent upon each other and had not noticed him as he drew back from a conversation which was clearly not to be interrupted.

He had not heard their words, but they had been so clearly a match, so close in intimate conversation, their postures conflicted and hopeful... He would not tell Tamaryl yet. His friend was occupied enough in finding their way home and grieving the loss of Parrin'sho. He did not need this fresh disappointment, too.

Maru hunched his mismatched wings and slipped up the stairs.

CHAPTER FIFTY-FOUR

Luca's head hurt, a hurt that reached down his spine and through his arms and about his stomach, so that if he moved he might be sick. Noise swirled about him dizzyingly.

His head itched somehow over the hurt, and he reached to touch it. But his motion was arrested by a blunt tug at his wrist, coinciding with another blunt tug at his other wrist.

Sharp fear raced through Luca, burning away pain and illness. He opened his eyes and stared at the iron shackles binding his arms. He lay on his side in straw, facing a wooden wall. A light chain snaked through the scuffed straw, connecting his shackles to a ring in the wall. About him he heard the now-recognizable sounds of a slaver's stable.

Luca's head pounded in fresh agony. He was a slave again—he didn't know what had happened, but he was a slave again. He closed his eyes and tried to think. He remembered the caravan stopping, yes. And then the bandits had attacked. He had seen the guards fighting, and at first he had not realized that they were fighting among themselves, that some were in league with the bandits. That was when he had run with—

Marla! He jerked upright to look for her. But the stall whirled about him and his vision blurred darkly.

Hands caught his shoulder. "Easy, master," whispered a familiar voice. "Be careful."

Luca could barely hear him over the blood pounding in his ears. "Cole?"

"Shh, I don't want them to hear. How's your head?"

"Where's Marla?"

"She got away, master. But we didn't. Isen's dead."

Luca choked down nausea, relieved for Marla, grieved for Isen, frightened for them. He blinked his vision clear. "What happened?"

"Slavers and bandits. I'm overseer for their new slaves they're selling off. You're one of them." Cole's voice sounded worried. "I tried to put you in the back where you wouldn't go as fast. I said no one would want to see you until your head was better. But they want a low

359

price sooner rather than a high price later, so you don't have much time."

Luca reached for his chest and realized his tunic was torn. He felt inside the unlaced shirt and groped futilely for the wallet that should have been there. "Where's—"

"They took it, master. You can't buy yourself out. They took it."

Luca's head throbbed. His inheritance... "You've got to get me out of here, Cole."

"I can't, master. They took you half-dead to the smith and put the cuffs on you. I was only just able to put you here."

Luca reached two-handed to probe gingerly at the swollen wound and sucked his breath. "I can't do anything. I'm chained to a wall. You have to do this."

"I can't! I'm an overseer. If they think I'm helping you to escape..."

Cole was terrified of losing his tenuous safety. Luca rubbed dried blood from his fingers. "You're an overseer, and I'm just another slave waiting to sell. Why do you still call me master?"

Cole hesitated. "I don't know. You promised me a chance to buy my freedom. I wish..."

Voices rose from the next aisle as two men began to argue over who had seen a particular slave first.

Luca looked at Cole. "You have to release me. You're an overseer, no one here will question you. We can walk out, as if you're taking me somewhere else, and we can hide."

"Hide?" repeated Cole incredulously. "We can't hide! We can't walk out—"

"We don't have any other choice."

"Cole!" boomed a voice. Cole straightened and jerked to face the end of the row, and slaves on either side shifted. A man came about the corner, tall and stern, and a few of the slaves ducked their heads. Luca recognized the traitor caravan guard who'd pursued him and Marla. Cole tensed as he started forward to meet him. "My lord."

"Where have you been—" He stopped and looked at Luca, sitting uncomfortably upright. "Oh, so he's more or less awake now. Been rubbing his nose in it, I guess? No harm in that, I suppose. But you've got other work." He jerked his head to indicate behind him. "There's a man eight rows down who keeps arguing he's a freeman, keeps demanding we let him go. It's disturbing the customers. Go and shut him up, whatever it takes."

"Yes, my lord."

The bandit glanced at Luca. "At least you're sitting quiet. That's smart. You'll bring a better price if we haven't had to hush you."

Cole ventured, "My lord, if you—"

"Shut up and move. I've got enough to do without teaching you your work too. Get him quiet and behaving. And you, be ready to show for prospective buyers. I'm not renting space for you to play sickbed, I want you out and paid for. If you don't sell today, you'll auction tomorrow, so look sharp. Keep your head up so you don't look half-dead." He turned on Cole. "What are you doing still here, you overgrown swine? I can have you in a train for Salfield in twenty minutes. Move!"

"Yes, my lord." Cole cast a quick desperate look at Luca and then started away.

Luca looked down at his chained wrists. It was as before— worse than before. What would happen to him now?

CHAPTER FIFTY-FIVE

"The calm continues. There have been no confirmed Ryuven attacks since Groom Lake," Ewan Hazelrig said to the assembled Circle. "If there are other Ryuven still within the shield, they are not showing themselves."

No, Tamaryl would not. Not to this dangerous foe.

He eased back from the Wheel's meeting room door and set off down the curved corridor. There would be maps in the Wheel's library, which as a famulus he could enter without question. Once he had located Groom Lake, he would set out. He had to reach it before Mage Hazelrig, who would undoubtedly have reached the same conclusion: The Ryuven carrying the broken piece of the Shard of Elan must have died in the last raid, so that no others could leap across through the shield since. And the broken chip must be at Groom Lake.

The library's maps showed him the town's location, tantalizingly close to Alham. He could reach it in a day's travel if he hurried.

He did not wait for a new day. No one questioned the fair-haired slave boy as he jogged out the city gates and along the coast road.

Groom Lake was a misnamed fishing village on the sea. Tamaryl did not know yet how a slave boy would ask for the bodies of the slain raiders, but he was closer now than before.

He had shivered through the night, not dressed for a late-winter trek, but he had arrived before Mage Hazelrig. He had to move quickly to keep his advantage. But now, on the outer edge of the town, he had no idea of how to start.

"Hello, boy, are you lost?" A little girl waved to him. "Are you a slave? Where's your master?"

Years of practice allowed Tamaryl to react without undue humiliation or resentment. "I've lost him. We were going down to the coast road and I fell behind in the dark. Is this the way to Alham?"

She shook her head. "You've come the wrong way."

Tam widened his eyes. "They'll think me a runaway! I walked

363

all through the night trying to catch up, and now your town elders will beat me!"

"I thought slaves didn't mind being beaten."

Tamaryl didn't want to sort out this confused idea. "Can I sleep in your barn, just until I can start back to Alham? I don't want anyone to see me. Or where are the slaves kept here?"

She looked puzzled. "Fergus has a slave who helps on his boat. And I think the herbalist has one?"

Not every town relied on the slave economy so prevalent in the rest of Chrenada. Fishing was a business which tended to favor skill and family cooperation, unlike plowing or road-laying or hauling. Tam had come to a community where he would stand out rather than blending in. "Can I sleep in your barn?" he repeated.

She nodded. "Don't frighten Duchess. She's going to have her baby soon."

Duchess was a brown and black goat with a suspicious eye. Tam fluffed her bed of straw and burrowed into it, ignoring her judgmental gaze. He was cold, and hungry, and now probably hunted, and no nearer finding the broken chip.

The pregnant goat was tethered in one corner of the barn with her straw, a bucket of water, and an armload of browse. Outside the reach of her tether, to her frustration, were a few bales of grass hay, set among barrels of fish and bundles of dried seaweed. One barrel had a large smear over the lid and side, where someone had spilled ink or paint.

Or blood.

Tamaryl sat up in his straw, earning another baleful look from Duchess. The Ryuven had raided here, and they had been in this barn, trying for the fish and seaweed. He got up and went to the stores, though of course no one would have left bodies to rot in the warehouse.

People had died here. His people, the Chrenadan fishermen, others. They had died for these barrels of fish.

"I brought you some bread."

He jumped, though it was only the girl, and then he felt foolish. "Thanks."

She looked past him to the fish and seaweed. "This is what the Ryuven wanted to steal."

He nodded, his mouth full.

"They killed my aunt Tabbie."

She said it too matter-of-factly, and it made Tamaryl's stomach twist. "I'm sorry."

She didn't answer. After a moment she said, "I thought you'd be asleep."

"I want to. I just was looking at the blood."

That made sense to her. She pointed at the rafters above. "One of them was caught up there. He was trying to fly in the barn, and Otser shot him with a crossbow, and he fell on the crossbeam. He hung there a moment, still flapping, and Otser shot him again and he fell onto the barrels. Scattered all over."

Tamaryl stared at her. "Did you hear about it? Or did you see this happen?"

She pointed to the far corner. "I was hiding back there in the feed bin. I watched it. Afterward, when they were dragging out the Ryuven, I went and looked. I kept some flowers and shells which fell out of his bag."

Tamaryl's breath caught. "Was there a crystal?"

"Just shells and some flowers."

Had the Ryuven raider picked up some pretty souvenirs of the human world to take home to a friend or lover?

"Where did they take the dead Ryuven?" If they had tossed the bodies into the ocean, hope was lost. Tamaryl couldn't hope to dive in the winter-cold sea, even if the bodies had miraculously not been carried away by tide or scavengers.

"To the midden pit, I think. They were wondering whether it would hurt the pigs if they got at them."

Tamaryl nodded numbly. He had known there would be no easy way to do this. Searching a midden for half-eaten, rotting corpses was no more than could be expected. He could bathe and vomit and bathe once he had recovered the fragment.

After a bit, the girl left, conversation exhausted. Tamaryl was exhausted too, but he wouldn't be able to sleep until he had searched where the Ryuven had fallen. He crawled around the area she had indicated, looking for any gleam. Would the fragment reflect in the dim light? What if it was covered in dust?

There was a rat burrow beneath one of the pallets of barrels. Did rats collect trinkets like crows did? Could the chip have fallen down the hole? Tamaryl was unwilling to push his hand into the dark hole, lest an occupying rat bite his probing fingers. He went to the grass hay and fished for a woody stem, bringing it back to stab around in the burrow. Hearing no squeaks of protest and feeling nothing move at its touch, he screwed up his face and reached into the hole, glad no one was there to see the vaunted Pairvyn flinch at a rat hole.

His fingers touched something hard, and he caught his breath. He caught it with his fingertips and coaxed it forward until he could grasp it, when his heart sank. It was curved, not angular. He drew it out anyway, revealing a tarnished brooch.

At least he had found something. He put his hand in again, just to be certain, and his fingers found another object. This one was planar and cool, and again his breath caught. He cupped the object in his fingers and rocked it into his grip.

It was a fragment of crystal, short enough to fit in his palm and wide enough to fill the fingers he closed protectively about it. It was salvation for Maru and Tamaryl.

He could not stay and sleep. He could not risk being found and detained now that he had the fragment. He set the brooch on a barrel for the girl to find and left, followed by Duchess's disapproving gaze.

Safe within his closed room, Tamaryl stared at the piece of crystal on his little table. He felt a measure of guilt in hiding his find; he knew the White Mage would give him nearly anything he asked.

At least, he would have believed that at one time. But that was before he learned Mage Hazelrig had hidden knowledge of Ryuven prisoners, before he had not saved the helpless Parrin'sho. Tamaryl was not wrong to keep the broken bit of the Shard of Elan to himself for a time.

Mage Hazelrig hadn't noticed his absence; he was on the road to Groom Lake. Tamaryl had hidden off the roadside every time he saw someone coming from the direction of Alham. Tomorrow, Mage Hazelrig would be supervising the excavation of the midden.

The jagged crystal seemed to glow with reflected candlelight. Though small, it absorbed much of the power used on it, and he would need to exert himself to affect it at all. But it would amplify the results of his magic, as well, if he could work it properly.

It galled him to be so weak.

It frightened him, more than he admitted to Maru or even to himself most days. What if he did not recover? The Pairvyn ni'Ai could not return without power. The sho would tear him apart politically, and then the che would do it physically.

And Maru... Tamaryl could sense little change in him as the days passed. It had been an awful, gut-wrenching shock to see his friend, broken and feeble.

He reached out to the fragment of crystal and spun it on the tabletop so that it threw back candlelight. Light gleamed off it in all directions and then winked out. A heartbeat later the crystal gleamed again, still spinning to a slow stop.

For a moment Tamaryl could not breathe, but he forced his hand to take up the fragment and turned it nearer the light. Yes, there, difficult to make out in the dimness but plain now that he was looking for it, a radial network of cracks in one plane of the piece. The light reflected off the other sides and refracted here, where the crystallized ether had been dropped or struck.

Light was energy, like magic. The cracks disrupted light; they would disrupt magic. The fragment of shard might not be enough to carry them through the shield.

For a long moment Tamaryl stared at the palm-sized betrayal, unable to think, unable to feel, numb with fear that he had stolen it for nothing, that there would be no fresh food for the Ai storehouses, no return home for Maru, nothing but his failure.

Someone tapped at the door. Tamaryl swept the crystal fragment from the table into his lap. "Who's there?"

"It's only Ariana."

He exhaled. "Please come, my lady mage."

She opened the door, pale in the weak light. "I saw the light beneath the door."

"I could not sleep." He looked at her. "Neither, it seems, could you."

She shook her head. "No, I was thinking. And then I wanted something to drink, I decided."

Tamaryl gave her a wan smile. "Then allow your servant to bring it, my lady."

She gave him a reproving look. "You are no servant now. You're the Pairvyn ni'Ai, as—"

"I am a mere shell of a Ryuven, without the strength of my kind or yours," he snapped. Then he looked away from Ariana's startled face, guilty. "I'm sorry. At least, when I was your servant, my power was comfortably sealed, rather than a raw, gaping wound, bleeding helplessness."

She moved toward him. "Does it hurt?"

He shook his head, upset with himself. "No. Well, yes, it hurts, I'm still healing physically. But my power—it's just not there. Dead. It does not hurt, it just does not exist." He swallowed. "Like waking to find that one's arm is missing."

She stood by his shoulder and laid a hand across the back of his neck, as she had done long ago when he was the human boy Tam. "I'm sorry." Her fingers were cool against his hot skin. "I... When I was in your world, at first, I woke to see Maru standing over me. I was afraid, I didn't know him, and I tried to repel him with magic—but nothing happened. The magic just didn't respond. And I was so afraid and so helpless—"

"And then, my lady mage, you found a way to use our own magical atmosphere, and you became powerful in both worlds." Tamaryl could hear the bitterness in his voice. "And you returned home, to acclaim and rejoicing."

Ariana's mouth firmed. "I returned home, where I discovered I had lost my magic here as well, and I have had to rebuild it from a child's skill."

"How diligent of you. But my power is not improving, and I am not healing, and I am trapped in his wretched place."

Ariana did not speak, but he could see the hurt in her eyes. He swallowed. "I'm sorry. I'll bring your drink."

Ariana stepped back, shaking her head. "I'll get it myself. Good night."

She closed the door behind her, and Tamaryl stared at it, feeling foolish and ashamed.

CHAPTER FIFTY-SIX

Soren was not glad to face the new day's issues of taxes and trade agreements and tariffs and border aggression. The last was his newest chore, since word had come of an upstart in the far west, some wastrel who'd somehow slain his warlord master and claimed power for himself. It was probably nothing serious—these wilderness bands mostly scuffled amongst themselves—but King Jerome had sent the reports on to Soren, so he was expected to formulate a response for his father's consideration.

He was grateful when Ethan rapped at the open door. "Ethan! Please, tell me something diverting."

"Not exactly, master. I've just had word that the Count of Bailaha requested an audience with His Majesty."

"What?"

"I'm told he will be admitted sometime late this afternoon."

Soren drummed his fingers on the desk between stacked papers. Shianan was trying, then. Given what he'd said before, he would venture an audience for no other reason. Despite the awkward display during the matches, he would risk it.

In a way, Soren was glad Shianan had swallowed his apprehension. But his timing, despite being Soren's suggestion, was poor; the king had been disgruntled at the unexpected and interrupted fight and had seemed in a foul mood since. If his irritation had its source in Shianan's unusual demonstration, it could not bode well for the commander's precious petition.

A vague unease filled Soren. He did not understand what passed between King Jerome and Shianan Becknam, but it did no one good. If the king were displeased with Shianan, Soren could not let him set himself for ill use—not the earnest, sober commander who'd sworn himself to Soren's service. Not his younger brother.

He pushed himself back from the desk decisively. "Lock up, Ethan. I'm going."

He wondered as he strode down the long corridors what he would tell Shianan. *Leave off, today; the king is not in a receptive mood.* Yes, that was probably best. Shianan did not need the burden of knowing the king had been displeased by his aborted demonstration, not when it seemed no one knew what exactly had happened.

The secretary frowned when Shianan appeared before his desk. "I'm sorry, my lord, but no one has sent for—"

"I know that," Shianan snapped, nerves making his voice curt. "I am the one requesting audience."

There was an awkward moment while the secretary tried to reconcile Shianan's request with the king's agenda, probably debating whether he should refuse outright or let the king himself deny it. Finally he rose with a sheaf of papers and went into the king's room, closing the door firmly behind him.

Shianan paced.

After what seemed an age, the secretary returned. He waved for a page and gave him quiet instructions before sending him off. Shianan chafed.

At last the secretary turned to him. "His Majesty will see you, but he must finish this present business first."

Shianan nodded, simultaneous relief and apprehension filling him. Now he would have his chance, and now there was no return. There would be no second chance.

"Thank you," he said gruffly. "I'll wait."

He paced, embarrassed by his nervous display but incapable of stopping. He tried to examine the painted portraits on the wall or the embroidered banners of antiquity. He saw nothing of them.

"His Majesty will see you."

Shianan jumped at the words and then silently rebuked himself. He nodded stiffly. "Thank you."

A servant held the door for several exiting ministers and then glanced expectantly at Shianan. He inhaled and walked through the door, keeping his eyes forward as it closed behind him.

King Jerome was seated at the narrow end of the heavy table, writing something. Shianan knelt beside him, awaiting acknowledgment. The king shoved away his paper. "I wasn't quite ready for you yet."

Shianan did not know whether this was apology or reproof. He kept silent.

"Rise, Bailaha. I'm told you want a few minutes. What is it?"

Shianan straightened, trying to form the words which had

been tumbling in his head since his sleepless night. "Your Majesty, I come with a request."

"A request?" The king's mouth twitched in an unreadable expression. He tipped his head to eye Shianan. "What is it you want?"

Shianan's pulse shook him. "I've come to ask permission to marry."

There was a long moment of silence. Shianan held his breath. The king sat immobile, looking at him.

"Bailaha," said Jerome at last, his words coming slowly, "why did you come to ask this?"

Shianan's heart leapt. Was this a promising sign? "Your Majesty, I—"

The door opened abruptly, and they turned together to see Soren brushing aside the flapping secretary. He shoved the door behind him and strode forward, bowing to his father. "Excuse me," he said, ignoring Shianan's startled expression. "I have some questions about the warlord—"

"Wait a bit, Soren," the king said shortly. "Bailaha has come with a petition."

Soren threw a hasty glance which Shianan could not interpret. "Perhaps, as he is already here, he would care to comment on the military situation—"

"Be quiet, Soren," snapped King Jerome.

Shianan looked from one to the other. Soren's sudden interruption seemed contrary to the prince's earlier urging. On the other hand, the king had silenced Soren to hear Shianan—something which had never happened before. A heady rush filled Shianan.

"Answer my question, Bailaha. Why did you come for permission to marry?"

Shianan glanced toward Soren, uncomfortable with his answer and doubly so before the prince. But this once, the king had set aside Soren for Shianan. "All my life has been yours to command, Your Majesty. My path has been chosen for me, and now I—"

"You understand you are not free to marry, or you would not have sought permission."

Shianan caught his breath. "I do."

"Then you already understand there are reasons why you cannot marry. Knowing these, you ask that I overlook them to accommodate your infatuation with some barmaid or merchant girl?" He shook his head. "You were right to ask, but I cannot grant the permission you seek." With an air of dismissal, he turned toward Soren. "Now, as you've come—"

"Wait!" The word burst from Shianan without thought, shocking him nearly as much as the king. "Wait. I've served you faithfully all my life. I've never questioned. This is the first time I've come with any kind of request at all."

The king raised an eyebrow. "That does not make it reasonable, nor obligate my favor."

"And what is unreasonable about wanting to marry?"

The king rose from his chair in disbelief to face Shianan's first defiance. "There is every reason you should not be allowed to marry! 'Soats, you're lucky you're weren't gelded—do you realize that? I stopped that—though if it had been done, I wouldn't have this trouble with you now."

It was the first time he had alluded to Shianan's birth, even obliquely. Hot terror and angry resentment ran mingled through Shianan.

Soren cut in hastily. "I think we can see a way through this—"

"Be quiet, Soren."

"Please, just listen a moment. What could be the harm in hearing him?"

"There is nothing else to be said. Bailaha, we've finished."

Shianan clenched his fists and bowed his head. "You are my father and you owe me—"

The slap caught him across the ear and jaw, knocking him staggering to one side. "I have never given you leave to call me that," snarled the king.

"Father!" Soren started forward and halted, uncertain and shocked. "What are you doing?"

"Keep out of this." King Jerome turned on Shianan, straightening with his ear ringing. "You presume too much. I see success and favor has clouded your judgment."

"Favor?"

The king's face twisted. "Insolent wretch of a—"

"Stop," urged Soren, extending his hands to soothe both of them. "Just wait—"

"Silence!" roared King Jerome. To Shianan he continued, "You ungrateful, arrogant whelp, don't think you are above punishment. I could have you in stocks or worse as a soldier, or imprisoned as a courtier. Reprobate!"

Shianan dug his nails fiercely into his palms and summoned the last of his fading courage. "I have been your most loyal servant. I have served you since I was but a boy. I had no mother, I had no father. I had no childhood. Now you tell me I may have no wife?"

"Not another word," Jerome snarled. "Open your mouth again, and I will have you strapped before your own troops. Get out of my sight, and put this ridiculous idea from your head. Get out."

Shianan swallowed hard, wanting to say more and yet aghast at his own rebellion. Words whirled through his mind with the gasping fear that he had ruined his only chance and was near to losing everything else. He bowed low and backed away silently, fumbling for a door.

The secretary and his pages were at the far side of the room, thumbing busily through sheaves or polishing the desk or studying the scrollwork at the side of the cabinet. None gave Shianan more than a glance. He blinked hard and left the room, fighting a swelling wave of frustration, humiliation, and fury.

Soren stared at the king. "Father, how—how could you—you hit him?"

Jerome looked away. "You saw how he was."

"That's no call to strike him! He was upset. You denied him the only thing he ever asked of you."

"He cannot be permitted to marry. And he cannot be permitted to rely on special favor, only because he is..."

"Because he is a royal bastard." Soren faced his father.

His father stared hard at him, as if trying to decide whether to protest his son's plain speech. Finally he exhaled. "Yes, of course that's what I mean. He cannot claim his birth for special favor."

"What special favor?" Soren demanded. "Any other courtier would have presented his marriage plans out of mere ritual courtesy, and you would have given approval without a thought. He truly wants your permission, because he doesn't have the rights of any other courtier." He grasped at logical argument, lacking time to make it cohesive but trying anyway. "If your bastard cannot marry, then it cannot be trading on bastard blood to ask to marry. But you've never acknowledged him, so he is a courtier and should be granted permission."

"Don't play lawyer's tricks with me. He carries royal blood, Soren. He—"

"And how often has he traded on that?" Soren gestured to where Shianan had stood. "How many times has he reminded you of that fact?"

"You don't see that—"

"How many times?"

King Jerome pressed his lips together. "This day only," he admitted at last. "This is the first time either of us have mentioned it." He sighed. "I'd never yet had to directly remind him to keep his place."

"Keep his place?" Soren gave him an incredulous look. "Shianan Becknam is the least ambitious man in Alham. He has no political aspirations whatsoever, and no one can accuse him of putting on airs. He practically grovels whenever he attends court—it's embarrassing. And why? Because he's reminded each time that he has no place here."

Jerome bristled. "I have given him lands and a title. He is a full member of my court, beside his military position."

"And do you make a habit of striking your nobles?"

Jerome's face reddened. "That's enough, Soren."

"He didn't demand the rights of a royal offspring. He only meant that a son should have his father's sanction—"

"Enough!" shouted Jerome, and Soren realized he had trespassed too far. The king looked hard at him, making it difficult for Soren to meet his eyes. "You came here knowing he'd ask, didn't you? You came to interrupt us?"

Soren nodded. "I knew he had requested an audience, yes."

"And you thought I would manage him badly."

Soren had no ready answer.

Jerome sighed. "What you fail to see, Soren, is that I am protecting you. A royal bastard is a dangerous thing, dangerous of himself and dangerous as a tool."

"Shianan Becknam has no political ambitions, Father. I've already said that, and you must know it yourself."

"I think you fail to understand the potential for trouble."

"I think you hold him to an impossible standard. What happens when he realizes at last that he cannot succeed? When he gives up entirely? When he no longer cares what you think of him?"

"I think you've said enough."

Soren bit his lip. He'd rarely argued with his father, and even more rarely with such indignant emotion. But he'd gone too far, perhaps. His father couldn't hear reason for the angry words which clouded it. He bowed. "Then I will go back to my own work."

He was nearly at the door when the king spoke again. "You tread a precarious path, Soren. You can be deceived. He may be using you to gain influence for the future. Shianan Becknam is dangerous."

Soren faced him again. "Which is more dangerous, Father— the man who resents and fears you, or the man who considers you an ally and a friend?"

"He will take advantage of your weakness."

"It isn't weakness, Father." Soren gave him a quick, sad look and bowed before exiting.

CHAPTER FIFTY-SEVEN

Ariana broke yet another of the fragile glass vials in which she was trying to capture a vapor, and with an exasperated syllable she flung her instruments down and took a few percussive steps from the workbench. Clearly, this was not a day for careful work, and she would have to find another, less painstaking task.

She had been growing aware of Shianan's feelings, and they pleased her, but she had been trying to keep a check on her own. Shianan did not have many friends; it was possible he was confusing friendship with romance. And she did not know if the bastard was even free to marry.

But when he had promised to speak to the king and return to her—that suggested he thought he could. And he had said he would come to her this afternoon or evening, with a tone quite unlike a friend's casual promise to meet again.

A hint of guilt corroded the edges of her flattered excitement. She wasn't certain yet of her own feelings. That is, she was fond of him and she admired him, but did she love him? Enough to marry him? Enough to face all that would come with marriage to the bastard?

She needed the vapor before her present project could proceed, and she was too agitated to handle the equipment safely. She was finished for today. She extinguished the athanor and began to clean and put away her equipment. She hummed a little; Shianan might not be to Bethia's refined taste, but Ariana liked him, anyway.

The surviving glass vials went on the high shelf, the glass and ceramic jars of ingredients on the lower. She left the athanor on the table, but the reference texts belonged in the cabinet in the corner.

As she replaced the books, she noted the small cloth bag she'd left there, not exactly hidden but out of the way of a casual glance. This was the remainder of her Ryuven medicine, a medley of dried herbs and other plant bits. Mage Parma had suggested that she examine the Ryuven herbs, but Ariana had suspected it was a ploy to occupy her anxious mind. Well, she needed something to occupy her now. She took down the bag and emptied it upon her work surface.

Some of the dried leaves looked familiar. This one was nearly ruegrass, and this one looked like a close cousin of wolf nettle. She began to sort them into piles. The sand sprig went here, and the trident-shaped leaves over there. Was this redleaf? She hadn't seen it often, but she thought that was its name. She brought a dusty book from the shelf and began scanning the sketches. She hadn't realized so many of the Ryuven plants had cousins in the human world. Mudvein, and lacy nettle—but wasn't that toxic?—and yellowroot...

There were a few that were too unfamiliar to place, but the fact that so many were recognizable prompted her to wonder if the rest might be included in a more complete herbal. Her father had a much larger volume. What if the Ryuven world did in fact share plants with hers? She didn't know what that might mean, but one could never discount new knowledge. And it was a far safer activity than handling glassware.

She folded several specimens into a sheet of paper and went to her father's office. He greeted her cheerfully, his eyes bright. "Hello, darling. Have you brought any news?"

"What do you mean?" The wretched man knew *everything*. She shook her head. "I came to borrow your herbal. Mine doesn't include these."

"Well, let me help you look. I can easily step away from this for a few moments. What are these? I don't recognize them, either."

"I brought them with me, from—over there. They were part of my medicine when I was ill."

"Interesting." He brought down a great book.

"The others look like plants I know, so I thought perhaps these could be here, too. But how could we share flora with the Ryuven world?"

"How can we share a language? Let's look." He flipped pages and began noting aspects of the dried leaf. "Three lobes, all pointed together... I wish I knew the color when fresh... A bit of woody stem..."

Ariana peered over his shoulder. "What's that one?"

He tapped the illustration with a finger. "Dall sweetbud."

Ariana made a face. "Dall sweetbud? It sounds like a whore's name."

"Ariana, darling, try to act the part of a lady, especially in front of your dear old father. Dall sweetbud was a precious herb, but it's not been harvested here for, oh, a couple of generations, at least."

"And this is it?"

"I don't—well, I wonder... I've never seen it, of course. It's very difficult to cultivate, and most of the wild plots were gathered too aggressively and exterminated."

"So this is valuable?"

"If it is dall sweetbud, it's quite valuable indeed. But I'm not sure that it is dall sweetbud." He set the trident leaf aside and picked another. "There can't be too many with this shape... Cliff bristle! This is also rare, though not like the dall sweetbud. It can be rendered a poison, though not one of the more efficient varieties. It affects the mind, dulling the senses and slowly killing the control of one's limbs. This was in your medicine?"

"It did blunt sensations..."

He shrugged. "Perhaps the dall sweetbud counteracted the greater damage."

"Then you think it is dall sweetbud?"

"I don't know." Ewan Hazelrig looked absorbed in thought, rubbing at his chin with a forefinger. "You could ask Tamaryl and Maru. I don't know that they'd know herbs, but it couldn't hurt to ask."

Ariana nodded. "All right. I'll make some sketches of all the different leaves, too, just in case."

Could that unusual specimen really be dall sweetbud? If it were, she mused, that could make it a valuable trading commodity, and with something to trade for crops, the Ryuven would have no need to raid and the long war might end.

And if their worlds shared plants, what else might they share? Could human crops end the Ryuven famine? Had the ancients drawn Ryuven when they painted wings on men? Her thoughts ran wild in uncontrolled speculation as her pencil moved, faithfully recording the specimen's details.

An hour passed, and then another. Ariana was absorbed in drawing the strange herbs, recording each specimen and annotating the sketch with remarks on color, consistency, the tiny cilia on the underside of a leaf, the way the veins came together. It was not difficult work, but it demanded concentration, and at last she realized it was late afternoon and Shianan had not yet come.

Had he forgotten her? Had he gone to her home instead of her office? Had he changed his mind? No, surely he would come. He had many duties and it was not yet evening. He would yet come.

But when she had finished documenting all of the Ryuven samples, he still had not appeared.

She would go to him, then. She wrapped herself in her cloak

against the winter chill and left the Wheel. But when she knocked at the commander's door, there was no answer.

She knocked again, not knowing what else to do. Surely she had not imagined it all? But still there was no response from within. She tested the door; it was locked.

"The commander's not there, my lady mage," offered a voice behind her.

Ariana spun, startled, and swallowed her surprise. "Do you know where I could find him?" she asked the soldier.

He shook his head. "I'm sorry, but he's not in Alham. He left this afternoon, we heard."

Left! Without speaking to her? "Did something happen? An emergency, something he had to see to?"

The soldier gave her an apologetic shrug. "I don't know. We were only told we wouldn't have evening training with him. If there's been a raid or something like, we didn't hear of it. He didn't take a company."

He left alone—left Alham, left her, left without saying a word. He had gone without soldiers, so it was not a military crisis. He was gone. It stuck her harder than she would have thought.

The soldier looked concerned at her distress. "Is there anything I can do for you, my lady mage?"

She shook her head. "No, I—no, thank you. I shall manage."

He nodded respectfully before moving on. Ariana swallowed against a tightening throat and began walking in the opposite direction. She drew up her hood as tears stung her eyes, surprising her further. She had only wondered, hadn't she? She hadn't counted upon his courtship, had she?

What had happened? Where had he gone?

CHAPTER FIFTY-EIGHT

There were more people in the stable now, looking over the stock. Luca leaned his aching head against the wooden wall and tried to think. Given the caravan's route, the nearest town large enough to support a trading stable of this size would be Cascais. It was a trade town, supplying caravans and providing a market for merchants to swap goods and balance their trains. Roads from Cascais led in all directions. If they could escape, they could find their way easily to Alham or Fhure—but Luca was chained to the wall.

Cole wanted to help, but he was afraid. He had been conditioned too long to obey orders, and he had paid for disobedience too dearly to risk gain. Luca was not sure he could count on the slave. But he had no other choice. Perhaps if he pledged Cole his freedom... Poor Isen. And Marla. What had become of her?

The sense honed under Ande alerted him, and he opened his eyes to see a man standing before his place in the aisle of waiting slaves. The man eyed Luca critically. "What're you?"

Luca hesitated. Should he present himself well, sell early and try to escape? But what if his new master chained him as Renner had done, and he stood a better chance here? "I'm just me," he answered, his voice deliberately slow. "I can carry things, when I'm not sick."

The man frowned and moved on.

Cole wove through the light traffic. "Master," he whispered, "they've listed you for auction in the morning."

Luca's heart sank. He wouldn't show well at auction and would sell for cheap labor—in this region, as likely the mines or salt valleys as anything else. "Take me from here. Release me, and we'll walk out."

Cole hesitated, conflict evident in his eyes. "Master, I..."

"You're an overseer; no one will question you leading a slave out."

"What about the cuffs? We'll just be taken again as runaways."

"We'll think of something. We'll have time for that when we're away from here. Cole!"

Cole looked down, eyebrows furrowed. "If we're caught..."

"If we're caught, you can claim you came after me."

"But they might see us leaving."

"They might not!" Luca could hear desperation in his voice. "Cole, you have to do this."

"Cole!" came a loud voice.

Cole stiffened. "It's Asher." He straightened and looked up and down the aisle, scanning the browsers. "I have to go."

"Cole, remember—"

Asher, the guard, appeared from the crowd. "Why aren't you ever where I need you?" He frowned and shifted his eyes to Luca. "You seem to be here a lot. Maybe you're not just rubbing his nose in it. You wouldn't be stupid enough to be planning something, would you?"

Cole blanched. "No! No, I wouldn't, my lord."

"No? Good. But if I see you here again without my direction, you'll be on the flats before you can blink. And you can pickle in the salt and sun and I'll be a thousand pias richer, so it's nothing to me. Now get to the east ring and get those wagons moved."

"Yes, my lord." Cole bobbed his head and started away without looking at Luca.

Asher bent close, scowling and making Luca's pulse race. "You're keeping quiet. Don't even think about planning anything. We can make it so you'll be glad to sell out of here. Auction in the morning, unless you sell tonight, so give up any dreams you had of running off."

Luca licked his lips. "I have brothers who can ransom me—"

"A nice thought! But do you really think I'll risk ransom and arrest when I can have the sale money safely now?" Asher grinned. "They can ransom you from your new master. Good luck with that."

He left, and Luca's heart sank. Cole would have even less courage now, and with Asher suspicious, they had less chance of success.

So near. He had been so near to happiness and freedom and a new life, and it had all been stolen by greedy treacherous bandits. He wanted to rail and kick, but his head hurt too much, and he knew too well protest would only accomplish ill.

Life had never been fair. It would be effort better spent to think on what he could do now.

Thir or Jarrick could ransom him, but few masters would give their newly purchased slaves paper and the coin to send a message. Luca would need to assure them of more than they'd paid, and he would have to explain somehow to his brothers that he had lost his inheritance and found himself enslaved again... That was a cheap price, compared to living a slave again, but he didn't relish the thought.

"Look at this lot," a man complained to his companion. "They look out of breath just sitting here. 'Soats, we'll never find a pair that can take the hills."

Luca registered the words dimly, used to casual insults and frank assessments. He kept his eyes down, not wanting to draw attention.

"You've got to take something. We can't go on with just two, no matter how you push them. And we want something left at the end of the trip, anyway, so we can't kill them on the road."

"I know, I know. But look at these."

"Look at that one. He'll know the road, he's old enough to have made it."

"King's oats."

The exclamation, uncommon on the Wakari Coast, caught Luca's ear. He lifted his aching head to scan for the speakers. "My lords!"

The short, wide man in front of him looked surprised at the slave's abrupt address. "Yes?"

"My lords are from Alham? Or near it?"

The man glanced skeptically at his partner but answered. "What is it to a slave?"

Luca gulped, trying to formulate his plan even as he spoke. *Home to Shianan.* "My lords, I need to get to Alham. If you take me there, there's profit in it for you."

"You need to get to Alham?" repeated the taller man incredulously.

He had only a moment to seize their interest. "I know it sounds ridiculous, but—I shouldn't be here. I was stolen. I have been stolen, more than once." He judged they would be suspicious of a freeman demanding his liberty; that could lead to legal troubles and they'd avoid the risk. "My rightful master is in Alham, and he will pay for my return."

"You're that important to him?"

"I am not just a draft slave, though that's what I'll sell as here. They don't know I'm trained." Education had saved him once, and it could save him again. "My master in Alham will pay twice my price here, making you a handsome profit."

"And if you're lying? Maybe you're just anxious to go to Alham because it's the opposite direction from the mines, and you'd rather we dump you back in the market there."

"No—no, there's a guarantee for you." Luca licked his lips. "I'm a clerk, an accountant, a good one. And I'm educated in other areas, too. I've been a tutor, when I wasn't accounting. If I'm not redeemed in Alham, you can sell a clerk or tutor for far more than what you paid for a draft slave."

The two men exchanged glances. "What if you're lying about being educated?"

"Test me. Ask me something of history, or ask me to reconcile some figures."

"'Soats, I wouldn't know if you were right about the history." The shorter man tipped his head to appraise Luca. "Twice what we pay? You're sure?"

Luca wasn't, but he hoped it would be true. "Twice. Or you sell me as a clerk."

"You know a clerk's price is more than twice that of a scrawny draft."

Luca's heart spasmed. He hadn't thought of that in his desperate grasping at straws. "You'd need proof that I had the training, my lord. I could refuse to give correct answers until you took me to Alham."

The man laughed. "Or maybe, if he needs you as much as you say, your master will pay more than twice." He gave a curt jerk of his head. "On your feet. I want to see you, and an educated slave should know enough to show some respect."

Luca rose carefully, turning to keep a hand against the wall. "I'm sorry, my lord. My head's not quite clear."

"What's wrong with you?"

"No fault of my own, I swear. I'm a good servant. But I took a knock to the head."

"So you're no good to us unless we find this master of yours."

"No! No, I'll be fine soon. I can earn my keep."

"How's a tutor at moving weight?" asked the taller of the two.

"I have been in harness before."

"Oh?" He frowned. "You're not much to look at."

"I took a single over the Faln Plateau. And if you're looking for a strong back, I can recommend one here. There's a slave called Cole, serving presently as an—"

"Oh, him? Broad fellow? They called him an overseer, asked an overseer's price."

Luca scrabbled mentally. "But I heard them mention the salt flats..."

"No, it's the auction for him, unless someone takes him first. Too pricey for my purse, anyway. What will they want for you?"

"As you say, my lord, I don't look like much for labor, and I've got a lump swelling out of my skull. Also, they'd rather be done with me quickly if they can. I'm stolen and they know it, but they're trying to turn a quick profit. Offer them four hundred to start."

The men exchanged glances, but Luca saw the gleam of interest in their eyes. "So that's eight hundred we'll have for you in Alham."

"Yes, my lord."

"And you'll work your way there."

"Yes, my lord."

"We don't need a clerk, we need a man in harness. We can't afford to take a slave on a pleasure trip. You'll give us good work."

Luca swallowed. "I'll do my best, my lord."

"All right, then. We'll see what they think you're worth."

CHAPTER FIFTY-NINE

Maru rubbed at his shoulder. It was his wing which hurt—it was always cold here, it seemed, and it made his mending bone ache—but that was awkward to reach without straining the injury, and sometimes if he rubbed his shoulder just so, it eased his wing for a short while.

Through the open door, he could see Tamaryl concentrating over the broken fragment of crystal, and Maru could feel occasional power fluctuations in the room. When Maru had asked how the reservoir was progressing, Tamaryl had snapped at him, and so Maru stayed outside. His friend had meant nothing by it, but Maru would not disturb his work again. He wanted Tamaryl to succeed. He wanted them to have a chance to return home.

His eyes shifted to the folded sheet resting on the table in the entry. The paper had slid beneath the door two hours or so before, and Maru had waited until the messenger had safely gone before collecting it.

He glanced back at Tamaryl's hunched form. His friend had a tender regard for the rika. But Tamaryl held little hope for winning Ariana'rika's love; he spoke of her only in removed tones, shielding himself. Even so, Maru could not bring himself to reveal that perhaps his friend's rival had already declared his love.

There was an abrupt rattle at the door and Maru leapt, fearful of discovery. But it was Ariana who entered, stumbling once on the hem of her dark robes. She pushed her cloak toward a wall hook but missed, and she stared at the puddled fabric as if confused.

"Ariana'rika?" Maru started toward her, softening his voice. "Are you well?"

She looked at him, and he was startled by the raw hurt in her expression. "I came home early..."

He adapted the easy tone of a conversant servant, soothing her with everyday familiarity. "Not so early," he returned, stooping to collect the fallen cloak. "The sho should be coming soon as well. Would you like something warm to drink? It looks chill out today."

"Yes, thank you," she answered, but the words were merely reflexive. No matter, he thought. Routine would relax her and help her recover from whatever affected her. He nodded and turned toward the kitchen. Her voice stopped him. "Did—" she began, but she seemed afraid to speak.

Maru hesitated. "Ariana'rika?"

"Did—did anyone—no one came here…"

He thought of the note. "There was a letter."

"Where is it?" she demanded, and he turned. He would have brought it to her, but she rushed past him and seized it. "Who brought this?"

"I don't know. It was left beneath the door. I could not answer, obviously."

She nodded distantly and opened the sheet, breaking the fragile seal. She stared at the page for a long moment, apparently reading and re-reading. At last she looked up with a shuddering breath and fixed her eyes on Maru. "My drink?"

He had been staring, waiting. "I'm sorry, Ariana'rika. I'll bring it now."

He hurried to the kitchen and pulled a pitcher of ale from its cool cabinet, mixing it with water from the pot kept near the fire. When he returned, he saw her drifting toward the room where Tamaryl worked, clutching the letter in one dangling hand. She hesitated at the open door. "Tamaryl…"

He hadn't heard her approach. His head jerked up as his hand shielded the crystal. "By the—don't you humans demand privacy for yourselves?"

Ariana recoiled. Maru winced. *Ryl, no—not now…*

Tamaryl's expression changed. He started up from the table, pushing the crystal piece behind him. But as his mouth opened, Ariana slammed the door.

She turned and nearly collided with Maru. She looked at him, and he thought she would cry. He extended the drink. "Ariana'rika," he said gently. "If you—"

She reached for him, embracing him awkwardly about the torso. He stiffened, startled, and then closed his free arm about her as she began to sob.

"He's gone," she cried. "He's gone, and he didn't even—and I was stupid enough to think—I was such a fool, and you're stuck here and I can't help you, and I can't do anything at all!"

Maru held her, ignoring the dull discomfort where she pinched a wing, while she fought to control her breathing, subduing the tears.

That was how Ewan Hazelrig found them as he entered.

Maru looked up anxiously, aware he was holding close the daughter of the highest human mage. But the White Mage only hurried to them with a gentle, concerned expression, easing her from Maru's grasp and enfolding her in his own arms more tightly. Confronted with fresh tenderness, she began to cry anew.

"Oh, Ariana," Hazelrig soothed, pulling her close. "I'm sorry."

Maru dropped his eyes uncomfortably, thinking he could back away and escape the humans' distress. His gaze landed on the note in her hand. It was almost certainly something concerning the commander—had something happened to him? Had he discarded his lover?

Hazelrig, though, seemed to know enough. His expression hardened over Ariana's shoulder. "Ariana, Ariana. It's all right, darling. I'll turn him into a cockroach."

Ariana sobbed, "No!" and Maru clenched his fists. It had been the commander indeed, he had toyed with the rika's heart, and Tamaryl had lost her to this.

Ariana pushed herself back to meet her father's eyes. "He didn't—it was my own fault."

"Was it?" Hazelrig's voice was gentle, but Maru could hear the steel within it. He glanced pointedly at the letter.

Ariana crumpled it in her fist. "I let myself—I talked myself into imagining—it was nothing."

"What, exactly, was this nothing?" The White Mage was roused at the wounding of his daughter.

Ariana only shook her head.

Hazelrig frowned and exhaled. "If not a cockroach, then will you allow a deformed gnome?"

Ariana sniffed. "Don't tease me, Father. Not now."

Maru gave a respectful nod, though he doubted either saw it, and retreated to the workroom. He slipped inside and jostled against Tamaryl, who waited stiffly behind the door, his head bowed and fists clenched. Maru watched him, his words caught in his throat.

"She..." It seemed Tamaryl couldn't say more.

Maru felt increasingly helpless. "Ryl... I'm sorry."

"No." Tamaryl shook his head. "No, I'm to blame. I did not... And then I snapped at her. And at you, my friend." He sighed. "I'm sorry."

"Ryl, I—"

"No. I'm sorry." He looked at Maru. "But I will not keep you here. I swear it. I won't let you be trapped here."

Maru regarded him suspiciously. "What about you?" He hadn't mentioned himself, and that was alarming. "You won't stay here!"

Tamaryl glanced toward the door, his eyes betraying his thoughts. "I hadn't thought..."

He was thinking of Ariana. Maru tensed. "I don't want to go without you."

"Do you want to stay in the human world for the rest of your life?"

"Do you?"

They stared at one another for a long moment, and then Tamaryl relented. "No, I don't want to stay here. I want to go home."

Maru didn't want to ask, but fear for his friend pushed him. "And what about her?"

"There's no use asking anything, is there? Not when she's crying for him and I have no claim on her?" His jaw set. "But anything might happen."

CHAPTER SIXTY

Luca dropped heavily to the roadside and closed his eyes, his pulse loud in his ears. He had found himself in far worse positions than now, but the rolling hills outside Cascais had been taxing, and his head throbbed with every step. Now that they had finally stopped, he wanted only to sleep and try to forget his headache and his new circumstance.

"Supper, you lot." Frangit banged a ladle against the pot, sending jarring waves through Luca's skull. "Eat up."

Luca's gut felt hollow, but his aching head overwhelmed what appetite he had. Still, he knew he needed food. He'd eaten nothing since the caravan's seizure and he would face more exertion the next day. He rolled slowly upright and shuffled toward the small cookfire where his new master warmed the meal.

His other new master, the more talkative Benton, was tugging at something in the rear of the wagon. He and his cousin Frangit had finished their business across the continent and were making their way slowly back home, trying to manage a few more coins along the route. They had lost two of their four slaves to illness, leaving them with a weighty cart and two weakened draft slaves. It was less costly, Luca had surmised from snatches of their conversation, to purchase two more slaves of mediocre quality than to sell their remaining goods at the discounted prices of glutted Cascais.

The supper, Luca discovered, was more substantial than the thin gruel of Trader Matteo's caravan. Each of them received a hot sausage and a handful of dried vegetables, reconstituted in boiling water. Benton and Frangit weren't careless of their labor, or perhaps they regretted the loss of their ill slaves and the expense of new ones. Regardless, Luca was encouraged at the sight, as well as the fact that neither cousin had lurked over the draft team with threats and a switch.

Perhaps, if he had to endure as a slave...

No. No, he would not remain a slave—at least, not in the hands of strangers. Benton and Frangit would take him to Alham, where he would be rescued by Master Shianan.

So near. So near to freedom and a new life.

A slave beside him with thin ginger-colored hair stared resentfully over his dish at Luca. Luca shifted uncomfortably and looked away, pulling his meal closer to his chest. He'd said little to his new companions on the road, busy with his work and his headache.

His sausage was cooling, and he pushed the rest into his mouth. He wished he knew what had become of Marla and Cole. Cole had thought Marla escaped, but where did that leave her—on the road with no shelter, no food, no protection? Anyone would think her a runaway or valuable property to be stolen and abused. And Cole might go anywhere, might well end up suffering in a salt flat or ore mine.

He finished the last of his tasteless vegetables and pushed his empty plate toward the fire. Hoping desperately they would not want him for further work such as scrubbing the cookware, he crawled toward the wagon and curled himself beneath it, tucked safely behind one of the wheels to blunt any casual kicks to rouse the slaves in the morning. Within seconds he was asleep.

"Your Highness, I do not know." General Septime shook his head unhappily. "I had no reason to think it important."

Torg looked back and forth between the prince-heir and the general. In truth, they had known instantly that something was wrong. Shianan Becknam had never requested leave in all his service, from Torg or Septime or any other. And why should he? He had no family, no home, nothing and no one to visit. His life was his work.

To Torg he had said only, "I'm going to see General Septime about some leave," and then walked away too quickly for Torg to question—wholly unlike his usual care.

Torg had followed him. "Sir! How long? What are your orders while you're away?"

But Shianan had not stopped until he reached the general's office and gestured to Petar that he wanted inside. He did not look at Torg. "I suppose you should hear," he said to the general's door. "Come in with me, then."

Petar held the door for them, and they went inside and saluted.

"I should like to take a leave of absence, sir." Shianan's eyes betrayed desperation over his carefully controlled voice. Torg could see it, and he guessed the general could as well.

Septime nodded. "Certainly you can have a few days. When will—"

"Now, sir. Immediately."

Septime looked surprised. "What about arranging for someone to take over your duties?"

"Captain Torg is more than capable, sir, and with the annual review finished and the Ryuven raids apparently ceased, he can see to things for the time I'm away."

Septime looked at Torg, but not critically, almost as if he were asking for information. "I am sure the captain is very capable, but there is no harm in taking a day to arrange things."

The commander glanced away. "It would be better for all concerned, sir, if I were to take a leave of absence now."

Torg's stomach clenched. The royal seal and the mercenaries hired to beat Shianan, and Septime's warning to avoid trouble with the royal house—and Torg's own memory of orders to let the bastard die in a tragic accident.

Torg could see that Septime was thinking something similar. "Go on then, of course, take some time to yourself. When can we expect you again?"

And a different man had answered, a Shianan Becknam Torg had never before seen. "I have a great deal of leave due me," he said in a tight voice. "I shall return when I can." And with a quick salute, he fled before the startled general could question or dismiss him, leaving Septime and Torg both staring at the closed door.

Torg jerked his eyes back to the general. Septime frowned. "Do you know anything about this?"

Torg shook his head. "No, sir. Only what happened at the fights, same as you."

The general shook his head. "If he's learned of something else, it would not be prudent to share it. Let's assume he is removing himself from a potentially awkward situation. Becknam is a good soldier, and he'll return when he can. In the meantime, please see to his duties, and tell me if you need assistance."

"Of course, sir." Captain Torg and General Septime had not spoken of it again.

But now Prince Soren was here in Septime's own office, asking them where Shianan Becknam had gone.

"I'm sorry, Your Highness, but he didn't say where he would go. I didn't think to ask. A man's leave is his own, after all."

"When will he return?"

Septime shifted. "I'm not exactly sure, my lord."

"What?" Prince Soren frowned. "Surely your officers may not take their leave in so slipshod a manner."

"No, Your Highness. That is, not generally." Septime's fingers twitched at his beard. "But Commander Becknam has not been in the habit of taking leave, you see, and as this was a particular case..."

Soren's eyes narrowed. "What do you mean?"

Septime took a careful breath. "He'd done a great deal of work preparing for the review and parade, and then there was that unexpected challenge by the mercenaries out to make a name for themselves. And of course, that business with the Shard and the Court of the High Star was not so long ago. No one could argue the man couldn't do with a reprieve."

"But where is he?" Prince Soren looked from Septime to Torg. "If Ryuven were sighted now, how would you contact him?"

Septime sighed and shook his head. "I don't know, Your Highness."

CHAPTER SIXTY-ONE

Ariana didn't know the Indigo Mage well, and in truth had avoided him, though she supposed he should be willing to see her. After all, her appointment as Black Mage had graduated him to his present position. She wasn't keen on asking for his help now, but her father had called him the foremost expert.

She raised her hand to knock again, and the dark blue door opened abruptly. Taev Callahan looked down at her, his marred face almost suspicious. "Yes? What do you want?"

Ariana's mouth went dry. "My father—er, the White Mage said you knew more of botany than anyone else."

He inclined his head slightly to one side. She wondered if it helped him to see her better or if it was just a reaction to the compliment. "Yes."

"I would like your opinion on some specimens."

He made a curt nod. "Come in, then." He stepped back and held the door.

His office was identical to hers, but strangely foreign with its unfamiliar clutter and different arrangement. She made her way to an open surface. "May I display them here?"

"Not there." He stacked two piles of notes into one on another table, nodding toward a chair. "Sit down." He took a half-dozen books from a second chair and brought it to the table for himself.

Ariana unbound the little bag and shook out the dried leaves. She began to sort them into groups.

"Not like that!" snapped Mage Callahan. "You'll damage them." He reached over the table, his fingers deftly separating the leaves into their various shapes and colors. "You keep them in that bag? They'll crumble—like this, see? They need to be kept flat."

"I'm sorry," Ariana interrupted. "This is how I got them, and I didn't think—"

"Obviously," he cut in. "One doesn't need to consider much when one is the daughter of the White Mage."

Ariana was stung. "I earned my place in the Circle," she protested, her voice failing to hide her pique.

"With your father on the panel."

"And he failed me the first time." She had never thought she would be eager to cite that.

He hesitated. "Then I suppose we can't assume that skill breeds true," he said, but the pause had betrayed him. "How is that apprentice magic coming along?"

"You heard that I broke up an exhibition match turned ugly?"

One corner of his mouth turned upward, and she couldn't guess if it was a smirk or what remained of his smile. "I suppose I did. All right, then, Mage Hazelrig. Let's see what you have."

"Thank you." Ariana took a breath. "Could you help me to identify these? I know dried leaves aren't best, but this is all I have."

"Clearly this is cliff bristle, which anyone should know. This one is mudvein, of course, and redleaf is obvious. And—" He stopped speaking, his finger poised over a crumbling leaf with three lobes. "What color was this when fresh?"

"I don't know. I never saw it but dried."

"Where did you find this?"

"It was given to me," she answered carefully. "It's not from a local source, if that's what you mean. I don't know exactly where it was picked." True enough, if incomplete, but she didn't know how much she wanted to share with the irascible Indigo.

"Hmm." He selected a book from the displaced stack and began paging through it, ignoring Ariana.

She sat back, trying not to look as if she were staring, but the livid scar across his face could not be ignored. He was intent on his book, his blue eyes flicking from page to page. She wondered if his eyes would look less blue if he were not in his deeply-colored robes. With his black hair and blue eyes, he must have looked quite striking before—before. The half-knitted line ran from his hairline across his face, over the bridge of his nose, and over his jaw before disappearing into his collar. No blade could have followed the curves of his skull so cleanly.

"Luenda," he said shortly, without looking up. The great and brutal battle which had obliterated their army, where her father had become the White Mage, where the boy Tam had been brought home from the battlefield.

She jumped in her seat. "I wasn't..."

"You were." He glanced up. "Of course you were looking. And how could you not? It's like sharing a room with a wyvern. One cannot not look."

She blew out her breath. "I'm sorry."

"For what? You were surely a mere child at the time." One corner of his mouth lifted. "I was not much more."

"I didn't realize you had been at Luenda."

"I wasn't a part of the Circle at the time, of course. I was far too young. I very nearly never became any older."

"It was magic, obviously."

"Obviously. A Ryuven bolt."

"You were fortunate to survive."

Again, the half smile. "You think?"

Ariana's chest tightened. "I don't..."

He sat forward and laid the open book on the table. "I'm very interested in your plant. I wish you'd brought a better specimen. This could be logorinum, or it could be dall sweetbud. Do you know what that is?"

"It's a valuable medicinal plant, now gathered to extinction or near extinction." Ariana was grateful that she could answer promptly.

His eyebrows rose slightly. "And logorinum?"

"I don't know it."

"That's because it is nearly worthless. It makes a passable seasoning if one's garden is otherwise empty." He frowned at the leaves.

"This was used in medicine," Ariana said. "Does that suggest that it might be dall sweetbud?"

His eyes shifted, though the rest of him remained still. "That does suggest such."

Ariana's pulse quickened. If the Ryuven had dall sweetbud—if they had such a valuable commodity, it could be used to open trade...

"Where did you find this?"

"It was given to me."

"By whom? From where?"

Ariana hesitated. All knew she had been to the Ryuven world, of course, but was it safe to mention their medicines? Did she want to reveal yet that they had precious dall sweetbud?

Taev Callahan sensed her indecision. "You wonder why I ask. I see no harm in explaining to you: I want the same advancement you seek." He sat back. "I am the Indigo, as you know. And that is not at first any great surprise, as I am young. Nearly as young as you. But I have been a part of the Circle for much longer than you have, my Black sister, and even after Addison Esparaciana was taken by the Ryuven,

I was not advanced to Indigo until you were admitted as the Black."

Ariana listened uncomfortably. What had this to do with her plants?

"Oh, they were quick enough to take me into the Circle—anyone who survived Luenda was valuable, after all, and at times we've been precious short of mages—but they're not keen to advance me." He turned his head, giving her a clear view of the scar. She wondered whether it was intentional. "No one could have survived such an injury. Anyone who did must therefore be a tapper right out of children's tales, or some other monster. Regardless of what he himself says on the matter."

Ariana shifted uncomfortably. "And you think discovering dall sweetbud will change what they think?"

He looked back at her and shrugged. "It can't hurt. Dall sweetbud would be an esteemed find, indeed." His blue eyes seemed to hold hers.

A man who identified a panacea and shared it with the world could not be a monster. But Ariana did not say this aloud.

Taev Callahan leaned forward. "Where did you obtain it? I will help you to confirm it."

He could not invade the Ryuven world in search of it. "I'm sorry, but I can't get more. I brought it with me from the Ryuven."

"The Ryuven?" He made a sour face. "What do they need of it? They have magic to heal them."

"Thank you for your help," she said, standing and brushing the leaves into a pile again. "I appreciate it."

"Be careful of that," he advised. "You have there enough, if it is indeed dall sweetbud, for a fever tea. It will go far if you guard it."

She nodded. "Thank you." She went to the door and hesitated, anxious to leave him but feeling oddly sorry for him. He didn't have to tell her why he wanted the plant.

"Goodbye." He gave her a bow of his head.

Ariana stood outside his door, bag of herbs in her hand. Long minutes passed, and she did not walk away.

The conversation had been intriguing, but not conclusive. It had distracted her, but accomplished nothing. What would be her next step? She couldn't do anything more until she knew if the herb was dall sweetbud. There was no point to delaying.

She knocked on the door.

Taev Callahan did not look pleased to be so immediately

disturbed, but his expression lightened when he recognized Ariana. "Well, our little Black sister and her herbs," he said in a tone which managed to be not quite condescending. "Back again so soon?"

"I need to know if it's dall sweetbud," Ariana said bluntly. "And if it is, I'm going to get more of it."

He raised an eyebrow. "How would you do that?"

"I'd go back for it."

His mocking skepticism returned. "You can cross the between-worlds?"

Ariana hesitated. "Not myself. But... if the shield should fail, if something happened and if Ryuven should come here, I would have him carry me back."

Now she had actually shocked him. "Carry you—but, my lady mage, he would as likely kill you."

"Not if I bargained with him."

He stared at her. "How little success may make one confident. At any rate, come inside, and let's test this plant of yours."

She seated herself at the table while he went to a cabinet and began browsing among vials and canisters. "Do you believe this is dall sweetbud?" he asked, his back to her.

She nodded before realizing he couldn't see her. "I think it must be."

He tipped a powder into a cup, poured a bit of liquid from a nearby pitcher over it, and sloshed it casually. "Then drink this."

She looked at the cup. "What is it?"

"It's a... purgative stimulant." He smiled with arrogant satisfaction. "You'll feel the effects within a few minutes. Then you'll take a tea of your specimen, and if it's dall sweetbud, you'll be fine again in another half hour or so."

She stared at him. "And if it's not?"

"Then you'll pass a miserable night, but it won't be fatal. Though there might be moments when you think that would be simpler."

She looked back at the cup. "And if it is dall sweetbud, then I'll be fine and we'll know the Ryuven have it."

"Yes."

She took a slow breath. "I hope this doesn't taste vile."

It wasn't as disgusting as she feared, but she imagined that it began to curdle as it reached her stomach. That was only her mind's trick, of course; it couldn't really react that quickly. She didn't think there were any purely herbal, non-magical potions which could take effect in only—

Her stomach gurgled and cramped abruptly. She folded her arms instinctively across her abdomen and glanced at Taev. "Is that right?"

"Oh, was that too strong a dose? I might have forgotten to take your slight feminine form into account." He grinned. "Sorry."

Ariana stared at him. "You—you unbelievable..." She couldn't use the word *bastard*. "You miserable dog."

He shook his head as he turned for the pitcher. "No, my lady mage, I'm afraid it is you who will be miserable—and, your pardon, as sick as a dog."

Ariana curled her fingers as her stomach clenched, and she felt a moment of indignant rage. "I can't believe that you—" Her bowel shifted and she froze with a sharp gasp.

Taev nodded toward the back. "In the back corner—"

She ran before he could finish speaking.

There was only a curtain separating the front office from his rear workroom, and she barely had time to close it before she dove for the homely but serviceable relief pot in the corner. Why did Taev Callahan have a privy in his workroom?

Her gut spasmed and she folded on the pot, feeling equal parts embarrassment, discomfort, and fury. And then with handfuls of robe crumpled in her fists, she felt her stomach heave in a different way, and a new fear shot through her.

The base of the curtain lifted, and an enameled bowl rattled across the floor toward her. "You'll want that in a moment," came Taev's indifferent voice.

Ariana seized the bowl and vomited, her innards roiling and twisting. For a long moment she could do nothing but squat and vomit. The hanging curtain was far too thin.

Horrid, worthless, detestable, beastly man...

The curtain shifted and the Indigo Mage began to enter. "I've got—"

"Get out!" shrieked Ariana, her face hot with sickness and humiliation.

He withdrew, but he did not leave. "I have the infusion. Do you want the dall sweetbud?"

She gritted her teeth, sour with puke. "Leave it. I'll get it."

"If you like." He brushed the curtain aside at the base and left a cup of dark liquid. "It should steep a few more minutes for full potency."

"Louse! Skunk! Why didn't you tell me it needed time to prepare? I could have waited before taking the first one!"

"You didn't ask," came the reply, and she could almost see the casual lift of his shoulders.

She moaned and rubbed at her watering eyes. If she lived through this, she would plot something truly awful for Taev Callahan.

During a moment of reprieve she eased to her hands and knees and crawled to the cup. *Sweet Holy One, I beg you, let this be dall sweetbud.* Her hands trembled as she lifted the cup, and she had to close her eyes and breathe slowly for a moment before she could calm her gagging and belching to swallow it.

It had a flat, peculiar taste, or perhaps that was just her impression after being ill. She had little time to think on it before scrambling back to the pot.

That curtain wasn't nearly heavy enough. *Misbegotten cur.* "How long will it take?" she called hoarsely.

"Until it begins to work? Perhaps half an hour or so, if it is indeed dall sweetbud."

I'll kill him. I'll transmute his blood to acid and pour maggots into his ears and invert a shield about him so that he can't even wriggle.

Ariana's stomach lurched again and she reached for the enameled bowl.

CHAPTER SIXTY-TWO

Ariana could not stop shivering violently. Every few minutes, borborygmus and dry heaves took her, but she had nothing left to vomit. Taev assured her the infusion of what she desperately hoped was dall sweetbud would be absorbed through her mouth and throat, so it would work despite the emetic—if it worked.

It had to be dall sweetbud. It had to be. She didn't think she could face a full night of this.

She lay on the floor, folded in half, her arms clenched over her stomach. Her muscles felt like water, but somehow her body kept trying to heave or expel more. She could only shiver and moan.

How long had it been since she took the dall sweetbud? He had promised half an hour. What if they were wrong, and it was only logorinum?

A spasm shook her and she wrenched upright, spitting.

"I didn't think you had anything left in you." Taev stepped over her and set a fresh bowl on the floor. "Here's this, if you need it."

She wanted to curse at him, but she hadn't the strength.

A chair creaked behind her as it took his weight. "Maybe you vomited too soon after drinking it. It might not have had time to be absorbed."

"You... you said..." she croaked.

"I know, I said it would be absorbed immediately. But I was trusting books, not experience. And that was an old sample, dried and stored with other herbs. Maybe it needs more time. Maybe it isn't dall sweetbud after all."

Maybe you gave me too much of the first. But it was too much effort to talk.

"Do you know how long it's been?"

"Eternity," she breathed.

He chuckled. "Nearer an hour or so."

Twice as long... It wasn't working.

He rose. "If it's not going to work, I'll mix something else for you."

She swallowed, hating the taste of her mouth. "How long?"

He hesitated. "Oh, not long."

403

Suspicion gave her strength, and she turned her head to eye him. "How long?"

He glanced away. "I can give you an antidote, but it will need a few hours to take effect."

A few hours...!

"It's a long time to have your stomach wambling, I'll grant, but it's better than waiting until this wears itself... What was that? Something about a cockroach?"

She clenched her fists, fighting nausea. "Get it."

She could hear Taev working behind her, grinding something fresh. How had she come to this? Why had she trusted Taev, when even the Circle did not welcome him wholeheartedly?

But he hadn't quite lied to her. Not yet, anyway. And at some point while she lay miserable on the floor, he had taken away the reeking pot and bowl. She was further humiliated by that, but she thought the task at least partial retribution.

She wished she could simply wake when it was all over.

"Try this," came Taev's voice from across the room. He walked toward her. "We'll hope it stays down long enough to have an effect."

She nodded weakly, pushing herself upright. "I should think so. I haven't vomited for a while."

He looked at her curiously. "No. No, you haven't." He tipped his head in his usual manner. "How long has it been?"

A spark of hope flared. "Since you started making whatever that is."

"That's a quarter hour. I had to time the infusion of ginger-tassel." He crouched beside her, holding the cup but not offering it. "And you haven't been—"

"Voiding," she interrupted, trying to give him a crushing glare but disappointingly certain it didn't have the impact she wanted. "It's humiliating enough, thank you. No, not in a while."

He pursed his lips. "I gave you enough bilgewort that you should have been sick all night, even empty. Perhaps the dall sweetbud is working, after all."

"Bilgewort?"

He shrugged. "That's not its true name, of course, but it's a colorful term." He smiled crookedly. "But it does seem our experiment was successful."

"Successful." She took a slow, shuddering breath. "When I can walk again, you had better run."

He laughed. "Come now, you'll be fine by this time tomorrow, and we've learned something wonderful. This is nothing to upset you."

"Nothing to upset—! Why wasn't it you, then, balancing on a pot with a bowl in your lap?"

"Because it was your question, not mine, and because I am the botanist and herbalist who could mix the remedy. But mostly, because I am the senior mage, of course." He grinned and stood, taking away the unnecessary remedy. "I'll bring you some water. We'll save celebrating with wine for another time."

She glared at him.

CHAPTER SIXTY-THREE

Sunlight struck Shianan as he emerged from the cover of the trees, making him wince and squint. His stride did not break. A soldier did not slow for things such as changing light.

He had chosen a route to run on his third day here, needing some outlet for his nervous energy. Running gave him a way to work his taut muscles without the need for an opponent, and he would find few fighters capable of challenging him here.

He did not know how many leagues he covered. He ran until he was too winded to continue, when he slowed to walk and regain his breath. Then he ran again. He ran through peasants' fields, past mills powered by streams or slaves, over greens where geese and pigs fed while tended by staring children, through unnaturally straight herb gardens. Hours passed before he made his way back to the large house of warm golden travertine. The over-sized oaken doors were open and he went directly inside.

Kraden was directing barrels to one storeroom or another when Shianan passed through, rubbing an arm over his damp face. The majordomo noted his arrival. "Good afternoon, my lord. Lisbeth! Something to drink for the master!"

Shianan waved away the ale the maid indicated first, nodding when she offered water instead. Fhure had excellent water, sweet from a spring which burbled forth in the cellar of the main house and then out through a channel into the yard. Shianan liked the taste of it.

It was good that he liked the water, for there was little enough else to like about Fhure. He had never really visited his county, as he had never been able to spare the time from his duties, and though the servants were obedient enough, even obsequious, he thought he detected an underlying resentment. He understood it—they had been long neglected—and he thought he could address it, had he the mind. But he could not face the challenge of another disapproving eye, and so he largely ignored them, peremptorily greeting the steward and promising curtly that they would go over the management at some later date. He went woodenly through the days, eating and drinking, pacing the corridors and exploring his property, running through his fields and the village down the hill from the main house.

He had heard nothing from Alham, not from Septime nor Ariana. He had not told them where he would go. He thought it would be simple enough to guess, if they wished, and he more than half hoped they wouldn't.

Tears of frustration burned at his eyes as emotion rose anew. He had tried his best, and it had not been enough. In the end, his desperate efforts to please were meaningless. He had offered his earnest service and received nothing in exchange. It was a market he would not enter again.

He blinked against the treacherous tears, feigning another wipe of his sweaty forehead to rub them away. Then he lifted a hand, bringing the maid. "I'm filthy," he said shortly. "I need a bath."

"I'll have one prepared, your lordship."

Maru bent over the table, observing the tiny structures Tamaryl was tracing in the broken crystal. "It cycles endlessly?" he asked skeptically.

"Not endlessly, of course," Tamaryl said. "It enhances, back and forth like a magnifying echo, and I think enough to allow us to leap across the between-worlds. We can use it for more than just harmonizing against the shield. The problem is, the fracture produces too much refraction, spilling energy out. It's an enormous energy sink to start—that's why the Shard is useful to the Circle, but not to a single mage—and to be truthful, I don't think I can generate enough power."

But Tamaryl would not have broken bad news in this manner. "So you have thought of another way."

"We can leech power from the Shard itself."

Maru caught his breath. "Can we?"

"I think I can channel it, even if I cannot generate it. I'll need to infuse a little at a time, what I can create now, storing enough to start the interaction. It should be able to accumulate enough that, with the inherent amplification, it will approximate typical power."

A typical che's power, Maru understood. Not the Pairvyn's. "Will it be enough?"

"We need only a few minutes, and then we should be able to jump before anyone comes to check on the fluctuation, if they even notice."

Maru nodded. The plan was dangerous, but it was the most

likely they'd found thus far. "You haven't told them yet. Perhaps the White Mage could help infuse—"

"I'll tell them later," Tamaryl interrupted, and his soft voice spoke more than his words.

"One more question," Maru ventured, as much to distract Tamaryl as anything else. "When we reach home—will we heal?"

Tamaryl's face clouded. "I think so." Then he looked at Maru with a more hopeful expression. "We find this world's magic a little more difficult to use. That's always been the case. When we are in our own atmosphere again, we should find it easier to draw our own power."

Maru nodded again. He was nim; if he never recovered from the Subduing, his social position would remain unchanged. He would remain crippled, bound to the earth instead of traveling freely, and he would find himself performing manual labor instead of magical tasks, but he would remain what he was.

Tamaryl, on the other hand, could not return without his power. He was already a figure of suspicion, having been condemned and exiled, having returned with a human mage, having demanded release from a long betrothal. He would need careful politicking to regain his stature again even with his restored title. It would happen, of course—Tamaryl was a good Ryuven, and with time the skills which had made him Pairvyn ni'Ai would win him respect once more——but it would take concentrated effort and display of magnificence.

However, if he returned wounded and empty of power, no different than the Subdued, he would be easy prey in Oniwe'aru's court.

Tamaryl smiled. "Cheer up, Maru. If we're careful, no one will come until it's too late to stop us, if at all."

Maru nodded, unconvinced.

Tamaryl looked at the crystalline chip. "It's our best hope. A few days more, so that I have enough power stored in the fragment, and we'll chance it."

CHAPTER SIXTY-FOUR

Marla rubbed her hands briskly across her arms, trying to warm herself. The afternoon sun helped, though the crisp breeze made her almost wish the trees grew nearer to the road to block the wind.

She was grateful for the cutback, though. The open space prevented easy ambushes, such as that which had snatched away Isen, Luca, and Cole. She shivered and glanced involuntarily over her shoulder, half watching for attack and half wishing irrationally for a glimpse of them.

Luca had shoved her ahead, telling her to run as he turned back. She had seen him reach for a staff, had known he would fight, and then she had run for the trees. When she looked back again, she had seen nothing but wagons—no Luca, no pursuing guard.

It had taken her a while to spot Isen's body, and she felt guilty for that. No doubt his resistance had helped her own escape, and she had not even seen him fall. She mourned him.

She'd hidden for what seemed a long time, watching what she could of the camp, until the wagons began to move. But she had not seen Luca among the shuffling chained prisoners.

Perhaps he had escaped. She hoped that was true, that he hadn't died there like Isen. She had not seen his body, she reminded herself. Perhaps he had escaped, and he had not been able to find her.

But he knew where she would go. If he was safe, he would come.

And it was the best place for her. Once at Fhure, she could claim she had returned to her previous position upon her master's death. Fhure was where she would find her mother, and it was where she might have word of Demario, and it was where she might find Luca if he lived.

So when she had given up waiting in the woods, hiding and hoping to see Luca or Cole returning down the road, she had made her way to the next town. She'd glanced through the slavers' stables, half-expecting to see familiar faces and at a loss as to what she would do if she did, and when she did not find Luca or Cole, she had asked directions and started on her way. She had no money to buy passage in a caravan, and she now distrusted their offer of safety, anyway. The

411

weather was not as mild as that they had left behind, and she missed the wagon and blankets she'd lost, but there was no choice. She had to press on to Fhure.

There was no leftover fruit to be found along the road, not in winter and within the reach of so many travelers. She approached camps a few times, offering to scrub pots in exchange for a meal. Once or twice she asked bread of kindly-looking strangers—women, she was careful to choose, though that was no guarantee—but for the most part she quelled her hunger with promises of hot, delicious meals when she reached her home. They would welcome her, she would dine well, she would sleep, and then she could begin to think on what had happened. Not yet.

She'd asked again this morning, and this road should lead her directly through the village and to the door of Fhure House. She quickened her pace, folding her cold arms against her growling stomach. She was nearly there. She was nearly there.

A man and dog appeared, guiding five placid sheep. The man nodded in a friendly manner and gestured behind him. "There's the village just over the hill if you want something to warm yourself."

"Thank you." That near! She wanted to run, but her tired legs warned against it.

She slowed as the road climbed, closing her eyes against the winter sun. A young girl drove a flock of geese down the road, and they honked and flapped about Marla's legs as they passed. She reached the crest of the hill and saw the distant house.

Fresh energy lifted her and she hurried down the hill, her eyes fixed on the hill beyond the village. Voices called to her as she passed through the market, offering dried fruits or woven baskets or warm clothing, but she ignored them and kept on toward the house.

When she reached the door, she rushed inside, looking about her and calling, "Mama! Mama, I've come back!" She caught a passing servant by a handful of sleeve. "Where's Marta?"

"She's upstairs," answered the servant, surprised.

"Upstairs?" Marla ran up the steps, ignoring her tired legs, and called as she hurried down the corridor. "Mama!"

Marta whirled out of an open doorway and snatched Marla as she ran. "What—" she gasped. "Dear sweet Holy One..."

"Mama!" Marla threw herself against her mother and held tight, as if they might be torn apart. "Mama, I'm home."

For a long time she didn't hear the words her mother was

saying, prayers of gratitude and questions and emphatic exclamations. Finally Marta loosened her embrace and moved back to see her daughter. "I'm glad—I'm so glad—but why are you here?"

Marla tried to think through the overwhelming rush of being at last home, at last secure after the awful journey. "I—I was—I came..." She stopped, emotion pressing at her. "Could we have some tea?"

"Of course we can!" Marta hugged her again. "No, better yet, you just answer one question for me and then we'll find you something warm to eat and a warm bed for a few hours. You look like the road nibbled at you all the way here. But are you here to stay, Marla? Are you staying?"

"Yes, Mama. I'm staying."

"Oh, thank the Holy One! Now come on, there'll be bread coming out of the oven about now."

"Mama." It had to be asked. "Have you heard anything of Demario?"

Marta's sympathetic eyes spoke the answer even before she shook her head.

Marla took a breath and nodded. That was enough for now. "Then, warm bread, please."

True to her word, Marta was good enough not to ask more questions, and after a meal of fresh bread, sliced pork, and melting cheese, Marla lay down on her mother's comfortable bed and slept soundly.

CHAPTER SIXTY-FIVE

It seemed to Luca that he even dreamed of sleep, his mind drifting into semi-consciousness as he walked unless Frangit's sharp voice jarred him to awareness. "Lean into it! Get moving! And you tutor clerk, we aren't taking you as a sight-seeing passenger. Put your back into it, or I'll find a switch and remind you where your back is."

The pain in his head had dulled to a steady, throbbing ache, a weight at his eyes which made him long for the brief rest stops and the glorious moment in the evenings when they halted. Then he lay still, savoring immobility, until their mash and sausage and bread were ready, when he joined the others and ate the bland but filling meal.

Tonight, though, he was only a few bites into his meal when the ginger-haired slave spoke to him. "Give me the sausage, chum."

Luca paused chewing, surprised. "What?"

"The meat, chum. Give it here."

Realization penetrated the haze of Luca's awareness. "No, I don't think I will." The other two slaves were already shifting away, shoving their own meals hurriedly into their mouths.

The slave leaned forward, his eyes glittering in the firelight. "Give it over, gimp. Sausage, now."

Years of conceding drew Luca's eyes down, made him turn away from the bowl in his hand—and then something in him resisted, and he felt his fingers tighten. He picked up the sausage and took a bite.

The slave moved quickly, snatching the meat and swinging at Luca with the other hand. The blow was clumsy as he pulled the sausage free, and Luca ducked away. The other slaves bolted, and Luca straightened. "Give that—"

The fist caught him across the eyebrow, sending waves of agony rippling through his skull. Luca dropped and clutched at his head, but it did not relent. Someone roared above him and he curled defensively as something struck him.

It never ended, king's blessed oats, flames, it never ended...

Frangit was yelling, and it hurt Luca's head. He kept his hands over his ears, his forehead to the grass, cringing.

Benton was speaking to him, Luca realized with a start. He

curled his fingers away from his scalp and tried to hear.

"...Scrambled? Can you hear a thing?"

"My lord," Luca said haltingly. "I..."

"Sit up, can you?" Benton sounded disgusted. "I thought you'd had the sense knocked from you, thought we were out our eight hundred. Frangit! Leave off him, he's got to pull tomorrow."

Frangit released the ginger-haired slave with a shake before growling a final revilement and stalking toward the wagon.

Benton sighed. "'Soats, now it'll be the work of tying you. You'd better be worth the trouble. Nalo, get over by the wheel. Luca, you on the other side. I won't have you ratting at each other through the night."

Luca sat up slowly, mindful of his head. "But I didn't—"

"Don't argue!" Benton snapped, and Luca flinched with the sound. "You were a part of it, whatever it was, and I can't afford to let you two damage each other when I need you working. Get over there."

"Yes, my lord," Luca whispered.

Frangit fastened Luca's left wrist cuff to the wagon wheel and walked away, grumbling. Luca slid around the wheel to the shelter of the wagon, leaving his arm awkwardly stretched, and kept his eyes from Nalo on the other side. He lay down and curled as best he could for warmth, cushioning his head on his outstretched arm. Behind him, the other slaves began cleaning up the supper mess, and Luca's stomach rumbled. Benton and Frangit talked in low voices as they arranged something on the wagon above, making it creak.

Luca turned as best he could and glanced toward the fire. "Anything left?"

One of the slaves shook his head. "Only what was stomped into the ground."

Luca settled again. At least he was not expected to do more work before sleeping. He was glad he'd gone away to relieve himself before eating; he'd had enough of that while chained to a wagon back with Renner. At least now he could sleep.

"Stupid gimp," came a harsh whisper. "If you're not going to pull your share, you can give us your meat, after all."

Luca didn't answer.

"I know you hear me. You'd better do your part tomorrow. Too sick to pull your share is too sick to eat your share."

Luca squeezed his eyes closed. *Only a little more,* he thought. *Only a little more to Alham...*

He slept.

CHAPTER SIXTY-SIX

Luca closed his eyes, steadying himself against the crossbar on the rough paving. Near Alham, the weather had cooled so that the slaves didn't sweat as they worked. He wondered how far it was now.

He wondered what had become of Marla. He wondered how Cole was faring, whether the bandits had sold him to the mines after all once they'd disposed of their other captives.

Something thudded into his arm. "Hey!"

"Nalo!" snapped Frangit's voice. "I saw that."

"Make him do his part!" protested the slave. "He's hardly pulling, like always!"

A little tremor ran through Luca. "That's not so. I—"

"You're coasting on us," Nalo growled. "Half-asleep."

"That's just my head—I'm still pulling—"

"He's right," Frangit interrupted. "You're loafing. Benton's doing as much in the back as you are in the shafts."

Luca's breath caught in his throat.

"I didn't want you anyway, but Benton thought we'd have free labor after selling you. Fat lot he guessed, heh? You lied about pulling before, didn't you?"

"No, my lord! I did take a tinker's single all over…"

"Heh. If your tinker didn't want to get anywhere, maybe." He turned to the wagon. "Benton! Your clerk is shirking!"

Benton was in the rear, watching the road and occasionally helping to push the wagon. "Well, move him," came his detached voice.

Frangit took a running stride and swung onto the moving wagon. Luca turned to look as he began to rummage through the packed cargo. Nalo hit him again. "Move it!"

"Nalo!" Frangit turned back and tapped the ginger-haired slave with a switch. "If you have the strength to be jabbing at your mate, you can be making better time yourself. Get to your own work. And you, Luca—your own work, too. You understand?"

"Yes, master." Nalo was subdued, but his voice held a resentful note.

"Yes, my lord." Luca clenched the bar and bent his head over it,

419

his pulse quickening. He felt faintly dizzy. He could push harder with a switch at his back, yes—at least for a time.

Shianan paused at the edge of the trees, keeping in the shade as he stretched and breathed deep. He had run most of his usual route and had only the last stage across the green and back to Fhure House. He bent low, bringing a pleasant pull across his hamstrings, and then set out on the last leg.

He passed a small herd of pigs, nodding at the pig boy who waved. There were several women chattering excitedly at the edge of the green, glancing from the village to the upper house to Shianan jogging toward them. "Your lordship, please tell us?" one called.

He altered his path to near them. "What's that?"

"The visitors! Who are they? We haven't seen horses on this road in months. Years!"

Shianan's chest tightened in a way that had nothing to do with his long run. "Visitors? On horses?"

"Yes!" The women were pleased to be the ones to deliver the news. "Yes, your lordship! They came up the road and right through the village, asking if you were at the house. They're up the hill right now."

Shianan sprinted, leaving the women behind. On horses—it was someone important, someone who knew where to seek him. Septime? King Jerome? No, the king would never come himself. Perhaps Ewan Hazelrig, come to punish the man who'd made unkept promises to his daughter?

Two horses stood in the yard before Fhure House, a cream color and a deep brown. At their heads Shianan recognized Philip, the royal horseman. He was pointing and calling instructions to a couple of servants, arranging water and fodder for his charges.

Horses and Philip meant someone with power. Perhaps the Ryuven had attacked, had raided Alham itself or another city, Septime had taken the army to meet them and someone had come by horse to order Shianan back into duty. Shianan hurried past Philip and went into the house.

Kraden was nowhere to be seen. He was probably in the kitchen, arranging service for the important visitor. Shianan rubbed a sleeve over his face and went into the main hall, ready to organize battle.

Prince Soren was seated at a table, examining his glove. He glanced up at the sound of Shianan's footstep. "See, I thought I'd find you here."

"Where are they?" Shianan asked breathlessly.

"I beg your pardon?"

"The Ryuven! Have they come? Is that why you've here? Where are they? How are our defenses?"

Soren shook his head. "I know of no Ryuven attack. I came to find you."

Shianan was checked. "To find me?"

"Yes. You'd disappeared from Alham, and no one knew where you were. I guessed you might be here." He gestured to the table and empty chairs. "Come and have a seat. Your steward has promised wine and refreshment."

Cold, efficient fight drained from Shianan, and anger rushed to fill the void. "You came from Alham—for me? Didn't you think I'd left Alham for a reason?" He gestured toward the door. "You rode from Alham on horses, drawing attention to yourself all the way—didn't you think of bandits and robbers? The Ryuven?"

Soren looked surprised. "Becknam—*z*"

"King's sweet oats, if I'd wanted to be at beck and call, I'd have stayed in Alham! I took my leave, the first leave of my life, so I could escape the barking and the staring and the scraping. I thought when I saw those horses that there must be a battle, another Luenda—but no, it's only my sovereign prince come out to risk his royal neck, and for no reason more than to drink my wine!"

Soren stared, and then his cheeks rounded. The corners of his mouth twitched, and he looked at the glove on the table.

Shianan's anger swelled. "What is it that amuses you?"

Soren gave in to the smile. "Not amused, no. But I think I am pleased." He made a small nod. "You've stopped distancing yourself with honorifics and planned speeches and little dances of etiquette." He shrugged. "I'm glad you trust me enough to shout at me."

Shianan's throat closed, and for a moment he could not respond. What had he done—shouting at the prince? His prince, and the lord he'd sworn to obey?

"As far as the bandits go, yes, I'd heard something about several new troubled roads. But I didn't think a day's ride from the city with Philip and my own sword was inviting too much trouble, not when we pay our army good wages to keep the roads safe." He pointed a finger. "And you're not the only one who might appreciate time away from Alham, either."

Shianan's voice was hoarse. "Your Highness, I shouldn't have—"

"Shianan," Soren interrupted, "come and sit."

Shianan obeyed. They sat shoulder to shoulder for a moment, keeping their eyes on the table, and then Kraden entered with a tray, followed by a young dark-eyed woman bearing another. "Ah, master, you're here! I'll bring another cup. My lords, here is the wine, and some excellent cheese, with seasoned pork and bread and fresh herbed butter, and I have apples and honey for you as well."

Neither of them answered, and Kraden made a nervous little bow before departing. The dark-eyed woman waited just a moment, looking at count and prince, before following.

"About what happened..." Soren began at last, his eyes on the food between them. "I meant to get there before you. I thought it might not be a propitious day. But I didn't know in time to warn you."

Shianan clenched his fists. He had spent most of the last few days determinedly not thinking of this. "Propitious... A foul mood might snap at a servant. A foul mood does not raise taxes or wage war. Important decisions reflect the man, not the mood." He shook his head. "The king does not intend to allow me to marry. I'll be fortunate if he doesn't have me gelded." He rested his forehead upon the heels of his hands. "He may even let Alasdair wield the knife."

Soren snorted. "Is that why you're hiding here?"

Shianan tensed. "I'm not hiding. This is my own estate."

Soren said nothing.

Shianan looked away. "If you came all this way only to tell me—"

"That I'm sorry?" Soren stared at the untouched food on the table. "I am. You didn't deserve that. And I'd encouraged you."

Shianan flexed his fingers. "I wish you hadn't been there."

Soren bowed his head. "I'm sorry."

"You said as much already."

"It's still true. I owe you a certain responsibility, you know, as sworn lord."

"You can do only what's in your power, my lord."

"And sometimes I wish it were more." Soren sighed. "This isn't finished, Shianan. I will solicit on your behalf."

Shianan cringed. "Don't make me a beggar."

"Never. But there might be a way to persuade him. You swore to serve me, and I intend to be a lord who serves his servants. And I promise I'll protect you from Alasdair." He grinned.

"Do you?" Shianan looked at him seriously. "Can you?"

Soren sobered. "Dear Holy One, what is he—is it something since he made you swear that stupid oath?"

Shianan looked at the table. "You know about the mercenaries at the public matches?"

"Of course. Some say you hired them to make a name for yourself, but the more common rumor is that the king wanted to surprise you and test your skill."

"It was Alasdair. Using the royal seal."

Soren blinked. "'Soats, maybe you should stay out here after all."

Shianan sighed. "In truth, I don't know where I should be. But I can't stay and see her day after day." He sank his head in his hands. "What if Alasdair learns? What if he torments her with her bastard admirer? I couldn't see her humiliated like that."

"Don't allow it. Won't your inexplicable absence permit more speculation on what drove you from the city? But if you're there, fulfilling your duty as always, that suggests there is less to the story."

Shianan cast him a sidelong glance. "And you want me to return, anyway."

"I do," confessed Soren. "And so, I think, does your lady. I'm told she passes by your office each night on her way home from the Wheel."

"You've had her watched?" demanded Shianan.

Soren held up a hand defensively. "Only, let us say, observed. You left suddenly and without word of where you were going, and we didn't know what had become of you. I thought you might have informed her, at least." He gave Shianan an accusing look. "But you didn't, did you." It was not a question.

"It would not have helped her. She was better not to expect me to return soon."

Soren shrugged. "If you say so. I don't pretend to know much of women. Perhaps they prefer their most ardent admirers to depart without warning."

Shianan flushed hotly. "And what would you have me do? Should I stay and bathe in the shame of being a slave, forbidden to love or marry where I choose?"

Soren looked away. "If that's how you think of it. But if you'd stayed, she wouldn't wonder."

Shianan rolled his eyes. "Ariana's sensible. She isn't going to mope and cry that I found her unworthy. Any man would be pleased to court a lady mage of her standing."

"You're sure she isn't shaken? That she wouldn't prefer you demonstrate your lasting affection by at least consulting her on a point which concerns the two of you so intimately?"

Shianan clenched his jaw. "You do have a way of stating things in your own light. Is that a skill taught to young royals?"

"With grammar and counting," snapped Soren.

"As it happens, I don't want to demonstrate my lasting affection," Shianan retorted. "I want her to be happy, and it's plain a tie to me would give her endless grief. I won't let her be hurt by Alasdair or anyone else. She's a beautiful and intelligent woman, well-placed; she was too grand a prize for me, anyway, and she'll find a better match elsewhere."

Soren hesitated. "You mean that?"

Shianan blew out his breath, his eyes fixed on the table, staring at nothing. "I mean that. I won't be selfish enough to bring her misery." There was a long moment of silence. At last, to occupy his hands, Shianan began to slice an apple. "My lord?"

"Thank you." Soren chewed the offered piece, keeping his eyes from Shianan. Finally he spoke. "You must tell me what it is like, loving someone enough to die for her, and then, to give her up."

Shianan drizzled honey over slabs of apple. "It's wretched."

"All those beautiful tales of unfulfilled love...?"

"They lie. Written by drunken bards who never loved anything but the sound of their own voices." Shianan took a bite, honey sweetness mixing with tart.

"I see." Soren took a piece of the honeyed apple.

They were silent a few moments, helping themselves to the food. Shianan rubbed fretfully at his sweat-slicked hair. The wine was good but not what he wanted after running.

At last Soren spoke. "If you won't come to quell rumor, then I should tell you to come to escape the plague."

"Plague?"

"There's plague starting—not in the city, but in villages and towns through the countryside. It's not one we've seen before. It's a terrible flux that leaves its victims weak and dry."

"Where is it?"

"In the central region, mostly, north and east of Alham, right where every trade caravan is going to carry it through to everywhere else." Soren shook his head. "We've been getting reports. Not many dead so far, only the weak—children and old ones—but that may change with time. And those it doesn't kill, it weakens, and if it spreads as planting comes... We won't have much of a harvest to feed those left."

Shianan licked his lips. "I suppose that next to a kingdom of starving sicklings, a refused match and a bullying young prince are insignificant."

"No! King's oats, that wasn't my meaning at all." Soren drummed his fingers on the table. "No, I only meant—never mind."

"I beg your pardon."

"It's only... I won't order you back. It's your leave, after all. But what are you doing here?"

"I'm not sure." Shianan rubbed at his forehead. "I had not really visited this place since... since it was mine. I like the quiet here. And it is good, I think, to be away from my duties for a time..."

Soren turned to regard him frankly. "Didn't I once say you were a poor liar?"

Shianan's shoulders drooped. "Abominable was the word, I think. But I don't think that's accurate."

"Regardless, I don't think you have any purpose here other than a desire to stay out of Alham—and that only because of the king's denial."

"And what if that's so? Isn't that enough?"

"Certainly, if you wish. After all, it is your leave." Soren took a breath. "But I'm asking you, and not as your prince and lord, but—I'm asking you, will you come again to Alham?"

Shianan stared at the pork, his mind curiously blank. What did it benefit him to be here, anyway? True, it would be difficult to see Ariana, but he was no stranger to having his failures flaunted. Rumor that he had overstepped his bounds might dog him, but that was no novelty, either. And in Alham he would not be reduced to running circles about his land like a mindsick animal.

And perhaps, maybe, Ariana would still welcome him to supper and to walks, and he could cherish what little he could claim.

"Yes," he said. "Yes, I'll come back, my lord."

"I didn't ask as your lord."

425

"I'll come regardless."

"I'm glad to hear it." Soren nodded. "I almost brought a horse for you, you know."

"What?"

Soren chuckled. "By the look of it, that would have made a worthy bribe."

Shianan flushed. "Yes, probably," he confessed.

"I'll keep that in mind the next time I need to fetch you." Soren reached for a piece of cheese. "So, my friend, will you share the hospitality of your house, or should Philip and I start back yet today?"

"I couldn't let you start on the road this late, even with horses. And I cannot have it said that I refused bed and board to my prince. You are of course welcome, though I am not certain our accommodations will be to my prince's custom. I have been a rather lax lord, I fear, and I hardly know my own house."

Soren shook his head. "After a day in the saddle, all I want is a bath and a soft bed. Philip must be made of leather and iron. I assume you country folk do have baths? A half-barrel of rainwater, perhaps?"

"Chilly rainwater, of course."

"Good enough."

CHAPTER SIXTY-SEVEN

Shianan sank into his familiar desk chair, feeling a vague despair.

There had been stares as he walked into the wide military yard, as he'd expected. No one had asked openly where he had been or why, but he could read the question in countless eyes. Still, that mattered little. It would be the king's next audience which would cost him the most.

But when he'd returned to his office and found his desk stacked high with accumulated paperwork, it was insult upon injury. It would take him a week or more to catch up.

With a sigh he began to sort the papers from their stacked chaos into a sort of organization. Briefly he considered requesting an orderly. He had previously declined one because he liked the privacy of his office and quarters, and because of a slight fear that one might report on him to officers or king, but he had found Luca's invasion less troublesome than he'd feared.

Of course, that had been Luca.

He missed Luca—missed his efficient organization and his steady friendship. He hoped his friend had found his footing in his homeland. Perhaps, when this piled work was finished, Shianan would send a letter to the Wakari Coast to confirm all was well.

He sighed. By the time this work was finished, Luca might have settled on the coast, started his own merchant house, and raised children.

He took a sheaf of training reports from Captain Alanz, flipped through them, and set them aside. The fourth squad needed work, but that was nothing new. Shianan would schedule a few extra hours with them when he had the chance. Torg could handle this request to help Sergeant Parr evaluate a handful of recruits who showed unusual promise. Shianan would see to this second group himself, though, as they had come from another company...

He had been working for a couple of hours when there was a knock at the door. "Come," he called.

It was Harl who entered. "Good evening, sir. Welcome back."

"Thank you, Harl. What do you need?"

427

"I was just to give you these, sir. That's all." He set a stack of papers on the desk.

Shianan eyed them resentfully. "I see." He glanced up at the soldier, still waiting behind the desk. "If that's all, Harl, then you may go. I have enough to keep me tonight."

Harl nodded slowly. "Sir..."

"Yes?"

"I just wanted to say, sir, that we, I mean, there's a lot of us who are glad to be under you, sir. If ever you need something, just say the word, sir."

Shianan looked at him for a moment in surprise. "Thank you, Harl."

The soldier nodded stiffly.

"Tell me, then." Shianan laced his fingers together. "What are they saying about my recent absence?"

"All of it, sir?" Harl looked up thoughtfully. "There's a few who said you left after seeing the king, so there was some trouble there. That's only a few, though. Others suppose the king gave you a mission of your own. Or it's said you went on another task for the Circle, as you've brought the Shard back twice."

It was better than he could have hoped. "I see. Thank you." He made himself smile. "If anyone asks, you may tell them on excellent authority that I'm not speaking on it."

Harl smiled and nodded. "Yes, sir."

"That's all, Harl. Thank you."

He sat for a moment after the soldier left, wondering if this quiet confidence from his men made him more valuable or more dangerous in the king's eyes. Finally he shook his head and bent again over the desk.

He had lit two candles against the deepening twilight when another knock sounded. "Come."

He caught a glimpse of three men as the door opened, but only one entered. He was difficult to see behind the candles placed to light the paperwork. "Come closer, please. What can I do for you?"

"You Shianan Becknam? Bailaha?"

The speaker was unfamiliar. Shianan slid his hand nearer the knife on his belt. "I am. Who are you?"

"I'm Benton Madden. I've come about a missing slave."

Shianan relaxed and tried to hide his annoyance. "If you're looking for a runaway, the officer you want to talk—"

"No, not mine, m'lord. Yours. Your own slave who's missing."

Apprehension washed over Shianan. Had someone finally noted that he'd stolen and sent away Luca? "I'm not missing any slaves."

Benton Madden gave a long, disappointed sigh. "I was afraid of that. I should have known better than to believe a slave trying to avoid the mines." He shook his head. "I wish he'd been yours, though. Frangit will be sharp, and we'll be lucky to get our own money out of him again. Sorry to bother you, m'lord." He turned to go.

Shianan watched him, wondering. A runaway slave had named Shianan Becknam as his master? Had someone fled Fhure? Only Luca had ever served him here in Alham, and Luca was safely with his brother across the border.

The door closed, and a few seconds passed. Then Shianan heard raised voices, a strained shout and then an angry retort.

The door was of heavy wood, but the tone caught Shianan's ear. It was probably just the suggestion, but... Impulsively he rose and went to the door.

Benton was a few paces into the yard. Beyond him, one man held another in a close grip, twisting his arm to control him as he protested and keeping a handful of hair at the back of the neck. He turned as the door opened, dragging the struggling figure with him, and Shianan's chest spasmed.

Three men looked at him, framed in the doorway, and a quick, eager voice urged, "Master Shianan!"

Even in the faint light Shianan could recognize the bent figure. "Let him up!" He reached for Luca, steadying him as he straightened. "King's sweet oats, Luca—what are you doing here?"

Luca gave him a wobbling tentative grin beneath a bloody nose. "I couldn't help it, master."

Benton Madden stepped forward again. "We found him in Cascais, m'lord, saying he was stolen and needed returned to you. He said you'd ransom him for a thousand pias."

"Eight hundred," Luca said quickly, and his eyes went to Shianan's. He looked uncertain, hopeful, afraid. "Eight hundred pias, to redeem me..."

Shianan's mind whirled, but the overwhelming thought was to secure Luca. "I don't have that much coin here. I can draw against my name tomorrow, if you'll come then."

Benton had cast a frowning look at Luca's correction. "That

429

will do, of course. We'll bring him in mid-morning, if you—"

"No," interrupted Shianan. "He stays, and you'll collect your fee in the morning."

Benton hesitated. "With all respect, m'lord—"

"I will write you a sale. Do you doubt I'm good for it? I will be working in this office all of tomorrow, so come at your leisure. I intend to set him on some of that work myself. And if he stays with you," Shianan added, pulling Luca away from his captor and looking darkly at his bloodied face, "it seems he won't be fit for service."

The second man bristled defensively. "He was lying, we thought, about belonging to you. And he got loud when we made to take him away. Why'd you say he wasn't yours?"

"I said I wasn't missing anyone," Shianan corrected. "Why didn't you mention his name? He told you he was stolen, yes? Well, I thought he was lost for good." He nodded toward the office door. "Go inside, Luca, and clean yourself up. If you two will step in, I'll write a sale for you."

He hastily scribbled a contract—"thank you, I'll see you in the morning"—and locked the door behind the traders. In the living quarters, Luca had set lights and was sponging at his nose. Shianan paused as Luca turned, and for a moment they stared at one another.

Luca broke the silence first. "I'm so sorry, Master Shianan. I couldn't think of anything else but to say that I was yours, and they never would have brought me this far without profit. I'll earn it back for you, I'll hire myself out—I'll make it up somehow."

Shianan ignored this. "Luca, what happened?"

"Eight hundred—it will take time, but I'll earn it back—"

"Luca," Shianan interrupted firmly. "I am not worried about the money. I would have paid far more. Didn't I tell you no one could afford your price?"

Luca looked at him with surprised eyes as he lowered the reddened rag.

He was too pale behind the blood. "Sit. Do you need something to drink?"

Luca gave a half-smile. "The irony, master."

Shianan cast him a reproving look. "I can handle a bottle myself, thank you."

"No, please, I'd better have water. I don't trust my head to anything stronger yet."

Shianan brought a cup and sat to face him. "What happened to your head?"

"I proved a few weeks of training with a staff does not enable me to hold my own." Luca reached to probe gently at the side of his head. "The swelling's mostly faded, I think, but I still have aches."

Shianan rose. "What kind of aches?"

"Dull, slow... I want to sleep. A constant dull fuzz, not coming and going."

"Give me that light." Shianan stood over him and parted his hair, frowning. "You have some bruising yet, but it's old. Look me in the eye." He studied the pupils, watched how they followed his movement. "I'll guess you didn't have a proper chance to recover?" He returned to his chair. "You'll sleep long tonight, see how that does for you. Tell me where you've been."

Luca laughed grimly. "Oh, Master Shianan, it's a tale worthy of song. I have been a draft slave and the enslaved master of a slave. I have been a stranger from the eastern desert and a leper. I have been the homecoming guest of honor and the impostor of a dead man. I have been abducted by bandits and sold into slavery. And I have now been over the table six times, which could surely earn a prize if there were one." He held up a hand tiredly to indicate the new wrist cuff.

Shianan stared, his heart twisting in his too-tight chest. "Didn't you go back with Jarrick?"

Luca took a breath. "I did. And I was freed, and I even went home. But—it was no home to me, that's the quickest way to say it. It's all I think I can say on that for now. And so I was coming back here, as a freeman."

"Here?"

"I wanted to take up business. I had a potential partner, or at least someone who might need an assistant." He stopped and dug the heels of his hands into his eyes. "I was so close. I had money, prospects, a place I wanted to go." He huffed a grim sob of a laugh. "Well, at least I got to where I wanted to go."

"What happened?"

"Our caravan was attacked. Hired guards were part of it. They took the cargo, the people, everything. We were sold as slaves. I didn't want to go to the salt flats, so I told those two I'd been stolen and you would pay double my purchase price." Luca paused. "Thank you."

Shianan shook his head. "I told you, I'm not worried about the money. But I'd meant for you to be a freeman. You had your family and your homeland."

Luca looked frustrated. "I told you, I chose to come. I wanted to find a place where no one knew me, where I could make a fresh start." He looked down at his cup. "I haven't made much of a start, have I?"

Shianan rose. "Finish your water and go to bed. You need rest, that's obvious, and the story can wait until morning." He reached beneath the bed and dragged out the rolled mattress. "Here."

Luca glanced at the mat. "You still have it?"

"What would I have done with it?" Shianan hesitated and looked at the returned slave. "You weren't supposed to need it again."

Luca made a half-hearted smile. "Sorry, master."

"King's sweet oats." Shianan shoved the mattress across the room, too fiercely. He lowered himself into a chair and rested his forehead against his hand. "Luca..."

He heard Luca shift in the chair. "I didn't want it to be this way. I didn't want to ask anything of you."

"That's not it at all." Shianan blinked away traitorous tears. "I'm angry with myself for being glad you're back."

Luca stared at him, and then Shianan saw the rigidity drain from his shoulders. "I'm glad to be here," he answered, his voice almost a whisper. He laced his fingers together and squeezed his knuckles white. "I have been a Furmelle slave, I have suffered daily abuse at the hands of the Gehrn, I have been a draft slave. I do not wish to be a slave, but this is the least of the three years of hell I have endured." He straightened and looked levelly at Shianan, drawing a breath. "But this I do say to you: do not sell me again, not even toward my freedom."

Shianan looked away. "I meant well by it. I thought you should go to your brother."

"It was not so simple as that." Luca's throat worked visibly in the candlelight. "You *sold me*. The only thing I ever asked, the only thing you promised."

Shianan sighed and rubbed his face. "I'm sorry, Luca. I am. I only... I meant well, believe me. That's all I can say."

"That was the only time you treated me as chattel, as a thing. I hadn't known that you could."

The words scorched Shianan like coals. The ground shifted beneath him, and he saw for the first time what it had been for Luca— not what Shianan had meant, but what had actually been. For a moment he couldn't breathe.

He struggled for a response, keenly aware nothing could be adequate, and found only self-loathing and questions. "Then—then why did you come here again?"

Luca looked steadily at him. "I had the idea that, if I did, you might say you were sorry for it."

For a moment Shianan could not answer. Words could not be sufficient. But at last he forced his mouth to work. "I'm sorry."

The short sentence burned. He had thought Luca was only hesitating to approach what he really wanted, just as Shianan did. He had not imagined Luca might not have wanted family and freedom, that he might have considered Shianan's liberation a betrayal. Sick horror filled him at what he had done, what Luca must have thought of him. "I thought it was the best thing for you."

"At first, I didn't see how you could," Luca said. "But then I realized why you had."

Shianan closed his eyes, as if that could stop Luca from penetrating his soul and seeing all. "I am sorry. Luca, I am so sorry."

"I understand it now, I think. But do not do it again."

Shianan opened his eyes and met Luca's gaze. "No."

The word hung between them, too small for its significance.

Shianan took a breath. "We can write to your brother, buy you passage—"

"Don't." Luca shook his head and winced as he moved too quickly. "I can't go back. Not yet. Not—not now."

Shianan wanted to ask, but there was too much laid bare tonight. Luca would explain when he could.

"All I could think of was making it to Alham. I can't think of what's next, not yet. I just needed somewhere before I could even think..." Luca raised his eyes and fixed them on Shianan. "It seems you have the keeping of me now."

Shianan's chest tightened. "You..." He placed his hands on his knees. "That is a heavy burden."

"It does not seem to be mine to manage." Luca smiled for the first time, grim and determined.

"You may not wish to stay near me, Luca. I'm a target for Prince Alasdair, I've angered the king, and Prince Soren himself had to root me out of my hiding hole. I don't know that I'll make a good master for either of us."

"Then I'll have to ferret out some more fraudulent accounts, I suppose."

Shianan smiled, his face flexing stiffly. "I'll be happy to have you to do it." He gestured. "Go to bed. You look like you were dragged the entire length of the road."

Luca nodded gingerly and started toward the mattress. He hesitated as he toed off his worn boots. "Master Shianan. The bandits near Cascais, are they—could someone be sent to—"

"A squad will be dispatched."

"They took other prisoners."

"We'll sort it out tomorrow, Luca. A night more won't make a difference. You need rest and I need—'soats, I don't even know what I need. Go to sleep."

"Good night, then."

Shianan went back to the unforgiving stack of paperwork, leaving the door to the living quarters ajar for no reason he could define. He was glad Luca had come back, glad beyond all excuse. King's oats, if Soren had not urged him back, if he had delayed only a few hours, he would have missed Luca entirely.

And how could he be pleased that Luca was a slave again?

But something Luca had said... Yes, it was good to have a friend near again. It was good to have someone nearby to trust wholly.

CHAPTER SIXTY-EIGHT

Luca slept late the next morning, later than Shianan had known him to do. He didn't wake until Shianan accidentally jostled a chest lid. Luca jolted awake, wincing. "Is it late?"

"No, no."

Luca squinted at the laundry. "Oh. Here, let me get those. I'll take them and—"

"Luca, let it be. How's your head?"

A knock at the door interrupted, and Shianan rolled his eyes. "They didn't wait long, did they? Wanted their coin, of course, and I can't argue that. But they could have given me time to reach a moneylender. No, stay in bed." He went to the door and pulled it roughly open.

Ariana looked at him with wide, staring eyes. He froze, startled. She took a breath and spoke first. "You've come back."

"I—yes, plainly. I'm back."

She waited a moment, as if expecting him to say something more. When he didn't, she lifted her chin slightly. "Weren't you even going to tell me you were in Alham again?"

Shianan flinched. The chill temperature of the outside yard began to creep through the open door.

"I overheard some soldiers talking in the yard. That's how I learned you'd returned."

Shianan made a vague gesture. "I came only yesterday. I haven't been here long..."

"Long enough for it to be gossip. And I had thought I might have a claim on you above that of a common soldier."

Shianan's heart stopped in his chest. He drew a quick breath, seeking an explanation to offer. "I have something to do, an errand. When I return—" He stopped himself. If Ariana would fare better without his dangerous influence, as he'd told himself, how could he justify going to her once more?

She opened her mouth as if to reply, but no sound came. Instead she looked at him levelly for a moment, and Shianan could not read her expression.

She pulled her cloak about her and adjusted the collar

435

minutely, the muscles of her jaw tightening as she held his eyes. "It seems we both have demands in our work. If you should want to speak with me later, you know where to find me." She turned and walked across the courtyard without looking back.

Something seized Shianan, clawing up his stomach and into his chest and through his lungs, making him sick and pained and breathless all at once. His limbs froze and he could not break his paralysis as he watched, speechless. Ariana passed the fountain and turned in the direction of the Wheel.

Luca came and gently shut the door, blocking the cold breeze which ruffled papers on the desk. "Master Shianan," he began, but he did not finish.

Shianan turned and walked away, sitting on the edge of the desk. He sighed. "I think we have long passed the point where I tell you to keep clear of your master's business."

Luca faced him and waited.

Shianan took a slow breath. "I suppose you know I stole the Shard for her? I expected to die then, I did. But I didn't, thanks to you, and I somehow got up the—I would have asked her hand. To marry Ariana Hazelrig! But I'm not really a free man, and I went to ask the king's leave..."

He glanced at Luca and saw he'd guessed the outcome. "No, it didn't go well. And I lost my temper, which is hardly wise before a king even if one is not a royal bastard." Shianan shook his head. "I said... I've never said such things before. And then I had no chance at all of being with her, and I couldn't—you see, don't you, that I couldn't stay and face her? Tell her that I'd ruined my only chance?" Shianan raked his fingers through his hair. "I am a fighting man by training and by trade, Luca. Why is it that I do not hesitate before a mortal opponent and yet I cannot move myself even to call back a woman?"

"You must write to her."

"What?"

"It's easier to write. Take the time to formulate the words exactly as you mean them, not as you think of them haphazardly and half-panicked, and put them on paper. Then let her see your thoughts with time to think on them and hear them, without the need to reply in the moment."

Shianan gave him a smile which mocked them both. "Did you spend your time wooing and winning fair hearts while you were away?"

Luca did not smile in return. "In my anger I called my sister a whore." He looked pained. "Those were my first words to her in years. I needed a careful letter to repair that damage. But she read it and heard me."

Shianan sobered. "I see." He nodded toward the courtyard. "But my lady mage is only as far as the Wheel. Will she read through a letter in place of hearing me?" He forced a shrug. "And I shouldn't taunt the both of us with what we cannot have."

"Can't you? You are a freeman. You may do as you wish."

A flash of anger went through Shianan. "I am not as free as that, Luca."

"Forgive me, but I've had opportunity to reflect on the nature of freedom recently, and you are freer than you think. The king influences law, but even he cannot break it, and marriage is binding. If you were to openly marry her—"

"After specific prohibition?" Shianan demanded. "'Soats, man, he already told me I was lucky to escape with my balls. They used to do that to bastards here, you know."

Luca stared at him incredulously. "With all respect, master, your line is barbaric."

"Heh. At one time it was probably considered judicious to visit the sins of the fathers upon accidental children. Rather like drowning unwanted kittens, I suppose." Shianan exhaled. "But regardless of what specific—act he intends, he is the king, and I am a bastard."

Luca nodded silently.

Shianan's voice faded hoarsely. "And so, what can I tell Ariana?"

"Tell her that for your part, you love her," answered Luca softly. "Don't leave her to wonder."

Shianan looked at him, wondering at Luca's unsaid reasons, and considered. It was not far from what Soren had advised. Yes, he owed Ariana that much. She was an intelligent woman, if idealistic, and she would understand.

His suit had been naturally clandestine, which was fortunate. He did not want any shame attached to her. And at least there had been no commitment, no arrangement between them.

He clenched a fist. Ariana would understand. She had the sense to see past her optimistic idealism and recognize necessity. He only had to explain.

He sighed. "I need paper."

Shianan pushed his fingers through his hair. His letter to Ariana was proving beyond difficult.

Luca bumped open the dividing door and carried a dustpan through the office. "Do you need anything?"

Shianan frowned at the half-filled sheet, marred with dripped ink and struck-out words. "Everything."

"It's not coming well?"

He sighed. "I don't want to pretend that she isn't everything she is, and she deserves better than simple rejection. But it's not as easy as it sounds to protest that she's my most precious thought and so I will not even pursue her friendship, now the king knows what I intended."

Luca gave him a sadly empathetic look.

Shianan looked down at his sheet and abruptly drew a savage line across it. "And whatever I write must be perfect, because she won't hear it once but again and again, each time she looks at it. And I cannot make it clear even to myself, so how to her?" He shook his head. "Sorry. Go ahead with whatever you were doing. I'm just arguing aloud."

Luca nodded and opened the office door, reaching around the frame to tip out the dust. Shianan set his chin in his hand, looking out into the courtyard. Two men crossing at a distance made him think of Luca's transport.

"I'm going to find a moneylender," he said aloud. "Holy One knows I need a break from this. If those two blockheads come for your payment before I return, tell them to wait. Take messages from anyone else but say to anyone but a general that I have quite a bit of work to catch up and I'll get to it as I can. Don't let on that I'll get to it when I've finished a letter to the wonderful girl I'm spurning." He shook his head. "'Soats, it's still morning, and I think I want a drink."

Luca tried to look encouraging.

Shianan blew out his breath. "I'll be back shortly." He reached for his cloak and went into the chilly morning.

Luca was waiting when he returned. "Don't take off your cloak."

Shianan set the money on the desk and tried to buffer his irritation with a weak joke. "I thought I said to tell anyone but a general to wait."

    Luca didn't smile. "Not a general. It's the king."

CHAPTER SIXTY-NINE

Generals Kannan and Septime were waiting with the king, as well as Chancellor Uilleam. The military and the council were both represented. This was not a private audience—but it was serious.

Shianan should have expected this. He steeled himself and knelt.

"So you've finally returned?"

"Yes, Your Majesty."

The words were in his voice, but they seemed strange to him. How different it was, now that he knew his coin would never be welcome in this market and he no longer sought to buy.

"You cannot just abandon your duties and flee to your country estate!"

"I abandoned nothing," Shianan answered as evenly as he could. "I had permission to take leave."

"Your Majesty, that is true." General Septime gestured apologetically but spoke in Shianan's defense. "It was a legitimate and reasonable leave-taking, if a bit sudden."

The king scowled. "Never mind that," he growled, turning away.

He would not admit the bastard had fled after a quarrel with his royal father. Shianan clenched his fists.

"You have duties to this kingdom," King Jerome said, turning back. "You cannot ignore them."

"They were not ignored, Your Majesty. You know I have only ever served you. I made my request appropriately."

It was a dangerous allusion, meant for the king's ears only. It reached them.

The king scowled. "I can strip Fhure from you."

Shianan's stomach clenched. He did not care so much for the estate itself, but it was the basis for his comital title. Without it, he was not nobility, not a member of the court.

But what did those benefit him now?

"If you feel you must." He swallowed against the thickness in his throat. "It was Your Majesty who bestowed the land and title upon me when you called me to Alham. You can of course take them back."

441

General Kannan nodded. General Septime looked pained. Chancellor Uilleam coughed.

"If it means so little to you, perhaps it should never have been granted in the first place," King Jerome said. "Perhaps you do not esteem the king's gifts."

"Whether I esteem them or not, they are yours to take." Shianan's voice was mostly steady, but his stomach was sinking. Without Fhure, without his title, he had less standing than ever to court Ariana or even to visit Soren. The king meant to strip him of status, but he was stripping him of friends.

"Your Majesty, I believe this sort of action is traditionally discussed with the council." Chancellor Uilleam said, without looking at Shianan.

King Jerome was not pleased to be interrupted. "I can manage my own court," he said curtly. "And it seems Bailaha—or rather, Becknam—is not anxious to keep his lands and title, so there seems to be little reason to debate it. The council can confirm this deprivation of title at our next convening."

Sweet all, it was done. Shianan could not tell whether he truly did not care for the loss or whether he was too numb with the shock to feel the cut.

"Have you nothing to say?" demanded King Jerome.

The words seemed distant, muted. "What would you have me say, Your Majesty? It is your court to manage."

"And if you were no longer commander?"

Ice shot through Shianan's chest and he couldn't draw breath. Not his military role—not the one thing he'd been raised to, excelled at, found purpose and respect in, not his one place in the world—

General Septime cleared his throat. "With respect, Your Majesty, that is under my authority, and I have no reason to remove Commander Becknam from his position."

"And if I should give you a reason?" The king turned his eyes on the general.

General Septime took a breath. "I would take any well-founded report into consideration."

King's sweet oats, Shianan had never guessed that General Septime might stand up to the king for him. But he didn't know if it would do any good. Could the king order him to demote Shianan?

He imagined for one moment going to his soldiers, the troops who trusted and followed him—or would there be a public ritual?—

shamed before all their staring eyes, and the thought was nauseating.

The king disliked General Septime's qualified answer. "We can discuss the military rank when we confirm the deprivation of title," he said gruffly. "And with that, I think we have finished here."

Shianan fled before General Septime or any of the others could call to him. He could not bear to face them, to answer the questions they would ask aloud or silently, to feel the shame of fresh rejection, derision, pity.

He slammed the door to his office as if he were pursued, and Luca looked up from his work. "Yes? What happened? Are you—all right?"

How humiliating that Luca knew even to ask. "The generals and chancellor were there. I—I'm losing Fhure. No longer a count."

"Oh..." Luca's dismay trailed away. "Why?"

"Because—well, he doesn't have much of a reason, really. He claims I abandoned my duties, but General Septime confirmed I'd requested leave. But really, it's because I dared to ask to marry, and because when he refused I said things I've never said and shouldn't have said."

"I'm sorry."

Shianan shook his head. "I can live without the title. It's not as if I make much of it now. But—sweet Holy One, I don't know if I can even—but he's trying to take the commandery too."

Luca's face showed he guessed the depth of this cut. "Oh, Master Shianan..." He started forward, and Shianan suddenly feared he was going to embrace him. He raised a hand to stave him off, regretting the gesture even as he made it. If ever anyone had earned the right—but no, Shianan couldn't take a kind touch just now, or he would shatter.

He closed his eyes. "I still have to explain to Ariana—and king's sweet oats, now I'm not even—" He drew a slow, shaking breath.

And suddenly, despite the shame of it, he wanted to see her. To hear her voice, let her bright idealism burn even briefly on his behalf before he accepted his losses.

He opened his eyes. "But then, no letter has ever compared to true groveling." He balled the half-filled sheet on his desk and tossed it into the glowing brazier. "If she won't hear me, then I suppose I've lost nothing in the end, and if she will, the best I can hope for is understanding. But this will take me some time, and I don't want to risk interruption." He buckled his swordbelt, removed for the royal audience, about his waist, occupying his hands with the familiar movement. "Tell no one where to find me, you understand? No one. This will be touchy enough without some sergeant pointing in to tell me the fourth squad still can't find the privies without help."

Luca nodded. "Tell no one, I understand. I'll say you are out with business and will return late."

Shianan gave him a quick, nervous glance. "I don't know how I'll explain, but I've abandoned my pride before now, and I have precious little to preserve today. I'll be back when I can." He whipped his cloak over his shoulders as he hurried out into the slanting sun.

Luca closed the door after him, wishing he could think of a solution. Barbaric, all of it. The Wakari Coast had its share of faults, but at least there slaves could be freed with a living master's manumission and royals did not brazenly beat or geld one another.

And Shianan's military commission—if he lost that, he lost himself.

Luca had napped again and his headache had nearly disappeared. He had to be careful, going slowly when he bent or straightened, but he could manage.

He suspected relief played as much a part as the blessed sleep. Perhaps the residual ache would fade when he learned what had become of Marla and Cole. Worry for them had nagged at him while he lay on his comfortable mattress, at last warm and satiated and safe.

But if Shianan no longer held Fhure, even if he found Marla, he would have no connection to her.

He went to the little kit of physic Shianan kept and took out the healing ointment. He shed his shirt and stretched to dab some along the welts and bruising across his shoulders. He was glad Shianan had not known of the switch marks. He'd been angry enough at the merchants for Luca's bloody nose and aching head and for having Luca at all. Luca didn't want his sympathy for more.

A knock sounded at the outer door. Luca dropped his shirt over his head and pulled at the laces. He opened the door, prepared to offer an apology on his master's behalf, and saw the prince.

Prince Soren stepped inside before Luca could collect himself enough to speak. "Brr," he commented, shifting his cloak. He looked at Luca. "Aren't you...?"

Luca bowed in hasty respect, wincing. "Luca, my lord. Your Highness."

"I thought you had gone."

The prince knew? "I've returned to serve my master."

Prince Soren seemed to consider this a moment, but he did not ask further. "I've come to speak with Bailaha. Isn't he here?"

Surely Shianan had not thought the prince himself would come to ask for him. "He is not, my lord. But I will tell him you would speak with him."

"Where is he now, then?"

The question was casual enough, but Luca's hesitation gave it unintended import. If the king were angry over Shianan's intended courtship, could Luca betray Shianan's mission to explain to Ariana?

Luca gathered himself. "I'm sorry, my lord, I cannot say."

"He didn't tell you where he went? Or is that not what you meant?" The prince's voice darkened. "Where is your master?"

Luca sank to one knee. "I cannot say, my lord."

A moment passed. When the prince spoke again, his tone was softer. "You doubt I mean well, and I suppose that's only reasonable. But whatever things may have been in the past, I consider Shianan Becknam now my friend as well as my liegeman."

Luca caught a breath, but he did not speak.

"Luca, I am your prince. Tell me where he is."

Luca gulped. "You are indeed a prince and so worthy of respect—but you are not my prince. I am a slave and no citizen, and therefore I have no prince. I have one master, and by his order I cannot say where to find him."

There was a long moment of silence, and Luca wondered desperately what he had done. How had he dared to speak so to the prince-heir? Would Luca even be here when Shianan returned?

But then, at last, he heard Soren chuckle. "You silver-tongued versifier! I knew you'd answered all but my own question the last time, but I had no idea what you could spin. King's sweet oats, it's good you're a slave and not a diplomat." He paused. "Stand, please, Luca. And don't worry. I told you once I wouldn't punish another man's slave, and certainly not this one."

Luca rose slowly, keeping his eyes low. There was no threat of imminent danger as he had felt from Ande and others, but he could not quite believe he had spoken so without repercussion.

"But hear me: all jests aside, I need to know your master is safe and yet in Alham. Tell me, very simply, if he has left the city again or if he intends to leave."

Luca licked his lips. "He has not, for my knowledge, left Alham, nor intends such."

A shout from the courtyard interrupted them. "To the Wheel! Ryuven in the Wheel! Hurry to the Shard!"

Soren spun, his cloak whipping about him. "In the Wheel? But the shield—how? The Wheel itself?"

Luca thought wildly of Shianan, going to the Black Mage.

CHAPTER SEVENTY

Tamaryl drew the borrowed cloak more tightly about him, flattening his wings to minimize their telltale shape. He hesitated in the shadow of the alley and glanced at Maru. "More."

Maru looked distressed. The uneven protrusion shifted beneath the cloak, but one knobbled angle still showed. He could not draw his broken wing any closer.

Tamaryl felt a quick flash of renewed anger for Maru's injury. "Do what you can," he whispered harshly. "Maybe they will think we carry packs beneath the cloaks." He knew even his own wings marred the shape of his back, filling the cloak from the back of the stretched hood to the ground. He looked something like a hunchbacked troll in a children's tale.

He flexed his fingers about the broken piece of crystal, reflecting the warmth of his hand. "We have to be quick. No hesitation, or we're lost. Are you ready?"

Maru nodded tightly.

Brave Maru. He carried as much risk on this venture, but without even a small pool of power to protect himself if they were discovered. Tamaryl gave him a hasty smile. "Let's go."

They hurried through the streets, keeping to the edges and lees, holding the ill-fitting cloaks close. There was not enough power between them to betray them to a mage sentry, but anything more than the most casual glance could reveal them.

But Tamaryl had traveled these streets a thousand times, a slave unworthy of notice, and he led Maru through the same paths and in the same humble manner, and somehow they arrived at the Wheel undiscovered.

Maru pressed close to a sheltering wall and released a long, quavering breath. "Safe thus far."

Tamaryl nodded. "This way. Stay quiet; there's nowhere to hide in these corridors."

They set off down the curving corridor, moving quickly past the closed workrooms. Only a little further until the stairs to the cellar...

A figure in violet robes came around the bend, her head bent

447

over a small book, and Tamaryl's heart quickened. Maru seemed to hesitate mid-step, but then he slid closer to the wall and kept moving. Tamaryl glanced away, as if the weight of his eyes could alert the mage, and he held his breath.

The figure in violet was nearly abreast of them when she raised her head. "Good evening," she commented, and then her eyes widened. "Who—dear Holy One—!"

Tamaryl formed a barrier and pulled Maru behind him as her power flared. He felt the cursory attack fail and bolted, hurrying around the curve before she could form a more powerful blow. "Ryuven!" the mage shouted behind them. Power billowed about them as she turned to pursue them. "Ryuven, here!"

Maru looked at him, fear shining in his eyes. Tamaryl slid to a halt. "I'll hold them off. Go and—"

"No! Ryl, no!"

"Go! I'll join you, I swear." He pushed Maru. "The next arch, the stairs down. Make the exchange—hurry. I'll come."

Maru gave him a steady, meaningful gaze. "Don't stay here."

Tamaryl shook his head. "I'm coming with you. But I'm covering our escape. Now go."

Maru ran, leaping into the archway as another mage came about the bending corridor. Tamaryl whirled with a flourish of cloak to draw the eye away from Maru and ran. *She'll be here... she'll be here...*

He reached the black door as Ariana tore it open. She stared at him. "Tamaryl—"

He lunged and seized her arm, pulling her to him. "Come with me," he said gruffly, turning her and holding her close. "I need you as a hostage."

"A hostage?"

"You're surety for our escape." He pushed her toward the stairs. "They can't kill us if you're our shield."

Any answer she made was lost as they suddenly faced two mages, Gold and Amber. Upon seeing Ariana they checked their arcane assault and hesitated. "Let her go!"

"I'm afraid I dare not," Tamaryl answered curtly. "Down the stairs, my lady mage." He descended first, keeping Ariana between himself and the following mages.

There was a faint tremor in the air about him—Maru's work. The distracted mages, focused on him and Ariana, did not seem to notice.

Tamaryl reached the base of the stairs and backed into the wide room, pulling Ariana with him. "Stay back!" he warned. "It would be tragic indeed to lose the Black Mage to one of the Circle's own."

There were more mages now, hurrying down the stairs and slowing as they saw Ariana held tightly to Tamaryl's chest, shielding him from any sort of arcane bolt. Tamaryl felt his cloak slipping but it no longer mattered. He had nothing to conceal now. He needed only a moment.

"The Shard!"

They had seen Maru behind the glossy crystal. He ducked behind it as the Amber Mage raised his arms. "No!" shouted another. "Not toward the Shard!"

Someone dashed into the cellar, light robes swirling, and Tamaryl swore. But it was neither silver nor white. He jerked Ariana nearer the Shard.

"How did they come here? How did they penetrate the shield?"

"Ariana, get out of the way!"

Tamaryl held her tightly. *Only a moment.*

But then another dark figure swept down the stairs, shoving aside mages as he charged to the front. Shianan Becknam glared across the cellar with blazing eyes. "Let her go!"

Tamaryl caught his breath. Becknam alone would guess Ariana was not in real danger. Still, he would not risk her... "Stay back, my lord commander."

Becknam leveled his sword toward Tamaryl's eyes. "I'm telling you to let her go." He started forward.

Tamaryl took a quick step backward, jerking Ariana with him and putting a hand to her throat. "Back! I'm not in a position to barter, commander. I need a shield of my own."

Becknam hesitated. "You wouldn't..." Tamaryl saw him hesitate, saw him realize he could not call Tamaryl's bluff without betraying Ariana's treason.

But Tamaryl had no need to protect Becknam's secrets. "I know what she is to you, and you know what you are to me. Keep well back."

Becknam paled. The mages were fanning about the room, but they still could not risk attack, not as long as Tamaryl and Maru kept Ariana and the Shard of Elan close.

Shianan Becknam stopped moving, but he kept his sword ready. "You snake-tongued dog," he snarled. "This has nothing to do with her. It's me you want dead. Come for me, then."

Maru shifted uneasily behind the Shard.

"Come on! Or can't you? Is the great Pairvyn ni'Ai reduced to hiding behind a girl?"

For a moment Tamaryl almost pitied the commander's position. His only hope lay in taunting Tamaryl into abandoning Ariana and fighting, and of course Tamaryl would not be so foolish.

"Pairvyn ni'Ai," the mages muttered. "How...?"

"Leave her, forget these mages, and face me. Champion against champion, without interference. It's me you want to hurt, not her."

"Shianan." Ariana's voice was nervous, uncertain. "Shianan, don't."

"I'm one man, Pairvyn! One man—not even a mage! Surely you can't fear me?"

"I'm leaving, my lord commander," Tamaryl said evenly. "I have no reason to fight you here."

The shield cracked invisibly, something shifting between Shard and fractured fragment, and the mages jumped and looked around as the magic wavered. That did not matter; if the shield fell for a few moments, that was a simpler escape for them.

Tamaryl turned his face toward Ariana's ear, breathing in the warm scent of her. "We're going, Maru and I. We're going now."

She did not hesitate. "Take me with you."

"What?"

"Take me with you!"

Tamaryl could not answer. He did not have the strength to carry both her and Maru, and there would not be a second chance. Why did she ask?

Power began to stream from the failing spell, making iridescent shifting ribbons in the air about them like translucent smoke. Shianan Becknam rushed through the pale colors, his expression murderous.

Tamaryl threw himself backward and twisted. "Shield!"

The blade sliced toward Ariana's throat, now where Tamaryl's shoulder had been. She flinched as her invisible barrier deflected the blade with a faint ring of steel. Ariana stared wide-eyed at the commander. "Shianan, no!"

He recoiled, horrified, and staggered backward.

More people crowded the stairs now—members of the Circle, grey mages, soldiers. Someone shouted and guards swarmed about one man, pushing him protesting up the stairs and out of sight.

Someone important, Tamaryl guessed, someone too valuable to risk near Ryuven. But he could not spare the attention.

Shianan was shaken by his near miss of Ariana, but he still faced Tamaryl determinedly, his sword ready. "Coward. Filthy lying treacherous coward."

And then the last of the shield faded, and there was nothing but glorious freedom between them and their home. Tamaryl's heart leapt.

"Stop them!" shouted several voices. "Stop them, no matter what!" Magic hummed.

"No!" howled Shianan, half-turning toward the mages.

"Ariana, down!" ordered Mage Parma, and power roared about her.

Maru turned toward Tamaryl, and Tamaryl pushed his feeble power toward the crystal and its reflected energy, fueling his own ability and preparing to leap the void.

"We have no choice! Sacrifice—"

"Wait!" Magic snapped through the cellar, disrupting Tamaryl, and Ewan Hazelrig shoved his way through the mass, panting for breath. "We can stop this! We can find an agreement—"

And then energy rolled through the cellar like rumbling thunder, resonating in Tamaryl's chest, and Ariana winced in his grip. With a whipcrack of displaced air, Oniwe'aru appeared.

Tamaryl caught his breath. That they would notice so promptly when the shield failed—

For an instant, no one moved, stunned at the appearance of the great Ryuven. Oniwe'aru swept the cellar with his gaze and smiled. "Nicely done, Pairvyn ni'Ai."

Ewan Hazelrig stepped forward, his face solemn. "May I—"

Oniwe'aru gestured. Energy shattered the air and lashed across the mage. Hazelrig reeled and fell.

Tamaryl stared in horror as his friend collapsed. He realized too late that Ariana was screaming, that she had torn free and rushed forward. Oniwe'aru easily deflected her bolt, which sparked into the gaping mages, and turned almost leisurely to face her—

Tamaryl shaped an inversion well and flung it about Ariana, bracing himself instinctively. Power from Oniwe shocked into the well's conduit and scorched through him. The room blurred about him as he took what should have killed Ariana.

Maru shouted distantly. "Hurry!"

Something struck Tamaryl—a magical blow, but this one from a human mage. They were attacking in force now, and he was far too weak for this. He blinked his vision clear.

Shianan Becknam was nearly upon him, his sword whipping forward. Tamaryl cupped magic in each hand and threw the first bolt, catching the commander in the chest. Becknam was lifted into the air, arcing backward with the force of it. Tamaryl hit him with the second bolt, and the commander jerked as if kicked, knocked aside mid-air.

Tamaryl heard Ariana screaming, and he reached desperately for her as with the last of his power he leapt the void.

CHAPTER SEVENTY-ONE

Ariana felt the cold dark of the between-worlds and then the abrupt shock of the Ryuven atmosphere pressing close upon her. She recoiled, but the thousand sensory darts hurled themselves at her— blades of grass shrieking as they rubbed in the howling breeze, fiery burning rays of twilight, stabbing thundering pain as someone spoke to her, touched her hypersensitive skin—

Ariana shrank away, curling into herself in an attempt to flee and block out the intrusive magic. But it battered down her feeble barriers, ran over her and through her, crushed her as she futilely struck at it...

Force begets force. She fought for control of her maddened thoughts, trying to focus through the shrilling pain. She had never been able to beat down the Ryuven magic; she had mastered it only when she had furiously used it. And she had spent the last weeks painstakingly practicing minute adjustments, obsessively rehearsing control.

With gasping, enormous effort she flung herself open to the foreign energy.

Power poured into her and overflowed, drowning her. She fiercely resisted the urge to clamp down on it—one could not withstand the tide—and instead channeled it outward, flooding through her hands and spiraling outward, whipping the air into wild eddies and making the grass ripple like the sea.

She opened her eyes, finally aware that she lay between Ryuven figures, and sat upright. Her hair waved in the upward breeze of her power and the cool leaves of the garden bent around her, though they only undulated gently a short distance away. She took a slow breath, feeling the power subside and obey her, and closed her tingling fists. She stood, and the ground was steady beneath her.

"Ariana," came a familiar voice. "Ariana, are you well?"

She turned to face Tamaryl, watching her closely, his expression worried as he held one hand tentatively toward her, as if afraid to touch her. She remembered how her touch had pained him after he had been sealed in her world, how traveling the between-worlds had torn him apart, how he'd caught her before leaping from the cellar.

She remembered everything.

Heat boiled through her and she slashed at him, energy crackling like striking lightning. Tamaryl threw himself backward as she advanced. "Murderer!" she snarled.

"Ariana!"

"How could you? How could you—you killed him!"

His hasty inversion well glowed as she struck at him. "No—"

"You killed him! And you used me—you used me to stop his sword. And Father—" She stumbled and went to her knees, rage and tears mingling in hot fury. "Oh, my father..."

"Your father, I think, is not dead," another voice answered. She whirled to her feet, but her quick attack was deflected. "My, Tamaryl'sho, what a spitfire she is when whole and well. And this was the mistress of your slavery?"

She straightened, trying to control her breathing. She could not, even with her new ability, hope to fight both Oniwe'aru and Tamaryl. She forced herself to take another measured breath and then seized on what he had said. "What about my father?"

"Is your father the White Mage?" Oniwe'aru flexed his wings behind him.

She nodded wordlessly, her throat closing.

One corner of Oniwe'aru's mouth lifted. "I should have guessed. I had assumed you were a mage of lesser ability, since you did not promptly die here, but you were in fact a great talent—like your father. He is very fast; one can see why he has been the White Mage for so long."

Her breath caught in her throat. "He's alive?"

"Unless your inelegant healers kill him, he may yet live. I doubt I was successful."

"But why did you attack him? He had done nothing! He had only—"

"Dear child," Oniwe'aru interrupted sternly, "it might have slipped your mind, but your people and mine are at war."

Someone else moved beside her, and she saw Maru shifting closer to Tamaryl, clutching the Shard of Elan.

"Tamaryl'sho destroyed the shield—excellent work, though I did not know to have our army ready. I came myself to view what he had done. But when I encountered a powerful enemy, I struck him down, just as he would have done to me."

She shook her head. "No—no, he wants to end the war..."

"Tamaryl'sho!"

Tamaryl straightened, a weary warrior answering his master's call. "Oniwe'aru."

"Take our prisoner to a secure place, and the crystallized ether as well," the Ryuven ordered. "I'll want to see them later."

Prisoner? Ariana stared. The ubiquitous magic began to prickle at her.

"As you say, Oniwe'aru. May I take personal responsibility for her?"

Oniwe'aru paused and gave him a long, steady look. "Before I grant that, Tamaryl'sho, tell me why you brought her here again. You did not spare her life from accident this time, and you had no further need of her as a hostage. Why did you carry her with you?"

Tamaryl hesitated. "She..."

"And you protected her." The Ryuven's eyes narrowed. "She attacked me, and you protected her."

Maru looked quickly at Tamaryl, alarmed. "Ryl'sho..."

Tamaryl went to one knee, and Maru promptly took two steps backward and knelt—differently, Ariana noted, upon two knees. Her pulse quickened again, and she felt the magic shift within its channels.

"Oniwe'aru," Tamaryl began, his head bowed. "I did protect Ariana'rika from your strike. But consider what chance of peace we might have if you were seen to kill a Mage of the Circle before—"

"You still talk of peace?" snapped Oniwe'aru. "Nim waited in line for a share of the last raid and were still waiting when our stores were exhausted. Will you be the one to go to them, to explain to the mothers of children that there will be no more food, no more supplies from a plentiful countryside, because you desire peace with the humans?"

"Oniwe'aru," Ariana made herself say, surprising them all. "I asked to come here."

He faced her, crossing his arms; he did not fear her or her ability. "You asked to be our prisoner here?"

"I am here, not as your prisoner, but as a diplomat." Her heart raced. She had no authority to do this, but it seemed to be the only chance for herself, for Tamaryl, for their kingdoms. "I have come to negotiate a truce and to suggest a profitable end to our hostility."

Tamaryl's bowed head rotated to stare open-mouthed at her.

She could not see Maru, as she dared not look away from the great Ryuven looking skeptically at her. Oniwe'aru took a step toward her, and it was all Ariana could do not to flinch. "You? You, the lowest of the Circle and no member of the court, you have come as negotiating diplomat?"

Ariana gulped. "If we can come to an arrangement, what does my ostensible position matter?"

Oniwe'aru gave a dismissive twitch of his head. "Maru is an intelligent and loyal nim, but I am not bound by whatever promises he might make to a human. Why should I accept your word?"

"You make war for food, for glory, for sport, for testing of your nobles—your sho and che," Ariana answered, hearing her voice quaver as she struggled for the correct words and tried to keep her fragile composure. Power surged in its artificial channels, threatening to overwhelm her again, and she fought for a steadying breath. "But it is food which drives you most strongly. If profitable trade were established, could the fighting end?"

Oniwe'aru did not blink. "There has been no profitable trade between our peoples in many, many generations. Even our traitors do not sell to one another."

"I believe that can change." She had not known to bring the little bag of herbs; it had been left in her workroom. "I—there is an herb in the medicine..."

Oniwe'aru smiled humorlessly. "The Ryuven have few medicines, compared to your easily-broken people. And we wish for food, a commodity which your countrymen are unlikely to share of their own will. If this is the negotiation you bring, we are finished. Tamaryl'sho—"

"No!" Ariana burst, frustration burning her. Pain stabbed at her. "No, you must—you monsters! You bereave me twice in a moment and then demand that I treat with you reasonably and clearly and—you're brutes, you're beasts! King's oats, I'm barely keeping control—your magic nearly killed me the last time I came here. Is this the honor of the Ryuven? Give me time to recover, to mourn, to master this magic which would end me, give me a proper audience and due consideration—and then, if you choose to continue this war, you will have tried every possibility and not wasted an opportunity to benefit your people and those children you claim to hold dear." She gasped, clutching her torso, and closed her eyes against the swelling sensations.

No, no, not here, not here. Breathe, breathe. Slowly. Let it move, let it pass through, channel it, let it run through... The pain began to gradually subside.

She realized no one was speaking. Carefully she straightened, breathing deeply, and looked at them.

Tamaryl and Maru still knelt, their heads bowed again. Oniwe'aru looked steadily at her. "Ariana'rika," he said at last. "That is, Tamaryl'sho called you by that name. Is that how you prefer to be addressed?"

"As I understand, that is an honorific," she answered. "I am pleased to accept it."

"Very well, then, Ariana'rika. As it was by your request that you came, I will receive you as an ambassador. Tamaryl'sho, you are charged with Ariana'rika's care and comfort until we meet to discuss this possibility of profitable trade and potential resolution." He paused. "But your coming cannot forestall our need to supply our people. Our harvest began a few days ago, and reports are troubling. We have very little, and there is unease and even assaults against our growers. I have set guards to protect the harvest workers from thieves. And so, Tamaryl'sho, you will also lead our warriors and bring more for our people."

Ariana swallowed her protest. She was in no position to argue, and she would never convince Oniwe'aru to let his people starve and fight amongst themselves.

Tamaryl inclined his head further. "As you command, Oniwe'aru."

Ariana looked at Tamaryl, at once familiar and foreign, and felt a fresh chill course through her. She had seen him kill Shianan. A tremor of pain rippled through her again.

Oniwe'aru looked harder at Tamaryl. "What happened to you? Are you even capable?"

Tamaryl wet his lips. "I recover, Oniwe'aru. I suffered some injury in the human world, but my power returns."

"I am glad I thought to bring Maru and the Shard. I had not expected to help you as well." The Ryuven lord looked at Maru. "And you? The same?" He shook his head. "I trust you will be of service soon, Tamaryl'sho?"

"I will, Oniwe'aru, and I will execute your command."

"Ariana'rika, I look forward to meeting with you at a more opportune time. I hope against my wiser judgment that you can offer

457

what generations have not found." Oniwe'aru turned. "Maru, you may leave the ether with any of my own guard."

He started toward the flowered walk, where two more Ryuven waited uncertainly, apparently drawn by the sudden arrival but unwilling to intrude upon their leader's conversation. They glanced from Oniwe'aru to the Ryuven and human still in the garden and then followed him toward the palace.

Tamaryl straightened and faced Ariana. "You think you can end this war?"

She tensed. "I'm trying." Her skin prickled painfully.

He looked at her and then glanced away. "Ariana..."

"You killed him." Her voice trembled, but with fury rather than tears. She had not yet allowed grief a foothold, nor worry for her father—she could not afford that now. "You killed him."

Tamaryl's jaw tightened. "He came at me with a sword—"

"And it would have been simple to deflect his attack! Simple! Far simpler than that kind of bolt. I know you had no power to spare—you meant to kill him."

Tamaryl's eyes flicked away. "I have fought for many years. Instinct takes—"

"Was it instinct that made you use me for your shield instead of casting your own? If you could not spare the power for that, how could you strike him twice with that kind of magic?" Tears stung her eyes and her blood burned with repressed energy.

Tamaryl looked back at her fiercely. "You call his death a bereavement? What is he really to you?"

Heat boiled through Ariana and she fought the urge to claw at her torso, fighting the awful sensation of her clothing biting her. She closed her eyes and took a steadying breath, and then another. Then she opened her eyes and started toward the flowered walk Oniwe'aru had taken.

"Ariana'rika!" Maru called. "Where are you going?"

"This is a palace," she snapped over her shoulder. "There will be a room where I can stay."

She followed the walk but saw only a solid wall, carved with intricate tessellating design. She did not hesitate but continued down it, keeping a steady pace. She would not return to ask direction, she would not allow them to see the hot tears spilling down her cheeks now. She did not seek the palace itself so much as she sought privacy.

A circle of flowering vines offered a screen, and she sank beside an upright boulder with a little sob. What had happened—how had this happened? She'd only wanted to pursue the dall sweetbud. She had never dreamed her friend would use her to shield himself, would allow harm to come to her father, would kill Shianan...

Would her father live? Did he even live now? Oniwe'aru had suggested he'd grounded himself, but there had been no time for the Ryuven to check his victim. Perhaps her father had not protected himself completely. Perhaps he had died in the moments afterward.

And she'd recognized the power of the bolts which struck Shianan. They would have broken through any mage's work, would have devastated any inversion well a mage dared to throw before them. She had seen his body thrown and broken. And her final words to him, their last encounter, when she had angrily chastised him and walked away...

She had fought down her emotions and found civilized speech for their murderers, saying what had to be said. She had made herself address them for the good of their peoples rather than for herself. She had played the part of a diplomat, though she was in fact a prisoner. But now, at least, she could give vent to her worry and fear and grief.

She wept, choking at first and then releasing herself to full cry. She struck at the boulder and welcomed the impact. She thought of her father, and of Shianan, and of her broken trust in Tamaryl, and she let magic rise and pound through her as she braced herself against the boulder and wailed.

CHAPTER SEVENTY-TWO

A little distance away through the sheltering plants, Maru shifted uneasily and tried to pretend he could not hear Ariana's sobs. He set down the heavy Shard and sat next to it, biting at his lip. An arm's reach away, Tamaryl rested his forehead against his arm, looking weary and frustrated.

Maru drew breath. "Are you injured?"

"No," Tamaryl answered curtly. He flexed a wing tentatively, betraying his words. The inversion well over Ariana had cost him, but not irreparably. He glanced toward Maru almost guiltily. "You?"

"No." The mages had not dared to risk harming the Shard, and then they had been wholly fixed on Tamaryl and Oniwe'aru.

Tamaryl looked away again. "She claimed him as a bereavement." His voice was bitter and resentful. "Did you hear that?"

Maru dropped his eyes, ashamed he had kept the secret. "He wanted to marry her."

"What?" Tamaryl's open expression hurt. "When?"

Maru felt miserable. "You were occupied with the Shard and shield. And I only overheard a bit, and I thought that you..."

Tamaryl looked sharply away. "You should have told me."

"And what good would it have done, Ryl? You had already purposed to come home. What would it have done, beyond torment you?"

Tamaryl said nothing, only clenched and unclenched his fist as he stared beyond the flowers.

Maru looked around at the twilit garden, looked at the Shard, looked at his hands. He asked at last, "Did you mean to kill him?"

Tamaryl took a long moment to respond. "I've killed many humans, Maru." The muscles of his jaw worked visibly. "I—I don't know."

Cold sorrow seeped through Maru.

"I've killed so many humans... And there are always more of them, always. And they come at you with not just magic, but with their steel and their unnatural muscles and their unreasonable covetous greed. They trade grain across the sea for gold but they shed their soldiers' blood to keep it from us." Tamaryl shook his head. "I don't

461

care anymore, Maru. I don't care if this war ends, I don't care if we let brainless reckless che advance through foolhardiness alone. I don't care to sacrifice myself any longer."

Maru's chest ached. "Ryl, don't. You don't mean that. You've had a very bad day—"

"I've had a very bad span of years," Tamaryl snapped. "Don't presume to correct me—I have spent fifteen years as a slave in the human world, sacrificed my position here, lost my betrothal, hid from my kin and my closest friend while I sought to end this war. And what have I done in the end? Daranai'rika is embittered and abandoned, she has lost her civility and her social standing. You were left to the nearest lord of obligation, you were abandoned to the furious mercy of a scorned female, and you were Subdued in a human household. Parrin'sho died to public jeers under a human axe. What of that fifteen years was profitable? In the end, there is no shield, there is no feast to end the famine, my friend is gravely wounded or dead, his daughter has seen me murder her lover, and we have won no peace at all. No, I think I am justified in resenting the entirety of this wretched affair."

Maru bit at his lip. He had no response.

"I just want to preserve what little I can, now. Bring you home, keep the hungry fed. If the stupid vainglorious che want to waste themselves against the stupid greedy humans, that's on all their own heads."

Maru shook his head silently, but there was no argument he could give which Tamaryl had not once held and surrendered.

Tamaryl rose abruptly, stretching his wings in the expanse of the garden as he had rarely been able to do in Hazelrig's home. "Come. We'll find Nori'bel and see what can be done for us."

Maru nodded. "What about Ariana'rika?"

Tamaryl faltered. "What would you have me do?" he asked softly. "You heard what she said."

"You are charged with her care."

"That will mean nothing at all to her. She thinks me a murderer, and I have no defense."

"Let me go," Maru offered. She had been weeping. She might speak to someone other than Tamaryl or Oniwe. "Let me talk with her."

Tamaryl nodded. "Yes. Try."

Maru left the Shard with his friend and made his way through the garden, listening for Ariana. He could not hear her now, but she could still be nearby. He peered behind bushes and within plantings, guessing she would have sought shelter.

A circle of flowering climbing vines seemed a likely place, and he ducked within it. Bent greenery showed where someone had rested for a time, but there was nothing in the circle but for an upright boulder, ordinary stone on one side and glassy slag on the other.

Maru's chest tightened. He reached cautiously to the boulder and felt the residual heat radiating from the stone. Ariana had done this.

All his old terror of human mages returned, sharpened by his imprisonment and Subduing. He had shrunk from her after she had raged at Daranai'rika—how much more now that he knew her capability and that she had every reason to view the Ryuven as enemies. He was suddenly very glad he had not found her in the garden.

CHAPTER SEVENTY-THREE

The Ryuven vanished from the cellar with a crack of closing air. Shianan Becknam's limp body slammed into the stone pavers and flipped once. It slid with momentum and did not move again.

Luca shoved through the crowd, heedless of the mages he elbowed, and threw himself beside his master. "No, no, please, no," he begged aloud. He seized Shianan's shoulder and turned him. Blood ran jaggedly over the unblinking left eye and down his slack face.

Luca could not move. "Help," he whispered. "Someone, help..."

The Silver Mage knelt beside Hazelrig, one hand rooting madly though the little bag at her waist. "Clear a space!" she snapped as others pressed close. She tore an amulet free of the bag and activated it, leaning over the white-robed form. "Don't you leave us, Ewan," she said fiercely. "Stay with me. Ewan, do you hear me?"

The White Mage groaned. "Ariana?"

Parma's relief was visible. "Thank the Holy One." She pressed the amulet against his torso and folded his hands over it, leaving hers atop his. "She's not here, Ewan. But she wasn't killed. She went to the Ryuven again, but we did not see her harmed."

Hazelrig blinked. "So many of you..."

Parma glanced around at the crowding mages. "It's not often we see you fall. You frightened us. Stand back, all of you, and give him some air."

As they shifted, Hazelrig looked blearily to the other figure on the floor. "Who's that?"

"None of us, Ewan. We're singed and sore, but you're the only serious injury. That's Bailaha. He's dead."

A man shook Becknam's body as if to wake him, his face twisted with shock and grief.

Hazelrig's voice cracked. "Dead?"

Parma hesitated. "He took two bolts directly, full bolts. If he's not dead yet, it's only because he wasn't mage enough to die instantly, but no ordinary man can take that and live, either."

"Save him." Hazelrig grasped for Parma's hand. "Luca... Call Luca."

The Silver Mage looked around uncertainly, knowing no one by that name, and guessed at the young man bending over the commander's sprawled body. "Luca!"

He did not respond, but he did not seem to hear anything as he wept. A friend, she supposed—no, she saw, a slave. A grieving slave.

"Help him, Elysia. Save him, for me."

"Ewan, it's impossible. He will be dead in a moment, if he's not already."

"It can be done." He drew breath, fighting for strength. "Help me up."

"Ewan! Lie still."

But he had rolled to his side and was struggling upright, and several hands reached to support him. "You must work as if you would create an amulet, but do it within him, at the site where the energy entered."

Parma shook her head. "It can't be done, Ewan."

"It can! It is possible, Elysia, for magical injury, trust me. I will—"

"You will do nothing! You will rest, Ewan, by all that's holy." She glared at a grey mage, who jumped and rushed forward to kneel behind the White Mage, taking his weight. "We'll try to help him."

"It will need multiple mages. Do it—do it for me." He squeezed her hand weakly.

She looked at the watching mages around them. "If several of us funnel power together as if to rapidly create a single amulet—but inside him? That could kill him itself." She hesitated, looked at Hazelrig, and then sighed. "But I suppose we have nothing to lose, right?"

"Save him, Elysia."

"You're unreasonable, Ewan." She gave his hand a quick encouraging pressure and then straightened. "Crimson, Forest, Amber, stay with the soldiers, in case they have need of you. There may be more Ryuven. We don't know how these came here, and they obviously had something to disguise their energy auras. Gold, Emerald, get to the royal family and keep them safe. Orange, stay with the White and keep him on the mend. Scarlet, Violet, come with me. You, grey—run and fetch some amulet gel, hurry!"

Luca twisted handfuls of Shianan's tunic and tugged weakly at it, making the body shift. "No…"

"Move aside," ordered a voice, and the Silver Mage knelt across from him. She placed a hand on Shianan's forehead and eyed him for a moment, finally shaking her head. "There's nearly nothing—but we'll try. Gather round!" She looked sharply at Luca. "Move aside, I said."

Luca stared at her, barely comprehending her words. "He's dead!"

"We're going to try to remedy that. Where's that amulet gel?" She pulled at Shianan's tunic, but the laces caught.

Luca blinked and then ripped at the cloth. "Save him! Please, my lady mage, save him!"

She snatched a jar from an extended grey arm and began smearing a fat globule over Shianan's bare chest. "Where's Callahan?" she demanded.

"Here," answered a scarred man in dark blue robes.

She gave him a hard look. "If you have any special skill," she said in a brittle voice, "this would be an ideal time to use it."

His marred face stiffened. "I've told you all again and again, I am no tapper," he snapped. "I do not know myself how I survived. And even in tales I've never heard of even a tapper drawing strength from one person and giving it to another."

"Then find another way to help. Hazelrig wants this one to live." She placed her spread hands across Shianan's chest. "I'll provide the focal point, and the rest of you feed power. Steadily, don't overwhelm me. Ready."

The Violet Mage began, "I don't understand—"

"Work exactly as you would set an amulet! But instead of using a reservoir token over months, we're going to pool it directly inside him now. Enough questions, now act."

The Indigo Mage knelt with the others. Luca waited, but it seemed nothing happened. They only sat around his master, doing nothing. A long moment passed, and he fought the urge to shout at them to get away, to let Shianan die in peace, at least…

"He's right," breathed the Silver Mage. "He's right, it could work, if it doesn't kill him. Easy, keep it steady."

Luca's lungs ached for air. He had forgotten to breathe.

"Parma…" warned the mage in red.

"I'm aware." She looked sharply at Luca. "You, be ready to hold—"

Shianan convulsed, his back arching high off the floor as he wheezed suddenly for air, a drowning man's gasp. Luca dove for his shoulders and pressed him to the floor.

"Hold him!" Parma snapped. She moved her hands slightly. "A little more, Callahan. Easy, Vana, keep it slow and steady."

"Right," the Violet Mage replied.

"Hold him steady, Luca." Hazelrig's voice was strained as he was lowered to the floor beside them. "This is uncharted magic. Some of the energy may touch things in his mind."

"My lord!" The sight of the White Mage infused Luca with irrational hope. He leaned into Shianan's shoulders as the commander's fingers jerked. "Can they save him?"

"Possibly." Hazelrig clutched a healing amulet closer to his chest. "I hope so."

Parma was sweating, lines of concentration etched into her face. Luca's attention was torn from her when Shianan spoke. "Bright round..."

"Master Shianan! Are you—can you hear me? What is it?"

"Give face for it," he muttered, staring upward with glassy eyes. "Bread quarrels."

Fresh horror shocked through Luca. "Shianan," he whispered. He looked beneath his arm at Hazelrig. "My lord, is that—?"

Hazelrig leaned heavily against a grey mage. "This isn't something we've done before."

Shianan shook, making Luca press harder, and his face crumpled into bloody tears. "It goes on... the race..." His body slackened. "Lonely grooming shiny metal, kissing clay feet."

"Concentrate!" ordered Parma. "Don't be distracted."

Luca's own cheeks were damp with tears. If they could not save him, or if he were left raving and mad...

Shianan giggled. "Hammer steely honied scripting." His eyes rolled loosely, unseeing. Luca wanted to wipe the bloody haze from the left eye but dared not release him.

Parma's breath was coming quick and shallow. "I'm tiring," she said levelly. "Callahan, I want you to take my place directing. Do you see it?"

The Indigo Mage nodded. "I don't believe it, but I see it. King's oats, has anyone ever done this before?"

"We don't have leisure to discuss that now. Take it."

She moved back as he cupped his own hands over Shianan's chest. She sat panting for a long moment, and then she spoke again. "Vana, you'll take it next. Soldier! Go and bring those of the Circle who aren't engaged elsewhere. We'll need rounds. And I want reports on the royal family." She shifted around Luca toward Hazelrig. "Ewan—how are you?"

"I'll live."

She looked toward the commander, dropping her voice for Hazelrig, though Luca could hear if he listened. "It's working. I don't know exactly how, but it's working. How did you know it would?"

Hazelrig shook his head. "I did not. I only hoped. I've seen it just once before." His voice trembled. "He's the bravest man I know, Elysia."

"There aren't many men who've singly challenged Pairvyn ni'Ai." She shook her head. "He tried to save her. After you fell, he tried to save her."

Hazelrig looked at Shianan, mumbling now about woven carpets. "I'd be proud to call him my son."

"Careful, Ewan, you've never been one to let your tongue slip." She rubbed her temple. "He's a very lucky fellow. A mage would have died instantly under that, and even a fit fighting man should not have lasted more than a few minutes. If he'd not had the whole of the Circle here to—"

"Not the whole of the Circle."

She took his hand. "Ewan... They returned her once. We'll pray they do so again."

CHAPTER SEVENTY-FOUR

Luenda, they called this place.

Tamaryl passed among the shattered bodies, human and Ryuven collapsed together in ugly, brutal death. He walked, going nowhere in particular but uncomfortable standing still in the midst of the dead.

He had told Oniwe'aru he would not fight this day, and he had stood unmoving in the center of the field, waiting, ignoring the shouts and pleas and threats of those around him. But it was not so simple for a Ryuven of such power to die. He had removed the bright sash marking his rank, and no one sought him out. Injuries from the incidental arrows and strikes and spells which reached him were healed almost involuntarily. It was hard to resist instinct, even when he expected to die.

It would have been better to die in battle. He was now a traitor, by the word of Oniwe'aru, and his life was forfeit. Even he could not overcome the concerted efforts of a dozen elite warriors. When he was found, he would die.

The sound of ragged breathing stopped him, and he looked down. He pushed aside a dead nim and uncovered a gasping human, folded and incoherent with pain. He had taken a magical bolt across the face, where it was killing him slowly. His grey robes marked him as a lesser mage, but beneath his scorched and boiling wound, he looked too young to be at war.

Tamaryl felt ill. Even if this were his enemy, he did not deserve lingering torture. He gathered a handful of energy and prepared to be merciful.

But he had warned Oniwe'aru he would not fight this day.

He knelt and shifted the young mage gently, exposing the injury. This was devastating to a human, but it would have been straightforward enough for Tamaryl to heal in himself. Why could it not be done in another? He made a decision and spread his hand over the boy's face. If he would not kill him and he would not leave him to suffer, he would heal him, or at least try. He did not know if humans could be helped magically, but the boy would be no worse for the effort, surely.

It took some time to find the right harmonization to allow the human mage to utilize the energy, but Tamaryl was in no hurry. It was strangely fascinating, in fact—if he focused the energy properly, the boy's body seemed to accept it as its own and began to heal normally, but at an accelerated rate, as if he were Ryuven. It took an incredible amount of energy, far more than it should for a Ryuven wound, but Tamaryl was Pairvyn and he had yet plenty this day.

When the raw wound closed, puffy and red but no longer seeping, Tamaryl straightened. The boy mage slept, exhausted from metabolic hyperactivity, and Tamaryl nodded to himself. He might be found by parties of either side searching for survivors, or he might wake and escape alone, but he had not died by Tamaryl's hand and had not been left to suffer.

Tamaryl walked on, noting absently how the reddening sun shed an appropriate hue. The scavengers had arrived already, ravens and wild dogs and others.

An overturned wagon sat on one edge, jutting upward and casting a long shadow in the evening light. The slaves which drew it had long since fled or died. Tamaryl looked beyond the wagon and wondered where the retreating human army had retired. He wondered how many of his own warriors had survived.

Something drew his attention to the wagon's shadow, and he saw a hunched figure with its back to the upraised wagon bed. Tamaryl moved closer and then froze. This was a mage, and he was neither dead nor insensible.

He was injured, though. The aura of power about him surged and flickered unevenly. Tamaryl knew better, but he was only passing time until his own death, and so he moved closer, curious and strangely unafraid.

The mage was watching him. He had probably hoped Tamaryl would pass without noting him. He was nearly beyond defending himself, now. Only his eyes moved as Tamaryl approached, looking at him steadily as he slumped in his blood-stained white robe.

Tamaryl's pulse quickened at the sight of the robe. "The great White Mage," he murmured. "How ironic—the one human who might give me what I sought, and too gravely wounded to do so."

The mage was afraid, but he had seen too much battle to allow it to rule him. "If you know me, then I ask that you do what you must with respectful speed."

This was the White Mage, leader of the Great Circle. If Tamaryl brought such a prisoner to Oniwe'aru, he might purchase his forgiveness.

But he would not fight this day, and he would not take prisoners. "I have come to kill no one," Tamaryl answered solemnly. He sighed. "I wish more could say the same."

"This is hardly the place for pacific speeches. There will be more killing tomorrow."

"I know. But I won't be a part of it." He glanced at the mage. "Nor, it seems, will you."

The human closed his eyes. "So you will not kill me, but you will watch me die."

Tamaryl lowered himself to the ground and crossed his arms over his knees, bracing his wings behind him. "Not with pleasure, White Mage. But if I help a boy too young to sacrifice his life, I spare only him. He will recover and go his way, perhaps wiser. If I help the White Mage of the Circle, I condemn many more of my own people—and while I do not wish them to fight, I would not aid their enemy."

"Bravely spoken," replied the mage weakly, "by one who invades our world. Enemy? We have never crossed to ransack and pillage your villages. We are not bloodthirsty beasts of prey, glorying in the kill."

The words were uncomfortably close to his own, and anger flashed through Tamaryl. "Is that how you see us?"

"Is there any reason to see you another way?"

"We fight to survive," Tamaryl snapped gruffly. "Without raids we would die."

The mage's gaze swept the littered field. "You're not doing so well with them, are you?" He winced as he shifted.

"I have done my part to end this war," Tamaryl said. "I have given my life to end it."

"I know Ryuven heal their wounds, but...." The White Mage's chuckle failed in a groan.

Tamaryl shook his head. "We are both dead," he replied. "You only look nearer it. When my people find me, I will not look so well." He glanced at the sky, expecting sho and che to appear at any moment.

"A traitor, are you? I wish we had met in better circumstances, then. I would have asked you how to end this war." He closed his eyes. "I've tried everything to find a different end; I would have gladly taken the words of a Ryuven."

Tamaryl caught his breath. The White Mage was highly placed

in human society. If he could be persuaded, then he might influence others. If Tamaryl could convince the humans that they were not monsters beneath consideration for trade, not horrors to be hated....

"White Mage," he ventured, "I saw a human boy healed today. He was dying, but slowly, and he could use focused energy as his own to recover."

The mage nodded wearily. "Mage healing, using artifacts of stored power." He closed his eyes. "I gave away the last I carried, though, fool that I am."

Tamaryl looked at him. "If I helped you to heal, White Mage, would you give me your word that you will seek to end this war?"

The human looked at him with sudden interest. "In what way? I will not go with you and help to crush our resistance."

"No, no—I want you to end this fighting by peaceful means, by engaging our peoples in trade and diplomacy. If we could purchase what we needed, there would be no need to reward vainglorious hotheads, no need for battle as a proving ground for young politicos. I can help you, if you will seek a more peaceful solution."

A grim, pained smile. "You ask me to pursue what I already hope for."

"Then you will swear to work toward its end?"

"By the most solemn oath I know," the human replied. "And you will be there to help bring it about."

Tamaryl smiled grimly. "I will be dead."

"You said they are seeking you. I can hide you, in our world, and you can help orchestrate our peace."

Now Tamaryl regarded him warily. "I will not be your prisoner, either."

"That is not what I intend."

Tamaryl considered. He had little to lose: ignoble death from his own kin and kind, or an uncertain future in the human world. If the human betrayed him, he could always fight to freedom or death, he reasoned, and be no worse in the end. He nodded. "So we save both our lives and set ourselves to saving our respective people?"

The mage smiled weakly. "You put it well."

Tamaryl reached forward and spread his fingers over the mage's bloody chest. "Then let us begin."

CHAPTER SEVENTY-FIVE

Shianan lay deep in a bed which was not his own. The sheets were smooth against his bare flesh, better than the military staples he expected. When he opened his eyes, he saw the shape and color of the ceiling over his bed were wrong, too. But a soft rustling near him brought a wash of familiarity; it was the subtle sound of Luca folding laundry.

He tried to roll to face him, but stiff pain knifed through his torso, stealing his breath.

"Master Shianan?" Luca came to the bed. "Can you hear me? Keep still, you're not healed yet." He leaned so Shianan could see him without twisting, eyebrows drawn close together. "You're in the Hazelrig house. My lord mage is recovering in his room, and you're in my lady Ariana's bed."

"Finally," Shianan murmured. "Although I'd rather hoped she would be in it, too."

Luca burst into relieved laughter. "Master Shianan! Thank all that's holy. I'm glad to hear you speaking sense—if a bit baldly."

He sounded almost giddy, and it worried Shianan. "What happened? And help me to sit up, would you?"

"You were struck by Pairvyn ni'Ai, do you remember? You—you weren't well." Luca turned and collected pillows from a corner trunk. "You should have been dead."

"I should have been dead since the Shard first was stolen," Shianan answered lightly. He wondered if he were a bit giddy himself. "What of it?"

Luca picked at a thread. "I thought—you had died. No one thought..."

Shianan sobered. "Luca..."

Luca shifted self-consciously and began to set the pillows. "But my lord mage instructed them on how to save you, and the mages took turns working their spell on you, and you lived." He grinned, embarrassed. "As you see."

"The mages saved me?"

Luca nodded. "Hazelrig insisted. It wasn't that they didn't wish to, but no one thought you could survive, only he knew a way. And

475

there was talk of how brave you were to face Pairvyn ni'Ai with only a sword."

Shianan blinked. "The Circle? Spoke of me?"

Luca reached behind Shianan's shoulder. "Let me lift you," he warned. "Don't try to hold yourself. From what I understand, your body thought it had been cut in half."

"My body thought..."

"You were attacked with magic. I cannot pretend to explain it, but I will say it most impressively nearly killed you." Luca pulled, making Shianan catch his breath as his torso shifted, and pushed the pillows behind him. "How's that?"

Shianan looked down at his bare chest. Had he lost weight? "I'm far too clean to hurt this much. Where's the mark?"

Luca shook his head. "Should a mage visit again, you might ask one of them. My lady Mage Parma has been here several times, and healers of course."

Shianan finally turned to the shadow his mind didn't want to acknowledge. "Where is Ariana? If I am here..."

Luca nodded unhappily. "She was taken with the Ryuven."

Sudden despair swelled in Shianan. "He isn't what he was before, Luca. I don't know how, but I know it. Something's changed in him. And the other one—that was a Ryuven lord, wasn't it? A clan king?"

A bell rang, and Luca jumped. "I'll be right back." He hurried out of the room.

Tamaryl was different, Shianan was certain. And the other had struck down Mage Hazelrig without a thought. *They won't hesitate to kill her.*

Shianan closed his eyes and tried to remember. He recalled Ariana's mad charge toward the Ryuven lord, and he remembered rushing Tamaryl, hoping the colored streams of light would distract his target. Then there had been a bright burst of agony and nothing else.

There were steps on the stairs, and then Soren entered the room. Shianan twitched upright, pain stabbing through him, and clutched at the sheets. "Your Highness!"

"Lie back, Becknam. I won't ask a wounded man to keep courtly etiquette. Luca, make him lie still."

Luca, following, straightened the blanket Shianan had pulled askew and then drew a chair for the prince.

"You see," Soren pronounced as he sat, "now we're both sitting comfortably. Well, I am, at least. I'll look in on Mage Hazelrig as well but Luca said you'd just awakened. How are you?"

"Better now than before, from what I hear. But what are you doing here? You can't come down the street—"

"Do not be so quick to tell a prince what he cannot do," Soren protested. "This is my city, after all, and if I cannot walk in safety down an affluent street to the house of our highest mage, then we have graver troubles than I'd thought. And I wore a hooded cloak. I came to see you, of course."

Shianan glanced away, uncomfortable in his weakened state.

"I came to the Wheel, when the alarm went out. But the cursed soldiers seized me and bore me away, for my own protection, they said, though I wouldn't be surprised if some of them weren't just as glad of a reason to leave. It was quite the scene." Soren smiled "And you, my friend, are the hero of it."

"Why?"

"You challenged Pairvyn ni'Ai yourself, even called him to fight you alone. While it might have been a bit presumptuous to call yourself the kingdom's champion, everyone agreed it was a splendid effort, and you nearly died in the attempt."

"I'd rather not think I must die to be in my duty."

"No. But we are very glad you'll be well enough, they say, to join in the coming battle." Soren's smile faded. "One is coming, we're sure of it. The Ryuven won't lose such an opportunity as this. The Circle—most of them, anyway—made some sort of temporary shield out of the fragment of Shard that was left, but they say it must fail soon. Then…"

Shianan's heart stilled in his chest. He was a soldier, raised a soldier, but he did not relish the idea of leading his men into battle and slaughter. "Can't they make the shield last?"

The prince nodded sadly. "The Silver Mage brought us a choice. We could protect Alham a bit longer if we did not shield the outlying lands as well. But what use is a guarded city if our fields are stripped bare? We told her to cast the shield wide."

Shianan clenched his fists beneath the concealing blankets. The shield prevented Ryuven attack but barred Ariana as effectively. If she could even return…

"The generals are arguing over where the attack will likely come. They're supposing somewhere on the plains, but that doesn't exactly narrow it down for efficient planning. The Ryuven will be—it will be another Luenda, they're saying." Soren glanced at the floor. "I'm sorry."

"It's been a long time without a real battle, just raids. We should have expected it."

Soren shook his head again, as if to dismiss the mood. "I didn't come to speak of that, and you'll have better information from your own sources, I expect. I came to see how you are. You sound quite well for a man who's only just awake."

Shianan made a gesture of indifference. "I've been better. I'm told the mages saved my life. I'll have to thank them." He glanced at his torso. "The thing about magic is that one either dies promptly or heals within a reasonably short time. I think I'll hang on for the few days it will take."

"I'm glad. I—I'm glad." Soren rubbed at his nose.

There was a moment of awkward silence. Luca cleared his throat. "Shall I bring refreshment for His Highness? And, master, you should have something. You haven't taken much."

"King's oats, Luca, let me at least pretend to decide myself."

Soren chuckled. "Your Luca has a most cheeky tongue in his clever head, I've noticed. If he has the chance to infect others, we'll have another Furmelle disaster on our hands, so be sure to keep him safely with you." He grinned.

Luca hurriedly bowed and retreated from the room.

Soren's grin faded. "I think I frighten him."

"There are moments when it doesn't need much," Shianan admitted. "And he was at Furmelle."

"Ah." Soren had the grace to look embarrassed. "Is that how you came by him?"

"No." Shianan let his head loll on the supporting pillows, glad he did not have to hold himself upright. "Can you keep a secret, Your Highness? I stole him."

Soren raised an eyebrow in mock severity. "Using your authority for gain, Becknam?"

"His master was arrested, and I took him from the prison before the guards sold him for profit." Shianan tried to shrug without much movement. "He was already stolen; I only stole him again."

"Where is his master now? His former master, I mean."

"Still in prison. It was the Gehrn priest who destroyed the shield."

"Ah. Well, commander, I think it should be perfectly acceptable to take a slave for questioning in such an incident. Did he know anything about it?"

"No, Your Highness. He was merely a tool of the priest—and one not highly regarded, at that."

"Then it is not unreasonable that, as he could not provide useful information, the state had finished with him and he could be disposed of in any convenient manner." Soren smiled. "I'm glad he went to you—and returned. I thought you had sent him to his family?"

"I have not even heard that story myself. He returned only last ni—'soats, what day is it? How long has it been?"

"Two days. You did worry us, you know." Soren laced his fingers together. "At least I don't have to visit you in your military quarters."

Shianan snorted. "Better than hiding in Fhure."

"But I so enjoyed my rustic visit there." Soren's grin faltered. "I'd like that, actually—visiting Fhure again. When all this is finished, when there's time, may I come?"

This was his way of expressing hope, Shianan realized. This was Soren's oblique wish that Shianan would return safely from the battle. Soren should have been fretting in conference with the king and advisers and generals, but here in Shianan's sickroom he was relaxed and even jesting, a different man. Shianan did not quite understand it.

He might not yet have Fhure, but that was not the point of the question.

Shianan quirked his mouth into a smile. "How could I refuse hospitality to my prince?"

Luca set a pile of fresh linens on the chest at the foot of the mage's bed and turned to go.

"Luca?"

"My lord! I had thought you asleep."

"I wish I were." Hazelrig shifted uncomfortably. "How is Bailaha?"

"He's awake now," Luca answered, pleased. "He's speaking. And the prince has just come to visit him, while you were sleeping."

"The prince here?" Hazelrig seemed startled. "I hope you've dusted."

"I've done my best, my lord, to keep—"

"Leave it, Luca, I was joking." The mage smiled tiredly. "You have the care of two invalids. I won't complain."

Luca nodded automatically. The healer who had visited yesterday had not been so generous, snapping at Luca about soiled linens changed only an hour before and irritable that no food was ready prepared. "Your indolence will cost them," he'd chastised over Shianan's still form. "That kind of regeneration requires an unreal amount of energy—see how he's wasted even now? How will he recover if you don't feed him properly?"

"I will set a pot of vegetables—"

"Diced bits, mind! And boiled soft. You don't want to choke him. And where is Mage Hazelrig's boy?"

"I don't know, my lord," Luca answered worriedly. "I haven't seen him at all."

"Run away in his master's illness? That won't go well for him, I imagine."

Luca kept the house himself, changing and laundering the bedding, cooking, carrying warm wash water upstairs, stocking the fireplaces with newly split wood to keep the invalids warm, sleeping in the corridor between their doors to listen for any need.

"The prince said the Circle—the others—made a temporary shield from the broken Shard."

Hazelrig smiled wearily. "Did they? Well done, Elysia."

Luca straightened the linens he'd brought, aware he was compulsively occupying his hands. "Shall I bring you anything, my lord?"

"I don't think so," Hazelrig admitted. His skin was sickly pale; the White Mage, indeed. He shook his head slowly, his eyes closing.

Luca nodded and made a small bow though the mage did not see him. "Yes, my lord."

CHAPTER SEVENTY-SIX

Ariana hated the open door. It was the local style, she knew, but she could not get past the feeling of exposure and vulnerability.

Ryuven passed her room frequently, casting glances at the strange human within, and no matter where she sat in the chamber she could feel their eyes. Even when no one walked the corridor, she could hear their voices plainly, hear their movements. She was never alone. She washed and dressed hastily, huddling in a corner and watching the door. At night she lay alternately with her face to the door, tensely alert for intruders, and with her back to it, trying to block it from her mind. She was never private.

She did not weep. She had given herself the single brief release in the garden, and then she had shut her grief away. Shianan was dead, her father was injured or dead—but grieving for them would squander the only opportunity she had. She could not afford distraction.

The nim who brought her meals and necessities was wary of her, and not without reason; the first human mage to survive their magic-infused atmosphere had caught his arm and asked boldly for a room, stunning him.

She could not face Tamaryl. Not yet. Not while she yet held her grief in check.

Oniwe'aru had not sent for her yet, though she questioned the nim often and even stopped higher ranking Ryuven in the corridor. Two days had passed without word from the Ai leader, and a faint panic warned that he was only toying with her, teasing his human prisoner before something much worse, that he had no intention of meeting with her or seeking to end the war. But she sharply pushed the thought away. Surely Oniwe'aru wanted peace as much as anyone. His people suffered with fighting, too.

She hardly slept at night, afraid in the Ryuven palace without a door, afraid to dream of her father jolting backwards, of Shianan's arched body hanging midair as she was torn away into another world—

She woke, her eyes burning, as someone moved outside her room. She jerked upright with a catch of breath and saw Tamaryl

481

facing her. They stared at one another a moment—only a few heartbeats, but it felt longer—and then he started forward.

Ariana flung magic at the archway, creating a shield. Tamaryl hesitated at the sudden flow of power and he stared into the empty air at the invisible shield, seeing it however Ryuven did. Then he wordlessly withdrew and went down the corridor again.

Ariana took a slow breath. What had made him come? Why hadn't he called to her, or knocked? He knew she was no Ryuven and preferred her guests to announce themselves. Why had he watched her as she slept?

Why had she erected a shield instead of speaking to him?

The magic crumbled, unmaintained. She realized she had created not just a physical shield, but the same variety the Circle had crafted to be powered by the Shard of Elan—a Ryuven-killing shield. It would not have merely stopped Tamaryl like an invisible wall, it would have torn him apart.

Guilty fear vied with indignant resentment and the ever-present struggle against sorrow. She hadn't meant to hurt him, only to stop him. She hadn't thought at all, only reacted. But...

A tentative knock interrupted her musing, and she caught at her blanket as she looked again at the open archway. "Yes?"

"Ariana'rika, you are called," said the nim, not quite entering. "Oniwe'aru will speak with you today."

Her stomach tightened. This was it, then. This was her chance, her only opportunity. "Thank you. How soon?"

"You have some time, Ariana'rika. I'll bring your breakfast."

"And could I have some clean clothing? Something more appropriate?" She still wore her workshop clothes.

"I will bring something for you, Ariana'rika."

"Thank you." She nodded. She did not know how much of the breakfast she would want—she had not eaten much since arriving, even without the fresh nervousness already twisting within her—but the Ryuven fruit was delicious and she would make herself take a little. She could not afford to be light-headed.

Shianan was sampling the lunch Luca had brought—soup with melted cheese, tempting despite his weakness—when a tap in the hall drew their attention. Luca leapt from his work. "My lord mage!"

"Stand back, Luca, I'll manage." Hazelrig eased himself into the room, leaning heavily upon a light-colored staff. "This makes me feel very venerable, like one of the legends of old."

Luca hurried to carry a chair. Shianan twitched helplessly in his bed. "Steady, my lord mage."

Hazelrig cast him a dark look. "Men in bed must not be too solicitous of those with a crutch."

Shianan acknowledged the reproof with a lift of his hand. "I beg your pardon, my lord mage. But I have done my walking this morning, twice about the room, with Luca's aid. And while I would never argue you aren't the peer of the great mages of the past, they are usually depicted wielding their staves, not leaning upon them."

Hazelrig chuckled as he sank into the chair Luca provided. "That is an artist's kindness. Do you know why the first mages had staves? We had not learned so much yet then, and magic did not use well those who would use it. Most mages aged poorly and died early. The staff was not a means to channel magic, as some claimed, but a walking stick." He paused, a bit winded from his effort. "Twice around, you said? That's very good for a man who should have been dead."

Shianan nodded. "I don't know how to express my thanks to the Circle."

"Leave the Circle for a moment. You know our shield is limited?"

Shianan nodded. "And then the Ryuven will come, yes. And we will meet them."

"You will go?"

"I cannot fail to go. And I'm feeling fitter even now."

Hazelrig smiled wanly. "You were nearly dead—you should have died. Most would take that as reason enough to avoid this battle." He sighed. "It will be another Luenda."

"That's what I have heard."

"If you go, Becknam, I want you to come back." Hazelrig looked evenly at him. "It will be carnage. But I want you to come home."

Shianan stared back at him. "I will not hide from my duty, my lord."

"I never believed you would, even if I were selfish and foolish enough to ask it, which I am not. No, you are one of the bravest men I know. I know that better than any other." He fingered the pale staff absently. "I meant—I want you to try to come back."

"My lord mage..."

Hazelrig glanced at Luca.

"Oh, you may say anything before Luca," Shianan assured him. "Luca knows all my secrets, even those I'd rather not know myself."

Hazelrig nodded. "Then I will say it plainly: You once intended to sacrifice your life for my daughter. Now that she is gone, I do not want you to sacrifice it again in retribution."

The words struck Shianan solidly in his chest. He straightened as best he could in the pillowed bed. "My lord mage, I do not intend to throw away my life on the field. If I fall in battle, I fall, but I will not give my life lightly to the Ryuven." Something stirred within him, stretching as it woke, angry and venomous.

Hazelrig looked at him narrowly and then nodded. "Good," he replied at last. "And, so it is clear between us, I do not know that Ariana is truly gone. He brought her home once before."

Shianan's throat closed with sudden force and he could not look at Hazelrig. That was before... that was before Tamaryl had learned Shianan loved her, before Shianan had guessed Tamaryl might desire her, too. That was before Tamaryl had used Ariana as a living shield, forcing Shianan to watch his own blade slice toward Ariana's neck as he struck for the Ryuven.

If Tamaryl had once respected and cared for Ariana enough to save her life, it could not be counted upon now. She might be captive even now, perhaps a prisoner in a silken prison, but nonetheless his captive—

"Becknam?"

Shianan gulped past the lump in his throat and made himself inhale. "I'm sorry." He could not crack before Hazelrig—not a mage, not her father. "I was only—I'm fine." Luca was staring at him worriedly, but Shianan looked deliberately at Hazelrig. "I mean to rejoin my officers soon. The healers said I should be capable within a few days."

Hazelrig smiled wanly. "Of course. Sometimes I envy you cleavers of meat."

Shianan looked at the mage, pale and still clutching his staff. "They said you were able to erect a shield. It's odd that mages are more susceptible to their own weapon."

"What is the difference in lightning striking a rock or a man? The man has a nervous system, and so he suffers greater injury. I don't mean you are a rock, my friend, but you do not have a magical nervous system, so to speak." Hazelrig glanced at Luca, silent in the corner. "I will miss your Luca. He has been very careful of me."

"Keep him after I've recovered," Shianan offered. "You have no one here, and he already knows your needs. Yes, Luca? You would help my lord mage, wouldn't you?"

"I would be glad to, if you will not need me," Luca answered with a small bow.

Hazelrig smiled at Luca. "I would be glad to have him, even for such a short period. Thank you both. Now, I think I will hobble my way back to my room for a nap. Being a mage of legend is not nearly as empowering as one might think."

"Shall I help you, my lord?"

"No, thank you. But if you should hear an unexpected thump, you might glance out for me." He chuckled and left.

Shianan looked at Luca. "You don't mind, do you?"

Luca shook his head. "I'm glad to help him. You'll be well enough?"

"I'll have no choice but to be. But I should be fine." He relaxed against the pillows. "I only feel so inexplicably exhausted."

"That's the mage healing, they say. You'll need another day or two of sleep."

"I've done nothing but sleep," complained Shianan. "And I haven't even dreamed anything worthwhile."

Luca smiled and then sobered. "Master Shianan, about the bandits..."

Shianan's eyes were already closed. "King's oats, them too. Write down what you know of it and I'll pass it along, though the Ryuven threat will take precedence."

"I will."

If Luca said anything more, Shianan did not hear it.

CHAPTER SEVENTY-SEVEN

Ariana was led through cool, intricately carved corridors to a mid-sized audience chamber, where the nim gestured her toward two tall female Ryuven who glanced indifferently at her but did not deign to greet her from their posts flanking the entry.

She saw Tamaryl standing just inside the chamber, and she hesitated. But he startled her by dropping to one knee. "My lady mage Ariana Hazelrig, Black Mage of the Great Circle," he pronounced solemnly, and she realized he was announcing her.

She stepped into the room, and Oniwe'aru rose from his high seat to face her. "Ariana'rika."

"Oniwe'aru, Altayr ni'Ai cin Celæno, Alcyon ni Pairvyn, Majja to Pleione," she answered. She had questioned the nim and practiced unceasingly as she waited. She curtsied deeply in her borrowed gown. The slits exposing her sides and back worried her slightly. She guessed the Ryuven would find no fault in the bared skin, but the garment designed to accommodate a broader torso lay loose on her slim frame. The statuesque female Ryuven outside the door did not show such draping fabric. "I am pleased to visit your court."

Oniwe'aru looked impressed as she straightened; she had surprised him by mastering his formal address. "Please, come and sit with me."

In this case, *with me* meant a seat just before and below his own, but Ariana was glad she would not have to stand for the length of the negotiations, or what she hoped would be negotiations. Edeiya'rika, the female champion, stood behind Oniwe. Beside the door, Tamaryl remained on one knee.

Oniwe'aru noted her curious glance. "Tamaryl'sho will remain to answer any questions or differences we may have, as he best understands our respective worlds and peoples. Please, make yourself comfortable."

Ariana sat in the backless chair, cool air brushing her spine. It gave her an unsettling sensation of being naked.

"I will begin the formalities," said the Ryuven. "I am Oniwe, aru of the Ai and not without influence among the other clans. My people have guarded our raids upon yours jealously and forbidden other clans to encroach, and any peace we reach will be guarded in the same way, as it must be equally profitable to us. Thus I pledge my worthiness to enter into negotiations and to uphold whatever agreement we conclude."

He looked at her significantly, as if he doubted her position. That was only reasonable, as she doubted it herself. But she had no choice but to make this venture.

She started by mimicking his declaration. "I am Ariana Alyssa Hazelrig, Black Mage of the Great Circle. I am the daughter of Ewan Hazelrig, the White Mage, and I know his mind in this affair, and I have confidence that what peace we may agree upon will be honored by him. He is not without influence in the Circle and in the court. I will not pretend I speak for our king, but I swear to you that I will do my best to have our agreement accepted and formalized by His Majesty King Jerome."

Oniwe'aru frowned faintly. "You have no personal word from your king?"

Ariana clenched her jaw. "With respect, my lord, my coming was somewhat impulsive. Had I known Tamaryl's intention, I might have previously sought an audience with His Majesty and brought letters of credential. But as we stand, I am afraid you have only my pledge that I will present and advocate your proposal as favorably as I can."

Oniwe'aru nodded. "I will accept that for our introductory negotiation, at least. But we cannot conclude an agreement without some token of good faith from your sovereign." He straightened in his low-backed chair, letting his wings shift behind him. "What suggestion for trade do you bring?"

Ariana took a bracing breath. "When I first came, the magic here nearly killed me. Your healer blended for me a potion to treat my illness. One of the ingredients is a precious medicinal herb in our world, gathered to extinction and priceless. We call it dall sweetbud, though I do not know by what name it is known here. But my proposal is this—medicine for food. We have nothing to rival dall sweetbud's healing properties, and if you have it in abundance, you could sell it at considerable profit. In exchange, you could barter or purchase grain and meat from our farmers' stores."

Beside the door, Tamaryl twitched and his eyes widened. She had surprised him.

Oniwe frowned thoughtfully. "You think your growers would

sell their crops for herbal medicine?"

"I do not pretend it would be so simple, no. The farmers and herdsmen would sell to their usual merchant buyers, some of whom could be approached by the Ryuven or their representatives. With all respect, the farmers have feared Ryuven attacks for generations, and I doubt they will be readily open to trade. But merchants are more inclined to new markets. And the promise of dall sweetbud should buy a more tolerant ear."

"And your merchants would purchase it? For coin, which they would then accept for foodstuffs?"

Ariana nodded, trying not to sound too eager. "There is a new sickness in the countryside. It has not gone far yet, but it is spreading, following the river. If there is a time to offer a lost legendary panacea, this is it."

"Hm." Oniwe'aru glanced toward Tamaryl. "Tamaryl'sho? What do you know of this?"

"Almost nothing, Oniwe'aru," Tamaryl answered, still kneeling. "I did not make a study of extinct flora during my stay. But I will agree that, if this herb is valuable to the humans, it is our most logical choice in trying another means."

"Better than your raids, you say."

Tamaryl stiffened. "I have always satisfied you, Oniwe'aru, in bringing supplies for our people. But it is no secret I would prefer a more pacific manner of securing a harvest."

Oniwe looked from one to the other. "And what is this sweetbud to us? What do we call it, and do we have it in plenty? Is it equally valuable to our healers?"

Ariana gestured uncertainly. "I don't know what you call it. I had a sample of it, but as I didn't know I was coming I did not have it with me... I could speak with a healer and try to identify it." She hoped desperately she could from among countless strange species.

Tamaryl rose and came forward, but he did not look toward her. "I could take her to Nori'bel, Oniwe'aru. It was she who blended the first medicine for her."

Oniwe'aru nodded. "Do that, and send word of what you learn. We can discuss this after you return."

Ariana was startled. "Return?" she repeated warily. She looked at Tamaryl, noting how his eyes shifted away from her. "Where are you going?"

His throat moved. "I am going to your world again."

489

The words chilled her. "You're fighting?!"

"You must understand our position, Ariana'rika," Oniwe'aru said. "We have no agreement of peace. We do not even have a formal agreement to seek an agreement. What I do have is a hungry clan and another failed harvest, and what you have is an idea for trade, its validity as yet unconfirmed, for a commodity we are not assured is even readily available. I cannot wait on so little. Your shield cost us dearly and we have used nearly all of our stores. We must have new supplies."

"You can't do this!"

"I must. Or do you think I could order starving nim not to cross on their own initiative? Do you think our sho, watching their estates falter, would not take it into their own hands to help their dependents?"

"You say the aru of the Ai cannot control his own subjects?"

"I say a wise leader does not ask the ridiculous, and I will not risk my people upon a mere chance offered by someone without authority to aid success."

"Someone—" Panic and anger rose simultaneously in Ariana. She could not lose this single, frail chance. "But you cannot attack us while we talk of peace!"

"I cannot talk of peace without evidence it is possible. Verify we have this herb in plenty and we will continue our negotiation."

She stood suddenly from her chair, clenching her jaw, prompting Edeiya'rika to shift forward. "You trust that we would still be willing to open trade after you raid us repeatedly."

"If the humans are suffering a new plague, as you say, they will be willing to trade for a miracle cure no matter who offered it." Oniwe'aru raised his eyebrow and regarded her flatly, disdainful of her changed posture. "I do not worry we will lose that opportunity."

They were sending more raids, greater raids, and she was powerless to stop it. She herself had given the assurance they had nothing to lose. She tried again, hearing desperation in her voice. "A raid won't win you enough supplies to replace a failed harvest. Why risk antagonizing those who might—"

"I know a village can't supply our clan," Oniwe'aru answered testily. "I will see my people fed, in whatever fashion I must, before I talk of experimenting."

Sweet Holy One, they were going to strip the countryside. The Shard's shield had frustrated and frightened them, and now they would fill their storehouses before even considering peace. She stared at each of them in turn. "You mean to destroy us."

He shook his head. "Never. Your growers are as valuable to us as to you. But we will take what we need."

"Can't you trust that we can share what you need? That we can share in a way that will not leave us to starve just as you fear for yourselves?"

Oniwe'aru did not change his expression. "I think, Ariana'rika, we have accomplished what we can today. Tamaryl'sho will take you to Nori'bel, where you may determine if there is a purpose to continuing our talk at some later date."

She couldn't breathe. Magic prickled at her, but she would not be dismissed. "No."

Tamaryl looked at her sharply. "Ariana'rika..."

"No. You must understand this—I will see our peoples at peace. I will do whatever is necessary, and I won't allow any more of us to be slaughtered or starved." She took a shuddering breath, hardly taking the time to choose her words. "I was raised under the shadow of this war. My father has fought Ryuven longer than I have been alive. My dear friend was raised a soldier to repel Ryuven and those who would take advantage of the Ryuven distraction. I myself was raised to aspire to the Great Circle, a function which today exists primarily to fight Ryuven.

"But I didn't truly see the awfulness of it all, perhaps because it had always been there. But I have now seen my father collapse and I have seen my suitor killed, by someone I loved as a brother, and—" she gulped and turned her voice to gleaming steel "—and I swear to you by all I hold holy that I will see this war end." She clenched her fists, pushing the foreign magic through her. "You say I have no authority, and indeed I have no title to command our kingdom—but if you will agree to try this trade, even for a time, I will swear to undertake it. If I were king, I would order a portion of the taxes supporting our army to secure grain, in goodwill and faith for peace, but as I cannot do that, I will pledge my dedication instead. If you venture this trade, I will not rest until you have what you need." She paused, licked her lips, tried to make her words sound considered and credible. "Please, trust me. Let me try to help you, to help all of us. Stop this."

Oniwe'aru looked at her steadily. "I cannot."

"You cannot?"

Oniwe'aru sighed, as if irritated. "Your mages remade your

shield, but as we have the crystallized ether, it is a weak thing, and weakening. We are observing it, and its decline. I have already given orders for our army to prepare. You make a very pretty speech, but I will not refuse them this opportunity for so slim a hope as you present."

Cold despair washed over her. "An army..."

Oniwe'aru looked almost sympathetic, though distantly. "I understand your dedication, Ariana'rika, and I can appreciate your efforts. But we must supply ourselves as we urgently need, and only then will we have the leisure to explore any merit in your suggested trade." He gestured. "I think it will be best if you remain here until our business in your world is finished. Tamaryl'sho, show her to Nori'bel now—unless she would prefer to return to her room at this time."

Ariana curtsied numbly, hardly aware of her movement, and backed toward the door as she would for human royalty. She had failed—she had accomplished nothing. Shianan was dead, her father dead or dying, and their kingdom was about to suffer another Luenda.

She became suddenly aware of Tamaryl walking at her shoulder, and she twitched aside. He looked away.

She tried to clear the lump in her throat. "Where can I find this healer Nori'bel?"

"I will send her to your room. That will be simplest."

Ariana wanted both to shrink away from Tamaryl and to reach to him for comfort. But the friendly boy had become a distant warrior who would not even meet her eyes as he prepared to murder her countrymen, in defiance of all he'd claimed to want. "And if she has dall sweetbud in plenty? You'll already be killing our soldiers and robbing our farmers."

He winced, surprising her. "Ariana..."

"Don't presume to call me by name," she snapped. "You used me as your shield, you killed—you said nothing in there, nothing! when you claimed for years you wanted peace. Why didn't you help me?"

"How could I help when I knew nothing of your suggestion?" he demanded. "I never knew of this herb. And I have done all I could by not speaking—would it help your cause if Oniwe'aru knew you'd meant to kill his Pairvyn?"

"What? How can you—" She stopped, realizing what he meant. "That shield—I didn't mean—I only locked my door, so to speak. It wasn't to kill you."

"Only because I was standing still. If I'd been even walking when you erected that..."

It would have shoved his organs out of place, even disemboweled him if he'd been moving quickly enough. She stared at him. "It wasn't like that."

"Wasn't it?"

"Of course not! You frightened me, I woke and I—what were you doing anyway? Pairvyn or no, you can't just walk in while I'm sleeping—"

Something changed, something in him went very still and hard. "I'm sorry I frightened you," he interrupted in a clipped, terse voice. "I will try not to disturb you again. And I will have Nori'bel come to you this afternoon." He nodded tightly and turned, leaving her in the corridor.

Magic converged on Ariana, stinging her and making her vision swim. She squeezed her eyes closed and fought to breathe slowly. Steady, steady... *Think of Father. Think of home. Think of—*

But every stable image was threatened now by thousands of Ryuven descending to pillage and litter the countryside with dead soldiers and starving survivors.

She seized the foreign magic and drove it through her, forcing it to her will and channeling it into a wind that poured from her hands, rebounding off the floor and whipping her clothing and hair about her. After a long moment the pressure eased as she regained control, and she opened her eyes. At the end of the corridor, two che stared at her.

Ariana was in no mood to be civil. "Go away," she snapped.

They did, startled. She strode to her room, wishing she had a door to slam.

She could not stop the Ryuven army. And when they arrived and found King Jerome's army waiting for them, there would be carnage.

She had to find dall sweetbud. It would not avert the coming disaster, but there was nothing she could do for that. Thinking on it could do no good. But if she could secure dall sweetbud, perhaps negotiate a truce... At the very least, it would give her occupation and some slight hope as she waited for opportunity.

She needed to sketch the dall sweetbud, to have its features firmly in her mind before examining new species which might be teasingly similar. If she identified the wrong herb, if the Ryuven tried to open trade with the wrong product, they would never have another chance. She tugged at the silken cord to summon a nim servant for paper and ink.

CHAPTER SEVENTY-EIGHT

Nori'bel seemed pleased as she entered. "You look well, Ariana'rika. I'm glad to see it."

She was short for a female Ryuven, Ariana guessed, only Tamaryl's height. It was a difference which still startled her. "You were the healer who cared for me before? I cannot express my thanks enough."

Nori'bel shook her head. "No, I should thank you. You made me the first healer to succeed in keeping a human mage alive. And now I am told I can do Oniwe'aru some service in helping you?"

Ariana nodded and presented the sheet on which she'd sketched her best memory of dall sweetbud. "When I came before, you mixed a medicine for me which included this herb. I took a sample back to my world, where we identified it as a plant we knew as dall sweetbud. What can you tell me about it here?"

Nori'bel took the paper. "Ah, this is samur," she identified easily. "That's simple enough."

"Samur." Ariana tried the word. "Is it common?"

Please, let it be a common herb. A weed, hardy, plentiful, and worthless. Please, let them be thrilled to find a use for surplus samur.

"Common? It's not uncommon, anyway, but it's hardly ubiquitous. We can grow it readily enough if we need it, if that's what you mean."

Ariana's heart quickened. "That will do, I hope. It's priceless in our world. It's a valuable medicine, or was until it was over-harvested and disappeared." She stopped herself, trying to control the anxious excitement in her voice. "I hope to establish a trade for it. Your samur, for our meat and grain."

Nori'bel looked at her sharply, eyes widening. "You think that's possible? You came to speak to Oniwe'aru about this?"

"Yes." Complaining of the aru's reluctance would help nothing. Letting rumors of hope build might force him to give trade an opportunity. "But we need to know if the Ryuven could supply enough samur to support trade."

Nori'bel considered. "We grow it in our medicinal plots. We don't grow much, as it is not particularly effective in itself, but it supplements more potent blends. I am surprised you say it is so useful to your kind. But if we could trade profitably for it, I am sure it could be grown in greater quantities."

The magic prickled at Ariana again, and she fought to control her rising excitement. "Could we—I mean—could I obtain some of it? To carry back and prove that it's available?"

Nori'bel pursed her lips. "I believe Inki'che should have a fresh crop of herbs for me this week. If you are comfortable leaving the palace, we could go to him and see if he has anything yet."

There was no hurry; Ariana would not be returning to her world soon. But she had to know if it was real. "Please!" She kept herself from reaching for the Ryuven's arm in eagerness. "Yes, let's go."

When Luca entered the sitting room, the White Mage's eyes were closed, though he sat upright in his chair, his staff beside him. Luca hesitated, but Hazelrig waved him in. "Come in," he said, opening his eyes. "I was only observing the shield."

Luca set down the tray and began to arrange the mage's lunch. "From here, my lord?" He never spoke so freely with anyone as he did with Master Shianan, but occasionally he startled himself while with Ewan Hazelrig, who had been so easy with the boy Tam.

The White Mage, however, did not seem to mind. "Yes, even here. The shield extends over the whole of Chrenada. It is quite as visible here as anywhere else in Alham." His smile blunted the gently mocking words.

Luca was chided nonetheless. "Forgive me, my lord. I know better than to question."

The mage seemed hurt. "Luca, have I been so strict as that?" But his attention returned to the shield, as he closed his eyes once more. "It is weakening," he said, though Luca did not presume it was to him. "It won't be much longer now."

Hazelrig had always been kind to him. Luca took a breath and ventured the question which worried him most. "Until what, my lord?"

Hazelrig opened his eyes. "Until the battle. When the shield fails, there will be a great and terrible battle." He sighed. "This will be no sudden raid. Don't fear to sleep, though. We will have fair warning. The movement of several thousand Ryuven is a difficult thing to miss." Luca's incomprehension must have been evident, for the mage raised an eyebrow. "Through the between-worlds?"

Luca shook his head.

"Ah. Well, you've not trained for magic or military. There is a certain amount of temporal realignment when a Ryuven crosses the void, relative to the Ryuven's power. Massed Ryuven increase this effect exponentially, so that when—" He stopped, looking at Luca.

"I'm sorry, my lord."

"No, I'm sorry, I will explain in layman's terms. What we had always believed—but perhaps I can make it simpler yet. Tam confirmed that the sho, the most powerful caste of Ryuven, may leap between worlds in a moment. They may also carry more matter with them, such as a lesser Ryuven, or even a human prisoner. The che need longer to leap, though it seems to them that they leap as quickly; that is the temporal realignment I mentioned. The che will arrive after the sho, if they leap simultaneously, but each will feel as if they spent only a moment in the void. And the nim, the least powerful, need what we would count as a handful of minutes to cross between worlds, and they may carry only themselves and a small additional weight, such as their weapons."

Luca stared at him, trying to understand while at the same time seizing wildly upon one phrase.

"When a number of Ryuven cross at once, there is a—well, let's say that the between-worlds void becomes warped. Can a void warp? I don't know, but it will do for our purposes. That effect means the length of time it takes for the crossing is multiplied. So a single sho may travel from his world to ours in a moment, while a half dozen che may need twenty minutes. Do you understand thus far?"

Luca bobbed his head.

"A watchful mage can detect the energy trace of traveling Ryuven, if near enough. A single sho gives us only a moment of warning. If a half dozen che were to come, we could have twenty minutes to prepare and meet them where they appear. A thousand nim give us a couple of days to present a stand." He sighed. "You see now?"

Luca nodded again.

"What is it? You look as if you have a question."

Luca opened his mouth and hesitated. But the question burst from him. "You said—you said Tam confirmed it for you?"

Hazelrig blinked at him. "Did I? I must be tired. I would have thought you... but no, he wouldn't endanger her. He'd trust you with his own life, but he wouldn't risk hers." He sighed. "Yes, Tam had a special knowledge of the Ryuven. Some might have considered it treasonous, so his role was never to be known."

Luca nodded. The boy somehow knew the Ryuven and assisted the White Mage. No wonder he had been used gently as a slave.

"But Tam wanted to end this war. He helped us to develop the shield. That is why I felt there was no treason in keeping his secret."

Luca was not sure why the mage felt the need to explain. A slave could not pass judgment on the White Mage, nor accuse him. He merely nodded again. "Yes, my lord."

Hazelrig slowly slumped. "I am not sure we will see Tam again."

So the slave had not fled, after all. He might have been taken by the Ryuven he betrayed. Luca nodded. "I'm sorry, my lord." It was easy to see the mage had been fond of him.

Hazelrig closed his eyes. "And Ariana... my daughter..."

Luca twitched uncomfortably as he saw tears brimming at the older man's lids. "Is there anything I can bring you, my lord?"

The White Mage shook his head. "No, Luca. Only, let me speak sometimes. It's good to explain things, to talk of something else, something known and simple and—I'm sorry, I'm not making much sense." He took a deep breath. "Thank you for the meal. Now you may go."

Luca bowed hastily. "Yes, my lord."

Taev Callahan adjusted the light cloth about his nose and mouth—there was little risk with inhalation, but with so much material, it did not hurt to be cautious—and raked the gathered leaves into a netted bag, tying it off. He set the bag aside and began filling another.

They had called him a tapper, as if such a thing existed outside of story, but long years had dulled their suspicion. They still regarded him at a distance, however.

But he could advance without their admiration. He could serve the kingdom and himself at once, just as they did, without playing their games of preference.

He set a third bag in the pile.

And if he carried a few others with him on his journey, well, that only made him more generous than those who would leave him behind. And if he seemed to be working for the greater good even as he helped himself, well, that couldn't always be helped. He cared nothing for the sheep who had abandoned him to Luenda and judged him for surviving. Certainly he felt nothing for the people the Circle allegedly served, did not care for the soldiers he shielded, never saw his child-brother's face in the refugees they passed after battles or imagined his dead tutor's face among the grey casualties.

He tied off another netted bag and settled them all into a larger unmarked burlap sack. The Black Mage was gone, carried off again to the Ryuven world, and who knew what she might find there. She hadn't the sense to make the best use of a situation, but he knew what to do.

CHAPTER SEVENTY-NINE

Ariana hated her decision and herself for making it. But she had no choice. She had to make every attempt to save her kingdom.

She could not convince Oniwe'aru herself; she needed the help of a powerful Ryuven. The only Ryuven likely to hear her was Tamaryl, and this meant she had to ingratiate herself to him once more.

She felt filthy even planning such a thing, as if she were whoring her friendship to gain what she wanted, making it currency in her desperate diplomacy. But she had no other options remaining. No one but a prince doniphan of the Ryuven—whatever that was—could forestall the coming disaster.

She prayed Tamaryl could.

She went to the archway opening onto the corridor and beckoned to the first nim she saw. "I would like to speak with Tamaryl'sho." She had wondered whether it would be more correct to go to him or to ask that he come to her and decided to leave it to the nim's interpretation.

The nim hesitated. "Er, Ariana'rika, that is, I'm not sure if you are to..." Apparently he was not certain, either, of protocol or Ariana's dubious privileges. He rallied and offered, "I will ask Maru to arrange a meeting."

Clever one, passing the responsibility. Ariana nodded. "I know Maru and would be glad of his help. Please speak to him as soon as you can."

She returned to her room and climbed onto the narrow bed— the design must have something to do with their wings—and pressed herself against the wall, her arms wrapped about her legs and her chin on her knees. The thought of falsely reconciling with Tamaryl was upsetting, but the thought of using Maru was even more so. Maru had cared for her when she was painfully ill, had become a prisoner in her world only through his concern for his friend, and had not joined in Oniwe's and Tamaryl's attack in the Wheel's cellar. He was a Ryuven, one of those who would ravage her world, but she did not want to lie to him.

501

She clenched her fists until her nails bit at her palms like the foreign magic gnawed at her mind. She would do what must be done.

Soren pushed himself from his desk and strode jerkily about the office, squeezing his fists. Like a wraith, Ethan appeared silently in the door, his eyes questioning.

Soren made a quick gesture. "No, I don't need anything. I just—king's oats, I have to move. Do something. I feel so—the shield is decaying around us, the Circle says there is nothing to extend it, and when it falls we will be overrun with Ryuven." He faced the servant. "I know you know all this. But 'soats, must we just wait for it?" He spun and moved across the room again.

Ethan said nothing.

Soren stopped and sank into his chair again, resting his head in his hands. "They're our people, Ethan. The farmers and herdsmen who will be raided, the soldiers who will fight and die, the merchants in the towns we'll guard... All of them are our people, my people, and I can't do anything to protect them."

"Not so, my lord. You direct and support those who can."

Soren looked at him disconsolately. "The Great Circle? Whose White Mage is still an invalid, whose Black Mage is abducted and perhaps, I pray not, tortured for our weaknesses? And I fear I'm stretching the Silver to limits. If I ask her once more about extending the shield, she might use me to fuel it."

"The Circle is more than its individuals, you have said," Ethan reminded him quietly. "And there are others."

"Yes, others—our army, our well-trained and well-equipped army." Soren did not mention Shianan Becknam, pale and wasted.

Ethan, though, knew what he thought as always. "His lordship is recovering."

Soren gave him a flat look. "In time to be sent to the next Luenda."

Ethan had no answer for that.

Soren sighed and looked at his desk. "I know there's nothing to be done. I'm only chafing here. Go back to your work. I'll get by."

Ethan did not retire but hesitated in the doorway.

"Oh, king's sweet oats," sighed Soren. "What now?"

"The Wakari contingent is en route and making good time. They will likely arrive to shelter in Alham while we are meeting the Ryuven."

"Good," Soren said curtly. "Then I won't be on hand to meet Princess Valetta, and that will be one less concern on my mind."

"Ariana'rika, may I enter?"

Ariana felt such a surge of gratitude at Maru's polite request that she sprang up and threw her arms around the startled Ryuven, bumping his recoiling wings and knocking them both off-balance. "Maru! I'm so glad to see you." She was surprised to realize she spoke honestly, not merely as part of her scheme to enlist help. "Really, I am."

He was moving away, carefully disentangling himself. "Ariana'rika, I did not know how to expect—I am glad you are..."

Ariana hesitated. "You thought I would be angry with you."

Maru avoided her eyes. "Possibly."

She took a breath and plunged ahead with her plan. "I want to speak with Tamaryl. We have to speak about what—what happened, and about what we can do to stop what may happen. Will he see me?" She guessed a sense of hesitation might carry her further.

"I'm sure he will. I will take you to him. Er, I don't suppose you have been given any, perhaps, suggestions as to where you might go?"

Ariana shook her head. "I have been to see Oniwe'aru, and I have otherwise stayed mostly here. No one has given me any restrictions that I know of. I don't much care for walking about alone, as you might understand."

Maru nodded. "If no one has directed otherwise, then we will go to his house. This way."

It seemed other Ryuven avoided them in the corridors. Ariana wondered whether this was due to her presence or if Maru, servant to the Pairvyn and a recent prisoner of humans, experienced it, too.

As they walked, she noticed a few furtive glances from Maru. "What is it?" she asked, shifting her Ryuven clothing self-consciously and tugging at the slits over her exposed back. "I know it's not exactly mine, but am I embarrassing myself?"

Maru, abashed, looked straight ahead. "I'm sorry, Ariana'rika. It is only—it is odd to see you so. I am accustomed to your own garb, but in Ryuven garments you look..."

Ariana stifled a giggle. "Startlingly attractive?"

"No! No, you look rather... deformed." Maru flushed. "I'm sorry, I—please, I did not mean that you—it's only that this emphasizes your slim torso and lack of wings. I mean, of course humans aren't meant to have..."

Ariana pushed past the apologizing Ryuven. "I understand." She strode briskly forward, keeping her eyes ahead. "Actually, a slim torso is considered desirable among humans."

She felt stupid. She had requested Ryuven garb to make herself more presentable to Oniwe'aru, and in fact she had only made herself ridiculous. Even ancient human art had added wings as an accoutrement of power and beauty. How could the Ryuven respect her when their clothing slipped and fell over her?

Maru called after her. "Ariana'rika, we turn here."

She stopped, bit fiercely at the inside of her cheek, and then turned back to Maru and the corner she'd ignored. He looked apologetic and uncomfortable. She paused beside him and swallowed her pride. "Should I return for my own clothes?"

Maru shook his head. "I am sorry for what I said. Some might find you quite exotic in your—humanness."

Ariana felt her expression slip. "Some? Might?"

Maru flushed again. "I do not seem to be able to speak without offense, Ariana'rika. Please trust that Tamaryl'sho is quite familiar with human standards of appearance."

But the Ryuven clothing emphasized her incompleteness, in Ryuven eyes. Ariana sighed. "As you say. Let's go."

CHAPTER EIGHTY

"Your Highness! The shield has fallen!"

Soren rolled from his mattress and landed already reaching for the tunic he'd abandoned for his nap. "How long ago?"

"Word only just came, my lord." Ethan was bringing Soren's boots. "Council is of course called."

"I'd supposed as much. Have the mages recognized anything?"

"I believe so," Ethan answered, "but it was unclear exactly what."

"It will be an invasion," Soren predicted flatly. "That's hardly in question. What we need to know is where and how soon."

Sweet all, this would be disastrous.

Shianan knew at the knock on the door, before Luca even admitted the soldier bearing urgent news. He knew the impermanent shield had at last collapsed, knew the Ryuven invasion had launched, knew he would lead his men to mortal battle. Thoughts unfamiliar in the face of combat jostled through his head—thoughts of Ariana, Soren, Luca.

He shoved them fiercely aside and met the soldier's and Luca's white-rimmed eyes. "What have the mages learned?"

The markings on the map seemed to blur into one another. Soren blinked and reached for his half-empty cup of tea.

"This ravine will be our primary handicap," General Septime continued, indicating on the map. "It will trap our men without hindering the Ryuven. But if we keep them to this side, our mages will be able to erect shields to disrupt their flight and give our archers a chance."

Mage Parma nodded and leaned over the map. "The Circle will be here and here, which will give us the best coverage of the area. We'll have grey mages on either side of us in each location."

"We'll need more greys to reinforce our soldiers here. And it wouldn't hurt to have a unit here, if we can. If we're pushed against that ravine, we've lost everything."

No one voiced aloud the truth, that they had already lost everything. Open battle against thousands of winged opponents, able to use magic from a safe distance, was all but useless. The army moved only to slow the slaughter of the countryside's populace and prevent an easy assault on the capital.

The army could save the kingdom, but it could not survive the attempt. Few had returned from Luenda.

"We'll want to approach from the east," Septime indicated. "The flux has spread, as of our last reports." He tapped a shallow valley. "It's moving downriver... It doesn't kill many, but it will render its victims utterly useless for fighting. We must avoid it."

Uilleam, Grand Chancellor of the Realm, frowned. "Our leaders in this battle... I'm sure I speak for everyone when I say we are concerned for the condition of Mage Hazelrig for his own sake and yet anxious for his presence in this time of need."

Soren gestured to draw their attention. "I saw the White Mage myself again yesterday. He is still weak, but he assures me he is convalescing. I do not think he will allow himself to stay behind, even if he is not completely recovered."

A few looked surprised that he had visited the mage, but that was their own concern. Soren owed no explanation for his visits to either Hazelrig or Becknam.

Uilleam nodded, and Chancellor Washe sat forward. "And what of Bailaha? I heard he was recovering in the mage's home."

"He was. I saw him as well." Soren kept his eyes from the head of the table, where King Jerome stared fixedly at the map. "He will be there too, I have no doubt."

"We might put the commander here," Kannan pointed, shifting the discussion back to strategy, "and the White Mage here with this group. The Silver Mage would be here, and our other divisions here, here, and south here. I could be here, Septime here, and His Highness along here. Your thoughts, my lords?"

Not long after, the council ended for the night. Soren stifled a yawn as they left the table; he was tired, and he did not expect to sleep much in the coming days. He wanted to go to bed. He hoped Ethan had kept something to eat in his room, to save sending to the kitchen.

"Soren."

He turned, straightening as he faced his father. The king placed a hand on Soren's shoulder and looked at him soberly. "Soren, I leave this in your hands. You will be the one to save our kingdom. I place this in your care."

Soren gaped. In his care? *Save the kingdom—or destroy it!* They faced an overwhelming challenge in the massing Ryuven, and now if—when—their army was devastated, the responsibility would lie on Soren's shoulders?

He shook his head. "No, I can't do this alone. You can't give me responsibility for this—"

"Whom else could I trust in my stead?" The king gave him a smile. "And when you succeed, of course, you will have a fine victory to display before the princess." He looked pleased with himself. "Go, Soren, and save our kingdom. Save us all."

Soren's throat closed, and he managed a quick bob before retreating. *In my hands! Sweet Holy One, save us—in my hands!*

Maru led Ariana through a gateway—she still thought them gateways, though she rarely saw actual gates—and into the airy patio where a cheerful fountain provided a quiet backdrop of sound. "Wait here, if you please, Ariana'rika. I will bring Tamaryl'sho."

"No need. I'm here." Tamaryl stepped from a portico and looked at them warily. "To what do I owe the pleasure of this... unexpected visit?"

Maru glanced at Ariana expectantly. She took a breath. "I wanted to speak with you."

Tamaryl made a tiny gesture. "On what point?"

"Perhaps there is a way we can help one another..."

Tamaryl raised an eyebrow, his expression cool. "And how is that, my lady mage, as our intended ends are quite different?"

"They're not!" she snapped. "You want to avoid fighting, and I want to avoid fighting. You want to find a peaceful resolution, and I want to find a means of trade. Only Oniwe's raid is—"

"I am commanded to see this raid done," Tamaryl interrupted. "Would you have a slave of so many years disobey his orders?"

Maru edged away, sensing the conversation would not improve.

Heat rose in Ariana and the air began to prickle at her bare skin. "Don't hide behind that, you hypocrite! That was your own bargain and you were no base slave. Do you or don't you wish to end this war?"

507

Tamaryl's expression flashed to something dangerous and then smoothed again. "I have been working to that end for the span of your life, Ariana'rika."

"How have you done so? By hiding in my world? By attacking my friend and my father?" She choked, startled by her own mention of the forbidden wounds. Foreign magic bit at her.

Somehow Tamaryl was suddenly close, very close, his breath scorching her as he leaned over her and snarled, "Do you somehow think that I do not grieve as well? Your father risked his life for me. I loved him too." He shook his head. "Your selfish mind cannot comprehend why I do what I do."

"Selfish? I only want to save lives! Why can't you see that?"

"You do not see half of what I wish you to see." He turned and started for the portico with long strides, his wings rigid and high.

The fountain was absurdly loud, drowning Ariana's hearing. She had failed, she had done everything wrong, she had driven him further and she was utterly alone and he would sacrifice her people for his own...

She choked out a word. "Tam." It was the hardest thing she'd ever said, calling him back, and she didn't know if she even wanted him to return. But the name came anyway. "Tam!"

He hesitated and half-turned. Ariana clenched her fists and tried to think, tried to breathe. Magic prickled over her, biting at her, making it impossible to focus on the whirling thoughts which had no form.

"My lady?"

He shouldn't have said that, shouldn't have called her by the familiar old address... If he had called her Ariana'rika, had kept a distance between them...

Ariana choked and dropped on the fountain's edge, scattering colorful fish. She ground her knuckles into the cool stone. "Beast! Monster! I hate what you did, I hate it, and yet you're the only friend I have in this—and I don't think I can trust you, I don't want you near me, and yet I want to turn to someone, some friend, after you've betrayed me—and I want you, you monster! I want to cry to you about *you!* Do you know how twisted that is?"

She couldn't see him. She stared at her knees through a clouding threat of tears as Ryuven magic jabbed savagely at her. She was aware of him moving toward her, but she could not think what to do about it, or even if she wanted to stop him. Already she was ashamed of her outburst, and already it was beyond her power to recall.

Tamaryl's hands gathered hers as he knelt beside the fountain. He took a moment to gather himself. "Ariana, my lady mage, please remember this—whatever else may be, I am still your friend. No matter what battles or magic or politics or else may come, I am your friend. I owe your father my life and I love you. I will not let you come to harm. If you believe nothing else of me, believe that."

Ariana jerked a hand free and slapped him across the face. "Is that why you shoved me in front of you as a living shield?"

Tamaryl didn't respond for a moment, one hand to his cheek, and Ariana tried to decide if she was glad or horrified at what she'd done. Then he looked at her with his lips compressed. "Do you know that among Ryuven, a physical blow is the very worst of insults?"

Ariana decided she was glad. "Did you know that among humans, hiding behind a female is viewed very poorly?"

"I did not hide behind you. And I might remind you it is no slight for a Ryuven male to let a female make a defense. Perhaps I should ask instead why you chose for your door a shield which might have killed me?"

"Why did you choose killing magic to defend yourself when you could simply escape without being followed?"

"I wanted—" Tamaryl stopped abruptly. He stood and stepped away. "Let us try this another way. What can I do to make you feel safe here?"

Ariana stared at him. "Safe?" she repeated. "Do you think I'm afraid?"

"You're shaking."

She was. Ariana ground her knuckles into the stone again. "And how could I feel safe?" she demanded. "I am alone in an enemy land, my friends are now my enemies, my father is injured or dead, my—" She choked off, uncertain what even to call Shianan and hardly able to speak of him or her father. Instead she gestured fiercely at the courtyard and beyond. "And I have no privacy here, no safety. Always there are eyes upon me, Ryuven coming to look at me or walk in on me. Even you, creeping in while I sleep."

"It's only because I was concerned—"

"I don't care what the reason, whether you were worried or guarding me or wanted to watch me sleep, it's disturbing and wrong! I just want to be able to sleep without worrying. Is that so much to ask? One night!"

Tamaryl's posture softened, and he nodded. "Stay here, and let me keep you."

She stared at him. "What?"

"I will watch for you. You will have a guard, so you may sleep safely."

Ariana set her jaw. "And who will guard me from my guard?"

He turned his head. "Never mind, then."

"Wait." Ariana inhaled, swallowed, exhaled. "I'm not—I don't know. You know this isn't... Look, just talk with me for a moment, all right? Don't tell me I can trust you—tell me why I can trust you. Tell me why you used me as a shield."

Rather than answering immediately, he fetched a chair from the shade and lowered himself into the backless seat. "My old wish for you to see me as a Ryuven has been fulfilled," he ventured after a moment. "You never hit me when I was a slave."

"You never hurt me when you were a slave."

Tamaryl sighed. "I knew the commander would not press an attack against you. Also, I trusted your ability to protect yourself without harming him or me."

"What if I had failed?"

"It never occurred to me you might fail," he answered simply, turning his palms upward. "A Mage of the Circle could create such a shield in the blink of an eye."

She eyed him dubiously. "I thank you for your confidence, but I do wish you'd found another way to express it." She hesitated. "And..."

Tamaryl rose and walked across the courtyard, his wings flexing restlessly. "I will be honest with you, Ariana'rika. I do not know why I used that magic. I reacted blindly, on instinct alone, while fighting. A human soldier attacked me, and I defended myself. I never thought consciously whether I would kill him or no. I only acted." He paused, standing still, and glanced back at Ariana. "It might have been the other way. You know Shianan Becknam meant to kill me. If he had, what would you have said to him?"

Ariana's gut twisted and she crumpled, tearing at the magical atmosphere and the clothing which chafed her and the utterly helpless rage she felt before it all. She fought the rising frustration and grief, suppressing all but a keening whine as she tore at her arms.

510

"Ariana!"

She sat up, drawing a deep breath which burned her lungs. "I'm—I'm all right. Don't. I just—it's only the magic." She choked and breathed again, slowly. It hurt. "I don't know, Tamaryl. I know he attacked you, but you know he was thinking of me."

"I know that." He turned away again.

She rubbed her eyes, feeling needles prick at them. "Sweet all, I just want to sleep. Maybe it won't all go away, but... at least I'd have slept."

He turned to face her. "Then you will stay?"

"How will that be seen? Will people think... whatever your people think? If everyone is talking of the Pairvyn and the human mage, how will that affect what we're trying to accomplish?"

Tamaryl chuckled, a bitter note souring the sound. "With all respect, my lady mage, you cannot accuse me of being a murderer and a lover at once. And if you recall, Oniwe'aru did charge me with your keeping. It would be expected."

"Fine, I'll stay. While you're at it, is there anything you can do about this cursed magic that's trying to peel away my skin?" She squeezed her eyes shut and drove her nails deep into her hands, trying to recall the calm control she had been losing steadily, worn weak by grief and fear.

Something brushed over her hair and cupped the back of her head. Before she could move, Tamaryl placed his other hand over her face, resting his fingertips softly on the bones surrounding her eyes. Something cool, like spring water which wasn't quite wet, poured over her skin and seemed to run into her.

"Let me try," he said softly.

Her head sank into his cradling hand as her rigid muscles relaxed, and the prickling of magic faded. "You blistered toad," she whispered. "Why didn't you do this when I first came here?"

"Before you'd mastered our magic, this would have done nothing."

She wanted to open her eyes but could not. "How exactly are you doing that?" Her speech was a bit slurred. Her body felt strangely limp and heavy, and she was now sinking deeper into his grasp. She might have been frightened, if she could recall the strength.

He chuckled. "If I did this with a bit more power, you would recognize it as an incapacitation."

She was torn between indignation and laughter, but she settled for a muddled, "Very funny."

"Should I continue?"

Either she did not trust him, or she did. "Yes, please."

The cool not-wet sensation rolled down her head and neck and over her shoulders. Now that he had given her a hint, she could see how it worked, blocking magic from the channels she'd created. She examined it, realized it was something she could allow or reject, and then let it pour through her in grateful relief.

"And, blistered toad?" He cradled her against himself as he sat. "Your invective has become a bit more colorful of late, my lady."

"Credit the Indigo for that." Ariana was suddenly sleepy, more sleepy than she'd felt in days. If it were true there would be no peering eyes—if only she would not dream of horrible things...

CHAPTER EIGHTY-ONE

Ariana awoke in a Ryuven sleeping room. Though the archway was open, she heard no household bustle nearby. She blinked and tentatively moved. She felt rested and whole, physically at least. She would think on the rest later. She rose and found scented water waiting on a stand.

"Ariana'rika? Are you awake?" Tamaryl tapped at the outside wall. "Good morning, my lady mage."

"Good morning. Do I have this wing to myself?"

"Mostly. I instructed that you were not to be disturbed, and as we had other guests, I kept watch myself for much of the night—but safely at the end of the corridor."

"Didn't you sleep?"

"It was not lost time. I thought on many things." Tamaryl smiled. "And you have no doubt heard, my lady, a slave needs no sleep."

"To the contrary, I have observed myself that one in particular certainly slept well, at any rate. Usually late into the mornings." It was so much easier to speak of the past, the safe past, when Tam was a mere boy and her father was well. She rubbed at her face. "Thank you."

Tamaryl looked at his fingers, then put them back on the wall. "Ariana, I am sorry. For what happened to Shianan Becknam. Whatever else he was, he was your friend, and I am truly sorry."

Ariana fought sudden hot tears, swallowing hard against the stone which swelled in her throat. She struggled to find an answer, but Tamaryl shook his head and retreated from the room, leaving her in abrupt solitude.

Shianan had been a good friend, in his way, and it seemed he wished to be more—but now that would not be, if ever it could have been. But that was why she had to convince Oniwe'aru, to prevent more such sad, senseless death. It hurt to think of Shianan, it hurt terribly, and she could not afford that distraction now. She had to close her mind again.

She stood still, breathing in slow rhythm, and made herself think of nothing for long minutes, until she had regained a tentative control.

She stretched long and deep, surprised at her physical recovery. She had not thought of using limited incapacitation as a means of relaxing muscles. That had been a clever idea. It required exquisite control, something Tamaryl plainly had alongside his great power... His great power, which had killed Shianan Becknam.

And she had so easily forgiven Shianan's murderer.

Her gut convulsed as horrific memory rushed at her again. Sweet Holy One, what had she done? Had she forgotten Shianan so quickly, to excuse Tamaryl so easily?

But Tamaryl's unanswered question remained: *If Shianan Becknam had killed me, what would you say to him?*

Shianan raised his hands overhead gingerly, his abdomen pulling tight. But there was no real pain, only the stretch of healing tissue—as if it had been a real wound, instead of the disturbingly odd magical injury—and his private practice with Torg had gone well enough. He was fit to go with his men, and he would be in condition again by the time the fighting began.

The outer door opened and closed, Luca returning from his visit to care for Hazelrig. "How is he?" Shianan called.

"Improving steadily," Luca answered, entering the living quarters. "He's talking of taking an apprentice after the battle."

"How improved?"

"He can manage the stairs now, with someone to steady him should he need it. He'll ride in a wagon to Arakidamia, but he says he'll be capable when he gets there."

Shianan shook his head. "It's a disturbing thing, magic. When honest steel cleaves a man, he stays cloven."

"You're in no position to protest, my lord," Luca answered pointedly. "And speaking of...?"

"I'm fine. I just returned from a private bout with Torg, who told me in respectfully certain terms he would not allow a crippled man to go to battle. I'm glad to say he was unable to prove me incapacitated." Shianan stretched again. "And whatever word has gone around regarding my involvement in the Wheel incident, it's done something to the men. They jumped the moment I spoke. More than usual."

Luca smiled. "The prince said as much."

"King's oats, though. I lost the Shard and the Black Mage at once, and they esteem me for it."

Luca crossed the room before Shianan could reflect on what he had said. "The flux is spreading, despite efforts to contain it. They say it's not where you're going, however."

"A blessing. Nothing like an army spraying its strength out its rearguard before it even sees the enemy."

"Is your cloak still repelling water satisfactorily?"

"It's fine. And that reminds me." Shianan jabbed a thumb toward a small coffer. "Go and buy yourself some more suitable clothing. That looks like you rolled down the road all the way from the Wakari Coast and," he added critically, "something like you stole it from a boy half your age. Don't they have enough material to make proper sleeves there?"

Luca glanced at the shortened sleeves sitting well above his wrist cuffs. "It's the latest fashion in Ivat."

"That's because Ivat is full of muddle-headed merchants with more style than sense," Shianan answered, skimming a report. "I know Alham winters are temperate compared to some, but you should still be decently clad."

Luca grinned. "Yes, Master Shianan." He nodded toward the table opposite. "I packed your things while you were with the troops."

Shianan crossed to the table and opened the pack there. Luca moved forward as he went through it methodically, touching each item and occasionally rearranging things. "Did I forget something?"

Shianan shook his head. "It's nothing you did. When my life depends upon laying my hand on exactly what I want within the span of a breath, I keep my own gear."

Luca nodded. "I've got my own—"

"You're not going."

Luca's eyes widened. "Not going?"

"You said yourself that a few weeks of training didn't serve you when you needed it. And here you won't face greedy highwaymen whose goal is your purse or to capture you alive to sell. These are Ryuven warriors, and they'll want to kill you, nothing less."

"But you began teaching me so I could help you! That's what you said!"

"What else could I say? What else could I tell anyone? Or you?" Shianan shook his head. "You haven't progressed nearly far enough to face real battle."

Luca's face had paled. "You cannot leave me here waiting for them to carry your body home."

Shianan gave a tiny laugh. "Luca, don't be absurd. They'd bury me where I fell."

"Shianan—!"

Shianan nearly smiled. "Then pray that I carry myself here again." Then he shrugged. "Or that I don't. I've written out a new death-will, and you'll be a free man and heir to whatever assets I leave. That won't include the title, I suspect, though the council has been too distracted to confirm the forfeiture, but it should leave enough to make you comfortable wherever you like. Holy One knows I've not spent any of it."

Luca stared at him, unspeaking.

Shianan sighed. "I have been into battle many times, Luca, and always come out again."

"And that raises the odds, doesn't it? How many times can you pass through fire and escape being burned?"

He shook his head. "You're staying here." He folded the pack together again and lifted it onto his shoulder. One hand fell automatically to his belt, checking sword and knife and small leather pouch. Then he leaned forward and embraced his friend, startling them both. "Goodbye, Luca."

He released the slave and went out the door, leaving a silent room behind him.

Ariana, freshly washed and dressed, found her way from the quiet wing to the courtyard, where a striking silver-haired Ryuven was humming as he scrubbed out the fountain. He glanced up, startled, as she came into the morning sunlight. "Ariana'rika! May I help you?"

"Can you direct me to the kitchen?"

"Oh, I will go if you like." He looked familiar, and he seemed nervous of her. No surprise there, though.

"No, there's no hurry." She sat in the backless chair Tamaryl had used. "What are you called?"

"I am Taro." He bent over the fountain again with a quick glance at her.

She felt guilty for his unease. Did he fear humans? What a foolish question; of course he feared humans, and human mages, and especially the human mage who had not succumbed to their native magic. "What were you humming?"

"I beg your pardon?"

"I thought you were singing when I interrupted you."

He smiled a little. "So I was. It's 'Ring Round the Moonflowers.' Do you know it?"

"No, not at all." She watched Taro abandon his brush and pick up a small bowl of assorted crumbs. "Oh! Are those for the fish? May I feed them?"

"If you like, of course, Ariana'rika."

She went to the fountain and began to sprinkle bits over the water's surface. The colorful fish emerged from the shadows where they'd hidden and began to gulp greedily. "If this is some breach of decorum, don't tell me anything about it," Ariana said cheerfully. "I've gotten to feed fish only a couple of times in my life."

Taro looked into the water. "Enjoy them, then. I do not know how much longer they will stay."

"You're sending the fish away?" Ariana laughed.

Taro did not laugh. "They are color and beauty, but they are meat when there is none. And I have seen nim fight or beg for the like of the bowl in your hand."

A cold, sobering weight settled over Ariana. "For this?" She knew nim might indenture themselves to escape hunger, but she had not guessed Tamaryl's own servants might have fled such a fate. Stores were failing, Oniwe'aru had said, but even then she had not imagined...

Taro glanced away. "I'm sorry, Ariana'rika. That was hardly fit speech for a sunny morning. If you like, I'll bring you something for breakfast."

"Yes, please," she answered, and then she felt renewed guilt for accepting the meal.

Taro departed, and she sat alone on the fountain's edge, watching fish chase one another and finish the crumbs. She wanted to simply watch them, her mind empty of all thoughts of Oniwe'aru and battle and Tamaryl and hunger and peace and herbs and her father, her dear father, and Shianan...

I knew the commander would not press an attack against you. I trusted your ability to protect yourself without harming him or me.

Tamaryl had acted for the least harm to anyone. He had tried to spare Shianan by using Ariana's defense. She could forgive him for that, surely.

The sunlight was bright, almost glaring after the winter grey of home. She trailed her fingers in the water, but the disappointed fish left her. She squeezed her eyes against the tears which suddenly formed. She needed to get away, to scream and sob and grieve, but she could not here, not yet...

"Ariana'rika?"

It was not Taro, but Tamaryl, standing at the edge of the patio with a bowl and cup. She blinked and forced a smile. "Hello."

"I heard you wanted breakfast." He set the fruit and juice beside her and then crossed to sit on her opposite side. "What's troubling you?"

She didn't meet his eyes. "I'll be fine. I'm only—I've a lot to think about. I'll be all right."

He sat very still. "Ariana, I meant it, when I said I was sorry. He was your friend. Do you see..."

"I understand," she whispered. "I know."

Tamaryl's arms wrapped about her and held her near his warm torso, buffering the sound of the fountain's splashing and the bright sunlight. Neither of them spoke or moved for a long while.

CHAPTER EIGHTY-TWO

Cold rain dogged the military train as they left Alham, soaking roads, equipment, and soldiers. Shianan's nerves were soon stretched to breaking, as he dealt with the thousand crises of mobilization and all plagued by the hated rain.

The rain did not cease as they went north but grew more vicious. After they crossed the river, two days out, an ice storm descended. Shianan lay in his tent and did not sleep, listening to icy pellets strike the cloth and trying to bury the cold, slow terror the sound woke in him. He wrapped his blankets about him and wished for more, trying to block out the rattle of falling ice. He angrily chastised himself for hearing it, for letting it touch him, for shivering at the mere sound, for failing to sleep. But resentment only glazed his unease. Though long accustomed to field quarters, that night he longed for stone walls, slate roofs, and burning braziers.

In the morning, already exhausted, he helped break wagons free of frozen puddles, shouting for burlap to be placed as footing for the draft slaves trying to start their loads on ice. The day stretched long and bitter, and by night Shianan was barely civil to his captains. "I don't care if they're tired," he snarled at Torg. "We're all tired, we're all cold. But if those wagons aren't on higher ground, they'll sink and freeze in the mud and never move in the morning."

Torg nodded, rubbing a streak of splashed mud from his face. "I know, sir. But the—"

"I don't care!" snapped Shianan. "Just get it done!"

He saw that slaves were shoveling channels to direct rain away from where they'd left some of the lighter wagons and muttered a few more instructions. He was hungry and cold, like the rest of his men. Now they were settling, he wanted supper and a warm bed. And the ruthless freezing rain continued to fall, ever dogging him with chilly unease.

Someone had already erected his tent—there were advantages to being a commander—and he slogged through frozen mud to the entrance. A lantern was lit inside, lending an artificial warmth to the interior. Shianan shook his head to disperse the melt-water inside his hood and pushed his damp hair back. Luca looked up from the tunic he

519

was mending and pointed. "I've brought your supper."

For a moment Shianan stared at him, afraid he had somehow fallen asleep on his feet and dreamed. But it was bitterly real. He drew a sharp, angry breath. "Luca! What are you doing here?"

"I followed you, as a good servant should."

"A good servant should do as he's told, and I told you to stay in Alham."

Luca took his time responding. He'd obviously schooled himself to present his argument reasonably. "I can help you. And I won't—"

"'Soats, Luca, don't you listen? You'll be killed out here. I told you not to come." Shianan's fury fueled his words through his weariness.

"I know what you said. But I won't stay in Alham and wait while—"

"Have you ever just done what I've said? Even once? Even when it would have protected you?" He turned, trying to put Luca out of sight, as if that would change anything, would keep him from this dangerous place.

"That's not what—"

"Can't you just do as you're told?" he demanded. "Listen and obey?"

"But—"

Shianan wheeled to face him and roared, "I own you!"

Shock struck each of them in the same instant, as the words hung almost tangible within the sagging cloth walls. Rain drummed out all remaining sound as they stared at one another.

Luca took a slow breath and arranged his features into a wry smile. "You owe me," he answered gently.

Shianan gulped, tried to move, couldn't. "Luca, I—I didn't..."

"You've said yourself that I've helped cover your back. I can do so again."

"Luca, I'm sorry. King's sweet oats, I'm sorry. I can't—I didn't—"

"Let me stay, then."

Shianan shook his head. "No." He dropped heavily to the low cot, heedless of the wet cloak soaking his bed. "If I die, Luca, and there is a chance of it, I die fighting, serving my country and my king. And you will grieve, and you will profit by my death, gaining your own self and a substantial sum of money."

"And that is worth your life?"

"Hear me out! If you die, Luca—and it is no chance but certainty, you cannot but die facing Ryuven—then I will grieve the loss of my closest friend, and I will carry forever the burden of knowing I did not prevent it."

Luca stared at him. "I came to help you."

"Your presence won't keep me safe. In truth, I'll be safer without the distraction of worrying over you." He smiled grimly.

"If you are—"

"There is one thing I have always done well," Shianan interrupted, "and that is to frustrate anyone trying to kill me. If death comes, I won't fear it; I have been a soldier all my life and I've known from boyhood what we faced. But know this, Luca—I do not go to search for death. I do not intend to throw away my life, nor to part with it lightly. I swear to you, I go to kill Ryuven." His jaw tightened. "More, I go to kill a Ryuven."

Luca's eyes gleamed wide in the lantern's light. "You can't— Pairvyn ni'Ai is nigh immortal. He's unstoppable. He's already nearly killed you!"

"Then he won't expect me again, will he?" Shianan's voice held no humor. "Leave that aside. Luca, I am truly sorry for what I said, I am. But I won't let you stay. If I cannot order you back, I'll order men to take you back. I won't have you die uselessly."

Luca looked away, his throat working visibly. "I understand. I'll go back in the morning."

Shianan eyed him closely. "You'll go?"

Luca's jaw spasmed. "I would not lie to you. I'll go back to Alham, and I will stay. And I will wait for you to return." He looked again toward Shianan.

Shianan nodded. "I'll come back." One corner of his mouth twitched. "And if I somehow fail, it will be the first time I have lied to you. But at least you will know it will also be the last."

Luca scowled. "That's poor comfort and poorer humor."

Shianan shrugged. "It's all I have." He glanced up at the roof, where water beaded ominously to show where the proofing was weak. "'Soats, I don't want to go out in that again."

Luca wordlessly passed him a cooled plate. Shianan unclasped his cloak with his free hand, tossing it to the slave, who hung it to drain as best it could overnight.

CHAPTER EIGHTY-THREE

Tamaryl's expression held only the barest shred of hope. "What have you learned?"

"There was nothing nearby. Nori'bel is flying to some more growers," Ariana explained. "She's sure we'll find some dall sweetbud—samur." She squeezed her fingers into balls of frustration. "Isn't there anything we can do?"

Tamaryl shook his head. "I've waited as long as I could."

"But what if she brings some?"

"The warriors leapt the moment the shield fell," Tamaryl said shortly. "Nothing can overtake so many in the between-worlds. And with so many in transition, I can't delay any longer." He took a breath. "Wish me well?"

"I will pray for you. For you, and for everyone else, and for an end."

Tamaryl embraced her and held her close, tightly, as if he feared to release her. His wings curved about them, nearly sealing them in a cocoon. Ariana gripped him tightly. "Come back to me."

"I will."

"I don't want to lose you, too."

"I will come." He clenched fingers in her hair. "I will come for you."

There was a soft cough from the side. Tamaryl's wing shifted enough for Ariana to see Maru standing awkwardly a few paces away.

Tamaryl took a breath. "I have to go, my lady."

Ariana's heart beat faster, but she did not move. This was Tam—Tam, the laughing boyish servant, Tam, the hidden Ryuven, Tam, who had killed Shianan as she watched... As he released her, she held her breath.

"My lady mage," he said softly. "I do not know if we will have a chance to speak again. But—please don't think ill of me."

"Tam..."

He smiled sadly. "I always liked it when you called me that, somehow." He looked at her hands, hesitating.

"Tamaryl, I..."

For a few heartbeats, neither of them moved. And then

Tamaryl grasped Ariana about the waist and pulled her close, meeting her surprised lips with his own. He kissed her deeply, fiercely, and she was taken by surprise. But she did not pull away. He tasted of power, of fire and lightning. His hand slipped along the slit in her back, tantalizing with the warmth of it.

He killed Shianan, a part of her mind whispered furiously. *You're kissing Shianan's murderer.*

He must have felt the shock ripple through her. He drew back slowly, reluctantly. She watched him, her eyes pulling wide, his hands sliding away from her to leave cool hollows on her skin. Surely he could hear her heart pounding.

"That's it, then?" he asked quietly. "Even if he is..." He straightened. "I'm sorry. I had no place... I'm sorry."

She reached for his hand, caught him. "I'm sorry. It's just that—it's too soon, and there's so much else."

"It was my error."

She squeezed his hand. "But—come back."

"I intend to." He gave her a little smile and then turned away.

Ariana swallowed hard against the lump in her throat. He would be safe. He was the Pairvyn ni'Ai. He would return.

Maru shook off his embarrassment and hurried to match Tamaryl's stride. "Well, that was encouraging," he ventured.

Tamaryl looked straight ahead. "She is uncertain."

"You can hardly blame her for that," Maru protested. He fingered the mace on his belt. "You told her you would return."

"Yes."

Tamaryl's voice was not quite right. Maru looked more closely at his friend. What he saw was not disappointment, but something darker and deeper. It frightened him. "Ryl, what are you thinking of doing?"

"She thinks of him," Tamaryl answered curtly. His tone was cool and detached. "Even though he is dead, she thinks of him."

"Ryl, she can't have forgotten her friend—"

"I told her I would return. And I will, after I have ended this war so there will be no more fighting hereafter."

"But we haven't even found her herbs—No, Ryl!" Realization poured over him like icy water. "No, you can't!"

"This war can't be ended by other means," Tamaryl snapped.

"Haven't I tried? And now she pins her hopes on a plant Nori'bel cannot even find, with no evidence any human merchant is willing to trade for it. Enough blind hope. I have seen my error, and it is time to save lives by crushing those who would kill us. If they cannot resist us, neither Ryuven nor humans will die after this battle."

Maru shook his head, horrified. "You can't—not all that you've worked for, not all that you've done—"

But Tamaryl took another step and leapt the void.

CHAPTER EIGHTY-FOUR

The rain had slowed them, and they had only hours to prepare to meet the Ryuven. Soldiers scrambled before barked orders, the weary draft slaves were threatened and prodded into final efforts as weapons and stockpiles of critical equipment were distributed. Shianan swerved from his path past an assembling group to pluck an arrow from a soldier's bundle. "What is this?"

"Arrow, sir," came the reply.

Shianan gave him a suitably deprecating look. "Thank you, soldier. Perhaps you'd care to tell me why it's not one of our Ryuven bolts?"

"I like these better, sir. I brought my own bow, too, to match the flexion. I use them for hunting at home, and I'm more accurate with these."

"Accuracy is not your chief concern here," Shianan replied curtly. It was shameful, how many unseasoned soldiers and locally raised troops had come for this. He held out his hand, and another soldier promptly gave him one of the standard heavy bolts. He held the two side by side, heads tipped toward his listeners. "What happens when your dainty hunting shaft goes through a Ryuven?"

The soldier blinked at him. "Er, if I've placed it well, it pierces a heart or lung or liver."

"Yes, perhaps. Or it might be you're releasing in the heat of battle, with your fellows jostling and screaming and falling all about you, and you're lucky to put it through a shoulder or thigh or anything at all. But let's be generous and say you put this arrow right through a Ryuven lung. What happens then?"

The soldier hesitated.

Shianan looked at another. "Your comrade appears to be confused or ignorant. Answer for him."

"The Ryuven will withdraw the arrow and heal himself, sir."

"Exactly right. The eerie winged monsters do just that. And that is why we have these." He angled the heavier bolt's wickedly barbed head toward the offending soldier's face. "Answer this one yourself—can a Ryuven pluck this out as easily as your pretty sewing needle?"

"No, sir."

"Will this shaft break as easily, letting him draw it out in two parts?"

"No, sir."

"Do you want your target to simply snap out your little sticking pin and then come to kill you for the inconvenience you've given?"

The soldier was squirming now. "No, sir."

"Do you think any of your fellow soldiers want you doing anything but your best for them?"

"No, sir."

"Then I suggest you stow away these toys and arm yourself appropriately. And if any of you should encounter anyone else who would put the rest of you at risk by not following orders, you might see that they re-arm as well."

"Yes, sir!"

Shianan went on, seeing that each of the squadrons was in their assigned place and ready. Grey mages hurried back and forth across the field. Shianan shaded his eyes and looked across the plain to where three of the Circle would make their stand. Hazelrig's white robes showed plainly.

At least Ariana won't be in the fighting. The thought did not cheer him; he was not glad to think of where she was now.

The thrice-cursed Ryuven had chosen their entry point well. The ravine limited the movement of the land-bound human soldiers, and the sloping plain led to some of Chrenada's richest farmland. When they fought down the defending human army, they would have easy plunder.

Well, not so easy, they hoped. Luenda had ravaged the Ryuven as well as the humans. And Shianan intended that even if the Ryuven moved on, they would not have their Pairvyn to lead them.

He went to the deep blue tent erected low on the hill—height was not a defense from the Ryuven—glancing about at the preparing army for final assurances that they were as ready as he could make them. He saw a contingent of archers set above the tent, busily grouping arrows for quick reloading. From that position, they would have the duty of protecting the tent below them from any Ryuven trying to reach it. Three horses shifted uneasily outside the tent, ignoring the soothing of their grooms. They were there in case of sudden need, to speed a general or prince to where their leadership was needed—or to safety.

Four more of the Circle passed Shianan, speaking quietly among themselves. He wondered briefly if any of them had been instrumental in the saving of his life, and then he brushed aside the tent door and bowed slightly as he entered.

Prince Soren, General Septime, and General Kannan looked up from their map. "Come in, commander," Kannan said. "You didn't see Vanguilder, did you?"

"No, sir," answered Shianan. He remained straight-backed near the door, the lowest-ranked of the assembly. He meant to maintain etiquette with the prince-heir before others.

Kannan swore under his breath. Soren started to speak, but the tent flap moved again, this time admitting Hazelrig and Parma. They nodded respectfully. "Your Highness, my lords."

"My lord and lady mage," Soren greeted. "Come in."

"We don't have long," Parma advised without ceremony. "They're very near to leaving the between-worlds."

Hazelrig nodded. "A couple of hours at most."

Kannan drummed his fingers on the table. "If your mages know their—"

"Sirs!" Marshal Vanguilder burst into the tent, his eyes bright with excitement. He checked himself, nodding to the prince, the generals, the mages. "Excuse me."

"What is it, marshal?"

"I've been to the crest of the hill and confirmed it—there's an orkanstorm coming."

Shianan's heart quickened. It was Septime, though, who asked first, "What? Are you certain?"

"The clouds are unmistakable," Vanguilder answered. "It's coming, and coming fast."

"Bless the Holy One who blesses," breathed Soren. "They'll drop right into it."

"It will play merry havoc with our archers," Kannon considered, "but the benefit will be well worth it. We need to utilize every advantage this brings. This will be quite a surprise to them. Becknam, I want your men on the downwind side, ready to close as the monsters arrive."

Shianan nodded. "Yes, sir." They would be fighting into the wind, but their odds had significantly improved. Orkanstorms brought ferocious winds, even whirlwinds, which would disable their archers and half-blind their soldiers—but the Ryuven would be thrown from the sky.

The meeting was intense but brief, and they scattered to adapt their deployment. Shianan could feel the stirring of air as the storm approached, though they were yet shielded by the gentle sweep of the hill. If they had to face the Ryuven, conditions could not be more ideal. He grinned savagely and shifted his belt.

Ariana let her head fall forward onto the table, cradled against her forearm. She was utterly empty. She had nothing left.

Beside her sat a full bushel of precious dall sweetbud, a full bushel of dried leaves—a lord's ransom at least in her own world, surely, and it had been gifted to her by the Ryuven who tended it in the hope she would use it to end the fighting and supply them with food.

And here she sat with a basket of wealth and peace, and she could not use it.

It was not that she had not tried—she had. She had begged Nori'bel, but the Ryuven healer was not strong enough to carry a human across the between-worlds. She had gone to petition Oniwe'aru, but he was closeted with other Ryuven for the battle and his guards had turned her away at the door, emphasizing their denial with slight movements of the ceremonial flanged maces they held. Ariana had angrily considered forcing her way into the aru's chamber, but Ryuven entrusted with guarding Oniwe would be formidable opponents, and even if she could overcome the Ryuven, violent demands could not lead to success in peace. The aru beyond would find her no challenge, and Oniwe'aru might be glad of the excuse to slay her.

She pressed her dry, burning eyes into her forearm. There would be a battle, an enormous battle, and she could stop it—if only she could go there.

CHAPTER EIGHTY-FIVE

Shianan adjusted his broad helmet so that he could see more easily through the upward-facing slits at the front crest. The rising wind whistled against the wide wedge spreading over his cheek guards and part of his shoulders. Their gear for Ryuven was awkward and odd-looking, but necessary for fighting an airborne opponent. Ryuven struck from above or dropped missiles which needed deflecting, and any arrow which missed a Ryuven target would descend to pierce a human just as easily.

But the Ryuven would not be airborne for long. Shianan blinked and rubbed grit from his eye. The wind was already noticeably rising. It wasn't a full orkanstorm, not yet, but it would aid them. He shifted the axe on his hip and set his spear into the ground, finding a firm place to brace it. Around him, two hundred soldiers did the same.

And then the nearest grey mage lifted his hand high. "They're here!"

Shianan glanced at the pale soldier beside him, a young man who had seen little combat outside of training. He slapped the man's back, leather palm against light steel, and grinned. "Don't be greedy now. Leave a few for the rest of us."

The man swallowed and nodded. "Kill the monsters."

"Right."

The air cracked open, thunder resounding with the splitting of atmosphere, and the sky was full of Ryuven. An instant later they spiraled away, grasping at their weapons and flailing with wings and arms as the wind took them. Some regained control and beat their way upward, others spun helplessly toward the bristling polearms.

Shianan sighted and adjusted forward, bracing the butt of his spear against the ground and his boot. A Ryuven struggled to catch the air but failed, thrashing onto Shianan's spear and sliding to the cross shaft with a jolt. He shrieked and lashed his hammer toward Shianan.

Shianan released the spear and moved backward, and the hammer passed harmlessly through air. The Ryuven grunted as he hit the ground, the spear through his torso, and Shianan stepped on the hammer as he drew his axe.

531

Ryuven were strong in magic, but their physical strength paled beside that of humans, nor could they burden themselves with heavy armor and keep their advantage of flight. The light steel cap crumpled easily beneath Shianan's axe.

Shianan braced his foot against the body and freed his spear. He glanced at the young soldier beside him, just completing a kill of his own. Shianan pushed him back from the dead Ryuven and snapped, "Take your spear! Now!" The soldier gulped and pulled it free, turning to reset himself for another Ryuven. *Don't give them time to think. If they take time to reflect on their first kill, they won't live to make a second. Make them fight. Make them survive.*

Another wave of Ryuven appeared, but these seemed to be coping better with the winds. One dropped stumbling to the ground before Shianan's front line, righting himself and flinging magic as he straightened.

Shianan felt the impact through his chest, and his abdomen screamed in remembered agony. He heard himself grunt as he set his spear and charged, ducking his head. A second bolt struck him, but there was weight on the end of his weapon as he faltered. He recovered and drove himself forward. If he could secure the Ryuven on the shaft, it would buy precious seconds and a chance at—

Someone rushed from the side and struck at the Ryuven warrior. There was a brief exchange of blows—Ryuven successfully fighting the wind were more skilled and more powerful—but the Ryuven had a spear in his abdomen and little could compensate for that. He died beneath the axe, and the young soldier looked wide-eyed at Shianan.

Shianan grinned breathlessly. "Well done. Now where's your spear? There are more of the monsters."

"Right, sir!"

Over them, a band of Ryuven had overcome the winds and climbed into the sky, moving fast toward the rear of Shianan's company. Suddenly they struck an invisible wall, flattening against it almost comically. Arrows showered through the sky, piercing the Ryuven as they struggled but bouncing away before reaching the mages holding the shield from below.

"Quarrels!" roared Shianan, and around him the men bunched together where they were not actively dispatching Ryuven, clustering shields to form larger shelters from the rain of arrows. Arrows and dying Ryuven fell, and the soldiers closed on the survivors.

They were faring well. They would hardly miss the Shard—after this massacre, there would not be enough Ryuven to seriously threaten them again for a long, long time. Shianan drove his axe into the neck of a Ryuven hammering a soldier's shield.

"Torg!" he called. "Move east!" With the wind, no Ryuven could flee the line and circle around to try the sky again. They would entrap the grounded and force them to fight hand to hand.

And then something shook the air and men gasped with impact. Shianan whirled with the others and saw a dozen men staggering backward, clutching at chests or throats with magical attack. A single Ryuven swept into the air over them, compensating for the wind and no doubt magically assisting himself in it. A bright crimson sash marked him, but Shianan knew his face.

He seized his spear and rushed forward, but Tamaryl was already winging away, striking at another group. Other Ryuven attacked, stronger warriors who were coping uncomfortably with the winds. Soldiers screamed as the fresh wave of Ryuven drove into them.

Ryuven were on the ground now, abandoning the treacherous sky for direct fighting. Magic stunned or disabled soldiers who could then be beaten with hammers which crushed armor into their wounds. Spears thudded into Ryuven to immobilize them as soldiers scrambled to kill them before they could escape and heal.

Shianan fell into his fighting, stabbing and hacking through the Ryuven. As the battle thickened, he abandoned his spear and used his sword, blocking magics and blows with his agile shield. "Alanz! Close that gap! Don't let them on your flanks!"

The orkanstorm worsened, sweeping the remaining Ryuven from the air. Shianan did not see even the Pairvyn ni'Ai. The grass was trampled and stained where humans and Ryuven had fallen, and loose dirt, blood, sweat, entrails, dung were whipped together into a darkening cloud. Wind shrieked over the hill and through the fighters, hindering all equally as they squinted to see and leaned into the gale.

Breathless screams marked the path of a whirlwind which drew human and Ryuven into its vortex, spinning them violently before dropping them upon their comrades. All scrambled out of its path, abandoning their individual fights, until it veered away and jumped the ravine, leaving the battle behind.

There was no time to think on the storm. Thousands of Ryuven came on relentlessly.

Shianan's arms were burning. He spun and caught a hammer's shaft with the flat of his sword, immediately lunging forward to cut from the shaft into the attacking Ryuven. Beside him another soldier fell as magic scorched across him. Shianan snatched a spear from the ground and flung it at the Ryuven who had killed him. Another Ryuven buried his hammer in a soldier's face.

Shianan repositioned his command several times, staying within the orders Kannan had given but adapting to the changing battle. How long had it been? He didn't know, and he couldn't risk searching for the clouded sun. Was the wind slowing? It seemed to be. Orkanstorms did not usually pass so quickly, but this one had not been particularly fierce, either. Perhaps they had felt only its edge as it swept over the plains. The Ryuven had recovered well from their disadvantage, and—

In the sky! Yes, the winds were definitely slackening, and the Ryuven had seized upon it. A winged shape dove at an angle, using the wind for additional speed, and struck a soldier from behind, crushing his neck and knocking him into the open ravine. Shianan shouted a warning, and another soldier tried to spear the next Ryuven, but the Ryuven used his hammer's shaft to deflect the spear and sent the soldier after the first.

And then Pairvyn ni'Ai was there again, sweeping through the humans. Shianan started forward, panting for air. Where were the mages? They knew no common soldier could withstand the Ryuven champion—joined magecraft was necessary to withstand him, said all the old veterans. Where were the mages?

Soldiers scattered, falling or fleeing before the forming wedge of Ryuven. Shianan snatched up a spear.

But Tamaryl rose into the air and, with a final disabling blast to discourage ambitious archers, sped across the field. He had given his warriors a foothold and would wreak his havoc elsewhere. Shianan snarled in frustrated hate.

Abruptly the Ryuven wedge shifted and turned. There was a pocket of soldiers trapped now between the Ryuven and the ravine. They fell into position as trained, the front line locking their shields as the second set their spears. The Ryuven magic blast struck mostly shields, but a few men cried and stumbled. Two more Ryuven swept down from above, killing a man who was looking forward. The group was pushed toward the ravine, and three more soldiers died.

"Alanz!" Shianan called, started forward. "Alanz! Through

their rear!" If they could strike at the back of the Ryuven, break their momentum, it would give the soldiers a chance to counter or escape.

And then a great shape came bounding across the field, charging into the side of the Ryuven wedge. Soren slashed from his horse, cleaving a wing and then a shoulder, and pushed on to the entrapped men. He wheeled the horse and plunged forward with the soldiers, who charged with their prince.

"No!" Shianan ran, no longer watching for Alanz or his men. He hit the Ryuven wedge where Soren had, cutting wings, boiled leather, arms. He pushed through fast, not pausing to face or finish any of them—that would be fatal. That would slow him. And he had to reach the prince—

Ryuven wings blocked out the light as Shianan swung his shield into an angry face. A flying pair dove toward the prince, who raised his sword to meet them. His horse flung its head and leapt aside wide-eyed as the winged monsters plunged toward it.

Shianan cut down a final opponent. Soren swung at the first Ryuven, who checked himself with a flip of wing and then caught Soren's arm. Soren raised a small shield reflexively and struck the hammer from the Ryuven's grasp. An instant later the shield cracked, failing beneath magical impact.

Soren spurred the frightened horse and twisted, wrenching himself and the Ryuven around as the soldiers swarmed about them. Someone jabbed a spear at the Ryuven, but the tip slid across leather armor. The panicked horse spun, knocking aside two soldiers, and leapt stiff-legged into the air. Soren, caught between horse and Ryuven, slid in the saddle.

Shianan shoved a human soldier out of his path.

The second Ryuven dove as the first lost his grip. He seized Soren's free arm and dragged him from the horse. Soren dropped but did not hit the ground as the two Ryuven together started for the ravine. Soren twisted as they sagged beneath his weight and slashed wildly with the sword he still held, missing his assailants. Shianan was close enough now to see the prince clench his jaw as he drew himself up by the arm they held, reaching with the sword again—

One Ryuven cried and lost his hold. The second dropped with the weight and Soren hit the ground, missing his feet. The prince struck again, his legs dragging, and the Ryuven yelped. They faltered and landed at the edge of the ravine. Shianan sprinted—so close!—and the Ryuven kicked the prince over the precipice.

"No!" Shianan cut at the escaping Ryuven and leapt after Soren.

The ravine wall was steep, but it was not sheer. Shianan had peered into it when they had first arrived. He landed on his heels and fell backward, sliding on the backs of his boots and leaning hard on his shield. Rocks and soil tumbled around him as he slid toward the bodies below.

He landed a short distance from Soren, who was mostly upright at the base of the wall, just above the obviously broken form of another soldier. His head hung forward, staring at the ground or his cuirass, but he had not fallen.

Shianan sheathed his sword and dropped the shield as he ran. "My lord!"

The prince lifted his head and looked at Shianan, his pupils unnaturally dilated. "Help." His voice sounded oddly flat.

Shianan slid on the rocky footing and came to a halt, staring. Soren had fallen down the wall and tumbled onto the waiting polearm of a dead soldier below. The spearhead had slid beneath the edge of his steel cuirass and stuck somewhere within.

Shianan drew a quick breath. "Sweet Holy One."

"I can't move," Soren said. "I can't—look out!"

Shianan whirled and drew his sword in one motion. A dozen paces from him stood Tamaryl, Pairvyn ni'Ai.

Shianan shifted in front of the prince, tipping his sword toward the Ryuven's eyes. He had no defense against the magic which should have killed him once before, and he could not throw himself recklessly forward while he had the prince to guard, but if opportunity came, he would seize it.

"I had thought you dead." The Ryuven's voice was almost surprised. His eyes narrowed, regarding them with the lazy gaze of a cat that has crippled a mouse. "By the Essence of all... but I suppose they liked you well enough to heal you." He swung a mace loosely from his right hand. "But there are no mages to heal you here."

Shianan's throat closed. "It's me you want, Pairvyn. Tamaryl. I offered to meet you before. Leave him."

Tamaryl's eyes shifted from Shianan to the motionless prince and back. "Always trying to protect someone, Becknam, and always failing. After I kill you, what is to stop me from killing your prince? After so much killing, why not kill those who ordered it?"

"Ryl!" Another Ryuven dropped from the sky, catching himself smoothly on the dry ravine floor. It was Maru, Shianan recognized, with his wing healed.

"Stay back, Maru," Tamaryl warned. "They say he is good with a weapon. One thing he does well, killing."

"You have no footing to speak of such things," snarled Shianan. He had to bait Tamaryl into using the mace instead of magic. Against magic of that strength, Shianan was nothing more than a temporary and useless shield for Soren. Against a mace, he had a chance.

Tamaryl continued, "It is the rulers who bring us to this bloodshed. It is Oniwe'aru's orders and King Jerome's. Better to cut off the head of the serpent."

"Ryl, stop." Maru moved slowly, as if afraid of startling the Pairvyn. "Think—you can't kill the prince."

"Can't I?"

"You can't, or this war will never end. It's only supplies, now—what will it be if you make it for royal blood? Think, Ryl. You don't want this bloodshed. It infuriates you even now. You gave so many years of your life to end this war—don't restart it now."

"They would kill our aru, given the chance."

"They would also leave us in peace, given the chance. But if you kill their prince, we'll never reach accord. Ryl..."

Tamaryl's eyes narrowed. "Fine! I'll leave the prince. He'll die shortly without my help, anyway."

"Then let's—"

"But Becknam has been so eager to face me. He offered to kick me off a parapet once, did you know? Even before our last meeting. He wants so to fight the Pairvyn, and I will oblige him."

Shianan let his knees flex another half inch.

"No, Ryl," Maru said softly. "Don't."

Tamaryl cupped his hand, and Shianan recognized the signs of forming magic. His pulse raced.

"Don't." This time Maru spoke to Shianan, as if warning him. Shianan stayed, though he could not explain why. Rushing Tamaryl would certainly kill him, but it might kill Tamaryl as well. If Shianan could destroy Pairvyn ni'Ai, he would have done all that he could have hoped. But Maru's single word stopped him.

Tamaryl's face hardened. "Maru..."

"If you kill him, she'll hate you, Ryl." Maru had one hand held low and partially extended, warning Shianan to keep his distance and wait. "Before, you struck in self-defense and in the heat of the moment. This will be thoughtful murder, Ryl, and she'll hate you for it." He hesitated, seemed to assess Tamaryl. He took a breath. "What if Daranai'rika killed Ariana'rika?"

Tamaryl exploded. "How dare you compare this?" He whirled, and Shianan's blade jerked—but Tamaryl's anger was for Maru. "How dare you?"

Maru's voice pleaded and bled. "Look where you are, look at what you're doing." His throat worked, and Shianan realized with a start he was near tears. "You wanted to end this fighting, Ryl. Look at yourself."

Tamaryl stared a long moment at the other Ryuven, his expression changing subtly but remaining unreadable. Maru seemed to be holding his breath. Then Tamaryl relaxed his fingers, letting the magic dissipate, and his wings sagged a few inches. "Maru," he said simply, and then with a crack of displaced air he disappeared.

Maru glanced at Shianan and then vanished as well.

Shianan stood still for a moment, not quite believing they were gone. Finally, slowly, he lowered his sword and replaced it, still alert for the sound of approaching Ryuven. He licked his lips, tasting sweat and blood. They had truly left.

He turned and hurried back to the prince. "Your Highness."

Soren breathed in short, quick gasps. "I think I can move my arms. 'Soats, what was that?"

"I hardly know." Shianan unbuckled the cuirass with strangely efficient fingers and pulled the breastplate away. There was little blood. That meant either the impalement was nearly bloodless or Soren was hemorrhaging internally, invisibly bleeding to death.

Shianan used a knife to slit the padding and shirt around the spear, drawing them apart to reveal the seeping wound. The cracked shaft of the spear had penetrated his left side and the steel head was clearly visible beneath the stretched flesh, wedged through his dislodged ribs. Soren glanced down and quickly squeezed his eyes closed, breathing curses. "I wish it had just pierced me," he panted hoarsely.

Shianan's hands were working even as his mind reeled. *No, no, no...* He cut the shirt from the dead soldier and twisted it loosely. "It will bleed when I break the shaft. Hold this—"

"When you what?" Soren stared at him with wide eyes. "No."

"You can't move with a polearm dragging from your ribs! I have to break the shaft here, just below the wound."

"Can't you—take it out?"

"You would die. That head is the plug holding in your guts. I can't remove that before we have you to a healer."

Soren stared at him. "Sweet, dear Holy One."

Shianan didn't want to think on it himself. Better to act. "It's already cracked, here." He indicated with a finger. "If I—"

Soren gasped and cried with pain. "No! No, don't touch it."

"I must, my lord."

"There must be another way."

"There's not! We have no choice."

"In tales," Soren panted, "I would conveniently faint. And when I woke, you would have packaged me neatly together and have made a delicious stew. And in between, I would dream of beautiful women, all dancing and smiling..."

"Don't talk," Shianan warned. He wrapped his fingers about the shaft.

Soren wailed at the touch. "No! No, please. Please." He panted for air, his face dangerously pale. "I can't do this. I can't stand this."

"You—"

"Look, can't you knock me out?"

Shianan gave him a level look. "I think I am about to."

"I mean, do it first. Hit me."

Shianan blinked. "My lord!"

Soren took quick, shallow breaths, flinching at each. Tears ran down his face. "Shianan—I am not a soldier. I'm not this brave." His whisper was nearly a cry.

"You're wounded—"

"I am telling you, Shianan Becknam, I do not want to be here when you break that thing out of me. Now by what oath do I need to order you to hit me?"

Shianan swallowed. "Yes, my lord."

Soren closed his eyes and clenched his jaw. Shianan stepped backward. For a moment he hesitated, unwilling, and then he gritted his teeth and struck.

Soren's head snapped hard, recoiling off the rock face behind him. His eyes fell open and rolled, and then he dragged his head around to glare hazily at Shianan.

Shianan stared in horror. "I..."

"I hate you," Soren croaked.

Shianan took a breath. "Not yet, but in a moment." He seized the shaft in two hands and wrenched it.

Soren gasped and screamed and writhed all at once. Shianan somehow made himself ignore it all and bore down on the shaft, trying to keep the end as stable as he could. An agonized howl tore from Soren's throat and then, mercifully, at last he stilled. Shianan did not allow himself to look at the prince. The shaft was proving stronger than he'd hoped.

He briefly considered his sword but immediately abandoned the idea; a breaking blow would rip the head through Soren's abdomen. He lifted his knee to the spear, bracing it as firmly as possible, and tried again. This time it cracked and shifted, and on the fourth try it finally broke away.

Shianan pressed the torn shirt against the wound, bleeding freshly with the movement. He wished he could just slit the skin and remove the head, but if the tip had lodged within an organ, that would be quick death for the prince. Better to leave it until the healers could take him.

Rather, until Shianan could take him to the healers... Shianan looked up with sudden despair. He had leapt over the slide in desperation, but it would be utterly impossible for a healthy man to climb, much less an injured one—or, he revised, a healthy man with an injured man on his back. He would have to hike up the ravine until he reached a point where he could climb out.

He looked at the unconscious prince. Carrying him would jar the piece in his side, but if he was careful he could avoid rubbing against it, and it would be no slower or more dangerous than watching Soren struggle up the ravine himself. And they would not lose time while the prince lay insensible.

There was not time for thought. If they didn't reach a healer soon, it would make no difference whether the spearhead were removed or whether Soren were carried. Shianan buckled the prince's swordbelt about his own waist, sliding the dropped blade into it and pushing it to the least inconvenient position. Then he unbuckled his own armor. The cuirass sat on his hips, and he would need to rest the prince's weight there if he were to carry him any distance. An unconscious man could hardly hold himself, but throwing Soren over his shoulder would be lethal. His gear shed, he took the prince's arms and pulled Soren's limp form onto his back, shifting him as gently as he could into balance as he took his legs, and started up the ravine.

CHAPTER EIGHTY-SIX

Torg ripped his axe free and spun to drive his shield into another Ryuven. A shower of sparks exploded beside him, brilliant and beautiful. Torg whirled, waited an instant as the sparks fell, and then struck through the collapsing inversion at the Ryuven who had meant to kill him. He nodded his thanks to the grey mage who had shielded him, who nodded back and turned to target a flying Ryuven.

Torg scanned the field, eyes running through the chaos. He had lost sight of Shianan some time before. That didn't necessarily mean anything. The commander could have shifted to another part of the field where reinforcement and command were needed, trusting Torg to keep his place.

There was no time to worry. The failing winds allowed Ryuven to take the sky again, and the archers were finally able to participate in full. Thick bolts slammed into Ryuven and dropped them onto the field, where soldiers rushed to finish them while avoiding missiles and hammer strikes from above.

Torg ran to where a Ryuven crumpled on the trampled field, groaning as he tried to extract a thick bolt from the wedge of flank muscle which powered his wing. The barbed head did its work, though, and he could not tear it free. He glanced up as Torg killed him.

Another form fell to earth and Torg whirled. But this one was human, his cuirass mangled and reddened.

A group of Ryuven wheeled overhead and flew east, apparently intent on escaping the battle and reaching the farms and warehouses they'd come to raid. But the mages threw another shield in their path and they struck it hard, falling as they lost position in the air. Some caught themselves as they landed and turned on the soldiers rushing to meet them.

Torg was tired, very tired. He lifted his axe and turned back to his men. Tired or not, they could only fight until the Ryuven fled or escaped or died.

Tamaryl entered above the Leaping Plain, breathing hard. He dropped to the ground and continued downward until he sat on the

541

long grass, resting his elbows on his knees and bending over them.

Maru, dear Maru, was right—Tamaryl could not kill Shianan simply to deny him Ariana. He could not kill the injured prince simply to purge his anger over the unceasing fighting. He could not betray himself and those who had suffered for his beliefs—Maru, Ariana, Ewan—in his rage.

He rested his forehead on a supporting knee. Almost he wished to return in time, to go back to being Tam, the unnoticed slave boy who carried the memories of the Pairvyn but had hope for a peaceful future. Exile had been hard, but he'd had friends and hope.

There was a soft pop behind him. Maru had followed him. Tamaryl didn't move. Maru came and sat beside him, plucking at the grass and shredding it.

Minutes passed, and neither of them spoke. The breeze moved about the plain, rustling the grass and gently toying with the pieces Maru dropped. The silence was disorienting after the deafening chaos of battle.

Tamaryl took a slow, deep breath. "You're right."

Maru continued to toy with the grass.

"Thank you."

Maru clenched a fistful of brown-green blades. "You weren't yourself, Ryl."

"No." Tamaryl flexed his wings behind him. "But I intend to be, now." He set a hand on his friend's shoulder. "Thank you for staying with me."

Maru shrugged. "You were missing for fifteen years. I didn't mean to lose you again."

"Hm." Tamaryl flexed his wings again and pushed himself upright. "Did you—see the White Mage?"

Maru nodded. "I saw him from a distance. I didn't go near him."

"Neither did I." Tamaryl took another slow breath. At least he had kept that much of himself in his madness. He had not wanted to face his friend, his partner in magic, his protector in the human world. "I hope he's all right."

Soren groaned, to Shianan's relief. At least he had not bled to death on Shianan's back. "Your Highness?"

Soren's voice came faintly to Shianan's ears, though his head hung close. "I thought I said I didn't want to be here for this."

"You weren't. But I have you back for now."

"I wish you didn't." Soren moved his arm weakly over Shianan's shoulder. "King's runny oats, this hurts. I think—I think I'll exile you to Damas, for this and for that punch earlier."

He was even jesting. That was a good sign. "Don't distract me with threats, Your Highness. I could drop you."

"Or I suppose I could have you paraded as a royal favorite." Soren gulped audibly. "Where are we?"

"We're following the ravine up, to find a way onto the plateau. Then we'll take you to the healers."

Soren sucked back a cry as Shianan stepped onto a boulder. "What—what do you think is happening up there?"

Shianan had not wanted to think on that, but it filled his mind each time he made himself stop wondering if the prince was dying. "We were doing well. We inflicted great losses, certainly. But now that the winds have slowed..."

"Carnage."

Shianan nodded reluctantly. "It will be like Luenda, as they said. We may stop them from stripping the countryside, but we will suffer for it. If they can take to the air now, and our soldiers are tiring..."

"You save me only for the wolves, then," Soren whispered hoarsely. "My father and the council will rend me."

Shianan had no ready answer. He did not know how the king saw the prince's failure—had not thought until recently there could be such a thing. And this failure would be grand, the loss of so many lives...

Shianan reached for the next firm step and eased himself up, trying to stay steady on the rocky foothold. 'Soats, but the man was heavy. His legs were trembling.

"What?" he protested at last. "And leave the kingdom to the little turd?"

"Heh." Soren offered what passed for a laugh. "You're sworn to serve that little turd. And he might prove a good king."

"He's an arrogant little cod and you know it," Shianan retorted, baiting the prince. He needed Soren to stay awake, to keep talking, so he could hear any faltering.

"Serves—right." Soren's voice was fading, but he kept speaking. "He'll have Lady Bethia Farlyle for queen."

"Her?" Shianan's surprise was genuine. "She's told everyone

she's your bride!"

"Not our fault," Soren managed. "We asked—marriage. What she put about..." Quick, shallow breaths punctuated his words. "Keeping me for a Wakari princess."

"I crave a boon, my lord. Promise you'll let me witness when it's announced which royal husband she'll have."

"'Soats, Becknam, have mercy. It hurts to laugh."

Good; he could still make weak jokes. "I'm sorry. I'll keep a respectful sobriety before my liege."

Shianan's legs burned. He did not know how far they'd come, but far enough to be well out of reach of the army camp. At least the walls were lessening, he thought. And they didn't need to reach the head of the ravine, if they could only find a place where the slope was gradual enough that Shianan could help Soren up the wall...

Now you're grasping at straws, he admonished himself. *Stay fixed on the task.*

He hesitated and then pushed himself up the next incline. Soren slipped on his hips and gasped. Shianan froze, trying to hold the prince steady. "Sorry."

Soren did not answer. Shianan turned his head, trying to see the dangling prince. "My lord?"

"Go 'way. 'M not here."

The moment of silence had worried Shianan. "Good. You should be ashamed of yourself, demonstrating such deficient swordsmanship publicly. Embarrassing."

"Are you just trying to keep me talking?"

"Yes." Shianan slipped on a loose stone.

"King's runny—! Take a rest. For both of us."

Shianan stopped. "I'm not sure how best to set you down."

"Don't I know that... No good way, I'm afraid."

"Then try to fall to your right, and I'll catch you."

There was a long pause, and then Soren's weight shifted slightly. Shianan grasped the prince's arms hard and let him slide, twisting so that he would fall clear and the spearhead still protruding from his ribs would not drag across Shianan's back. Soren's legs hit the ground and did not support him. Shianan staggered and lowered him.

Soren seemed frozen, his hands hovering near the wound, his bruised face tight and pale. "King's runny oats," he ground between clenched teeth, "why don't you just punch me again, Becknam?"

Shianan sat down more heavily than he'd intended. "If I

thought it would do any good, I might."

Soren blinked at him, no longer angry. "You—you don't look—you look worried."

"I am." Quickly he added, "But if you had a bellyful of blood, you wouldn't be speaking to me now, and you might be dead already. So we just need to keep anything else from tearing inside."

"You know how to cheer a man." Soren eased himself onto one arm. "I keep feeling that if I only shift the right way, it won't hurt so much. And then I look down, and I just want to puke."

Shianan was drawing slow, deep breaths, trying to conceal his fatigue. "Don't look."

"Anything to drink?"

"You shouldn't have any alcohol."

"I meant water, and I meant for you. Though I'd like some water myself—if I didn't think it would run right out again." He winced.

"Water's gone. I dropped my kit, for the weight. So we'll have to reach the camp soon." *Holy One, let us find help.* "How are you managing?"

"I'd be fine if only I didn't have to breathe." Soren closed his eyes. "All jesting aside, I feel like there's a shaft of wood and steel laced through my ribs, and if you won't let me go unconscious on your back, then I want to find someone who will take it out."

"I'll do my best, my lord."

"I know that. I didn't mean anything else."

A few moments passed while Shianan greedily gulped air. He wanted to stay, wanted to let both of them rest. But if he didn't move soon, he would stiffen. He wished—but there was no advantage to wishing. He pushed himself to his feet, his legs burning. "Time to go."

"Demon commander," muttered Soren. "Will you think less of me if I pass out when you lift me?"

Shianan picked up a sturdy dry stick, broke it to a handsbreadth in length, and dusted it against his trousers before passing it to Soren. "I swear I won't note a thing."

Soren grimaced. He placed the stick between his teeth and slowly, resolutely, lifted a hand toward Shianan.

CHAPTER EIGHTY-SEVEN

Ariana clutched the bushel basket in her arms, the edges of the woven strips cutting her skin. She had no idea how to attempt this, nor what would happen if she succeeded—but she had to try. There was nothing left but to try.

She closed her eyes. *Visualize. See what you want.* She thought of the bright sky over the Ryuven world, of the brilliant blue over her own. *No, no—that's no winter sky.* The sky would be grey, blustery. There would be rain, even snow. Grey, cloudy... *Now connect them.*

She hardly knew how to think of the between-worlds. It was one of the greatest mysteries remaining to the Circle, and if her father had learned anything of it from his knowledgeable famulus, he had not shared it.

But there was a way between the worlds. She concentrated. It had been cold, and black, and terrifying—but she could not think of the fear. It was easier to imagine a starfield, cool and dark but with a glimpse of her own sky just beyond it. If she *willed* herself there, if she forced the magic to carry her...

Power burned through her, but she did not feel anything change around her. She did not know how to open the—gate? Rift? Channel?

It didn't matter what it was called; she needed to pass through it. And she commanded the power to do so. She gripped her bushel and focused her arcane strength on ripping apart the air about her.

Energy raced over and through her, scalding the air she breathed. The basket trembled in her arms. She saw in her mind's eye the motes swirling about her, the material of the atmosphere, and with immaterial fingers she seized handfuls and tore it in two.

There was a faint clap of thunder, quiet as a gently closing door, as the air split and rushed to replace itself. Ariana opened her eyes in wondrous anticipation, but saw only the Ryuven bedchamber about her.

She had disturbed the air, at least. She could do more.

She tried again, forcing the magic into place. Power swirled around her, raking her hair and her skin, tugging at the basket. It whipped at her with cyclonic force, rending the air of her little chamber. She felt her breath sucked away as it stretched at the air, pulled at the fabric of the world.

There was something wrong, something immobile near her. It did not bend with the rushing energy. She looked at it and saw a pillar of brilliant, burning power, like a wellspring of magic.

"Tamaryl!" Her magic failed and spiraled outward, and belatedly she realized the centrifugal inertia of it within the room. Before she could capture it, Tamaryl had erected a barrier to contain the snapping strands of energy.

She opened her eyes to look at him, standing in the doorway. Maru stood behind him, blinking at her.

"Ariana'rika, what were you doing?"

She stood erect. "I was trying to return to my world."

He stared, and for the first time she saw him speechless. "I—by the—holy Essence within, do you know what you could have done?"

Anger flared. "I could have gone back! I could have tried to stop the battle!"

"You could have been lost forever in the between-worlds, and what would that have helped anyone?" Tamaryl was nearly breathless. "Do you even know how to manage the negentropic momentum of—"

"If I had any choice but to—"

"We've come to help," Maru interjected over both of them.

She checked herself and stared at them.

Tamaryl looked at Maru and then nodded. "Ariana, I've come to help you, if you'll let me. I've come to take you back, and I pray they'll hear your suggestion."

She caught herself. "You'll help me?"

"If you recall," he said wryly, "I wanted to end this war before you did." He nodded toward the bushel basket in her arms. "You have what you need?"

"An inexpensive herb for you, a precious medicine for us. Oh, I hope it works."

Tamaryl turned to Maru. "We'll be arriving in the middle of the battlefield, and I'd rather not be pierced full of barbed arrows upon arrival. I want you to form a shield just below us."

Maru nodded. "But I can't hold—"

"You won't need to maintain it, I hope. It's just to protect our arrival. After that, Ariana'rika and I will do the rest." He turned back to Ariana, adjusting his leather breastplate. "We'll have to interrupt the fighting."

"Stop an entire battle? Of armies? No pretty display of colored sparks is going to distract an entire army."

"You're going to strike them, and hard. Hard enough that they can't immediately jump up and carry on, hard enough that we'll have an opening."

"I can't. Even a Mage of the Circle can't spread an effect so wide as that would need, and I don't want to kill my own soldiers." She shook her head. "I wish I could take the magic from here with me. It's so plentiful, I could be much more effective."

Tamaryl's eyes widened, and she saw the boy Tam she had known grow gleeful with excitement. "Maru, go and bring the Shard."

"What?"

"Go! Hurry!" He turned back to Ariana to explain. "We'll use the Shard to hold an opening here. You'll be able to pull through that line to our magic. If a human mage can draw our intense power for use in your thin-magicked world..."

Ariana gasped. "It will be an enormous reserve. Like ten thousand amulets at once."

"You can strike the fighting soldiers. You needn't reach the entire field at once. If we can stop the center, the others will note the disruption and slow on their own to hear your new orders."

"*My* orders... I can't order an army!"

"You will today. As will I. This is our sacrifice for peace, presuming authority long enough to make them realize it's possible. You'll have to sound convincing." Tamaryl's eyes held hers, bright with intensity. "I'll need you to cast, as I'll be wholly occupied in holding the channel."

She nodded. "I'll do it."

"It's going to be difficult."

That much raw power pouring through her would use her hard. It would be difficult, and it would hurt. "I'll do it."

"Good."

He hesitated, looking at her intently. It unnerved her, and she searched for something to say.

He spoke first. "Your father is alive."

Ariana gaped, and her knees went weak. "Alive? You saw him?"

"He's fighting—well. He's fine." Tamaryl's hands caught her

arms. "Don't lose your focus, now."

She nodded through her rising tears. "I know. I will do it. I'm only—oh, sweet all, I've been trying so hard not to believe he was dead."

Tamaryl slid his arms about her and she clutched him, choking as she tried to suppress her sobs of joyous relief. "Later," she sniffed, trembling. "I can think on it later. First we have to stop the fighting." Pent grief threatened to burst through her thinning restraint in its abrupt negation, and she could not afford to be crippled with emotion when she would need all her skill and control. "Just—don't speak, not yet. Later."

Tamaryl's wings shifted restlessly, but he said nothing, and after a moment he withdrew, arms and wings pulling back from her. She rubbed at her eyes and nose and tried to fight down her joyful agitation by pressing her hands against her too-tight chest.

Maru returned breathless with the Shard of Elan cradled in his arms. "I am certain I should not have this. Where are we taking it?"

"You will hold a shield below us," Tamaryl explained rapidly. "I'll use the Shard to keep the path behind us open, so Ariana may draw energy here to fuel her magic there."

Maru's eyes popped wide. "Will that work?"

"We hope it will." Tamaryl looked at Ariana. "Are you ready?"

She had stopped trembling, her feelings locked away for later. She took a long sash from the wardrobe and fashioned a makeshift harness for the bushel basket to hang from her neck. "I'll need my hands for whatever magic I'll be working."

Tamaryl stepped behind her and wrapped his arms beneath hers, nestling against her body. "So your hands remain free." She could feel the warmth of him through the opening at her back. "Ready."

It was black, deep black, and the cold plucked at her like a living thing. How could she have thought to come here on her own? There was nothing, nothing to guide them, nothing to help them find their way to the next world or back to the first. It was all void, all chill, all terribly *naught*...

And then light burst around them and they were in the sky, even the grey clouds dazzling after the deep dark of the between-worlds. Immediately she felt the shift in power as Maru erected his shield, a frail hemisphere of protection against the hundreds of warriors directly beneath them. A black arrow snapped against the shield and, deflected by the curved shield, flew off into the sky.

Tamaryl's arms squeezed about her as he strained to keep them in the air. His great wings beat over them, rocking her as his muscles flexed. She lifted her arms and felt for the magic.

There! Tamaryl had done it, somehow—a river of power poured into the sky with them, drenching them with arcane energy. Tamaryl was pulling some to himself, lending strength to his overtaxed wings, but what he needed was only a fraction of what tumbled through the rift.

She breathed deep of the cool, clean power and closed her eyes, drawing it inward. It tasted faintly of the void, she could not say how, and it swirled tightly around her as if unwilling to spread into the foreign atmosphere. She gathered it and channeled it, compressing it as it spun. More she gathered, and more.

There was the faint sound of shouting, as from a great distance, but she ignored it. Magic spun about her in a clear stream, a whirling vortex of raw energy, burning hotter and hotter as she forced it upon itself and compressed the spiral further into a disc.

It burned her. It whirled about her and through her as when she healed Tamaryl, roaring into her like the sea in storm, filling her, stretching her, crushing her from within. It blinded her with scorching light and tried to consume her.

Maru's shield was failing, but now she was ready. She gasped a final, bracing breath and released the pent magic.

It exploded around her, blasting outward from her torso with devastating intensity. The air shattered before it and Ariana crushed her hands against her ears as it thundered with force enough to hurt her closed eyes. Tamaryl wrenched away from the deadly tide of power, faltering, but the thinning stream bore them up, whipping their clothing and hair and stinging skin.

Ariana opened her eyes and saw the wave roll across the plane, staggering humans and Ryuven alike. On all sides, battle slowed.

She could not give them a chance to resume. "Hear me!" she shouted, letting the magic echo through her lungs. "Stand, now, and hear me!"

She looked at the battlefield now for the first time, and she abhorred it. So many... She had known she would face battle one day as the Black Mage, and she had studied it and spoken of it and prepared for it, but there was still so much in the actual sight of it...

And it had all been unnecessary.

Anger lanced through her next words. "Drop your arms! You

will not brandish a weapon while I speak. Stop, now!"

The magic roared in her voice, and they stared at her. Then they actually lowered their weapons, though they did not release them entirely, eying the wary soldiers and warriors about them suspiciously. Beyond the reach of her magic, the fighting seemed to slow, as the stillness rippled outward and the combatants paused to stare at the trio midair.

"This is ended." Sweet Holy One, the more she looked about, the more dead and dying she saw... Fury writhed within her. "You are like animals—no, for animals cease when there is nothing left to gain by fighting. You are less than animals! Monsters!"

She could not feel Tamaryl's arms now, numb where the magic poured through her. They were sinking toward the ground.

"This fighting has ended. It is *finished*. Go back to your leaders and clear this field. We have a new way of treating now, and it does not need weapons." She looked across the field but could not recognize faces. "Where is Taev Callahan? The Indigo Mage?"

She had not realized how still the field had become until she saw Callahan walking toward her, the only movement among hundreds of staring eyes.

She jerked the knot in the sash so that it fell free. "We have—"

And then another movement flashed across her vision, and she spun midair as a human soldier and Ryuven warrior lunged toward one another. She did not know what had triggered them, but they could not be allowed to fight, the entire field would rush to join—

She felt the tingle of released magic an instant before she unleashed her own, and twin bolts, human and Ryuven, cracked into the pair, blasting through them and dropping them already dead. Ariana saw them crumple, saw those around them recoil, saw the field blur through tears of rage.

"You stupid fools!" Magic seethed through her. "Don't you see that we could be done with all this?"

The ground rose to meet her, and she shoved the basket at the breathless Taev Callahan. "Look there!" she demanded, her voice choking. "Do you see what that is?"

He took a handful of the dried herbs and stared wide-eyed.

"Tell them! Tell them now!"

His voice was not backed by furious magic. "It's dall sweetbud. It's an entire bushel of dall sweetbud." He lifted his head. "This can stop the plague."

"It's medicine, priceless medicine. And that is our gift to seal peace." She turned her enraged glare on the field, looking around at humans and Ryuven and seeing them flinch from her gaze. "The Ryuven will not fight for food, but trade for it. We will not repel them, but welcome their commerce. And there will be no more fighting this day."

Angry tears blurred her vision. *Not now!* But she had just helped to kill two fighters, and she had yet to mourn and celebrate, and her body burned and ached with raw power, and all that she had clung to finishing was here, was now, was done...

She stepped past Callahan, leaving him holding the precious basket, and started across the field. Someone moved toward her, and with a flick of her hand she sent him stumbling backward. After that no one approached her, or even remained in her path as she strode across the trampled field, blinking and squeezing her eyes shut and hoping no one could see her weeping.

CHAPTER EIGHTY-EIGHT

Luca used the first of the money Shianan left him to send an ashamed letter to his siblings, breaking the news of Isen's death, explaining how he had been robbed of his inheritance and enslaved once more. It would take time to reach Ivat, but they deserved to know. It was possible Thir could send around to cancel the letter of credit, so the thieves could not bleed their house. And it was possible Jarrick might come for him again, if he dared return to Alham. Despite what Luca had told Shianan... He did not want to go home again; it was home no longer. He did not know what he did want. But he would not refuse to see his siblings again.

Then, as Luca had once wished his family had searched for him, he searched for Marla and Cole. He did not have the resources of a merchant house, but he'd sent letters to traders near where they had been attacked. Even if he did not reach the trader who had one or the other, another might note the described slaves if there were profit in it. Luca could earn back their price for Shianan.

He was kneeling beside the fountain, scrubbing out Shianan's water pitcher, when a soldier came running across the courtyard, stumbling with weariness. Luca moved aside as the soldier approached the fountain. But immediately others crowded about, trapping Luca close. "What word? How's the battle? How do we stand? The horse messenger didn't tell us a thing."

"We're stopped," panted the soldier, cupping water with his hands. Someone pulled Luca's pitcher away to fill, and he took it gratefully. "Black Mage and Pairvyn ni'Ai together ordered a truce, surprised everyone. There's talk of peace—but nothing's sworn. We need royal word for that." He gulped more water.

Luca breathed for the first time since the soldier's appearance. A truce! That was the best he could imagine.

"The king has to ratify Prince Soren's word?" someone asked.

The soldier lowered the pitcher, beard dripping. "No, and that's a sticking point—the prince is missing."

"Missing!" gasped a half-dozen voices.

He nodded and rubbed the back of his hand across his wet beard. "Not dead—missing. There's some that say the Ryuven took

555

him."

"A hostage to hold the peace?"

"Maybe. But they're not claiming him, if they have him."

There was a moment of muttering while the listeners considered this.

"The Black Mage?" someone asked skeptically. "That's lowest in the Circle. How does the Black Mage order a truce?"

"She pops into the sky like a seeding Ryuven, floating with Pairvyn ni'Ai and cracking magic to deafen everyone within half a league, and she kills the first man to heft a weapon, that's how." He nodded significantly. "It's going to be messy, I'll gamble—if she did arrange a peace with the Ryuven, ending the raids, that's one thing, but if she took authority what wasn't hers to do it..."

"She doesn't know where the prince is?"

"Who knows? She's not there. She just *walked away*. She and Pairvyn both—they just vanished. Went their separate ways and left the generals and the Ryuven lords, whatever they are, to kind of sidle up to each other, scratching their heads."

Luca kept his face low, listening intently. Ariana Hazelrig had returned safely from the Ryuven, at least. But what had become of the prince? And where was Shianan?

"What now?"

"The horse messenger is to be getting the king's word on whether we'll hold to the Black Mage's peace. No one's guess what that will be—she's got no authority to treat at all, but she brought a faith-gift from the Ryuven. The Indigo Mage is gibbering about it, some sort of priceless medicine he says will stop the spreading flux and anything else, it seems. So they don't want to just throw it back in their winged faces, anyway. And no one knows where Pairvyn ni'Ai is again, and that's to be considered." He took another drink. "It's twisted wrong—but they're saying the Ryuven will pay in coin for what they want. If the monsters could be trusted, I suppose."

"Trade with the Ryuven," someone mused. "They've never traded. They've stolen and left blood-debts years long."

"I've got to go for the chancellors," said the soldier. "I need a breather after that." He dropped the pitcher into the fountain, where it filled and sank, and started away. A few followed him, clapping hands on his shoulders, while others consulted and debated.

Luca stared at the pitcher, watching it drift to the fountain's floor. Then he summoned his courage and ran after the soldier. "I beg your pardon, my lord, but do you have any word of Commander Becknam? Count of Bailaha?"

The soldier looked at him. "Becknam the bastard?"

This man wasn't one of Shianan's men, wasn't from Alham's garrison at all. "Yes, my lord, that commander. My master."

"Well, did you want him dead or alive? You can't be glad for either just yet. He's missing from the field."

Luca's heart stilled.

"Not found dead, but he's not answering, either. Like the prince, and maybe the Ryuven stole others, too. Men are swearing blue he wouldn't have run off the field like a whipped Furmelle, that he had to have been taken. So you've got a bit of time before you go on the block. Enjoy it." He walked on.

Shianan was missing. They couldn't even find his body—but there would be no reason to take Shianan. He wouldn't be a valuable hostage like Prince Soren. He was missing—wounded, perhaps, beneath brush or behind a boulder or unrecognizably maimed. He was dead or in trouble, and no one knew to help him.

Dear Holy One. Luca turned back to the commander's quarters, numbness spreading through him. He passed through the front office into the sleeping room. He hesitated a moment, and then he went to the coffer Shianan had indicated. Within it lay several folded papers, a few sealed packets, and a small bag of coins. Luca lifted out the bag and slipped it into his clothing.

Ewan Hazelrig's head throbbed with each heartbeat, and it seemed as though everyone were speaking from a distance, though they were gathered close about the camp table. He closed his eyes and concentrated on the sensation of cloth beneath his sweating palms. He could feel Elysia's gaze on him.

"Without the prince, we haven't the royal authority," insisted Kannan, his tone barely civil. "And without the prince, we aren't inclined to make any promises that might preclude our having him back."

The Ryuven opposite flexed his fingers into the table. He sat sideways on his chair to accommodate his trailing wings, twitching in his frustration. "As I have said, I do not know where your prince may be. I did not order his capture and I have had no word of him."

"But you did not know of this truce, either."

The Ryuven scowled. "No. And the Pairvyn has—leave that aside. But we cannot wait upon your masters' approval. My warriors are impatient and hungry."

"And what of your own master?" demanded Kannan.

"He will not attend himself," came the level answer. "He is occupied."

"We can ease the wait," Septime offered, "for all our troops. We will share our meal tonight as evidence of our good faith. None of us want to break truce tonight, while we wait for word. Let's feed our soldiers and hope that eases some of the tension outside."

"My lords," Hazelrig said, "I think that is the best suggestion we could hear. Let's send word out quickly that meals are to be prepared and shared—from the same pots, so there is no question of faith."

"And we will continue to wait upon word from your king and council?"

"Yes, we will. We can do nothing but that."

CHAPTER EIGHTY-NINE

Soren had fallen silent long ago. Shianan was grateful the prince was no longer awake for his pain, but he worried the prince might die on his back and he would not realize it.

Darkness fell quickly in the ravine, and the moonlight did little to alleviate it. He would have to stop. He dared not risk stumbling with the prince. A fall could be fatal.

He reached a broad, flat sheet of rock and squatted painfully until the prince's legs dragged the ground, and then he eased the arms over his shoulders. His clenched fingers seemed locked. Once Soren was safely lowered, Shianan let himself fall to the stone, limbs shaking.

The walls were much lower now, perhaps only twelve or fifteen feet to the lip. Hours before, he might have been able to climb out and devise a way to bring Soren out safely. But Shianan was too exhausted now to make the climb himself, much less with the injured prince.

He was damp with sweat, even in the cold air. He needed to start a fire soon. There was nothing for shelter, but the walls blocked much of the wind, at least. He looked at the scattered wood wedged among the rocks, left from spring floods and damp with recent rain, and forced himself to move.

He gathered a collection of driftwood to the side of their slab, where the heat would reflect off the stone wall to augment the warmth, and was attempting unsuccessfully to light it when he heard a sound from the lower part of the ravine. He froze, listening, and then slid his sword from its sheath as he moved between the faint noise and the unconscious prince.

The sound came again. Sick fear twisted Shianan's gut. A search party would be calling for the prince, not moving in near silence.

He leveled the sword into the darkness. "Who's there? Declare yourself."

There was a soft, leathery rustle—shifting Ryuven wings.

Shianan resolutely forced away his weariness. "That man is Soren, the prince-heir of this kingdom. He is injured and no danger to you. If you can save him, he will make a valuable hostage. But save him. Do what you like with me—but help him."

"You regard your life less than any man I've ever met," drawled a familiar voice, "and at the same time, you have such incredible arrogance. What makes you think your life is worth his?"

Shianan stared into the darkness. "Pairvyn!"

"But I will take neither of your lives tonight. We are under truce." Tamaryl's eyes glittered as he moved forward, faintly illumined by the thin moonlight. "Though if ever I wished to kill you... She has already seen you die. She already grieves you, and she already sees me as your murderer. I could lose nothing by killing you a second time."

"You could gain nothing, either. I am the bastard, and I may not wed a Mage of the Circle. In killing me you would spare me a lifetime of seeing her without knowing her."

"And you are so quick to throw that away." Tamaryl's lip curled in disgust. "Have some small respect for your opponents, at least. Do you believe I would kill an injured man purely for spite? Do you think, if I would, my mercy could be bought with your life?" He shook his head. "I cannot stay long; I am not at liberty—"

"Wait." Shianan lowered his sword. "Wait, please." He sucked air through his lips and called upon long practice of humiliation. "The mages were able to heal me without amulets, after—after the Shard was taken. I know I have nothing of value to offer you, but... Please, can you help him? With your magic?"

"I cannot."

Rage flared in Shianan. "Monster! I will give you anything you ask, and you refuse to help him!"

Tamaryl's face twisted and he shook his head. "I'm sorry. It is not that I will not, but that I cannot. Your injury was magical; that is wood and steel." His tone was nearly an apology. "I can explain it—"

"I don't want you to explain it, I want you to save his life!" He choked, his flash of fury fading to despair. "Please. Save him."

"I am sorry. I cannot." Tamaryl gestured. "But I will leave you this."

The reluctant wood flared into sudden, vigorous flame. Shianan sidestepped and jerked the sword into defense, never taking his eye from the enemy.

Tamaryl crossed his arms, disdainful of Shianan's threat. "We are indeed under truce, my lord commander. Keep that in mind if you should come across any of my warriors." And with a soft disturbance of air, he disappeared.

Shianan let the sword drop. At least he had not needed to defend the prince, had not needed to fight. He wasn't sure he could have.

"What was that?" Soren's words were indistinct.

"Nothing now, my lord," Shianan answered. "It's gone."

The firelight showed Soren closing his eyes again.

Shianan started toward him. "I need to move you between the fire and the wall, my lord. For warmth. Just once, and then you can lie still."

Soren's face did not change. "Do it and be done."

The sardonic jests had ended. His acquiescence worried Shianan, but there was nothing more he could do. He lifted the prince as carefully as he could and set him, moaning, against the sloping wall, the fire at his feet. Soren let his head fall backward, pale even in the firelight.

Shianan left the sword out; any damage from dew was insignificant compared to the utility of having it ready. He wished briefly for water or meat. He was too tired to feel hunger, but he knew he'd need the energy. But as there was no likely prospect of either, he moved to Soren's intact side and sat as close as he could without jarring the prince, to share warmth.

Luca hesitated in the doorway. He had not heard that slaves were disallowed within temples, but prescripts were often more strict in Alham. No one challenged him, though, and he slipped inside, edging along the rear wall.

He passed several alcoves for private petition, but his target on the far side was smaller and less grand, more suitable for a slave. Beside it was a wide coffer with a slit in the locked lid.

Luca waited until a well-dressed woman deposited several shining coins before moving close. He brought out the small purse of coins Shianan had left. The bag would not fit through the slit, and he began to untie the drawstring.

"You come with a notable offering," said a voice behind him. Luca jumped and spun, clenching the bag to him. The priest held up his hands in a soothing gesture. "Forgive me. I didn't mean to startle you."

Luca struggled for words. "I may pray here, yes?"

"Certainly. The Holy One welcomes and hears all." He glanced at the bag in Luca's fist. Did he wonder if Luca had stolen it?

"It's mine to spend," Luca defended quickly. He pushed the bag at the priest. "It wouldn't fit, but I want to give it all."

The priest raised his eyebrows at Luca's earnestness. "Of course. Thank you." He accepted the bag and loosened the string as he stepped nearer the coffer. "Would you like someone to hear your mind? Counsel with you?"

Luca looked down. "I'm here to ask assistance."

"You need the strength of the Holy One? His protection?"

"Both." Luca bit the inside of his lip. *And so you may hope.* "My master is at the battle. Word came he is missing, and I want to pray that he is well. That he is safe and will come home."

The priest studied Luca, who stared self-consciously at the priest's robed knees. "You are most sincere in your petition."

Luca nodded stiffly, embarrassingly close to tears. If he were to lose Shianan as well... "He has his sins, but—but I will pray most solemnly for his safety."

The priest nodded. He pulled the drawstring tight about the little bag's neck. "Take this back," he said gently.

"But..."

"Go and pray, and may the Holy One bless you as he sees best. When you see his hand, you may bring an offering if you wish. But one cannot bribe the One who created all things."

Luca nodded uncertainly. The priest gestured toward the nearby alcove. "Stay as long as you like."

Luca entered the narrow alcove and looked at the trio of candles burning at the head of it. No other decoration broke the expanse of smooth plastered walls. He sank to his knees and bent forward, a familiar position of abasement.

No, that did not feel right. He had knelt countless times before Ande to beg mercy, but he would never have petitioned the priest in earnest hope. If the Holy One was truly all-knowing and all-powerful, Luca owed him respect and fear, but if he were also merciful, Luca need not approach him as he had the Gehrn priest.

He shifted to a seated position, crossing his folded legs before him and bowing his head. This felt nearer a solemn conversation and less a futile grovel.

Holy One, I mean no dishonor. Please hear me. He clenched his fists. *Please, Master Shianan is—he's all I have now. Please... have a plan for him. Let him yet breathe, and let him return safely. Please bring him home.*

CHAPTER NINETY

The soldiers shifted uneasily as they stood. The Ryuven officers had left the generals' meeting tent some time ago, but the air of suspicion remained. All were painfully aware they were under a truce neither side had anticipated, or even welcomed, and which might at any moment collapse into renewed warfare.

The grey mage with them stiffened suddenly. "Ryuven!"

The soldiers leapt to rigid alert, jerking their crossbows into readiness. A second later there was a faint pop of disturbed air, and a new shape stood in the darkness outside the torchlight.

"Who's there? Stand and declare yourself!"

The Ryuven did not stand but walked forward into the light. "I haven't much time. I must speak with your—"

"Pairvyn!" breathed several soldiers, staring at the crimson sash. The grey mage blanched and took a step backward, and someone released a crossbow.

A shield arose about the Ryuven. The bolt ricocheted off the invisible surface and shot toward another soldier, whose eyes barely had time to widen—

Flame erupted about the arrow, scorching it out of existence, and only a wave of heat washed over the soldier's stunned face. "Tamaryl'sho," rebuked Hazelrig, leaving the tent, "a spherical shield? In the midst of a group?"

Tamaryl inclined his head. "I apologize, my lord mage. I reacted without thinking."

The two generals and the Silver Mage exited the tent. Hazelrig stepped through the startled soldiers, leaving them watching, and approached the Ryuven. He hesitated, looking as if he wanted to speak but could not find the right words.

Tamaryl faced him steadily. "I can't stay long. But if you wish to find your prince, send men up the ravine, to the northwest. Hurry, he's not well."

There was a moment of shock as the others absorbed this information, and then Septime began issuing orders. "Gleston! I want two search parties, each with a healer and supplies. You'll need litters from the physic tent and rope, if he's to be brought up from the ravine.

Have them assembled in ten minutes. And which man released that arrow?"

Eyes shifted to one soldier, who looked as if he'd have preferred to sink through the destroyed grass. "Sir..."

"Give your weapon to the man beside you, and get yourself to the rear of this tent."

Tamaryl's wings twitched. "I cannot wait. But Mage Hazelrig, have you spoken with the Black Mage?"

"She left the field, and no one has seen her."

"But she will be well?" His throat worked visibly.

Hazelrig opened his mouth. "You're—"

But Tamaryl made a quick, shallow nod. "Thank you, my lord mage. I wish you speed in recovering your prince." And he vanished into the between-worlds, air rushing to fill his place.

Kannan moved forward to stand beside Hazelrig, who stared where the Ryuven had been. "He was quite well-spoken, for what he is. Showed a proper respect to you and all."

Hazelrig did not answer.

"And 'soats, I don't know if I could have reprimanded Pairvyn ni'Ai." Kannan chuckled. "You spoke with him as if he were just one of your grey mages. You must have 'nads of brass."

Hazelrig spoke at last. "Reles'sho said Oniwe'aru would not be attending to ratify the peace."

"Right. That's fair enough, as we wouldn't bring our king out here, either—but he said he was busy, which is odd. What keeps a ruler busy when he needs to be treating for peace?"

Hazelrig licked his lips. "We should find the prince quickly, and have him validate this peace. And we need someone to go to the nearest city and inform the merchants that dall sweetbud will be available for purchase, in limited quantities. The herbalists and healers will fight in the streets for it, but we want a good price, because there must be no question whether the Ryuven can afford our grain. And we need this trade to open tomorrow morning."

Shianan had not meant to sleep, but he woke to voices calling across the ravine. Searchers!

He rose, sword in hand, and checked the prince. Soren was still and pale, but breathing. Shianan moved down the ravine the way they'd come, where he could hear voices echoing. "Hello!" he shouted.

"Here's someone!" a voice reported excitedly. Shianan waited as they wound their way to him, lighting the walls distantly and then coming around the last bend with bright torches and shining armor. "Commander Becknam!"

He nodded wearily. "Thank all that's holy," he breathed.

"Are you injured? We're seeking His Highness—"

"He's there." Shianan gestured behind him. "Wounded."

Several men nodded and ran on, and Shianan noted two had poles strapped to their backs. They were prepared for a litter, then. Another remained, looking at him closely. "Here, sir," he offered, extending a leather bottle. "Something to drink?"

Shianan seized it and gulped eagerly.

"Are you all right, sir?"

"I'll be fine. See to the prince."

"We've brought a healer, sir, and there's another party on the rim. We'll have him back for care. If you're not injured...?"

"I think," Shianan said, sinking gratefully against a near boulder, "I will sit here while you see to the prince."

Soren did not wake under the care of the camp healers or the three healing amulets they strapped to him. He was promptly rushed to Alham, drawn by rotating teams of the fastest slaves while others suspended his litter in the wagon, absorbing the worst of the rattling shocks.

It was not Soren, then, but Grand Chancellor Uilleam who approved and signed the hasty peace, agreeing to a treaty of trial. The Ryuven would bring the precious herb for market, and they would purchase foodstuffs at the same time. Soldiers would see that there was no disturbance in the market area and that the Ryuven had a fair chance to purchase goods just as any merchant. The truce would last four weeks, and then the leaders would consult as to its success.

Shianan learned this when he finally hiked back to camp, all his body aching. He accepted the news, stumbled into his tent, and wished fervently for a warm bath.

The army broke camp. Progress was slow. Alanz was one of a number of officers who had died on the field, and many of the soldiers were wounded or gone. Wagons, loaded with armor, weapons, and the dead, began their slow way back to Alham.

When at last they neared the city, they were cheered by people gathering at the roadside to welcome and praise them. These were the soldiers who had fought to save them from the Ryuven—these were the ones who had bought at least a temporary peace! And enough remembered Luenda to exhibit real gratitude.

They entered the city itself, and volunteers appeared to help push the wagons up the sloping roads. Groups split and wound toward the various stations, and Shianan limped toward the Naziar with his command. They passed through the open gate before the sober cheers of the townspeople.

He was trudging across the courtyard, one hand on the side of a wagon he wasn't really helping to push, when a figure flew toward him. Luca struck him forcefully, knocking him into the wagon as he embraced him and then recoiling as if suddenly recalling his position and their audience. "Master Shianan," he tried breathlessly. "Master Shianan! Are you well?"

"Well enough, and a hot meal, a steaming bath, and a warm bed should do for the rest." Shianan clasped his friend's arms, feeling a real smile spread across his face. "It's good to see you, Luca. Very good." He grinned tiredly. "I told you I would return."

"Don't play so arrogant. They said you were missing!"

"I suppose that's true. But I'm found. Come with us; you can lend a hand." It was clear the slave would not leave, anyway.

The caravan made its way to the warehouses, where tired men and slaves pushed the wagons into line. "Leave the weapons loaded," Shianan ordered. "They'll be here in the morning, and I don't want a bunch of sleepy half-wits trying to clean and oil them tonight." And if the truce went suddenly sour, it would be best to have them ready. "Just take care of the others. There will be a place in the south building."

It was a somber business, laying out the dead. Those who had died early or in the care of the camp healers had received at least a cursory cleaning, while those who had died late or on the road still showed the signs of their last distress. Grey mages had done something arcane which kept the bodies a few days longer than strictly natural. This night and the next day would see many families collecting their own and taking them for rituals. Those left, with no one near enough to claim them, would be taken outside the city and interred.

Shianan turned to Torg, who was easing himself out of a wagon, careful not to jar the arm hanging in a sling. "How are you?"

"Managing. Better than I could be, as I've been napping on and off. Go and get some rest yourself."

Shianan nodded. "I will. Just let me see things started."

As he moved away, Torg met Luca's eyes, and he twitched his head sharply toward Shianan's back.

Luca gave a respectful nod to the captain and moved after his master. "What can I do to help? What must be finished before you can leave?"

"Hm? The dead have to be laid out for claiming, and the wagons need ordering so that they can be drawn out again quickly, and someone will need to stand for the kin coming to—"

Luca circled and stepped into his path. "Master Shianan, with all respect, you look like week-old vomit. What must be finished by you yourself, before you can leave this to others?"

Shianan stared. "'Soats, I think I went wrong in teaching you the staff."

Luca gave him a smile.

Shianan nodded tiredly. "Right. If Torg's been sleeping, he can see to the claiming kin. And these may be a bunch of turnip-headed mutton-brains, but they're my mutton-brains, and they know enough to handle a wagon without my holding their hands. Let's go home."

In his quarters, Shianan sank into a chair, staring at his stockinged feet. "I don't know whether I want to sleep directly, or take that steaming bath and then sleep. Maybe sleep in a bath. And I'm certain I should eat somewhere in there as well." He looked at Luca. "The prince was injured. Badly. What have you heard?"

"Not much, only that he was wounded, but no details of it."

"It's bad, Luca. I was there. I—I don't know if he'll make it." He closed his eyes and took an unsteady breath. When he opened them again, something had shut within him, sealing what he dared not touch. He ran a hand through his hair. "I ought to have that bath, I think."

"I'll get fresh clothes."

The soldiers' bath was not yet busy, as most of the men were either still at the warehouses or too tired to bathe, but a number of men were taking advantage of the water. There was no steam, as the fires had been allowed to die and it would take a day or two to heat the water again.

Shianan made a face as he filled a bucket from the tepid pool. "Well, it will rinse off the grit, anyway." He upended the bucket over himself to sluice the worst of the sweat and grime.

Luca cast a furtive glance at the other soldiers and retreated to the wall, well out of the way, where he began folding Shianan's discarded clothing to occupy his hands.

Shianan did not bother with the soaking pool. He craved warmth and rest, and the cool water offered neither. He scrubbed at his skin and scalp and then, finally clean, pushed himself wearily back from bucket and brush. Almost before he straightened, Luca offered him a towel. "No hurry, then?"

"I'd like to see you fed and sleeping. It's only good sense, really, as the better my master fares, the better I'll fare." Luca grinned.

"Your sympathy is touching." Shianan buffed his body, shaking his head. "Maybe I'll try the Kalen baths later." He squeezed water from his hair and reached for his clothes. "What I'd give for a good aelipto just now."

He slid his braies over his legs and tied the laces. Then he tugged at the shirt in Luca's stack, but it slid reluctantly over the slave's stiff arms. He looked up and prompted, "Luca?"

The slave blinked and looked down at the shirt. "Oh. Sorry."

Shianan dropped the loose shirt over his head. "I just thought I'd like to have the worst of the aches pressed out of me." He left the shirt unlaced and took the tunic. "But I suppose we haven't had good luck with the place, after all."

Luca stared at his empty hands. "Master Shianan..."

"Yes?"

Luca seemed to startle, scanning the wide room about them. "It can wait."

Shianan exhaled. "Good enough. Will you bring something to eat? I'm going back."

But he was asleep atop his blankets before Luca returned.

CHAPTER NINETY-ONE

The cord shifted about Tamaryl's throat as he swallowed. His arms, crossed at the wrists behind his neck and bound by the cord, were growing heavy, but he could relieve the strain somewhat by bowing his head. That, he thought, was appropriate.

Where was Maru? Was he similarly bound in another cell, awaiting Oniwe'aru's judgment? It would have been easy to take him. It would not have needed Oniwe'aru himself to trail Maru through the between-worlds.

Tamaryl could have fought, could have resisted his arrest. But fighting would have wounded them both and ultimately profited nothing.

The following sho and che had spread about him and closed, ready to fight but leaving the first blow to him. Tamaryl didn't look at them but at Oniwe'aru, who stared evenly back at him. "Tamaryl'sho."

As if by an unseen signal, the sho and che moved. Cords and chains settled about Tamaryl, making him wince as they drew tight and fed on him. He could have repelled them, could have fought them, but it would only delay the inevitable. And he did not want to appear a rebellious traitor when he did not consider himself one. He hoped to explain, to make them understand, and they would not hear him if he fought them.

Oniwe'aru stepped forward, and the others shifted so that they faced one another. "Is this what you wanted?" Oniwe'aru asked heavily.

"I knew it might come to this," Tamaryl answered. "But I hoped it would not."

Oniwe'aru's expression did not change. "Still, this was by your choice."

Tamaryl felt one brief moment of panic—*no!*—but he hardly had time to struggle before Oniwe'aru stretched out his hand. The effect struck him like hot irons as Oniwe'aru ripped the inherent magic from every fiber of his body. It was like having the power drawn from him for his binding in the human world, condensed and distilled into pure, unnatural agony. He arced rigidly backward, jerking in the hands of the Ryuven holding him, and begged for blackness.

It finally, belatedly, came.

Now, he was bound and imprisoned, drained of his power like any criminal. He hoped Maru had been shown mercy. He had only obeyed his lord of obligation, and that provided a measure of protection to nim. Surely he would not be punished too harshly.

A bolt rattled loudly, and Tamaryl raised his head, pulling at his shoulders. It was a che who came through the door, not Oniwe'aru. He carried a long, forked rod; they were taking no chances with the Pairvyn ni'Ai. He closed the door behind him and faced Tamaryl. "What did the humans offer you?"

The question surprised Tamaryl. He had not expected the accusation of being bought. "They offered me nothing." He shifted and the chains across his chest, holding his wings close and immobile, bit at him. "Where is Maru?"

The che scowled. "You're in no position to ask questions, or haven't you noticed?"

Tamaryl gave him a sardonic half-smile. "Oh, and I thought the luxury of a locked door was due to my rank and honor."

The bolt came fast. Tamaryl sensed it and tried to protect himself, but there was no real power left in him, and the energy sizzled through his weak defense and seared into his face. He gasped with the shock of it.

The che's eyes widened slightly as he realized he had just struck the Pairvyn and would suffer no consequence. He stopped forward. "So you say you were not enticed to betray Oniwe'aru? You turned for the simple pleasure of it?"

Tamaryl could feel the weal swelling on his cheek. It would not heal without his power, and the implication of letting the che's injury remain galled him as much as the pain. "I have always served Oniwe'aru and our clan to the best of my ability."

"You fled the field and then interrupted a battle which had turned to our advantage!"

"I gave our people a chance to survive!" Tamaryl checked himself; he owed no defense to this che. "We can purchase what we need without risk to our own. Surely you can see the benefit in that."

"I see you've closed opportunity for anyone below you to improve his station," growled the che. "You shielded your own shank, afraid we would outshine you soon. But see where it got you? What is your position now?"

He advanced on Tamaryl, the forked stick ready in his hand,

but Tamaryl could do nothing. At best it would be days before he regained his former strength, but his chains were fup-forged, burning away any returning power. He could only watch as the che moved forward. Grinning at his own manic daring, the che kicked Tamaryl—in his unprotected gut, first, and then again in his face as he grunted and folded.

The che laughed. "But I might profit yet by your attempts. I was one of those who captured the traitor. You've only aided me."

The cell spun about him. A physical blow—the worst of insults. *Two* of them. And Tamaryl could only sit and bleed before him, like a chastised nim or even a human slave. By the Essence, he had not known he was so proud.

But why couldn't they see what he had done? Didn't Oniwe'aru know the good of it? Was he truly too offended at the slighting of his orders to recognize the greater gain?

The che regarded him with a disdainful sneer. "You're not much now, are you?" He turned his back and went to the door. "What a sad end for a Pairvyn. But a fitting one for a traitor."

Had they repealed the truce? Made it all for nothing? *No, please, no—Essence within, let something have come of all this...*

The iron bolt slid with an echoing finality, leaving him in the dark again.

Taev Callahan glanced around once more, assuring himself no one was near. It was falling dark, and anyone observing would be as difficult to see as he would be. But he was far from the road and near a rocky, unused part of the river, quite alone.

He stepped carefully onto a river rock and picked his way across the first third of the fast-moving water. Then he crouched and felt for a stick, wedged across two large stones, where it held firm a rope and the attached net. He withdrew it all, watching the netted leaves shed water.

The first bushel of dall sweetbud had been sold, and at stunning prices. The spreading plague had frightened those with coin enough to buy protection. It would not do for any of them to become ill after taking the new herb.

This was the eighth of the dispensers he'd destroyed. He would leave the others, as a few remaining pockets of flux would make the sickness more believable and spur a steady demand for the cure. He laid the dripping net across a flat rock and, with a moment of concentration to counter the wetness, set it aflame. He was careful to stay upwind, for bilgewort smoke could do unpleasant things.

When the flames had died, leaving only unrecognizable ashes, he kicked them smoking into the river and turned back toward the road.

TO BE CONTINUED
Kin & Kind

GET A FREE STORY AND MORE

The website has everything from background research and inspiration to story glossaries and book club discussion guides, as well as an infrequent newsletter for events and releases. Go to **www.LauraVAB.com** to receive bonus stories and sneak peeks, special or advance offers, and release information.

Thank you for reading, and please be sure to review *Blood & Bond* at your favorite site. I read every review! and I'd love to hear from you.